"COMPELLING . . . *RAMPAGE* HAS THE MAKINGS OF ANOTHER OSCAR-WINNER MOVIE . . . AN ACTION-PACKED THRILLER FROM PAGE ONE."

—*King Features Syndicate*

Chris Taggart: With his bare hands and fierce ambition, he's changed the skyline of New York. Now he's made the Mafia an offer they can't refuse—and the only one who can stop his one-man war is the woman he can never have . . .

Tony Taglione: Chris's brother, he's kept the family name and its code of honor. He's fighting his own blood—but he'll use the law to bring down the Mob, and anyone who gets in his way . . .

Helen Rizzolo: On the surface she's legitimate Ivy-League, a lady of grace and sophistication. But the fire in her heart is Mafia-bred—and when the shooting starts, she'll take charge . . .

"VIOLENCE, MONEY, POLITICAL CHICANERY, POWER, SEX . . . JUSTIN SCOTT SETS OUT TO TELL A SLAM-BANG YARN AND DOES PRECISELY THAT. . . . IF YOU ARE LOOKING FOR ESCAPIST FARE, LOOK NO FURTHER."

—*Baltimore Sun*

(more . . .)

"*RAMPAGE* IS VIOLENT AND SUSPENSEFUL
... LOTS OF ACTION AND INTRIGUE. ..."

—*Pasadena Star-News*

Reggie Rand: An ex-Scotland Yard man, he's made a
career of hunting IRA killers. Now he's Taggart's
right-hand man—specializing in assassination
and terrorism ...

Jack Warner: An N.Y.P.D. detective on the take, he'll
betray anyone to save his stash, his badge—and
his own skin ...

Sal Ponte: Consigliere of the powerful Cirillo family,
his moment of weakness dooms his own Don ...

Frank and Eddie Rizzolo: Helen's brothers and the
muscle of her family, they're enforcers no one can
take out—until they come up against Chris Taggart's men ...

"JUSTIN SCOTT'S *RAMPAGE* GIVES A NEW
TWIST TO THE EXPRESSION 'WAR ON CRIME.'
THE ACTION RANGES FROM MANHATTAN'S
TOWERING SPIRES TO THE LABYRINTHS OF
THE CITY'S UNDERWORLD; ITS PLOT HAS
THE SPEED AND IMPACT OF A JACKHAM-
MER!"

—David Morrell, author of
First Blood

RAMPAGE

"SCOTT'S NEW THRILLER WILL STRIKE READERS AS ALL TOO PLAUSIBLE. . . . THE STORY KEEPS MOVING AND INDUCES ONE TO STICK WITH THE VIOLENT, BLOODY SCENARIO UNTIL ITS . . . CLOSE."

—*Publishers Weekly*

RAMPAGE

"CRUNCHING VENGEANCE ON CRIME . . . SCOTT IS AS LIVELY A STORYTELLER AS EVER, HERE INCLUDING CONVINCING DETAIL FROM THE BUILDING TRADES AND THE SONG OF THE HIGH IRON, AND ENTERTAINING PEDANTRY ABOUT THE MAFIA AND TERRORISTS. . . . FINELY RENDERED SETTINGS."

—*Kirkus Reviews*

RAMPAGE

"A SPELLBINDING BOOK—ONE OF THOSE RARE NOVELS YOU CAN'T PUT DOWN UNTIL YOU'VE FINISHED THE LAST PAGE, AND WHICH DELIVER ALL THE WAY THROUGH IN EXCITEMENT AND HIGH DRAMA."

—Fred Mustard Stewart, author of *Ellis Island* and *The Titan*

RAMPAGE

A NOVEL BY
Justin Scott

POCKET BOOKS

New York   London   Toronto   Sydney   Tokyo

a Gloria Hoye
mio amore, mia bellezza, mia amica

This novel is a work of fiction. Names, characters, places and incidents are either the product of the author's imagination or are used fictitiously. Any resemblance to actual events or locales or persons, living or dead, is entirely coincidental.

POCKET BOOKS, a division of Simon & Schuster, Inc.
1230 Avenue of the Americas, New York, N.Y. 10020

Published by arrangement with Simon & Schuster, Inc.
Library of Congress Catalog Card Number: 85-27824

ISBN: 0-671-64852-7

First Pocket Books printing March 1988

10 9 8 7 6 5 4 3 2 1

POCKET and colophon are trademarks of
Simon & Schuster, Inc.

Printed in the U.S.A.

Prologue

The Privateer

THE WITNESS BEFORE the President's Commission on Organized Crime wore a hood over his new face. Metal detectors had greeted spectators entering the columned rotunda of Federal Hall in Lower Manhattan and U.S. marshals had erected screens to shield him from the TV cameras. He testified through an electronic voice distorter, which made him sound like a cheerful child in another room.

The commissioners—business people, criminal justice professors, congressmen and -women, and law enforcement experts—faced him from tiered tables covered by periwinkle-blue cloth. Counsel directed questions from the center of the front table. A grizzled old judge chaired from the back.

Christopher Taggart, the youngest commissioner by far, sat in front. The seal of the commission, prominently displayed, had a Latin motto that meant, the lawyers told him, Pluck Out Evil by Its Roots. He was armed for the task with a pad for the notes he kept in a clear hand, a gold pen that he began tapping impatiently, and a microphone, which he seized with sudden exasperation.

"Mr. Counsel? This witness isn't telling anything about the Mafia that Jimmy Breslin hasn't already published in the *Daily News*."

Members of the press laughed, and counsel, an urbane former federal prosecutor vaulting the rungs of government service two at a time, doled out a smile with the correct proportions of respect and superiority. Christopher Taggart seemed to have forgotten again that he asked the questions, witnesses answered under threat of contempt citations, and commissioners listened politely.

"Be assured, Commissioner Taggart, that this witness is eminently qualified to assess the effect of the Federal Organized Crime Strikeforce on the Mafia."

The witness, a bold man with the garrote before he entered the Federal Witness Protection Program, hastened to agree with the chief counsel. Taggart assumed he enjoyed these occasional outings and wanted to be invited back. The mouth hole in his hood flapped and the cheery child sounded earnest. "Two years ago I was a *capo* in the Cirillo family here in New York."

"But you were already in the slammer last year when the Strikeforce indicted every boss of the Mafia's ruling council," Taggart shot back. "The important question is, who's taking their place? I don't see New York's Mafiosi lining up for unemployment."

"You're gonna see more and more surprising guys testifying for immunity," the mobster promised. "The Strikeforce is flipping some heavy hitters. They're scared shitless—excuse my French—about who's going to inform undercover. Even the Cirillos. Every place they move, the FBI or the Drug Enforcement Agency's waiting with an army because they've infiltrated the street crews. It's *war* out there and the mob is losing."

Taggart interrupted again. "The agents are doing a great job. But the mob still controls heroin, cocaine, unions, extortion, hijacking, and gambling. When the Strikeforce puts one leader away, five more step up to replace him. Who's taking over, Mr. Witness?"

"Hey, you don't knock 'em off in a year or two—or even ten. But don't think it's a bed of roses for the bosses. It's not like changing mayors. They gotta fight each other for the job."

"As a businessman, I'd like to see my law enforcement tax dollars going to more than making Cosa Nostra mobsters uncomfortable."

"I just wanna say I never heard the words 'Cosa Nostra' except on television. What I was in, we called it the rackets."

"And I'm calling a recess," Judge Katzoff interrupted. "Would the marshals clear the room?"

A dozen marshals escorted the man in the black hood from the witness table, cordoning him with their bodies. An easel displaying a chart of organized crime leadership in New York City crashed to the marble floor with a loud bang. Federal agents plunged anxious hands into their jackets and handbags.

Taggart smiled. He was dressed like a rich, busy man blessed with a stylish woman or two who looked after him; his navy-blue suit, expensive and conservative, off the rack from Paul Stuart, was greatly enlivened by an interesting shirt that enhanced his blue eyes, and an Italian silk tie and handkerchief. His blond hair was short and fashionably groomed in the style he called stockbroker punk. The harsh television lights revealed a faint scar that creased both his lips, and another that furrowed his brow.

"Mr. Taggart," the chairman said, when reporters, technicians, and elderly spectators had trooped from the rotunda, "I'm on a tight schedule."

"I've got four Manhattan skyscrapers on tight schedules, Your Honor. For all I know, they've fallen down. I haven't seen 'em since our dog-and-pony act hit town Monday. I didn't volunteer to showboat. I joined this commission to expose organized crime and find ways to hit back. But all we're doing is rehashing old news for the benefit of TV. We're asking this turkey to tell us what we already know about old men who've already been arrested."

The old judge, who had made a name for himself jailing Vietnam war protesters while Taggart was in junior high school, flushed.

"What about the new ones?" Taggart demanded. "Do you know how smart they're getting? Last night, the New York State Organized Crime guys busted a Cirillo bodyguard who was carrying more antibugging equipment than a KGB agent. They buy the same sophisticated surveillance receivers, bug alerts, and telephone analyzers that the government does. There's a new breed, as vicious as the old, but hipper, and getting harder to catch. These guys are not going to fall for a mike in their girlfriend's panties."

"I'll instruct counsel to schedule a technical witness," the judge replied dryly.

"I'd rather hear about the government leak on that Sicilian deal."

"What leak?"

Katzoff looked at the staff members who had collected around his chair at the center of the rear table. They looked at each other in panic.

"Who told the press that the Strikeforce had asked the Coast Guard to surveille a Greek freighter? The ship happened to be carrying Sicilian heroin, which the smugglers moved to another ship when the story broke."

"I can explain, Your Honor," said the commission's chief investigator, a slick New York Irishman in his thirties, who had been temporarily detached from the Drug Enforcement Agency. He circled the witness screen, shaking his head at Taggart. "Your Honor, somebody in the Treasury Department wanted to be sure he got credit for his agency. It was a stupid bureaucratic screwup, but those things happen. What I want to know is how the hell did Commissioner Taggart find out about it? It wasn't in the paper about the dope."

"I do my homework," Taggart shot back. He turned around and faced his fellow commissioners. "Look, when I asked my friend Governor Costanza—or should I say my father's friend?" —he hesitated, and those who knew him best glanced away. "When I asked Governor Costanza, 'Get me on this crime commission, get the President to appoint me,' I did it because I believe that the Mafia, or the rackets, or call it what the hell you want to, threatens everyone in the country. I build buildings and I see Mafia extortion every day. They'll kill construction like they killed the New York harbor. The investigation I was talking about that got leaked would have been the biggest Cirillo bust since the Strikeforce got their last underboss. What can our commission recommend to prevent such fuckups? You'll notice, unlike our tame witness, I'm not asking you to excuse my French."

"All right," said the judge. "Let's break for noon recess."

Taggart stuffed the morning's press releases in his briefcase and hailed the chief investigator. "Hey, Barney. Lunch?"

"You paying?"

"Sure. You got it last time. How 'bout Windows on the World?"

"Last time was Blarney Stone."

"So live a little."

"Seriously, Chris. How the hell did you know about the leak? Did your brother tell you?"

The smile went out of Taggart's eyes and he said coolly, "You know damned well Tony never leaks. Especially to me."

"I didn't mean it that way," Barney apologized hastily.

Taggart threw his arm around Barney's shoulder, gave him a slow grin and a friendly finger. "Hey, I'm just a business-man."

"I know, I know. And you hear things."

"From guys like you who talk too much. Hoods and cops, you're all the same, you can't keep your mouths shut."

At the restaurant atop the World Trade Center, Taggart took a table facing uptown. It was a muggy May day and the sky-line appeared hazy and distant. Taggart's gaze fixed on it nonetheless, and in the powerful north light Barney noticed that his big hands were impeccably manicured, the nails buffed to a satiny sheen.

"What's it like looking out there and seeing your own build-ings?"

Taggart's glittering eyes, powerful Italian nose, and sensual mouth gathered in one of his infectious grins, reminding Bar-ney that he was barely thirty years old. "Almost as much fun as being a cop."

While they were drinking their second martinis Taggart asked casually, "Did they really find the leak?"

"Better. They found the dope."

"Nice going. How?"

"Criminal intelligence."

Taggart laughed. "In other words, you turkeys got a tip."

"Hey, hey. Who's this?"

Jack Warner, a burly police detective attached to the Strikeforce, opened one eye at the whisper in the dark. When the camera clicked, he opened the other and heaved himself out of the musty chair where he had dozed intermittently through the long night. Another car was approaching the abandoned parking garage that he and three federal agents were watching from a defunct metalworking shop on the other side of Forty-fifth Street. Thirty pounds of Sicilian heroin that the Strikeforce had lost track of earlier had surfaced in the garage, or so said a tipster.

The FBI agent in charge fired off a second round of film and stepped back to give his partner from the Drug Enforcement Agency a look. The telescope was aimed through a hole they had peeled in the tin that covered the door. A street lamp glinting between the boards that covered the window lit the room dimly.

"I don't know him," the DEA agent said.

Warner waited his turn while an IRS criminal investigator stooped over the telescope and adjusted the focus. He too shook his head. "Never seen him before."

"Jack will know," the FBI man said. "Warner, get your ass here. Who's this guy?"

Jack knows. Damned right Jack knows! Thirty-eight years old, eighteen on the New York police force, with fourteen in Organized Crime Control, Jack Warner knows more than anybody about the Mafia. He knows who's up, who's down. He knows wiseguys their own mothers don't know. But he especially knows that tonight's hot tip is very hot indeed, because he phoned it in himself.

Warner rotated the eyepiece a quarter turn to compensate for the nearsighted IRS man. A car's image hardened in the lens —a black 1986 Chevy Caprice straddling the sidewalk, with New York plates 801-BD. The driver in profile, big nose and pompadour hair, was checking the block. The door of the supposedly empty building slid up and the car moved into darkness. At four o'clock in the morning, during false dawn before the Memorial Day weekend, the street was so quiet they could hear the metal door rattling in its tracks.

"You know him?" the FBI agent asked.

Warner yawned. "That's a Cirillo hitter who runs security for their stash pads. He's been moving up lately. Started out bouncing in their clubs."

His Strikeforce "colleagues," as Warner enjoyed dubbing the Feds, exchanged testy looks. All night the cop had been batting a thousand.

"Is there any hood in New York you *don't* know?"

"That's what your local policeman's for."

And no help from the tip, thank you, for he was proud that he had recognized the hood legitimately. It was a point of honor with him that he knew more about the Mafia than the Feds. He practically lived with the wiseguys, one jump ahead of the Mafia—two jumps ahead of the cops. Like his brother the priest who complained that he served two masters, God and the bishop, Detective Warner also had two bosses, the New York City Police Department and another who paid better.

"You know you look like one of them?" the IRS man grouched. "How do you pay for that shit you're wearing?"

Good question, Warner thought; and if you don't like my clothes, you'd hate my Swiss bank account. It was a hot, muggy night and Warner had removed his suit jacket, exposing, in addition to his belly gun, a pure cotton shirt tailored to his girth, gold-nugget cufflinks, and a brand-new black-and-gold Baum and Mercier wristwatch. His shoes, handmade in Italy, had set him back three hundred bucks each.

"I been a cop eighteen years, so I make a decent buck. All I got to spend my salary on is one rent-controlled room. But don't worry, Internal Affairs gets on my case every time I take a girl to dinner, so if I ever go on the take, they'll be the first to tell you." Good answer, he thought.

"It always looks funny on a cop around dope."

"But at least I don't look like a cop," Warner replied mildly, "Half the wiseguys in town figure I'm on their side. Guys like to talk and I listen."

"I don't look like a cop, either."

Warner's quick eyes catalogued the hair too long over the ears, the tie that had turned up at Christmas, and the shoes cracking under the shine. "You look like a guy paying bills for a wife and three kids in the suburbs. Good cover. Suits you."

He peeked through the crack in the tin, but the street was empty. It was dumb to piss off anyone who might know something useful some day. "Hey," he apologized, "when you love this city you want to own it—*hold* it! Like in your hand. Guys try different ways. A politician runs to be mayor. An actress wants her name on Broadway. Big builders like Trump and

Taggart, they change how the sky looks. But the only way a cop can own the city is *know* it. Knowing who's who makes me feel like New York is mine."

The telephone rang. They jumped. Ma Bell had come across. The FBI agent answered, listened, covered the phone, and asked Warner, "Would you mind, Jack?"

An assistant United States attorney, one of the Strikeforce prosecutors, was writing warrants for the bust. Warner gave the kid the background, street names, and home addresses of the heroin traffickers they had spotted going in the garage.

"You wearing a computer?" the lawyer asked.

"Yeah. The FBI gave it to me. Fits in my heel."

It was an axiom of the drug trade that deals and dealers were always late. But the arrival of a stash-pad guard suggested to Warner that things were going to break, so he offered to relieve the man on the telescope. He knew, of course, the general drift of what was going down, but it was impossible to know everything, because lately strange things were going on in the rackets and a lot of people on both sides seemed to be running around with a bag on their head.

The phone rang again. It was the FBI agent's supervisor pressing his man for a prediction. Warner motioned for the agent to cover the mouthpiece. "He's worried about holding a ton of agents over the holiday, isn't he?"

"For one maybe tip."

"Yeah, well, I figure the Maf probably wants to take the weekend off, too. Tell him it's coming down any minute."

"Are you *sure?*"

"We've busted so many suppliers they're hurting for product. They're not going to sit on that stuff."

The agent promised his supervisor an imminent bust and hung up gingerly. "Jesus, I hope you're right."

"Hey, hey! Here we go." A van was turning onto the sidewalk; its horn blew and the door opened. Warner stepped back to let the Feds look through the telescope. "That's the lab I told you about."

The Strikeforce backed a theatrical hauler's truck into the garage's Forty-fourth Street driveway, where it looked in place, if thoughtlessly parked, just down the street from the banners of the New Dramatists Guild and The Actors Studio.

On Forty-fifth, the agents blocked one garage door with a Con Ed truck and the second with barricades behind which they started to drill holes in the street. Forty agents in bullet-proof vests crouched inside the vans, with cutting tools and battering rams. When the police had quietly saturated the Ninth and Tenth Avenue ends of both blocks, the FBI man in the metal shop started to call the shots, with Jack Warner watching over his shoulder.

Both vans reported they were set, as were the cops. "Okay, let's—" the FBI agent started to say.

But Jack Warner seized the telephone. A blue Buick was rolling toward the garage. "Hold it! We want this guy."

"Who's that?"

"That's Nino Vetere's car, but it can't be him. One of his geeps, in case somebody needs to be killed." The Buick blew its horn at the barricades. The driver shouted not to block the entrance, and the agents attired in workboots and yellow Con Ed hardhats obligingly lifted their saw horses.

"Give him a minute to check the stuff out," Warner cautioned. "Maybe the bastards'll get some on their fingers."

Then, in an act of bravery that gave Warner the shivers to think about, an athletic DEA agent had herself lowered silently from the roof, five stories down a shaft into the car elevator. She wrapped her ample thighs around the head of the hitter guarding the entrance, stuck a gun in his ear, and asked him to throw the switch that raised the door. Twenty agents piled into the building while the drug distributors were occupied running chemical tests in the back of their van.

For a minute it looked like a clean bust.

Then the blue Buick came screaming out of the darkness, scattering the agents in the doorway and flinging the young woman over its hood. The car skidded on howling tires onto Forty-fifth Street and raced for Tenth Avenue. Warner, who ordinarily stayed out of the action to maintain his cover, charged after it. Somebody in that car was either very stupid or very desperate, and he had to know which.

The Buick ran onto the sidewalk when it reached the Corrections Department bus blocking the intersection. A quick-thinking patrolman filled the space with his prowl car and the Buick crashed into it, bounced off a wall, and stopped.

Cops with riot guns surrounded the wreck. They pulled a bloodied figure out in handcuffs, and Warner was astonished to see that it was Nino Vetere himself. A heavy-duty Cirillo crew leader, maybe number one, Vetere reported directly to underboss Nicholas, the elder son and heir apparent of Don Richard, the chief of the clan.

Agents were staring with their mouths open in disbelief. One did not find major Mafia guys on the street. No wonder he had run. Vetere was already in deep, deep trouble, awaiting trial on federal racketeering charges. Now, with a major heroin arrest, he was looking at the rest of his life in jail, and the Strikeforce prosecutors were going to pound his balls to flip.

His testimony would be golden, Warner knew, since he knew how the Cirillos ran their family. If they convicted Nicholas on Vetere's testimony, old Don Richard, who was trying to retire, had no one left to control the family but Crazy Mikey, his younger son, who was aptly nicknamed.

Warner approached an FBI agent he knew well. "Better get his family into protection or he won't deal."

"We're miles ahead of you, Jack. The marshals are on their way."

"Great! What about his girlfriend?"

"What?"

"His girlfriend. It's not enough protecting his wife and kids. He won't testify if the Cirillos can get to his mistress."

"I didn't know he had one."

Warner wrote down her name and address.

But he was baffled by what in hell Vetere was doing at a heroin buy in the first place. Mobsters as high as him were supposed to stay miles above the product. They dealt in money twice removed—and even that they didn't actually *touch*.

Someone had set him up; Warner had a feeling he knew who.

Blue shades of evening darkened the city. At the base of the Taggart Spire a bare bulb was already burning in the gate shack, as were Park Avenue's street lamps and lights in the surrounding buildings, but so tall was the partially built skyscraper that the upper works still blazed red and gold in the sun.

The construction site was quiet with the workmen gone. A tall plywood fence muffled the sound of traffic and the sweet clicking of high heels on the sidewalk, and the job seemed deserted except for the night watchman and his German shepherd, which closed its eyes when it recognized a perspiring Jack Warner as he swaggered through the gate.

"You believe this weather?"

"Radio said cooler tonight."

"Yeah? What kind of Memorial Day they gonna sell us? Gimme a hardhat."

Warner knew that the watchman was a retired cement-truck driver. The old guy probably figured him for a Taggart Construction front-office superintendent or a union boss, or even one of the mob hoods who stopped by for their payoffs.

"We'll keep the elevator."

It rose noisily through the cavernous lobby shell, ten stories of empty space—Taggart's big "fuck you," Warner thought, to the price of square footage in midtown Manhattan and to Taggart's nearest competitors, the smaller Trump and Olympia towers on Fifth Avenue, the IBM and AT&T buildings on Madison, and the Citicorp complex to the east. The Spire's interior walls were taking shape on the lower office floors. Higher up, the floors were open to the glass skin. The fiftieth to seventieth floors were not yet sheathed and their decks were bare concrete, while the very top floors—destined to be apartments, and still sprouting three V-shaped derricks—stood wide open, raw lattices of steel through which the wind gusted freely.

A figure waited on the highest girder, a thousand feet above Manhattan. His narrow steel perch, cantilevered beyond the columns that supported it, thrust thirty feet into empty air. He swayed at the end, on the very edge, leaning into the wind.

Christopher Taggart turned from the sunset, half his face shining, half in darkness. "Join me."

Warner shivered. He looked down and regretted it instantly. This side of the building dropped sheer to the sidewalk, and they were too high to distinguish people in the dusk. The taxis were specks chasing hairs of light.

"How about you meeting me halfway, Mr. Taggart?"

"Chicken?"

"If I were, at least I'd have wings."

Taggart laughed appreciatively and headed in from the precipice. His light, rolling gait, broad shoulders, and lean waist reminded Warner of a boxer's. Warner edged out to the pillar and by the time he had closed grateful fingers around the nearby upright, Taggart was leaning casually on the other side.

"Don't move!"

Taggart swung around the pillar and expertly patted Warner's chest, back, and legs; next he felt his waist for a Nagra recorder inside his belt. Warner, who took the same precautions with his contacts, submitted without complaint.

"How in hell do you stand it up here?"

"One time when my brother and I were feeling our oats, my father hired us out as ironworkers. We were scared shitless, but more scared he'd belt us with a two-by-four if we didn't have the balls for it."

"My old man beat the shit out of me, too," Warner said. "Musta been seventeen before I was big enough to deck the bastard. . . . I still don't mind saying I'd like to meet elsewhere."

"Elsewhere? How about one of the tables the Strikeforce bugs at the Brasserie?"

"You know what I mean."

Taggart swung back to his side, peered around the column, and looked Warner in the face. "I know this is the most private place in New York, Detective Warner. Start talking."

"I was all day with the prosecutors breaking down Nino Vetere. Nino said he wanted to score big to take care of his children before he got convicted on the RICO charge." The reference was to the Racketeer Influenced Corrupt Organization act; RICO, for short, cost twenty years and the Strikeforce lawyers brushed their teeth with it every morning. "Nino was looking at life or damned close, so he sings and turns in his crews. 'No way, Barf Brain, that's not enough. Give us more. Give us the guy running the Cirillos. Give us Nicholas Cirillo.' And he finally says, 'Okay, get me out of this and I'll show you how old Don Cirillo's still running the family through Nicholas.'"

Warner looked at Taggart to gauge his reaction; Taggart stared through him. "I know most of this from the radio. I can guess the rest."

Guess this, Warner thought, again watching closely for reaction. "Nobody knows where the dope came from. The original Sicilian stuff went south when the Feds leaked. The street says it was sold in Florida. Which sounds like somebody brought in new stuff and *gave* it to the Cirillos, pretending it was the stuff they had paid for. Who the hell gives away five million bucks of heroin?"

"Who cares?" Taggart snapped impatiently. "Vetere and Nicky Cirillo are old news. What did you find on the Rizzolos?"

"The Rizzolos are being their usual weird selves."

Taggart had some particular interest in the Rizzolos, which Warner hadn't figured out yet. They were a small Brooklyn family who were sort of odd man out, the smallest of the New York crime groups—maybe a hundred "made" members and four hundred soldiers—and also the tightest, and very independent. They had broken from the Cirillos, and when the Cirillos had hit back, the clan had made what came to be called the Rizzolo War so bloody that the Cirillos had finally backed off and left them alone. Their response to the Strikeforce had been just as unpredictable.

"Strikeforce hits their bookie joints, but nobody's there. They just went out of business—empty storefronts, not even a piece of paper. They even took the phone jacks. It's the same with the numbers bank. So the Strikeforce hits that big coke operation I told you about that Eddie Rizzolo stole from the Colombians. *Nada.* Like their street guys are bus drivers and waiters, period. 'Course they can't shut down forever."

Gazing at the setting sun, Taggart asked, "Have you figured out who's running the Rizzolos?"

Warner shrugged, uncomfortable with the idea, yet moved by the evidence. "Maybe you figured right. The sister might be the real boss. Eddie 'the Cop' and Frank are just plain dumb guys. Like you said, since the Strikeforce put old Don Eddie away, somebody's been running the Rizzolos just fine."

"She sounds like an interesting woman."

"Listen, Mr. Taggart." Jack was getting used to the height, as he did each time. So long as he could hold on to something solid.

Taggart turned his head, alert to a new note in Warner's voice. "What?"

Warner took a determined breath. "Things are moving real smooth on my end."

"Then what's your problem?"

"The thing is, Mr. Taggart. I think I been with you from the start on this, right?"

"Early on."

"And I think you'll agree I'm pulling my weight and then some. What you know of the mob, you know through me. I been your expert. I been your man in the field, your contact. I—"

"You want a gold star, Jack?"

Warner took another deep breath. "I know what you're doing."

Taggart waited.

"The bust this morning was a setup," Warner said.

"So?"

"What do you say we cut the shit? I know what's going on. You been using my information to turn in the bosses."

"*Your* information? You're a cop. If your information is so good, why don't you arrest them yourself?"

"You're getting information from other people, too. The Crime Commission, other cops you hang out with, federal agents, and connected guys you're tight with—yeah, I know about them—and construction guys you do business with. Maybe even your brother."

"Not my brother!" Taggart said sharply. "Tony is one hundred percent straight. He always has been and he always will be."

"But yes to the others?"

"What do you want?"

Warner was startled; Taggart's question was as good as a confession. He said, "I want in."

"In?"

"Share. I want a piece of it."

Taggart's reply was deceptively soft, but Warner wasn't fooled. The builder's whole body seemed rigid with tension; he could almost feel him stiffening though the pillar. "What if I told you I'm not doing it for the money?"

"You're not doing it for the money?" Warner shrugged. "You're so rich you don't want money? Then you won't mind sharing the profits."

"What if there are no profits?"

"No profits? Who you kidding? Crime pays, man. It pays big—I figure half 's fair. Huh?"

Taggart stared across the Hudson for a full minute. The sun slipped into an envelope of cloud and the sky flamed behind the New Jersey hills. Warner looked around anxiously. The air was clearing as the humid heat lifted. To the east, stars were rising over Long Island. In the southeast, the lights of a single freighter plowed into the black spread of the Atlantic Ocean. The wind was accelerating, dry and cool. His perspiration-dampened shirt felt suddenly cold.

"Jack, you still carry that money clip I gave you?"

"What? Money clip? Yeah."

"Let me see it."

Warner pulled a gold Tiffany clip from his trousers. His initials, in diamonds, spelled how well he had done over the years selling information to Christopher Taggart. Taggart pulled his own clip from his pocket and transferred five folded C-notes to Warner's. "Cab fare," he said with a fathomless smile. "Let me see your wallet."

As Warner passed Taggart his pigskin wallet, he flipped it open to flash his tin—a blunt warning not to try to buy him off cheap. Eighteen years and he still felt the surge. An NYPD shield asked a potent question: Do you want to fuck with a man who has twenty thousand partners?

Taggart put wallet and shield in his pocket.

"Why—?"

"So you don't drop 'em."

A long arm streaked out of the sky as Taggart whirled around the pillar and his big hand fell like a hammer. The blow enveloped Warner's face and with two hundred pounds behind it flung him into the air.

Warner felt the column wrenched from his hand. Then he

was falling. The black sky whirled into city lights, building tops, blazing windows. The street looked like a dark ribbon and nothing was between it and his falling body. He screamed.

He was brought up short, hanging upside down by one foot. Warner looked up through his flailing legs and saw Taggart's immense hand clamped around his ankle. His blue eyes had turned dark with fury.

"Don't you ever hit me for a payoff!"

"Please."

"You got that?"

"Please, Mr. Taggart."

"Say *yes.*"

"Yes. Yes. Yes."

"You *are* doing a good job, Jack. But not good enough to shake me down." He pulled him toward the girder. Warner reached and stretched and at last touched the sun-warmed steel with his fingertips. But Taggart jerked him away.

"Jack, maybe I ought to let you go." Taggart jerked him up in the air.

"No!"

"Like this!"

To Warner's disbelief, Taggart opened his hand. He fell, screaming. It seemed he was falling forever. But Taggart grabbed him again, swung him back and forth. Warner's head was bursting with blood, his chest pounding with fear. Somehow, Taggart must have learned about his files. If he didn't admit to them, Taggart would drop him.

"I got notes," he screamed.

"Blackmail?"

"No. No. I wouldn't use them. It's just my information."

"Where?"

"In my room."

"Where in your room?"

"In the wall behind the fridge. I wasn't going to use them. Honest."

Viewed upside down, shaded scarlet by the sunset, the broad angles of Taggart's face seemed to soften sympathetically. The swinging slowed, the awful arc diminished.

"I know, Jack. You only want more money. Don't worry

about it, I'll be buying plenty of information. You'll give me the notes?"

"God, yes."

He felt himself swung in from space and laid prone on the steel. He wrapped both arms around the girder and moaned his relief. Taggart knelt beside him, shaking his head. "You damned fool," he said, not unkindly, "you've wet your pants."

When he could walk again, Taggart helped him off the girder and led him solicitously toward the elevator. Warner couldn't stop shaking. His brain was roaring with blood and fear. "I thought I was dead," he mumbled.

Taggart laughed. "Jack, how could I throw an NYPD detective off my own building?" He clapped Warner on the shoulder and handed him his shield and money clip. "Go home and get those notes. And Jack . . . I don't give second chances."

Warner took that as fair warning not to voice the question that was still driving him crazy.

If Christopher Taggart wasn't in it for the money, what the fuck was he doing with the Mafia?

Book I

Slaughtered Saints
(1976–1984)

Chapter 1

CHRISTOPHER TAGLIONE REMEMBERED the day for its crisp heat and its promise. Nothing, it seemed, could be better, and nothing could ever go wrong. He bounded out of the hole, the enormous pit they were excavating between two buildings in midtown Manhattan, and hit the sidewalk running, signaling the next truck. Sweat glistened on his bare chest, poured between the cement spatters that spotted him like a gray leopard. His hair was long then, gold flying from the rim of his hardhat. A great-looking woman smiled at his exuberance and he grinned back—a star, twenty-one years old and future partner in Taglione Concrete and Construction.

His father's trucks filled Fifty-sixth Street, enormous concrete ready-mixers that towered over the taxis inching past and thundered at the pedestrians scuttling between their lofty wheels and the plywood construction fence that rimmed the hole. It was the summer of the American Bicentennial and Mike Taglione had painted his fleet patriotically in grateful celebration. Red and white stripes swirled around their chassis, and white stars spangled the blue mixers, rising in a jaunty heaven as the huge barrel-shaped tanks rotated half-turns to make the concrete flow.

Tony Taglione, Chris's dark and slender brother, who was two years older and sixty pounds lighter, came charging up the ramp hot on Chris's heels. Tony's jet-black hair, long like Chris's and that of the younger men on the job, was held out of his eyes by a sweatband fashioned from a Tall Ships T-shirt, which had started the morning white but was now as gray as his jeans, his heavy, laced construction boots, his bat-

23

tered gloves, and his skinny chest. They were working side by side and, as usual, in a race.

"That's my truck."

"You're next."

The woman who had enjoyed the sight of Chris's youthful exuberance stopped and stared at the dark-eyed Tony with frank and open interest. Tony slowed to return a practiced smile and Chris stepped into the street, pumping his fist, and reestablished his claim to the lead mixer. The driver was leaning half out the window to express admiration for another lady in a loose summer dress.

"Frankie! Move that truck!"

The behemoth swung ponderously across the sidewalk, splintering the planks wedged against the curb, and groaned down the steep earthen ramp, with its air lines sighing and brake drums protesting the weight. Chris harried it into the pit, exhorting the driver and impatiently tugging the massive bumper.

Posters on the ramp gate depicted the emerald-green office building taking life . . . Taglione Tower; Thirty Stories; Michael Taglione, Owner-Builder. Down the ramp, men and machines were deepening the hole and erecting wooden forms for the concrete footings. A chain saw blared, the forest sound incongruous until the city walls banged it back like shrapnel.

"Let's go, let's go, let's go. You're good. Come on!"

His father was experimenting with a new building concept called fast-tracking, in which the stages of construction were overlapped to save time. Thus Chris and Tony were pouring foundation piers in the middle of the hole even as excavation continued around the edges. Beside the ramp a tread-mounted pneumatic drill drove a long steely tongue into a granite ledge, tearing the stone apart with a quick-time *bang-bang-bang*. Back hoes seized shattered granite, chunks of old cellar walls, and rusty pipes from the former building, and hoisted them into dump trucks, which drove out of the hole on flattened springs. Half a block away, the blasters' whistle blew, the ground shook, and steel mats jumped like startled dogs.

Chris guided the mixer into position and jumped for the chute as the driver climbed down from the cab and started the barrel spinning. The big truck roared; the concrete hissed, tumbling inside, and the stars on the barrel spun in a blur. Chris manhandled the chute over the dark maw of the pier hole, which was bored deep into the bedrock. A wooden frame that rimmed the hole would contain the wet concrete until it set, forming the top pads on which the ironworkers would raise the building's steel columns.

Thirty feet away, Tony was furiously urging his truck to the next pier. "Come back, Rocco. Back her up. Come back, come back. Whoa!"

Chris grinned at his brother's expression as Tony watched Rocco, bull-necked and bullet-headed, descend ponderously, the live ashes of a hangover smoldering dangerously in his eyes. Rocco squinted at the sun, rubbed his temples, belched, and strolled to the back of the truck, where the mixer controls and the pour lever were located. Tony waited, exasperated, and when Rocco paused again to relight his stogie, brushed past him and, goosed the throttle himself.

"Don't strain yourself, speedy."

"Watch the mouth, kid."

"Get off your fat ass if you don't want to hear it. We got schedules."

"Frankie, take over," Chris snapped, breaking into a lithe run.

Rocco reddened to his bristly scalp and lunged for Tony, who had turned his back to nurse the machine. Just as he reached him, he felt an arm drop on his own shoulder, a firm tug, and then Christopher Taglione was walking him away from his truck, asking amiably, "So, Rocco, you getting married or not?"

Rocco looked at the big, rangy kid with the arm wrapped around his shoulder like a length of hoist cable. If he really wanted to dig in, he might have stopped their forward march, but then what? Chris, who had been full-grown since he was fourteen, seemed to have added a few more inches this past year at college.

"You know, one of these days Tony's gonna get his mouth handed to him."

"No," Chris countered, still gripping Rocco's shoulder, still steering him away, still smiling. "He's got *me* to look out for him. That's what brothers are for. Right?"

"Yeah, well, he's gonna pull that shit on the wrong guy when you ain't around and he's gonna get his ass busted."

Hardly a thing about Chris changed, Rocco noticed. His grip was firm, and his smile friendly. Maybe his eyes turned a little gray, though it could have been the way the hot sun crossed them as he faced Rocco with utter conviction.

"If you ever run into that guy, Rocco, tell him for me he's going to have the kind of trouble that never forgets."

Rocco was surprised at how much he believed Chris. He wished he hadn't gotten into this. Somehow, he'd done more than threaten the guy's brother; he had blundered into some private territory where Chris was dangerous.

"Forget it. My head's killing me."

Chris's eyes flashed in the sunlight, bright blue again. "Hey, there's a reason to get married—no more hangovers. I'll have your truck out in a second. Take a break."

Rocco sat down on a form, muttering that if his old man owned the company he'd be at the beach. Chris ran to help Tony with the chute.

"I can fight my own battles, Bro."

"I know you can fight them. Winning them worries me."

"I can take him."

"Oh, yeah, Godzilla? Then who drives the truck? Go!"

Tony scampered to the pour lever and Chris shot him a triumphant grin as twelve cubic yards of cement, broken stone, sand, and water erupted from the mixer. Tony threw him a shovel to speed it along. The concrete rattled down the trough and cascaded fifty feet to Manhattan's core.

"Not bad for college kids."

"Hey, Pop! Hey, look at you. Tony, check out the threads."

Tony peered over the chute. "Goes great with the hardhat."

Mike Taglione dodged a puddle of the spilled concrete that splattered his sons, planted his fists on his hips, and beamed at the pour. He was decked out in his blue "meeting suit," a fine old gabardine whose broad lapels had come back into style around 1970 and was ordinarily unearthed for nothing less than contract signings and permit hearings. Chris spotted a silky new tie, fashionably wide and probably bought by his secretary, who had the hots for him, a ceremonial white hand-kerchief in his breast pocket from the same source, and a whiff of the aftershave lotion dispensed at the Waldorf barber shop. He was even wearing his gold watch; the last time Chris and Tony had seen that had been at their mother's funeral.

"Where the hell are you going?"

Mike Taglione drew an old red handkerchief from its hiding place in his back pocket and pretended to flick the dust off his shoes. "While you college geniuses hump concrete, your dumb hod-carrier old man's been invited to testify before a United States Congressional Housing Committee."

"You been indicted?" Chris said, ducking futilely as his father belted his hardhat with a lightning hand.

"I'll indict you, wise guy. Congressman Costanza called up. Could I *please* catch the first plane to Washington to tell 'em about the new concrete?"

"I guess those contributions paid off," Tony said quietly.

Proud and thrilled for his father, Chris said, "Congratulations," and reached to hug him.

"Hands off the clean suit, you dirty guinea. Jeez, if only Irish could see me now." Irish had been his pet name for their mother, Kathleen Taggart. "I'll be back tomorrow. Arnie's watching the job, so you guys watch Arnie."

"We got it, Pop. Secretary know where you're staying?"

"Yeah, well, uh, Sylvia's gonna fly down with me to . . ."

Chris laughed. "Take notes? It's about time, Pop. Three years."

"Yeah, well, no big deal."

Tony's face clouded and Chris shot him a warning glance. When his brother turned judgmental, as he had now, his dark, intelligent eyes burned beneath his pale high brow as surely and sternly as a Jesuit priest's. "Have a good time." Chris fired a second warning look at Tony, who went along, muttering, "Sure, Pop. Have fun."

Mike grinned and cast a satisfied eye on the bustling foundation site. Suddenly his expression changed. "Here comes that greaseball Rendini."

Chris saw Joey Rendini, a heavyset man in a business suit, standing just inside the gate. He looked about, spotted them, and swaggered down the ramp. Chris knew that Joey Rendini was in the rackets. He controlled a Teamsters local and was connected to the Cirillos, the biggest of the New York Mafia

27

families. He was, as Chris had often heard his father yell, a pig when it came to payoffs, abusing to the hilt the power that the Cirillo connection gave him.

"The greaseball walks like he owns my job." In Mike Taglione's Brooklyn-tuned lexicon, "wops" and "guineas" were fellow countrymen, respectable Italians or Sicilians, but "greaseballs" were the greedy, hard types of any nationality who tried to horn in on legitimate businessmen.

"Until you say no," Tony said, "you'll pay him forever."

Keyed up by his father's anger, and frustrated because he couldn't do anything about it, Chris turned on his brother. "Grow up! A little grease is a sensible investment. It gives people incentive to do a good job."

Tony, who seemed to have inherited their mother's strict Irish-Catholic morals, said flatly, "It's illegal."

"There's a middle ground," Mike Taglione said. "The trouble with Rendini is he's so greedy he turns grease into blackmail."

"No, Pop. It's like Watergate. You're straight or you're crooked. There's no middle."

When his father turned away, Chris leaped to his defense. "That's cool for you, if you're going to be a lawyer. But me and Pop, we gotta face the fact that Rendini can pull the drivers off any job we contract." Alarmed by the angry flush darkening his father's face, he stopped arguing with Tony and said, "Take it easy, Pop."

Rendini picked his way across the beaten earth, grimacing at the dust and splashed cement. He was a darkly handsome man in his thirties, overweight and perspiring freely. Mopping his plump face with his sleeve, he called, "Hey, Mike, we had a meeting."

"Something better came up. What do you want?"

"We gotta talk." The mobster glanced at Chris and Tony. Chris gave him a cold nod, but Tony glared.

Mike Taglione addressed Rocco, who was hosing his chute. "Get that truck out of here." He waited, silent, while Rocco hastily coiled his hose and drove away. "Okay. Talk. My boys and me got no secrets. Chris is going to work with me when he's done with college, and Tony's going to be my lawyer."

"Yeah, well, this wildcat strike looks like it's heating up."

"Spell that another payoff?"

"Spell it how you like, Mike. You know the rules."

Mike Taglione shook his head. "Rules change. This time it's *my* building. Thirty years I been pouring foundations, and general contracting. But this time I'm the developer, and this job is all Taglione from the doorknobs in the crapper to the peastone on the roof."

"Mike, what are you busting my balls for? So you're moving up in the world. Congratulations."

"You know where I'm going right now? I'm going to the United States House of Representatives in Washington, D.C."

"So?"

"So I think I earned the right to say 'Go fuck yourself.'"

"Don't be dumb, Mike. I don't know if I can control my drivers."

"Rendini, if you tell the poor bastards to squat, all they can ask is what color."

"My drivers—"

"Hold it! They're *your* union members, 'cause they got no choice, but they're *my* drivers."

Rendini shrugged. "I don't care if you're going to Washington. I don't care if you're eating supper with President Gerald T. Fucking Ford. You know the rules. You wanna play, you pay."

Chris shot a glance at Tony, who was regarding Rendini with open hatred, apparently unaware their father was rising onto the balls of his feet, telegraphing his sometimes violent temper. Yet his voice stayed calm, so detached that Chris wondered if he had somehow convinced himself that he had finally risen above the dirty side of the business. "You pull one driver off my job and I'm going straight to the U.S. Attorney."

"You nuts?" Rendini blurted.

Chris was dumbfounded. The New York cement business was a collusive industry, with bidding often controlled by the few outfits that ran it. Quality material got delivered on time, but the U.S. Attorney had more than once expressed the government's interest in how they had arrived at the price; whoever visited his office for a frank talk stood a chance of leaving in handcuffs.

"You nuts?" Rendini repeated, his mouth agape, and Chris wondered what in hell his father had in mind.

Mike Taglione laughed, suddenly enjoying himself, and grinned at Tony. "Maybe I'll take the advice of number one son here and ask for immunity. Maybe I'll answer every question the U.S. Attorney can think up."

Tony clapped him on the back, leaving a gray handprint. "Nice going, Pop."

Frightened, Chris cautioned, "Pop—"

Rendini cut him off with quiet menace. "While you're there, Mike, ask for protection. You and your kids might need it."

His father threw a lightning right cross, faster than the eye. Chris barely sensed a blur before he heard the impact. Rendini flew backward and landed flat in the mud, blood spouting from his nose. Mike Taglione advanced, his balled fists floating like wire springs. *Get off my job."

Men came running. Chris and Tony moved shoulder to shoulder, Chris in the boxer's crouch his father had taught him and Tony seizing a length of reinforcing rod. But by then it was over. A driver, one of Rendini's clique, helped the union man up, and he staggered away, holding his sleeve to his face. Taglione watched, rubbing his hand, until they disappeared behind the street fence at the top of the ramp.

Chris said, "That wasn't too bright," and Tony said, "Pop, I didn't mean to push you into—"

"Nobody pushed me. Rendini got what he deserved. Should have done it years ago." He looked at the men who had gathered. "All right, fellas. Show's over."

"Pop?" Tony looked awed. "Where'd you learn to punch like that?"

Mike Taglione gave Chris a wink that warmed his heart in the hard years to come, and explained gently, "Nobody *gave* me the concrete business, Tony." Then he laughed, and the laugh stayed with Chris a long time, like an echo in an empty room. "I must be getting old, I hurt my hand." He fanned it in the air and sucked a knuckle. "Shit, hurts like a son of bitch. Hey, what's wrong with you?"

Chris said, "Why don't we ride out to the airport with you?"

"Bodyguard? That's all I need." This time he winked at Tony. "You hit some hood with *that* fist and Tony'll spend his law career defending you from a murder rap. No. I'm paying you guys to pour concrete. Back to work."

"Pop. Please."

"I'll be fine. Take care, both of you. Go home together. Take a couple of your buddies with you. This'll blow over. I'll get Congressman Costanza to talk to some people. Don't worry about it. Okay?"

He pulled out his watch and started across the excavation with his head held high and shoulders thrust forward like an adventurous bull.

"Look at him," said Chris. "Looks like he just got laid."

Mike Taglione turned and waved at the bottom of the ramp. Then he cupped his hands and yelled over the clatter of the pneumatic rock drill. "Keep an eye on Arnie. Takes him one day to throw a job off a week."

A mixer rounded the turn and started down quickly.

"Where the hell's he going?" Chris said. "Pop! *Move!*"

Freewheeling, with brakes and engine silent, the concrete mixer hurtled down the ramp, pushed by its tremendous load to twenty miles an hour in the short space between the street and the rock drill at the bottom.

"Pop!"

Chris raced toward him, shouting and waving his arms. Mike Taglione whirled, saw the danger. His reflexes were superb. He gathered his legs, pivoted and jumped in an astonishing liquid motion. Chris thought his father had made it, and had he been wearing his regular workboots instead of what he called "cab-catching shoes," he would have escaped. But the smooth soles skidded on the earthen ramp and he stumbled. The trunk's bumper slammed into his chest. His head snapped back and his hardhat disappeared under the wheels with a loud crack.

He fell to the dirt, rolled a short distance, and reached to ward Chris, who was running full tilt. Chris seized his outstretched hand. They locked fingers, as he reversed his headlong plunge, dug his heels in, and pulled. He felt the shocks reverberate through their straining arms as the truck ground his father's body beneath its wheels.

Chapter 2

THROUGH THE LONG burial Mass, Christopher Taglione fixed his eye on a stained-glass window his mother had contributed to her church. It was fashioned after Giotto's "Lamentation Over Christ"; weeping disciples and angels hovering in a stone-blue sky mourned a naked, bleeding Jesus. Before his father's murder, Chris thought the window looked a little silly with its gaudy stigma. Now, it seemed false. None of the haloed mourners looked angry. Where was their rage? His own fury was gorging his throat.

The sun came out as the priest droned on, streamed through the window, and laid a cold blue shroud over their father's casket. The two halves of the family sat separately, as at a wedding—Italian construction workers and Irish cops. All the Tagliones were on the left. On the right were the Taggarts, led by Uncle Eamon in the dress uniform of a police captain.

Chris could hardly breathe. His anger burned like a hungry fire, shooting jagged heat-bolts that attacked the air itself in a ruthless search for fuel. He hated this church. His anger struck during the homily. When the Irish priest mispronounced their name Taglion*ee*, Chris felt Tony stir beside him. Then he compounded the insult by remarking that Mike Taglion*ee* had died cruelly in his prime.

"Mike Taglione didn't die," Chris retorted in the front pew. "He didn't *die*. He was murdered."

A woman screamed, their Aunt Marie, who heaved her grief like something palpable caught in her body. Her cry unleashed a storm of bereavement and Mike's sisters shrieking the family's loss, for death to these women was a thief. Their men sat silent, as they had been expected to sit for centuries, their faces like dark stone, and hearts bound against the whims of a capricious Nature.

An old man glanced curiously at Chris and Tony, for in his vanished world the sons sought vengeance. He hardly expected a vendetta in America in 1976, and certainly not from college students, but old ideas lived in his memory as the ancient perfume of Sicily's dry soil and hot sun lingered in his nostrils.

Chris looked across the aisle at Eamon Taggart, his mother's brother. He was a broad-shouldered, handsome Irishman with salt-and-pepper hair, pale blue eyes, and the noncommittal gaze of a man who knew how to get along. Uncle Eamon nodded back, which Chris interpreted as Eamon's promise that Mike Taglione had friends among the cops who would not take his murder lightly.

They carried Mike's casket—Chris, Tony, Uncle Eamon, Uncle Vinnie, Arnie Markowitz, and Mike's brothers, Uncle Pete, Uncle Johnny, Uncle Tom—to a grave beside his wife's in the churchyard. Only a block from Queens Boulevard, the cemetery was sheltered by the church, a brick rectory, and a high wall of reddish stone—a quiet place that seemed to be miles away from the city. Chris took Tony's hand and felt him trembling. Except for a clear report to the police, his brother had been virtually silent since the killing. Yet he joined the Hail Marys and Our Fathers with a strong voice as they lowered Mike's casket into the ground.

Uncle Vinnie, Mike's favorite brother-in-law, rode home with Chris and Tony in the lead car. At times Mike's rival, often his partner, he was a prosperously fat man and the most "Italian-Italian" of the family. He had stayed the longest in his old neighborhood, in a Little Italy railroad flat, years after the others had left Brooklyn and lower Manhattan for the comforts of detached houses in Queens and nearby Long Island. Chris had always looked to him for a tenuous link with an ethnic past which was more vivid in the movies than in his parents' house. His jowly face looked doughy.

Outside the house the street was filling up with the businessmen's late-model Lincolns and Cadillacs, and the civil servants' old Chevies and Plymouths. The feast would be a huge gathering and Chris didn't think he could handle it yet. "Tony, cover for me, okay?"

"Where you going?"

"The job."

Uncle Vinnie said, "You shouldn't, Chris. Everybody's coming."

"It's okay, Uncle Vinnie," Tony said. "We'll cover."

He thought that the rock drills, the dozers and backhoes in action, and the endless line of churning mixers might make his father seem less dead, and his departure, as Father Frye had euphemized it, less final. But when he arrived at the job he realized why Uncle Vinnie had tried to stop him. The hole was deserted.

Chris ran from the limousine. Inside the ramp gate he found a guard and Arnie Markowitz, his father's long-time project manager, who had come directly from the funeral and stood now on the ramp, gazing sadly at the raw mud where Chris's father had choked out his life. There was a deathly stillness about the excavation which even the drone of mid-Manhattan could not penetrate.

"What happened?"

"The bank pulled out."

"What the hell for?"

"Your pop ran a one-man show. What's Taglione Concrete and Construction without Mike Taglione?"

"Me. I'm here. Me and Tony."

"Tony's going back to school. And you should too. Hey! Where you going?"

Chris spun on his heel, his barely controlled rage suddenly directed at a specific target. "To the goddamned bank. I'm going to finish my father's building."

"Forget it. The bank doesn't know you. They'll make you fill out forms." Arnie seized his arm. "Why don't you talk to your Pop's friends? He's owed a lot of favors. Come on, we'll go to your house and eat."

Chris stood stiffly atop the ramp.

"Come on, Chris."

"Get in the car. I'll be with you in a minute. I want to be alone a second." Arnie walked toward the car and Chris looked at the silent machines. A man in a business suit approached from the sidewalk. "I just want to say I'm sorry about your father, Chris. We talked when he was trying to get his building started. If you have any problems give me a ring. Maybe I can help." He handed him his card.

"Like what?"

"I heard about the bank. I can set you up with a short-term bridge loan till you wrap up your regular financing."

"How much?"

"Short term runs about twenty-four percent. But I'd need a fella to sit in and keep an eye on things."

"Fuck you."

He turned his back—it was that or hit the guy—and slammed the door of the limousine with an eerie sensation of reliving his father's early days when Mike Taglione had forged his iron rules of survival. No loan sharks. No silent partners. "You believe that guy?" he asked Arnie. "Fucking shylock hits on me the day of the funeral?"

"He's a criminal. You want nice manners?"

Lambs' heads made the funeral feast. In the morning Uncle Vinnie had brought the cloven skulls from the Manhattan markets, wrapped in newspaper; now, hot and savory, they steamed on the sideboard with bowls of tripe and macaroni. So many leaves had been inserted in the dining table to accommodate the mourners that the lower end thrust into the living room, where a second crowd were balancing plates on their laps. The house was hot and alive with the babble of talk his father had loved.

Chris's Uncle Pete, a teacher, greeted him tearfully. "There are some guys make you feel you're part of something big. When they go, you wonder what it's all about."

Chris wondered which of the men hunched over their plates could help get credit for the job. Their bond with Mike was strong. Other uncles spied him, kissed his cheeks, and led him to the head of the table. Tony, ignoring a full plate and deaf to the blandishments of his aunts, was deep in conversation with Uncle Eamon. The police captain jumped up as if relieved by the interruption and said, "There you are, boy. Take my chair."

The women brought Chris a plate. Uncle Eamon flinched

from the *contadino* food and retreated to the bar, a table of bottles in the living room, leaving Chris and Tony in the care of Uncle Vinnie, who squeezed between the brothers with a refill.

"Eat."

Chris took a bite, couldn't swallow, and pushed his plate away. "The fucking bank shut us down."

"It figures."

"What should I do?"

"That's a tough one, Chris."

"Can you help me get money?"

"Black money."

"Pop always said no shylocks. I already told this one to get lost." He showed Vinnie the loan shark's business card. "Know him?"

"Shit, yes. He's a Cirillo shylock."

"He said he knew Pop."

"He knew *Pop?*" asked Tony.

Uncle Vinnie said, "You know how it is. Mob guys cozy up to legit businessmen." He glanced around and lowered his voice. "They know they're shit; they want someone important to tell 'em they're not. But don't forget, they also want a piece of your action. A couple of years ago, when you father was putting the Manhattan building together, everywhere he went this guy showed up with a big smile."

"What did Pop do?" Tony asked.

"What could he do? As nice as he could, he ignored him. You don't want a guy like that thinking you insulted him. He probably bought your father a drink and now he goes around saying they're buddies. You were right to stay away from him."

"I guess so, but I still have to raise the money."

"You sure you want to get involved at all? You're going to have your hands full with the cement, unless you want to consolidate the cement. Why don't you come in with me?"

Chris caught the flash in Tony's eyes. His brother knew shit about the business, but he was sharp enough to warn him that Uncle Vinnie's offer, part *famiglia*—looking out for family interests—was also the sort of sharp, cold act practiced by survivors in the New York cement business.

"If I don't finish Pop's building," Chris said, "the grease-balls win."

"There will always be wiseguys," said Uncle Vinnie.

"Not always," said Tony.

"The rackets have been around a long time," Uncle Vinnie retorted sternly. He chewed a forkful of tripe and said to Chris, "Aren't you going to finish college?"

"Fuck college. You think I'm going to study business so I can get a job working for somebody else? We already got a business. I'm a lucky guy. My pop built a business." His eyes filled and Uncle Vinnie looked away.

"Let me talk to some guys."

Later he led Chris into the living room, where a gray-haired patrician banker was waiting with Arnie. Both the banker and the Taglione project manager looked uncomfortable. "This is Pete Stock, Chris. He's a real estate officer at the bank."

"We've met. Thanks for coming today, Mr. Stock."

"Of course I came. I've dealt for years with your father on his Queens projects. I'm sorry that the bank had to withdraw credit on the big building."

"I want to finish my father's building."

Stock shook his head. "Chris, you're plunging head first into a deeply troubled market. Manhattan's getting overbuilt."

"We're preleased. And Aetna's pledged to buy it in two years."

"That's fine for Aetna. They don't risk a dime until you've finished the building and actually filled it with tenants."

"But we're preleased. We've got tenants."

"You've got tenants *signed*, which is how your father got Aetna. But you still have to get them in. So, in other words, the bank is taking the risk on your performance—*your* ability, now that your father is gone, to meet schedules and contain costs and control labor. It's a big job for a college student."

"I can do it. I've worked with my father since I was fourteen. We had big plans to move Taglione Construction into Manhattan development."

Stock swished the ice in his drink. "Chris, Manhattan real estate is even tighter than the cement business. It's been controlled by a handful of developers for decades. Men who can walk down Fifth Avenue, or Second Avenue, or Eighth Avenue, and tell you the history of every building on the street, from the day the land was assembled to who built it, financed it, bought and sold it, leased it, renovated it, and tore it down and built a new one. . . . I hope you understand that I'm trying every way I know to discourage you."

"We were going to be guys like that. . . . Can you give me credit?"

"We'll bring in a man to run the job."

"*No.* Then it's not our job. No way. I can do it. My father must have told you he was going to make me a partner."

"At least fifty times." Stock looked pained. "Listen, your father's friends are leaning hard on me, very hard. But if you insist on going alone—"

"I do."

"Then the best I can do is persuade the bank to extend interim financing for two months. If you haven't performed by then, it's all over."

"I can do it."

"But you have to agree to put the trucks up as collateral—"

"The trucks?" Chris echoed, dismayed. "We've already put up all our property."

Stock sighed, clearly uncomfortable with his own terms. "That's what my superiors will demand. I'm sorry. If you still feel this way Monday, come by the office and we'll do the paperwork. But at this point I want you to listen to your father's project manager."

"Don't do it," said Arnie. "Without the trucks you got nothing."

"Yeah, I know, but—"

"Your father's trucks. That's all you got."

In his mind Chris saw them parked in rows at their East River plant, astonishing in their number. By the time he had been old enough to count there had been enough to be called the fleet. "I have to think, Mr. Stock."

"That's precisely what I want you to do. Goodbye. Good luck. And again, I'm so sorry we've lost your father."

"I'll walk you out," said Arnie.

Chris stood where he was, his mind reeling.

A tiny old man tugged his sleeve. He looked down at Alphonse Castellone, who gave him a toothless grin. "Leesa trucks."

Alphonse Castellone was unbelievably old, totally uneducated, and as primitive as a Sicilian cowherd. But he had pioneered heavy-equipment rental in New York and was very rich because of it, which Chris and everyone else in the room respected mightily. Already his aunts and uncles were watching with relief and pleasure the private conversation of the grieving son and the wise elder.

"They're my father's trucks, Alphonse."

Alphonse replied with the bluntness of age, "Your pop was the last dummy in the city to own equipment. So what you lose your trucks? I buy 'em from the bank and leesa back. I leesa ya anything. I leesa shovel, I leesa grader. I leesa whole goddam tower crane. But I canna leesa *contacts*. I canna leesa smarts.

"Sellin' cement is knowin' who's who and what's what. You already got that from your pop." He looked around the living room, nodded at the people watching respectfully, and said, "Fuck the trucks."

Chris felt his lips part in his first smile in three days. The old man was right. Arnie had utterly no understanding that his father's contacts were the real value of Taglione Concrete. Alphonse patted his arm. "You did a good funeral. Your father woulda liked it. It's over now. Go do some business."

Chris tore after Stock and cornered him in the foyer. They talked over the details for a few minutes and the banker reluctantly honored his offer. Then Stock left amid a general exodus of business associates and friends. Shortly, the family too began to trickle away, the few Irish first, Italian cousins next, and finally teary aunts and sad-faced uncles. The women instructed Chris how to heat up the food they had left in the refrigerator, and the men clasped the young brothers in their arms.

Uncle Vinnie was the last to leave. He sent Aunt Marie ahead to the car, which was parked down the short front walk at the curb. "You need anything, anything at all, you telephone. I'll stop by the job Monday, Chris."

"I'll be at the bank."

"So I'll walk you over. See you early. Hey, Tony. You call if you need me, right?"

"Thanks, Uncle Vinnie."

Chris stood with Tony in the front door, holding each moment like a heartbeat. Uncle Vinnie gripped the iron railing as he climbed down the front step. His shoes clicked on the walk. The street was quiet but for night bugs humming in the trees; the sidewalk was softly lit by street lamps which cast dull pools of light filtered by the leaves. Far off a highway murmured like a river.

Uncle Vinnie's Cadillac settled deeply on its springs. His door thunked shut, blacking the courtesy lights which had shined briefly on Aunt Marie's unhappy face. He started the engine and turned on the headlights. The power steering whined as he slowly pulled away and around the corner, the taillights blinking through the neighbor's privet hedge. Tony turned into the house and Chris followed, holding the door open a moment longer before he closed it.

They were alone.

"Look how they cleaned up. Like nobody was here."

"Aunt Marie had the vacuum going."

They stood looking around the empty living room, then at each other. "Want a drink?"

"Yeah."

Tony poured Johnny Walker Black at the table set up as a bar. The ice bucket, a gold plastic container made to look like a barrel, was empty. They headed for the kitchen. The big refrigerator icemaker was empty, and the crushed-ice dispenser in the door was out of ice as well. Chris found an old tray in the freezer. He smacked the shrunken cubes out in the sink, filled their glasses with a handful, and headed for the living room.

"Want to go downstairs?"

Downstairs was a wood-paneled family room where, since their mother died, they usually ate supper on trays, watching the TV news with their father. Tony started to turn off the living-room lights.

"Leave it, man."

Chris settled on a puffed couch, beige like the carpet and

covered in a shiny cloth. This had been their mother's room, her special place for special events. It had a big glass coffee table, couches, and chairs flanked by enormous lamps. Shortly before she died, she had hung a picture of the Pope over the fireplace.

Before the cancer, she had enjoyed giving parties, and their father had knocked out a wall so the living room elled into the dining room, like a suburban house. Her grand piano filled the other end; it had been unplayed for years, although Tony had once taken lessons. The polished brown top was down and on it stood a realistic model of the Fifty-sixth Street building as it would look nearing the end of construction; the lower floors were sheathed in soft green glass and most of the steel frame was erected. On top was a little derrick hoisting a steel beam from a miniature truck with "Taglione" written on the side.

"Remember when he got the model?"

"That was one smart architect. That toy gave him Pop's business for life. . . ."

They sat silently, looking around the room.

"Life," Tony repeated bitterly. "We said dumb things like that when Mom died too."

Chris said, "You know what I never got until now? He protected us when she died. When did *he* cry?"

"Ask Sylvia."

"Get off it, man. That just started."

"Chris, you are so fucking naive. Pop was balling her for years."

"No way," Chris retorted firmly. "She had a guy until after Mom died. She told me once. They were both lonely."

Tony softened abruptly. "Hell, she's a good-looking woman. Pop was lucky to find her."

"Speaking of good-looking, did you check out Cousin Mary Jane?"

Tony grinned. "I wanted to jump on her right in the church. Remember when we met her at Uncle Eamon's the first time? What was she, six? I was eight. You were six? We had the most incredible fight in the car on the way home."

"Pop called us horny bastards. I thought Mom would croak. . . . Shit, now I'm saying it."

"Remember when he caught us at Uncle Vinnie's?"

42

"Everybody at the kitchen table eating spaghetti."

"Except us in the front room with what's-her-name."

"I don't think he ever told Mom."

Chris went to the piano and reached behind the model for a picture in a tarnished silver frame. "Mom when she met Pop. Is that Mary Jane today?"

Tony took the frame and studied her picture. "The Mick side is dynamite."

"Tagliones aren't bad. You notice Lucille?"

"The *elephant?*"

"No. Not Uncle Vinnie's Lucille. *Little* Lucille Taglione." Every branch of the Tagliones had a Lucille, named for their great-grandmother, a mythic figure from the old country who had died a year ago at age one hundred. Little Lucille belonged to Uncle Pete.

"What are you robbing, cradles? She's fifteen."

"I'm not saying *jump* on her, but in a couple years she's going to melt some eyeballs."

"A little bottom-heavy."

"Baby fat. It goes away when they have sex."

"It does?" Tony looked at him. "Oh, bullshit. Christ, you had me believing you."

"Remember the time you asked Pop if it was true when I told you that dragonflies fuck flying?"

"He belted me for saying 'fuck'—"

"For an older brother you were pretty dumb."

"I didn't now how else to say it. Then he came out to the pond with us. Remember?"

That was upstate in the Catskills, where they spent summers with their mother. Mike drove up on weekends; Chris and Tony would lead him barefoot and sinking in the wet grass around the pond Saturday mornings to show him the frog eggs, snakes, and baby fish they had discovered during the week. Chris remembered the water squelching around his father's toes, the way he rolled up his pants and how white were his feet and legs, while theirs were brown from playing in the sun.

Tony threw his head back and gazed at the ceiling as if he were seeing the mountain sky. "Dragonflies swooping together twosies and threesies, really getting it on, laying eggs in the water and having a fine time. Pop watched about ten minutes, not saying a word. Finally he looked at you—real serious, his eyebrows got thick—looked at you, looked at me, and he said, 'They're dancing.'"

"When he walked back to the house we heard Mom laughing. God, I wish . . ."

"What did Uncle Vinnie say about the building?"

"He set me up with a guy at the bank. They want the trucks for collateral."

Tony shrugged. "You going to?"

"Would you come in with me?"

"I'm going to law school."

Chris wandered back to the piano and stared at the model of his father's building. He twined his fingers through the threads that represented derrick guys, the cables that supported the derrick mast. The model builder was a nut for detail, right down to the spider, the round fitting atop the mast where the guy lines converged.

The funeral day began rushing though his memory—the window, the priest he didn't like, the shylock, and the stilled machines. His hand clutched and snapped a cable. He put down his glass and tried to tie it. But his fingers were clumsy from the scotch and trembling from his exhaustion, and he snapped another. The mast started to lean; before he could stop it, it snapped a third thread, of its own weight.

"What are you doing to Pop's model?"

"Nothing." Chris gave up and released a fourth and fifth cable and laid the derrick gently on its side, resolving to repair it when he was sober. "What did Uncle Eamon say?"

"They're investigating."

"That's what the cops tell strangers."

"He'll stay on it."

"I wish I had stopped Pop! I saw he was mad. I should have pulled him back. I could have stepped between them."

"It was too late. It was over in a second."

"I didn't think."

Tony crossed the room and removed Chris's hand from the model. "Pop was too fast. I didn't even see that punch. Did you?"

"I saw him go up on his feet. I should of known when I saw him go up on his feet. He was so fucking fast."

"I wish he had taught me to box," Tony said sadly. "He'd always say I was too light, wait till I got bigger. Said he was afraid he'd hurt me. He never taught me. You were younger and he taught you."

"I had the weight," Chris said lamely. "He knew if he slipped that I could take a punch."

"He waited too long."

"What are we going to do about Rendini?"

"What do you mean?"

"He killed Pop."

"I told you, Uncle Eamon—"

"Aren't sons suppose to avenge their fathers?"

"Avenge?" Tony looked at him like he was nuts. "Sons sleeping in sheep shit in Sicily, maybe. Not Americans."

His brother's hand fell away from his and Chris suddenly felt so alone that he started to cry. "I should have stopped him."

"You couldn't."

"If I'd moved a second sooner I'd have pulled him away from the truck."

"You got there ahead of me."

Chris shuddered. He could still feel his father's grip go dead in his hand.

Tony said, "I'm going to bed."

"Oh, stay up, man."

"I can't. I'm crashing."

Chris watched his brother ascend the stairs; Tony was self-contained, a small, tight package, like a sealed, permanently lubricated electric motor humming along forever. Chris laughed. Tony turned. "What?"

"The last thing Pop said was to take care of you."

"Hey, Bro? He said the same thing to me about you. Good night."

"How soon before you have to leave for school?"

"I'm leaving the job tomorrow."

"*What?* I thought you had two months."

"Congressman Costanza stopped by before you got back."

"He did? Hey, that's really nice of him."

"He said he was sorry he couldn't make the Mass, asked about you, said all the right things. Anyway, I hit him up for a job."

"Doing what? Hey, I need you this summer at least."

"He's recommending me for a student internship in the criminal division of the U.S. Attorney's office. I'm going over tomorrow for an interview."

"Tomorrow's Saturday."

"They don't punch a time clock. I'm sorry about the timing, Chris. It's a great shot for me. If I get in there now, I'll have a leg up when I graduate."

"But you were going to be Pop's lawyer. Not some Fed's."

"That was Pop's idea, not mine. Good night."

"Jesus Christ, Tony. We always thought—"

"You always thought and *he* always thought. Nobody asked me."

"It's our company. Pop made it into something big."

"I don't care about making money. I want to serve."

"Serve? Serving fucking who? Serve us."

"I'm going to serve the law. I want to be part of it. Not just dodge around it."

"I don't believe you. You sound like a goddamned priest."

"Chris, I'm sorry. This is a fight I was supposed to have with Pop two years from now. Good night."

Stunned, Chris got up and took a slug of scotch from the bottle. It burned going down. He tipped the bottle again, but he knew he wasn't going to get any higher tonight. Just a headache in the morning. He turned out the lights and climbed the stairs. Tony's door was closed. Chris had left his bed unmade but an aunt had made it. He flopped on top of it and stared at the ceiling. He got up and went down the hall and looked at his parents' bed. Then he took a shower and climbed into bed.

He lay awake in the dark and for some reason thought of Greenpoint—their taste of the street the end of his junior year of high school, a few months after their mother had died. They had started hanging out with a group who had an apartment in Greenpoint—a "crash pad" in the dated parlance of the middle-class American hippie drug scene that had finally seeped down to the Italians and Irish of Queens, even as the originals were getting haircuts and going back to school. Grass and acid and 'ludes fueled the scene, coke or the Procaine mixes that passed for it, and whispers of heroin nearby; couples joined, split, realigned, like the dragonflies. Chris and Tony, fleeing their mother's death, had plunged into the free-and-easy difference of it all, the obliteration of time, and the dull kick of working angles dealing dope.

It hadn't taken their widowed father long to realize something was wrong. His reaction had been typical Mike Taglione. He had driven to Greenpoint early one morning and collared his sons, who had crashed on a mattress with a girl from the Bronx. "You want to get high? I'll make you high." Clamping a big hand around each neck, he marched them down the stairs, tossed them into the Lincoln, drove to Wall Street, where one of his friends was superintendent on a sixty-story tower. He pulled tools and gear from his trunk, shiny new stuff, straight from the supplier.

"Here's your hardhat, spud wrench, bolt bag, gloves, and shoes. Put 'em on." He handed his friend papers from the Ironworkers' Union. "Here's their tickets. This guy's your boss. I'll pick you up at quitting time."

"Hey, Pop," Tony protested.

"You want to go college, you're going to pay for it. You can see your friends on the weekend. Meanwhile, a lot of people did a favor for this. Don't make me look like an asshole."

Chris, too, started to resist, until he was stunned to see fear on his father's face—it flickered in his eyes and made his jaw work. The special bond they had always shared helped him understand that tough Mike Taglione was alone and helpless, and was desperately trying the only thing he knew how. Chris told Tony to shut up.

The super pointed at a spot five hundred feet in the sky. "Dougherty's your pusher. Boss of the raising gang. Grab a keg of bolts on your way up."

The keg weighed two hundred pounds. They manhandled it to the top, where Dougherty, a grizzled veteran of thirty-five, and some six inches taller than Chris, put them to work carrying small beams for the detail crew. It had been a turning point, forging a new family out of the lost sheep "Irish" Kathleen Taggart Taglione had left alone. They got hooked on the macho work, and by the end of the summer were bulging with muscle and had been promoted to bolter-ups, installing the final bolts where headers and columns joined over the city. Next summer they had advanced to connecting the girders. Only this year they had come back to the concrete to pour foundations because it was their father's special building.

And in Greenpoint, Chris thought, as he drifted off, most of the kids they'd hung out with were still hanging out. A few had overdosed, and one had gotten shot while making a buy in Harlem.

He was asleep when the phone rang. He came up groggy, felt around on the floor, found it under his extra pillow. The luminous clock said three.

"Chris?"

"Yeah?"

"Uncle Eamon. You awake?"

"What's the matter?"

"I had to call you before you read it in the paper."

Chris sat up. "What happened?"

"We found the driver in a garbage can."

"Dead?"

"What do you think?"

"What about Rendini? He's the one who told the driver to do it."

"He didn't tell him in front of witnesses. So with the driver dead, the scum bag is scot-free."

Eamon Taggart and Mike Taglione had met in Korea; after the war, Eamon had introduced Mike to his sister. In the sheer ignorance of his bigotry, he had never dreamed that the tall, blond Kathleen could be attracted to his dark, barrel-chested Italian war buddy, and he had been stunned, even betrayed, when Mike and "Irish" married. But they had stayed friends of a sort, and when she died, it was Eamon who brought a bottle and sat with Mike through the night.

Now he perched on the edge of their father's chair with his captain's cap on his knees, and tried to explain why the police couldn't arrest Mike Taglione's killer. Tony listened silently. Chris hammered him with questions he could not answer.

"How can you believe that driver lost his air brakes?"

"The driver said he did. By the time we got to the truck, they weren't working."

"There were fifty men hanging around that truck! Rendini's people had time to mess up the lines."

"*You* know that. *I* know that. But we can't *prove* it."

"But the driver was one of Rendini's hoods. Didn't you say he had a record?"

"He's *dead*. We can't offer immunity to a dead man. I wish I could say we'll bring Rendini to trial. But we won't. We can't, as much as we want to. But it'll be a long while before they hit you for another payoff, I guarantee it."

"But Rendini had the motive to kill my father."

Uncle Eamon sighed. "Chris, just between you, me, and Tony, Rendini didn't likely act on his own. A Cirillo crew leader might have been waiting in the car. He might have okayed killing your father. But I'll bet even he called upstairs to an underboss on the mobile phone."

"The Cirillos gave orders to kill my father on the *CB radio?*"

"They don't come right out and say it."

"I can't believe they'd say it on the radio," Chris protested, fighting the idea that the murder went above Rendini. It was too complicated. How many names and faces could he hate?

"Chris. They talk carefully." Chris glared stubbornly and Eamon sighed again. "Look, when your pop and your Uncle Vinnie get together to sell cement, do they—*did* they—come right out and say, 'I'll bid so and so and you bid such and such less?' No. They talk around it."

Chris started to protest the slur. Eamon ignored him. "Same thing here," he continued blandly. "You know what I'm saying. Take my word for it—Rendini's just one little link in a long, long chain. You wouldn't believe the command charts the organized-crime squad has drawn. They look exactly like a corporation's."

"Show us," Tony said.

"Beg pardon?"

"Let's see them."

Eamon drove them to One Police Plaza.

The Mafia's command charts drawn by the Organized

Crime Control Bureau were draped on easels like architectural renderings. Chris recalled how his father had practically danced with anticipation at the first plans presentation for his Manhattan tower. A young, heavyset detective was waiting for Eamon.

"This guy knows more than anybody, right, Jack? Jack Warner, my nephews Tony and Chris Taglione. Show 'em what you do here."

"Yes, Captain." Warner did not mention their father, but it was clear by the chart he chose to illustrate that he knew what had happened. "Here's the Cirillos, the biggest of the New York families. The family Joey Rendini answers to. Rendini is here, pretty high up 'cause that union local is a real money earner. I'm pretty sure he's a soldier, a "made" guy, but maybe just an associate. These guys here are what they used to call *capos;* the young ones call 'em crew leaders. Above 'em are underbosses. This Salvatore Ponte, called Sally Smarts, is *consigliere,* counselor to the boss himself, old man Cirillo. 'Don Richard,' he calls himself, but he used to be just 'Little Richie,' 'cause he's a runt."

"Who are these two?" Tony pointed at blocks beside Don Richard.

"Michael, 'Crazy Mikey,' is Don Richard's younger son and chief enforcer. He acts as his father's personal, private hitter. Crazy Mikey loves his work. Wears a little coke spoon around his neck shaped like a sawed-off shotgun—sort of his badge of office. Nicholas is his older brother—the one with the brains. They're Don Richard's heirs. When he retires, they inherit, *if* they can hold off the underbosses. But you gotta remember the chart's only about half right."

"Why?"

Uncle Eamon said, "You're part Italian. You know how tight your families are. How do we infiltrate? Even using Italian cops is tough. Everybody knows who everybody is. It goes back to the old neighborhoods."

"It sounds like you're saying we're criminals because we're Italian, Eamon," Chris interrupted. This was nothing new from the Irish side of the family; nor, he wanted Eamon to know, had he missed the sideswipe about bid rigging.

"Your people are tight," Eamon continued blandly. "They

know who went to jail, who went into the service, who went to college, who stayed home, who joined the Force. Isn't that right, Jack?"

Chris noted that Jack Warner tactfully dodged Eamon's question. "Also, the balance of power is constantly changing. When we do infiltrate, or persuade an informant, we often find we've connected with people who've already been edged out of power. The Cirillos are getting stronger and stronger with alliances and takeovers."

When a telephone rang, Warner answered, excused himself, and left the room quickly.

Uncle Eamon said, "It's a long chain. And tough for the law to break."

"The law sucks."

"Often," Eamon agreed.

"I'd like to kill them with my own hands."

"That's a normal reaction."

"I mean it. I feel like sawing the barrels off a shotgun—"

"I'll not hear that talk, Chris."

Chris's mind leaped to an old untraceable weapon he had bought at a country tag sale. His father's workbench at their Catskill cabin had a heavy vise; hacksaw the barrels, throw away the blades, vacuum the metal filings, dump the vacuum bag . . . He looked his uncle in the eye and made what he knew was the most careful decision of his life. "Sorry, Eamon. I just feel so angry."

"Revenge is a normal desire. Of course, you want to get even."

Tony had been studying the chart intently, tracing names with his finger. "That's precisely the same stupid thing Rendini did," he said. "Instead of suing Pop for a punch in the nose."

"What?" At this new resistance from another quarter—his own brother—Chris felt himself starting to lose control again, felt rage searing his throat.

"Revenge is crazy," Tony replied coolly. "That's what courts are for. The law is the only civilized way to get even."

Chris spewed the rage at his brother. "Didn't you hear Uncle Eamon say the law can't touch them?"

"It's practical, too. Not just civilized. If you take revenge on a killer, the killer's friends will take revenge on you, and back and forth and back and forth. But when the *law* catches a killer, the whole bloody chain is broken."

"You sound like a fucking textbook. Jesus Christ, Tony, I'm talking about *Pop*."

"So am I."

Uncle Eamon said, "Tony's right. You go ahead. You live, you forget."

"I'll never forget." The brothers locked eyes, the gray-blue and the dark in somber harmony. They had spoken as one.

He put up the trucks as collateral for a sixty-day bank note. But even as he signed the paper on Pete Stock's desk, he saw the future in a terrible instant—even if he could finish his father's building, he would never lose his rage.

The bank advanced him two million dollars to bring men and suppliers back to the job. The final construction cost required over twenty million. A brief respite, but the sharks smelled blood in the water. A second Cirillo shylock called with the same offer of short-term money at 24 percent.

The accountant who was steering Taglione Concrete and Construction over the mud flats of probate joined with Arnie to advise that he abandon the project. "You want I should tell you something, Chris? Your *father* shouldn't have gone into that fucking building. There's another recession coming, and we're still not out of the last one. Real estate's dead."

"Real estate goes up and down in cycles."

"Three blocks away that turkey on Fifty-seventh Street's been standing half-built for six months. Jobs are shutting down all over Manhattan."

"Not this one."

"How you going pay for it?"

"I don't know yet." He was too angry to be worried. And he had much grimmer thoughts in his mind. Business and the dreams he had dreamed with his father were one thing—but murder was another.

He called a staff meeting. Arnie, Ed the accountant, the bookkeeper, the foreman of the mixing plant, and Sylvia Marx filed gloomily into his father's office. Their faces and the silence reflected their doubts that Taglione Concrete and Construction really existed without Mike at the steering wheel. Chris had to admit he felt a little silly sitting at the scratched metal desk.

"We got some pretty screwy files," the accountant reported. "Your dad kept a lot in his head."

Chris knew his father had run a one-man show. He was haunted by his father's arcane business habits, yet instincts he had never tapped were welling up from memory. First and foremost, his father always had an answer. Chris stood up, put his hands in his pockets, sat on the desk, and told the sad-faced accountant, "Start new files."

Ed exchanged an incredulous look with the bookkeeper.

"Buy one of those little computers. We had one in business class at school. They run about thirty grand and they're great for keeping track."

"*Buy* a computer? With what? A lot of your dad's customers figure with him gone there's no rush to pay their bills. We're crunched for cash. I don't even know if we can make the payroll."

"Sell a truck."

"You mortgaged them."

"Thirty-four, thirty-seven, eighty-six, and one fourteen were in the shop. I forget to tell the bank we owned them."

The accountant smiled.

"Sell it to old Alphonse. *Lease* a computer. Feed it our delivery invoices for the last six months. Give me a list of who owes us what by the end of the week."

As they filed out, Sylvia Marx hung back. His father's secretary was a statuesque fiftyish blonde, a former Copa dancer with stunning legs. At the funeral she had stood off to the side, not sure of her place. Grief had cut hard lines in her pretty face.

"What's up, Sylvia?"

"I know the accounts that owe us the most."

Chris visited the worst of the worst at a job site in the financial district. The steel was halfway to the sky, which meant they had owed on the foundation pour for a long time. He pushed into the main office trailer and introduced himself to the project manager.

"Sorry about your father, kid. What can I do for you?"

"I'm collecting our outstanding accounts."

"And I'll bet we're standing way out. Right?"

"Right."

"And you're pressed for cash?"

Chris admitted he was.

"Well, I know exactly what you're going through, because so am I. . . . Tell you what. You want to clear things up? I can try and raise maybe about forty cents on the dollar."

"Forty cents? But—"

"Help me out and help you too, right?"

"No. That's not even cost."

"That's the best I can do for you."

"Forty cents is ridiculous. You owe me a legitimate debt."

The project manager stopped smiling. "You want to settle for thirty-five?"

Defeated, Chris returned to the office and told Sylvia what had happened.

"Get a haircut."

"Nobody cares about long hair anymore, Sylvia."

"Sure. All the builders' kids look like you."

"So?"

"You can't afford to look like a kid. It's show biz. You gotta look the part."

"It wasn't looks with my father."

"Your pop was born with a part. Anybody looking at Mike Taglione knew this was one tough, smart, straight guy. Looking at you they see a nice college kid with long hair. You're big, but you look a little too sweet to hit anybody."

"They could be wrong about that."

Sylvia gave him a shrewd look. "Maybe."

"I don't even *know* a barber. Girls at school cut my hair."

"That I can believe. Why don't I make an appointment with your pop's barber? And meet me at Paul Stuart's afterwards."

Chris watched his image change in the Waldorf-Astoria barber shop mirror as his hair slid down the satiny sheet like yellow straw. He looked a little like a stranger and a lot like his father. His nose seemed bigger, and his brow grew broad and high. Freed of the shadow of long locks, his glittering blue eyes became the most prominent feature in his face.

Chris went to the colored bottles in front of the mirror, opened one after another, sniffing the contents. "This one."

"That's what your father liked."

"Right."

"Very nice," Sylvia said when he walked into Paul Stuart's. She took his arm and led him to the second floor.

"People are staring at me."

"They think you're my gigolo."

"Christ, Sylvia."

"I used to take all my fellas shopping, but your father, God bless him, absolutely refused to buy clothes."

He bought a suit and Sylvia chose a half-dozen shirt-and-tie combinations.

"French cuffs are not really appropriate for daytime wear, madam," the sales clerk remarked.

"The guys on his dance card aren't up on their Emily Post." Later she revealed why she had insisted on the French cuffs. "I already bought these for your pop's birthday. I want you to have them."

Chris opened the unmarked box. Two big cuff links burned white on a black velvet bed. "Are these diamonds?"

"Don't worry about it. I know a guy." She worked them into his cuffs. "Kinda loud, but your pop woulda liked them." She stood back and admired the effect. "You'll probably outgrow 'em, turn conservative when you're a big success. Now go get 'em!"

Chris visited the next job on the debtors' list, found the project manager's office in a tenement across the street, and presented his bill.

"Hurting for cash, are you?"

"I'm just straightening up some loose ends before I start a new building."

"What new building?"

Chris shot a French cuff, exposing a flash of diamond. "I can't go into it yet. My father's partners are very nervous— afraid somebody'll bust in on the deal. Now if you can just give me a check."

"Is that the same building your father started?"

"Another," he embroidered the lie, looking hard at the guy. "I want to clear things up with you."

The guy scratched his head. "It's a kind of a heavy number."

Chris shrugged. "I won't bust your balls. I'll let you give me half now and half next month."

Heart in his throat, he sat back as if he had the day to spend, and watched the man actually write a check. He forced himself to straighten his other cuff instead of lunging for it.

"Dinner," he told Sylvia. "To celebrate and thank you."

He chose the Palm because he remembered his father mentioning it, but the restaurant was one Mike had taken her to and the evening turned somber. They talked about how much they missed him. Sylvia got drunk, but covered well until the cab, where she cried. Chris said he wished he could kill the bastards. At her door she kissed his cheek and said, "Finish your pop's building. That's the best revenge."

"You have only one month left and no way to raise more money, and Arnie's already behind schedule." The accountant nudged the bookkeeper, who nodded grave agreement. "But you did great on collections and we're billing like a real business. So you don't need banks. You're fine if you just get out of that fucking building."

Two problems. And both were Arnie. His father's old project manager couldn't hack it. And to make things worse, the bank knew. He went back to the best run of the jobs he had dunned to talk to the project managers, who ran the business end, and the superintendents, who bossed the field. Ben Riley was the first he clicked with, a blunt-spoken, middle-aged superintendent who reminded him a little of his father. Riley was sufficiently charmed by his brash approach to repair with him to a bar, where he ordered milk for his ulcer—a common superintendent affliction—lit a cigarette, and passed one to Chris. Nervous, Chris dropped it. Riley ground it under his boot and gave Chris another. "The building business is bids and schedules. You know diddley about bids, zip about managing supplies, and zilch about labor. How do you expect the banks to lend money to somebody who can't guarantee a schedule?"

"I know a lot about building. I know that labor's going to

try to fuck me over and suppliers are going to try to steal me blind because they think they can. I think I know from my father how to control them, but the bank doesn't believe it, so I need help."

"You sure do."

"I'll top what these clowns are paying you by ten percent, including your incentives. Plus I'll pay you a two-month bonus up front in cash."

"You're not kidding?"

"I'm too young to kid. I'll be at the job tomorrow morning."

Again and again, he raided his competitors until he had hired four top managers to do the job his father and Arnie had done alone—two top field men and two in the office.

"Fancy window dressing," Arnie grumped. "They're tripping over each other. You got enough bosses on the payroll to build the fucking pyramids."

"Window dressing for the banks' sake," Chris mollified him. "With all these heavy hitters running the job, they can't bitch about Taglione Construction being one kid. Now you gotta make me look good by whipping the cement into shape."

"Hey, wait a minute—"

"Arnie, you were a week behind schedule."

He moved the Brooklyn headquarters into trailers at the foundation site so he could personally oversee the project. When the staff complained that his father never made them work under such rough conditions, Chris dipped again into Mike's reserves of good will. "The sooner we finish the building, the sooner we get indoors. Besides, how can I learn to build Manhattan skyscrapers in Brooklyn?"

When his notes came due, his new managers had the foundation poured ahead of schedule and steel rising out of the hole. He put on his new suit and went to the bank, confident that Taglione Construction's performance had proved itself creditworthy, and proud that the interest check in his pocket proved he had put Taglione Concrete in the black. He failed to register that Pete Stock's receptionist was emptying her desk drawers into a shoulderbag.

"Chris Taglione to see Pete Stock."

"Mr. Stock is no longer with the bank."

"What? Where'd he go?"

She looked up, her face bitter. "Where do you think? The unemployment line."

"Fired? Christ . . . Well, can I see his boss? Who's his boss? Sphunt?"

"Sphunt's fired, too. *Everybody's* fired."

Chris looked around, noting belatedly that the corridors were in disarray, with pictures off the walls and boxes on the carpet. "Who's in charge?"

"Mr. Bunker."

Through the open door Chris saw a man about his age unpacking a cardboard box. He wore shirt sleeves, a narrow tie loose at the neck, and wire-rimmed glasses. Chris knocked on the door frame and stepped in. Bunker said, "You're late."

"No, I'm not."

"You're from Wharton."

"Taglione Construction."

"I'm looking for my assistant."

"I'm looking to roll a note. Taglione Construction. You're backing my Fifty-sixth Street tower."

"Was this one of Stock's deals?"

"Sure. My father dealt with Mr. Stock for fifteen years."

"Bye-bye."

Bunker pulled a framed diploma from a cardboard box and hung it on one of the many picture hooks Stock had left on his wall. It said that Bunker had graduated from the Harvard Business School three months ago.

"You mind telling me what's going on?"

"The bank has eaten too many loans," Bunker replied, straightening his diploma. "About two hundred million dollars' worth, to be precise. So they're cleaning house. They fired everybody in the real estate department and hired me to pick up the pieces."

Chris sank in a chair and stared in disbelief.

"My bank has to do this now?"

"Well, it's obvious you possess one quality a builder needs —total egocentricity. Not just *your* bank. *Every* bank."

"What?"

"Every bank in New York has, as of this morning—or will, as of tomorrow—fired its entire real estate department. It seems some very cozy relationships have sprung up between real estate officers and developers."

"How the fuck do you think we got buildings built?"

"You got too many of them built. Nobody said, 'Stop.' So you've got twenty million square feet unused, empty, and unrentable."

"My building's preleased."

"There's another recession coming. Are you sure your tenants can afford the space?"

"We can't just stop. We've promised to supply the space."

Bunker reached into his box and pulled out a coffee mug. "It suddenly hits me, this is what I went to school for. Guys like you and Stock get so cozy nobody asks the hard questions."

Chris stared at him. "So you're going to run an uncozy department?"

"Right. Nobody's pulling friendship to jolly me into dumb loans."

Bunker removed the last item from his box, a Hewlett-Packard calculator, and set it beside the mug.

"Let me ask you something."

"And then I must excuse myself."

"How are you going to know who's honest?"

"Credentials."

"And who keeps their word?"

"Track record."

"That's the past. Track records and credentials only tell you what's *already* happened. Cozy is knowing about it now." A childhood and adolescence of conversations half heard at family dinners and job-site trailer offices started galloping onto his tongue. "How do you know who's maybe getting into trouble with some building inspector? And who's about to get slapped with a mechanics' lien 'cause he stiffed his employees? And whose contractor is overbooked? Who's undercapitalized? Who's got union problems? Who can't hack it anymore? Whose subs are about to go broke? Cozy pays, man. You gotta be in touch. Otherwise you miss the good deals and only the people everyone else knows to avoid will come to you. Now I'm bringing you a good deal. I am preleased, thank God, and I'm running ahead of schedule. The slowdown means I'm getting breaks on everything. And my building is small enough so even if some of my tenants back out, I won't be killed."

"So what's your problem?"

"I need money. My old man was—died, and everyone thinks I'm a kid. All I'm asking for is the money they agreed to loan him."

Bunker looked at him for a full and silent thirty seconds. Chris glared back. Couldn't anybody see what he knew was true?

"Preleased?"

"Fully."

"Let me find your file."

Bunker returned with a thick folder which he spread on his desk and read for five minutes. Finally he looked up. "This is a bitch."

"I don't owe that much," Chris protested.

"That's the bitch. You don't owe us enough money to have any leverage."

"What?"

"This morning I told a developer he owed us forty-six million dollars. He said he was aware of that. I asked when he proposed to pay it. He said as soon as the market gets better. I said that's not good enough. He said, Then take my building. Then he said, Fuck you, and hung up. Because he knows as well as I know that the bank doesn't have any use for a half-built unleased building."

"But he *will* pay you," Chris said. "If you were ballsy, you'd lend him the money to finish his building."

"You say ballsy and I think twenty million unused square feet."

"He's not a deadbeat, he's just temporarily in trouble. Like me."

"Unfortunately for you, Mr. Taglione, you don't owe anywhere near forty-six million dollars. So your troubles aren't the bank's."

"But I do have leases if I can just get the thing built."

Bunker tapped the papers with his pencil and poked his calculator again. "The fact is, your father does seem to have minimized the risk. It's a fairly creative financial structure."

"Pretty good for a hod carrier."

"Beg your pardon?"

"Something he used to say."

"It's obvious he was more interested in completing a building than reaping a large profit."

"He wanted to get his foot in the door."

"Yes, I can see that. It's a good location, too. It's this goddamned market that worries me. . . . Do you mind my asking how your father died?"

Every instinct screamed that this slick Presbyterian would not lend money to a wop in a Mafia feud.

Bunker looked at him. "You said he died."

"A construction accident," Chris murmured, the lie burning in his stomach. "A truck. Never knew what hit him." Another lie, to lay him to rest. If only that were true, he might not hate so much; but Mike Taglione had known exactly what had hit him and why.

Bunker removed his glasses, covered his face with his hands, and peered between his fingers. "I don't believe I'm doing this, but provided everything you say checks out, we'll roll your notes another sixty days, and extend the next stage of credit."

"Just like that?"

"Why not? I'm the entire real estate department, except for my assistant from Wharton, who apparently can't find the building."

Chris felt like a door had opened on a sunny room. He reached across the desk. "Thank you. I'll never forget."

Bunker shook hands mechanically, as if they had told him at school he was expected to indulge native customs.

Chapter 3

THE BROTHERS WENT out for a farewell supper the chilly September night before the day Tony returned to Cambridge for his first year at Harvard Law School. Chris suggested driving into the city, but Tony insisted on his favorite, Abatelli's, an Italian restaurant on Woodhaven Boulevard. While Tony drove their father's Lincoln, Chris stared moodily at the sidewalks; children were running home from the neighborhood shops with loaves of bread, milk, and the evening paper. He dreaded living in the empty house without his brother. He knew already that he would sleep most nights on a couch in the office trailer.

"Why do you think Pop did it?" Chris asked. "Why'd he tell Rendini to go fuck himself? After all those years of paying off."

"I don't want to talk about Pop."

"Yeah, but why? I gotta know why."

Tony sighed. "Why'd he suddenly go from building Queens apartment houses to a Manhattan office tower?"

"I think Pop made a mistake by not paying."

"No, he didn't. Will you get off it?"

"You mean that? He didn't make a mistake?"

"He did the right thing. His only mistake was doing it too late."

Chris clung silently to his brother's judgment.

Tony laughed softly. "You know, we're switching roles at last. Here I am twenty-four years old, starting law school, and I'm finally becoming big brother, and you're becoming the dumb kid."

"It took you long enough, runt."

The restaurant was deep and narrow, with three long rows of tables set with white tablecloths under replica Tiffany lamps. Joe Abatelli greeted them as regulars, for Tony had insisted on eating here two or three times a week, but tonight the expression on Joe's square, fleshy face seemed guarded, Chris thought, and his greeting an ambivalent-sounding "Back so soon?"

"Tony can't stay away and my pop always said this was the best guinea meal in the city."

Joe put them at a table far in the back, Tony facing the door, and Chris the service bar. He beckoned a waiter and hurried away.

"What's his problem?"

"Knife fight in the kitchen, maybe."

They drank two fast scotches, as the restaurant filled up, and Chris started to relax. Hunting their waiter for another refill, he happened to be glancing toward the entrance when a sensual, dark-haired girl glided in on the crest of a large family.

His throat tightened and his mouth went dry; for one clear, icy moment he forgot his father, the job, everything. She was very young, in her middle teens, slight, with pretty legs and small, round breasts. Her lips were full, her eyes large and very still. Her dark skin seemed to glow and her hair was like a long, silky drift of black night.

Tony looked up from his menu. "Check it out!"

"I saw her first—she's mine!"

Tony gave his sharp tone a look. Then he smiled and said, "We'll see."

"I'm not kidding, Bro. This is one time you keep your hands off or I'll break your head."

"Oh yeah?" Tony said with another teasing smile. "You might have to get on line. Catch her big brother. He looks like an ape somebody shaved. Christ, she has two of them. And look at her old man!"

Her father was shorter than his sons, but easily as broad, and despite his fear that Tony would move in on him, Chris laughed. "Alphonse could lease those guys to chew rocks. Hey, her mom's cute."

"Kind of like Sylvia." She had Sylvia's carefully made up

and dressed look, as if she too had been in show business, but she was petite like her daughter.

"Mom must have some genes to hold off daddy's. That has got to be the most beautiful girl in Queens. Let's trade seats."

"I wouldn't give you this seat for three hundred dollars. Turn around and stop staring."

Joe Abatelli sat the family near the front. The parents placed the girl between them, while the brothers sat with their backs to Chris and Tony.

Tony flashed his best smile.

"What was that for?"

"She looked at me."

Chris glanced over his shoulder. Her enormous eyes were violet. "I am definitely in love."

"She's only about fifteen."

"I will sleep in her garage for three years." He stopped Joe as the owner went by calling orders to his bartender. "Hey, Joe, you got a line on those people?"

"What people?"

"The far-out girl with the huge ugly guys."

Joe pulled away. "I hear he owns the Blue Bus Line," he said coolly.

"She's his daughter?"

"I don't know 'em. They're from Brooklyn."

"What are they doing here?"

"What are you, a detective? They came to my restaurant. I'm very complimented. I hear they own restaurants, too. In Canarsie."

Chris grinned. He felt spacey, high on the scotch, and abruptly happy, as if a weight had lifted and he could be twenty-one for a night instead of businessman of the year. "I'll pay you eight hundred bucks for her phone number."

"I'm busy." Joe hurried off.

"What's with him?"

Tony shrugged.

"How about another drink?"

"Is she looking?"

"At me. What are you gonna eat?"

"Cheesecake on her breasts."

Tony waved for the waiter. "How you doin'? Veal chop for Chris. Steak for me. Split a caesar salad?"

"Big one. And clams. Want to have clams first?"

Tony said, "We'll start with clams. And we'll have another drink."

"Doubles."

The waiter wrote it down and left.

"What's she doing?"

"They just got company."

"Who?" Chris didn't want to waste a turn around when she was distracted. "Who came in?"

"I'm not sure." Tony looked tense, alert, like a hunter sniffing the wind.

"What's going on?"

"I said I'm not sure."

"I'm checking this out. I'll get some cigarettes."

"No! Stay there. Have one of mine. I'll tell you what's happening."

"Who came in?"

"Another family. I'll tell you when to look. Papa, Mama, and a guy about our age. Joe's pulled the tables together. Everybody's up, shaking hands. Now!"

Chris pretended to wave for a waiter. The new arrivals were Italian, too, but looked like out-of-towners. The father was wearing a pastel leisure suit with a lot of gold, and the woman, suntanned to a mahogany brown, bulged in pink slacks and a flowered blouse. The son, a quiet-looking kid with troubled eyes, said hello shyly to the beautiful girl, who replied without a smile.

Their waiter came back with the scotch. Tony asked, "Who just came in?"

"I don't know 'em."

"Joe knew they were coming. What'd the reservation say?"

"I don't know, man," he replied, hurrying away.

"What's Miss Universe doing?" Chris asked.

"Reading her menu."

"You think they'd sell us their daughter?"

"Lease her."

"We could say we're orphans starting a new family. We need a sister."

"Funny."

Their waiter returned with raw cherrystone clams and hot bread. Chris started to turn around again. Tony said, "I'll watch, you tell me how the job's going."

Chris filled Tony in briefly on his loans from Bunker and the latest scheduling victories achieved by the managers he had hired for credibility. Tony's dark eyes kept flickering toward the front of the restaurant. "It sounds like you know what you're doing."

"No. But no one else seems to, either. So I keep moving and they keep running after me. Funny thing is, I know now that's how Pop operated. He always seemed to know what he was doing, but he couldn't. Nobody could. It's all a moving target. Sure you won't join me?"

"I told you, I'm going to be a prosecutor."

Chris glanced over his shoulder. She was looking down at her precisely folded small hands, her face shielded by her long, shiny hair. The second time he looked she was nibbling like a cat from a plate of antipasto. There were several big platters of the hot antipasto on the table and the group seemed to be prolonging it as an icebreaker. When he looked a third time, her father said something, and her brothers turned around and gave him a hard look. Their waiter rescued him with a thick veal chop that covered most of the plate.

Later, halfway through his steak, Tony said, "I can't figure it out."

"What?"

"That's a meet of some sort."

Chris turned around again. She looked up, straight at him, her violet eyes blazing defiance. Then she surprised him with a small, private smile, and he smiled back. Her brother noticed and Chris turned away before he caused her problems. Tony was smiling too, and Chris suddenly realized he didn't know which of them she had smiled at.

"It's about her," he said. "They're marrying her off."

"What?"

"And she's fighting it."

"Nobody does that shit anymore. Order some wine. I gotta make a call."

Tony was gone a long time. Chris buttered breadsticks,

picked at his salad, and stole glances at the girl. She got up as if to go to the ladies' room. The same direction, he thought enviously, that Tony had gone. She was gone awhile, and when she came back, she gave Chris a stoned smile and he realized she had escaped to smoke a joint. Tony returned and Chris asked, "She come by the phone?"

"Yeah, she's going to spend the weekend with me at the cabin. After I teach her what to do with it, she'll marry you."

"You didn't even say hello."

"Actually, I was too busy talking to the guys at the office."

He clinked his glass to Chris's and said through his smile, "There *is* a meet going on at that table. They're connected."

"Bullshit. Racket guys don't meet with their wives."

"I thought the Blue Line Bus sounded familiar. Miss Universe's father is Eddie Rizzolo. He runs South Brooklyn and chunks of Queens. Gambling mostly, books and numbers, and he's got his paws in freight forwarding at Kennedy and LaGuardia. A little hijacking on the side. He's got a kind of loose partnership with the Cirillos. I keep hearing that this is a mob joint. Now we get to see the bastards."

"Fuck," Chris blurted, his emotions flip-flopping as they had all summer. "What are you taking us to a mob place for?"

"I want to see these fuckers with my own eyes—hey, who's this?"

A little man in his sixties scuttled in the door and made for the joined tables, apologizing profusely in a voice that carried. "I'm so sorry. Business. I couldn't get away."

His thin ginger hair looked dyed. His suit was too large and his face sagged as if he had lost weight recently; his movements, however, were quick with nervous energy. Chris thought of a tiny shrew he had seen in the country, flinging itself on giant beetles, which it ripped apart with teeth and claws.

The fathers and the brothers shot to their feet, protesting that they themselves had just arrived. The mothers bobbed their heads with confirming smiles. The girl watched gravely, still as granite. Joe came running and solicitously guided the newcomer to the head of the table.

"Sit, sit." The little man smiled, and they dropped like stones.

"Somebody big," Tony said needlessly, and then, more to the point, *"Turn around, Chris."*

He did, his heart pounding. "Hey, Joe!" Joe was hurrying toward the bar again, calling for another Pinot Grigio. "Who's that came in?"

"I don't know." He passed by again, the wine bottle in his hand. While he was fumbling with the foil and cork, the waiter dropped a check on Chris and Tony's table.

"What's this? We haven't even finished. We're going to have dessert."

"Joe wants you to pay."

"What are you talking about?"

"You're bugging him with all your questions. He's got a big night going and he doesn't have time for it. The drinks were on the house."

"What is this? All I'm asking is about a girl—"

The waiter leaned closer. "You ought to shut up, Chris. Do you know who just came in? You ever hear of Don Richard Cirillo?"

"Bullshit," said Tony. "He never comes out."

"He's out now, man. Sitting right there. So why don't you both shut up."

Chris turned completely around and stared at the man who controlled the biggest single piece of the rackets in New York: narcotics, gambling, extortion, and a number of union locals that his father—and now he—had to deal with. And one Teamsters local in particular, run by Joey Rendini.

Tony pinned his arm to the table. "No."

"I'll kill that fucker."

The waiter backed away—"Jesus, what did I say?"—and Joe Abatelli raced to their table. "Please, Chris. I don't need this kind of trouble."

Chris started to stand up. Tony wrestled his arm with both hands and muttered through his teeth to Joe, "You know what happened to my father. Why the hell didn't you say something when we came in?"

The restaurateur looked wild with panic. "I didn't know. I just knew these people were meeting. Neutral territory or some fucking thing. I didn't know *he'd* set it up. Gimme a break, Chris. Let me get through the night. Don't start trouble."

"We're leaving," Tony said. "I don't want to be in the same room with those creeps."

"Thank you, Tony. Thank you. Thank you very much. I'm sorry about this, Chris."

"What's the meeting about?" Chris asked.

"Hey, come on."

Tony turned on him harshly, "Joe, a second ago you're thanking me. You owe me. Answer Chris. What's it about?" Their father's credo: Take nothing for nothing. *Give* nothing for nothing.

Joe whispered, "I think it's two families been fighting. Don Richard brought 'em together. I appreciate your leaving now."

"I want dessert," Chris said.

"Chris, Tony, please. Here, I got this." He snapped the check off the table, crumpled it in his hand. "You just take care of the tip."

Chris repeated his request in the firm but polite voice he employed on the job, and he was quite suddenly not a twenty-one-year-old kid to be shooed out of a restaurant. "I want dessert. My father ate here. Tony and I come two and three times a week. This is our place. You can't kick us out for some rackets guy."

Joe went white. "Get him what he wants."

The waiter ran for the pastry trolley and rolled it swiftly to their table, silver serving pieces ringing against the platters. Chris stared at the dark cakes, the cannoli flecked with red and green citron, the striped Napoleons. A single crumb would choke him. "Forget it. Let's get out of here."

"Too late," Tony muttered. Cirillo's party was staring as Don Richard got up and walked toward them. He picked up a chair in his wiry, brown-spotted hands, set it between Chris and Tony, and sat down. He looked straight at Chris with eyes like coal. "They told me you been bothering the girl."

Tony said, "We did not bother the girl."

Don Richard ignored him. "Now you're bothering me," he said to Chris.

"Do you know who I am?" Chris asked, controlling the

impulse to hit him only because he was so small and old enough to be his grandfather.

"No. I want you behave in this restaurant or leave."

"Behave? You tell *us* to behave? Your people—"

"I didn't come here to talk. I came here to ask you nicely to stop bothering a family party."

"Your people—"

Don Richard cut him off with a savage gesture. "Outside!"

Chris surged to his feet. "Let's go."

"I'll catch up," said Tony. He headed quickly for the men's room.

The Cirillo leader paused at his own table. "Excuse me a minute."

Chris kept going, the girl's level stare a hard diamond light in the center of the red haze boiling across everything he saw. He pushed through the foyer and onto the dark street, and turned to face Cirillo as he came out the door. "Your people—"

"Kid, I don't know what your problem is, but I'm telling you nice to leave us alone."

"You tell me to *behave?* Your hoods *killed* my father."

"What?" The little old man propped his spotted hands on his skinny hips and looked up innocently at Chris. "What are you talking about? Who's your father?"

"Mike Taglione."

"Never heard of him."

"Joey Rendini killed him."

"Who?"

"He works for you and did it on your orders."

"Sonny, the last guy I killed was before you were born. I ain't in that business no more."

"Now you pay people—"

"Hey! I been nice. You're attackin' me. Fuck you." Cirillo pointed a finger toward the street. Two strong-arm men came swiftly from a car. "He's not allowed back in the restaurant."

Cirillo turned on his heel and went inside.

"Get out of here, kid," one of the men said.

Chris had ceased to think. It never occurred to him that the scotch had gone to his head, that Tony had disappeared, or that even one on one either of these men was formidable.

They were as tall as he, heavy in the belly, and eight or ten years older; the restaurant neon flickering red and green highlighted thin lines of scar tissue which creased their brows and spelled heavyweight hopeful.

"Fuck you." He started back to the restaurant.

The two men glanced up and down deserted Woodhaven Boulevard, calculated the distance to the nearest pedestrians, and moved swiftly in concert. One stepped lightly behind him. The other tossed a sharp jab at his face. Enraged, Chris blocked it, feinted with his left, and threw a hard right cross, the first combination Mike had ever taught him.

The strong-arm hit the sidewalk with a surprised grunt, shook his head, and bounced back to his feet like a rubber ball. "Good hands, kid."

His partner rabbit-punched Chris in the back of the neck and sunk a fist into his kidney. The pain staggered him. They pinned his arms behind him and shoved him around the corner where thick trees darkened the streetlights. A tall, rangy man stepped out of the car, flexing his hands, and sauntered after them.

"We can handle it," said one of the men holding Chris, and his partner cautioned deferentially, "It's okay, Mikey. Maybe you better go back to the car."

"Shut up!" The man they called Mikey stepped closer, fingering a gold coke spoon, which was fashioned in the form of a miniature sawed-off shotgun. Chris couldn't see his face in the shadows, but the soft profile of blow-dried hair and the slick-looking leather jacket might have belonged to a rich young Italian-American bachelor cruising the discos—one of the new young entrepreneurs who had perhaps expanded the family grocery store or restaurant into a high-profit fast-food joint. Chris's eyes locked, however, on the finely tooled spoon dangling from a gold chain. Mikey. *Crazy* Mikey? Don Richard Cirillo's enforcer son.

A bony fist, studded with rings, flickered out of the night and smashed his mouth. Chris levered himself against the men holding him and kicked back. Mikey dodged most of it and attacked like a whirlwind, punching and kicking. Chris tried to protect his balls with his legs and braced his work-hardened stomach muscles to absorb the body punches; Mikey changed tactics, and all the heavy work in the world wasn't worth a damn against the flurry of hard jabs that tore Chris's cheek, blackened his eyes, and cut his lips.

Dizzy with pain, he sensed Mikey pause, planting his feet, and knew he was winding up to hurl a deliberate roundhouse to break his nose. It flew from the shadows like a stone. Chris managed to slip it partially, but it still tore a furrow along his cheek and banged his ear. Mikey kicked him in the stomach. The air whooshed out of his lungs and he hung helplessly between the two men holding him. Mikey fished a set of chrome knuckles from his pocket, swiftly removed his rings, and worked the knuckles onto his fist.

"Chris!" Tony yelled from the street.

"Get away!"

Tony skidded around the corner, launched himself, and hit Mikey airborne, dragging him down in a cursing tangle. They both got up and Tony swung wildly. Mikey doubled him over with a punch in the stomach and whirled on Chris, who was kicking in another futile effort to break the hold the other men had on his arms. A police siren screamed suddenly, drawing close. Light flashed on the knuckles. Cold metal tore into his face. The three men smashed him to the sidewalk, and ran.

Chris crawled toward Tony. When he saw the streetlight through the trees he was vaguely aware that Tony was turning him onto his back. Then there were red lights and cops and Tony was announcing calmly, "I'm Tony Taglione. I called Captain Taggart."

On the way home from the hospital in the car, Eamon said, "The trouble with you is you're arrogant."

"He killed my father," Chris slurred through battered lips. It had taken ten stiches to close a cut on his mouth and three on the rim of his eye. He ached everywhere and the teeth on the left side of his mouth felt loose.

"Let the law do its job—no buts!" Eamon retorted angrily. "I don't care who he is, or who you think he is, he's got the same rights as anybody else. The only person allowed to disturb his dinner is a police officer with a warrant."

"But no cops are doing that. Cirillo's free."

"You want to pull a *Death Wish?*" Tony interrupted scornfully. "Bronson blows away the Mafia boss? Bullshit. The Mafia's a system. It's not one guy. The law's a system for that job."

"The one punching me was called Mikey. Isn't that Cirillo's son? The one they call Crazy Mikey? Eamon, I couldn't see much of his face, but he had a little coke spoon like a gun. Remember? Show me pictures."

"Go to bed," said Eamon. "Sleep it off."

"I'm not drunk!"

"Then you've got no excuse."

He vowed never again to blunder into a fight he couldn't win.

Ten weeks later they tested him.

The Teamsters' shop steward who spoke for Joey Rendini asked for a private meeting. Chris knew, despite Uncle Eamon's assurances to the contrary, that the Cirillos were about to end their self-imposed period of respect for the dead. He sat at his desk trying to control the expression on his face while the shop steward spelled it out.

"We got a problem with the ready-mix drivers, Chris."

"How bad?"

"There's wildcat talk."

Chris picked up a pencil and slowly drew a circle around the date on his calendar. It was four and a half months since his father had been murdered. He had been waiting for this, wondering how long they would wait—and how he would react.

Chapter 4

THEIR TIMING WAS no mystery. His building was precisely at the level, sixteen stories, when he had to start pouring the concrete decks to stiffen the steel frame. Without that "diaphragm" to hold it together, the structure would wobble and rack as he built higher.

Concrete was his own product, and yet he was powerless to supply it if the Mafia made his drivers walk. He shoved his hands under the desk to hide them. He was learning to control his face, almost without effort, but he couldn't stop his fingers from curling into fists. He wanted to break the shop steward's arms. Then he heard his own voice coolly expanding his options, declining to fight when he couldn't win.

Since the fight at Abatelli's, he was constantly surprised by the cold-bloodedness of his rage. It still surged wildly out of his heart, like the jagged bolts of an electrical storm, but he was developing somewhere in his mind a sort of transformer, which channeled his anger into usable energy and protected him from its deadly backflash.

"Why don't you work up a list of your men's demands?" he asked calmly, maintaining the charade of labor relations. "Then see what your needs are." The bribe. "And I'll talk to my people." A warning not to make it too expensive. "I'll get back to you." A second warning—that he might not pay. And then, buzzing Sylvia on the intercom, a blunt threat. "Sylvia, call Riley. Tell him to bring in that truck of cable we got in Long Island City."

This was to let the shop steward know that if worst came to worst, Chris could keep working by guying the steel frame with cable and turnbuckles until he got concrete. His ironworkers could continue to erect steel, and he could even prepare the decks to pour when the strike was over. Not that he wanted to; cabling cost a ton in time and labor and was only a temporary expedient. But it served to remind the shop steward that they were all in this together. He dismissed him with a curt "Get back to me," and sagged behind his desk, physically ill.

You pay to play. He knew now, he thought bleakly, why his father had lost his cool with Rendini; he had been simply unable to stand paying bribes anymore. Grease, sensible investment, and incentive were all bullshit words to pretend it didn't tear a man to pieces to be forced to give away his work for nothing.

He was still shaking that afternoon as he drove Tony to Kennedy Airport to go back to school after an uncomfortable Thanksgiving break. "I swear, if Rendini had come himself, I would have killed him."

"Tell 'em to go fuck themselves."

"That might work in Harvard, kiddo. But I have to deal with these people."

"That's the same mistake Pop made."

"I gotta follow my gut. And my gut is stuff I learned from Pop."

"You're perpetuating the system that killed him," Tony replied coldly.

"And you're getting high and mighty about a scene you don't understand and have never worked in. This isn't hopping around atop the building with a spud wrench. I'm talking about keeping the job alive."

"Maybe distance gives me a clearer eye. Maybe the reasons for the excuses don't show up at long range. Maybe you're too close to it to understand what you're doing to the rest of us."

"Doing to the rest of who?"

"The whole city. The country. Democracy is fragile. You undermine it with your payoffs and bribes."

"I'm talking about business."

"Business? Look at the water." They were driving on the Belt Parkway, skirting the lower bay of New York. A tug plowed seaward and a few rusty freighters stood at anchor. Otherwise, the broad blue bay looked as empty as the sea.

"What about it?"

"Where'd the ships go?"

"What ships?"

"Remember when we were kids Pop would drive us around the docks, show us the ships? The harbor was full of ships. Remember the Erie Basin, the Atlantic Basin, the whole West Side? They're all gone. The mob's longshoremen's unions wrecked the shipping business. The best harbor in the world is empty. How would you like to see that happen to construction?"

"I don't know what you're talking about."

"I'm saying, if you don't like moral reasons for honesty and responsibility, look at the practical. Responsibility works better."

"I'm *taking* responsibility. I'm trying to save Pop's company."

"Parading around in a fancy suit? You're just picking up where Pop left off. Compromise."

"Are you blaming Pop for what happened?"

"Pop fed the Mafia just like you are. Bribe money is power. People like you and Pop give the Mafia its power. They grow on guys like you and Pop."

"I'm going to knock your fucking head off if you don't stop talking about Pop that way."

"Why don't you stop the car and try it?" Tony shot back. "But it won't change the issue. If you pay those bastards, you're going to cross a line and you can never come back. They'll own you forever. And you and I are going to end up on opposite sides."

"We're family."

"Don't pull that shit on me. Family's the same excuse Pop used! Got himself killed, didn't he? Left us—"

Tony slammed his hand against the door, and for a second Chris saw beyond his own anger to the grief Tony was finally allowing to well up. "Can't you see," he continued with a trembling mouth, "that the one thing that makes this country safe to live in is that citizens are more important than families?"

"Including brothers?"

"Especially brothers. People with every opportunity like you and me, we have a responsibility to make things better, not worse."

"What is it with you? You only see things *your* way. Who the hell appointed *you* judge of better and worse?"

"It's not an appointment," Tony said coldly. "The job's there for the asking."

"Maybe the job ought to have tougher requirements. Compassion, maybe. A little understanding of ordinary people."

"Ordinary people have the same responsibility as the rest of us. Truth, honesty, no compromise."

"How'd you get so hard-assed?"

"Watching you suck up to the people who killed my father."

Chris swung hard, a backhand blow heavy with rage. Tony snapped his head away, fast, but Chris's high school ring tore across his cheekbone. When Chris saw the blood on his face he froze, squeezing the wheel, despising himself.

"I'm sorry," he said, begging forgiveness, burning to kill Rendini. And Rendini's bosses and their bosses. Right up to Don Richard. Make them lose what he had lost.

"You're bleeding . . . it hurt?"

"Just get me to my plane." Tony found a tissue in the glove compartment and pressed it to the cut.

"I'm sorry I hit you."

"Yeah."

"You shouldn't have said that."

"You got a problem with the truth?"

Chris drove slowly the last mile and a half, past the color-coded parking lots. He remarked upon a Boeing 747 crossing an overpass they drove under, but Tony was silent. Chris passed the last lot and drove straight to the departure door.

"Aren't you going to park?"

"You got any more to say, write me a letter."

Tony looked hurt, but it quickly turned to anger. "Let's get something straight. I'm going into public service. You're going to be a problem for me if you're illegal."

"I won't be any more problem than Pop was."

Tony shoved his way out of the car and through the terminal doors. Chris watched his form fade into the mass of shadows rushing beyond the glass. He ran into the terminal and found Tony on the check-in line. "Hey, we're all we got left. . . . I want to hug you goodbye."

Tony forced a smile. "Hands off, you dirty guinea. You want the women on the plane to think I'm gay?"

Chris embraced him, surprised how small Tony felt. "Get good marks."

"And you straighten out your act."

"Maybe I'll change my name."

"That'll fool everybody but you and me."

Chris backed away. "See you at Christmas?"

He waited for some sign that the two of them were more important than an argument about payoffs, but all Tony gave him was a high-beam stare and a remote "Sure. Christmas."

Hurt and mad, lonely and sick with remorse, Chris stopped at the churchyard. He sat beside the thin grass covering the new plot and stroked the turf on his mother's grave. He wondered if the aching he felt for his father would subside the way it had when she had died. But no one had killed her; there had been no one to blame but God and disease, no target for rage.

"Pop, what should I do?"

Stupid question. Pop had always said, "Pay the bastards if you got no choice."

When the shop steward reached for the banded, used twenties, Chris clamped his hand on his wrist. "Pass the word—no pigs. I'll follow the rules, if you guys do. But if you take too much, or threaten me or my brother, you'll kill the goose that lays the golden eggs."

"Hey, Chris, I think—"

"Tell your people what I said. They already killed my father. I got nothing to lose."

The air lay still behind the cemetery walls, cold and sweet with wood smoke from the rectory. Dew glistened on the fallen leaves. He had stopped as he often did early in the morning on his way to work. He knelt and brushed the leaves from the grave, and he tried to commune with his father.

"How are you getting on, Chris?"

He jumped. Father Frye, his mother's priest, had crept out

of the rectory and stood over him. Chris kept his head down and continued brushing the leaves with his hands.

"Tony's gone back to school, Father. I've dropped out to run the company."

"I'm sure your dad would be pleased. I'm told your building is progressing nicely." His breath hung in the cold air, like cartoon balloons.

"On schedule."

"You must be the youngest general contractor in New York."

It had been a dry fall and the new grass was taking slowly. He rejected the notion of hiring a gardener. Let it follow its own course. "What can I do for you, Father? I'd like to be alone here."

"I was going to visit you soon. We should have a talk."

"About what?"

"Your mother, you may not know, was a faithful supporter of Sinn Fein in the years before she died."

"I know she contributed money to Irish causes near the end of her life."

"Enormous sums."

"Penance," said Chris. "Because she couldn't get my father to take your church seriously." His mother had embraced the Catholic hierarchy in the Irish-American manner, cherishing the belief that a direct line existed from priest to pope to God; she had fallen deeply in its thrall as she lay dying. Chris's father had been the opposite, heir to the Southern Italian peasant or *contadino* tradition of family first and damn all outside authority, be it government or the Catholic church; he had had little patience and less respect for priests and bishops.

The priest ignored the jibe. "I've been asked to convey the sympathies of certain parties. They want you to know that they understand it was your father's money your mother contributed and are grateful."

"She was dying. How was my father going to stop her?"

"Perhaps he found it easier than accepting the church." The priest smiled. "It all works out in the end."

"By certain parties, you mean Provos, don't you? Terrorists. She had some strange types visiting the hospital. My mother's money went for guns, did it?"

"Your mother believed in—getting the job done."

"My mother was half nuts with pain and fear. She could just as easily have left her money to a cat."

"Your mother knew exactly what she was doing."

"No, she didn't. But the point is, now they're wondering if the money's going to continue flowing to the Old Sod?"

"I imagine the thought crossed their minds," Father Frye admitted with another sly smile. "You *are* executor of your parents' wills."

He had never surrendered the idea of revenge. It sustained him that one day, somehow, he would destroy Rendini. Privately embracing his vision, even rehearsing the steps at odd moments, made the act seem real.

But his experience in business—distancing himself from the day-to-day details—shouted louder than before that the *method* he imagined was foolish. Were he to actually pull the trigger, he would set the entire police apparatus against himself; detectives, patient men with decades of learning, like Uncle Eamon. Surely he could be clever, put his quick mind to bright invention, stack the details—yet the odds were with the cops.

He looked at the priest and found himself on familiar ground. Why not hire a professional just as he hired superintendents, project managers, lawyers? Even interior decorators, he thought with a thin smile that made the priest squirm. A professional outside American organized crime? Chris loaded his voice with heavy insult and asked the priest, "How do I know my money will ever get to the IRA?"

"Are you suggesting—"

"You've got a great setup for a con game here. Wrap the church in the Irish flag to shake down the orphans of dead contributors."

Father Frye bristled, but he kept icy control—a man above insult when serving his cause. "If you came to my church, my parishioners would set you straight about my dedication to Ireland."

"I want *proof*."

"Proof?"

Chris took a breath, acutely aware that he was on the edge of changing his life. "Bring me proof."

"What sort of proof did you have in mind?"

"Bring me someone convincing."

The priest puffed up. Chris thought of a mean little boy playing soldier. "Convincing is it you want? All right, Chris. I'll convince you."

John Ryan, quiet-spoken, middle-aged, ordinary-looking but for his icy blue eyes, was in the country illegally. He met Chris, as the priest had promised, in an Irish bar on Second Avenue, where British liquor bottles were marked off-limits with a diagonal red stripe. Chris took him to a Jets game and spent the afternoon and a long supper feeling him out. Late that night, he dropped him back at the rectory, still unsure how to rate a killer.

"You're looking for something," said Ryan.

"Maybe."

"Father Frye told me what happened. I think I can guess."

"Meet me at Charley O's for lunch tomorrow."

He drove to the job, climbed into the control cab of a crawler crane, and sat the rest of the night trying to assess how capable John Ryan was. At dawn, when the gleaming black-and-chrome commercial garbage trucks were racing down the street and he still hadn't made up his mind, he realized that he now put less time and thought into the gambles that were thrusting his father's building out of the ground.

At lunch he showed John Ryan a photograph of Joey Rendini. "He lives in Brooklyn. When the papers say he's dead, the IRA collects five thousand dollars."

The gunman ran his blunt fingers over the face. Three days later Rendini was sprawled across the front page of the New York *Post,* shot twice in the knees and once in the back of his head.

Nursing an Irish coffee in the smoky, warm winter-afternoon gloom of Charley O's, Christopher Taglione waited with one heel hooked firmly on the bar rail, his eyes set just as firmly in the middle distance. He looked reflective and older than his years, but he was in fact gravely confused.

A glance at the handful of regular customers who reigned between the end of lunch and the start of the cocktail hour roused his fleeting concern; he should have been more careful where he chose to pay the gunman. But fear and cunning were far from his mind. Why, he wondered, was he not supremely satisfied that he had righted a terrible wrong?

He shivered and swallowed more of the hot, sweet, boozy coffee. He had to admit he felt less triumphant than sick. Yes, he had wanted to erase Joey Rendini, but the shooting in the knees amounted to torture, and his images of vengeance—the sawed-off shotgun barrels clinking to the workshop floor, Rendini's face disappearing in a torrent of pellets—had not encompassed pain. He realized, too late, that he didn't even want Rendini killed so much as made to suffer terrible loss, as he had suffered loss.

Ryan came in at last, his lined cheeks ruddy from the cold. Blowing on his thick workman's hands to warm them, he nodded hello to several drinkers. The bartender poured Murphy's, no ice, without having to ask. Again, Chris was reminded that this association could be dangerous. Yet Ryan was no fool. He pretended not to notice Chris at first, and when he did he said casually, "Well, young fella, how are you?" and drew him just as casually toward an unoccupied corner.

Chris took fifty one-hundred dollar bills in an envelope from his breast pocket, passed the envelope under the table. What should he say? he wondered. Congratulations?

Ryan went to the men's room, presumably to count the money. Chris waited in turmoil. His father's murderer was dead. What was wrong? Ryan looked surprised to see him still there when he came back.

"Tell me what happened," Chris demanded.

"The man begged for his life. He swore he wanted only to beat up your father. He claimed that the order to kill your father came right from the top."

"Who on top?" Chris asked angrily, his earlier misgivings forgotten. "Who gave the order?" Ryan could be drumming up business. But Uncle Eamon had raised exactly the same possibility. Wasn't a Mafia murder an endless chain of wrongs?

"He would not say," John Ryan replied, adding simply, "I believe he was in fear."

* * *

Taglione Construction topped out Mike Taglione's tower with an American flag he had bought a year before he was killed. When Tony came down from school for the bittersweet topping-out party, Chris showed him the newspaper clipping about Rendini and waited anxiously while Tony read the story. He longed to share his revenge.

"Yeah, I heard. Too bad."

"What do you mean?"

Tony sighed. "This might sound strange to you, but I've been running on a sort of fantasy that after I graduated law school I'd get Rendini in court." He smiled thinly. "I guess I'll have to settle for his bosses."

"Aren't you glad he's dead?"

"I wish he were in prison."

"That never would have happened."

"Now we'll never know."

Chris clung to the rightness of his less than satisfying efforts. "At least Pop can rest easy."

Tony's face was a cold mask. Up came the highbeam stare. "Don't you think Pop deserves more than one scumbag shooting another scumbag?"

Chapter 5

R AND," THE ENGLISH policeman introduced himself. Chris settled warily behind his father's old desk.

Inspector Reginald Rand—according to his card, which Chris started rolling between his fingers—appeared to be in his forties. His black hair was graying at the temples and he wore a trim mustache, also graying, and a tailored suit. He had a powerful grip for a slim man. His eyes were remote flat pools shielded by reflections.

"What can I do for you?"

"Scotland Yard's Special Branch has killed an IRA terrorist."

"So?"

Rand took out a Charley O's matchbook. Chris shoved an ashtray in his direction. The policeman gave it a thin smile, opened the matchbook, and showed him the inside. It had two matches left. Two more lights and John Ryan would have thrown it away, along with Chris's telephone number scrawled in pencil.

Chris touched the desk for strength. Through his fingers he could feel the building pulsing as the tower crane hoisted concrete to the upper decks.

"Maybe he was looking for a job."

Rand cast a dubious eye at the six-button phone anchoring the twenty-fifth-story floor plan.

"Do your workmen ordinarily contact you directly, Mr. Taglione?"

"Taggart."

"Beg pardon?"

"I'm changing my name to Taggart. My brother may go into politics, and building can be a dirty business."

"Very well, Mr. . . . Taggart. I repeat, do your workmen ordinarily contact you directly?"

"I don't know if you've ever worked with your hands, Inspector, but workmen pass the word on jobs. Maybe my name fell into the grapevine."

"Oh, I'm sure it did." He smiled. "But *which* grapevine?"

"What was his trade?"

Rand's smile went out like a light. It was a definitive announcement that he was taking the gloves off, and Chris felt his second rush of panic.

"Understand, Mr. *Taggart,* my interest is not casual. I *must* know what he was doing in this country. And I will before I leave."

Chris started to protest. Rand cut him off. "Sir, your father was killed in a—questionable, shall we say?—'traffic accident.' A union officer with whom your father had feuded was subsequently kneecapped and shot dead. Now I find your telephone number in the possession of an Irish terrorist."

Chris thought crazy things, even killing the cop and running away, or denying everything. He felt young and scared, very stupid, but most of all, he felt hot panic coursing through his limbs and leaving devastation in its wake.

Rand raised his hand as if to ward off a wild blow. "You realize I'm here unofficially. I only just got off the plane and took a taxi into Manhattan. If I make it official I'll have to confer with all sorts of United States immigration agents, the FBI, police, what have you. . . ."

Had he heard right? Christopher Taggart stared inquiringly into the flat pools of the Englishman's eyes, trying to pierce them for meaning. Had he heard what he thought he heard? He rose unsteadily and went to the iron safe where he kept grease. He came back and stacked five grand on his father's desk. Fifty used one-hundred-dollar bills.

Rand looked at it a long time. He held up two fingers. Chris doubled it, with a deeply relieved smile. Rand stepped to the desk, stroked the surface, traced squares around the money with his finger. But he didn't touch it.

"I'm not yet convinced this would be in my best interest.

You see, I know your mother contributed generously to the IRA, but *you* haven't. I'm hopeful that means you can help me perform my duty, which is to protect the British public from Irish terrorism. If so, we can shake hands on this transaction and part as gentlemen."

Chris nodded; they were nicely in synch. Rand was saying, Convince me you are not an IRA supporter; then, for ten thousand dollars, I will forget that you paid a terrorist to kill the man who murdered your father.

"The guy did a job for me," he admitted. "Private. Nothing political. Nothing to do with England or Ireland."

"An entirely private matter? I *will* enquire further, you know."

"It was exactly what you guessed."

Rand inspected him with a hard, penetrating stare. Abruptly he nodded. "Excellent. I was concerned, of course, that the IRA was preparing political attacks in the States. One has desires"—he smiled at the money—"but one also has obligations. Well, I think this has worked out very nicely all around, don't you?"

"Has anyone else made the connection?"

"Your police certainly haven't. And my sources indicate the mob hasn't either."

"What kind of sources does a British cop have in America?"

"The same sort of cutthroats I cultivate in Europe, Africa, and Asia," Rand answered with a modest smile.

"Then I'm in the clear?"

Rand stuffed the money into his raincoat. "Completely."

Impulsively Chris thrust out his hand. "My name is Chris."

Rand hesitated, finally took it. "Reggie. But may I say something, Chris?"

"Sure. This is the classiest shakedown I ever had."

"Thank you. You've been a damned fool, though. Be more circumspect next time you need such assistance. Make your arrangements through a third party. It was sheer luck I killed your gunman, you know. If I'd arrested him instead, he'd have sold you in a flash to save his own skin."

"I hadn't thought of that."

The remoteness in Reggie's eyes dissolved a little and he looked genuinely concerned. "And now you're trusting *me*.

What if I were wired? For God's sake, man, what if I were a homicide detective with a phony British accent?"

"What makes you think my office isn't wired? What makes you think this shakedown isn't on tape?"

Reggie reached under his belt and pulled out what looked like a telephone beeper. "This. It pulses if that sort of thing is going on."

Chris stared, secretly delighted by the older man. His spectacular success in the building trade had stifled his father's friends, and even the bankers were treading softly. No one dared push advice on a man with the magic touch. He hadn't realized how lonely he had become, or how young he sometimes felt.

"I guess I've been kind of stupid," he admitted.

Reggie returned a long, hard, calculating look. Chris shivered with anticipation, sensing that in Reggie's world his magic touch meant nothing. "You're not stupid so much as very young and, please forgive me, appallingly arrogant. If you persist in acting as if you can walk on water, you'll end up either in prison or dead."

"Want a job?" Chris asked.

"Thank you, no. I have a job."

"How about dinner?"

Rand shook his head. "I think I'll just fly on home before anyone notices I'm missing."

"I'll drive you to the airport. There's a good restaurant on top of the International Building."

Reggie looked dubious but agreed to a ride. He was booked on an eight o'clock British Airways flight, but fate intervened in the form of a two-hour delay caused by a Heathrow baggage-handlers' slowdown. So he let Chris take him to dinner. In the car Chris had pumped him about his work but had found out little. At dinner Reggie asked about the construction business and seemed intrigued. Finally, over coffee, Chris blurted, "I want to kill them all."

"Impossible."

Chris blinked. Unlike Uncle Eamon's policeman's lectures, Reggie Rand was merely making a practical comment.

"I want to get them all," Chris repeated.

"Shooting them isn't the answer. 'They,' as you call them, are a system. A society. A shadow government."

"How do you get a society?"

Reggie hailed a waiter.

"No, no, this is on me," Chris protested.

"Thank you. I thought I'd have a glass of port. Would you like a brandy?"

"No. I'll try the port. Never had it."

Reggie asked what brands the waiter had.

"Sandeman, Harvey's—"

"Croft?"

"Maybe."

"Excellent, tawny for myself, ruby for the gentleman. You'll like that better first time." When it came, Chris tasted it and said, "Like Marsala."

"Yes, very much so. . . . Have you ever wondered why ports and sherrys come from Portugal and Spain yet have English names?"

"Never thought about it," said Chris, anxious to return to the subject of revenge.

"Two systems collided. In the eighteenth century, English wine merchants started buying the Spanish and Portuguese product in quantity. A small portion of a vineyard's output, at first; more the next year, as the taste for it grew in England; and more after that, paying whatever price the grower asked. Eventually they bought the entire crop. That went on for a few years. Suddenly the merchants refused to pay the price. The vineyards had nowhere else to sell, because the wine merchants had seized control of the entire market."

"Why'd they change the names?"

"They married their sons to the Spaniards' beautiful daughters. Just bloody absorbed them." Reggie raised his glass, gazed through it at the mile-long blue lines of runway lights beyond the window, and smiled at Chris. "Of course, it was all legitimate business. Neither society was evil, and indeed both benefited. . . . Now, the society you propose to attack is evil. And it has the strength of evil, which is the strength that comes from answering to no one."

"There's gotta be a way to beat them."

"There *are* ways," Reggie said mildly. "Mussolini did it in Sicily. But are you willing to be evil to beat evil?"

"I'm willing to do anything."

"Then you ought to very seriously consider doing nothing."

His rage grew cold, intense as laser fire. He kept waiting for his achievements to be enough, but they never were. Every time he paid off, he paid the Mafia system that had killed his father. For it was his father crushed by his own truck who remained the center of his existence; the minutes holding his father's hand as life seeped away were the source of his rage; and Mike Taglione's tears were the fuel of Chris's determination to wreak terrible vengeance.

Atop the tower one evening, he compared the Mafia to a construction derrick that at night kept working, secretly snatching materials off the street, and building them into the tower, making itself part of the tower. Cables guyed the derrick mast, each guy like a New York Mafia family. Cut enough guys and the derrick would topple into the street.

Six months after Reggie Rand shook him down—almost a year to the day since his father had been murdered—Chris's accountant came in while he was watching the evening television news. The accountant had a list of reasons why Taggart Construction shouldn't bid to general-contract a new corporate headquarters on Madison Avenue, a job which would begin about the time they finished Mike's building.

"I know your father, God rest his soul, would be very proud of you, Chris, but this time you could blow the whole shooting match. The architect's gone bananas and the client knows it, so the late penalties are like Stalin's."

"It's a class project," Chris retorted wearily. "If I pull it off, I'll draw class clients." The fact was, with his father's building nearing completion, he didn't know what he wanted to do next. Despite a full year since the murder, his mind still replayed it as vividly as if his father had been killed this morning.

"If you don't pull it off we'll be selling pencils on the IRT."

Suddenly Chris gestured for silence.

A Belfast riot was big on the television news. A Special Branch inspector was accused of murdering an Irish prisoner, and Chris had recognized Reggie Rand marching in grand silence through a gauntlet of reporters outside Scotland Yard.

He bought British newspapers and followed the story. Reggie had surprised two IRA Provos in a remote cottage outside Londonderry and in the ensuing gun battle he had shot both. Later, a third man hiding in the eaves claimed upon his arrest that he had seen Reggie gun down a man who had already surrendered. The London *Times* took no sides, the mass-circulation *Sun* demanded a medal for the Special Branch officer, but the moderate *Guardian* spoke what was likely to be the government line, praising "the officer's resourcefulness and bravery, which are, however, not licence to take the law into his own hands."

Chris announced a vacation. His accountant blinked. "What?"

"I'm dead tired. I got to get away."

"It's about time. This has been a hell of a year."

Chris nodded vaguely. "Yeah. Just don't fuck it up while I'm gone."

He telephoned Tony to ask if he would watch things for him, but Tony had been invited back for another summer internship in the U.S. Attorney's office. "Where are you going?"

"London."

He found Reggie Rand in a Victoria Street pub near Scotland Yard. As at their first meeting, they operated in complementary modes. Chris left when Reggie spotted him, walked to the Thames Enbankment, and stuffed a train ticket to Cambridge behind a pay phone.

The following afternoon he waited in a student beer garden on the Cam, slouched before a pint at the scarred wooden table in an open window. The place was packed with Americans over for the summer semester. The low ceiling echoed the roar of conversation, the air was thick with cigarette smoke, and the floor smelled of beer. The students looked like ghosts; it seemed much more than just a year since he had lived like this, talking, drinking, smoking too many Marlboros, and making notes on thoughts he no longer had time nor inclination to think.

Reggie wandered through the crowd with a Newcastle Brown Ale. He had dressed his part in rumpled corduroys and a heavy knit tie, looking like a don on the prowl for a student bedmate.

"Thanks for coming."

"You seem at home here."

Chris patted his faded Fordham sweatshirt. "School is school. I saw your problem on television. Sit down."

Reggie sat and trickled his ale from the bottle into his glass. "Decent of you to remember."

"It's going against you," Chris said. "What are you going to do?"

"Not to worry. The Yard is delighted to give me my full pension if I'll only retire. Friends have offered some interesting armaments work."

"Selling guns?"

"Something like that."

"Do you still have your 'cutthroat' sources?"

"They weren't issued by Her Majesty's government, if that's what you mean."

"I'll top those offers."

"Oh?"

"I'm looking for that 'third party.'"

"You still demand revenge?"

"I have to. The law can't."

Reggie lowered his ale, untouched. Somebody started banging a guitar and he leaned closer so Chris could hear. "Yesterday I made inquiries. Your business is thriving. You're on your way to becoming a man of wealth and power. Why court these 'darker enterprises'? Your enemies are mired in the gutter. The sky is yours. Isn't completing your father's building revenge enough?"

"Not when my father can't stand on the sidewalk and look up at it."

Reggie shook his head and said gently, "I'm afraid I'm somewhat overqualified to contract gunmen. No, Chris. You set this meeting up very well. In fact, I rather admire your flair for the clandestine; you've read your Le Carré. Though I'd have chosen a less conspicuous shirt. But I've no interest in finding you another gunman."

"You think it's beneath you?"

"It's as if I hired Taggart Construction to erect a garden shed."

"No, no, no. I'm looking for more than gunmen."

"How's that?" Reggie glanced idly out the open window, where the shallow river lapped the beer-garden terrace, and picked up his ale.

"I'm building an organization."

"What sort of organization?"

"An organization to destroy the Mafia."

"You don't say?"

"I didn't fly three thousand miles to fuck around," Chris snapped angrily. "Or crack jokes. I'm making a legit proposal."

Reggie deflected his glare with a mild apology. "Terribly sorry. But the Mafia employs, shall we say, perhaps thirteen thousand men in America—the majority in the so-called five families of New York—and its power has grown for four generations."

"Nine thousand associates in New York," Chris said, "and less than nine hundred made members. They're not as strong as they seem, nor as organized. They have as much trouble getting along with each other as they do with the cops. But their real weakness is that they're city kids—street fighters—not soldiers. Their leaders are wide-open, vulnerable to the kind of terrorist violence common in the rest of the world—car bombs, rockets, automatic weapons."

"They control their streets."

"Listen. I got in a fight with Cirillo's strong-arms last year. I was too mad to be scared of two on one, and I took one guy out right off. So they brought in another, made it three on one, and beat my head in. That's how the mob intimidates its victims and protects itself from competitors, but ganging up on somebody is about as far as they go. They depend upon the protections of a free society. The Police Commissioner is not allowed to send tanks to level their homes or hang them from lampposts the way Mussolini did. He beat them because they weren't soldiers. Look what I did with a single IRA man."

"Let's say you manage to identify and slaughter their

leaders. New leaders take over. That's hardly destroying the Mafia."

"I know that! That's why I came to you."

"You may hold an exaggerated opinion of my talents."

"I have a plan, Reggie."

"And I suspect you're going to tell it to me."

"If you're trying to piss me off, you're doing a good job of it. Will you shut up and listen?"

The flat pools which were Reggie's eyes glazed over like ice.

"In one sentence, young man, what is your plan?"

"Support one Mafia family in a takeover war against the other four."

Reggie looked at him and the pools began to glisten. "Destroying all five in the process?"

"Right."

"What are your weapons?"

"Three weapons. Imported violence. Drugs. The law."

"What do you want from me?"

"Number one, violence. I want you to hire soldiers we can slip in and out of New York on a one-time basis—IRA gunmen, Palestinian bombers, French mercenaries, professional fighters, terrorists."

"A Shadow Mafia?"

"Exactly." He liked Reggie's phrase. "A Shadow Mafia to destroy the real one. Number two, drugs. Drugs are Mafia currency. I need a big, steady supply of heroin as a weapon to burrow into their networks. They want it, man. They need it. They're as addicted as the guy who shoots up with a needle. I'm going to hook them to me, then cut 'em off."

"*À la* our wine merchants? What's your third weapon?"

"The law. You'll do international, Interpol and whatever else you know. I'll do New York. I'm going to set them up and turn them in. And I'll use the law for information. I'll put Organized Crime Control cops on *my* payroll for intelligence information."

"Never trust a crooked policeman," Reggie said, and smiled.

"I'm trusting you. Every man has his price."

"Don't ever forget his limits. He also has a magic number,

that amount after which he will·cease to work for you—another thing not to forget when establishing risky contacts."

Taggart smiled back. "That's the kind of expertise I want from you. Along with violence, drugs, and risky contacts."

"Recruit a Mafia family. Take over the Mafia. Destroy the Mafia. Then what?"

"Hand the leftovers to the cops."

"The leftovers being the family you provoke against the others?"

"What's left of them."

"Then close down shop and walk away?"

"Of course."

Reggie smiled and his eyes flattened with private knowledge. He started to say something, but juggled it first in his mind; obsessed with revenge, Taggart seemed a little naive on the subject of walking away. Instead of pursuing it, Reggie stated the obvious. "It would take years."

"I've got years," Taggart shot back. "Everybody's always telling me how young I am. So I've got plenty of time."

"And money."

"I'm starting to make money."

"And of course," Reggie mused, "at some point your operation will start to generate money itself."

"Maybe it would. I guess so."

Again Reggie was struck by Taggart's blind side. Did he really not consider the mind-boggling profits, the millions for thousands, that successfully smuggling large of amounts of heroin would yield? Apparently not, for he was forging determinedly ahead again, like a tank skirting the observation points on the high ground in favor of a direct route to its target.

"But I need your international cutthroats, Reggie. I need your fighters, smugglers, informers, thieves, hijackers—"

"Killers."

Chris met Reggie's eye. The flat pools had formed again and he felt his own gaze reflected. "I'm hunting killers. Nobody knows that better than you."

"The odds are against you. By a great margin."

"I'm going to beat them."

"A very great margin."

94

"I'm still going to beat them. They took my father. I'll take away what they care about—power."

"But they didn't kill *my* father, more's the pity. You'll forgive me if I ask what is in it for me."

"Exactly what you want."

The Englishman's brow rose sharply. "And what is that?"

"The way you're heading—gun salesman, security expert —you'll end up so bored you'll shove a thirty-eight in your mouth. I read about you. You've done it all. You've been in action your whole life. You're the best. I'm offering you a shot at—"

"What is it you think I want?" Reggie's soft voice turned softer and quieter, pulsing with menace. Having turned the tables with a shrewd guess that broached the Englishman's reserve, Chris had also loosed demons. Demons that convinced him that Reggie was the man to direct his war.

"Roam the world. Write your own rules."

"A privateer?" Reggie sounded amused.

"Backed to the hilt! No one to answer to . . . but me."

"That would make you the privateer, and me merely your vessel."

"Come on, Reggie. Let's stop dicking around."

"Why, may I ask, not just hire a competent killer to eliminate the top dons?"

"Because I realized you were right. It's the system more than single men." Ironically, his brother's diatribes against revenge had finally convinced him, though not in the way Tony intended.

"New criminal groups will pop up. And remnants of the old."

"But not institutions. The new groups will be weak and the law will beat them."

Reggie nodded agreement. "I'm told your FBI is gearing up for a major campaign against organized crime."

"Glad to hear it." Taggart grinned. "I'll take all the help I can get. Nobody ever said this was going to be easy."

"They'll crack down on you, too, if you're not careful."

"But I am careful. I hire only the best. Welcome aboard, Reggie."

Reggie sighed. "One million dollars per year."

"What?"

"My price. Cash."

"A million—"

"I don't intend to haggle with a businessman. That is my price. Out of that I'll foot the initial expenses. Cutthroats do expect to be paid, you know."

"Wait a minute. I'm not saying you're not worth it. But I don't have it now. I'll pay it, but in the future. Give me, say, five years. That's a lot of money to make disappear from a legitimate business."

"Generate it out of your drug smuggling," Reggie replied, suddenly sarcastic. He pushed back his chair.

"I'll pay you a hundred grand a year," Chris countered, wondering where in God he would get it. "And pay you the rest once we're rolling."

"You're missing the point, mate. I seriously doubt you'll still have this crazy idea in your head by the time you're earning that sort of money."

He stood up, his ale untouched. Shaking his head in disbelief, he said, "I suppose I should be complimented you thought of me."

"It's not crazy. It'll work—look. Imagine a construction derrick atop a building. The building's society. Right? Now imagine it at night. Everybody's gone home, but the derrick keeps working when nobody sees it—like the Mafia—snatching things off the street and building them into the building, making it part of the building, part of society. Cables guy the derrick mast. Each guy holding the mast is a New York family. Let's say five guys, five families. We're going to cut one guy after another, and when we cut the last one the derrick's going to fall into the street."

"I don't intend to be standing under it when it lands."

"We'll be on top of the building looking down."

"If you still believe that when you can afford me," Reggie replied dryly, "we'll chat."

Stunned, Chris watched him walk out of the pub. Disappointment turned swiftly to anger and he hurried to the train station, heading for London and the airport, seething that the Englishman had treated him like a nut. Reggie was already on the platform, waiting for the same train. Taggart took it as an omen. He went up to him and promised, "I'll be back, you son of a bitch. And we *will* chat—if you're still the best."

Reggie sighed. "For a hundred thousand dollars I'm sure I can find someone to shoot Don Richard and a few others."

"*No*. I want to take more than their lives. I want to take their *belief* they can do it. I want to make it too tough to start over, too hard to be in the rackets. Too dangerous, too risky, and too scary. I want them to cease to exist."

Chapter 6

HE COSTED OUT his attack on the office computer, as if he were estimating a bid on a building, and discovered logic behind Reggie's demand; perhaps his fee wasn't out of line. In fact, it appeared that Reggie Rand's million dollars a year would be only a small portion of what revenge upon the Mafia might cost. And between raising the money and creating the Shadow Mafia, it would take years; perhaps a decade. In a sudden leap of the imagination—grim in its concept, but exciting in that he could indeed conceive it—he embraced the reality that he might be well into his thirties before his father was fully laid to rest.

The only way he knew to raise the fortune he needed—every penny of which he would have to hide from the IRS—was to succeed as a major developer on a scale that his father had never dared dream. He had to build many buildings, not just one at a time, and also had to extract a much bigger profit than bank financing would allow. The answer was joint ventures. But to attract joint-venture investors, he initially had to make his name with some big buildings on bank mortgages. He set up a meeting with his best and probably only hope, Henry Bunker, who behind his prickly facade was a cautious man.

After greeting Chris in his office, Henry Bunker removed his wire-rimmed glasses and gave him a tart glower. "You took a vacation."

"You make 'vacation' sound like Legionnaires' disease."

"Is your building on schedule?"

"No."

"What?"

"Two weeks *ahead*, as if your little spies hadn't told you. Pittsburgh fucked up or we'd be up three weeks. Where do I sign?"

Bunker called his secretary for the notes due and wiped his eyeglasses while Chris signed them. After she left to make copies, Chris sat back and smiled. "Let's get down to the real reason I came by today."

"The *real* reason?" Bunker put his glasses back on. "What do you mean, the real reason? I thought you're trying to finish your father's building."

"I'm top-heavy in management. My guys have expensive time on their hands."

"Fire them."

"I hate to break up a hot team. Why don't we work out something with the people who hold the mortgage on that Fifty-seventh Street building?"

The banker gasped. "Chris, you came in here to try and save your father's building in the midst of the worst real estate depression in memory, and now you're trying to start another?"

"You know the one I mean?"

"Yes. It's standing there like a half-built tombstone."

"Let's finish it."

"Have you any idea how much money they're owed?" *He* apparently did, because he started scribbling numbers and pecking at his Hewlett-Packard.

"If you were stuck with that mortgage," Chris replied, "you'd sell your sister to get out of it."

"I would not sell my sister during a recession," the banker replied dryly. "And we are most definitely looking at a recession."

"*They're* looking at a recession," Chris shot back. "They screwed up the building. But I've got the top people to run the job right. We'll close it in before winter and start renting in the spring. You've got the cash. We can buy it for a song."

"There's no one to rent it to when it's done," Bunker objected. "Who's going to live in it?"

"If we can't rent it, we'll sell it as cooperatives."

"To whom? I'm frankly not sure that this is the right time to invest heavily in Manhattan real estate."

"Real estate is cycles. We're in a down cycle. Now's the time to get in before the next up cycle."

"Cycle theories are dreamed up to generate sufficient hope to prevail over intelligence."

Chris surged toward the door and Bunker flinched at his size in sudden motion. "Come on," Chris barked, his father echoing in his voice. "Let's take a walk."

"Now?"

"I'm going to show you the next cycle."

"How old are you, Chris?"

"You want to come with me? Please."

"The reason I ask is I'm too young to be here and something tells me I'm older than you."

"Just a half-hour walk. I'll buy you lunch."

"You can't afford it."

But he agreed to let Chris tour him up Sixth Avenue. It was a crisp, clear summer day, the avenue thronged with people walking during lunch hour, and New York—thank God for his sales pitch—sparkled.

"What am I supposed to be looking at?"

"Faces and buildings. All these young executives. Guys and girls like us. All these office towers just finished."

"And half empty."

"I'll talk about that in a minute. But all these people are commuting for hours to get here."

"From the suburbs."

"You want to live in the suburbs?"

Bunker shuddered.

"Neither do they. They want to live here. They want to walk to work."

"You can't write off the suburbs."

"I don't have to. The Arabs have done it for me. The suburbs have passed their high point and can't grow anymore. The roads are clogged. Nearby land is running out. And single-family housing costs are going crazy. But at the same time there are more people. My class at Fordham had twice as many students as ten years ago. The baby boom kids are coming up. They're going to flood this city and need places to live, starting with that tower on Fifth-seventh Street."

"Are you sure it's big enough?" Bunker asked sarcastically.

"As soon as we finish it, let's go to Columbus Avenue. It's just waiting to be developed."

"If Lincoln Center didn't get that wasteland developed, nothing will."

"Sixth Avenue will," Chris promised. "These people have to live somewhere."

"Chris, your theory depends upon renting these office buildings, and right now it's more likely we're going to see deer in Times Square."

"No. Money's coming this way."

"That's news to my bank."

"The world is going to hell. Half of it's shaky dictatorships, and the other half's already in revolution—right?"

"Basically."

"But even the most miserable places have people with money. Where they going to put it?"

"Hong Kong."

"So the Chinese Communists can take it?"

"Beirut."

"Which will blow up if things get worse with Israel?"

"London."

"With England nationalizing anything not in running shoes?"

"Geneva."

"Swiss vaults, while inflation whipsaws it? Definitely not. They gotta make their money work someplace they can count on. That leaves the only stable democracy where the government has a healthy respect for money—the U.S. And where will these money people buy apartments, start businesses, and rent offices? The money capital of the safest country in the world—*New York*. So let me ask you—"

"What were you studying in college?" Bunker interrupted.

"My father told me I could study anything as long as I read the newspaper. Let me ask you something."

"What?"

"Why don't you and me get in on the ground floor before the safe and easy boys come back into the market?"

"Dammit, how old are you?"

"I'm twenty-two, for crissake. How old are you?"

"Twenty-three."

"Wanna shake on it?"

On Thursday nights the cops picking up college credit at Fordham's Manhattan campus gathered after class in Jimmy Armstrong's Saloon on Ninth Avenue. They ran the New York Police Department gamut from sergeants hoping to become lieutenants to lieutenants gunning for captain to detectives in homicide, burglary, and organized crime control. Christopher Taggart took to waiting for them around ten o'clock, his big hand wrapped around a glass of Murphy's from which he drank sparingly.

Having been reared around his Uncle Eamon, he was comfortable with cops and knew how to put them at ease. One trick was to honor partners and treat the sour, unfriendly, gloomy cop as politely as his cheerful, outgoing buddy. Another was not to ask questions. But the best device was to seem so rich and powerful as to not need anything from them.

When they asked, "What course are you taking?" the answer, "I'm putting up a building over on Fifty-sixth," did wonders.

"Office building?"

Taggart shrugged. "Thirty stories."

"My brother's in construction. He's an electrician."

"Is he good?"

"Busts his ass."

"If he ever needs work, send him over. I'm Chris Taggart." He shook hands.

"Nick Pomodoro. My partner, Charley Dobson."

Dobson glowered.

"Chris is building a building over on Fifty-sixth."

"Oh, yeah? When are they going to do something about that one on Fifty-seventh? There's planks blowing off in the wind."

"I just took it over."

"Oh, yeah?"

"I'll have her closed in by fall. What do you guys do?"

"Homicide." This was worthless in terms of Mafia intelligence, but it was an opening to more cops.

"Nice work if you can get it."

"Steady," Nick agreed, and even Dobson ascended from his gloom to remark, "It's a fucking growth industry."

Taggart returned Thursday night after Thursday night, gaining their confidence until he was less cop buff than one of the boys. A street-crimes sergeant needed a bridge loan to close on a new house before he sold his old one; Taggart obliged. A mounted patrol sergeant everybody liked was forced to retire at sixty-five; Taglione Concrete put him and his horse in charge of security at its sprawling East River plant.

On Wednesdays he regularly hit a cop bar behind the new police headquarters downtown. Tuesdays, a spaghetti joint next to the Fifth Precinct. On Fridays, religiously, he joined Uncle Eamon for end-of-the-week drinks with his brass hat cronies. And Monday nights it was back to Armstrong's Saloon to catch the captains trickling in from the John Jay College of Criminal Justice.

That summer, just before night classes ended, Taggart Construction contributed to the PBA's widows' fund. Taggart loaned the Taglione family's Catskill acreage to several PAL-supported Boy Scout troops for wilderness camping. And in the fall, he formed the Mike Taglione Memorial Foundation, which bought a thousand bullet-proof vests for the NYPD.

He borrowed a leaf from Sylvia's show-biz book and invested serious money in his business image. He toyed with the idea of an elegant car like a Rolls-Royce, but settled instead upon what he described to his decorators as a "blow 'em away" office in the partially completed Fifty-seventh Street tower. Unfortunately, he didn't make clear who his image was aimed at, so he scrapped it and tried to explain again. "My old man always drove a big white Lincoln Continental."

"So what?"

Chryl Chamberlain zipped her drawing case shut with a vicious buzz. Her partner, Victoria Matthews, glared angrily and gripped a clump of her red hair as if to yank it out. A year out of Pratt Institute of Design, they were outraged that a

Taggart demolition crew was stuffing their first effort into dumpsters.

"I still think you're tops. I'm trying to explain what I need."

"Not very clearly," Chryl replied icily.

Taggart wondered whether he would toss them out with their design if they weren't two of the most beautiful girls he had seen in his life—women, actually, in their late twenties, who had retired from modeling to study architecture. But for hair color—Chryl was blond—they might have been sisters, with their lovely, lean faces, straight noses, and long bodies that seemed to drape over furniture as if each piece had been built with them in mind and gently placed underneath. They had a habit that enchanted Taggart; one would lightly rap the other with the back of her half-closed hand, their heads would bob, and a word, a look, or a laugh would flicker between them. Today, however, they weren't laughing.

"My pop used to say, 'Most guys humping a guinea Cadillac'—that's a wheelbarrow—'think they're smarter than the boss. My car makes 'em wonder.'"

"But you just threw half our job into a goddamned dumpster."

"And handed you a check for your full commission."

"It's not just the money."

"That's right. I won't smile at something that doesn't work. Do you get what I'm saying about my father's car? Forget taste. What you did looked great, beautiful." He cracked a small smile and tweaked the dragon's tail. "Soho chic—"

"You son of a bitch!"

"But it doesn't work for me. At this point I gotta go for impact. I've got a problem making money people believe me. I've got great ideas, but they think I'm a kid. I have to get their attention before they'll listen. Can you try again? Can you design me an office that makes a joint venturer scratch his hard head and wonder, Maybe we should be nice to this kid?"

"What's a joint venturer?"

"A guy in control of a hundred million dollars, such as the assets of an insurance company. An investor I gotta convince to go in with me on a new project."

"How old are you?"

"Old enough to take you both home and screw your brains out."

"That's offensive."

"Asking my age is offensive. I just *paid* you for a job I didn't like. Now I'm giving you a blank check for your biggest commission since you graduated. And you're still bugging me about how old I am? Just like the joint venturers."

"That doesn't give you the right to act like a clod."

"And speaking of brains, it shouldn't take too many to figure out that if your design gets me more buildings to build, you'll get commissions for lobbies and plazas and offices. That doesn't give me clod rights either, but it would be a hell of a lot of fun. We can do some good buildings."

Victoria rapped Chryl's shoulder, and they exchanged a speculative glance. They were very tight, so finely tuned to each other that Taggart couldn't read them.

"Okay, I'm twenty-two."

"Sounds old enough to me," Chryl said. "We'll put our heads together for a boyish fantasy."

"One more thing."

"What?"

"It has to be movable. I'm a builder, and I want my office where I'm at."

"We'll make you a new one."

"No. I want that image to come with me. You know how kings used to move from castle to castle to keep an eye on things?"

"Carrying their tapestries with them," said Victoria. "Right. Okay, we'll come up with a *royal* boyish fantasy."

Chryl touched her with her knuckles. "Do we call him Your Majesty?"

"Clod will do," said Taggart, and they were friends.

He got lucky and connected with a federal agent who would serve him for years. An assistant business agent of the Cement and Concrete Workers Union hit Arnie Markowitz for a payoff at the East River plant, and Arnie, who could be very street smart, sensed something was wrong and passed the guy up to Chris. The business agent started talking in circles, trying to get Chris to finish his sentences for him.

"I don't understand," Chris finally interrupted. "Do I have a labor problem or don't I?"

"I think it's fixable."

At that point, custom deemed it appropriate to lay money on the table. But Arnie's warning, and the heightened senses Chris had begun to cultivate while scheming his revenge, told him something wasn't kosher.

"So fix it."

The business agent backed out with a frustrated look. Chris went down the stairs after him and followed him around the corner. A sedan was double-parked on Eighth Avenue. It had long, whip radio antennas. Inside was a man, barely visible behind tinted glass. The business agent shook his head as he passed. Taggart leaned on the roof of the car and knocked on the window until the glass was lowered an inch.

"Was that prick wired?"

"What?"

"I'm Chris Taggart. You're trying to sting me for bribery. What are you, FBI?"

The agent tried to look serious.

"If this is what my taxes go for, I'd rather buy an aircraft carrier."

"Take it up with the IRS. What did I do wrong?"

"You sent the wrong guy. The turkey can't act. Every time he opened his mouth he was reading from your script, and then he expected me to read it back. If I changed one word, he almost dropped his teeth. What did you get on him?"

"None of your fucking business."

"Hey. I just helped you do your job better next time and you're yelling at me. I'll tell you something else. You're wasting your time. I don't pay bribes."

"Can I quote you on that?"

"I'll sign an affidavit."

"Better discuss that with your lawyer."

"I'll ask my brother. He's interning with the U.S. Attorney's office. Well, this blows the afternoon. How about a beer?"

"Close your eyes."

Long, perfumed fingers closed his eyes. Chryl took one

hand, Victoria the other, and they led him into his new office. He heard the door close firmly.

"Ready? Open."

"Outta sight!"

"We can't decide whether to call it 'Clod Chic,' or 'Guinea Cadillac.' What do you think?"

"I love it."

"You would."

They had mingled Japanese electronics and expensive-looking European antiques. An entire wall sported the latest executive toys: stereo, multiscreen television, and video games. In the center a leather ottoman faced burled-walnut bookshelves. Anchoring the business end was an art-nouveau desk with lines that flowed like a river.

"The carpet's for class," said Chryl, as Victoria demonstrated the electric curtains and multilevel lighting. "John D. Rockefeller bought it second-hand."

Victoria touched another button. The bookshelves opened and a king-sized bed was lowered with a sigh.

"I love it." He walked around, toying with the electronic control panels. "What happened to my books?"

"Since you persist in putting your own books in the shelves, we've had them leather-bound. As you get new ones, your secretary will send them to the bindery. Including those tacky paperbacks."

The first electrical contractor to set eyes on the desk said, "No wonder you're jewing me down. What did that fucker cost?"

"Somebody's got to pay for it."

A Morgan Guaranty vice president Bunker had introduced him to said, "I saw that piece in Christie's last month. I wondered what lucky devil would get it. Very nice, Chris. Very, very nice."

Even the cold-eyed Bunker was impressed. "Yet another reason to get richer sooner."

Chris reported to Chryl and Victoria that it was working. "For a ten-thousand-buck desk the guy's talking about syndicating a sixty-million-dollar condo. People want to believe."

"Did he ask how old you are?"

Chris touched her mouth. "I said you two could vouch for me."

Victoria sprawled on the leather ottoman and laid three lines of coke in the etched grooves of a gold thirties Dunhill cigarette case. She held it toward him.

He shook his head.

"Do you guys ever try sex without dope?"

Chryl peeled off her designer jeans, stepped out of her panties, and pressed a button that simultaneously closed the drapes and lowered the bed. "Chris, you're a credit to your gender, but often nobody's home. Something's in your head. So we put something in ours."

"What do you mean?"

Their ménage dated from the night they celebrated finishing the office. They had taken a sort of possession of him, like a mutual Christmas gift, and the several years they had on him often made him feel like a kid. He watched Victoria squirm out of her slacks and tried to concentrate on saying, "Hey, I resent that. I really like you. I'm half in love with both of you."

Chryl touched another switch and the light turned golden, flickering on her shapely legs as she crossed the carpet and stretched over the ottoman with a silver straw.

"There are times I don't know where one of you begins and the other ends."

Victoria smiled over her shoulder. "Don't think we're complaining. We're quite capable of filling in the spaces. We also like you dearly."

"I get lost with you."

Victoria looked unusually serious and said quietly, "I wish that were true, Chris. We'd make you a bigamist. But you're lost in something else."

For fiery moments, time disappeared with them, and memory dissolved. Their first night he had lain spent, unable to remember why he had gone to England. But the next day, when they showed the office to their parents, he had ached that these well-dressed strangers should see what his father would have loved.

Chapter 7

*H*E BEGAN TO revel in his work, moving surely and swiftly again, as when he first took over his father's building, fueled by the larger goal. Now everything he did served the single purpose of creating wealth and power to destroy the Mafia.

Uncle Vinnie offered to bid partners for a Newark Airport runway contract if Chris would front the project. Chris suspected Vinnie was holding hands with somebody in the Port Authority who had foreknowledge of the bids, but he didn't ask because he needed the money. He bid what Vinnie told him; Taglione Concrete undercut the local competition and landed the contract.

He rescued another half-built derelict on upper Broadway for a song, and he continued scouting Columbus Avenue properties between Lincoln Center and Seventy-second Street. When his accountant iterated the banker's contention that it was "a wasteland," he extended the search to Eighty-sixth Street.

"I have heard," Henry Bunker complained when Chris hit him up for mortgage money, "that the one decent restaurant above Seventy-second Street maintains an armored car for its customers' convenience."

"How about another walk?"

After a twenty-minute walk from Bunker's Sixth Avenue office, and an excellent meal, Chris showed him the bill. "Expensive restaurants mean expensive apartments. The waitress says the armored car's in the shop for reloading, but I want to show you something."

He led Bunker up grim-looking blocks of Columbus to a basement bar he had discovered on Eighty-sixth Street. The bar was called Strykers, and Chico Hamilton was playing that night. Bunker, who regretted admitting to Chris that he had a severe weakness for jazz, agreed to stay for a few beers. After three sets he was making noises about getting up in the morning, when Chet Baker walked in with his trumpet.

Baker played "The Thrill Is Gone." Then he put down his instrument and sang it. And Henry Bunker, wiping his eyes and complaining about the cigarette smoke, promised to review Taggart Construction's proposal for a Columbus Avenue apartment tower.

On the way out they ran into a black narcotics detective-sergeant Chris knew who invited them to a narc party in a Village loft. The detective shared a bottle of Southern Comfort she had in her purse in the cab downtown, and they landed thoroughly ripped on Washington Street at two o'clock in the morning. Upstairs was wall-to-wall cops—NYPD, DEA, Treasury. Taggart introduced Bunker to some friends. Suddenly he stared at a group laughing loudly.

"What's the matter?" asked Bunker.

"Want to meet my brother?"

Tony had a beer bottle in his hand and a sharp grin on his face. He said something and four cops cracked up. When Chris approached him, his grin faded and he looked as astonished as Chris had felt. "What the fuck are you doing here?"

"What about you?"

"I'm a guest of that lady over there. This here's Bunker, my banker. Bunker, meet Tony Taglione, first-class prosecutor on the make and number one brother."

Later, when they were alone in an all-night coffee shop on West Fourth, he asked Tony, "Are you on a case with these guys?"

"Cops bring their investigations to prosecutors they want to work with," Tony said. "I'm making friends."

"Drugs?"

"Drugs make the best cases. The wise guys get crazy around the money. And freaked by the prison terms."

* * *

From the night they bumped into each other wooing the cops, Christopher Taggart followed his brother's law career with wary fascination. Tony, it seemed, was advancing in a sort of legal parallel with Chris's his own march for revenge. Congressman Costanza had helped get him the summer internship in the Southern District U.S. Attorney's Office and Tony had been asked back the next summer. By that time he had transferred from Harvard to Columbia Law School, claiming he wanted to be near the New York action. The next summer he had interned with the public defender. He worked for the Manhattan DA, ground out good enough grades to clerk for a federal judge, a former crusading organized-crime prosecutor, passed the New York Bar examination, and then landed a job with the Justice Department in Washington.

For two years the brothers met at Christmas and weddings and funerals. Then one day Tony telephoned from Washington, as excited as Chris had ever heard him, and announced he was coming back to New York.

"Gonna work for me, Bro?"

"No way! Criminal Division of the Southern District. I want you to come to my swearing-in."

Taggart managed to stammer congratulations, but when he hung up the telephone his heart was pounding. He went to the window. As usual, Chryl and Victoria had moved his office to the building he was currently erecting. Madison Avenue was streaked cement-gray a hundred feet in both directions from the gate. His heart was still going like a jackhammer. He saw a dangerous opportunity, risky as hell, but too good to resist.

He was clear in his conscience that he had never pushed Tony in this direction, that his brother had arrived in the U.S. Attorney's office of his own free will. But he had promised his father he would take care of him, so he said, the morning of Tony's swearing-in, "Before you go and pledge your life away, I'm asking you again—please join up with me as general counsel and a full partner in Taggart Construction."

Tony looked at him with fiery eyes.

"Four hundred grand a year," Taggart persisted. "Hot and cold running secretaries. We'll make a great team, man."

"No! You've asked me before and I've told you before, I don't want corporate practice. I'm a prosecutor."

"Still gunning for the Mafia?"

"Don't ask me again."

"I promise," said Taggart. He threw his arm around Tony's shoulders and they went upstairs to the executive floor for photographs with the U.S. Attorney.

Taggart had met Arthur Finch at the last Al Smith dinner and had been impressed. Scion of an old New York railroad family, Finch had ignored the careers of foundation directorships, Foreign Service, or Ivy League academia traditionally favored by inheritors of huge private incomes. And though he looked like a clubman in his staid Brooks Brothers suits and dull neckties, and spoke in a voice that evoked elite boarding schools, he had waded into government lawyering with a steely determination the equal of any striving Italian or Irishman. The youthful prosecutor regarded himself as conservator of his office's eighty-year-old tradition of disinterested law enforcement. He was famous for icily correct rages when confronted by incompetence, laziness, or any hint of political subversion of the legal process. He was also, persistent rumor had it, running like a cheetah for governor of New York State.

Finch administered Tony's oath of office before a hundred assistants in the office library. Taggart's eyes filled as Tony pledged to uphold the United States Constitution and the laws of the land. The casual gathering of the prosecutors to welcome another to their band was strangely moving, but the source of his emotion was a sudden fantastic vision of his father alive beside him, wearing his blue meeting suit and a broad grin and stage-whispering proudly that from now on they had better be damned careful talking business around the breakfast table.

Finch announced that Tony would be specializing in organized crime business extortion, then joked, with a wink at Taggart, that any plans to convert the U.S. Attorney's St. Andrews Square offices to a high-rise condominium had to be cleared by Washington.

Chris saw Tony's face mask up and the mark his ring had

gouged on his cheek turn angry red. Tony had long ago put his inherited share of the company in the blind trust required of public servants, but Christopher Taggart had become too flamboyant a New York character for his name change to distance Taggart Construction from Tony Taglione. The delicious irony was that from the day he took his first job with the Justice Department, few wise guys dared demand a payoff from Tony Taglione's brother.

They went down to Tony's new office. It was cluttered with cartons of books, his backpack, and the former occupant's desk, chairs, and telephone. Tony told his paralegal assistant he would greatly appreciate a typewriter before lunch, and turned to Chris. "Lunch is out. I have to get to work."

Taggart handed him a gold-wrapped package he had stashed with the receptionist. "Happy new job."

"Since I'm on the public payroll, I gotta be careful what I accept from rich businessmen." It sounded like a joke, so Chris kidded back dutifully, "If you report it on your income tax, it's going to knock you into another bracket. Go on, open it."

Tentatively, Tony removed the wrapping and opened the box, revealing a dark leather briefcase with solid gold corners. He turned it slowly in his hands.

"I figured it's time you stop carrying a backpack," Chris said. He pointed out the combination locks and Tony's initials, A.M.T, embossed in gold. "The hinges suck, like on all of them, but Saks'll fix 'em. Do you like it?"

Tony set it on his desk, crossed his arms, and stared. "I'll look like a defense counsel."

"Look inside."

"Cheri and Vicky pick it out?"

"*I* did."

"Seems more their style."

Stung, Taggart said, "Hey, what do you have against Chryl and Victoria?"

"Nothing."

"You hit on every other girl I had since I was twelve," he said heatedly. "Why won't you even talk to them?"

"I don't do that stuff anymore," Tony replied seriously. He

startled Chris by putting a hand on his arm. "Chris, I'm not as crazy as I used to be."

"If anyone in this family is crazy it's me, not you."

"Chris, they all see me straight arrow, but you know. Come on, Bro, we've been places."

It was as intimate an exchange as they had shared since the night of their father's funeral, six years ago, and Chris shook his head in disbelief. Tony was such an innocent—Kathleen Taggart's altar boy son—thinking that their Greenpoint escapade and the occasional Queens Boulevard drag race was heavy-duty sin.

"But I'm over that," Tony continued earnestly. "Now when I have to prove something to myself I do it right here at this desk and in that courthouse across the plaza. Kicking criminal ass beats stealing my little brother's girlfriends."

Tony took his stunned silence for argument. "Bro, it doesn't matter anymore that you're bigger than me now, or Pop liked you better, or I didn't want the business. Okay? We have our own lives. Our own women."

"Pop didn't—"

"Drop it. Please. Pop's not here to defend himself and you can't speak for him."

"Okay. But would you do me one favor?"

"What's that?"

"Try to be nice to Chryl and Victoria? Whatever you think, they are magical women and they're very, very important to me. Like, I would have really liked to bring them here today."

Tony flashed a teasing grin that flung him back to childhood. "Do they switch mother and playmate roles? I mean who makes breakfast and who stays in bed?"

"Is rapping a brand-new Assistant United States Attorney in the mouth against federal or city law?"

"God's law." Tony glanced at his watch. "Listen, this is a real nice briefcase, but I gotta get to work."

"Not yet." Chris shut Tony's door and locked it. "Open the briefcase, Bro. Look inside."

Tony gave him a puzzled look and shrugged. The catches released with a soft click.

"Calfskin, so wrap your lunch in plastic. The salesguy said

they taught you at law school what to put in the pockets. See the secret compartment?"

Tony traced a line of stitching that rimmed the inside of the lid. His finger went unerringly to the release, the maker's seal, and it popped open.

"How the hell did you figure that?"

"I'm a sneaky guy. What's this?" Tony pulled a manila envelope from the compartment.

"Your real gift. Check it out."

Tony opened the envelope and spread a half-dozen sheets of typed paper on his desk. "What *is* this?"

"Your first case."

"What are you talking about?"

"Names."

"I can see that."

"With addresses and phone numbers."

"Who are these people?"

"Guys in the Concrete Workers and the Teamsters who've been hitting contractors for payoffs and kickbacks; and contractors who're buying sweetheart contracts."

"Where'd you get it?"

"And they're hitting on the union pension funds."

"I said, Where'd you get it?"

"I'm around. I hear stuff."

"Rumors."

"It's better than rumors. I hear one thing, I hear another. I put a few pieces together. Sometimes they add up." He picked up the last sheet of paper. "See this?"

"What is it?"

"Codes."

"For what?"

"I don't know. But this guy, I'm told, imports heroin."

"This says anchovies."

"Look who he sells the anchovies to."

Tony turned the page. "Vitelli Pasta 'n' Things. Atlantic Avenue."

"Owned, I hear, by a guy named Eddie Rizzolo."

Tony reached for the phone. "Let's sit down with my boss."

"No."

"What do you mean, no?"

"Keep me out of it."

"I can't just take this."

"Why not?"

"I have to tell the Crim Div chief where I'm getting it."

"No, you don't."

"You're telling me the rules?"

"Wait a minute," said Chris. "Just hold it a second." Even if the chief of the Criminal Division didn't throw him out on his ear, his plan to betray certain mobsters to the U.S. Attorney required a degree of secrecy that only Tony could supply him. "What if I were a street hood who you turned stoolie? You think I'd risk talking to more than just you? What would you do if I said, 'I ain't talking to no boss.' You must have some method of protecting a confidential informant."

"'Deep Throat,'" Tony admitted. "No attribution, no testimony."

"Call me your Deep Throat. If I hear anything else, I'll inform you, and only you. In the meantime, maybe you can get probable cause on this. Maybe get a wire up."

"Kind of cozy with the vernacular, aren't you?" Tony asked shrewdly, and Taggart realized he had gotten to him just in time. Two years tougher and his brother wouldn't buy it.

"Treat this like when an agent brings you a case. All you have to ask is, 'How can I make a case?'"

Tony looked at the door. "Chris."

"What's the matter? I'm a legitimate source. You can vouch for me if they ask. Tell 'em you've known me your whole life. I'm sure there are plenty other noncriminals who pass information to your office."

"But usually with a reason. Like they want to get even or knock off a competitor. Or they want what someone has."

"Clowns like these killed Pop."

"I remember."

"So I'm getting even. What's the matter with that?"

Tony divided the papers into two piles, crossed his arms, and stared at them as he had at the briefcase. "I'll tell you what's the matter. The construction stuff is one thing. I imagine you get hit for payoffs. I pray to God you're not paying them. But I understand that you know who's crooked and who's straight."

"I know who's crooked," Taggart agreed with a smile.

"But this dope stuff." Tony picked up a typewritten sheet. "This is like an agent affidavit. How do you know this?"

"I'm around."

"Around criminals?"

"Guys talk. I listen."

"Who are you hanging out with?"

"What is this, the third degree?"

Tony looked at him. He was dead serious. "You better believe it."

"Hey, I'm just a businessman."

"Businessmen don't come in here with dope deals."

"Bullshit. Guys with money are offered deals all the time."

"Not straight guys."

"Wait a minute. I'm just a businessman. But I got two reps around the city. One for being honest. And one for live and let live." He clasped his hands together, doubled his index fingers, and pointed them at Tony. "But *you* know, and *I* know, that they owe us."

"They owe the law."

"In this case it's the same thing."

"Where'd you hear this?"

"I'm in a bar one night. Somebody starts bragging he knows a guy who knows another guy who opened the wrong crate of anchovies, and he nearly got shot for it by the Rizzolos. . . . Doesn't the name ring a bell?"

"Sure, Eddie Rizzolo runs South Brooklyn. He used to be linked to the Cirillos."

"What else? Don't you remember? Blue Bus Line?

"Yeah, they own a legitimate bus company. It gives them enough profit to file real tax returns."

"Restaurants? Canarsie? Remember the little doll in Abatelli's?"

"Miss Universe. The night you got your head beat in."

"Her father. When I heard the name I remembered the connection between Eddie Rizzolo and Don Cirillo, so I started paying attention. I paid a guy for the codes he overheard in the Rizzolos' restaurant. And now, whenever I hear something I listen. Real close. When I get home I write it down. I write down his name, what they called him—'Bugsy' or 'The

Beast' or 'Eddie the Cop,' whatever the fuck. I write down where he's from and what family somebody whispered he was connected to. I got a research guy in my office who checks things out for me. My secretary looks up addresses and businesses. Then I talk to my friends in the cops. Sometimes what they say fits what I heard someplace else. When I get the same rumor from two sides I end up knowing more than either side."

"How'd you find the guy who sold you the codes?"

"What are you busting my hump for?"

"How'd you find him?"

"They killed Pop, goddammit. I got a right."

"How'd you find the guy who sold you the codes?"

Chris contrived to look embarrassed. He turned to the window, gazed awhile at the ramps looping onto the Brooklyn Bridge, and finally admitted in a low voice, "I hired detectives."

"Detectives?" Tony asked scornfully. "Are you nuts? What are you, a one-man gangbusters?"

"Hey! I'll spend my money the way I want to. I'm not breaking any laws."

"Okay, okay." It was Tony's turn to study the bridge. Finally he said, "What do you expect? You waltz in here with a name and I'll authorize the FBI to arrest the guy?"

"Tony, you know and I know the FBI has tons of organized crime investigations going. So does the DEA. So does the NYPD, State Police, Labor Department, IRS, Customs. The agents and cops do the planting and the prosecutors harvest. All I'm doing is pointing you toward some wise guy you might not know about. If it looks like the beginning of a case, use it."

"Do you mind me asking why you didn't give it to the cops?"

"Cops? Why should I give it to strangers when my brother's in the Criminal Division of the Southern District U.S. Attorney's office?"

"Uncle Eamon—"

"He's ready to retire. Besides, cops don't have the clout that your office does. What's your problem, Bro? Are you telling me you don't want me messing around in your career?"

"I'll take any source I can get," Tony replied hastily. "But I just got here. It took you time to put this together."

Taggart laughed. "I waited for you. I had faith you'd get where you were going. Tony, what do you got to lose? Put Rizzolo away and they might even invite you to join the Strikeforce."

Three office buildings, a midtown hotel, and a Westchester shopping center later, Christopher Taggart returned to England. He stayed at the Savoy because Chryl and Victoria told him he would like it. He visited the British foreign office to discuss building a new British consulate in Manhattan. He met with the managers of the Royal Family's estates to pitch erecting a hotel tower on one of their valuable and vastly underutilized midtown Manhattan properties. He wrote Tony a postcard: "London's picking up. Might buy it. Congratulations on making Strikeforce. (signed) Deep Throat."

Although he was now twenty-nine years old, when he stepped out of his hotel on the last day of the trip with a knapsack slung over one shoulder, he still looked more like a professional graduate student than a Manhattan developer that *New York* magazine had dubbed—quoting a rival builder—"the slickest new dude in the Big Apple."

He drove southeast of London to a country pub outside Maidstone that Reggie Rand frequented for lunch the rare times he was in England. The bar was thick with young car salesmen and insurance agents, but the former Scotland Yarder was seated alone at a table in the bay window, reading his newspaper by the rain-filtered light and smoking an expensive cigar. A plate of cheese and pickled onions sat untouched beside a freshly poured Newcastle Brown Ale.

He looked prosperous; the Burberry trenchcoat folded on the bench beside him was new, and his blue suit looked like a twelve-hundred-dollar job Chryl and Victoria had talked Chris into having made at Kilgour, French and Stanbury. The British racing-green Jag parked in front, Chris had learned, was registered to the arms trader that employed him.

Seven years had passed since Chris had shared his plan with Reggie in the student pub on the River Cam, but physically, Chris was relieved to see, the Englishman appeared not to have aged. He had a little more gray in his hair, perhaps, but he was still thin as a knife and appeared either remote or dangerous, depending upon how the light caught his eyes.

Chris tossed his knapsack on the Burberry. "Remember me?"

"I certainly do. What's this?"

"Open it."

Reggie unzipped the flap, turning the opening to the window, and closed it again. "It appears to be money."

"Your first year's salary. A million bucks. Cash."

Reggie looked at him, the flat pools of his eyes seeming to ripple. His mustache twitched as he shook his head with a rueful smile. "I'm rather taken aback. You passed my little test."

"Let's get something straight, Reg. When you work for me, I don't pass your tests. You pass mine."

Reggie Rand might have bridled, but he could not help smiling at Christopher Taggart's earnest audacity. "How long has it been since your father died? Eight years?"

"Eight years since the Mafia murdered Mike Taglione."

What a strange young man, Reggie thought; equally strange were his own emotions. Widowed for decades by the last German V-2 to fall on London, he had learned to enjoy his life alone and the dalliances that went with it. But of late, as he rocketed through his fifties, he had begun to take notice of children, and he wished sometimes that he had fathered a son.

Then along came this driven, vengeful, frightfully clever American—and an orphan to boot. It was too bizarre. "I made no promise to work for you."

"You need a job."

"You're misinformed." He thrust a proprietary hand toward the window, indicating boundless opportunity to the south and east—Africa, the Levant, a festering Orient. "There's a world full of angry natives out there, many of them violent. I'm doing very well arming them, thank you."

"Your business card says Hovercraft, but in fact you're the senior rep with Breech Arms Limited of Slough."

Reggie's eyes narrowed fractionally. "That's not common knowledge."

"I just bought an interest in Breech."

"I beg your pardon?"

"I'm a director through a Luxembourg holding company. I thought it might be handy for writing end-user documents for buying weapons. I'm going to get you fired. So like I say, Reggie, you'll need a job."

"What have I done to deserve your largesse?"

"There are four men in the world I could have hired, but each of them told me you're the best. We want only the best."

"We."

"I've got a great start on cop contacts and a pretty good intelligence profile on the current state of the mob. The feds are starting to romp all over them. We're going to finish the job. I'm nearly ready for your cutthroats. But first, we've got to get some dope flowing. The American market imports about four tons of uncut heroin a year. We need a ton for bait."

"Two thousand pounds of heroin? Why, if I had the ability to get rich importing heroin into America, would I do it for you?"

"You *can* do it. I checked. Selling guns, your contacts are even better than when you were a cop. You're tight with people from Amsterdam to the Golden Triangle. You know the Chinese Triads and their Swiss bankers and the shippers and airlines that mule the dope in and the money out. But you never run dope. Remember, when you shook me down in my office you said, 'One has desires, but one has obligations.' You seem to be a guy with a code, Reggie."

"And you're still prepared to spend millions and years more for revenge?"

"I'm projecting three years. Two more to get ready and a year to fight."

Reggie drained his ale in measured swallows. He pulled a cotton handkerchief from his pocket and dabbed his mustache, which was perfectly dry. Then he smiled like a man who had seen the future and liked the look of it.

"You appear to have matured, Mr. Taggart."

Two years separated the day in Kent that Taggart hired Reggie from the night on Forty-fifth Street when they betrayed Nino Vetere to the Strikeforce. In that time Taggart had laid the groundwork for his Shadow Mafia. He strengthened his political connections and boosted the prestige of Taggart Construction by starting the Spire; he continued playing Deep Throat for his brother Tony, and he penetrated the heart of law enforcement via the President's Organized Crime Commission. Reggie shuttled tirelessly between Europe and Asia, forging links to terrorists and mercenaries and connecting with international heroin merchants. Under Taggart's direction he established financial conduits in Switzerland, Luxembourg, Singapore, and the Cayman Islands and corporate fronts to shield Taggart's legitimate business. The Englishman subverted Mafia spies in Sicily and New York and formalized Taggart's cop and agent friendships by placing the officers on his own payroll; when the two years were over, the cops were still friends with Taggart, but worked, secretly they thought, for the Englishman with the bulging wallet and the empty eyes.

Taggart's opening gambit—the setup of Nino Vetere—appeared to be a success. Nino Vetere cooperated with the Strikeforce prosecutors that hot Memorial Day weekend and turned in Nicky Cirillo; New York's most powerful crime family was thrown into sudden disarray. But it was only the beginning, and that night, when Taggart suspended the treacherous Jack Warner from the top of his Spire, he already knew that his biggest challenge loomed. He still had to seduce a Mafia family into waging his war of vengeance.

Book II

Sweet Kiss of Revenge
(The Present)

Chapter 8

A WHITE DRESS of soft jersey, which never quite touched her hips though it moved as if it might, high-heeled shoes, and silken jet hair turned heads when Helen Rizzolo jumped down from her chartered Cessna. The pilot, who had made no headway with his silent passenger, tried again, but his eager smile got lost in the off-putting solemnity of her gaze. She refused help with her bag and hurried toward the hangar, where a lone taxi waited.

The driver didn't ask her destination. There was only one place to go—the federal prison, whose colorless stone walls dominated these remote western New York flatlands just as a castle cowed a medieval town. They hassled her at the main gate, as usual, but once inside, a guard captain on her payroll showed Helen into an attorney-consulting cell and made a show of closing the barred spy hole. Her father stuffed his cap between the bars anyway and scooped her into his huge arms.

"Sweetheart." Eddie Rizzolo buried his face in her hair, and she stroked his head until at last he stepped back, holding her shoulders in his hands, shaking his head, and grinning delightedly. As always, he stared at her face as if desperate to memorize her features for the long days to come. She noticed that he hadn't shaved in days, which wasn't like him.

"You look tired, Pop."

"But you look gorgeous. Jesus, it's good to see your face. How's your mother?"

"Okay."

"Hey." He took her chin in his thick fingers. "What's the matter?"

She couldn't say that his hair seemed thinner than at the

time of her last visit, or that it had turned nearly white since his conviction, so she forced a big smile. "Everything's okay. I just wish you were coming home."

"You live to gain," he replied, seriously. "And to gain you sacrifice. Right? It's the only choice we can live with."

"I know. I'm not complaining."

"How are your brothers?"

"We'll talk."

"Trouble?"

She shrugged. "I can handle it. It's you I worry about. Are they treating you all right?"

He looked away.

"What's wrong?"

"A guy pulled a knife on me." He raised his sleeve. His forearm was bandaged from his wrist to his elbow.

"What? We paid——"

"Maybe we paid the wrong ones," he said quietly. All of a sudden he looked frightened, and she had never seen that before. Her throat gorged with helpless anger. "We'll get on it, Pop," she promised fiercely. "We'll take care of it."

He looked away again, his brows working. She took his hand. "Does it hurt?"

"No. Yes! I don't know." Then his expression relaxed and he gave her a strange smile. "I'm doing fine. I'll be home any day now."

"Home? What do you mean, home? What happened?"

He glanced at the steel door and shook his head. No bribe could guarantee they weren't being bugged. Wives and daughters were, after all, time-honored couriers, and sometimes she suspected that the Feds ordered the guards to accept the bribes to trick her father into speaking freely. She made him sit so she could lean close to his ear and whisper, "What do you mean, *home?"*

Even in his prison uniform, even using prison soap, he still had the sweet smell which was her earliest memory of him. But it was odd that he hadn't shaved. He was usually as neat and precise as she.

He smiled vaguely. "I'll be home as soon as I'm better."

"Better? They didn't tell us you were sick."

"My . . . my. As soon as my . . . my . . . my . . . gets better."

"You mean your arm?"

"No. No. My . . ."

"Pop? *What* gets better? What are you talking about?"

"My, my, you *know!* When the doctor says my, my, my . . . So I can go home from the hospital."

She felt fear seep into her body. She shivered. "What hospital? What do you mean?"

"Well, you know, this hospital. This . . . I . . ." His eyes roved over the room and settled on the bars in the door. His voice trailed off. Suddenly he looked afraid again, as if he had finally heard the empty ring of his own words in the crazy way she was hearing them. He blinked, walked around the table, and stared at her. Then he asked in a small, puzzled voice, "Why are you crying, sweetheart?"

"What is wrong with him?" she screamed at the guard captain.

"I don't know, miss. I really don't."

"Has he been to a doctor?"

"Couple of times. Said he felt funny. We took him there right away. Don Eddie has no troubles here."

"What about that knife?"

"We took care of the guy. It was just a scratch."

"It frightened him. He's different. I want to talk to that doctor."

"I don't know if he's around today."

"Find him, goddammit!"

She paced in the captain's office, running her nails through her hair, sinking into helpless terror. When the captain returned with the news that the doctor would see her, she said, "I don't know what, but something's wrong. He's confused; he doesn't know where he is."

"Like a little senile?"

"I didn't say that! He's only sixty years old."

She tore frantically through her bag and hurled a roll of hundred-dollar bills on the captain's desk. "Listen, you take care of him until he gets better. If he gets confused like that, he can't defend himself."

"I'll watch him as close as I can. It might help if I had a little money to pay a few more guards."

"You'll get it tomorrow. As much as you need. But if anything happens to him . . . you'll die."

"Hey, listen, lady—"

"You want to try me?" She stepped toward the captain, the blood rising in her face, her lungs filling, and he backed up. Helen took a deep breath. "Pass the word. Whoever hurts my father dies! I don't want him *touched!* Now, please, take me to the doctor."

The doctor, who had not been bribed, treated Helen as he would have the relative of any inmate. "What's wrong with him?" he repeated her question casually. "I would guess arteriosclerosis. Hardening of the arteries."

"He's not even sixty."

"Then call it Alzheimer's disease. That strikes men young. I don't know a darned thing about it except I can promise that it's never going to get better."

"But that's crazy. You don't understand. He's always been healthy. He doesn't smoke. He hardly ever drinks and then only wine and—"

The doctor glanced at his watch. He was young, and he managed to look sour and bored simultaneously. "If you look back a few years you might see flashes of strange behavior started then."

Memories slammed into her. Little lapses, apparently unimportant in the daily rush of events—lost in Manhattan, one time; failing to recognize a bodyguard, another.

"Can I get him out on this?"

"I'm not the warden. But it's an easy thing to fake."

"He's not faking."

"I'm not a judge either, miss. Or a parole board."

He was enjoying her agony. She collected her strength, putting her thoughts in simple order. She spoke to this monster as if he were a child. "You're a doctor—and under these circumstances, my father's only doctor. My family has influence. What can my family do for you in return for taking excellent care of my father?"

The young man laughed. "How about getting me on the staff of a real hospital?"

"The day my father comes home on a medical."

"Are you kidding? You should see my record."

"I don't care if you carry AIDS. Take care of him and I'll put you in the best hospital in the country."

She left the prison, stunned and grieving for her father. Only after her plane had been airborne for hours and they were heading down the Hudson River at eight hundred feet altitude was she able to admit that whatever happened next, from now on she could count only on herself.

When she saw the city spires beginning to thrust through the murk, she tapped the pilot's shoulder. "Westport."

"Connecticut?"

"Yeah. And I want to call Brooklyn."

She found her Uncle Frank haranguing his "boys." He greeted her with a big, surprised smile, then resumed his pep talk, gesticulating with a baseball bat and strutting like a rooster with a round belly and a balding head.

"I know they're big," he bellowed, "so you gotta hit hard. Back each other up. And please, please, please think before you throw!"

He thrust the bat into their circle. Nine young men with "Frank's Excavating" emblazoned on their uniforms piled hands on it and gave a throaty cheer. Frank sat beside her as they found their mitts and trotted onto the field in the fading light of a Westport evening.

"They're going to kill us," he confided. "You picked a hell of a day to come. Stubby's is romping the league."

Stubby's Bar and Grill's leadoff batters, full-bellied mustachioed men, each bigger than the last, were warming up. Fifty or sixty people watched from the low bleachers, while on the sidelines Greenman's Olds and The Car Store teams rehashed their game just ended. Lights came on, turning the brown infield mocha and the grass emerald; the air was warm and heavy.

Gloomily Uncle Frank watched his pitcher lob slowball warmup pitches. "Move back!" he yelled at his shortstop and motioned his outfielders to move farther out. He huddled with his line coaches, then returned to the first row of the bleachers, which served as his dugout.

"Beer?"

He pulled two from the cooler at his feet and popped the tops.

"What brings you to the country?"

"Softball?"

He eyed her shrewdly. "Oh yeah? What's wrong? Have you seen your father?"

"Play ball!" The umpire stepped behind the catcher. Stubby himself addressed the plate, cast a condescending eye on Frank's pitcher's first effort, and fouled it over the left field line, through the dense weeping willows that bordered the field, and across four lanes of Route One. Frank's pitcher threw four balls in a row, and Stubby walked.

"Is it your father? Hey, hey, sweetie, what's wrong?" She was crying and he put his arm around her. "What's the matter, sweetie?"

"He's sick. He got stabbed. Not badly, but it seemed to set him off. . . . It might be Alzheimer's disease."

"They letting him out for it?" Frank asked coolly.

Frank was her mother's eldest brother. He hated the rackets and had violently opposed the marriage of Helen's parents; he hadn't spoken to her father in thirty-five years.

"They said he's faking. I'll get lawyers on it. He acts like he's eighty-five or something. He can't protect himself."

They sat awhile in silence, watching Stubby's runners circle the bases. Finally Uncle Frank sighed. "Is there anything I can do?"

Helen shook her head. "I just had to tell you."

"How's your mother taking it?"

"She doesn't know. I've got enough on my hands without her going crazy. I'm not going to tell her. Don't you."

"You two still fighting?"

"You know how it is."

"Yeah." Uncle Frank dried her eyes with his handkerchief. Then he teased her knee, making her squirm. "Like mother, like daughter."

"She's *your* sister."

"Sweetie. When are you going to get out?"

"What out?" Helen asked coldly, on guard now and her tears forgotten. "I'm not in."

"This is Uncle Frank, so don't tell me you're not in. Those lunkhead brothers of yours couldn't empty a can of tomatoes with instructions on it. If your father's really sick, it's all going to fall on you."

"Restaurants don't run themselves, Uncle Frank."

"I'm not talking about the joints," he snapped fiercely. "And I'm not talking about the bus company. I'm talking about—" He glanced at the crowded bleachers and lowered his voice. "You know what I'm talking about. Get out. Get out while you can." His eyes glistened as he took her hands. She pulled away, but he seized them again, hard, and tugged her around to face him. "You're not even my kid, but you're my favorite kid. You know? Since you was this high. You was *my* little girl."

For as long as she could remember, she had come up here with her mother. In Uncle Frank's house—much more than in her own home, where her father often disappeared unpredictably—she felt treasured. Her uncle adored her as only a man with no daughters could love a niece. Here she felt safe. Even though he was leaning on her, she was glad she had come tonight.

"I've seen this coming," he said. "You're getting sucked into it worse every day. And your goddamned father has allowed it."

"My brothers need me."

"Screw your brothers!"

"I have a duty. What is the saying?" She whispered in Sicilian, "'A wife is one thing. A sister something more.'"

"Don't give me that peasant crap. Get out of it! Make a life for yourself. Be some kind of real person. Like you almost did when you went to college."

"I didn't fit in there."

"I know it was hard. What do you think I gave you the car for?"

She smiled; her parents had refused to let her live in a dorm the first semester, and had her driven every day from Canarsie to Bronxville and home again at night. When Uncle Frank found out, he gave her a red Fiat Spider.

"I needed wheels."

"You had wheels, driven by a gorilla. I gave you your own

131

car to make you feel like one of the regular kids. You almost did it before they dragged you back."

"They sent him to jail. I had to come home. Mama was—"

"Your mother—who I love—was as bad as him. She should of told you never to come home. Go to school. Be a person."

"That's the past."

"It's not too late. Do it!"

Helen tried to meet his eye. He was no fool and he knew her well enough to suspect that it wasn't only for her brothers and mother that she served her father. That perhaps she was tempted by the power that masqueraded as responsibility—and even relished it.

She pretended to watch the game and Uncle Frank pretended to change the subject. "Hey, what do you think of my pitcher? Nice-looking guy?"

"He's gorgeous." She had noticed him before the game began; he was tall and dark with thick black hair, sleepy eyes, and a body to dream upon. Which raised the problem she had faced since her father went to jail—if she dated a guy who wasn't connected she had to hide her true life, and if he was connected he would try to steal her business.

"Thirty years old, divorced. She was a bimbo. A guy that good-looking gets bimbos when he's too young to know better. He got the kid, a beautiful child you could die for."

Helen indulged herself with a long look. He was absolutely beautiful, an Adonis compared to the beer-bellies fielding. He pursed his lips slightly each time he wound up, a nice movement, like a probing kiss. Uncle Frank nudged her, grinned slyly, and apparently changed the subject again. "Did I tell you? Your cousin is finally going to be a dentist."

"How long has he been in college?"

"Longer than Enrico Fermi."

"Congratulations."

"Congratulations? Now I got no kid to take the business. . . . But this guy pitching? I send him out to dig a septic, I know he's going to bring the machine back in one piece. I'm thinking maybe I should make him a partner."

"Who takes care of his little kid?"

"His mother. Real Italian. Good family. But it would be nicer if he was *my* family."

"Sure. Who gives their business to *stranieri?*"

"Lemme introduce you."

"What? Frank—"

"He's a husband for an Italian girl. Strong when he should be, but a pussycat inside. What do you say?"

"He's in Westport. My business is in Brooklyn."

"You make a clean break. You sell the joints. You sell the buses. You leave your brothers the other stuff. You move up here, buy new businesses, and live in my house till you see if you like this guy."

The funny thing was how easy he made it sound. "What about my mother?"

"Connecticut's not Hong Kong, you know. It's an hour's drive, you can visit. Besides, you make bambinos with that fella and your mother'll be here like a rocket."

"Frank, what are we talking about? I don't even know this guy."

"I'll introduce you. You don't like him, I know others. Nice people—straight."

"Like you."

"Fucking A straight. I want to see the stars at night I look out the window; there's the sky, not a bunch of security lights. I hear a noise in the backyard and the cops come. It's a raccoon. I got a stranger at the door, he's waving a brush, not a gun. It's the real world. You pay your taxes. You do a little better than your parents did. You have some fun."

"What's fun? I have fun."

"Yeah? Tell me about it. If you take a guy like my pitcher to bed and it feels like something special, you don't worry about him being busted selling dope."

She gave him a smile, teasing. "All this bed, you make it sound tempting."

"What do you think I moved my family for?"

"You're in another world."

"It's a *better* world. See my boys playing? They graduated high school. They married their girlfriends."

"Just like Canarsie. So?"

"But *you* can't do that in Canarsie. Everybody knows

you're on the wrong side. Here you can start new." He nodded the length of the low bleachers at the people watching Stubby's massacre his team. "See their parents. Look at those girls, younger than you, with pretty babies."

He jumped up. *"Hey! Nice out.* Watch the first baseman when he comes in."

Stubby's team took the field and Frank's Excavating trotted to bat. The first baseman kissed a pretty girl and scooped their two-year-old into his arms.

"See? This is what real people do, Helen. They have fun, they work hard. They don't kill, they don't hurt, they don't push dope."

A blond all-American sort of guy with the name "Brace" stitched on his uniform greeted the couple, took the giggling child, and held him overhead. "How's the bambino?"

"Hear that? They even talk Italian. Let me introduce you."

"Uncle Frank, what are you doing to me?"

It was make-believe. At home she was bogged down in a seemingly endless war with the other families, while the Strikeforce prowled the edges, picking off the weak and growing stronger everyday. But here, tonight, with the air so soft and warm and the colors perfect, anything seemed possible. She looked again and wet her lips.

"Okay. Introduce me."

Uncle Frank motioned his pitcher over and gave him some unnecessary advice. Dark eyes flickered toward hers, filled with humor, maybe knowing passion. Helen smiled back.

Uncle Frank, transparent as a windshield, abruptly took notice. "Hey, Rudy. Ever meet my niece, Helen?"

Rudy cocked his head, obviously comfortable with women who enjoyed his looks, and just as obviously enjoying hers. "Hi."

"How you doing?"

Rudy shook his head at the scoreboard where the umpire was arranging double digits. "We're not always this bad. You up from the city?"

As if she needed confirmation that this was not a sudden impulse on Uncle Frank's part. "Canarsie. Are you always the pitcher?"

"The other guy ran the backhoe over his foot."

"How'd he do that?"

Rudy glanced at Uncle Frank, winked at Helen. "I don't know if your uncle wants to hear this again."

"Tell her," Frank grouched, then wandered off to confer with his leadoff batter. Rudy sat beside her and leaned close. "Your uncle sends him to dig a pool at a big rich house down by the water. The homeowner's daughter comes out sunbathing. He lifts the pods and starts moving the machine a little closer to the deck. She 'forgets' she loosened her top and starts to sit up. He forgets he's still in gear. She goes 'Oooh,' grabs her top, misses by three inches, and he creams his foot."

Helen laughed. "Is that true?"

"Oh, yeah. See, everybody sits in their own house here and Hubby or Daddy goes to work, and in comes this guy with no shirt on a machine. Happens all the time."

"Where's your cast?"

Rudy grinned. "I'm too old for kid stuff."

"Rudy! Rudy!"

"You're up."

"Excuse me. Gotta get a hit. Hey, we're going out for pizza after. Wanta come?"

She looked at him, liked his arms, liked his eyes, and thought, What the hell. She could stay the night at Uncle Frank's if it got late and run the country streets in the morning. "Sure."

"Later."

He hefted his bat and swaggered to the plate. The umpire called the first ball a strike and she booed with the crowd. Uncle Frank returned to the bleachers, his face troubled.

"He's really nice."

"I told you."

"What's wrong?"

"Don't look now, but your hood brother is here."

"What? Where?"

"He's in a van, over there."

Her stomach clutched. Eddie here without warning meant there'd been more trouble.

"I gotta go."

"Get rid of him. We're going for pizza after the game."

"I can't. . . . I'm sorry."

"Get out. Get out." Frank grabbed her hand. Helen pulled away and hurried toward the driveway.

Eddie's van was black with smoked-glass windows, a little beat up, and consequently as ordinary as the thousands of vans that plied the outer boroughs and suburbs. Even the beefed-up tires to support its bombproofing looked like last winter's snow tires. She spotted a second van Uncle Frank hadn't noticed, and, parked at a distance, a car with three guys who looked like federal agents.

Behind her she heard Rudy connect with the sharp crack of a solid base hit. The little crowd cheered and she wanted to turn around and see how he did. But Pauly, her brother's bodyguard, seemed very nervous; he gunned the engine and popped open a door for her. She got in and they started to roll.

Her brother, Eddie "the Cop" Rizzolo, was a strapping man in his thirties with fine jet hair and an open, sensual face swelled by food and wine. Physically he looked like a bigger, younger version of their father, but he had neither the shrewd intelligence nor the ambition that made Eddie Senior a leader —*had* made him a leader, she reminded herself. Those days were gone.

Eddie's ordinary-looking van was luxuriously appointed, with leather seats, a bar, a TV, and a partition between the passenger compartment and the driver. He put down his Johnny Walker Black, pulled her close with a kiss on the cheek, and turned up the sound on the Cable News.

"Just in time for the bullshit. President's Commission on Organized Crime."

"What's wrong? Why'd you come up here?"

"Catch this first."

"What happened?"

"I'll tell you in a minute. Look at this."

She and her brothers had already concluded that the Commission's witnesses were way out of it; they described the past while the Federal Organized Crime Strikeforce was breaking down doors in the present. The camera panned the men and women at the periwinkle-blue tables while the chairman closed the hearing and thanked them for their work. They looked like they thought they should look, serious—all but a smiling blond guy in front who seemed familiar.

She tapped the screen with a red nail. "Who's that?"

"Taggart. The builder."

"Taglione's brother?"

"That's him. You musta seen him at the trial."

She said nothing, but she had seen him long before her father's trial. In fact, he'd never been at the trial. The camera cut back to the chairman, who scheduled the next hearing in Atlantic City. Eddie laughed, flipping it off. "So next month they'll get laid and play craps."

"Hey, you're white as a ghost. Are you okay?"

Eddie raised the hand he'd been hiding. It was pillowed to his elbow in an enormous gauze bandage.

"Oh, my God! Eddie."

"Fucking Cirillos sent some blacks to hit one of our numbers on Knickerbocker. Too bad for me I was there. Blew my fingers off. Two of 'em."

She stared at the bandage, her stomach churning.

"No big deal. I'm checking out who did it."

"That's why there's Feds in the car behind us."

"There are? I guess they figure I'm going to shoot somebody back. They figure right."

"No. We don't want another war."

"What do you think this is?"

"Later. After the Strikeforce."

"Later? The rate the Cirillos are sucking up Brooklyn, they're going to be charging us rent on the house."

Helen glanced at Pauly. He was driving nervously and watching them in the mirror. "I thought the Strikeforce getting Nicky Cirillo would slow them down."

"Not if Crazy Mikey comes up on top." Eddie promised with grim relish. "Then we'll see a real fight."

Her brothers still couldn't understand that it took more than guts, muscle, and snap decisions to fill Don Eddie's shoes. They were like proud, brave bears, ferocious in battle, yet doomed to be puzzled by the events which led to the fight, and mind-blown by the diplomacy which would end it.

She closed her suede bomber jacket because the van was ice-cold. Eddie noticed right away. "Cold?" He turned down the air-conditioning, threw his arm around her, and snuggled her close, like her father. Her heart flew to him.

"How's Pop?" he asked.

"Not so good."

"I wish he'd let me and Frank visit."

"He can't stand to see you guys inside. You know that. It's like you're convicted, too."

"Yeah, I know. So how is he?"

"Some guy pulled a knife on him."

"What?"

"It was taken care of."

"It goddammed better be."

"It's tough. The blacks own the prison."

She realized with an almost giddy sense of triumph that she had already decided not to tell Eddie and Frank about his condition. She kept a private place within her where she told the truth about things of the heart, but this was business. Her family simply could not survive her brothers' leadership, so she had lied about her father, so they could all survive.

"We got black friends," said Eddie. "Spanish, too."

"Maybe you better talk to them again. There's a limit to what we can buy from the guards. I think maybe we should—"

She had a funny feeling that Pauly was listening. She pressed the partition button. The glass hummed shut.

"Wha'd you do that for? Pauly's like my right hand." Eddie flourished the bandage with an ironic laugh.

"There's some things to talk about."

"Sit on it till we're home with Frank. You sure they took care of the knife?"

She started to reply, but Pauly was still bothering her. Like most no-class Italian guys she knew, Pauly took his image from the movies. *Saturday Night Fever* almost a decade gone, he was still failing hard at a John Travolta image in a black leather jacket, white shirt, black pants. A real *cafone*. Who else would drive her brother around for ten years? But why so nervous tonight—the tense set of his shoulders? This wasn't his first war. He kept cocking his ear toward the intercom. She touched the switch. It appeared to be off.

She looked at him. Pauly's eyes were flickering like snake

tongues in the rearview mirror, and suddenly Helen felt herself reeling from her third sickening jolt of the day. What if the Strikeforce had turned Pauly? That was their style. Get right to the top. What if her brother's bodyguard were wired? What if he had fixed the intercom so that he was transmitting every word that she and Eddie spoke to the federal agents tailing the van?

Helen opened the vanity, lighted the mirror, and calmly examined her makeup.

"Pop was wondering if you want to promote Pauly."

"What? Since when does Pop get into running my crews?"

"He says Pauly's earned it."

Pauly, the dumb *cafone*, proudly squared his shoulders.

Early the next morning, Eddie Rizzolo entered the Florida room in the back of the house that Helen used as an office. She was dolled up in a tight silk blouse, tighter jeans, and the open-toe, high-heeled shoes with thin straps that Eddie's girlfriend, who was jealous, called "fuck me shoes."

Helen looked up from a computer screen she was filling with financial spread sheets, swiveled her chair, stretched her perfect legs, and gave him her full attention. He knew she weighed a hundred pounds and stood all of five one without her spikes, and he towered over her, but when she fixed her violet eyes on him, he felt as if she filled the room.

"Was Pauly wired?"

Eddie nodded.

"Feds?"

"Southern District Strikeforce."

"What are they doing over here in Brooklyn?"

"They cut a deal with the Eastern District—joint investigations."

"Great. Was he alone?" Meaning, had the Strikeforce wired other Rizzolo lieutenants to transmit conversations with their bosses?

"Guaranteed. We had a little talk, first. It's a bitch with somebody you like."

"How long was it going on?"

"It just started, thank God."

"Thank God. How'd they get him?"

Eddie rubbed his mouth. He saw where she was going and didn't like it. "Pauly had a little heroin action on the side."

Her eyes flashed. "So they waved twenty years at him and he flipped?"

"His little cousin was in on it. That nice kid, Joey? The Feds told him they'd get the kid, too. Pauly got scared what the fags in jail would do to little Joey, so he flipped. They had him by the balls."

"Did you know about Pauly's heroin action?"

"I didn't really know. . . ."

She leveled her gaze on him, cold, silent, watching.

"I guessed, but I stayed out of it."

"Eddie. We've agreed—no heroin! It's how they got Pop. It's not worth the heat. You've got to stop acting like one of the boys. You make 'em think you're just another guy, so there's no respect, there's no fear. You think Pauly would have dared pull that on Pop?"

"Yeah, well, maybe they know I'm not that smart."

She made a face, motioned him over, pulled his head down to her, and kissed his cheek. "Do me a favor? Remember something?"

"What?"

"Remember you're not alone, okay? It's you and Frank and Pop. And me."

Yesterday's unseasonably muggy heat had given way to a clear, chilly morning. After dead-heading some pansies in the backyard, she glanced up and surprised her smoky reflection in the bullet-proof plastic that her brothers had attached to the jalousie windows. A trick of the light made her face appear clear against a murky background, like an old-fashioned studio portrait of a passionate girl with serious eyes. She moved to touch it, but the shift caused the glass behind the plastic to appear, and the narrow slats seemed to slice her face into many parts. She shivered, shook her head violently, dropped the petals on the grass, and went back inside.

She cleared the computer in which resided the legitimate books for the Rizzolos' bus company, wedding palaces, and dance clubs. The blank screen stared back, another mirror. She got up to tend her house plants, but excess water was standing in their drain saucers, turning the jade leaves yellow. She punched some Corelli out of her stereo, but it did not soothe her and she turned it off. She stared at the oil portrait of Joannes Baptista Guadagnini that she had bought when she went to Italy to help after a big earthquake there. Her "patron saint"—but even the great trickster of the Cremonese violin makers could not make her smile today.

The light was making her crazy; it looked dirty because of the bullet-proofing. Her brothers were proud of the offset mountings which allowed her to crank the slatted windows to let in air, but, as with many things Frank and Eddie did, execution never quite matched intention. The special plastic had grown cloudy since her father had led them through the last mob war, when they had broken away from the Cirillos. It was so murky that her Canarsie neighborhood appeared to be underwater, while at night the glare of the security floodlights on the postage-stamp front lawn, the driveway, backyard, and alley was diffused like a snowstorm.

Ordinarily, when she felt trapped, she had many escapes—the old farm their grandfather had bought upstate in Westchester, a whaler's mansion on the north fork of Long Island which the connected side of her mother's family had owned since Prohibition, and a summer cabin in the Adirondacks. Cousins, people she liked, lived on handsome estates in the New Jersey hunt country, where she was welcome, even courted; for even the best Sicilian families had divorced sons in need of remarriage. And there was always, of course, Uncle Frank in Westport; and now, his handsome pitcher.

Once, when she got the itch to really break loose, she had boarded a plane alone to an isolated Club Med on Martinique, and for a week that still shimmered in memory she lived like somebody else. But since the Strikeforce, nothing was ordinary, and she wasn't going anywhere until things got a lot better, which didn't look to be soon.

She fled upstairs, removed her spike-heeled shoes, and peeled out of her jeans and blouse. She hung up her clothes, put her shoes in a shoe bag, and tossed her panties in the hamper. She confronted the mirror on her high school dressing table and regarded her body with pleasure. She was slight yet strong, fine rather than delicate. She chose a gray sweatsuit piped with lavender and tied a matching lavender sweatband around her head.

Eddie and Frank fell silent when she strode into the family room. Frank was even bigger than Eddie, a quiet, robust man of great and often indiscriminate appetites—quick to anger, quick to forget. They looked guilty about something, and Frank, who, unlike Eddie, could never lie to her, glanced anxiously at the unlisted telephone.

"I'm going running."

"It's dangerous to make it a habit, Helen. You set up a pattern and they're waiting."

"I have to get out."

Frank, whose street crews were responsible for the Canarsie area, sent reluctantly for her bodyguards. He cast another guilty glance at the telephone.

"What are you two up to?"

"Nothing."

"Come on."

Eddie looked obstinate, but Frank said, "This guy got in touch."

"No dope deals."

"Fifty keys," Eddie shouted, waving his bandage.

Frank said, "The price is going through the ceiling with the shortage. We could use the cash, Helen. Let me go upstate and dig up some bread."

"You guys! You got a Strikeforce just waiting to nail you. Did it ever occur to you that phone's probably bugged?"

"I swept it this morning," Eddie retorted, and Frank added, "We didn't say nothing."

"Besides," Eddie said, "the Feds can't just call us up to buy it. That's entrapment."

"Now you're lawyers. Listen, lawyers—you buy, you possess. Then you say hello to some guy the Feds wired and you're conspiring to sell it. I told you, no deals, no business."

"But this is different."

"We have an agreement, Eddie. You and Frank and me. When they put Pop inside we agreed. You and Frank run the business, but I make the decisions."

"I'm talking about running the business. You're moving into our territory now."

Eddie looked very determined and started pacing. Frank pushed his closed fists together, causing muscle to swell in his upper arms—his way of shrugging. Eddie, as usual, was the problem.

"Frank, did we have a deal?"

"Yes."

"Would you tell Eddie, please?"

"Come on." He pushed harder and his knuckles turned white.

"Eddie. Did you agree, too?"

Eddie broke off pacing. "Yeah."

"Did Pop go along?"

"Sure. He knew we was a couple of dummies."

"Hey." She went to Eddie, her heart filling. She tugged him toward Frank, and put her arms around both of them. "This is us. Right?" Teasing, she dug her nails into the rolls around their waists. "You want to come running? Get rid of those guts?"

Eddie pulled away. "What if we rip it off? This guy's a schmuck."

"Yeah," Frank said. "How about it, Helen? Can't we just steal it?"

The listed telephone rang in the kitchen. They waited, glaring at each other. Their mother appeared in the doorway, holding a towel, and Helen thought, as she often did, I'll never be that beautiful when I'm her age. Despite ribbons of gray in her hair, she had a showgirl's body and a face every boy in the family fell in love with as he came of age. Helen was never sure whether her mother really missed her father or preferred being sole boss of the house. She must miss sex—not that they ever talked about it. Like they didn't talk about business, either. Even the time the Cirillos blasted the picture window with shotguns, and the *Post* had Don Eddie's picture on the front page, she had clung to the fiction that her husband was a bus company executive.

"Some girl named Marcy on the telephone."

"Marcy Goldsmith?"

"Some Jewish name." Her mother shrugged. "She says she was your roommate in college."

"Tell her I'm out."

"Don't you want to say hello?"

"Mom. Please."

"Okay. I'll lie."

"Thanks."

Eddie started to speak as soon as she left, but Helen stopped him with a gesture. "Wait. She'll be back."

"How do you—?"

"I know."

Her mother returned, perplexed. "Marcy says you're alumnae."

"Didn't you tell her I'm out?"

"We got talking. She sounds like a nice girl."

"Tell her I'll send a check."

"Don't yell at me." She turned to Eddie and Frank. "You guys hungry?"

"Yeah, Mom. Sure."

"I'll bring something."

Eddie waited until their mother had gone again. "What do you say, Helen?"

"No."

Outside, two of her best men waited in a car. A third, a young zip from Sicily, warmed up in running shoes. She flopped beside him on the grass and did stretches, aware that grandmothers and widowed aunts were fluttering curtains up and down the block—Helen, the wild one, was at it again. The houses to the left and right were occupied by Rizzolo lieutenants, as were those that backed on them from the next street. The grouping offered a sense of security, but the street was no fortress if the Cirillos provoked a really bloody war.

"Let's go!"

Helen jogged out of the neighborhood, trailed by the car and the young zip, and took a road that cut across a marsh, through the park, and onto a path beside the Belt Parkway. The clear sun sparkled on Jamaica Bay. A land breeze, dry and chill, swept the shore. When the car had to cut ahead to intercept her at the next entrance, she motioned the zip to catch up. He was cute, with a little angel smile; but appropriately tough. What a way to blow a family apart, Helen thought; sleeping with a bodyguard. Brought up by decent people, he knew his place and never once threw anything remotely like a pass. Respecting that, she treated him with the same cool remoteness as she did all her family's retainers, and when she ran with him she wore baggy sweats to play fair.

She wished, as she often did, that there was some way of getting regularly and happily laid without jeopardizing her empire. A sudden dazzling-white smile made her look like a gypsy girl; in a few more good years she could afford to buy Club Med. But then the handsome French kids would be employees and it wouldn't be the same. Besides, thanks to the Strikeforce, the Rizzolo enterprises had stopped growing for the first time since she had taken over.

"Pennsylvania Avenue."

Two miles and she was feeling good, up for the long way back, another three miles. The bodyguard tinkered with his Walkman, which had been altered to serve as a radio connection with the car, and he repeated the direction into a dummy earphone.

Two runners came the other way.

Helen and her bodyguard automatically closed ranks to make them split and go around. They were jocks, big and muscular. The one on her side—a handsome Irish guy who looked like a fireman—gave her an appreciative grin, which she fell for hook, line, and sinker, smiling back even as his partner practically tore her bodyguard in half with a fist to the stomach.

The zip went down with an explosion of breath, blood, and vomit, clawing for the gun in his sweats. They were ready for that, too. One of them got to it first, pulled the gun, and ripped the wire out of the radio. The other caught Helen as she lunged toward the highway. She screamed for help. A car screeched to a stop. Two men were inside. It seemed like a miracle until they held the back door open while the runners forced her onto the seat.

She fought, kicking, biting, screaming. One threw himself on top of her. She levered her knee into his groin. He yelled and rolled off. His partner grabbed her by the shoulders. She laced into his wrist with her teeth, kicked a third man in the face, and threw herself at the door. She got the handle open. But they pulled her back and slammed her face down on the seat, where they pinned her bucking hips and jabbed her with a needle.

Chapter 9

T WELVE MILES TO the northwest, as Helen Rizzolo's captors sped toward Kennedy Airport, Christopher Taggart's White Rolls-Royce Silver Spur rounded a Harlem street corner, crunching broken glass beneath its tires. Reggie, his face hidden by doper shades and the polished visor of his hat, drove slowly down the block of derelict houses and dusty trees. Taggart sat stock-still in back, staring at the one-way bronze windows that made Harlem appear to bask in a golden sun.

Heroin addicts gazed at the corner, waiting for their man. Some were crying; some waited stoically in holes battered through the cinder blocks that sealed the gutted brownstones; the strongest clambered up rickety stairs for a better view. All stared in the same direction, like spring flowers tracking the sun on a cold day, and no one gave the gleaming car a second glance. Their man would come on foot, and he was late, if he was coming at all, for junk was getting short.

Reggie repeatedly checked Taggart in the mirror, but his regular smile had died, and he hadn't barbed him with a joke all morning.

"You know, sir, heroin trafficking is like child molesting in that one takes the most advantage of those least able to resist. On the other hand, you're not likely to entice Mr. Cirillo with butterscotch and toffee."

The first rule of the dope trade was never do business with anyone recommended by the person with whom you were already doing business; your associate has turned informer and his new friend is a cop. Taggart had to get Crazy Mikey Cirillo to break that rule.

"This sounded a lot better in theory." He had crossed lines by the very nature of his vengeance and expected to cross many more before he had destroyed the Mafia, but dealing junk was less like crossing a line than changing sides. The thing that kept rattling in his head was whether, if by some miracle they were to meet, his father would accept his goal as justification.

Reggie gave him a look, a reminder that heroin was Mafia currency, and Mafia power was wired to supply. Which made the Mafia just as dependent as the addicts on the street, and as ripe for exploitation.

A shiver ripped up the block, the junkies stirring as one, like grass in the wind. Taggart turned to the back window, expecting to see their dealer, but Reggie, alert to his mirrors, said, "We have a police car overtaking us. Two officers driving a brass hat."

The NYPD blue-and-white sedan shot alongside. The siren blipped and the cop in front gestured to pull over.

Taggart lowered his window. "Hi there, Captain. Hunting pussy?"

"Chris! What the *hell* are you doing here? I thought you were some damned pimp." The precinct commander stuck his arm out and they shook hands from car to car. "You trying to get killed riding around in that?"

"This baby's a lot safer than yours. I look like a local hero. You look like the enemy."

"What are you shopping for, a place to build a parking lot?"

Taggart winked. "Captain, if you were a very rich man I'd take you for a tour of the Columbus Avenue properties I bought in 1977. Harlem's getting hot. Now's the time to buy."

"Get your checkbook. I'll sell you my station house."

The cars moved off.

At last the dealer came, carrying a gun, because the shortage had driven the price of a "dime" bag up to fifteen dollars. His own connection had been an hour late with half the bundles he had promised, and his price had risen to one hundred and twenty dollars for ten bags, up from the normal seventy.

* * *

Downtown, Harlem's biggest black heroin distributor gazed mournfully through the iron bars of Gramercy Park as he discussed the dope situation with a Cirillo family crew leader. "If your people don't connect with my people soon, I'm going elsewhere for product." He was lying, in that he was already looking. The Cirillo *capo* repeated that he would have heroin soon. He nodded at the statue of Edwin Booth for something to say. "What's the line on this guy?"

"His brother shot Abraham Lincoln for freeing the slaves."

Beyond the park, through the far fence, the distributor noticed a beautiful Rolls Royce Silver Spur cruising past the Gramercy Park hotel. He had to get one of those; he had two cars already, a black limo and a red Corniche convertible, but neither booked like that white sucker with bronzed windows.

The *capo* tracked Crazy Mikey Cirillo to one of the family's whorehouses, a Flushing brothel that catered to a big afternoon crowd. Mikey, who should have been attending to business, in the crew leader's opinion, was putting on a show—a boxing match in a small ring in the basement. His hard-edged, handsome face was flushed with excitement, and the *capo* presumed he had just had a hit from the little gold sawed-off shotgun dangling around his neck. Shouldering through the mob around the ring, he reported the black distributor's threat. Mikey's expression turned menacing.

"Later."

"Mikey, the guy's not kidding."

Mikey cut him off. "I'm taking bets. Sherry or Rita?"

Two naked women were warming up on the ropes, a big buxom blonde and a smaller brunette. Reluctantly the *capo* appraised them. "The blonde."

"You'll lose." Mikey grinned. "Little Rita's a killer."

"This trouble can't wait, Mikey."

Mikey hit the bell with a ball-peen hammer. Thirty johns in suits and sports jackets cheered, and the girls tripped into the ring.

Because the light gloves hurt, Sherry and Rita had a long-standing agreement to pull punches. The johns didn't give a damn. They were happy with spread-legged falls and undulating struggles to rise from the canvas. Besides, as Sherry had explained to Rita, if anybody got bored, they could go upstairs and get laid, which was what they had come for in the first place; the nude boxers were only a floor show. But today, Crazy Mikey made one of his unpredictable visits and tumbled to their arrangement.

His face clouded as he watched Rita pretend she had taken a roundhouse to the jaw. She flung her arms high, flopped to the canvas, crawled to the ropes, writhing like a snake, and dragged herself back to her feet with the enthusiastic support of the johns. Mikey rang the bell signaling them into their corners.

The johns crowded around, toweling them down, plunging champagne bottles between their lips, spilling the stuff on their breasts. Mikey leaned close to Sherry and whispered, "A big one for first blood."

"You're kidding."

He crossed the ring to Rita, a tough little Spanish brunette with pointy breasts, and repeated the offer. Her eyes widened. "A thousand dollars?"

"All you got to do is make her bleed."

He hit the bell again and the girls bounded out of their corners, the webbing of the rattan stools imprinted on their flesh. Sherry, the blonde, still seemed reluctant to really punch, but Rita went for the face. Sherry peekabooed. The smaller Rita flailed at her gloves.

"Go for the body!" Mikey yelled.

Rita stepped back, planted her feet, and sank her glove into Sherry's belly. Sherry dropped her hands with an astonished gasp.

"Hit her!!"

Rita swung again, slugged Sherry in the face. Sherry sat down hard on the mat, crying. Blood trickled from her lip.

Rita pranced, clasping her hands over head and shouting, "I get the grand. I get the grand. Pay me, Mikey. Pay me."

"Hey, Sherry's not out," her champions protested.

"Don't worry," Mikey assured them. "Fight's just getting started."

The johns piled into the ring, heaved Sherry onto her stool, and poured champagne over her head. Mikey inspected her lip.

"You all right, sweetheart?"

"I can't believe she hit me," Sherry sobbed, wincing as the champagne stung the cut.

"What are you, nuts?" Mikey laughed. "For a thousand bucks she would have blown a monkey."

"It's one thing to fuck for money. It's another thing to hurt your friends."

"Everybody's got their price."

"I don't."

"Sure you do. The winner gets five grand."

"Forget it."

"The loser spends a month on the third floor."

Sherry gaped at him. "A month?"

"Every night. All night. Go for it, doll."

He whispered the same to Rita and the happy grin slid off her face. The third floor serviced rich kinks. A gorilla stood guard to make sure none of the girls went to the hospital, but short of that the customers got to do what they paid for; ordinarily the girls rotated. Neither Rita nor Sherry *had* to obey Mikey and his manager, but if either left the Cirillo brothel she would find the rest of New York—the bottomless bars, the sex clubs, and the porn flicks—locked tight, which left the option of getting lucky and marrying a doctor or, failing that, working the trucks in Long Island City.

They came out slowly, measuring each other.

"Mikey!" the *capo* protested. "We need product!"

Mikey turned, cold and deadly, and the *capo* recoiled, realizing too late that he had made a mistake. Crazy Mikey was no fool just because he happened to act like a spoiled rich kid. Goading a couple of girls into maiming each other might be merely a distraction while his brain shifted to overdrive to fathom what had gone wrong in the dope trade.

He reached for the gold coke spoon. Though barely an inch and a half long, it broke at the breech like a real shotgun, revealing a tiny cache of white crystals. Mikey snorted, closed the breech, and let it fall against his chest. "I'm doing it," he said softly. "Now get the fuck out of here."

As he watched the girls pummel each other's faces, Crazy

Mikey realized he had begun to get over the shock of his brother Nicky's arrest by the Strikeforce. Three days ago he had been pulping a bookie who had screwed the family when the word came and a bunch of long-faced guys had whisked him away like he was suddenly President of the United States. His father, Don Richard, had commanded him to take over Nicky's duties. He said he had faith in him. Later, the crew leaders told him bluntly how bad the dope shortage really was.

There was something going on that Mikey didn't understand. Everybody said the shortage stemmed from two years of Strikeforce busts. They had included the Pizza Connection, the Anchovy Connection, the Sicilian Connection, the Pizza Connections Two and Three—even the fucking Nepal Connection. And now the Forty-fifth Street Garage Connection, which had led to the crew leader Vetere's turning in Nicky. The arrests of wholesalers and importers had begun to squeeze New York's heroin supply just as the junkie population had increased. That's what everybody said.

Except that the Cirillos had been major importers and distributors for thirty years, and Mikey knew a lot of smugglers. Many who hadn't been busted complained of hijackings, unexplained accidents, and mysterious betrayals. Add those stories up and something weird was going on. What, nobody knew. All that was sure was that product was short and getting shorter. He opened the gold sawed-off coke spoon again, raised it to his nose, thought twice, and emptied the coke on the floor. Fucking up his head wasn't going to make his problems go away.

News of Mikey's plight flowed relentlessly to his father, despite the fact that the old man was, in theory at least, retired. Within hours, his *consigliere* reported the threatened defection of the black Harlem distributor. They discussed it over iced tea on the patio of Don Richard's home on a Staten Island hilltop. His thin red hair had lost some color in the decade since his dispute at Abatelli's with Christopher Taggart, and he stooped a little, making his shrunken frame seem smaller.

Manhattan lay across an empty harbor. The shining Wall Street towers hid the Metropolitan Correctional Center, but in his mind's eye Don Richard could see his older son's prison as if the towers weren't there. Forget the lawyers' promises. They were bluffing. His elder son was going away for years; in terms of controlling the vast family—the only terms that counted—Nicky was as good as dead.

Don Richard's *consigliere* warned that dozens of Cirillo *capos* were itching to fill his shoes.

"Mikey can handle it."

"You know I love Mikey like he was my own," the *consigliere* argued, "but he's not ready."

Don Richard shook his head. "He's a fast learner and he wants it. That's the most important thing. Even if he don't know it yet, he wants it. Like I wanted it."

"He's the baby, your youngest," the *consigliere* countered. "We expected less of him and he grew more slowly for it."

"Bullshit," said Don Richard. "That's nut doctor talk." He denied he had a soft spot for his youngest son—he was simply too hard and ambitious a man himself to admit such a weakness. In fact, his faith was rooted in memories of himself when he was Mikey's age. Surely he had been as silly and arrogant, and look how far he had come *without* the advantage of the tall and handsome looks of a natural leader.

Mikey would perform when he had to, despite a soft childhood as the son of a rich and powerful boss. Don Richard was so sure that he decided to stay aloof of the heroin-supply problem. His *consigliere* repeated that rebuilding their shattered import network was too stern a test for Mikey, that Don Richard must come out of retirement to help. Don Richard ignored that advice, as Christopher Taggart was betting he would.

The old man noticed, through the chain-link fence on the road, a huge white Rolls-Royce. He glared, offended that some cheap Colombian cocaine dealer was house hunting in *his* neighborhood.

In the car, Taggart said, "Head for the airport. Let's see what Miss Rizzolo has to say for herself."

Chapter 10

"Τ HE SHOT'S WORN off again," Reggie said. "I ought to give her another before she hurts herself."

"Wait."

Fascinated and a little awed, Christopher Taggart studied Helen Rizzolo through a one-way glass. Reggie's women had strapped her ankles and wrists to an oak chair, which was bolted to the stone floor. They had been careful not to hurt her, but no one had imagined the ferocity with which she would fight the unyielding leather, wrenching and twisting, her slight figure corded with straining tendons, and her face a mask of finely controlled rage. Her eyes met their own reflection in the mirror that camouflaged the view port, but she just kept struggling, as unselfconscious and determined as a leopard in a trap.

"I'm ready," Taggart said.

Reggie touched his arm. "I beg you to reconsider."

"We've been through this. She controls the Rizzolos. I can control the Rizzolos through her. They are tough, ambitious, and hate the Cirillos. As we hit the Cirillos, her family will pick up the pieces and recruit their soldiers."

"Ask yourself why you've chosen this woman."

"She had no criminal record. Her family's attracted the least Strikeforce heat since Tony jailed her father. She's innovative; she's against drugs and is perfect to take over gambling. Plus, she needs help."

All true. Starting with the thin lead Taggart had given his brother, Tony Taglione had made his name at the Southern District by convicting Don Eddie Rizzolo. When the Cirillos tried to move in on their territory, Helen's brothers fought

154

back in a bloody struggle which still smoldered and was exacerbated by mutual accusations of Strikeforce informing. The latest round had been the Cirillos' shotgunning of Eddie, Jr., who had, as was his wont, survived.

"She's also very beautiful. You've had your eye on her since her father's trial."

Before, thought Taggart, studying her through the glass. *Long before.* Like a sketch that captured the essence of the painting to come, the woman Helen Rizzolo had become had lived in the face of the girl Taggart had seen ten years ago in Abatelli's restaurant. She had grown an inch or so taller, perhaps, and womanhood had made her arresting beauty even more exotic, but her qualities already had been there—the power in her deep, still eyes, her fierce pride, and her heart-stopping sensuality. He was unwilling to admit to Reggie that he was as smitten at the sight of her today as he had been when he was only twenty-one. Yet he was confident that in the past ten astonishing years he had grown capable of savoring her at a safe distance.

"I'm not going to blow my whole scam 'cause I like the way she looks."

"Chris, while I was making our Sicilian arrangements, I had the great privilege of a love affair with a woman there. They never forget, they never forgive. If she ever realizes how you plan to use her family, she will destroy you."

"I'm Sicilian, too."

"One-quarter."

"That quarter's working overtime."

He pulled a black ski mask over his face and entered the room. She stopped struggling the instant she saw him and Taggart thought again of an animal, a predator whose every move embodied the dual purposes of attack and defense. She acted like an animal conserving strength while assessing a new threat; patience replaced the rage in her dark violet eyes.

"Helen, no one's going to hurt you."

"Take these things off me."

"Will you listen?"

Her eyes flickered over the stone walls, the small shuttered window, the solid plank door he had shut behind him, and his mask. If she was frightened, it didn't show. "Do I have a choice?"

"No."

"I'll listen."

Taggart unbuckled her ankles and then her wrists, prepared to defend himself if she kicked. She stood up, quietly massaging her wrists. "My clothes are clean and I've been bathed. Who touched me?"

"A nurse and a doctor, both female, were with you all the time."

"I'm thirsty."

Taggart poured water from a pitcher on a rough table by the door. She drank half and continued to draw small sips from the glass as they talked. "Who are you?"

"A friend."

"Listen, *friend*, do you know who I am?"

"Helen Rizzolo. You're here because I admire how you run your business."

"Ransom?" Helen laughed. "You grabbed the wrong person. I don't run anything. My family owns restaurants and a bus line—neither of which are doing well enough to pay ransom. My brothers run them. I handle the books, which is why I know they're not doing too well."

"It's a good story, Miss Rizzolo. The Feds believe it—at least the part about you not running things. More to the point, so do your rivals—the other New York families. They can't believe a woman could head a tough Mafia family. But the truth is that *you*, and you alone, control the Rizzolo betting parlors, the numbers, the extortion, and the hijacking. Your brothers just carry out *your* orders."

"Are you crazy?"

"*You* shut down the bookie joints when the Strikeforce hit. *You* stopped the war with the Cirillos. Yesterday, *you* ordered that one of your soldiers be, shall we say, 'terminated,' when he was discovered with a Strikeforce transmitter."

"I don't know what—"

"Your brother Eddie's crew leaders beat his head in with a baseball bat after Eddie was done questioning him."

"I don't—" She reeled suddenly and dropped the water glass. It shattered on the stone. Taggart caught her as she sank to one knee amid the shards. Her body, which appeared delicate, was in fact as firm and resilient as a finely braided wire rope. She wrenched loose and bowed her head. "I'm okay. I'm okay."

"I'll get the doctor."

"No. Just let me rest." She knelt, shaking her head. Taggart kicked the large shards of broken glass into a corner.

Helen tried to stand, pulling herself hand over hand up the chair. Taggart reached again to help, encircling her in one arm. She stiffened and shrugged him off coldly.

"Why do I get the feeling that you're FBI?"

"Come here." Taggart stepped to the window and opened the shutters. The whitewashed stone wall was two feet thick. Outside, sheep dotted brilliant green hills under a lowering sky. "Look."

"Where are we?"

"The west of Ireland."

"Ireland?"

"It's not FBI territory."

She touched the thick, wavy window glass. "How long was I out?"

"Sixteen hours."

"Do you realize my brothers are tearing New York apart looking for me?"

"They started to, but we convinced them to wait quietly."

"We? What is this?"

Taggart left the shutters open. "Let's talk business."

"What kind of business?"

"Organized crime."

Helen walked unsteadily to the chair and sat down. "I don't know who you are. I don't know what you want. I don't even know what you're talking about."

"I'll talk and you listen. There's no risk. . . . The government has busted the council, and the situation in New York is that the old Mafia is nearly washed up. The Federal Strikeforce is winning. I give you five years, tops."

"If I ever meet someone in the Mafia, I'll tell 'em what you said."

"It's going to take you a while to get this," Taggart replied patiently. "Just listen. Demographics were killing you even before the Strikeforce. You haven't enough soldiers anymore to run your operations and protect them from your enemies. Italians are the new Jews in New York. Their kids are going to college, so they're no longer cannon fodder for Sicilian warlords."

Helen looked up. "I don't know who you are or what you want, but don't you think that college-educated Sicilians might be more capable Mafiosi?"

"You've become too organized. All your lawyers and MBAs and accountants make you an easy target for the Strikeforce. Just like tax evasion got Al Capone, RICO and dope convictions are getting a better-organized generation. The old dons never adapted to the changes. Their heirs, your father's generation, aren't much better—sitting around swapping stories as if electronic bugging didn't exist. And your generation is hopeless. Maybe they're smarter about bugs, but when they get arrested for something, they talk to the cops. So who's going to replace them?"

"I don't know what this has to do with me."

"Your father, for example."

Her eyes flashed and Taggart was surprised to see pain in their depths. The next instant, however, they went blank again, revealing nothing.

"Don Eddie," he continued, "is a long-term resident in federal prison because the modern veneer he adopted played right into the government's hands. He let a smart accountant talk him into laundering heroin profits—which was theoretically a better idea than burying them in a hole in the ground. Your father was right to try it, but the Feds found the records. So even though they couldn't pin the heroin on him, they got him on the heroin profits. I don't mean to make light of your father's situation, but his misfortune might help you and me understand each other."

"What's your point?"

"Do you agree that the *system* is a mess?"

"Whatever you say."

"But the *market* is still growing. Ordinary people's appetite for criminal services is insatiable. They still want to borrow money, get high, gamble, and pay strangers to lay them.

These services are currently earning one hundred billion dollars a year."

She fixed him with an intent and somber gaze. Her extraordinary beauty pulled him like a whirlpool. Taggart felt himself sucked down, getting lost in her eyes. He turned away. She said, "That's an exaggerated figure."

"Settle for eighty? Eighty billion dollars a year is the gross national product of Austria. Or the total gross of General Motors."

"What do you mean, *settle?*"

"I'm taking over."

"Taking over what?"

"Organized crime. All of it—everything. I'm filling the vacuum left by the Strikeforce."

"With what?"

"That's where you come in. The Rizzolos will run the street in New York, Long Island, Westchester, Fairfield County, Jersey. Everything the five families currently control is yours. I'll protect and supply you from the top."

"What are you talking about?"

"On the street level, you will subcontract, as it were, supplying the labor for extortion, shylocking, numbers running, whorehouses, porn, and muscle for the unions. On the upper level, I will eliminate your rivals and provide banking services and protection."

"You're dreaming."

"Am I?"

Helen stood up and started pacing from one stone wall to the other. Taggart sat down in the chair to put her at ease. She stepped behind him and massaged his wrists, a pretense to draw out the long sliver of glass she had secreted in her sweatshirt sleeve when she had dropped the drinking glass. She held one end in the cloth, slipped her other arm around his throat, and slid the point of the shard through the right eye of his mask.

Taggart froze. The glass glittered a centimeter from his eyeball.

"Who are you?"

"You can't get out of here."

"The hell I can't. You're walking me through the front door. Who *are* you?"

"Don't you see what I'm offering?"

"You're crazy. This whole thing's crazy. You can't just move in. There's a war in New York. Strikeforce on one side, the rackets on the other. And you think there's room in the middle? *Don't move!*"

He had started to reach for her hand.

"I've already done it. Trial runs. Smuggling, wholesaling, money laundering. And today, kidnapping."

"You can't—"

"Miss Rizzolo, you're the leader of the most secure, best-run crime family in New York. A few hours ago you were jogging in your own neighborhood surrounded by your best bodyguards. You woke up tied to a chair in Ireland."

"How?"

"I hired an experienced IRA kidnap team to subcontract the job. A second contractor brought you here. When you've agreed, you'll be sent home, having crossed international borders *four times* without anyone the wiser. I've done all this without maintaining armies the way you do. Don't tell me there's no room in the middle."

"You're stalling me. I don't believe you. Tell the truth!"

She sliced the skin that rimmed his eye. Blood trickled down the mask.

"My subcontractor thought you were a piece of cake compared to the British politicians they've snatched. He said your security was a big joke."

"The truth!" She cut deeper. He jerked from the pain. She moved the sliver to the surface of his eyeball.

"Reggie!"

Reggie, who was watching through the one-way glass, had waited for Taggart's signal. Now he stepped into the room, his Remington P51 cocked like an eleventh finger between his clasped hands.

Taggart said, "Reggie will be the richest retired Special Branch officer in the history of the British Empire—provided I remain alive—which makes him, among other things, the best bodyguard in the world. He's been a killer for thirty years. He's going to kill you in one second if you try to hurt me."

Helen Rizzolo let the glass sliver fall to the floor, where it broke again. Reggie backed out of the room and closed the door. Taggart stood up.

She eyed him fearlessly.

He seized the sleeve of her sweatsuit, pulled it to his face, and dabbed the blood.

"Don't worry, I won't hit you."

"I'm not worried."

"I won't hit you, for the same reason your kidnappers were ordered not to rape you. The job I'm offering demands respect."

"May I ask what a non-rapeable Sicilian-American girl is worth to the Irish Republican Army?"

"Fifty M1's and enough ammunition to slaughter a British regiment."

"You got a bargain."

"Damned right I did! That's what I'm trying to tell you. Sicily isn't the only source of drugs and murderers. Helen, there are cities in Asia and Africa whose names we'll never know, where millions of people play the lottery every day and the prize is a ticket to America. The whole Third World is an endless supply of hungry sons and daughters. They'll fight, they'll kill, they'll fuck, they'll mule drugs. They'll do anything for a meal or a lucky break. Don't you see it? I can *import* violence—when and where I need it."

Taggart released her sleeve, but neither he nor she moved.

"The world is much more violent than we Americans are. If a Conforti or a Cirillo, or even a *Strikeforce*, messes with my people, I can hire a subcontractor to blow them up, machine-gun them, or kill them quietly with a knife. Radicals, mercenaries, whatever the job calls for. When my murderers are done they go home, clutching whatever little treasure they wanted—guns, explosives, money."

"Then what do you need me for?"

"The *street*. I'm not going to hire Palestinian bombers or South African guerrilla fighters to slap around a welsher. That's where your family comes in. Your people take the street. I'll attack the other families' leaders. You'll never worry again about a rival family. Your soldiers can concentrate on business instead of defense." He smiled suddenly, hot on his own juices, because he was getting through to her.

"You're wasting your time and mine. You know your answer."

"Don't push me!"

She went to the window, rested her chin on her folded hands on the stone sill, and gazed out at the fields of sheep. A mackerel sky was drifting in from the sea and the sunset was tingeing it pink. The scene looked like a holy card the nuns gave for being good. She hungered suddenly to be out-of-doors.

Taggart asked, "Why don't we go for a walk?"

"All right. I'd like that."

She gave him an ironic smile when he handed her a lavender windbreaker in her size. "Thought of everything?"

A stone path gave onto the fields, where deepening grass rippled in the steady sea breeze. She held her face to the wind and the sun and picked up speed. Taggart strode easily beside her, learning her moods. The fields spread along a crumbling rim of cliffs. Whitecaps dotted the dark-blue sea lough below. Miles to the west, the Atlantic stirred. Helen drank it in, pausing now and again to stare with frank pleasure. Her silky black hair fluttered about her cheeks. The wind swept it back.

Taggart feasted on the remarkable beauty of her profile, the richness of her mouth. Sexually the heat shimmered off her, yet he felt an enchantment more complex, brushed by forces unknown in his experience.

Reggie trailed at a distance, flourishing a walking stick that concealed a four-ten squirrel gun loaded with buckshot.

"Does he think I'm going to throw you off the cliff?"

"Reggie assumes the worst, always."

"I already took my best shot."

Taggart grinned. "He's a little put out because he missed you palming the glass. Did they teach you that in your father-in-law's casino?"

"You know too much about me."

"You heard about my offer. You think I'd make it blind?"

"If Reggie is English, why would he give the IRA guns and ammunition?"

"Reggie makes his own arrangements—just like you will —but if I know Reggie, that particular branch of the IRA is going to have a problem. Make up your mind, Helen."

"What about the Strikeforce?"

"I'll take care of the Strikeforce. You won't have to worry about them anymore."

"That's a little hard to believe. The Strikeforce belongs to the U.S. Attorney."

"I can handle them."

"Let me explain something, mister. If the Brooklyn or Manhattan District Attorney comes after my brothers, our lawyers handle it. One way or another, they can deal with it. But if the United States Attorney for the Southern District of New York gets on their case, it's 'Oh shit.' Who do you think got my father?"

"Tell your brothers to stop using the phone in the bus barn. The Strikeforce is tapping it from a street vault on the corner."

"You're *inside?*"

"I can also assure you that the Rizzolos are low down on their hit list at the moment. Taglione is concentrating on the Cirillos."

They found a sheep path worn to the stone and followed it toward a promontory. "You must give me a sign," she said thoughtfully. "Something by which I can trust you."

There was a rhythm to this dance and Taggart knew suddenly and surely that the time had come. He led her to a lichen-covered rock wall and sank to one knee before her. Then he pulled off his mask and placed it in her hand.

"Look at my face, Helen."

Helen Rizzolo stared. At last he had astonished her.

"I know you!"

"My name is Christopher Taggart. I build skyscrapers. I own Taggart Construction and Taggart Realty. I am a director of the Association for a Better New York. I'm a charter member of the Mayor's Commission for Growth in the Eighties. My new Park Avenue spire will make Trump Tower look like a box of Saran Wrap. When you get back to New York you can look at my picture in the newspaper and my address in the telephone book."

"I know," she whispered.

"Maybe you saw me on TV," Taggart said, wondering whether she remembered their brief encounter ten years ago at Abatelli's. "I happen to be a member of the President's Commission on Organized Crime."

Helen's face turned blank with distrust and she asked harshly, "How'd you get appointed? Your brother? Your name isn't Taggart. It's Taglione. You changed it when Tony Taglione became a prosecutor. Who do you think you're kidding? Your brother put my father in prison."

"And now I've just put my entire life in your hands," Taggart countered. "Until you say yes, I am at your mercy."

"No," she said, with devastating accuracy. "Your *plan* may be at my mercy—maybe. But not you. I can't touch you. Who would ever believe this conversation?"

"Only you have to believe it. I'm all your prayers answered. I'll free you to operate by your best instinct and observation, instead of fighting a hundred years of Sicilian history."

"What are you doing this for?" she asked suspiciously. "You're a rich man. You run things."

"I intend to be richer." Taggart had concluded that only wealth and power were motives that would make sense to this empress of the Rizzolo clan. Certainly, if he were she, he would not throw his lot in with an avenger. "A lot richer. Which is what you're going to be if you join me. A lot richer. And a lot more powerful."

She searched his face, hunting God knew what. But while Taggart waited, quelling his impatience, Helen was, in fact, less concerned with his motives than with the opportunities he offered her family, and the risks. *His* family was the problem. Tony Taglione.

"Is your brother in on this?"

"Christ, no." Taggart shook his head emphatically. "If my brother had a tape of this conversation, he would send me to the electric chair."

She believed him, but didn't understand. "Why does he hate you?"

"He doesn't hate me. He loves me, deep down somewhere, but he's a law-and-order guy. He's what used to be called a moralist."

"Yeah, fine, but you're his brother."

"Tony sees life like two tunnels. Right and wrong. Once you're in one, you can't transfer to the other."

"I don't get it. He's your brother."

"It's his way," Taggart said simply. "Our family is half construction workers, and half cops. Tony got the cop half."

She still didn't understand and knew she never would. "Then who do you have inside his Strikeforce?"

"I have many contacts in many agencies, and in many families. That's all you have to know. *Capish?* Do we have a deal?"

"I expect trust from a partner."

"Subcontractor. I don't take partners."

"I'm not interested in being a subcontractor," Helen replied coldly.

"I'm not doing business that way. I've chosen you over the Cirillos, the Bonos, the Imperiales, or the Confortis. The Rizzolo family will survive the Strikeforce and prosper. But on my terms."

"What if I refuse?"

"It's a deal breaker."

"You're asking a lot."

"I'm offering the whole goddamned city of New York."

"You're asking me to put my family under your control."

"No. I will tell you what needs to be done. *You* will control your family."

"And you will control me. I don't like it."

Angrily Helen faced the now darkening sea lough. Yet her anger was merely from pride, which she could not afford to indulge. Her father, she knew, would never make a deal with an outsider. But he was weak now, helpless, while she, beset by the other families and the Strikeforce, was on her own; for if the power of the Rizzolos was not yet all hers, the responsibility surely was. She had little to lose and much to gain; besides, a deal was a deal only as long as it served both sides. She faced Taggart with a smile. As her father used to say, it was a choice she could live with.

Taggart saw that patience had again curtained the diamond-hard light in her eyes, which he suddenly realized was not at all at odds with her extraordinary beauty, but its foundation.

For an eerie second he saw something else that almost made him shiver, but the feeling evaporated when she stretched her sleeve over her thumb, wet it with her tongue, and dabbed his face where the cut had opened up again. "We're going to have to find a better way to meet."

Taggart laughed. "Is that a yes?"

"Your terms *sound* generous, but you're asking a lot back. . . . My family is very fortunate to put such a powerful friend in our debt."

Taggart smiled at the old-fashioned Sicilian belief and thrust out his hand. Gravely she slipped her fine and pliant fingers between his. He held them for a moment, savoring the victory. He had won an army.

Chapter 11

O N A WARM June night, two weeks after returning from
Ireland, Taggart met Reggie high atop the bare steel of the
Taggart Spire to assess their response to the heroin shortage.
Work lights illuminated the columns and headers that framed
the space Taggart had chosen for his triplex penthouse, and
the great derricks stood silent against the stars. Below and beyond, New York sprawled, its lights a dense carpet in the
center, thinning gradually north and west and south into the
suburbs. Easterly they stopped abruptly at the dark wall of
the sea. Jets descended on the edges and long trains flowed
in measured procession.

Taggart walked into the wind; Reggie trailed like a cat,
reporting on feelers extended into the Cirillos' heroin pipeline.
Taggart listened with a heady feeling that for each light scattered in their millions there was a switch that he and he alone
could turn on or off as he pleased. For in the dark between the
lights, the men and women of his Shadow Mafia were making
temptingly generous overtures to the hard-pressed Cirillo drug
traffickers.

Among them, Taggart and Reggie decided that night, a Cal-
ifornian named Ronnie Wald looked best.

"We're talking pure," Ronnie Wald told the Cirillo soldiers
sent to check him out. "Pure and plentiful."

Reggie Rand's agents had discovered the slick West Coast
dude in a California prison. Essentially a con man, and a good
actor as any con man had to be, Wald was tough enough to
survive fourteen of his twenty-eight years inside. He wore
three broad rings on his right hand, which served as knuckles

in a pinch, and was good with the knife he carried in his alligator boot.

The Cirillo soldiers didn't like him, his suntan, his fancy boots, or his bleached jeans, and didn't trust him. But the street said he had stuff to sell in heavy-hitter quantity.

"Ninety-four point eight percent. Run it through your box."

Wald opened his hand and flashed a generous sample in a baggie. "If you like it, we can talk numbers."

The Cirillos recoiled. The Strikeforce, the DEA, the Federal Organized Crime Drug Enforcement Taskforce, the NYPD and State Police, half the fucking world, were busting wholesalers left and right, and this Wald clown was flaunting heroin in broad daylight like it was coke in a pitch-dark disco and they were a couple of girls who'd fuck for it.

They looked up and down the West Side block for the fourth time in a minute. It was a hot, sticky evening; the Puerto Ricans were drinking beer on the stoops and young executives were walking home with paper bags of takeout food and their jackets slung over their shoulders. Half the buildings on the block were being renovated and the gaping windows and lattice scaffolding made a thousand hiding places for Feds with binoculars and gun mikes.

"Let's go for a ride."

Wald shrugged. "If you got the time, I got the time."

They got in the Cirillos' car, a rented T-bird, and headed up Amsterdam, outta there before the Puerto Ricans and junior executives whipped out machine guns and FBI badges. Wald took his bag out again and dangled it like he was pushing Carvel flavors. "This'll stand forty. You know?"

"I know how to cut junk."

"So what's your problem?"

The soldiers exchanged looks. The one not driving said, "I'm gonna pat you for a wire."

Wald showed his teeth. "You can't be too careful." He leaned forward while one of them hung over the seat and frisked his back and waist and legs. When he was done, Wald dropped the baggie on the front seat. "Check it out. Meet me at a Hundred-fourth and Broadway tomorrow."

"If it's good."

"If it's good," Wald mimicked amiably. "Listen, my men,

you better get used to dealing with class." He got out and walked away, glad to put space between him and the dope; Reggie's guarantee that the street he had met the Cirillos on was free of cops had ended when he got in their car.

"Gotta be a Fed," was the Cirillo reaction.

Wald's sample checked through the hot box at ninety-four point eight on the nose. The Cirillo soldiers discussed Wald and his dope with their *capo,* who relayed the information in veiled terms to Mikey Cirillo. Crazy Mikey drove around Manhattan half the night, cruising the clubs, worrying. Even the heroin's purity seemed damning. If Wald was a Fed, wouldn't he supply a top sample? On the other hand, Wald's name had popped up in other deals and no one yet had a bad word for the prick. What it came down to, Mikey knew, was he needed product. The whole fabric of supply was falling apart like a rotten towel, and his distributors were looking elsewhere. He telephoned the *capo:* "Keep going."

"Keep going" meant find out how much Wald could deliver. And if it all hit the fan and the *capo* got caught and the Feds waved twenty years in his face, what could he testify? Crazy Mikey Cirillo said, "Keep going"? Maybe his smart brother, Nicky, should have been this careful.

Taggart and Reggie concluded that Wald had tapped a direct line through the Cirillo insulation, which just might lead to Mikey Cirillo himself. While others continued courting Cirillos, they decided to let Wald sell five kilos of heroin at one hundred and fifty thousand dollars a kilo, and repeat the sale in a few days.

Then the Cirillos soldiers asked Wald if he could supply larger amounts.

"Five keys a pop is plenty private enterprise for me, thank you. My boss hears I'm diddling around with these little side deals and I'm in trouble."

The Cirillo soldiers looked at each other. "Side deals?"

"Hey, don't get me wrong. I don't mean he doesn't know I did it. But enough's enough."

"We'd like to meet this guy."

Wald laughed. "Forget it."

"Well, maybe my boss would like to meet him."

"If your boss can buy fifty keys a pop, you send him around."

"Tomorrow."

Wald looked surprised.

"Tomorrow," the soldier repeated. Who the hell did Wald think the Cirillos were?

"I'll see what I can do. Riverside and a Hundred-sixth."

Their *capo* was wary and insisted on cruising the meeting spot for an hour ahead of time. He didn't like the spot. It was a busy intersection at the wide junction of 106th, Riverside Drive, and a service road. Tough to keep track of the traffic and sidewalks and the park. He said, "Drop me off at Broadway. Pick them up, make sure they got no tail, then come back for me."

"What if they won't come?"

"Fuck 'em. This looks like a setup. Don't say anything stupid. And if he has stuff with him, leave."

The Cirillo soldiers dropped their boss on Broadway and drove back to Riverside. Wald was waiting, "Where's your guy?" he asked.

"Where's yours?"

"Waiting for us." Wald waved up a cab. "We figured you for this paranoid shit."

Reggie Rand stepped out of the cab wearing light slacks, a shirt unbuttoned down his hairless chest, a gold chain, sunglasses, and a gray-flecked beard. He slipped into the Cirillo car, too quickly for a photograph. Wald climbed in front. The soldier floored it and raced up Riverside on the yellows, scattering pedestrians.

Wald said, "You're gonna get a ticket."

"Funny." He doubled back and picked up his *capo* on Broadway. The *capo* got in back next to Reggie. "Pull onto a side street," he told the driver. "Check 'em out for wires."

"Wait," said Reggie.

"What?"

"I said wait."

Shortly after he had joined up with Christopher Taggart, he had studied with one of the New York theater's top voice coaches to call up a flat American accent on occasions like this. "Let's shake hands hello first."

He extended his hand. The *capo* took it warily, trying to probe his sunglasses with his glittering black eyes. Reggie smiled. The whole purpose of this meeting, and of the transactions to follow, was to impress the Cirillo hierarchy with his ability to import heroin on the top level. If this *capo* didn't eventually lead Taggart to Crazy Mikey, the whole scheme was a waste.

"Okay. Frisk us and get it over with."

The *capo* patted him down thoroughly. When he found the gun on his ankle, Reggie said, "Look, but don't touch."

"Mine's clean too," said the soldier at the wheel.

"Drive."

"How much do you want?" Reggie asked bluntly.

"Huh?"

"How much do you want to buy? What quantity?"

"Fifty . . . uh . . . units."

"Sir. This is your car and you've taken the liberty of frisking me. Do me the coutesy of saying kilos."

"Are you crazy?"

"Stop the car. Stop it, I said!" It eased to the curb at 152nd Street. "Would you be more comfortable if we walk around the block? Just the two of us?"

The *capo* nodded.

"Have your man follow. This neighborhood's a bitch."

They started down the steep slope to Riverside, trailed by the car. They walked a block, and finally, as they trudged back to Broadway, the Cirillo *capo* admitted that he wanted to buy fifty kilos of heroin.

At the corner, Reggie said, "Excellent. Come up with six million two hundred and twenty-five thousand dollars and it's yours."

"We gotta work out a consignment deal. A third down?"

"I don't mean to sound rude, but consignment is for friends, and I don't even know you."

"Who the fuck are you to say you don't know me? You know who I represent. Who are *you?*"

"I'm a man with fifty kilos whenever you can pay for it, sir. Good evening." He signaled Wald, aware that England had crept tartly into his voice. The Cirillo *capo* did not appear to notice.

"Hold it. For cash? Four million."

"At one twenty-five a kilo you've already got your break."

"Four and a half million."

Reggie pretended to ponder the offer. "Can you save me laundry bills?"

"Bearer bonds."

"Five million in bearer bonds. Have your chap work it out with mine."

The *capo* blinked and Reggie concealed a smile. Considering the terrible shortage on the street, both the price and, equally important, the quantity were golden. The Cirillos had reason to rejoice.

The next afternoon, Wald and the Cirillo soldier checked in separately to the Palace Hotel carrying identical Lark suitcases. In Wald's room the Cirillo soldier set up a portable lab in the bathroom, spooned random samples of the fifty kilos from Taggart's stockpile, and heated them in test tubes. The heroin melted at 230 degrees and remained white, indicating it was at least 90 percent pure. When he signaled that he was satisfied, Wald scrutinized the stolen bearer bonds under infrared and ultraviolet light and, when *he* was satisfied, counted the negotiable paper with the fastest hands the soldier had seen outside Atlantic City.

That same night a Nigerian United Nations envoy in Reggie's pay delivered the bearer bonds in his diplomatic pouch to Switzerland, where Taggart's full system of international contacts went into play.

The diplomat turned the bearer bonds over to a broker who sold them as previously instructed and delivered the proceeds to an officer of Geneva's Union Bank with instructions to deposit them to various accounts. Upon confirming receipt of those deposits, a Chinese heroin distributor with Dutch citizenship—a member of the Triad, Green Pangs—arranged for three hundred kilos of processed Burmese heroin to be released at a remote landing field near the Thai border in the Golden Triangle.

A Thai air taxi brought it to Bangkok airport, where it docked alongside an AirVac twin-jet air ambulance diverted from a legitimate medical run. Resuming its legitimate journey, the AirVac plane picked up a Mobil executive who had broken his back on an Indonesian oil rig and flew the injured man to American facilities in the Philippines.

AirVac was owned by a consortium of American corporations based in Luxembourg and controlled by Euroland, a real estate company held, through a string of holding companies, by Christopher Taggart. Taggart had bought the ambulance business secretly when the recession of '83 had sharply reduced the market for extremely expensive corporate-executive emergency medical care. Routinely engaged in legitimate medical evacuations, the silver jets with the green cross on the tail were a common sight in the private aviation sections of major airports. No one bothered them other than to ascertain that hospital-bound patients weren't carrying plague, and they crossed borders with a minimum of customs inspection. Thus had Helen Rizzolo been smuggled out of Newark Airport disguised as a rich Belgian in a coma and brought into Ireland as an oil executive injured in a North Sea drilling accident.

In Manila, a fresh crew, ignorant of the jet's hidden cargo, continued east with a New York executive in the glove trade who had been shot in a brothel. In New York the jet was visited briefly at Newark Airport by Reggie Rand, a director of AirVac Holding, who left with a panel truck full of heroin sealed in body bags worth hundreds of millions to Crazy Mikey Cirillo.

Chapter 12

Visions—The Club, on Queens Boulevard in Forest Hills, was an expensively redecorated movie theater with chairs in the balcony, a main dance floor of glass, and a second showcase dance floor on the raised stage. Taggart paid twenty bucks at the door and bought a five-dollar beer at a glass bar which was filled with water and goldfish and changed colors with the lights. A hot-looking joint, yet for this space and the money spent, Chryl and Victoria, who kept threatening to design a club, could have done a knockout.

It was early and the place was overrun with women who got in for half price before eleven. He danced with several who asked him to, while he located the peephole where the owner kept an eye on the action. Taggart traced it to her office, guarded by a well-dressed bouncer in a silk shirt and heavy gold chain, the kind which, Reggie said, had a weak link to break away in case somebody made the mistake of fighting the guy.

"Can I help you?"

"Tell Miss Rizzolo Chris is here."

Her office was stark white, clean, and soundproof but for the insistent bass thumping through the wall. As the bouncer ushered him in, Helen stood up behind a table desk, which was cocked toward the smoked-glass window Taggart had spotted over the music station. She wore tight jeans and a shimmering white blouse and spike heels. Taggart wanted to tell her she had beautiful feet, but the alarm bells that had gone off in his head the moment he entered the club were clamoring that he was playing with fire.

"Come in, Chris. With you in a minute. That's okay, Sal. Thanks."

Sal backed out and shut the door, and she said, astonished, "What are you doing here?" She gave no sign whether she had seen him at the bar.

"You said we had to find a better way to meet."

"I've been meeting with Reggie for a month. I thought that was the deal. What's happening?"

Acutely uncomfortable wherever a tap could be installed, he asked, "Is the room clean?"

"It is and you know it."

"What do you mean, I know it?"

"I found out who Reggie had among my people."

"Reggie said I shouldn't come," Taggart replied with a smile, doubting she had found all of Reggie's spies.

"Like another beer?"

"No, thanks. We have to talk, but not here."

"Where should I meet you?"

He felt lightheaded and wanted to show off. "Park and Fifty-sixth. I'll be at the main gate."

"I'll be in a cab."

Taggart turned to leave. "Nice-looking club."

"It's okay."

He felt her eyes on him as he crossed the dance floor. His hands were shaking. This was crazy, but he couldn't help it—or didn't want to. He felt like he was back in school, romping around after a pretty girl the major thing on his mind.

When she got out of the cab at the Taggart Spire, he led her into the dark work site and aboard a freight hoist. "Afraid of heights?"

"No."

The lights blossomed like a flower the higher the hoist rose. At the top, Taggart took her arm and walked her to the edge of the plank floor. Overhead, the derricks soared, enormous dark Vs against the sky. She looked around as if she liked it, and he was glad he had brought her.

Taggart stroked a steel column. "This is a dinosaur. They'll all be cement soon."

"What did you want to talk about?"

"Are your brothers still buying it?"

Helen hesitated and Taggart tensed. He needed them desperately. "Are they?" he repeated. "Reggie says he's not sure."

She looked out at the lights. It was a month since Taggart's people had flown her back from Ireland, but she could still see the expression of astonished relief on Eddie's face when she walked in the front door, trailed by the FBI agents who had been waiting outside. Eddie threw them out, hugged her, and listened dubiously as she promised to explain everything after a bath. While she was still in the tub, they sent her mother to ask the big question: Had she been raped?

"No, Mom."

"Are you sure?"

"Mom!"

"Then what happened? What did they want?"

"They had a message for Frank and Eddie."

"That's all?"

"Would you send them up, please? I have to talk to them."

Her mother changed the subject as only she could. "Do you have to work so much with your brothers? Don't you miss having a guy?"

"You mean a guy to get laid?"

"Helen, do you have to talk that way?"

"Yeah, Mom. I miss having a guy. I miss it a lot. You want to send up Eddie and Frank?"

She could have added, but didn't because she didn't want to make her mother miserable, that she couldn't have a straight guy because her life would be secret from him, and she couldn't have a rackets guy because he would try to take it away from her.

Her brothers trooped into her bedroom, closed the door, and stood around the bed looking very uncomfortable, as she intended them to. She had set the stage, propped up against the pillows in a fluffy bed jacket, sipping a glass of white wine.

"What happened?"

"Have you swept the house?"

"This morning, like always. No bugs. What happened? Who grabbed you?"

"The whole thing was a setup. They just wanted to talk."

"Talk?" Eddie exploded. "They grab a girl off the street to talk?"

"Who are they?" Frank asked quietly.

Taggart had suggested an explanation. Helen modified it, hoping that a promise of independence linked to an opportunity to destroy the Cirillos would prove so tempting to Eddie and Frank that they would accept dealing with people they didn't know. She said, "You know what the Italian police are doing to the Sicilians."

"I know they got a big guy to squeal."

"And what the Sicilians are doing to each other."

"They're killing each other, just like the Cirillos are killing us. What does it have to do with who the fuck snatched you?"

"There's a new group of Sicilians who survived. They're getting out of Italy and going international. They're setting up the money in Switzerland and Luxembourg. They're recruiting the best from each country to join them. Italy, France, England, Jamaica, Canada, the United States."

"Recruiting?" Eddie asked belligerently. "Who the fuck they think they are?"

"The future." She held his gaze until he looked away. "They don't trust the Cirillos. They want us to take New York."

"Tomorrow soon enough?" Frank asked.

"They'll back us with everything we need. Hitters. Weapons. Information on the cops. Laundry—"

"Dope?"

"No dope. There are better ways to make money."

"What do they want from us?"

"Partners they can count on; a door into legit corporations; and a skim on the laundry. But first we have to get rid of the competition. That means the Cirillos and everybody else."

"The rest will fall in line after the Cirillos," said Frank.

"Whadyou tell 'em?"

"I told them I would tell you guys what they said. That's all."

"What if me and Frank don't agree?"

She shrugged. "I guess no deal."

"But why'd they grab *you?*" Eddie demanded. "Why not me or Frank?"

"They knew about me seeing Pop. I think they had contacts up in the jail. So they knew I knew the business."

"I know the business, too. So does Frank."

Helen hung her head and replied contritely. "But you weren't dumb enough to go running every day. I was easy. Sorry."

"It's a trick," said Eddie. "They're Feds."

"They took me to *Ireland*, Eddie. They kidnapped me. They're not Feds."

"It still could be a trick."

Helen had leaped at that opening, ensuring that they would never deal with Christopher Taggart. "I'm the go-between. If it's a trick, what do they get? Me. As long as I'm the only one who talks to them, they can't touch you guys or the family."

"I'm not letting my sister take a rap."

"Nobody's taking a rap. It's no risk."

Eddie made a face. "Pop wouldn't buy that."

"He already has," she lied smoothly—her second lie about her father in less than a week. "I went to the jail before I came home. I ran the whole thing by him and he said, go for it. Eddie, don't you see? These are smart people and they like the kind of tight family we are. We're natural partners."

"I know we're good. What are they going to do *for* us?"

"We can tap into an international cash-and-information system," she answered, embroidering the lie with details that might actually come to pass in the future when her family controlled New York. Christopher Taggart was right. Internationally organized activities were the future. "They've got scams going with government money that make heroin look like sand."

"What kind of information?"

Helen had paused to sip from her glass. "They warned me the Strikeforce has a tap on the bus phone. They're in the street vault on the corner."

Eddie and Frank had liked that, had liked it a lot. . . .

She turned now to Taggart. The wind drew a silken veil of black hair across her face. "They're still going along, but they're getting impatient. They want results damned soon."

"Tomorrow," he promised, gazing with satisfaction at the shimmering city.

"Tomorrow?"

"Do you know the new Cirillo Brooklyn underboss?"

"He tried to kill my brother Eddie."

"Do you know Tommy Lucia?"

"I know he's a Cirillo crew leader. A gambler. Number two to the Brooklyn underboss."

"Tell your brother Eddie to make a deal with Tommy."

"What kind of deal?"

"Ask him to join the Rizzolos."

"You're crazy. Tommy Lucia won't talk to Eddie."

"It would double your book and numbers."

Helen considered it. "Yes, but only if Tommy Lucia brings the right people with him. What makes you think he'll break with the Cirillos?"

"Can Eddie handle it?"

"Of course he can handle it," she said sharply. And then, in softer tones, "I'll stay close. We'll be ready. . . . How do I get down?"

"I'll take you."

In the elevator he asked, "Would you like a drink?"

"No, I gotta go."

Taggart found her a cab, and she was gone.

Slightly dazed by his own audacity, he walked slowly toward Third Avenue to the Old Stand, where he could usually count on finding some off-duty cops from the Seventeenth Precinct. He stood at the bar, sipping an Irish coffee and thinking that he was glad he had done it.

Helen's cab driver was not pleased with a fare to Canarsie, and less so when she told him to take the Belt Parkway. "Lady, we're a lot better off going from Flatbush to Eastern Parkway to Rockaway Parkway."

"I want to see the water," she said, staring out the window and ignoring his surly remark about the ferry.

Christopher Taggart was shaping up as a very lucky break. He had given her a chance to protect her family from the Cirillos, even as she consolidated her own power with her brothers. She would call the shots, and by the time she got her

179

father home on a medical and Eddie and Frank finally realized he was no longer capable of being the boss, they would have already accepted that she was in charge.

When her cab crossed the Manhattan Bridge, the driver headed for Flatbush Avenue.

"I said I want to go on the Belt."

"Screw you, lady. I don't make anything riding around Canarsie. And I can tell just looking at you you're not gonna tip."

"Because I'm a woman?"

He slammed on the breaks, reached back, and opened the door. "Hop out. I don't need this shit."

Helen glanced up and down the barren stretch of shops with closed gates and thought, This guy would really throw me out of the cab and leave me here if he could. She supposed she would be frightened if she were alone; but she was never alone and she said in a voice low with suppressed anger, "Call your dispatcher, please. Tell him I'm a friend of Johnny Carroccio."

The driver looked at her and the sheer certainty in her voice made him do it.

"Be nice," the dispatcher radioed back. "Be very nice." The driver turned the car around and took the Belt Parkway. When the harbor came into view, he asked politely, "Who's Johnny Carroccio?"

"He lends money for taxi medallions to people who can't go to the bank."

"Good friend?"

"He works for my brother," she replied and the driver fell into a profound and lasting silence.

Yes, Taggart had come along at a good time. Though tonight, she had to admit, he had worried her. He was lunatic to come and see her, and she wondered whether he was an amateur playing at the rackets. But the kidnapping had been masterful precision work by a powerful international enterprise.

Belatedly it occurred to her that she should have said yes to his drink invitation to find out what was going on in his head. Nice-looking guy; nice manners. And he moved gently for a man his size. She had said no automatically. It was habit by now.

* * *

Tommy Lucia was a tough survivor of the Brooklyn gambling rackets. Longevity being one route to power in an unstable world, patience another, Tommy had gotten ahead by going along and by choosing his opponents carefully. His long career with the Cirillos reminded Taggart of his own Uncle Eamon's successes in the Police Department. But while his uncle had retired after thirty years, Tommy Lucia still reported daily at the Caffè di Tullio on Knickerbocker Street in the Bushwick section of Brooklyn.

The di Tullio had a front room with a long, clean counter, a modern espresso-cappuccino machine, and four-color posters of the Italian World Cup soccer team. In the back was a second, larger room where the regulars played cards at round tables. At six in the evening it was like a village square as Sicilian men from all walks of life stopped in on their way home from work. Among them was the new Brooklyn underboss of the Cirillo family.

Tommy, his number one crew leader, stood by, pleased. With the RICO conviction of the underboss's older brother, the mantle of Brooklyn leadership had fallen on powerful shoulders. A handsome man in his sixties, Tommy's boss wore a fine blue suit, and a ring of snowy white hair circled his otherwise bald head. He greeted friends and neighbors amiably, embraced an old baker—laughing with him at the flour marks pressed on his suit—and sat down at a card game while younger men scrambled to bring him espresso.

Tommy knew a winner. Their gambling enterprises were flourishing as the new man extended books and numbers into parts of Brooklyn which were previously Rizzolo territory. When the hotheaded Eddie "the Cop" had struck back, the new underboss's counterpunch had been masterful—suckering the greedy slob with a phony cocaine deal to lower his guard.

The fact that Eddie had lost only his fingers instead of his life could fairly be attributed to luck, and luck, Tommy Lucia knew, was never more than a brief lowering of house odds. In the end, the new underboss would destroy Eddie and reclaim the rest of Brooklyn from the breakaway Rizzolo clan. He might even edge out Crazy Mikey for boss of the underbosses, and from there? Maybe when Old Don Richard died, overall boss—carrying Tommy on his coattails.

The pay phone between the front and back room rang. A kid leaped to answer and handed it to Tommy. He listened, went back to the card table, and whispered, "Somebody torched one of the Rizzolos' Blue Line buses."

"Call your friend in the Rizzolos. Say I'm concerned they might misunderstand. Tell them we are sorry, and we had nothing to do with it. And put a couple of men out front, in case they don't believe you."

Tommy dispatched some men to the sidewalk, then got on the phone. He had just made contact with his "friend," who sounded skeptical, when the front door opened on three blond men in blue suits. "The fucking FBI just walked in. I'll call you back."

The men stepped up to the counter, set their briefcases on the floor, and ordered cappuccino.

"To go?" the counterman asked hopefully.

"Here. You got a men's room?"

"Middle door in the back."

One of them strolled between the card games, went into the bathroom, and strolled back a few minutes later. He and his companions spooned sugar into the cappuccino and sipped it until a black sedan with a government seal on the door double-parked in front. Moving in swift concert, the men in blue suits opened their briefcases and unfolded stock-mounted machine pistols. Two stepped into the rear room and shot the underboss. A bodyguard tried to pull a weapon from his jacket and they blew him across the room. The third gunman turned his automatic on Lucia, who pressed against the wall and opened both hands, palms out; he thought he was dead for sure.

"On the floor."

Tommy dropped to the linoleum, waiting for the bullets. But the guy just looked at him like he was covering him, while his partners sprayed the walls. When everyone else alive was flat on the floor they backed out to the waiting car, from which protruded a gun covering Tommy's men on the sidewalk. The car pulled away, running red lights and speeding north.

The Italian neighborhood gave way to Spanish. Then Knickerbocker Avenue entered a barren industrial district of canals and railroads. Less than a mile from the shooting, the driver turned into a deserted rail yard, raced alongside a string of flatcars, and stopped behind a warehouse. The men in blue suits got out, climbed into a shiny steel shipping container on a flatcar. The automobile drove away. Shortly, a switch engine coupled onto the flatcars and hauled them through Brooklyn to the Atlantic Basin, where cranes swung the containers aboard a Swedish Mersk Line container ship, which sailed on the evening tide.

Tommy wasn't too surprised to get a message that evening from his "friend" in the Rizzolos. He returned the call expecting threats. His friend sounded bewildered. "I don't know what's going down. But I got messages for you."

"What?"

"First, Eddie Rizzolo says he didn't do it."

"Yeah? What's second?"

"There's a guy wants to eat dinner with you. Ten o'clock. Café des Sports."

"Never heard of it," Lucia said suspiciously.

"Neither has Crazy Mikey or the Strikeforce. It's on West Fifty-first between Eighth and Ninth."

Lucia figured that the name meant sports, and a trophy cabinet in the brightly lit front bar confirmed it. A big guy, who acted like the owner and looked like an ex–soccer player, said, *"Oui, monsieur,* your friend is waiting."

A self-assured blonde led him past customers who looked like show-biz people. Nobody connected in the joint—just people. She showed him into a cubicle couched between brick walls. Lucia was just thinking he liked the way she walked, when his eye fell on his host. There, at a table set for three in the privatemost corner of the restaurant, his back to two brick walls, his enormous hand cupping a fragile-looking wineglass, was Eddie "the Cop" Rizzolo.

Which made no sense at all to Tommy Lucia. Eddie waved him into the empty chair across the table. "How you doing?"

"What is this?"

Eddie started to extend his right hand, smiled at his missing fingers, and asked instead, "You want a drink? I got a bottle of wine. If you don't mind French."

The self-assured blonde produced a glass, poured, and asked if they would like to hear the specials. Eddie, apparently on his best behavior, said to Lucia, "Mind if I order? We talked about it earlier."

Lucia glanced at the third place set beside Eddie, but apparently they weren't waiting. "Go ahead."

"We'll share the pâté and the celery rémoulade."

Lucia was impressed until he remembered that Eddie had his hooks into a lot of restaurants.

"Sound good?"

"Sure." He wanted to throw the woman out of the cubicle, grab Eddie by his lapels, and scream, What the fuck is going on?

"What can you tell us about the scallops provençale?" Eddie asked.

Lucia listened to his head roar while she described the dish and Eddie interrupted repeatedly. He was getting the shakes, recalling the gunfire of several hours ago. One second his boss was alive, the next, dead on the floor.

"How about you?"

"You got steak?"

"*Au poivre?*"

"Go for it!" Eddie exulted. "Double french fries for both of us. They got these good-looking skinny ones—kind of like you, doll." He grinned at the hostess. "And maybe some red wine for my friend when his steak comes."

She left, and, as it was a large table, a comfortable space separated them from the nearest diners. Eddie grinned, inviting his questions. Lucia caught his breath and stalled. No way Eddie Rizzolo was going to make him look like an idiot.

"Classy-looking girl."

"Her father's the owner."

"It shows."

"Always."

Eddie sipped his wine and broke off a piece of bread. He was displaying patience he had never been known for, acting like he could sit there all night. Lucia couldn't stand it anymore. "So what's going on?"

"We're all well. My sister's home safe, no harm done. My hand don't hurt no more. Are *you* all right?"

"Better than this afternoon."

"Good. My father always says things can always get better; for worst there is no end."

Lucia forced a smile and asked, as was proper, "How are they treating Don Eddie?"

"My sister says he's fine. She sees him regular."

"You said she's well. Who took her?"

Eddie looked embarrassed. "A thing in the family. Can you imagine? It was good, of course, that they didn't hurt her. Not like getting snatched by Colombians." He shook his head. "Would our grandfathers have imagined the things we have to worry about?"

"It's a strange world," Lucia agreed. He sipped the thin white wine, buying time, wondering how Eddie "the Cop" got so smart so fast. Eddie had apparently gone to a lot of expense to advance him, Lucia, up the Cirillo hierarchy by blowing away his boss. Thank you very much. But Eddie Rizzolo wasn't smart enough, tricky enough, or even greedy enough to put such a scam together. He and his brother, Frank, had the slob tastes of your ordinary street hood—a full belly, a fast car, and friendly broads. Somebody was backing them.

The restaurant owner passed the cubicle and gave Eddie a nod. He waved back, and Lucia wondered what next. "I hope you don't mind," Eddie said. "My sister's in the city and I told her to meet me here. Okay if she joins us?"

She arrived like a windstorm, black mane flying, arms laden with packages, perfumed, flashing eyes. A rich little Italian princess, and one hell of a piece of ass.

Lucia smiled at her. "How you doing?"

She gave him a cool nod. Sex might be written all over her, if you knew how to read it, but she wasn't giving any away. Dropping her packages on the empty chair, she sat beside Eddie and kissed him.

Tommy Lucia smiled again. She was his answer! Daddy's little go-between. Old Don Eddie was dealing from jail. His daughter would report. Must gall the hell out of Eddie to have a woman sit in on his meet. Relieved that at least he had an idea who was leaning on him, Lucia said, "I think I'd like that red wine now, Eddie, if you don't mind."

"No problem." Eddie flagged down a waitress and asked for the wine list. "How about you, hon? Something to eat?" Helen took her brother's arm like a little kid. "Can I have an espresso?"

"If they don't got it," said Eddie, "I'll make 'em send out."

Tommy figured Eddie would surely turn to business when he had finished ordering, but to his annoyance, Helen resumed the amenities that her brother had stalled with. "We hear Don Richard is well."

"Don Richard amazes us all."

"Aren't the old guys great?" Eddie asked innocently.

"They're not old when they have their health," Lucia parried, for he saw clearly where this was going. Fucking Rizzolos.

"Health is all," Eddie agreed.

"And freedom," said Lucia, jabbing Eddie with a reminder that his father was in prison.

A dark shadow floated over Eddie's broad face and he looked dangerous. But Helen nudged him lightly and he controlled himself. Lucia grinned; in the clubs the coke dealers' girlfriends used to hold the drugs to fool the cops, but now the girls sold the stuff themselves. Eddie better watch it or Helen might take over, he thought. Wondering whether she would join the discussion or merely report to her father, he said, "There's a lot going down I don't understand."

"Look at it this way," said Eddie, tearing off another piece of bread and passing the basket to Lucia. "If I wanted to kill you, I've had two chances today. Atlantic Avenue, where you had breakfast, and Woodhaven Boulevard, lunch.

"Knickerbocker Avenue."

"I already told you, that wasn't me."

"Guys have found out I'm not so easy to kill."

"Three, if you count I coulda gotten you on the sidewalk a minute ago. Four, if I cut your head off with this butter knife."

"So you're doing me favors. Why?"

"I want to talk."

Lucia made his face blank. No way he was going to put himself in the position of dealing with the Rizzolos behind the

Cirillos' backs. Bad enough sitting in public with them. "You're talking to the wrong guy. Don Richard—"

Eddie cut him off, switching to Sicilian, a language that conveyed multiple possibilities. "Why don't we talk about Don Richard later? . . . Funny thing. Your boss getting shot kind of clears your way to running Brooklyn for the Cirillos. Doesn't it?"

"It'll go to Mikey," Lucia replied in English, still wary.

Helen's Sicilian was as fluent as Eddie's, and more subtlely insinuating. "Crazy Mikey is busy selling dope in the city. What does he care about making book?"

Lucia couldn't help but nod agreement. Gambling was big and steady money; they had built empires on it, but it didn't turn guys on like dope. Mikey was hooked on the insane profits.

The restaurateur brought the wine Eddie had ordered, a '71 Bordeaux as rich as cream, and confided it was one of his last. Eddie waited until a waitress brought his sister's espresso. Then he tilted his glass toward Lucia. "The future."

"What future?" Tommy asked coldly, determined to stop their advance before it got out of hand.

"Our future. We're in the same business, by and large. So we're dumb to compete when we could pull together. We got the same problems with the blacks and Spanish throwing their weight around. We got the same problems turning dollar bills into clean C-notes. We got the same problems laying off bets."

"Russia and China got the same problems too. I don't see their future together."

"Books and numbers," Helen interjected quietly, "don't do well in a war."

"What war?"

Eddie held up his maimed hand. "We got nothing but trouble if we keep shooting up each other's stores."

"So what do you want, Eddie?"

"You."

"Me? You want me to work for you?"

"We're looking for good people, Tommy."

"I appreciate the compliment. But I am content where I am. What would I get that I don't already have?"

187

"Better than the Cirillos gave your boss," Eddie answered. "And better protection, too."

"But only if you bring the best people with you," Helen added. "That's important. You must deliver your best. We'll take good care of them. Nobody will lose."

"Except my friends the Cirillos."

"The Cirillos are going to lose anyway," Eddie sneered. "Brooklyn, for openers."

Lucia hid his contempt. The boast was Eddie Rizzolo at his loudmouthed worst. A man shouldn't talk about it, a man should simply do it. Nor should he give away his whole plan. He said, "You're talking about a big step. I could lose everything. The Cirillos are big, and you're not. I don't see them giving Brooklyn to you or anybody else."

"Think about it," said Eddie. "Think about it till Tuesday."

Lucia had a sudden, funny thought. If he were legit, this would be extortion. He stared at Helen, who was watching him intently. "Give your tough brother's mouth a rest," he said coldly. "Why don't *you* tell me what happens Tuesday?"

She touched Eddie's beefy forearm, silencing him, and held Lucia's gaze so hard and so long that he felt a strange shiver in his spine. He knew three kinds of women in the world—whores, wives, and mothers. But there was something dark in Helen Rizzolo's eyes that said she was a thousand years old, the fourth kind—*maghe*, a witch.

"Somebody might not tell you to lie on the floor Tuesday."

Don Eddie couldn't have put it better, Tommy Lucia conceded grudgingly; the old bastard had himself one hell of a go-between. "You're strong-arming me," he protested, "like I was a fruit stand buying protection."

Helen returned a smile and the dark years receded slightly into the cool depths of her eyes. "Look at it this way, Tommy. We're offering a choice you can live with."

Taggart and Reggie watched the Café des Sports from a rented limousine, parked in a row of similar black, white, and silver cars waiting for the theaters to let out. They were in a block of tenements hung with fire escapes. Several had restaurants on the ground floor. An hour after Helen had gone into the café, Taggart noticed a man come out of a neighboring building, glance up and down the street, and hurry toward Eighth Avenue, swinging his attaché case as if proud of a good day's work.

"Reggie, hand me the phone, please."

Reggie gave it to him, shooting looks up and down the street for the source of the trouble. "What's wrong?"

"Not a thing." Taggart swiftly dialed the home number of a real estate broker who worked for him. "Elliot, you're going to make us both rich. I just saw a broker for Wootten coming out of a tenement on West Fifty-first near Eighth. Unless he's screwing a hooker, they're doing an assemblage. Buy me a store with a long lease."

Reggie retrieved the phone with a broad smile. In the past two years with Taggart he had learned enough of the Manhattan land business to know that when the developer-clients of Jones Lang Wootten had almost got their parcel assembled, they would find Christopher Taggart owning a leasehold in the middle of it, ready to negotiate a sale, a construction contract, or a trade for a deal on some other property they were developing elsewhere in Manhattan.

Moments later Tommy Lucia emerged from the restaurant followed by Eddie Rizzolo with his sister holding his arm. Taggart watched Helen, whose gaze wandered about the street as she closed her cape against the evening chill of a midsummer Canadian high. Eddie and Lucia shook hands to conclude their business.

"It's working," Reggie marveled.

"Of course it's working. They're like sharks. All they know is to keep moving. . . . Okay. It's time to make Crazy Mikey crazier. Have somebody drop a hint that the *capo* we're supplying is a big money earner."

Chapter 13

A CIRILLO BODYGUARD was paid four thousand dollars to drop the hint, and Reggie promised to double his fee if Crazy Mikey got demonstrably angry. At the risk of overkill, the spy chose a moment when they were snorting cocaine in the stalls of Sunsets, an oceanfront Hampton Bays summer dance club. He knew Mikey to get a little paranoid scaling Colombian heights, and indeed, when he mentioned casually that a certain *capo* was making some very impressive heroin buys, Mikey turned white through his suntan, the golden spoon fell from his fingers, and he bolted out the men's-room door. Seconds later, his big black Mercedes convertible was scattering parking-lot attendants and burning rubber onto Dune Road. He sped back to New York, shouting on the car phone that the *capo* in question had better join him at the Flushing brothel if he knew what was good for him.

"I want to meet your man's boss."

"I don't know if he's got a boss."

"He's got a boss. Just like you have a boss. Set it up!"

Reggie seemed appalled when the *capo* approached him with Mikey's demands. "Such a thing just isn't possible."

The point of being a boss, he explained with infuriating deliberation, was that one did not take risks one could pay others to take. Why would his boss want to get involved?

The *capo* said, "Mr. Cirillo wants to buy a hundred keys a shot. But he don't want to pay up front. He agrees consignments are for friends, so he wants to make friends."

"And he's a little touchy about you getting all the action, too, isn't he?" Reggie asked innocently.

The *capo* shrugged, but his dark eyes turned private.

Reggie decided he might be a man with a future in Mr. Taggart's service. He held him off two weeks before announcing that his boss had agreed. "But with tighter security than the Pope. Your boss is allowed one companion. I will be with my boss. If they have anything to discuss they will do it alone. Third Avenue and Sixty-eighth."

Reggie's spy reported that Mikey was having second thoughts; he was worried that Reggie might be an undercover FBI agent and that the buys, as big as they had been, could all be part of a huge government sting operation. At the same time, Reggie learned from his British sources that Mikey's people were expecting an immense heroin shipment from London. Thus neither he nor Taggart was surprised when Crazy Mikey did not show for their meeting.

Taggart sent Reggie to Paris. He had befriended Kurt Spielman in the aftermath of the massacre during the 1972 Munich Olympics when eleven Israeli athletes were killed by Palestinian terrorists. The disillusioned Israeli had left Mossad to freelance. Like Reggie, he had kept his body in shape and his contacts current. He had a deep affection for the dapper Englishman based on mutual tastes and Reggie's kindnesses over the lean years. Somehow, whenever things were hard, Reggie Rand could be counted upon for a job.

Summoned to Versailles, Spielman met his friend in a tourist restaurant which served an astonishingly good lunch. After they helped the waiter recalculate a bill equally astonishing for its creative currency exchange, they went for a walk in the palace gardens.

"What mayhem?" Spielman smiled.

"A hijacking . . . with a twist."

Reggie gave him details, airline tickets, expense money, and passports, and wished him luck.

Two days later, Spielman found himself with two hired hands in a bogus yellow taxicab trailing an Emory Air Freight truck around Kennedy Airport at two in the morning. Slipping out of the North Freight Terminal, the step van stopped at British Airways, then sped out of the airport onto the Belt Parkway and into the streets of Brooklyn. Spielman spotted a Mercedes leading the truck and an Oldsmobile taking up the rear, and he had his doubts about the dirty van following his own car. His men were veterans he had used often; nonetheless he repeated his orders to keep the violence to a minimum. "Chase them, don't kill them, unless you have to."

The car and the weapons—pump shotguns and automatic pistols—had been waiting in a long-term parking lot when they got off the plane. God willing, they'd be back in Europe in less than twelve hours. Ahead was a mile-long straight road that cut between bulldozed blocks of abandoned factories. There were few lights and no traffic.

Spielman's driver blinked his high beams and pulled ahead of the Oldsmobile, the air freight truck, and the Mercedes. Spielman and his partner rolled down their windows. A quarter-mile along, the driver jammed on the brakes, slewed screaming through a U-turn, and sped back toward the convoy. Spielman and his partner shotgunned the Mercedes, shot out the truck's windshield and tires. Then, while the Oldsmobile fled, Spielman climbed out, shot the padlock off the back of the truck, and lifted the door.

"Chara!"

The smugglers had buried their heroin in a legitimate truckload. There were easily a hundred packages, stacked floor to ceiling. At that moment, the van he had wondered about raced up, decanting men with guns.

Spielman jumped to the road, firing his automatic, while his men laid down accurate fire to hold the Mafiosi at bay. Spielman opened the taxicab door. A bullet tore through it, inches from his hand. He tossed a thermite grenade into the back of the freight truck and got in the cab. "Go!"

He heard the familiar dull thud, and when he looked back the truck and its contents were an orange pillar of flame.

When he heard about the explosion, Mikey Cirillo went crazy. "They burned up the whole fucking truck!" he screamed. "What kind of fucks do that?"

The *capos* who had to explain things to their Harlem and Bed-Stuy distributors gazed back silently. None of them had ever heard of a hijacker destroying what he couldn't take, but that mystery mattered not at all. Two hundred irreplaceable kilos—a quarter-ton, or two months' supply—had gone up in smoke. The Strikeforce bust at the West Forty-fifth Street garage, arrests in Sicily, more Pizza Connection indictments, several hijackings around the world, and now this. It might not all be Crazy Mikey's fault, but what, they wondered, would Crazy Mike promise next?

"Mikey, the blacks aren't standing still for this. Another few weeks I won't be able to park my car on the street up there."

The *capo* Reggie had been selling to took the blame for the screwup. His boss, Crazy Mikey, really did want to meet Reggie's boss. Reggie said he would try to set another meeting. He made them wait a week. This time, Mikey showed. It was Reggie's first close look, and he wondered if Taggart had bitten off more than he could chew.

Despite his reputation for impulsive violence, Mikey had the self-assured air of a man who had grown up around power. His father, the elderly Don Richard, had been securely in command when Mikey was born, and this showed in the arrogant set of his thin lips, the seemingly blasé expression in his dark eyes, the authoritative manner of a man used to getting his way. Rather, Reggie thought, like the English public school boy who breezed on to Sandhurst and an Army command.

It was easy to believe the underworld rumor that Mikey was growing into the job of chief underboss, and Reggie was reminded of how young Christopher Taggart still was. In fact, he thought with a thin smile as he climbed into Mikey's car, Mikey reminded him of Chris's hard-eyed brother Tony, who might be better suited to deal with this sort.

"Tell him where to go." Mikey greeted him coldly.

His driver's broad shoulders were bulked out by a fourteen-ply Kevlar bullet-proof vest; his heavy hands and attentive, intelligent eyes told Reggie he was the best bodyguard the Cirillo clan employed.

"Turn the corner . . . into that parking garage . . . down the ramp to the end. Park there."

Mikey looked at the silver-gray Citroën-Maserati. "No way I'm getting in your car."

"I'm sorry. It's the only way."

Crazy Mikey's eyes turned black and glittery. Reggie found himself hoping he would change his mind again. But he said,

"No bullshit," then snapped some Sicilian at his driver, who lifted a powerful signal analyzer from under the seat. Reggie unlocked the Citroën-Maserati, started the engine, and warmed it up. The bodyguard sat in front with the analyzer on his lap, and Mikey sat in back.

Reggie drove up the ramp onto the street, around the block, and north on Third Avenue, searching his mirrors for the Cirillo chase car. It was a yellow cab, ideal camouflage in midtown, but less so as they passed Ninety-sixth Street and entered Harlem. He turned on the radio, which emitted a shrill beep. "Turn your transmitter off, please."

The bodyguard looked at Mikey, who nodded.

"We agreed two on two," Reggie said mildly. Mikey looked out the window. Reggie reduced speed until he was crossing intersections on the yellow light. The chase car followed suit, two blocks behind. Reggie nudged the accelerator; the Citroën burst to sixty. He crossed 125th, careened right down a long, dark block past the city bus barn, took another right and a sudden sharp left, hooking across three lanes of traffic into the northbound lane of the Willis Avenue Bridge. A moment later he turned onto the Major Deegan Expressway, accelerated to ninety mph, exited onto the westbound Cross Bronx Expressway, and then drove south onto the Henry Hudson Parkway. Gliding sedately into a riverside parking area at 125th, he got out of the car and motioned for them to follow.

Mikey came warily, sticking close to the bodyguard, who handed him the signal analyzer and walked with his hand in his pocket. Reggie was impressed; too few people realized a bodyguard wasn't a servant. He led them to the edge where the Hudson River lapped a crumbling bulkhead. A big open Cigarette-type ocean racer waited in the shadows beneath a broken light, guarded at a distance by several heavyset black men with fishing poles.

"What is this?"

"A boat."

He had taken her from people in the Long Island cocaine run, and she was uniquely fitted for the night shuttle between the Patchogue River and points two hundred miles seaward of Fire Island. Her numbers were readily changed, and each set was backed by forged documentation, but her real defenses against hijackers and the law were speed, stealth, and, if these failed, a unique capacity for suicide. She was built of fiberglass, and all metal fittings—rails, chocks, wheel, even the steering linkage—had been replaced with epoxy and graphite composites to offer the least radar target. The only metal aboard was in her engines, which were mostly below the waterline. If the boat were trapped, the hull was wired to blow a hole the length of the keel.

"Mind your footing."

He showed the way with a penlight to the deep bucket seats set four abreast in the broad open cockpit, which was sheltered by a massive wraparound windshield, and started the engines. The bodyguard checked his signal analyzer, but again detected no transmitters. Reggie loosened the single line which held the bow to the current and flipped it off the dock cleat. When the river drew her off, he engaged the engines and she murmured quietly toward the dark.

He let her go for a half-mile into mid-channel and turned upstream toward the George Washington Bridge. Blue garlands of catenary lights draped the orange line of the roadways; their reflections painted the water the breadth of the river. He opened the throttles. Now she thundered, her propellers cutting a luminous froth as she drove hard into a chilly wind.

"You're gonna drown us if you hit something."

Reggie ignored him. The deep-V hull drove debris down and away from her shielded propellers. He turned off his running lights as the boat passed beneath the bridge. He continued upstream a mile, veering toward New Jersey. An eighth of a mile from the black wall of the Palisades he stopped the engines, and the boat glided and slowed, then drifted. When current and momentum held her in limbo, Reggie released the anchor winch and let her fall back, setting the hook in the muddy bottom.

"Gentlemen?"

He unlocked the cabin door and lighted the step with his penlight. He closed the door when they were inside and turned on a single lamp, which lit the small compartment with a dim red light. The cabin was surprisingly large, with a gleaming galley. Mikey glimpsed a bidet in the mirrored bathroom. He saw that it had been a real pussy barge until the bunks had been replaced with deep leather swivel chairs bolted to the deck. Now it looked like a conference room on a corporate jet.

Christopher Taggart had his back wedged in the U-shaped bow seat, his face deep in shadow, and Reggie noticed his hands were folded tightly.

"Sit down."

A goddamned nigger, thought Mikey. But as he sank warily into the chair nearest the bow seat, he realized that Taggart was wearing a black ski mask and leather gloves; his skin could have been green for all he could see.

"What's with the mask?"

"If I were you, Mikey, I'd expect the man who sells me a hundred keys a pop to be very careful. In fact, I'd demand it."

"You got a name?"

"No."

"I don't like this."

"We've made every effort to arrange a safe meeting. No one followed our car or our boat. Your own equipment guarantees no one is wired. No one can see us or hear us. What don't you like?"

Mikey looked around the cabin and repeated loudly for the benefit of a bug. "I don't like this. I don't know what you're talking about. Let me outta here."

"Mikey."

"You're fucking Feds. Fuck you. I ain't done nothing but gone for a boat ride."

Taggart turned his slit-eyed mask to the bodyguard. "What's your name, fella?"

Surprised, he answered, "Buddy."

"Well, I'm awful sorry, Buddy." He nodded at Reggie, who pulled the gun from his ankle.

Mikey couldn't believe his eyes. *What is this?*

Reggie repeated Taggart's "Sorry," and shot the bodyguard.

The Teflon bullet tore through Buddy's bullet-proof vest and threw him out of the chair onto the deck. Mikey's ears were ringing, and smoke burned his nostrils. He gaped at Buddy, whose face was dead white. He was moaning softly. Blood was spreading from his shoulder, soaking the front of his shirt. Reggie pounced on the wounded man and pulled Buddy's gun from his shoulder holster.

"*What?*" yelled Mikey unbelieving. "What the fuck did you do that for?"

"Would the Feds shoot Buddy?" Taggart asked him calmly.

"Why—?"

"Now you know we're not federal officers."

"You just shot a guy to show me you're not a cop?"

"You can trust us."

"But—"

"We mean business, Mikey. We're looking for good men we can trust. We do not give second chances."

Slowly Taggart's purpose sank in on Mikey. He figured the guy for a Sicilian, though he was big for one and had no accent at all. One thing for damn sure, he wasn't a cop. And people called *him* crazy! "But what about the stuff?"

"Let's step outside and talk. Take care of Buddy," he said to Reggie. "Tell him again we're real sorry." Taggart knelt beside the wounded gangster, peeling bills off a roll. "Hey, Buddy? You hear me? Sorry, man. Mikey will get you to the hospital soon as we're done talking. Here's five grand." Taggart stuffed the money in Buddy's shirt. "You'll be out in a couple of weeks. Take a vacation and recuperate—okay?" Taggart stood up and motioned for Mikey to follow him. "Let's take a look at the stars."

They stepped up to the cockpit and closed the door. Mikey could hear the river sliding past the tethered hull. Overhead were pale stars. Upriver it was black, with sweet woodsmoke on the breeze; downriver were the lighted bridge, the glittering towers of Manhattan, and the scattered lights of the Jersey condos.

"You guys are nuts."

"That's how we stay alive. What do you want to talk about?"

"Well, how much can you supply me?"

"A hundred keys a week."

"What's it gonna cost me on consignment?"

"When I can deal on consignment, one hundred fifty thousand a kilo."

"I paid one ten last time."

"That was last time. Figure one fifteen for cash at the present rate."

"What do you mean, present rate?"

"In my experience, prices fluctuate in every area, from source to freight."

"I don't know about that. I have to talk to my people."

"Look, man. I don't want to dick around with you. *You* are your people. Mikey Cirillo doesn't have to ask anybody's permission. Your guys are having problems getting stuff. I got plenty."

"One fifteen?"

"For cash. Those bearer bonds are fine, but I guess you don't get them that often. One fifty on consignment."

"Gold? Jewels?"

"I'm not a fence."

"Steady supply?"

"Guaranteed. That's what you're paying for."

"Don't leave me hanging."

"You and me deal direct. Our people can handle the stuff and the cash, but you personally come to me when you want to buy. No chance of stings."

"I can go with that."

"And one more thing?"

"What?"

Taggart couched it as a threat, but it was really an invitation to Mikey to expand the Cirillo heroin operations. "If you want to bring in another guy, *you* sell to him. I don't want to know from any third parties. No partners. I'm telling you right now, up front. If you come with a guy you know since you were in reform school and he's the son of a don who runs the Bronx, and he's made his bones and served ten years because he told the cops to fuck off, I'll kill him. Then I'll kill you. Clear? You deal with who you want to. I will only deal with you."

"I don't like threats," Mikey said quietly, thinking no Sicilian would ever be so blunt, and wondering exactly how much this guy could deliver.

"Then don't do anything to make me repeat them. . . . Hey, what are we arguing about? Your worries are over. I'm your man. You get your hundred keys a week you can count on. You get a fair price. We oughta shake on it. . . . Then we can take poor Buddy to the hospital before he bleeds to death."

Mikey silently extended his hand and Taggart gripped it firmly. The guy talked like a mick, Mikey suddenly realized —a hearty Irishman.

"And who knows? Some day soon you might even want more than a hundred keys." Taggart had his back to the bridge and saw the light glitter in Mikey's eyes.

Crazy Mikey was hooked—just as hooked as if he were shooting the junk himself.

Taggart and Reggie Rand cruised Mulberry Street in a ten-year-old Cadillac with rusted rocker panels and a tear in the vinyl roof. Reggie slouched behind the wheel in sneakers, greasy jeans, and a Moosehead T-shirt; Taggart wore jeans and a leather vest, flashing bare muscle through the open window. If they looked like anything, he thought, it was a couple of out-of-town dopers too dumb to know it was almost impossible to score in Little Italy. Twice they passed Paletti's, the steakhouse where Crazy Mikey's rival heroin distributor, Joe Reina, ate lunch, but they were early. Reggie turned onto Kenmare and parked with the engine running.

Taggart cocked his ear to the potently burbling dual exhaust. "Rhapsody of a misspent childhood. We used to sneak my old man's Lincoln to the drag races. Two cars off the line."

"Straight track?"

"Queens Boulevard. Tony and me would pull the mufflers and resonators to reduce back pressure. You should have heard it—six hundred cubes cooking. That car hauled freight."

"I presume you tuned the carburetors to compensate."

"Carbs, timing. Tony had a beautiful touch. Then we'd stash the mufflers in the trunk and find some turkey with a hopped-up muscle car. Cameros were big that year. Also Chevel SS's, even Vets; Chevy was turning them into pigs those years. I'd bet twenty bucks and blow them away. We'd make two hundred bucks a night, then put the whole muffler system back together before we got home. I'll bet you had a souped-up Jag when you were a kid."

"A Lancaster."

"What the hell's that?"

"Four-engined heavy bomber."

"In the Second World War? What, you lied about your age?"

"Among other things."

"Okay, head up Mulberry again. . . . My father used to take us down here on Sundays. It was jammed with families like ours coming in from Queens and Long Island and Jersey to look at Grandma's old neighborhood. See the clam house? Cars would cruise by all day, people saying, 'Hey, where was Joey Gallo shot?' They still do, I guess." He laughed. "What a fucking heritage."

As they crossed Grand Street, Taggart glanced east. "There's our boys."

"Jews everywhere!" The Palestinian laughed. "Why are we killing Italians?"

His friend driving the truck returned an indulgent smile. Perhaps his own eye was less obsessed, or perhaps it was just that he had lived once in New York. Surely Grand Street on the Lower East Side teemed with Jews, but among the shoppers and shopkeepers were as many Chinese, Spanish, and blacks, not to mention bargain-hunting East Side matrons, West Side actresses, and suburban housewives of many hues and persuasions. "I suppose," he said, "to fry an egg, we milk a cow for butter."

They drove carefully west, obeying traffic lights and waiting patiently when cars parking and garbage trucks blocked the street. Ahead was Little Italy, Mulberry Street, and Paletti's Steak House, where Joe Reina, the Conforti narcotics importer, was having his customary late lunch.

Neither Palestinian knew Reggie Rand or Rand's agent who had contracted their mission. Reggie had hammered out the bargain—four perfect, blank British passports—with their unit leader in Algiers. All they knew was that after years of exile in a dusty training camp two hundred miles from Algiers, they were suddenly back in action.

They double-parked across the street from Joe Reina's limousine, took the radio transmitter, and unloaded some fish crates for appearances' sake.

* * *

On their next pass Taggart directed Reggie to a parking space two blocks down Mulberry, from where he could see the sidewalk in front of Paletti's Steak House. It seemed to him that the limousine driver was eyeing the truck suspiciously, and he checked them with binoculars. The Palestinians were three blocks farther up by a pay phone.

Reggie dialed from his cellular phone. One of them answered in French and Reggie told him to sit tight.

Taggart watched the sidewalk; next to the restaurant was an Italian social club with a blank window, and up from it a plumber's shop, a funeral home, another restaurant, and a hardware store. Below Paletti's, nearest their parking spot, was an empty storefront from the cellar of which, he had learned from an agent he trusted, the Strikeforce conducted electronic surveillance of the steak house. Below the storefront were a laundry and a bakery. Across the street a row of tenements was being renovated. Sometimes the sidewalks were empty, but suddenly they would fill with people.

"You sure those clowns won't jump the gun?"

"Positive, Mr. Taggart."

"I don't want to kill a bunch of innocent people."

"Not to worry, sir. The detonator requires two radio signals —theirs and mine. It won't go off by accident if some child comes down the block with a remote-control Cabbage Patch Doll." He opened his hand; in his palm lay a dull black box.

Joe Reina's lunch guests were a Sicilian importer and the *capo* who headed Reina's network in the South Bronx. Everybody knew the Strikeforce had the restaurant bugged, but the steaks were tops and the fact that the Feds were listening made it off-limits for war.

This was a good thing because the current dope shortage, which was becoming the longest one Reina could remember, was making people crazy. Hijackings were becoming routine, and get-rich-quick freelancers were screwing people all over the place, so erroneous revenge couldn't be far behind. Conversation, of course, was casual, although personal contact was very helpful in understanding each other later on the telephone. Reina had observed that it helped to know a man's

201

voice and face when he was trying to talk a problem around a wiretap.

After they finished the meal with coffee and anisette, Reina said casually to his *capo,* "You wanna order the check? I need a breath of air."

He got up and thanked the restaurateur for a good lunch. The Sicilian followed him out the door. Reina paused on the sidewalk for a moment. Too many people were walking by. His driver hopped out of the limousine, but Reina waved him off and led the Sicilian down Mulberry and around the corner.

"So? Where's the stuff?" Reina asked.

"Already what I have is on the road," the Sicilian said.

"By now it was supposed to be God, already," Reina replied testily, referring to a twenty-kilo shipment of heroin due weeks ago, which should have been long sold and turned into money.

"This guy in Florida's giving me a big headache."

"If this keeps up much longer I'm going to shrug my shoulders."

"No, no. It's gonna work out. They just wanted that I should take this little walk."

"Delivery is not your affair. It's their affair. You don't have to take a walk. They have to." He stopped at a pay phone. "Call them now. Tell 'em you want delivery, now!"

The Sicilian dialed the number of a pay phone outside the Collins Avenue Pizzeria in Miami and pumped in quarters. When it was answered, he spoke in Sicilian and in code as well, because the FBI had Sicilian-speaking agents on their taps.

"How's the weather?"

"The weather got bad. It started to rain hard. Everyone went to take cover."

The Sicilian covered the mouthpiece. "He says cops again." And into the phone, "Is it still raining?"

"It is sleeting. Damned weather, it never ends."

"Can we expect our tomatoes soon?"

"Soon. It would be better if you came down . . . to the . . . parking lot."

"I can't do that this time. We have the documents."

When he heard "documents," Reina nodded gloomily.

Money was not the problem; he had bags of the stuff, but never enough dope.

"We're waiting on you."

"We will speak Sunday. Then I will know who is coming and when."

"Excellent. It's my pleasure to have spoke with you. I wish you a world of good. . . . I embrace you. . . . Give my regards to everyone. . . . Goodbye. Many things. Good things. . . . "

The Sicilian hung up the phone, a thoughtful light in his eyes. "He's lying. I don't think the stuff is ever coming unless I pick it up myself."

Reina shrugged. "You two guys have to decide this thing—and soon!"

They walked back to the restaurant and stopped on the sidewalk. Reina waved to his *capo,* who threw money on the table and hurried out. Reina heard the telephone ring as the door opened. The owner answered it, waving goodbye through the window.

"Paletti's."

"Listen," said an electronically distorted voice. "I'm going to say this once. Get your waiters and busboys in the back. You got five seconds. Do you understand?"

Paletti looked out his front window. Through the sheer curtains he saw Joe Reina and the Sicilian talking while Reina's driver held the door. Beside the limo was a dark van. He said, "Jesus Ch—"

"Five seconds."

Paletti snapped his fingers. The busboy and the waiters hurried to him.

"Into the kitchen! Hurry!"

Paletti followed them. Outside, Reina shook hands with his importer, who gave the *capo* a nod.

"We'll talk Sunday."

Fire blew across the street. Window glass disintegrated for a block on either side of the restaurant. A dust cloud filled Mulberry Street. When it cleared, the van and Reina's limousine were smoldering wrecks.

The Palestinians dropped their binoculars and transmitter into a sewer and walked to the subway station on West Broadway, where a girl who worked for one of Reggie Rand's agents led them onto the E train and helped them change to the JFK Express at West Fourth Street. At the airport, the Palestinians boarded the seven o'clock Northwest Airlines flight to Hamburg.

In New Jersey, a rival heroin importer named Vito Imperiale was crawling around his lawn uprooting crabgrass when he heard the news on the radio. The bombing sounded to him like a Cirillo move since Reina had covered maybe a fifth of the New York market. Imperiale figured he would pick up some of the slack, but Crazy Mikey Cirillo was bound to take most. On the other hand, Mikey's eyes were bigger than his stomach, and soon he would be short of product. When that happened, Mikey would have several options: He could go out to Kennedy to meet the Lebanese and Pakistanis who stepped off the airplane with dope in their burnooses, he could buy synthetic stuff and kill half his customers, or he could do business with old reliable Vito Imperiale.

As the radio reports got more specific throughout the afternoon, Imperiale was surprised to hear it had been a car bomb, which had caused damage up and down the block. That was pretty heavy-duty stuff, but then, it paid to remember that Crazy Mikey Cirillo wasn't called crazy for nothing. Imperiale had mixed feelings about his prospects. Being needed by Mikey Cirillo wasn't necessarily wonderful.

That evening a crew leader arrived at the heavily guarded suburban mansion. Imperiale was on the patio, slapping mosquitos and frowning at tufts of grass he had pulled from the lawn; it had separated like straw because the Japanese beetle grubs were tearing up the roots.

"A Cirillo guy called me," the crew leader reported. "He said that Mikey says he didn't have nothing to do with the bomb."

"Right."

"He says Mikey might be interested in buying from us."

"Sell the greedy bastard what you can, but keep him away from my sources."

Chapter 14

THE UPPER DECKS of the Taggart Spire were still bare steel, reddish and dull in the cold light of an autumn morning, but now, at the very top, a shiny ribbon of glass wrapped Taggart's penthouse and its cantilevered living room. Capped by glass, the tall, slim spire impaled Park Avenue like a diamond stickpin.

Taggart inspected the penthouse work, trailed by Ben Riley, the superintendent, who was taking notes and eyeing his watch as if it were a poisonous snake. Riley wore a quilted vest against the cold; Taggart had on a three-quarter coat of leather by Claude Montana. Steel girders shook as one of the V-shaped roof derricks fetched up another huge plate of reinforced insulated glass from a truck on Park Avenue.

"The city ain't gonna give you a CO until the building's done," Riley protested, trying to get him to change his mind about finishing the apartment early. He was having kittens while trying to sheath, wire, and lay pipes in the penthouse before that work was completed on the lower floors. "You can't live up here till the building's done anyway."

"Fuck a certificate of occupancy," Taggart shot back. "It's my building and it's my apartment. The Mayor can shove his paperwork. All that's standing between me and living in my apartment is you."

Across the city Taggart could see his current projects in varying states of completion—a half-erected frame of an apartment tower on upper Madison, another rising above Central Park on Columbus, and a dark hole on East Forty-seventh Street where a poured concrete substructure was nearing street level like a stack of bones. Those notches on the skyline were ordinarily a deeply satisfying sight, but this morning he was more interested in Reggie Rand, who had stationed himself behind the elevator and was dialing calls on a car phone he had brought up from the street.

The elevator clanged its arrival and Chryl and Victoria stepped off in hardhats, blue jeans, and black leather jackets, capturing the full attention of the glaziers and riggers who were manhandling a ten-by-twenty-foot sheet of glass that the derrick had hoisted alongside the deck. "Christ on a crutch, the decorating broads," groaned Riley. "That's all I need." He fled to the edge of the roof, bellowing at the riggers to steady the glass.

Taggart distractedly kissed each cheek offered. "Ben's falling behind. Are you ready to decorate?"

"Decorate?" asked Chryl.

Victoria gazed thoughtfully into the glass room, framed it with her gloved hands. "I see a single picture frame on that wall."

"Off-center," Chryl agreed.

"Empty."

"Not another stick of furniture."

"Oh God, no! Total minimal."

"A very thin frame."

Knuckles rapped a shoulder; heads bobbed. "An icy black line."

"All right, all right," Taggart said. "I'm sorry, I meant design."

Victoria slipped her hand inside his coat.

"Mr. Taggart!" Reggie called.

Taggart hurried to his side. Reggie unhooked a pager from his belt and showed him the number on its one-line screen. "Bronx exchange. This might be my chap in Joe Cirillo's crew. I'm running down to find a coin box."

"But if he's calling from a pay phone," Taggart demanded impatiently, "can't you use the car phone?"

"You pay me not to take chances."

While Taggart had penetrated the heart of Crazy Mikey's heroin distribution, his parallel, and equally vital, campaign to overthrow Cirillo bookies and loan sharks and to replace them with Helen Rizzolo's people was moving more slowly because gambling and shylocking were less centralized than heroin. The betrayals and apparently random attacks that Reggie had engineered had begun to unsettle the numerous Cirillo bookies and shylocks, but not yet sufficiently to convince many to shift allegiance to the Rizzolos. Taggart had called for another attack on the scale of the Caffè di Tullio shooting that had induced Tommy Lucia to change sides. Reggie selected the biggest Cirillo shylock enforcer in the Bronx, and the most vicious—Crazy Mikey's cousin Joe.

When Reggie returned, Taggart joined him again at the elevator. "What's up?"

"Joe Cirillo is planning a sort of public punishment for a Bronx industrialist. I think it's for us. With your permission, I'll bring in soldiers. I need a top team. No bolshies or starving natives."

"That's your decision. But I'm coming along to watch."

"I don't recommend that."

"I'm coming anyway," Taggart snapped, unaware that he had used the same tone of voice in overriding his superintendent.

Joe Cirillo slid his fingers into a chrome knuckle-duster. Working himself up, he ran the razor edge along the fleshy part of his other hand, drawing a thin line of blood which he tasted with his tongue.

"I'm making an example of this guy," he told the six hitters crammed shoulder to shoulder behind him. "When you borrow from us, you pay."

A second van was parked behind them, awaiting his signal. Across the street was a long, low, mustard-yellow brick factory, a modern windowless building. It was just after the lunch hour and they had watched from a distance until the employees had finished their stickball game and had gone back to work.

The hitters were big, well-dressed men nearing middle age, trusted soldiers, who were ordinarily years senior to a routine beatup. But in the past few weeks half a dozen Cirillo enforcers had been arrested while collecting outstanding debts, doubtlessly set up by informers, so until they somehow cleared their street crews of Strikeforce informers, a job like this was best done by guys who had a stake in the family.

"When money was tighter than virgin twat," Joe reminded his soldiers, "this joker borrows to build his factory. When he has union trouble, we get him a sweetheart contract. When he's got chemical shit, we make it disappear. But now he tries to fuck us."

The factory owner was expected to carry a dozen Cirillo soldiers on his payroll, supply specially hollowed-out plastic toys to ship heroin, and make off-the-books cash interest payments weekly. He had performed until he got suckered into a high-stakes poker game in Atlantic City. The rest was history, to the tune of two hundred grand outstanding, and, finally, a weekly interest he could not pay.

"The whole Bronx is gonna hear him scream."

Joe's men looked as if they wished to discuss the fact that suddenly it was getting unhealthy to enforce collections. Not only were guys being arrested right and left; others were attacked in the streets. Two days ago a Cirillo crew leader overseeing a beating had been attacked himself by a black street gang; from his hospital bed he swore that it was a setup. They were waiting for him. Nor had the gang come to the defense of the welsher, who was a roundly hated white landlord.

One of the hitters summoned up the courage to say, "Something's going on, Joe."

Joe Cirillo looked at the guy. "You got a problem?"

"Maybe it's more than bad luck that everyone's getting hit at once. Our guys are—"

"You want to go home early? You can leave now."

"Joe, what if somebody's moving in on us? I keep hearing about the Rizzolos. I'm seeing Rizzolos where they shouldn't be."

Joe stared him down. Then he motioned the others out of the van. "Okay, get him ready. Remember, nobody leaves till I'm done pulping the bastard."

Twelve men entered the factory simultaneously, converging on the front door and the side and rear loading bays. In the bright carpeted lobby, the receptionist looked up with a smile that faded uncertainly. A burly black security guard dropped his magazine and went for his gun.

Joe Cirillo's men mobbed him, took his revolver away, and locked him to a railing with his own handcuffs. The factory owner heard the scuffle and stepped out of his office in shirtsleeves and loosened necktie. When he saw the hoods, he fled back through his door, which he locked, and pawed desperately at the telephone. They kicked the door open, rounded his desk, and slapped the telephone out of his hand. He backed against the wall, pleading and covering his face. Two Cirillos seized his fleshy arms and marched him out. Another dragged the receptionist along. Leaving a man at the door, they burst onto the low balcony that overlooked the main workroom.

The plant, covering nearly a half acre, was washed white as a desert by overhead fluorescent lights, and it reeked of the sweet, cloying odor of hot plastic. Fifty men and women were working the extruder machines, presses, and bench drills. They looked up at their boss cringing between the large men holding his arms, and a dark wave of apprehension washed over the room until they and their machines stood motionless and silent. Workers in the back started to retreat to the rear doors, but the Cirillos were there too, herding the rest of the guards, whom they had surprised at lunch.

From the front entrance the arrogant click of heel taps on linoleum broke the quiet, and Joe Cirillo strolled in. He removed his wedding ring as he surveyed the silent black and Spanish faces, and made a show of working his fingers into the chrome knucks. Then he nodded and his men lifted the factory owner off the floor. He squealed in terror. But before Joe could go to work, one of the Spanish girls, a kid eighteen or nineteen, charged up the stairs screaming and swinging a monkey wrench.

"Let her through," Joe instructed.

"Rosa. No!" the owner cried, but she came anyway, swinging the wrench. Joe ducked under it. Her momentum dragged her to him, her hands locked on the wrench, the whole side of her body exposed from her ankles to her face. Joe measured his target and backhanded her with the knuckles, and she went down, her cheek a bloody smear. The joker actually tried to hit him!

"Balling the help?" Joe sneered. His men heaved the guy

into the air again. Joe stepped between his flailing legs, the knuckles cocked.

A block away, atop a three-story bakery, the tallest building in the industrial park, Reggie Rand, who knew the police patrols down to the minute, watched his men go into action. They were French mercenaries, two brothers, and their protégé, a young German boy. Reggie had flown them in, supplied the weapons they had asked for, and tonight would fly them back to France.

Taggart stood beside him, with hands in pockets and eyes like ice. From this vantage point they could see the plastics factory's front entrance and driveway, the Cirillos' vans, and a lower rooftop directly across the street from the factory. Reggie had pleaded that Taggart shouldn't be here, that his enterprise was so risky that he ought to take every opportunity to minimize his risks, but Taggart seemed more and more bent on taking chances.

Suddenly, on the low roof across from the factory, there was a hint of motion in the shadows. A moment later, shooting started inside the factory. Muffled by the cinderblock walls, the rapid-firing automatic weapon had the muffled buzzing of a high-speed printer. A year ago Taggart had ordered Reggie to put him through a basic weapons survival course, and the noise, he recalled, was terrifying. Inside the factory, Taggart knew, the shattering reports of an unsilenced Uzi on full automatic sounded like a war.

"Surprise."

He watched the doors with grim satisfaction. A few more attacks like this and the Cirillo loan sharks were out of business. The Cirillo soldiers came boiling out the doors, white-faced, arms and legs pinwheeling as they fled. Some trailed, staggering, and one collapsed on the sidewalk. Those who could, raced to their vans. Reggie pointed to the rooftop across the street. "Watch the German. He's superb."

A figure popped over the parapet and leveled a short, blunt weapon on his shoulder. His captain arose easily beside him, covering with a stock-mounted automatic pistol in the unlikely event the boy should need help.

Whooom! A rocket struck the rear van, blowing the Cirillo enforcers back just as they lunged for the doors. The explosion hurled them to the street, where they writhed, burned, or were too stunned to seek cover. Joe Cirillo, the last man out of the building, gaped incredulously at the inferno. His bullet-shattered arm hung like a stick, the chrome knuckles still attached to his fingers. He shambled into his own van screaming, "Go. Go!"

The van leaped forward, scattering the men who tried to get in after Joe, and squealed for the corner. *Whooom!* The van turned to flame, slewed across the street, leaped the curb, and crashed into the factory wall. Joe Cirillo rolled out of the passenger door and crawled into the gutter. The burning van exploded thunderously. The explosion threw him across the street, where he lay, twitching feebly, as the flames reflected red off the chrome knucks still attached to his hand.

That night, after the police and fire department had left and he had picked up Rosa in the emergency room and put her in a cab, the owner of the plastics factory propped his feet on his desk and figured things were looking up. He was clear. Whoever had attacked Joey Cirillo had done him a big favor. Everyone knew that he had had nothing to do with it. But with all the cops around, the Cirillos couldn't take a chance on trying to hurt him again. One of the security guards knocked on his door. He still looked embarrassed for screwing up, and the company had doubled the guard at no extra cost.

"Guy out here wants to see you."

"Sure." More cops, detectives, Feds; the more the better.

But he wasn't a cop. He looked like an accountant. He opened a briefcase, revealing rows of shiny metal toggle switches, which he jiggled back and forth for an electronic sweep. Satisfied, the guy closed his briefcase and said, "I represent people who are assuming Cirillo obligations in this area."

"What are you talking about?"

"I'll be back next week to collect."

"What are you talking about?"

"God is not coming down to save your ass a second time."

* * *

Taggart insisted on meeting the new collector.

"On this, I put my foot down," Reggie replied.

"I'll wear a mask. I've got to watch my people."

"But that's what I'm here for."

Taggart insisted. Reggie told himself that he wanted to retain strict control, but he wondered whether Taggart simply couldn't resist daring the odds. It was one thing to meet face to face, masked, with Mikey Cirillo to consummate the heroin deal, but it was frivolous to tempt fate. Had Reggie the time he might have worried more about Taggart's walk-on-water attitude, but he was too busy. Events were accelerating. No sooner had he displayed the new Rizzolo shylock to a masked Christopher Taggart than he had a meet, alone, with the outside leader of an upstate prison gang.

"I don't get it," said the gang leader as he counted the money that consummated their deal. "South Bronx numbers used to be strictly Cirillo territory."

"That's right."

"But now the Confortis and Bonos are stirring the kiddie gangs against them, trying to take over."

"Correct."

"So who the hell are you?"

"I'm gentrifying the neighborhood," Reggie replied blandly.

Bumpy Fredricks, or "Bump" to his clients, worried more about robbers than cops as he made his rounds collecting bets and noting the numbers on flimsy cigarette paper. But when a dark van started following him he didn't know what to think. Cirillo numbers runners all over New York were getting taken off. Up until now, he had liked working for the Cirillos because they kept order. Now he wasn't so sure, because when a Mafia family started fighting its rivals, the neighborhood gangs got bold.

The van hung back, stopped when he went into a store, started up when he came out. Being an optimist, Bumpy decided the big boys had sent the van to look out for him as he made his rounds. The dry cleaner played his regular 234 and repeated his refrain that it had to come in someday. The liquor-store clerks next door slid 285 and 314 through the money slot of their bullet-proof glass, the former for his girl-friend's apartment number, the latter for somebody's tag scrawled on an IRT car. The girls on the hotel stoop picked numbers out of the air—417, 630, 555, 259—like leaves were falling on them, and pressed the dollars in his hand.

Bumpy rounded a corner and said, "Oh, shit."

Three kids from a gang called the Spanish Main were lean-ing on a storefront. They straightened up when they saw him, as if they'd been waiting. They rarely ventured up to this side of Third Avenue, because it was Devils' territory and the Devils had a protection agreement with the Cirillos. Trouble was, Bumpy thought, the Devils had been getting their asses kicked lately and there wasn't a Devil in sight. Then he real-ized there were more Spanish Main waiting up the block. He turned back, figuring to head for the more populated Morris Avenue, but two more kids were rounding the corner behind him, at which point he stopped worrying about the money and the slips because his real problem was going to be getting out of this alive. At twenty-eight and nursing a tubercular leg, he was too old to run and too tired to fight. God, send me a cop, he thought. But there were none. He looked for the van which had been following him, but there was suddenly no one on the burned-out block but him and them, and they were walking his way.

Bumpy stepped to a parked car, reached carefully into his pockets, and started piling dollar bills on the hood. The wind caught them and he lunged, crumpling them in his fists. The kids formed a half-circle on the sidewalk around the car, watching with dead eyes, and Bumpy felt an anger he seldom indulged begin to well up inside him, a boiling frustration. All he was trying to do was make a small living and these little bastards half his age made him walk in fear. He was not a violent man, though he had seen as much violence as anyone who had grown up in a poor city, but suddenly, if he could, he would shoot them all like Bernie Goetz, the subway vigilante. Not that he could shoot them—he had no gun, just a knife, which he really could not use well enough to defend himself one on one, much less against the six guys now circling him and watching him try to keep his money from blowing away.

"Here. Take it."

He had made the worst possible mistake—not that he had any choice—by admitting he was defenseless. Their leader, a kid with a three-whisker mustache, said, "Somebody pop him."

Two of them pulled guns, huge, rusty forty-fives with barrels big around as sewer pipes. Forget a flesh wound. They were going to tear holes through his body. He felt like screaming, Go away, leave me alone! "Here's the money," he repeated softly.

"Pop him."

Bumpy closed his eyes.

"Whoa! Who be that?"

An engine raced close by and Bumpy opened his eyes. The van was coming. It stopped short beside the car and two black guys in suits and raincoats got out quickly. He thought they were cops, canceled that, and thought again; maybe, by their business suits and cold faces, they were Black Muslims. But maybe not; maybe something else. They gave the street a quick look and one pulled out a big plastic garbage bag, the other a sawed-off shotgun.

"Pieces in here. You first."

The thirteen-year-old with the forty-five looked at the sawed-off double barrels and gingerly dropped his gun into the sack.

"Now you. Don't drop it. Just lay it in gentle." His partner turned the shotgun on the leader. "Tell your men to open their colors. The rest of the guns. Then the knives."

"Hey, man, who the fuck—?"

"Who the fuck? What do you *mean*, who the fuck?"

Bumpy saw the dude's polished shoe blur up from the sidewalk high as his shoulder. The steel toe cracked the kid's jawbone and he fell hard and silent to the cement. The dude wiped the blood off his shoe on the Spanish Main leader's pants. "Anybody else say who the fuck?"

He collected the rest of their weapons and told them to pick up their leader. Then he pointed at Bumpy. "You mark this man? You remember him. If he *ever* has a problem—any kind of problem at all—we'll come back and cut your balls off." He looked at each kid, straight in the face. "So that means if you see anybody *else* giving him a problem, you look out for him. Right? He's your friend. Got that? Okay, go on now—git!"

When they had gone, he turned to Bumpy. "There's been some changes made."

"Yes, sir."

"You'll be delivering your bets to someone else."

"Yes, *sir*."

"Mikey, we got trouble."

Crazy Mikey waited, working his coke spoon with his fingers, repeatedly opening and shutting the miniature breech. Had the bearer of more bad news been anyone but Sally Smarts Ponte, he might have thrown him down the stairs of the Jackson Heights videogame warehouse he used for meetings. But although troubles were multiplying faster than he could keep up, he still couldn't yell at *Consigliere* Ponte. As far back as his childhood, the *consigliere* had been there, his father's closest adviser and his own godfather, a firm, quiet man whose advice always cut to the heart of a problem.

"It sounds like something everyone's afraid to tell me, so they sent you."

Ponte, a darkly handsome lawyer in his fifties, gave him a smile. He wasn't a warm man; were he, Mikey couldn't have trusted him. But he was a man who lent his full attention to whomever he served. "You're right. They're afraid."

Mikey thought that it was incredible that just when the dope business was going so well, everything else started falling apart. First they had lost Brooklyn books and numbers to the Rizzolos. Now the bastards were moving into the Bronx. But the other families accused the Cirillos of moving in on *them*. Everybody thought he had bombed Joe Reina in retaliation for the Caffè di Tullio shooting. Vito Imperiale was barely talking to him, and the Bonos and Confortis had announced that Cirillos were not welcome on their streets—which put all of them one angry Sicilian from open warfare.

"Now what?" he asked Ponte.

"They hit the Chelsea club. Robbed the customers and the take."

"Who?"

"Looks like freelances."

"Find out who and get them."

"That's not the problem. After they left and the customers were leaving, some people came up to the high rollers and said they had caught the guys and had their stuff. They brought the high rollers to another club in the next block and helped them sort out coats and jewelry and even some cash."

"What other club?"

"A new joint opened during the summer down the street from Limelight. Tommy Lucia's friends had it ready to go. Wheels, booze, broads dealing blackjack—the whole thing. Most of our best customers stayed the rest of the night."

"In other words, the Rizzolos have moved into Chelsea." Mikey started playing with the little shotgun model again; Ponte watched anxiously, but Mikey, he was relieved to see, never went near the coke. At last, he said, "It's time to hit back."

"I wouldn't rush into anything, Mikey."

"I ain't rushing. I been thinking about this for weeks."

"Tommy's just a dumb guinea in the middle."

Crazy Mikey said, "Yeah. He's in the middle of Frank and Eddie Rizzolo."

"We can't afford a war with the Strikeforce on our backs," *Consigliere* Ponte protested.

"It'll be a short one," Mikey promised grimly.

"What if it's not the Rizzolos?"

"Then who?"

"I don't know. I think something's going on."

"What?"

"I don't know."

"Here's what I know: Memorial Day, somebody turned Vetere in to the Strikeforce and Vetere ratted on Nicky, so my father told me to take over. Everybody thought I couldn't handle the family past Fourth of July, but by the end of the summer I got the dope flowing again. But while I'm busy doing that, three guys walked into the Caffè di Tullio and blasted our Brooklyn underboss, and pretty soon we lost most of his books. By Labor Day they were hitting us in the Bronx. Now, it isn't even Halloween and Tommy Lucia is holding hands in Manhattan with Frank and Eddie Rizzolo. We're going to be dead by Christmas if we don't do something about the Rizzolos."

"Warn Helen and have your people watch her club," Taggart ordered when Reggie reported what his spies were picking up in the Cirillo camp. "Follow her when she goes to the restaurants."

"First of all, they're not likely to attack a woman, especially when they don't know she's the real brains of her family. Secondly, the Rizzolos were defending their enterprises when your father was pushing a wheelbarrow."

"I'm not taking chances. I don't want her hurt."

Chapter 15

THE RIZZOLOS' BLUE Line bus barn was a steep-gabled wooden structure built in 1893 to house trolleys. It sheltered an area of Long Island City two blocks long and three wide. Skylights dimpled its vast roofs like mountain villages of little houses clinging to their slopes. Inside it resounded with idling engines, shrieking air guns, and low-gear whine as drivers jockeyed the buses into the maintenance bays. The air reeked of diesel exhaust.

Helen Rizzolo had always loved the smell. The sharp bite reminded her of rare visits as a little girl to see her father at work in his white shirtsleeves rolled up his thick forearms, a dark vest, and a loosened tie. Once, to her brothers' dismay, he had let her steer a bus while seated on his lap. It was a place that made her happy, and when she came to do the payroll, she always entered through the wooden gingerbread embellishments around the front door. She turned on her headlights and beeped the horn to warn the hustling mechanics, and her Fiat skittered past the bays, dodging the buses like a busy, bright-eyed red bug.

The office was a hut in the back, partitioned by thin plywood walls that barely muffled the noise. She could tell by the quiet when the mechanics were on lunch or coffee break. The office had a much lower ceiling than the rest of the barn, windows that looked out on a junk-filled yard, and a back door. Eddie and Frank hung out here, since the company was their legitimate employer; Eddie was president, Frank vice-president, and she the treasurer.

She kissed them, took her desk, and opened a container of tea she had bought at the deli. Eddie, head in hands, was staring at a sheaf of papers from the city. "Why the fuck did Pop make us a bus business in Long Island?"

"Now what's wrong?"

"We can't go interstate. The buses in Westchester, they run the route through two *inches* of Connecticut so they can tell the city to go fuck itself 'cause crossing the state line makes 'em interstate commerce. But we gotta obey every local law the city makes up. Can't use this street, can't use that, no noise, no idling."

While talking, Eddie was writing a note; they had installed a new telephone line in response to Taggart's warning about the Strikeforce tap, but with the buses coming and going they couldn't count on sweeping every bug. He slipped the note to her: "Three more Cirillo books came our way last night. We got Brooklyn numbers wrapped up and a lot of the Bronx."

Helen smiled and Eddie returned a grin which seemed, she thought, almost deferential. Thanks to her deal with Taggart, Eddie and Frank were giving her credit for their new prosperity.

"Why don't we go through Jersey?" she asked aloud, writing back, "Any word on how Mikey's taking it?"

Eddie showed it to Frank, then touched a match to the paper. It burned in his ashtray.

"Well?"

He shrugged. Helen looked at Frank. He shrugged, too, and she realized her brothers were embarrassed to admit that whatever spies they had managed to infiltrate among the Cirillos didn't know. She reminded herself that her new power was a two-edged sword. She had to be careful not to undercut their pride. They would do something foolish to get it back.

She started in on the computer, but her mind stayed on Christopher Taggart and his scheme. It was going almost *too* well. Between the Strikeforce tearing pieces out of the Cirillos on the legal side and Taggart gnawing away from inside, the huge, powerful family seemed almost paralyzed.

The telephone rang. Eddie picked it up, listened a moment, and glanced her way. Helen pretended she didn't notice when he nodded to Frank and said into the phone. "I'll be here."

"Who was that?"

"Nothing."

"Are you guys dealing again?"

"Shhhh! Jesus, Helen. What if—?"

"'Cause if you are, I want you to stop it. I told you no dope."

Eddie scrabbled about his desk for a piece of paper and wrote, "Shut up! It's just a little coke deal on the side. Guy's been talking it up for months."

"I don't *believe* you," she protested, thinking, How could they risk blowing everything for a stupid dope deal? But she blamed herself; she had pushed them too hard. It was like they had to prove something to themselves, like they didn't really need her. Godammit, they did. And she needed them.

Eddie wrote, "We're just going to set up a meeting," folded his arms, and stared obstinately at his desk top. Even Frank wouldn't meet her eye. Seething, as angry at herself as she was at them, Helen pounded the computer keys like an old-fashioned typewriter.

Twenty minutes passed and the phone rang again. Eddie snatched it up. His eyes widened and he motioned to Frank to pick up too. Helen grabbed her extension and covered the mouthpiece as the caller repeated, "I said, You recognize my voice?"

It was Crazy Mikey Cirillo.

"Yeah, I know you. What's up?"

"I just want you to know who this is coming from."

"What's coming?"

"This."

Helen looked at Frank, who sprang to his feet like a panther, reaching into the locker where he kept a brace of legally owned hunting rifles. Then the wall seemed to get suddenly very big as it flew at her. An explosion thundered through the barn.

She found herself on the floor, pinned under the wall, which was propped up by her desk. The computer lay beside her; the winking green cursor blanketed the screen with squiggly shapes she had never seen before. The mechanics were yelling in the barn and something was roaring. A liquid—her own blood, she realized when she touched it—was running down her face.

"Frank! Eddie!"

"Stay there, baby. You okay?"

"Frank!"

"Yeah, I'm fine. Don't move, hon. They might be shooting."

She heard Eddie crawl past in the dark and yell, "There's a fire!"

Helen saw the flickering of the flames. The mechanics and drivers were yelling; somewhere a man was screaming. She found the telephone wire on the floor, reeled in the phone, and dialed the lighted dial. When 911 answered she said, "Fire and explosion. Blue Line bus barn. Ambulance."

She freed her leg and crawled out of the shelter formed by the wall and her desk. She was surprised to see daylight pouring in the skylights brighter than ever because the glass had been broken. The far end of the barn, the front, was filled with black smoke. The dense, greasy smoke had trapped some forty buses inside. She tried to stand and found she could. Frank grabbed her, his face horrified. "You're bleeding."

She wiped at it with her hand. Her head hurt. "I'm okay."

Eddie came back with a gun in his hand. "They're gone."

Frank yelled, "I'll drive a bus through the wall there to make a hole for the others."

"No," said Helen. "Help the men out! Leave the buses."

Frank was wild-eyed. "But I can save 'em!"

"We'll do better on the insurance."

Her legs started to collapse under her own weight and Frank scooped her into his huge arms. A million sirens seemed to scream at once. Eddie led Frank through the office door. Cradled in his arms, she saw the first plumes of water cascading into the flames. Frank carried her to the paramedics, who swabbed a gash in her scalp. She sat on the back of the ambulance watching the flames disintegrate the gingerbread front of the barn. By then the police were there, plainclothesmen and uniformed cops, and they were questioning Eddie and Frank, who were shrugging a lot.

"Okay, lie down, dear," a paramedic said. "We're going to take you to the hospital."

"No, I'm fine."

"You might have a concussion."

She tried to argue, but her hands were shaking and she had the weirdest urge to cry.

She passed out in the ambulance and awakened in bed to hear a doctor saying, "Even a slight concussion is a helluva lot worse than no concussion. . . . Hello there! Follow my finger, please."

He held it a foot from her face, moved it slowly above her forehead and down to her chin. "Good. Nauseous?"

"No."

"Good. Now this way, left to right." She focused and followed his finger to the right, saw it cross his middle-aged face. Behind him were a nurse, a television hanging from the ceiling, an IV rack at the corner of her bed, the bathroom door and wardrobe, a hundred red roses on a table—and Taggart standing in the doorway.

His face was working. He brushed past the doctor, took her hand, and knelt beside the bed so they were face to face, inches apart. He seemed barely able to speak. "Are you okay?"

"Mr. Taggart," the doctor interrupted. "If I could finish—"

"Is she okay?" He was holding her hand as gently as a kitten.

"I'm not making any promises. But the CAT scan shows no bleeding."

Helen tugged him closer and whispered, "What are you doing here?"

"I was driving around my jobs; heard it on the radio."

"You're taking chances."

"Don't worry about it. How do you feel?"

"Okay. Where's my brothers?"

"Answering cops' questions."

"My mother?"

"They didn't want to tell her till they knew how you were. Shall I get her?"

She still felt like crying. "I want to see my mother."

Taggart signaled someone she couldn't see and turned back to her again and whispered, "I'm really sorry. I told Reggie to watch out for you."

"We can take care of ourselves. Isn't that what you're using me for?"

"I figured the fighting would stay at street level."

"You figured wrong—but *we* got hurt."

Her head hurt and it was hard to think while the room made circles, but it seemed important to make him understand what was going on in the rackets. She closed her eyes and pretended to cry. The ruse worked. Taggart leaned closer and the doctor backed away to let him comfort her. "Why are you surprised?" she whispered. "Crazy Mikey knows he didn't bomb Joe Reina or shoot Al Conforti, or burn down that fortress Harry Bono had in Westchester. He knows he didn't sell Vito Imperiale's underbosses to the Strikeforce; he knows he didn't chase the other families out of Kennedy Airport. And he knows he didn't attack his own enforcers. We've always been enemies and now he sees us getting stronger at his expense. What would you do if you were Mikey?"

Taggart stood up, his face turning cold. "I'm sorry," he repeated. "I'll take care of it. You have nothing else to worry about."

"Don't fight with Mikey," she warned him. "That's our job."

"I'll be in touch." His hand tightened on hers, his lips parted, and she thought for a second he would plunge to her mouth. Her body coiled and she started to lift her head from the pillow. But instead of kissing her, he backed away and let go of her hand with a little squeeze.

The room started whirling faster. The doctor reappeared and shined a light in her eyes. Helen raised her throbbing head and looked past him at Taggart, who, thinking he was out of sight, had stopped hiding the fury that seared his face.

She saw in that raw expression a side he had hidden last spring on the Irish cliffs, and again the summer night atop his building. Yet it recalled vividly the night ten years ago at Abatelli's when he stormed out after Don Richard Cirillo. Christopher Taggart was a man capable of embracing an all-consuming hatred.

It was frightening, and all the more so today because the attack on her had provoked his rage, as if Taggart wanted more than his stated intention that the Rizzolos seize the street. Coming to her club, and now racing to the hospital, he seemed to want to possess her. Helen tried to weigh coolly the additional opportunities that this might present for her family, but deep in her heart she began to fear the price. And she sagged back on the sheets, terrified by her own impulse, when he had taken her hand, to pull him down on top of her.

Outside the hospital, Reggie was waiting in Taggart's car. "Did the police see you?" he asked.

"Set up a meet with Mikey."

"But you're to meet on the boat next week."

"*Now.*"

"There's only one way he'll agree to meet."

"I know. Cut him off!"

They boarded the boat in Tarrytown at one of Taggart's several boathouses scattered about New York, and headed downriver as night fell. The tide was receding, the Hudson flowed swiftly, and the offshore racer skimmed the water on muted engines. Reggie steered silently until he had concluded the electronic sweeps.

"You surprise me, Mr. Taggart."

"How's that?"

"You certainly didn't expect the Cirillos not to fight back."

"Right."

"Is it possible you're overreacting because the girl happened to be there?"

"Anything's possible," Taggart replied easily, and Reggie felt better until Taggart added, "He almost killed her."

"What do you intend?"

"To make sure it doesn't happen again."

"But you're forgetting—"

"I forget nothing."

When the boat passed under the George Washington Bridge, Taggart went below and locked himself in the cabin. He wedged his back into the forward V-bunk and waited, while Reggie steered into a private marina at the foot of a New Jersey condo. His anger was rising; he could taste it in his mouth. He listened to two men board and felt the boat turn and gradually pull away. A while later the engines stopped, and he heard the anchor chain rasp out of the winch. Taggart pulled the ski mask over his head just as Reggie unlocked the door.

Their meetings were ritual performances by now. Reggie came first, checked to see that only the red navigation lights were burning, and waited just inside the cabin door. Mikey's bodyguard, a heavyset Sicilian who had replaced the wounded Buddy, made sure Taggart was alone and ran a quick electronic check, augmenting what he had already done on deck. Then he stood on the other side of the three-step companionway.

Mikey stepped between them and ducked to clear the door. His thin lips formed hard lines in his bony face. He faced Taggart with dark, angry eyes. Taggart stared back.

"Get out!" Mikey told his bodyguard.

Reggie closed the door as he and the Sicilian went on deck.

"Your people are fucking me up."

"Sit down," Taggart said.

"Why are they doing this?"

"People I know have a problem."

"I'll listen. But before I do, you listen to me. Don't jerk me around. You promise to deliver, you better deliver."

Taggart returned his stare and made no reply. Finally Mikey asked, "All right. What's your friends' problem?"

"Somebody threw ten sticks of dynamite at their bus barn."

"That thing in the papers?"

"The Blue Line in Long Island City."

"What do you want me to do?"

"Guarantee such a thing never happens again."

"Guarantee? How can I do that?"

"Put out the word."

"To who? I don't know those people. I don't know what they're fighting about."

Taggart felt like he was falling backward, plunging ten years into the past. It was the night on the sidewalk in front of Abatelli's again. Don Richard denied he had killed Taggart's father and had joked that he hadn't killed anybody in thirty years. He hadn't even known the name Mike Taglione. As if it were happening now, he saw the skinny old man turn his back, heard the order, "He's not allowed in," and felt this same Crazy Mikey pound his face as he joined the Mafia bonebreakers in the fun. Sorrow, rage, and guilt overwhelmed his heart and overcame his mind. He could hardly form the words: "You hurt a friend of mine. Your people threw the dynamite."

Mikey didn't deny it. "That's none of your fucking business. That's got nothing to do with dope."

"It's got everything to do with dope."

Mikey looked intrigued. "How's that? The Rizzolos are gamblers and shylocks. They got freight at Kennedy?"

"If you ever go near them again, I'll cut your heroin supply for good. That's what it has to do with dope."

"They're none of your business," Mikey repeated.

"I'm making it my business. Don't ever go near her—ever! Or you're dead."

"*Her?* Hey, nobody knew the girl was there . . . is that it?" Mikey sneered. "You got the hots for their kid sister?"

Taggart bounded off the bunk, flew the length of the cabin, and clawed at Mikey's throat. But Mikey was fast, and hit him with a vicious right to the face. Frenzied, Taggart barely felt it as he threw Mikey against the door, which fell off its hinges. Mikey dropped to the companionway, half in the cabin, half in the cockpit. Punching and kicking furiously, Taggart drove him up the companionway, dragged him to his feet, and clubbed him back to the deck in the second it took the Cirillo bodyguard to act.

Reggie and the Sicilian had been standing in the stern, as far from the cabin as possible to allow the bosses to do their business without corroborating witnesses. The tide had turned and the boat was pulling downstream against its anchor, so that the George Washington Bridge lights shown on Taggart and Crazy Mikey. The Sicilian drew a weapon in a fluid motion as he moved closer and dropped into a crouch. Reggie chopped his neck. He fell to the deck but slammed Reggie with a scissors kick, which threw the Englishman hard against the gunnel.

Reggie cried out and staggered as he tried to stand. Astonished—in two years Taggart had never seen him hurt, much less stumble—and frightened for him, Taggart turned to help. Mikey used the distraction to kick him in the groin. He collapsed in searing pain, trying to cover up as the mobster hit him with a flurry of kicks and punches. The Sicilian picked up his gun and aimed it with two hands. He shouted for Mikey to move aside, that he had Taggart covered.

Taggart drove the pain from his consciousness, like a debt he would pay later. He seized Mikey with both hands, and held him like a shield. Mikey fought back. The Sicilian looked for an opening. Reggie, hunched over, breathing hard and holding his ribs, moved in sudden swift silence and chopped the Sicilian's neck again. This time the Sicilian collapsed on the deck with a helpless whimper.

"He tricked you," Reggie said bleakly, after they had dropped Cirillo and his bodyguard and the boat was pulling away from the Mill Basin pier on a creamy wake. "You told him too much."

"Fuck him."

"You've gone too far. Until now you had the heroin as a club over him. By showing your concern for Helen Rizzolo, you've given Mikey a club over you."

Taggart saw he was right, but caught an answer on the wing. "Maybe so, Reg, but if he thinks I have the hots for her, he won't make the real connection."

Reggie leaned back heavily in the padded seat, holding his ribs, angrily waving Taggart off when he tried to help. Taggart brought the boat back toward the light on Staten Island that he had been steering for. Reggie drew a handkerchief from his pocket.

"He is going to go looking elsewhere for reliable sources."

"Then we'll take care of elsewhere."

"Which takes you further away from your goal."

"Relax, Reg. You're getting way down."

Reggie put the handkerchief to his mouth, spat, and examined it dispassionately by the red glow of the instrument lights.

"You okay?"

"Maybe I am getting 'down,' as you put it. The real trouble is, I'm getting old and you're getting out of control."

Chapter 16

*J*UST AS REGGIE predicted, Crazy Mikey asked for a meeting with the narcotics importer Vito Imperiale. He suggested some sort of neutral ground like a Manhattan restaurant, but the word came back: No way was Vito Imperiale coming into the city while a war was on. Instead, Crazy Mikey was invited to Imperiale's house. For Mikey to call on a lesser figure violated protocol, but his father and *Consigliere* Ponte urged him to accept.

"Give a little now, take later," said Ponte.

Imperiale's driver delivered a garage-door opener folded in a map of Alpine, New Jersey.

"What the fuck is this?"

"The garage is attached. You drive inside, nobody sees you."

Mikey and his bodyguard drove up the Palisades Parkway in a rented Honda. Twenty minutes north of the George Washington Bridge they exited into the bedroom community and found Imperiale's house in a maze of broad and empty suburban streets lined with maple trees that had turned bright yellow. It was a new three-story, Tudor-style house with bright white stucco and dark brown beams, set on a fenced four-acre lawn. Across the street a telephone truck was parked beside a stanchion on the grassy shoulder.

The fence reminded Mikey of his father's place on Staten Island, which was bigger and finer-looking, being constructed of brick and marble. Nonetheless, Vito was doing all right. They drove into the driveway, pressed the garage-door opener, and Imperiale's garage door, which was disguised to look like a stable entrance, opened.

After they drove in and the door rumbled shut, Vito stepped into the garage with a friendly smile. He was a fat, pear-shaped man, with a big nose, widely set dark eyes that appeared darker yet because his skin was so white, and shiny black hair. Crazy Mikey left his man in the kitchen with Vito's men and followed his host into the living room. At no point, he noticed, did Imperiale address him by name. He led Mikey through a big living room cluttered with overstuffed beige couches and chairs, and out french doors onto a big stone patio. A high, whitewashed brick wall shielded the patio on three sides. The house blocked the fourth. Overhead were blue sky and the noonday sun, which had warmed the furniture cushions.

"No windows to vibrate when we talk," Imperiale explained. "No bugs and taps out here. But shut up if a balloon comes over!" He laughed and poured espresso from a wet bar set in stone.

"What about that telephone truck we passed on the way in?"

"Feds. I leave 'em one phone line to keep 'em busy. Whenever I see the truck, I have a man talk nonsense. "Here we're safe."

"You mind if I check?"

"Be my guest."

Mikey opened his briefcase and checked for transmitters and recorders. When he closed it, Imperiale said, "So what brings you to the country?"

Mikey's father kept telling him to open negotiations slowly, but it was an old-fashioned, stupid thing to do when both of them knew exactly what he came for. "I want to buy."

"I figured that, with Joe Reina gone. How much?"

"Much as you can. Two, three hundred kilos a week."

"That's a lot of product."

"It'll save you a lot of trouble if you sell it all to me."

"What makes you think I got trouble selling it where I do?"

"The FBI, the DEA, and the Strikeforce are doing a number on my middle guys. If my middle guys are getting busted, so are yours. The thing is, I'm bigger and I got more guys, so I can roll with the punches longer than you. And another thing, you're what, fifty-five?"

Vito said, "Sixty-five," with a smile, and Mikey felt proud he had scored on that one. "So what?"

"I'm only thirty. A guy my age is supposed to fight, likes to fight. A guy fifty-five or sixty, maybe he deserves to slow down a little."

"Maybe," Vito conceded. "What makes you think I import so much stuff?"

Crazy Mikey smiled. "My father says you do."

"You'll need more than me to fill your needs. I don't have that much."

"My father thinks you might know sources."

Imperiale covered his annoyance. "How is Don Richard?"

"Never been better."

"Forgive me, I say with all respect that I think your brother getting arrested was good for your father. It makes an old man young to work again."

Mikey's expression turned complex, and Imperiale hastened to soothe him. "Particularly if he has another son to help him."

"What do you say?"

Imperiale's patio seemed less secure than usual. The world had tracked him down again. The Cirillos must have lost a big supplier. There'd been rumors Mikey had wired into somebody really big. Then suddenly, the street supply had dried up again, as if Mikey had lost that supplier. So now Mikey was leaning on him.

He shrugged. "I been thinking of easing up a bit. Maybe if I supply you exclusively, I'd get off the street."

"It's an easier living," Mikey replied, amazed by some of the things he heard himself say these days. Six months ago he would have said that if Vito didn't get off the street, he could kiss his street crews goodbye. Today he took his father's advice and spoke softly.

And the amazing thing was that Vito took the hint.

Taggart was in the telephone repair van across the street from Imperiale's house. The white stanchion was the wire closet for the immediate area, which was serviced by underground lines. Reggie focused a laser listening gun on Imperiale's kitchen window. A conversation played through the van's speakers.

"The bodyguards," said Reggie. "Mikey and Vito will talk on the patio, where we can't hear."

"But at least we know they're meeting."

"Yes."

"Just don't hurt Mikey."

"Not to worry. No one shoots his pilot."

He turned off the laser, which picked up the vibrations of voices rattling the kitchen window, and drove away before the phone company or the Feds came along on their business.

Each new battle of what Vito Imperiale called the Strike-force War—the Bronx shootout, the Mulberry Street bombing, the Rizzolo bus barn bombing, and the vengeance-fueled street fights that followed—reminded Vito how glad he was that he had moved his family to the suburbs. They lived like kings in Alpine and didn't have to worry about day-to-day shit. Let his *capos* fight it out in the city. When he was home, he was home free. The house was lighted and guarded in case some Bronx asshole tried to track him down out here. Even the Feds were cooperating, hanging around outside in their phone truck.

Not that it was all a bed of roses. There was always some damned thing going wrong with the house, and out here there was no super to raise hell with or neighborhood handyman to set things straight. If a faucet leaked you called a plumber and paid thirty bucks just to have him drive in your driveway. No hot water? Up drive the electrician and the plumber, and you kiss goodbye to four or five hundred bucks for a new heater. This morning, he realized, after Mikey had left, the lawn mowers were late. And those who finally did come a little before lunch were new guys who didn't know the property. And as this late-fall morning would be the last mowing before winter, it was doubly important that it be cut right.

They were the blackest blacks Vito Imperiale had ever seen; their skin was so black it was almost gray. He called from the door, "Where's the regular guys? What's his name, Washington?"

"Washington, his wife be sick."

Funny accent; maybe from the Caribbean. "I hope they told you what to do."

"We know, boss."

Imperiale closed the door, scratching his head. "Boss?" Funny accent. He watched suspiciously from the picture window. His wife called him for lunch. "What's the matter?"

"The landscaper changed the lawn guys. They're going to screw up. They're going to miss the lights." He had yelled all summer to teach the regular crew to trim the grass around the security lights.

They ate lunch in the kitchen with the bodyguards; his wife was always fussing after them, like they were sons or nephews. He was irritable. Mikey was offering a pretty good deal, but he didn't like having to take it. Since the first request for a meeting, he had known this was coming and had decided not to fight. But with one headache out of the way, he was going to have another—keeping the supply up. Three hundred kilos a week were not smuggled past customs without risk. It took a lot of people, and the better they were, the more they tried to lean on him. If he thought about the future, it would get overwhelming, so he shifted his worries to the lawn again. It was flourishing so late in the year, thanks to a wet, warm autumn, and he knew the substitute lawn guys were going to screw up.

Sure enough, after lunch, ragged wisps of grass stood around the high-intensity security lights embedded at strategic points around the lawn. He called again from the door. "Hey, trim those lights!"

"Yo, boss."

The one driving the big winged Lock mower swung it around and started mowing a six-foot swatch toward the nearest light.

"Not with that, for Christ's sake! Use the weed eater." He gestured at their truck where the trimmer was kept. The dumb fuck waved and kept going.

"Oh, shit. *No!* You're going to hit—"

The machine ran over the light, mangling the fixture and exploding the bulb with a vaporous *bang*. The Lock mower kept going, yanking the wires right out of the ground. Before it finally stopped, thirty feet of Romex cable was tangled in the blades and Imperiale's lawn was gouged like some monster mole had gone berserk.

"Jesus fucking Christ!"

Imperiale leaped off the back step and ran across his new-mown lawn. The blacks were walking toward their truck, shaking their heads. The ripped-up earth smelled richer and wetter than the cut grass. New seed would never sprout before winter. It would be mud all winter and frozen ruts.

"You dumb fucks!"

All four turned to face him—crouching, hands extended, cocking the slides on little pistols. They fired in unison.

"I'm told," Reggie Rand reported with a smile, "that Mikey beat up the *capo* who brought the news. At any rate, his people are asking to buy from ours again."

"Not until he agrees to no more attacks against the Rizzolos."

"He agrees."

"Good. Raise the price again."

"I already have. They asked for five hundred kilos. I think they were just a little surprised we had that much."

"Do we?"

"Barely. We agreed to give it to them at two hundred fifty thousand a kilo, on consignment. Twenty percent down and two percent interest a week, with a month's grace. Next month Mikey Cirillo will owe you one hundred million dollars plus five hundred thousand dollars interest."

"Half a million interest a week? That makes me the biggest shylock in the country."

"Soon you'll have to be the biggest enforcer."

"Unless he pays me back."

Reggie smiled again. "Which isn't likely."

Chapter 17

U NCLE VINNIE'S ANNUAL contractors' party was going full blast when Christopher Taggart rushed in late. Thirty men in tuxedos were grouped around the spacious Waldorf-Astoria suite, laughing, trading jokes and gossip, drinking at the well-stocked bar, and ignoring the elaborate crabmeat, smoked salmon, and caviar hors d'oeuvres. Pier glasses reflected towering arrangements of autumn flowers—chrysanthemums, asters, and purple anemones that stood on consoles at either end of the main room, while the hotel windows offered splendid scenes of night advancing on the city. Bedrooms were available down a long hall—a dozen barelegged girls in T-shirts and high heels circulated—and the party was, traditionally, a mostly Italian and strictly-no-wives affair. When Taggart entered, a group of men near the door pounced on him as if they had stationed themselves there for his arrival.

"Chris! Hey, Chris!"

A cement supplier who had slugged it out with his father pumped his hand; and an electrical contractor who had tried to stiff him in the early days seized his arms, still begging forgiveness for a slight ten years old. Other contractors, suppliers, bankers, and fellow developers crowded around, slapping his back, as if by bouncing their hands off his flesh some of the Taggart touch might stick to them.

Uncle Vinnie bounded across the suite, his bulging chest and belly resplendent in a ruffled white shirt and jet-black cummerbund. His round face was alight with a proud smile because his star nephew had come. "Hey!" They embraced.

"Sorry, I got held up. Fucking Board of Estimate. I'm going to kill the mayor one of these days."

"Nice a ya to come. I know you're busy."

"Would I miss this?"

"Have a drink. Sweetheart, bring my nephew a drink. Whatcha gonna have, Chris?"

"Perrier."

She started toward the bar, but Uncle Vinnie grabbed the hem of her T-shirt, baring her taut behind. "Bullshit. Bring him a CC on the rocks." He let her go with a pat. "That's what your old man drank."

"My pop drank red wine like any decent guinea."

"Yeah, but he knew to drink CC in the Waldorf. Wanna meet some of the guys?"

As Uncle Vinnie led him to an expectant group, Chris experienced again the eerie sensation of having men twice his age hang on his every word. Were he to suggest dynamiting the Empire State Building to build a new one with bigger windows, they would nod sagely, and one or two would probably offer their services. "Hey, what's the matter?" Uncle Vinnie asked, as he herded him toward the next group.

"At these things I think of Pop. He'd still be younger than a lot of these guys."

"I know. Me, too. I think about him all the time. Ten years? Like yesterday. What are you gonna do?"

Uncle Vinnie beckoned a pretty girl. She hurried over, her nipples pointing through thin cotton. Uncle Vinnie handed her a room key and nodded at a man standing alone. "Sweetie, there's a fellow there who'd love to talk to you."

She gave Uncle Vinnie a stoned smile, Chris another, looped the key ring over her little finger, and pranced off. Uncle Vinnie watched until the connection looked secure, then turned back to Chris. "Funny thing about your pop. He wouldn't go with the girls. Never when your mother was alive."

"Really?"

"Only guy I knew never had girl friends. How about you? Want some? There's a blonde with legs right up to her tongue."

"Naw. I'm fine." He averted his gaze from a dark girl with a pretty body who looked a little like Helen Rizzolo. Uncle

Vinnie noticed and said, "See how ya feel later. Here's Alphonse."

Chris shook the ancient Sicilian's hand and bowed his head with respect. "Hello, Alphonse. We did good with your trucks."

Alphonse beamed. "Howsa repairs? Like I promise?"

"My people say, no problem."

"Listen, Chris." Alphonse took his elbow and lowered his voice. Uncle Vinnie stepped closer and Chris encircled his shoulder with a conspiratorial grin. A concrete man did not fill a Waldorf suite with nalf-naked women purely for the pleasure of getting his friends laid. Alphonse had trucks, Vinnie had cement, and the big jobs Taggart Construction did these days often required more cement than Taglione Concrete produced in house. "What is this talk about a stadium in Manhattan?"

"Well, there's still some spaces around."

"Who owns them?"

Chris shrugged. "People who control that kind of property tend to keep quiet until they're ready to build."

He winked at Uncle Vinnie because the city was suddenly giving him serious resistance, and a little optimistic rumor in the business couldn't hurt.

Alphonse smiled happily, his sleepy old eyes alight. "I was thinking that if someday somebody built such a stadium—and it happened to be near some old railroad tracks—we put the concrete trucks on trains."

"That would certainly eliminate access problems," Chris agreed, confirming Alphonse's guess, and wondering how in hell he had found out the location. "As usual, Alphonse, it is profitable to see you. How is your grandson?"

"*Aggh*. Another goddamned *studente*. Shit on the business."

"Hey, hey! The food!"

The company mobbed the door as four of Uncle Vinnie's sons bustled in with giant suitcases of food they had smuggled by the Waldorf staff. They spread it out on the conference table: garlic, tomatoes, onions, pork, veal, and Gorgonzola filled the air with a pungency no hotel caterer would dare permit.

Chris sat on a couch surrounded by contractors and devoured a plate of calves' brains, sausage, and eggplant. A very pretty redhead kept leaning over the back of the couch, refilling their wineglasses and brushing her breasts against his cheek. "Can I get you anything else? More pasta?"

A cool voice beside her said, "Pasta's a *New York Times* word. My brother eats macaroni."

"Jesus Christ," Uncle Vinnie blurted, sounding equally astonished and embarrassed. "It's Tony."

When Chris finally got his head disconnected from the girl's breast, he saw his brother standing there in a dark suit, briefcase in hand, surveying the party with a fathomless gaze.

"I hope I'm not interrupting, Uncle Vinnie."

"What do ya mean, interrupting? You're my nephew." Uncle Vinnie barreled around the couch, kissed Tony's cheeks, and embraced him. "Hey, everybody. My nephew Tony's here."

There was a moment's startled silence before the men put their plates aside and stepped over and shook hands, mumbling pleasantries. Tony looked each in the eye and replied with a word for each that implied he remembered not only their names, but their businesses.

"Hey, it's really great to see you," Uncle Vinnie repeated when the parade had ended.

Chris pulled Tony down beside him. "You killed this party faster than herpes."

"Hungry?" asked Uncle Vinnie. "Honey. Get him some—"

"I'll get it." Tony went to the table and filled a plate with small portions from each dish, while the others conversed quietly and pretended not to watch an Assistant United States Attorney in their midst. He returned to the couch and picked at the food.

"I was looking for you, Chris. Gotta talk. I didn't realize you were having this kind of party, Uncle Vinnie. I might not have come."

Uncle Vinnie grinned. "Hey, can I tell 'em you're off duty?"

Tony looked his uncle in the face. "No. But I will leave— Chris, when you're ready."

"Hey, you don't gotta run."

Tony Taglione said, "I don't patronize hookers and nobody

in this room will talk to me without a lawyer. So I don't see much point in staying."

"Now wait a minute, these are legit businessmen."

"So why do they freak when I walk in?"

"You got a rep. But these are straight guys your father worked with."

"As they'll be the first to remind me. Chris, let's go."

Chris stood up and embraced his uncle. "I'm sorry. Tell the blonde with the legs to her tongue that I feel I know her even though we've never met."

Uncle Vinnie laughed, smacked them each affectionately on the back of the head, and walked them to the front door. Chris waited until they were alone in the elevator.

"Was that necessary?"

"I've saved you a lot of trouble," Tony replied with a thin smile. "They'll think twice before they ask for kickbacks and payoffs from Taggart Construction."

"Was it necessary to fuck up Uncle Vinnie's party?"

"I need to see you. I called your office and Sylvia said you were here. I didn't realize what was going on till I got inside. Once in, there's no way I'm pretending I don't have eyes."

"It's just a party, for crissake."

"Chris, do you think those girls come from the Nightingale-Bamford School?"

"What's the big deal if a girl wants to pick up a couple of C-notes blowing businessmen? They're home by ten o'clock."

"They are supplied by the Mafia. You think Vinnie calls up twelve girls he happens to know?"

"Yeah, or his secretary does. Who knows?"

"The hell he does. He pays a guy with a regular circuit and the guy brings them in from upstate, Atlantic City, New England. The guy is either connected or pays connected people for protection. The Mafia gets the money. The girls get drugs and tips."

"What you want to see me about?"

"Your new girlfriend."

"What girlfriend?"

"Are you aware you're involved with a Mafia person?"

Taggart laughed. This had to happen sometime, but he had himself to blame for accelerating events by blundering into the hospital. "A Mafia 'person'? Hey, listen, man, I don't know what you're talking about."

"I'm talking about Helen Rizzolo."

"How'd you hear about that?"

"My agents keep track of criminals."

"I'll bet they were afraid to tell you they saw me."

"Chris, are you fucking crazy? You know damn well that Helen Rizzolo's brothers are two of the most vicious bone-breakers in Brooklyn."

Taggart tried another small joke, while he gauged how much else Tony knew. He would be himself and needle his brother for being so serious, but that resolve lasted for only the briefest exchange.

"Isn't Brooklyn out of your territory?"

"Not anymore. You plan to keep seeing her?"

"Hey, what is this?"

"I'd appreciate it if you didn't."

"It's partly up to her. I'm not that sure she likes me. As a matter of fact, since the hospital she's been avoiding me."

"Good. Keep it that way."

"It's already rolling, man. What happens happens."

"What about Pop?"

"Get off my back."

"Chris, take it to its logical conclusion. You going to bring her home to the family?" Like many trial lawyers, Tony was a great mimic and could paint a scene with his voice. "'Uncle Vinnie, I want you to meet my Mafia girlfriend. You remember the Mafia, they killed my father. And Helen, meet my brother Tony—he sent your father to jail and is hoping to do the same to your scumbag brothers.'"

"Am I supposed to laugh?"

"You're supposed to *think*, you asshole."

Silent, they walked through the lobby and onto the sidewalk.

"Cab, sir?" asked the doorman, signaling the empty street.

"Two," Chris snapped, angry that Tony had put him into the false position of pretending he didn't care about his father, when it was his father who lay behind everything he was doing.

It was about eight-thirty and the evening rush for the theater

239

had ended, but cabs were sparse. They waited in stiff silence. Finally the doorman got one, but as they argued who would wait for the next, a couple raced out of the hotel, screaming at each other in Texas accents that they were goddamned late.

"Ah told you you should of called the theater to hold the show."

Chris stepped back from the cab. "Be our guest."

"That's right nice of you boys," the man said. "You all have a good evening—"

"Get in!" his wife yelled, and the cab raced off.

They looked at each other and couldn't help smiling. Chris nodded up Park Avenue where the Taggart Spire sent a lonely line of work lights straight into the sky. "Want to see the job?"

Tony hesitated. "Okay."

Silent still, they walked up Park Avenue and onto the site. Chris waved off a superintendent, who was still working with some subs and who looked alarmed that the boss had appeared, and made directly for the elevator. Tony stopped him and pointed at a spindly pipe frame outside the building. "How about the hoist?"

"You got it! Hey," he called to the watchman, "send us up."

They climbed onto the platform. The lift engine roared and the open material hoist climbed up the side of the building, high above the amber lights of Park Avenue.

Chris saw a grin dance on the ridges of Tony's face. "You miss this, don't you?"

"Don't you? When's the last time you worked the iron? God, look at it. . . ."

"How you been?"

"Working my ass off. Double eights six days a week. You?"

"Same. It gets more every day. . . . Hey, Tony?"

"What?" They had climbed to the point where they were looking down on the lower building's roof. The noise from the hoist engine grew soft and a cool breeze sighed in the frame.

"My offers still stand. Offer number one is if you want to be a lawyer, be my general counsel."

"I told you general counsel's like an employment agent. You end up hiring real lawyers to do your work."

"Offer number two—and my favorite—is if you prefer to really work hard for living, be my partner."

"I already have a job."

"You're not going to be a prosecutor your whole life."

"It *is* my life."

"Ever peek at your blind trust?"

"You know damned well I don't."

"You're doing good."

"You push me on that and I'll contribute the whole thing to curing the common cold."

"Okay, okay. Forget it. But the offers stand, anytime. What was I up to last time? Six hundred thousand and hot and cold running secretaries?"

"I got a job. And that's what I want to talk to you about. Very seriously. What is going on?"

"Nothing."

"You visited her in the hospital. You hired three specialists for a bump on her gorgeous head. Sounds more than nothing to me."

"What can I say? I flipped, man."

"But you know who she is."

"I know about her family. But she's not a hood."

"But Pop . . ."

"Whatever her brothers are doesn't make her a criminal."

Was it a setup? he wondered. Was Tony onto his Shadow Mafia? Or had surveillance just made the connection at the hospital?

The hoist stopped and Tony swung onto the plank floor. Chris watched him wrap an arm around a column and gaze up at Manhattan's pink-black night sky. A forest of columns rose two stories above the wooden floor, boxed by headers and beams, and dwarfed by three enormous stiff-legged derricks. Their vertical masts and slanting booms, which were jointed at the floor, veered apart as they soared twenty-five stories above the building to cast V-shaped shadows, as if the Spire herself were flashing jubilant victory signs at the stars.

He wasn't sure he wanted to show Tony the glass apartment. Tony derided anything lavish and sneered at the idea that extravagant design paid back tenfold in free publicity. Taggart thought he had had enough condemnation for one night and it was better to play the Helen thing through to the end. He asked, "How tough are the brothers?"

241

"The worst."

"It's not your problem."

"You've already made it my problem. How'd you meet her?"

"At a fundraiser for a new parochial school. She was on the building committee."

"What were you doing there?"

"The church was hitting me for a low bid. She was hosting the party."

True and verifiable. It was a jampacked cocktail party in one of her family's wedding palaces. He had gone for a final look before choosing the Rizzolos for his plan, and had not, of course, actually spoken to her. That came weeks later, after the kidnapping, when he visited her at her club and brought her here to the Spire.

"Didn't you know who she was?"

He made himself sound contrite. "Yeah, I remembered, you know, from when she was a kid. Remember her that night?"

"I sure do. I also remember her glaring at me when I put her father away."

"Well, I wanted a closer look. I was intrigued. When I got a closer look I liked what I saw. There's a person there who's more than just a Mafia goon's daughter. She's tough, sure. She's strong, she's intensely independent, she's lonely as hell. She loves music and she's beautiful enough to kill for. What else can I say?"

"When was that?"

"I don't know. Around the middle of May."

"Did you know she was kidnapped about a week later?"

"Kidnapped? What do you mean?"

"Kidnapped. Snatched. She didn't tell you?"

"I told you, we're not that close."

"Not close? The nurses said you were throwing hundred-dollar bills around the emergency room. How'd you hear she was in the hospital?

"Wait a minute. What do you mean, kidnapped? Who kidnapped her?"

Tony shrugged. "It was some kind of family thing."

"Was she hurt?"

"She was back in a few days and it settled down quickly, so I assume they worked it out among themselves."

"Does it have anything to do with the bombing?"

Tony shrugged again. Taggart could not guess whether he was denying he knew or was declining to answer.

"How'd you hear she was in the hospital? I'm told you were there twenty minutes after they brought her in."

"I heard it on the radio. I called the bus barn. The cops told me." Verifiable again, because it had happened precisely that way. He heard the news in the car, called, and got to the hospital less than half an hour after she had.

Tony said, "Can I ask you something?"

"Nothing's stopped you so far."

"Why don't you marry Chryl or Vicky?"

Chris grinned. "I couldn't marry just one of them; then you'd be back bitching about bigamy."

"Marry *somebody*, for Christ's sake. Settle down a little."

"Me? What about you?"

"I'm too busy."

"What if I married Helen Rizzolo?"

"You can go along when she visits her father in jail. Do you know she's the go-between for him and her brothers?"

"I don't know that. And you're probably just guessing."

"Does she know you helped me send him up?"

"You gonna tell her?"

"I'd love to because it would end it. But I won't."

"Thanks for the break."

"It's not a break. You were a confidential source. I promised not to blow your cover."

"A man of your word."

"Besides, if I did, her brothers would kill you. And I love you too much for that to happen."

Tony removed his jacket and necktie, loosened his shirt, and mounted the column, planting his feet against the inside flange and gripping the outside with his hands.

"Where you going?"

Tony climbed straight up to the header, climbed on it, and attacked the next column. Taggart lost him in the dark. He tore off his own bow tie and tuxedo jacket, and started after him. Tony was sitting astride the top header, thirty feet above the plank floor and ninety-six stories over Manhattan.

"You really believe that about Uncle Vinnie's hookers? That they're just picking up a little spare bread?"

Relieved for any subject change, Taggart leaped into the argument. "I just can't get on everybody's morality case."

"Chris, Chris, Chris. You know, sometimes I think you really are what you pretend to be."

"What's that?"

"Just a businessman. A genius at building skyscrapers and otherwise just a dumb, happy-go-lucky idiot. No offense?"

"Sure. No offense."

They sat, Tony silently gazing at the city, and Chris wondering. Had Tony found himself lonely, as he himself sometimes did, when the action stopped a moment? Was this one of Tony's rare lapses, when he tried to patch things up, feeling a little lonely and seeking to repair the tatters of their family? Did he just want to talk? And had used the excuse of Helen Rizzolo?

Tony had no confidants in the U.S. Attorney's office—not with the iceman reputation he cultivated to mask his youth. He worked too hard to have close friends outside of the office. Women were drawn to him, as they had been as far back as Taggart could remember; the nymphs were lured by his power, the mothers touched when they convinced themselves they saw something vulnerable at his core. He had almost married in college, the year their father was killed, and again in Washington, when he worked for the Attorney General. Since then, Tony had retreated from involvements, like an old-fashioned athlete who feared women would suck away his strength. He bounced from woman to woman, dating professionals who were as career-oriented as himself, much the way—Chris had to admit—he himself would have done, too, if it weren't for Chryl and Victoria, who in their way stabilized his life. Until now, of course, because connecting with Helen Rizzolo had unhinged everything.

Tony stood up and started across along the header that rimmed the thousand-foot structure.

"Take it easy. It's dark and you've got heels on your shoes."

Tony walked sure-footedly along the twelve-inch steel

girder toward the nearest derrick. Chris followed his brother's dim shadow, feeling a little crazy, a little daring, and more than a little paranoid.

Somehow, tonight Tony did not seem lonely. In fact he was aloof, in charge, and even more pleased with himself than usual. Chris caught up at the derrick, which leaned so close he could almost touch it, and sat down again; straddling the header. The ironworkers had left the boom in a nearly vertical position, so the V between boom and mast was tight, the two arms almost parallel.

Chris reminded himself that devious, convoluted plots were *his* way, not Tony's. Tony constructed his court cases in a straightforward manner, much the same way ironworkers erected a steel frame, raising columns, connecting them with headers and beams, laying a floor, hoisting their derricks, and raising more columns. If Tony had an inkling of what he was doing, Chris knew, he would attack head on.

Without warning, Tony stepped off the header.

"Wha—?"

"You're playing with fire." Tony's voice came out of the dark, several feet away on the derrick. He had jumped to the derrick and Taggart heard him ascending. He jumped to the derrick himself and climbed after him, although he couldn't see Tony in the pale light cast up from the city and down from the stars. "Where the hell are you?"

"Hang on, I got a penlight."

The little white light blinked to the side. Chris laughed. They had climbed the opposing arms of the derrick. Tony clung to the slightly slanted boom; Chris was on the mast, six or eight feet away. They held silently to their respective perches as the wind sighed through the steel. Chris remembered something Tony had dodged earlier. "What did you mean that Brooklyn's not out of your territory?"

"The Attorney General has amalgamated a new *joint* Federal Organized Crime Strikeforce. It now covers the whole city, Long Island, Connecticut, and New Jersey."

"Who's the new boss?"

"It comes under the U.S. Attorney for the Southern District, so Arthur Finch controls it."

"But who runs it?"

"He offered it to me."

Taggart stared across the space that separated them. As neither Reggie nor Jack Warner had told him yet, it must just have happened. So that's what Tony was sitting on; no tricks —something unthinkably worse. A new agency in the vengeful hands of his brother posed a deadly threat to his Shadow Mafia.

"Aren't you a little young?"

"I'm connected in Washington from when I worked for the AG. They figure I knew enough of the right people to make the agencies cooperate."

"Have you accepted?"

"We're working out the details. I'm negotiating for as much autonomy as Arthur will give up."

"Would you please come to work with me?"

"What? Are you nuts? I've fought for this Strikeforce for ten years."

"Tony, you want to stay in public service and that's good. But you've got to broaden yourself, get more experience, learn business, find what makes things tick."

"You'd be surprised how much business you learn prosecuting crooked businessmen."

"But get some managerial experience."

"Chris, I have forty people working directly for me and hundreds of federal agents on tap. With this new thing, I'm running an army."

Which was precisely what worried Taggert. "What about politics?" he asked, still searching for a way to separate his brother from the new Strikeforce.

"What about 'em?"

"A guy like you should go into politics."

"Maybe someday. But I've got other things first."

"A stint in business would really set you up with the right people. Hell, the mayor of New York calls me a couple of times a week, I talk to the governor—I know you do, too, but more as Pop's friend. I'm talking about *hondling* with them. I can put you in the same room with senators and congressmen, the party leaders. You need them to run for office. I really want you to work with me."

"But the U.S. Attorney has offered me everything I need to destroy the Mafia."

"It can't be done that way."

"You know a better way?"

"Of course not," Chris said hastily. "But—"

"So it's the only way."

Taggart laid his cheek against the cold metal. He looked down and felt a sudden stab of fear. Anyone could fall.

"Is this why you barged in at Uncle Vinnie's?"

"Sure. I had to tell somebody."

The emotion soared between the derrick arms. It felt like Tony had flung him a net. "Stay there!"

"Wait!"

But Chris had already locked his eyes on the black edge of the boom, gathered his legs, and launched himself into the dark. Something brushed his shoulder and cold steel banged into his bare hands. Then he was clinging to the boom. He set his feet, sucked his palm where he had cut it, and looked around the dark.

"Tony? Where the hell'd you go?"

"Over here."

His brother's voice came from behind him, on the mast Chris had just left. "I told you to wait. I jumped, too."

Chris sagged against the metal, his heart pounding.

"Get rid of that woman," Tony called.

"What, you got the hots for her too?"

"I'm not joking."

"Tony, I've got it bad. I'm going to play it out, see what happens. I'm going to do everything I can to turn her on to me."

"She's trouble."

"Not for me. Maybe for you, and if that's so, I'm sorry."

"What if I bust her brothers? Can you imagine what the papers will do when they find out the connection?"

"I suppose it would knock 'Nuns Staff Abortion Clinic' off the front page of the *Post*. Are you going to bust her brothers?"

"That's exactly what I'm talking about. It puts a barrier between us."

"No more Deep Throat?"

"I can't talk to you anymore because I'm an Assistant United States Attorney."

"But I'm your brother."

"Sharing pillow talk with Don Eddie Rizzolo's daughter."

"You want to listen in?"

"Don't fuck with me. This is serious, Bro. If I could stop it, I would."

"When we were kids you stopped a lot by dating my girls. Why not Helen?"

"I already have."

"What?"

"The summer we met her, for crissake, dummy. We went out."

"Bullshit. You went back to Harvard the next day."

"I came down from Boston to see her."

"You prick!"

"Hey, it was ten years ago."

Taggart was surprised how much it hurt, and he felt like a total ass asking, "Did you hit on her?"

"None of your fucking business."

"You son of a bitch."

"What are you mad at me for? She was there too."

"She has nothing to do with it. I asked *you* not to touch her. You ripped me off, Bro."

"It was ten years ago," Tony repeated. "Forget it."

"I wish you believed in what was right as much as you believe in the fucking law."

To his surprise, Tony apologized. "I'm sorry. That's the last time I did something like that. I told you a few years ago, I don't do that anymore."

"It must have been weird when you prosecuted her father."

"Very. I cleared it with Arthur first, of course."

"Of course."

"The point I'm trying to make now is, Helen Rizzolo is trouble, and until you dump her we can't talk about anything that concerns my office."

Taggart smiled in the dark. The most important thing was to protect his connection to the Strikeforce, but he couldn't resist making Tony squirm for betraying him. "We can't talk? What if I told you I heard about a heroin deal going down next week?"

"Call nine one one."

"Five hundred kilos."

"Five *hundred?*"

"That's what I hear."

"From whom?"

"Not her, and that's all I'm going to tell you. Good night, Bro."

"Wait a minute."

"I thought we can't talk."

"Five hundred kilos? Where?"

Taggart smiled again. Reggie's people had been pumping the rumor through the law-enforcement agencies, and Tony's staff would surely have heard it by now. "Park Avenue."

249

Chapter 18

*I'*M SO GLAD you could come, Chris."

Taggart's host, an elfin man with a gentle handshake and a reputation as the liveliest music scholar of the last two generations, greeted him warmly in the crowded foyer of the East Side apartment he used for an art gallery and a music room. Taggart had read his textbook in college, never imagining that years later he would be one of forty or fifty people invited by him to a musicale. The host introduced him to the composer, who looked equally nervous and happy, and to the soprano in a long green dress who would sing the new work. They raced off and Taggart confessed, "I've never been asked to something like this before."

"Dear boy, brace yourself for an avalanche when the word gets out that Taggart Realty is supporting young performers." He glanced at the foyer where more guests were pouring out of the elevator and inquired politely, "Do you know anyone here?"

His guests included young men and women Taggart assumed were musicians, elderly wealthy-looking patrons with dour escorts, and some famous faces—a feminist, an architect, a writer, and a City Hall luminary, the deputy mayor for capital construction who was giving him grief on his stadium project.

"Who is that?"

"Isn't she exotic? I was lecturing at Sarah Lawrence. She came up to me, enchanted by a conspiracy theory that a Cremonese scoundrel named Guadignini might have tricked two centuries of violin makers into believing that Stradivari, Amati, and Guarnari used untreated wood."

"What's her name?"

"Helen Rizzolo. She always comes alone. Shall I introduce you?"

"No, that's okay. You've got more people coming."

"Well, the bar's in the bedroom. They'll bring some munchies and then I'll ask you young men to carry chairs in for the performance."

Taggart found a white wine and made his way back into the living room. Helen was wearing a black cocktail dress—just a touch hookerish, he thought. Her jet hair was shorter than when he had seen her at the hospital and was swept back at the sides in a sleek, stylish manner that Victoria and Chryl would approve. Diamond studs flashed from her ears and when she pivoted toward him, her attention fixed on one of the many paintings, Taggart saw a single large diamond suspended between her breasts.

Working his way closer, he amended his opinion about the dress. Other women were similarly attired, but she was doing more for hers. A slick-looking European used the painting as an opening, and when she gazed up at him, listening attentively, Taggart felt a powerful jolt of jealousy.

He wandered about the room, waiting for the right moment to bump into her to ask if she would sit with him during the performance. The deputy mayor hailed him with a smirk. "Since when are you a patron of the arts, Chris?"

"I'm getting the inside track on the Carnegie Hall demolition."

The deputy mayor's wife went rigid in the second it took her husband to laugh, at which she drifted determinedly toward the wine room. Her place was taken immediately by Kenny Adler, a PR man whom Taggart had learned to treat as a member of the mayor's administration. With one eye on Helen, who hadn't noticed him yet, he asked, "So what are you guys waiting for on my stadium?"

"Reassessing the risk," the deputy mayor replied blandly.

"It's not your money. For crissake, can't you get it through his bald head that all I need is the city's enthusiastic permission? I'll raise the money. Just give me a break by making me look good."

"And if you blow it, the mayor looks like a schmuck."

"Have I ever blown a building?"

"His Honor doesn't want to be in on the first. This is a lot bigger than just a building. And a lot more exposed."

"You're telling me a Manhattan stadium won't go? Next door to the convention center? Accessed by a federally subsidized subway link? What is your problem?"

The deputy mayor glanced around. "I'm not saying I'm saying this. But there is a feeling that an indoor 'Polo Grounds' with million-dollar sky boxes is a bread-and-circuses sort of thing."

"It *is* an election year," Adler chimed in. "Again."

"What does His Honor want from me? A low-income high-rise on top?"

Helen was still paying rapt attention to the European, who was leading her toward a second painting. Taggart whipped out his wallet, turned to the notepad. "Mr. Deputy, you just gave me a great idea. You want something really hot? Something the mayor can sell? Look." He drew a round ball with his gold pen. "This is the stadium, right?"

"The famous white basketball."

"Now." He drew a tall, slim triangle on top of the ball.

"What's that?"

"The tallest building in the world."

The idea had popped full-blown into his head. He should have thought of it ages ago—would have if he weren't living half and half. "A supertall building *atop* the dome. Two hundred floors. Convention-center hotel on the lower levels, condos and executive suites on top. Even some City space in between so the mayor can shack up when the home teams are in town."

"There's no economies in a supertall," the deputy mayor protested.

"Don't talk to me about elevators. There are values in a project like this more than the money. Ask Kenny. New York needs the biggest."

"How much?"

"Think billions instead of millions," Taggart admitted, "but it has the pizzazz to draw the money. I'll bet I could pull it off without the Urban Development Corporation. Screw the state. We can do it right here in the city."

The deputy mayor looked interested because, as Taggart

well knew, the mayor hated ceding control to independent like the UDC.

Adler asked, "Does it have a name?"

"It has a name that team franchises will sell their mothers to broadcast from. The Manhattan Super-Spire."

Adler smiled. "The mayor would love nothing more than to turn the Jersey Meadowlands Arena back into landfill."

"Maybe we ought to have lunch sometime," said the deputy to Chris.

"I am having *dinner* with the governor next week. Just remember I gave you first shot—catch you later."

He cut swiftly across the room. The European had been pressed into carrying folding chairs, and Helen was inspecting the hors d'oeuvres. When she reached for a shrimp, Taggart speared it first.

"Excuse me."

"That is mine," she said icily. "And you are a prick for moving in on me like this."

"I want to see you."

"I came to hear music. Not for business."

"Reggie handles that."

"Leave me alone. My brothers are going nuts waiting for the Cirillos to drive up the street in a tank, and you're jerking my strings like a puppet. I really have to get away sometimes."

"It cost me a hundred thousand dollars to get invited tonight."

"What do you mean?"

"You've been dodging me. When I heard you were coming here, I established a lunch-hour performance fund for chamber music in my new building. I hired our host to select the performers."

Helen gave him a slow smile. "Just to see me?"

"Worth every penny."

"And tax deductible."

"Would you like to have dinner after?"

"No, thanks. The guys in my car get nervous if I stay too long."

Sunlight, stirred by the river, snaked through the tall french ballroom doors of an estate house south of Croton-on-Hudson, rippled on the ornate ceiling, and bounced softly into a humiditycontrolled vault where it played on a perfect cone of near-pure heroin. An icy, malevolent mountain, four feet across and a yard high, the heroin looked like enough flour to bake fifty cakes or enough snow to build a backyard fort.

The art dealer from whom Taggart's agents had bought the house had turned the ballroom into a painting gallery and installed the walk-in safe, which Reggie Rand had booby-trapped in case thieves or cops broke in. They had burned the various wrappings that might give clues to the drug's diverse sources—Reggie's Burmese, Chinese, and Indian connections—and had blended it all in one anonymous heap. Now, wearing surgical masks, rubber gloves, and hospital gowns, they worked with the door open for relief from the fumes as they bagged it for Crazy Mikey.

Reggie thrust the nozzle of an Electrolux vacuum cleaner into the mountain. A deep pucker appeared, as if a mine had caved in inside it, and the slope began to collapse. The grains hissed through the hose. When the filter bag was full, the motor shut off automatically. Reggie opened the machine and gently removed the plump sack, which weighed almost exactly a kilogram.

Choosing a bag at random, midway through the job, Taggart slipped an electronic tracker through the bag's slitted rubber diaphragm. The tracker was an RF signal-emitting device sold to businessmen worried about kidnapping; it could be secreted in a briefcase, affixed to a car, or, in a miniature nuclear-powered version, implanted surgically under the skin. Reggie's device was modified with a remote-controlled on-off switch; it would enable Taggart to turn on the beeping radio signal from a distance—*after* the Cirillos had finished sweeping the heroin for hidden electronics—and to tell the Strike-force exactly where Crazy Mikey's dope was headed.

Reggie encased the vacuum-cleaner bag in plastic, using a heat-sealing food wrapper, and laid it beside the others on a dolly. When the dolly was full they wheeled it aboard a silver straight-back truck which bore the name of a Long Island produce wholesaler.

Taggart knew the risk of dealing personally in heroin, but the risks were even greater with hired hands, because everybody, even professionals, went crazy over the profits. As

Reggie liked to remind him, every man carries a number in his head above which he suspends the rules. Thus, as a matter of course, Reggie would park the truck at the Hunts Point Market before informing his people where it was and where to deliver it, just in case they were getting ideas; nor would he tell them that tonight they were trafficking in treachery.

In the hours before dawn, Taggart and Reggie waited on a narrow sliver of upper Park Avenue that flanked the Metro North Amtrack rails. The street was crowded with trucks and vans heading uptown to the market. A truck bristling with radio antennas pulled into the archway that carried 104th Street under the tracks.

"That's the Cirillo escort," said Reggie. The men inside it were sweeping the area for police radios and tracking devices. It pulled out and headed uptown, trailed by a battered van. "Mobile laboratory and the money."

Next came Ronnie Wald driving the silver truck that Taggart and Reggie had loaded in Croton. It bore the name "Sam Gordon Purveyors" on its side. A sleek gypsy cab trailed it closely, and the cab in turn was followed by another. Reggie eyed the precautions approvingly. "I like Wald."

He eased his own gypsy cab onto Park. Taggart sat in the passenger seat, watching the rear. A truism that ruled the lives of Taggart's enemies now ruled his too: when it came to selling heroin, he worried less about the cops than the criminals. Getting ripped off or killed was the real danger of the life, and a far more likely consequence than arrest.

Wald's truck stopped at the 112th Street market entrance under a brightly painted sign, "La Marqueta," as the Park Avenue Market, a vast food and clothing emporium housed under the railroad tracks, was known in East Harlem. Wald backed the truck into the building. His men from the gypsy cab followed. The Cirillos, already inside, would analyze the heroin while Wald inspected the down payment—twenty million dollars in cash and bearer bonds.

"Time," Taggart said, "to make Jack Warner a hero."

Reggie drove to a pay phone on Lexington Avenue. Taggart dialed the U.S. Attorney's office and pressed an "electronic handkerchief"—a portable model of the voice distorter that his secret witnesses used at the President's Commission on Organized Crime—against the mouthpiece.

"Put Jack Warner on the phone. Tell him it's CI Twelve."

Confidential Informant Twelve was the designation Warner had assigned the scramble-voiced informant who had telephoned a week ago about a supposed Cirillo heroin buy. He had no way of knowing it was Taggart, or that Taggart and Reggie had carefully spread the rumor by priming numerous agents with a variety of informants. Precise details about the buy, the time, and the participants differed from story to story, but each informant had named Park Avenue as the locale and five hundred kilos as the amount. The hastily formed Strikeforce intercept had been code-named "Park Avenue," Reggie had learned, though it was anyone's guess on exactly which of Park Avenue's one hundred and eighteen blocks the deal was going down.

"It's on the truck," Taggart said when Warner picked up. His own voice, disguised in the earpiece, sounded as if a third person were on the line. "I'll call back in ten or fifteen minutes."

"Any idea where, yet?" came the suspicious reply.

"Not yet. But I know it's going to be five hundred keys."

Silkily Warner inquired, "Want to tell me why you're performing this public service, fella?"

After a long night of sitting around smoking too many cigarettes, Warner and his fellow agents were beginning to suspect they were being jerked around. As he hung up, Taggart gave an answer the bent cop could believe in. "They ripped me off."

They drove back to La Marqueta, where dozens of trucks were unloading produce. Five minutes later, Ronnie Wald appeared driving the battered van. Wald lowered the window, the signal that it contained the down payment for the heroin, and drove west guarded by his gypsy cabs.

"Are you sure Wald'll deliver the money?" Taggart asked.

"No, I'm not," Reggie replied cheerfully. "Twenty million dollars is the most tempting amount he's carried yet, though I think I've convinced him that I'm not a man he would want to worry about in the middle of the night. More important than the money is that he simply gets away from here."

The next moment, the Sam Gordon Purveyors truck full of heroin came out and headed east. Reggie trailed it. But several blocks along, he had to stop for a red light, because a police car was on the corner. The heroin truck kept going, around a corner and out of sight.

"Pray that they've stopped sweeping." Taggart flipped the tracker switch, and the location device they had buried in the heroin broadcast a loud beep. He unfolded a New York City street map and when the light changed, Reggie steered by the frequency intensity of the sound. They continued east. Taggart compared their route to the street map.

"Phone!"

He dialed Warner again from the corner of First Avenue and 125th.

"The stuff's heading for the Triborough Bridge."

Jack Warner was dismayed. "You said Park Avenue! We're all over Park Avenue."

"They were on Park. Now they're going for the bridge. It's a silver truck with Sam Gordon Purveyors on the side. If I don't read about this in the papers tomorrow, I'm calling the Strikeforce chief to tell him you screwed up."

He ran to the car. "Catch up, in case they blow it."

They tore across the lightly trafficked approaches to the bridge. The truck was pulling out of the toll booth area. It continued onto the approach, across the span, and turned onto Astoria Boulevard. There was still no sign of the Feds. Taggart reached for the cellular phone.

"Wait."

A black car shot past, winking a little red FBI light on the roof. The truck sped up and a second car passed Taggart and Reggie. When a NYPD patrol car came screaming out of La-Guardia airport, the truck cut across three lanes of traffic, shot through a police turnaround in the median barrier, and stopped suddenly by the narrow park beside the water. The doors flew open; two men hit the grass running and disappeared in the dark.

Police sirens howled and Reggie pulled onto the shoulder to let them race by. Cruisers ablaze in blue and red light were converging from east and west and pouring from the airport, and shortly it seemed as if every third car on the highway had an intent-looking DEA agent holding a red flasher on its roof.

Taggart stabbed a switch, which sent the destruct signal. The beeping turned to a shrill whistle and ceased abruptly as, somewhere in the half ton of heroin, the tracker burned. When the Strikeforce examined the dope that they had seized from the Cirillos, the only evidence of treachery would be a knot of charred metal in a glaze of melted heroin.

"I wonder how Mikey's going to pay me back."

The driveway to Don Richard's house had never seemed longer, and Crazy Mikey felt like crawling the distance. His father's summons had been curt. A car had glided up to Mikey's Bayside condo and the driver had said, "Your father wants to see you."

Mikey, still awake after a long grim night of assessing damage, had shaved and dressed hurriedly and ridden across Queens wishing he had taken the time for a cup of coffee. When he told the driver to stop at a diner, the driver said he wasn't allowed. Mikey snorted a hit off his little shotgun instead.

"If I didn't know better, I'd think you were taking me for a ride," he joked sourly, to which the taciturn driver had replied, "Not yet."

Now the driveway yawned ahead. The car pulled around the circle. The house hulked somberly in the morning mist. Mikey got out and a servant opened the front door, itself a lousy sign. When things were okay he used the kitchen door. But today he felt more like an employee than like family—an employee who had screwed up. His mother didn't even come out of the kitchen to greet him. Instead, a cousin, who worked as his father's secretary, waited in the center hall.

"Where's my mother?"

"Florida."

"That bad?"

"Sorry, Mikey."

He led him to the library, a room with shelves full of knick-knacks and photos. His father was sitting in a wing chair, his shrunken profile toward the fire, his eyes on the harbor and the city beyond. He faced Mikey with a cool smile and motioned him to a straight-back chair.

"I hear you got trouble."

"What do you got, spies?"

"Spies?" Don Richard asked scornfully. "I read the newspaper. Biggest heroin bust in history. Who else but you?"

"Us."

"*No*. We share the loss—not the blame."

"Pop."

"What the fuck did you do?"

Mikey hung his head and worked his big hands. "I don't know."

"Did you agree to a vig?"

"Two percent a week."

"Half a million dollars a week?"

Mikey looked up. His father had found out the numbers already. There were people still going behind his back. "A month free."

"Wonderful. A whole month. Why did you agree to a vig?"

"I needed the stuff. I—"

"How you going to pay?"

"I don't know."

"How you going to get more stuff?"

"I got everybody looking. There's stuff around. It's in little pieces. This guy had big pieces. You know?"

Don Richard sighed. "Tell me about this guy."

Mikey told his father the little he knew about the guy in the mask, and about the boat, the Brit who fronted for him, the way he shot his bodyguard, and the enormous amounts of heroin he was able to supply. When he was done, his father said, "That's all?"

"I think so."

"Has he ever done anything strange?"

"Like what?" asked Mikey. He didn't want to talk about the night he and his best bodyguard got beat up.

"Does he shoot dope?"

"I don't think so."

"Sniff cocaine?"

Mikey squirmed as his father's gaze burned into his golden spoon. "No."

"Nothing?"

"One thing, maybe. . . . He's got the hots for Helen Rizzolo."

"He *knows* her?"

"I think so."

"I wonder if Helen Rizzolo knows what he does."

"Pop, this guy is more secret than the Russians. His own mother doesn't know."

Don Richard touched his fingertips together, sighted the Wall Street skyline over them, let his gaze drift over the harbor, and finally brought his old eyes to bear on Mikey's face. "But *you* should know when you deal with somebody. You should know who he is."

"How? I tried, for crissake. Nobody had one bit of postage on him or the Brit. It's like they're from another planet."

"Maybe you don't concentrate. Maybe you sniff too much dope. . . ."

"I'm not stupid about it."

"Then maybe you waste your mind on boxing matches. . . ."

"That was five months ago!" Mikey protested, wondering who in hell had told him. "Memorial Day weekend. What does that have to do with now? It was just—"

"You put two girls out of work for weeks."

"Come on, there were guys paying extra to fuck 'em right there in the blood—Pop, we're running a billion-dollar business. Why are we arguing about a couple of whores? Christ, is there anything they don't tell you?"

"That's what I'm trying to teach you. If you don't keep track of details, all you got is empty dreams. I want to know everything. Guys know that. They ain't afraid to tell me what they think I should hear. They know Don Richard doesn't shoot the messenger."

Mikey looked away, out the window, across the water where the city waited to test him again and again. "I really fucked up, didn't I?" he asked at last.

Don Richard returned a kindly smile; Mikey flinched. It meant his father was resigned to the fact that his kid was not as smart as he had hoped. Don Richard confirmed Mikey's fear with an airy "Don't worry about it."

"What do I do?"

"Order your people to find new suppliers. But you stay clear, because the Strikeforce'll be all over them. Tony Taglione has tasted blood."

Mikey hung his head. "You're coming back in, aren't you?" You're going to run the business."

Don Richard shrugged his scrawny shoulders. "Maybe I retired too soon. Maybe I'm tired of sitting around."

"What about this guy I owe?"

"I'll get a line on him."

Don Richard ordered *Consigliere* Salvatore Ponte, "Sally Smarts," to the Staten Island house. He had recruited the handsome middle-aged attorney while Ponte was still a college student and had made him his protégé, eventually his counselor, and finally, when he retired, mentor to his children. Ponte's fortunes had risen with the family's, and as he was so much younger than the Don, he had stayed on as adviser, first with Nicky and then with Crazy Mikey. If he was disturbed that Don Richard was back, he did not show it, although he took any opportunity he discovered to defend Mikey, for Crazy Mikey was still his best shot at the future. But, as the Don put it so well, if they didn't resolve Mikey's screwup there would be no future.

Summonses were issued and a stream of taxis and unremarkable automobiles began decanting visitors who were ushered into the library with the view of the harbor. There Ponte greeted them with the degree of cordiality their station deserved and presented them to the Don, who sat behind a huge desk and peppered them with questions. Strikeforce agents, alert to the traffic, parked outside Don Richard's fence and wondered what was going on. But the visitors kept their counsel, so no one beyond Don Richard's circle knew that the Cirillo family leader was asking precisely the same question: What's going on?

Unlike Crazy Mikey, who had come of age after the Cirillos had seized control of New York narcotics and knew little beyond the fabulously profitable heroin trade, Don Richard had an overview acquired in fifty years of profiting at a great variety of violent, illegal enterprises. He saw the rackets in the broader sense of a second government. He saw the unions as concentrations of money and power, and the gambling public as his own taxpayers. He understood loansharking as the foot in the door of legitimate business. He saw where he fit into the society in ways Mikey could not, and saw himself as a wily servant, whereas Mikey, subconsciously at least, was a marauder. Thus Don Richard's visitors hailed from many regions.

His questions, too, were couched in broader terms. To Ponte's surprise, he seemed to ignore the heroin bust. He was much more curious about the Rizzolo rebellion in Brooklyn. Why, he asked a bookmaker, are the Rizzolos daring to take over South Brooklyn numbers? Why, he asked a Bronx loan shark, have the loans you've written since the summer dropped by half? Why, he demanded of a union treasurer, haven't you pressed certain builders to open their payrolls to more Cirillo soldiers? He inquired in detail about the recent killings of Joe Reina, Vito Imperiale, and Harry Bono. And he astonished *Consigliere* Ponte with his knowledge of seemingly trivial events—shootouts in the Bronx, street attacks, a firebombing.

Because he confined his questions to loyal associates, the answers were as blunt as they were disturbing. Finally, he confided to Ponte that he was considering demanding a meeting with the Rizzolo brothers, but hated the thought that even the coldest demand would elevate those two *cafone* to higher planes than they deserved.

"Perhaps," he mused, "I could send someone to see Don Eddie in prison."

Consigliere Ponte objected vehemently. "Don Eddie's as bad as his sons. Where do you think they learned it?"

"Maybe they're beyond his control. Maybe he doesn't know what they're doing. Maybe it's a simple matter of telling Don Eddie what they're doing. He can stop them with a word."

"But the Rizzolo brothers aren't smart enough to set this up themselves. Don Eddie's got to be behind it."

"I'm not sure how smart this all is," Cirillo mused. "All these attacks—while the Strikeforce is hitting too—are kind of stupid, when you think about it. Who wins? Taglione and his Feds. I don't think Don Eddie's stupid. I think these sons of his got a crazy idea while their old man was locked up."

"Don Eddie betrayed you years ago," Ponte objected.

Don Richard brushed the air with a bony hand. "Less betrayal than wanting to be on his own. I can understand that. I can't forgive, but I can understand. . . . Look into it."

Consigliere Ponte knew the difference between a discussion and an order. He shut his mouth and assigned people to look into the best way to make contact with the imprisoned Don Eddie Rizzolo. It had to be somebody who could get past the government, get permission to visit the Don, yet of high enough rank so Rizzolo would listen. This was no time for insult, perceived or real; a prisoner's perception would be rutted with suspicion.

The government couldn't deny Don Eddie a visit by a lawyer. Ponte considered going himself, but it seemed foolish to bring such attention to the Cirillos. Besides, Don Eddie knew Ponte hated him for betraying Don Richard and might not see him. That would be a joke, going all the way upstate nearly to Canada, to be told by smirking guards that Mr. Rizzolo wouldn't see him. Then he got an idea and went back to Don Richard to propose it.

"His daughter."

"Helen?"

"Why not? Invite her here. Treat her respectfully; ask her to carry your message."

Don Richard thought about it. The last contact he had had with Helen Rizzolo was arranging her marriage to a Conforti Las Vegas casino owner's son some ten years ago, when she was only sixteen. He had tried to enhance his own power by stopping a war between the Confortis and the Rizzolos. But the marriage hadn't worked, which had made him look the fool.

"She won't come. Even if she would, I doubt her brothers would let her. They probably blame us for the kidnapping."

"No. They've told people it was something in their own family."

"I'll think about it."

When Ponte returned the next day, he was astonished to see a black man in Don Richard's library pacing before the windows and staring at the view as if he were a guest on a space station. He was a hard-looking man in his thirties; he wore a suit without a tie, and his hands glittered with heavy rings. Ponte was sure he was the first black man to ever set foot in the house; another reminder that Don Richard was always unpredictable. Don Richard made no introductions, saying to the black man merely, "Tell him what you told me."

"He's crazy as a bedbug."

"Who?" asked Ponte.

"Old man Eddie Rizzolo. He's flipped out."

It hadn't occurred to Ponte that Eddie Rizzolo was operating irrationally. "What do you mean? How do you know?"

"Mr. Cirillo asked me to see how he's doing in the pen. My people checked him out. He's nuts. Like his brain's gone, like he's senile." The black pointed at a large manila envelope on Don Richard's desk. "My people stole a copy of Rizzolo's medical report. It's all there."

Don Richard gave the envelope a grim smile. "Read it."

Ponte couldn't believe his eyes. "Alzheimer's disease!"

"He's gone, man. There's no one home."

Don Richard ushered the black man out personally, with a gnarled hand on his big arm and a warm nod as they shook hands. Ponte turned away to keep from staring. Seventy-five years old and reluctantly back from retirement, Don Richard was adapting to the changing world better than his sons. And he seemed to thrive on it: his appetite was enormous, beaming servants had confided.

The door closed and they were alone again. Don Richard hummed a tune he remembered from the Glen Island Casino. His first job was breaking fingers when musicians welshed on bets and loans; a neighborhood kid named Oxie held the guy, whose replacement had to cough up initiation fees and dues to the union local. A nice little racket.

"So who's behind it?" Ponte asked.

"The brothers aren't smart enough," Don Richard answered.

"Then who's running the Rizzolos?"

"I think I'm beginning to understand."

Taggart tracked the Cirillo visits through Reggie's spies in the family, his own friendships with cops and federal agents, and his contacts on the President's Organized Crime Commission. Everyone in law enforcement was intrigued by the meetings. Their subject remained a mystery, however, though a lucky break offered a confusing hint when a retired Brooklyn *capo* limped into the Don's house, leaning on a cane in the silver head of which an enterprising FBI agent had secreted a bug; all they discussed, however, was the Rizzolo takeover of some candy store books on Ocean Parkway.

But Taggart noted that old Don Richard was conducting the meetings himself. While Cirillo soldiers and allies were Staten Island bound on the Verrazano Bridge, Crazy Mikey, supposedly the acting boss of the family, was scouring the scummier sections of the Bronx, Brooklyn, and Manhattan for narcotics importers. Taggart concluded that Don Richard was resuming command.

He met Reggie atop the Spire and Reggie agreed, warning, "He'll attack."

"No. Crazy Mikey would attack. But the old man will be more careful. He's old and he's tired."

"But what if he's old and vicious?"

Taggart walked away from Reggie and looked down at the city. It was evening, the night still at bay, and a late-autumn haze was drifting into the streets. It carried a cold bite and a memory of football practice after school, pumping up for the Thanksgiving Day game.

"No, Reg. First of all, he doesn't know who to attack. Second, he knows damned well that when Tony and the Strikeforce find out he's back in control, they'll come gunning for him."

"He may simply attack the nearest irritant," Reggie countered. "The Rizzolos. Very well, that's what we recruited them for, after all. As for your brother and the law, don't forget that the Strikeforce is merely *one* of Don Richard's concerns. He's the last of the old dons and he's regained control of the last of the old Mafia empires. And you've attacked it."

Chapter 19

*H*ELEN COULDN'T GET Taggart out of her thoughts.

Tax deductible or not, the man had spent a hundred thousand dollars to sit beside her at the musicale. And he didn't even act resentful when she left early, though a deeply disappointed smile had showed how much he liked her. She liked him too, she had to admit; when she tried to talk about the music, he had listened. And despite his blond looks and Manhattan-businessman clothes, he was Italian through and through; how had her Uncle Frank described a guy for an Italian girl? Strong where he should be, but a pussycat inside? She touched the heart-shaped diamond ring she had put on her finger this morning. Taggart was making her a little crazy.

Suddenly, alerted by a familiar clanging noise in the backyard, she ran to the window. Old Mario, her mother's great-uncle, had come to bury the fig tree. Every November he arrived wearing his blue suit and heavy shoes, with a shovel, a rope, and a big iron stake. He drove the stake into the ground with the shovel. Then he tied the rope as high up the trunk as he could reach, and bent the tree to the ground. It seemed a miracle it didn't snap. Tying it to the stake, he started digging earth out of the lawn, which he threw on the tree.

She watched proudly. In a city where poor people slept in the street, her family had room for a simple old man who would never fear or want for anything simply because her parents had reared her and her brothers to take responsibility. When they were children the old man's presence had made them feel secure. Now it was his turn. By the same token, when her lawyers finally convinced the government that her father was truly sick, she would bring him home and they would care for him here, in his own bed, until he died.

The old man worked for an hour—unhurried, heedless of the bodyguards passing between the houses. He worked until the fig tree's branches were buried under a blanket of soil which would protect it through the winter. Come spring he would return, unearth the tree, and straighten it up. Every summer it bore fruit.

Taggart riddled her thoughts. Could she have it all with him—a guy *and* her business? He was no ordinary rackets guy out to rip her off. But what about that other thing she had seen—Taggart's hatred? Combined with his strength, it could make him a dangerous opponent.

She went to the kitchen. Uncle Mario's muddy shoes were at the back door. Her mother was serving him coffee and cheesecake. Helen greeted him in Sicilian, his only language, and he grunted a reply. Her own Sicilian was good, polished when she had gone to Italy to help with the earthquake relief. Thousands of peasants had died in the wreckage of ancient walls. The disaster had marked her with a powerful fear of chaos, and left her with few illusions about the primitive life; there, in the morning a woman milked the cow, cleaned the stable, and cooked breakfast before she woke her husband, which Helen saw as proof that women with no better means to serve their families served them as slaves.

Her mother poured her coffee. "That guy Chris called again."

"What did he say?"

"Same. Wants to talk to you. Who is he?"

"A guy."

"What's wrong with him?"

Helen shrugged.

"He sounds really nice."

"You'd love him, Mom. He's a builder."

"A real builder?" she asked sharply. Helen looked at her. Occasionally her mother dropped her pretenses and admitted that they lived in a world where men who called themselves builders needed a front.

"Yeah. In the city."

"So what's wrong with him?"

"He's great-looking. Real nice manners."

"So what's wrong?" she repeated.

Helen turned away and engaged Mario in Sicilian. The old man was convinced a cold winter was coming. He wanted to wrap the rhododendron with burlap. She shared a smile with her mother; what Uncle Mario really wanted was to turn the front lawn into a zucchini patch. She half listened, thinking of Taggart, fantasizing that maybe at last she had found a way to have a guy without jeopardizing her empire.

The telephone rang. It was the listed line so her mother answered. She thrust the receiver at Helen.

"It's him again."

"I'm not here."

"Yes, you are." She put the receiver on the table in front of Helen and retreated to the coffeepot.

Helen picked it up with a black look for her mother. "Hello?"

"It's Chris. The guys get you home okay the other night?"

"No problem."

"Hey, listen, you want to go to the Governor's Ball?"

"The *what?*"

"The Governor's Ball. It's a big fundraiser at the Waldorf. They'll have a good band."

"That sounds a little heavy-duty. You know?"

"Let me talk you into it at lunch. Are you free tomorrow?"

He's asking me for a date, she thought. Like we're two real people. She held the phone, shaking her head, and wondering what Taggart wanted.

"Go on," whispered her mother. "What do you got to lose?"

"I'll call you tomorrow," she said, and hung up.

Her mother looked dismayed. "I don't understand. What's wrong with him?"

"Bad timing."

"What, do you think God delivers everything perfect the day you want it?"

Helen cupped her mother's soft cheek in her palm, an unusual gesture because the mother and daughter rarely touched. "Mom. Take my word for it. God didn't make this delivery."

* * *

Tony Taglione's expanded joint Strikeforce hit again, raiding a Kennedy Airport hotel room where a big Sicilian smuggler was concluding a sale. They seized forty keys of heroin and millions in cash, arrested the Sicilian and, remarkably, one of Crazy Mikey's crew leaders. Taggart tracked the U.S. Attorney's press conference on the evening news in his office, which Chryl and Victoria had moved to the third floor of the partially completed Spire. Reggie sat beside him, sipping a neat whiskey.

"Mikey is desperate. That man shouldn't have been there."

Taggart flipped the sound from channel to channel as he hunted for shots of his brother. Tony, as usual, dodged the camera, sitting quietly at the press conference, while Arthur Finch did the talking and introduced the agent supervisors who had led the sweep. When he introduced Tony, Tony's expression said he couldn't wait to get back to his office.

"Come on," Taggart urged the image on the screen. "Sell yourself a little. Hey, hey, look at Tony!" He turned up the sound. A Channel Four minicam crew had cornered him in an elevator and the reporter was asking with concern, "As Strikeforce chief, are you aware there is a heroin panic in the streets?"

"I'm aware that methadone and detox programs are serving double the clientele of a year ago. I am aware that schoolchildren don't shoot dope that isn't readily available. I am aware that availability is a major factor in drug abuse."

"What does it mean in terms of the Mafia?"

"They're losing."

Taggart clapped his hands. "Go for it, Tony!"

"He certainly has a way with words," Reggie observed dryly.

"Is it true your office is preparing indictments against the leadership of the Cirillo family?"

Taggart looked at Reggie, whose narrow shoulders lifted in an elegant shrug.

"If it were true," Tony answered, "I couldn't comment."

All three stations went to commercials and Taggart turned them off. "That's news to me."

"Ultimately," Reggie said, "the Cirillos have to be his target. Who's left?"

"I want the Cirillos myself." He walked around the room, made a drink and a new one for Reggie, and stared out at Park Avenue. The broad median was ablaze in Christmas trees. Reggie was right; of course, the government was after the Cirillos. But they were his, first.

"I had lunch with Helen today. She says you're bugging her," he said.

Reggie looked appalled. "How did she happen to get through to you without me knowing?"

"She didn't. I called her." He had, in fact, called every day for a week before she agreed to lunch. "Relax. We met alone at a pizza joint on Ocean Boulevard. Just the two of us. She didn't want her brothers to know."

"Alone?"

"She slipped her bodyguards."

"Did you notice anyone following her?"

"I didn't see anybody."

She had waited in her little red car when he got the slices. While they ate, she revved the engine like Mario Andretti. Taggart had made small talk and had gotten her to smile by mimicking contractors complaining about his brother's office investigating bid-rigging on a Navy job. Then she had fixed him in her serious gaze and asked, "Why?"

"Why what?"

"Why did you choose me? Forget all that bull you said in Ireland."

"Why not choose you? I've always worked with women in my business. Why shouldn't I work with one in this business?"

"That's not a reason."

"Okay, I'm enchanted."

"That's not a good reason."

"Oh, it's a good reason," he replied. "Maybe not a *smart* reason." And to his surprise she had smiled again and even touched his arm with her long nails. . . .

He could still feel them, electric on his skin. "It wasn't a major date, Reg. But a beginning."

"You are foolhardy."

Taggart grinned. "I'm indulging a normal human desire to—"

On occasion Reggie had scared Taggart, and this was suddenly one of those occasions when he skewered him with eyes that had seen it all and hated much of it. "Human? You can't be *human* when you take revenge. You can't risk indulging yourself in a lover or—now that we're on it—your temper, as you did with Mikey, or your arrogance, which you're indulging daily."

"I remember. Be evil to beat evil?"

"The Devil is organized and disciplined, or he wouldn't have lasted as long as he has. . . . Chris, haven't you any concept of the danger?"

"My brother already found out about Helen. What's he gonna do? Indict me for falling for a moll?"

"It's not funny. Being near her doubles your risk. You're forgetting why you recruited the Rizzolos."

"Reg, you're looking wired. You could do with a rest."

"I'm quite all right."

"Take a vacation."

"Vacations are for amateurs."

Taggart shrugged and closed the subject. "I'm taking her to the Governor's Ball. It's a fundraiser. Taggart Construction's buying a table."

"May I ask why—without your telling me to go on holiday?"

"Because I want to. . . . Hey, it's better being in open contact. Things are breaking faster and faster. Nobody has to know I'm giving her orders while we're dancing."

Still, he had to consider Tony. If Governor Costanza did go for the Presidency and Arthur Finch managed to beat the mayor out for the governorship, Tony, the leader of the Strikeforce and the man who had the Mafia on the run, had a shot at replacing Arthur as U.S. Attorney. There was no pressure Taggart could exert on Tony's behalf—the office had been fiercely nonpolitical for eighty years—but having a brother publicly dating a mafioso's daughter wouldn't help his appointment. So he telephoned Alphonse and asked the old man, "Will you lease me a grandson?"

"I've done girls plenty times," the Vegas hit man assured Sal Ponte at their first meeting. "But never for you guys."

Don Richard's handsome *consigliere* was too sharp to go by appearances, but he worried nonetheless that the hit man did not appear formidable. Indeed, nothing about Eddie Berger was threatening except his reputation. Hand to hand, anyone over five six and one hundred and forty pounds could have knocked him down easily. And were he knocked down, nothing in his demeanor would reveal that Eddie Berger would be back shortly to kill by whatever means available.

Reggie Rand would have spotted him instantly for that peculiar brand of crazy who had mastered the details of day-to-day life—a lunatic who knew that cops never noticed a little guy pushing a broom—and therefore roamed at will. Abandoned at age three in an Arizona diner, raised as a ward of the state, Eddie Berger had learned early that a child who appeared to obey rules was rewarded. Neatly lettered book reports handed in on time returned praise and affection from teachers, guards, and foster parents; his schoolmates were less delighted; unlike the adults, the children sensed that Eddie Berger was dangerous.

By nineteen, the ordinary-looking little man was an accomplished serial killer, well on his way to his third dozen random murders. Still a rule follower, neat, clean, well-mannered, he wandered the country, working hard at whatever menial job he drifted into. He had a car, kept up the payments, and neither drank nor smoked. Nothing stood between him and killing people for the rest of a long life. When he learned he could get paid for it, he had turned pro and had, Ponte knew, zapped some very tough people.

"They made me," he admitted to *Consigliere* Ponte at their second meeting.

"Who made you?"

"Some guy she met by the water. Maybe they heard I'm around, but they don't know why."

Ponte passed a direct order from Don Richard. "Do it tomorrow night."

"Don't take this the wrong way, but I want my fee doubled."

Ponte's dark face closed up, and his eyes went blank. To those who knew him the look meant danger.

Berger didn't know him and didn't care. "The reason is," he explained, "I'm going to have to drop out after. The word'll get back to her brothers."

"Don't worry about her brothers."

"Nobody fools the street. Double or nothing."

Ponte gave in. It was smarter to pay than to explain that for Helen Rizzolo's brothers to avenge her death they would have to do it from their own graves.

Chapter 20

"Nice table," said Helen.

"At two grand a plate it ought to be," Uncle Vinnie agreed proudly. "Chris's father was the same way. Nothing was ever too much for Costanza, even when he was just starting in Congress."

Taggart's party was sitting at a table next to the dance floor, directly across from Peter Duchin's orchestra. On their right was the mayor's entourage, to the left Governor Costanza, whose popularity with New York's Italian-Americans had filled the Waldorf's Grand Ballroom to capacity. Television cameras, quiescent while the faithful ate, were stationed against the back wall. Strategically sprinkled among the heavy contributors were former New York mayors and a governor, to whom the passage of time had affixed, like moss, the affection reserved for bold men unlikely to cause any more trouble.

The present mayor was working the room in the hope Costanza's Presidential ambitions would open up the governor's mansion. He deadpanned that Taggart's Spire was four stories higher than zoning allowed. And when the governor stepped by for a word about Taggart's stadium proposal, and for a look at the women, the mayor bounded back.

"I could build a high school with the taxes he's saving on the Spire."

Governor Costanza, who maintained privately that privilege was Manhattan's hottest industry, looked like he wished a *New Yorker* friend wasn't hovering.

"Schools?" Taggart threw his long arms around the politicians. "I'm already providing jobs, business opportunities, and space for tax-paying tenants. Can't you guys do *anything?*"

He grinned at Helen, who smiled back, and winked at his beaming publicist, who was already rising for a private chat with the lady from *The New Yorker*. He was having a ball. The wine was Italian, and Peter Duchin was seducing hundreds into dancing between courses. But the best part was Helen Rizzolo, whose solemn eyes had widened appreciably when he had introduced her to the governor and the mayor. She sat at Taggart's left in diamonds and a red dress that bared her shoulders, and had made, even in the incandescent presence of Victoria and Chryl, an impression. Alphonse's accommodating grandson—Taggart's beard—had apparently fallen in love during the limousine trip. Strait-laced Henry Bunker looked so intrigued that his wife started holding his hand.

Uncle Vinnie loved her, but what man wouldn't? Interestingly, so did Aunt Marie, who wasn't fooled by the beard. That Taggart and Tony weren't married was not her fault. For ten years, since Mike Taglione had been killed, she had herded toward them legions of every conceivable variety of Italian girl that Queens and Brooklyn had to offer: old-fashioned family-bred Italian girls; rich Italian girls; eighties-slick Italian girls; glossy, college-educated Italian girls with their provocative blend of femininity and iron will. As she had no idea that Helen's family was "connected," to her eye Helen was all the wonderful sorts of Italian girls rolled up in one classy little package that might persuade her bachelor nephew to finally make a family.

Chryl and Victoria were rampantly curious; they were thus far behaving themselves, Taggart noted, though repeatedly rapping shoulders and bobbing heads for swift and secret thoughts. Finally, Victoria, who was sitting on his right, beckoned him closer and anounced quietly, "Maybe this isn't one of your bimbos."

"Do you approve?"

She leaned across her escort—a bearded critic from an architectural magazine who routinely savaged Taggart's buildings and seemed disappointed that the brash builder hadn't broken a champagne bottle over his head—and said to Chryl, "He's serious."

Chryl asked him to dance. In his arms she said, "In our opinion, you have fallen in love, you bastard."

"You think so?" he asked earnestly. If they thought so, it

was true. They were in every way his best friends. Only Reggie knew him better. "She makes me a little crazy."

"That's a good sign. . . . We'll miss you. We'll miss you a lot."

"I'll be around."

"Not like that, you won't. A woman like her would cut your heart out for messing around."

Taggart kissed her. "Who's telling who to be careful?"

"Not us, kiddo. She'll know who to blame." She kissed his cheek, clung to him a moment, and led him off the dance floor. "Come on, back to your party."

When Helen excused herself to go to the ladies' room, Chryl and Victoria arose smiling to join her and Henry Bunker remarked, "Nothing they talk about can possibly be to your advantage."

Taggart excused himself. In the lobby he found a telephone booth, closed the door, and dialed a number Reggie had obtained from a NYNEX supervisor.

"Let me speak to Crazy Mikey."

"Who is this? How the fuck did you get this number?"

"I bought it. A thousand bucks a digit. I already knew your area code. Put Mikey on."

A hand covered the receiver. Then Mikey came on.

"It's your man from the boat, Mikey."

There was silence.

"I want to remind you we've got a payment coming due."

"Hey, man, you're pushing the wrong guy. When I got it, you'll get paid."

"That's not good enough. I'm not selling you another ounce until you pay up."

"How the fuck am I supposed to earn the money with nothing to sell?"

"That's your problem."

"Oh, yeah? What are you going to do about it?"

"Mikey, you've been a collector. Like the song says, 'You can run, but you can't hide.' Do I have to send somebody to break your legs?"

"Who the fuck do you think you're talking to?"

Taggart hung up, combed his hair in the men's room, and strolled back to his table. Helen, Victoria, and Chryl returned, too. Helen, who had directed most of her attention toward Alphonse's nephew and Aunt Marie, put her hand on Chris's arm, jolting him as she had a week ago in the car, and said with a private smile only he could fully appreciate, "Your friends made me an offer I couldn't refuse."

"What's that?"

"They're going to design me a club."

"You're kidding!"

"You told them I have clubs. They said they've always wanted to do one. We made a deal."

Victoria, Taggart realized belatedly, had assumed the business look she wore when the design house of Matthews and Chamberlain negotiated a contract.

"Where?" he asked her.

"The lobby of the Taggart Spire."

"My lobby? But it's an office-building lobby."

"Can you imagine a ten-story-high dance club? Can you imagine the sound—the *lights* in that incredible space? Ten stories of music? It's going to be drop-dead fantastic. Hey, Helen, you want to call it that? Drop Dead Fantastic? Maybe just Drop Dead."

"No."

"How about Death," said Victoria. "That would be nice. Death. I like that."

Helen said no again, and Victoria said, "You're right, it's a downer."

Taggart repeated, "It's an office building."

"Not at night. Chryl's got this great idea. Fly the lights and mirrors like stage sets. At night, lower them for the club. In the morning, winch them up out of sight." Her shapely hand rose airily to the upper tiers.

"Do you know what that will cost, even if you can get it past the city?"

"You can afford it."

"Me?"

"It's your building."

"What if I don't want a disco in my lobby?"

Victoria reached over and patted Helen's hand. "Don't worry, dear. We'll go to Donald Trump."

"Okay, okay," Taggart said. "I'll look into it."

Victoria showed her teeth. "Go bounce it off the mayor. Now."

On his return he saw the party was about to go to hell as the TV crews turned on their lights and eight hundred people who had been having a good time dancing started waving to neighbors stuck home in their rec rooms. Taggart plowed through the madness, demanded Helen's coat check from Alphonse's vastly disappointed grandson, and grabbed her hand. "Let's get out of here."

"What about my date?"

"He's got classes in the morning. Come on, I want to show you something."

Taggart helped her into her black mink, and through the lobby. A nod to one of the many bodyguards Reggie had insisted on secreting about the hotel had produced his white Rolls at the canopy. The clock on the Helmsley Building read one o'clock. Park Avenue was nearly empty, as were the side streets, but for a sprinkling of taxis and limousines that converged on the Waldorf.

The Spire's Park Avenue and downtown faces were decorated with five-story trees of hanging work lights, topped by Stars of David to honor Chanukah. "Next year, when we're occupied, we'll control the lights on a computer to make patterns with the windows—trees at Christmas; hearts on Valentine's Day; rabbits at Easter."

"What if someone wants to work late in a blacked-out office?"

"He'd better bring a flashlight. It's in his lease."

The car stopped in front of the construction gate. "Would you like to see my apartment?"

"The building isn't done."

Taggart pointed up, out the back window. A solitary gold light shone at the top of the dark tower. "I finished my place first."

Helen took his hand in both of hers. He felt her warmth through her kid gloves. "Could we do something first?"

"Sure. What?"

"Could we look at the Christmas windows?"

"Now? I don't know if they're going; it's after midnight."

"They are," she said eagerly. "My father used to take me late at night—just the two of us. Every Christmas we saw

Saks, Lord and Taylor, and Altman's. Sometimes, if it was late enough, we'd be the only people there. Could we?"

"Sure."

The big car headed west, tailed by an old cab, which Taggart didn't notice. When the Rolls pulled to the curb in front of Saks, the cab stopped two blocks back. Station wagons were parked in front of the department store; couples were leading small children along the windows. "Just like we used to," said Helen. They got out of the car to look.

Saks had done a thirties New York Christmas scene. The first window showed a sleek man and woman going off to a party, bidding good night to nanny-tended children in pajamas; outside the elaborate model house a miniature Duesenberg waited at the curb.

"The thirties." Helen smiled. "My grandfather was starving. Repeal played hell with the liquor business."

"Mine was a bricklayer. He got laid off when they finished the Empire State Building."

She glanced up at him. "Why do you keep asking me out?"

"Honestly?"

"If you can."

"I kind of flipped for you."

"Mr. Taggart, I have microphones in my bars to keep my employees from dealing dope. The mikes pick up the customers' conversations, too. I hear that line thirty times a night."

"It's guys hoping you're listening."

She laughed, thinking that his compliments always sounded like he meant them. They moved to the next window, where the sleek couple were now dancing at the grand ball. "Seriously, why? What's going on with you?"

"Just like I told you."

"We are in different worlds, man. I met people tonight who if they knew who I was would spit on me."

"Not in front of me they wouldn't," Taggart promised in a hard, low voice and Helen saw for a second that capacity for hatred again. It was never far from the surface; yet neither, she had to admit, were his exuberant warmth and the tenderness he radiated toward her. Both made her wary. She doubted he would ever hurt her, but he might someday make her hurt herself.

She said, "I don't know what's going on. I don't know

where you are. And I don't know where you and your scam come together."

"Do you remember the first time we met?"

She glanced around but no one was near. "Me tied to a chair and you strutting around in a mask?"

"No. In the restaurant."

"What restaurant?"

"Abatelli's on Woodhaven Boulevard. I saw you on a summer night with your family about ten years ago."

"My 'betrothal,'" she acknowledged with an ironic smile. She hesitated—for she had good reason not to discuss that night further—but by now she cared enough about him to be as straight as possible and wanted to speak the truth in her heart. "I was wondering when you would mention it."

"You remember?"

"Of course. You stared at me all night. You gave me a really nice smile. I wondered who you were."

"You blew me away. I couldn't get you out of my head."

Helen smiled. Honesty's "reward" had paid off quickly; Chris's happy expression proved he really meant he liked her, and that he was courting her for more than his scam. She felt like she had for a brief second last spring at Uncle Frank's ball game, wondering if a special door could be opened that she thought forever closed. But the pitcher, whatever his name was, was a guy in that other world, whereas Chris and she had much in common.

"What was going on with you?" she asked. "What were you doing there?"

"Eating, until I got in an argument with Don Richard Cirillo. Remember?"

"I remember you went out with him. He came back alone."

Taggart's expression grayed; he looked away a moment, touched the scar on his mouth. Then looked back at her, the gray look erased by one of his easy grins. "You got stoned in the ladies' room."

Helen smiled. "No. I got stoned before I came. I got stoned *again* in the bathroom."

"I guessed they were giving you away."

"You guessed right."

"I didn't think that happened anymore."

"My parents had their reasons."

"Later I heard that Cirillo was brokering peace between your family and the Confortis."

"It was much more complicated than that. My parents would not have 'sold' me for peace, I can assure you. They're real Italian-Italian in some ways, but they're not low class."

"Then why'd they do it?"

Helen shrugged, looked around the sidewalk, stared at a little girl holding her father's hand. "Marrying me off killed a lot of birds with one stone. I was kind of wild. They knew I'd be nothing but trouble if they kept me home. I was nowhere in school. I was *ready*, you know? Sixteen, and everything looked better outside the house."

"You seemed younger."

"I was hell on wheels. I had thirty-year-old guys calling me up." She laughed easily and Taggart decided there was no question he loved her. "My brothers were spending half their time threatening my boyfriends."

"What happened?"

"Oh, Christ! What didn't happen! First of all, the whole thing was a Cirillo trick, which I found out later. Second, the poor kid I married was really messed up."

She moved to the next window and Taggart followed. Here the sleek couple were bidding their host and hostess good night, maids were ladling eggnog for the diehards, and outside it was snowing and the Duesenberg had miraculously been transformed into a horse-drawn sleigh.

"My husband was beautiful. A really good person. But he couldn't hack his father, his whole family, all the pressuring. He didn't want the rackets. So he was a doper. Just like with real kids when the parents try to make them be a doctor, so they drop out? I didn't know it at first. I smoked and did a little of this and that, so I didn't think it was any different for him. But it was." She pushed her hair from her face and shook her head violently. "The trouble with being married to a druggie is it's so lonely. He was always telling me he loved me, and he did, but three-quarters of the time he was flying."

"You didn't fly with him?"

"I tried. But I'm not a druggie. I get bored if I get stoned more

281

than a weekend. Two days and I want my head back. So I'd get straight and he was still flying. I was alone till I made a friend."

She moved again and Taggart followed. The sleek couple were tearing across Central Park in the sleigh. Helen looked at Taggart and her eyes glistened. "You know so much about me—you know who the friend was, don't you?"

Taggart shook his head.

"Come on, you must know."

"I guess somebody in the casino."

"Sure. Where else would I meet somebody in Vegas. Guess who?"

"Somebody you fell in love with?"

"Yeah."

"Then I'll guess his father, the owner."

"Jackpot. You knew it was my father-in-law—I wish you wouldn't lie to me. I've been straight, more so than with anybody I ever talked to. I want you to be straight with me."

"I'm sorry," he said, and Helen thrilled to his chagrined smile. "I'm out of practice. We'll work on it."

"Thanks. That's nice. That's real nice. . . . Did you know I got pregnant by him?"

"No."

She looked up at him sharply, nodded to herself. "No, no one did. I didn't know what to do. Then I figured, okay, I'll pretend it's my husband's. All I'd have to do was get him off the dope long enough to get it up."

"Logical," Taggart replied lightly, finding it hard to handle how harsh she sounded.

"The baby's grandfather would have really been his father. And the baby's father would really have been his brother. Family, right?"

"You make it sound easy."

"It could have been. Only my father-in-law lover got shot by the goddamned Cirillos."

She went to the last window, and when a ten-year-old girl smiled up at her, she lightly touched her hair. The girl moved on. Taggart joined Helen again. The couple were on their knees on their drawing-room carpet, hastily wrapping toys. Champagne was in a bucket and the man was holding the knot while the woman tied the bow. They looked about to kiss.

"So I went home and I told my parents, You owe me! You get me an annulment and an abortion. And they did. I don't know what it cost, but they got the marriage annulled. I had my abortion. I made them let me go to college. . . . That was funny, Sarah Lawrence College. You should have seen it. This little Italian girl in perfect makeup with hair washed every day, while the real girls are dressing down to look like our kitchen help. . . . In college they taught me about music. They gave me a 'don,' this woman who played the violin like an angel, and for one whole semester I studied an Italian composer I had never heard of named Corelli. Then your fucking brother sent my father to jail, and I had to come home to help Eddie and Frank run the business. . . ."

Taggart wished he had not chosen her family to be his instrument of revenge. "You keep calling other people real. You're real."

"Not like them. They can make all the mistakes they want. In the rackets, one mistake and you're caught. But who can live a perfect life? . . . Why were you fighting with Don Richard?"

She had caught him off balance. "I thought he killed my father."

"Did he?"

Taggart shook his head. "Somebody got mad and flew off the handle. It took me a while to see it that way."

She touched his throat. "Your pulse is pounding like you're going to explode."

Taggart escaped the necessary lie by kissing her mouth.

She kissed him back, her lips opening and molding softly to his; he felt her fingers on the back of his head, exploring his hair and drawing him harder against her mouth. Their tongues met. She broke away with a satisfied smile.

"Hey. Merry Christmas."

Taggart felt like he would float across Fifth Avenue if she weren't holding his hand. "Why don't we go someplace and exchange presents or something?"

She was still holding his hand. She probed his face, her violet eyes dark with wonderment. "I really don't know."

"Want to see my new apartment?"

She shrugged, as if so sure of herself in most things, Taggart thought, that being unsure about him didn't matter. She almost seemed to revel in the luxury of not deciding. "Why?" she marveled. "Why did I tell you all that?"

"You figured I knew it anyhow."

She gave him a lopsided smile. "God, would my mother love you. A nice, rich Italian boy not in the rackets."

"Half."

She arose on tiptoe and whispered harshly and bitterly, "Whose brother put my father in the slammer and who's moving in on the Mafia? Just wonderful!"

"Leave out the last part."

"Chris, you're crazy."

"Want to go play?"

"I'll look."

"Come on."

They got back in the car, which headed toward Park Avenue. Helen leaned against the door on her side as if debating whether to jump out. Then, to his delight, she moved closer and laid her head on his shoulder. Her hair was shiny and lightly perfumed; when he kissed it it felt like dense folds of silk. Taggart sat back, happy to watch the city slide by the bronzed windows. He hadn't felt like this since—but there was no since. He had never felt like this in his life.

The Rolls drew up to the Spire. A timid-looking little guy in a ragged army jacket was huddled by the construction fence. As Taggart and Helen got out of the car, he started toward them with his hands in his pockets. "Sir, you got change for coffee, sir?"

The building guard hurried from the gate, saluting. "Good evening, Mr. Taggart."

"Evening, Johnny. They get my elevator working again?"

"Yes, sir."

The little guy, backing warily from the guard and Taggart's chauffeur, was shivering, so Taggart slid a pair of C-notes out of his money clip. "Cold," he said, his father's rough voice echoing in his head. "Get yourself a coat."

Helen followed him into the chaos of the lobby. The cement floor and steel supports were lit by bare bulbs; cables and scaffolds cast shadow webs on the poured concrete walls and the lofty ceiling. "Your club, madame."

"Can Victoria and Chryl really do it?"

"Given a sufficiently blank check, they could arrange tasteful sunsets in the east."

"Don't worry about the money. You'll make a fortune."

"Oh, yeah?"

"When John Gere's PR man pays a hundred and fifty bucks cash for a bottle in the Champagne Room, a hundred and twenty of that is cash in your pocket."

"Right this way, partner."

She hesitated again. "You really like them, don't you?"

"We're real friends."

"More than friends?"

"We've become family. I met them right after my father died. I gave them away at their weddings. When they got tired of the bozos, I provided shark divorce lawyers. Sometimes they're like mothers to me and sometimes I'm like a father to them."

"They showed me pictures. Victoria's little girl looks a lot like you."

"That's Annie. Tony says she looks exactly like our mother."

"Do you—?"

"The kids carry the names of rich, old Wasp families. There isn't a door in America that will be closed to them. And until then, they've all got Uncle Chris whenever Mummy needs a man around the house."

"Do you still get it on with them?"

"Sometimes."

"Both of them?"

"Chryl and Victoria are a couple. It's both or neither, which was one of the problems in their marriages."

"It's not something I can get with, but they seem very happy."

"They're hot in their field, they're getting rich by their own hand, and the jerks they married gave them beautiful children. Damned right they're happy."

"Will you ever have your own children?"

"Funny you should ask. Shall we go up?"

The elevator shaft was still an open frame, but the car itself was finished in lacquer and chrome. In the corners were crystal flower vases filled with white freesia which perfumed the air, a silver umbrella stand, and a bottle of Moët chilling in a silver bucket.

"Won't they steal this stuff?"

"Private car, straight to the owner's suite. Champagne?" Taggart removed the foil, gripped the cork, twisted the bottle, and filled two tulip glasses. "Cheers."

"Per cent 'anni." She smiled at the bubbles boiling from the hollow stem as the elevator started to ascend. . . . "Chris, how rich are you?"

"Never quite as rich as I look, but doing pretty good the last couple of years. And thanks to a maniacally confused city government, I get enough tax credits to keep most of it. . . . Swallow if your ears hurt."

She said in deep seriousness, "What are you doing it for?"

"What do you do what you do for?"

"I'm protecting my family."

"Me, too."

"I find that hard to believe."

Let this tiger go? Taggart thought. Get out somehow, take Helen and get out. And spend the rest of his life remembering a broken promise? Not while Mike Taglione's killers ruled New York. But afterwards? He shivered, unable to complete the thought, and was saved from further unsettling introspection by the doors opening. He took Helen's hand, which she slipped naturally into his, and led her into the foyer. The doors hissed shut behind them. The air smelled of fresh paint, brand-new lacquer, and roses.

"You live well," she said, and he felt obliged to explain.

"It didn't really cost anything because it's worth a fortune in free advertising. My publicist will get articles about the apartment published in all the magazines. Everybody will hear about the building being the newest and most incredible. That makes it a hot building. Which means I sell an eight-hundred-thousand-dollar condo for a million two and promise the owner he'll be able to sell it for a million five next year because the building has my name on it."

"I'm in the wrong business."

"Well, if you ever want to go straight—" He smiled.

"This is yours, not mine."

She was impressed, he realized, yet not impressed, as if

trendy opulence was of the world of *stranieri,* too far from her own to have a lure. He showed her the downstairs bedrooms, the kitchen, dining room, and library on the lower levels. On the top floor, down a long hall, appeared a room with glass walls. As they neared it, views of the night leaped from the city.

"Look at the ceiling," he said, leading her inside.

And for the second time—the first being six months ago when he removed his mask on the Irish cliffs—he astonished her. She looked up; twenty feet overhead the stars shimmered in the glass ceiling. She circled, staring up at them. Her gaze descended through the glass walls and finally to the floor.

She screamed, and Taggart caught her in his arm. *"Easy.* I've got you."

She brought a hand to her chest, gasping, "Oh, my God!"

They were standing on a glass floor, a thousand feet above Manhattan. The city sprang at them like a monster rising from the dark with a million gleaming teeth.

"Feel my heart." She laughed. "I thought we were falling. Oh, this is fantastic!"

Taggart leaned against a column—the same column from which he had dangled Jack Warner last spring—and watched Helen prowl the room. It occurred to him that all this stuff was suddenly fun in ways he had never been inclined to notice before. She drifted among the furniture islands, stroking fabrics and polished surfaces, drinking in the views, and looking down repeatedly. At one point she sank into a chair, leaned over the arm, and stared through the floor.

"It still makes me shiver."

"I know. It took me a week to make my legs behave."

She prowled again until, near the outer wall, she stopped in a space between two groupings. "What are these lines?" she asked, pointing at evenly spaced wires in the floor, so thin as to be almost invisible.

Taggart started toward her. "Touch it."

She knelt, her gown puddling around her, and felt the glass. "It's warm."

"Heaters."

She stared at the building tops between her spread fingers and suddenly glanced at him with a grin. "Oh, wow! I just got this incredible idea."

"I was hoping you would."

"Have you done it?" she asked.

"Not yet."

"Truth?"

Taggart sat on the floor beside her. "Truth. You're my first guest. The place was finished today. Only problem is the floor's hard as a rock. I drove my engineers crazy trying to come up with a soft floor, but everything they tried was cloudy."

"Will anyone see us?"

"That's up to you." Taggart handed her a remote-control switch. She toyed with the dimmer, smiling, and lowered the lights until the room went black.

"It's like we're floating in the sky," she breathed.

Above, below, and around them were black night, stars, and lights. Taggart's eyes adjusted and her face took form in the glow from the city. He kissed the soft skin on her shoulder. She moved against him, and he traced the strap of her gown with his lips and tongued her breasts.

"Chris? . . . What do you want of me?"

"How about your body for ten years? Then we'll talk."

"Don't joke. We're in business."

Instinctively, though there couldn't possibly be a bug in range, she had whispered the last in his ear. Taggart replied in kind. "The fact that we're beating the Mafia only makes it better."

"Beating? You sound like a cop."

"Making it ours," he amended, alert to the razors in her voice. "*Look!*" He swept his hand across the floor as if caressing the lights below. "We're like barbarians, you and me, galloping our horses over a rise—there's the city, waiting to be taken. It's ours because we want it."

"You're drunk," she said unsteadily.

He brought his mouth to hers again, kissed her deeply, and when he stopped they were both shaking. "Drunks can't kiss. Am I drunk?"

Helen pulled away and sat up. "You're scaring the hell out of me."

"You've scared the hell out of me since the day I first saw you."

"Chris, you can't believe that. It was ten years ago. I was sixteen."

"I make things real by wanting them."

"You're crazy."

"Since my father was killed, I haven't done a thing that people didn't say was crazy. But if I'm crazy, then we're floating here with no floor under us. There's no Taggart Spire, just air over some old wreck of a building I had to knock down to build this one. So if I'm crazy, I don't know how we got up here, but we're falling fast."

She looked at the prize sparkling beneath them. "Hold me."

"I can't. We're falling."

"I have a parachute." In a swift, graceful motion, she unzipped her gown, slid out of it, and raised it over her head.

Taggart stared. The city glow penetrated the floor and spread soft light on her breasts, which were small, round, and tipped with dusky nipples. Her legs unfolding beside him were long, slim, and shapely. She wore stockings, a garter belt through which her strong thighs flashed like neon, and lace panties taut about her hips. She looked back, a little defiant, a little proud.

"You're not real. We're still falling."

They came together gently at first, almost tentatively, as Taggart, awkwardly aware of his size, held himself in check because he was afraid to crush her in his excitement. Then dream and reality merged and in the heat of reality, the dream evaporated. She was suddenly and totally three-dimensional, her mouth sure, her breasts soft and warm, her legs strong, engulfing.

Eddie Berger wore black under the army jacket, which he jettisoned in a subceller—black high-top sneakers, black socks, black sweatsuit, black watch cap, and black makeup base on his face. Nearly invisible in the shadows of the concrete stairs but for the narrow whites of his slitted eyes, and silent on rubber soles, he climbed ninety-six flights to the top of the Taggart Spire. He had jogged thirty miles a week to prepare for jobs like this, and he consequently scaled the last flight still breathing lightly.

The top level was a plank floor, apparently destined to become the roof, and there he waited, still as a wall, while his eyes adjusted to the dark. Gradually he became aware of the construction derricks looming overhead and a glow on the south side of the building. When his eyes could distinguish the girders scattered about, he moved silently among them, heading for the glow. At the edge of the plank floor he found the top of the glass cube jutting from the side of the building—Taggart's cantilevered living room.

It puzzled him at first; he knew they'd come up here, but he hadn't realized that the incomplete building was habitable. Expecting to find Helen Rizzolo holding hands with her playboy boyfriend on the roof, he had discovered instead a luxurious apartment floating in the sky. It took a moment to realize he was looking down at them through a glass roof. Just then the lights dimmed and went out and the glow disappeared. He was left staring at the dark.

Again he waited until his eyes adjusted. Finally he saw the stars reflected in black glass, like lights on a river. Moving cautiously, careful not to make a sound, he worked his way to the edge of the glass and looked down.

His gut wrenched and he felt his balance going. Beneath the glass, where he least expected it, was the city. He gradually figured out what he was looking at: a cube-shaped room, perhaps thirty feet square, with a glass roof, three glass sides, and a glass floor. He could make out dark clumps of furniture here and there. In the center was movement. As his eyes grew accustomed to the dark, he saw them in silhouette over the city lights—Helen Rizzolo and the playboy-builder, making love on the floor.

Eddie Berger lowered himself to the glass, found it strong, and inched across it. They were little more than outlines in motion, but there was something profoundly erotic about the way they floated in the sky, twenty feet under his perch, as if they and he were the last three people in the world. He watched for a long time, fascinated by the slowness of their movements and the balletic exchanges of position, as if they were indeed floating, adrift in a warm, buoyant liquid. He wished he could hear them, and he was surprised at how much he loved them.

Light from Park Avenue below and the heavens above revealed tantalizing glimpses—her thighs flickering as she rolled over, his golden hair, her teeth suddenly agleam in passion, as if a single star were lighting her gasping mouth. Suddenly, they went rigid. He thought they had seen him. A scream pierced the thick glass, another, a long silence, then laughter, and they collapsed, spilling over each other.

He laid his face on the cold glass roof and caught his own breath. But he had watched too long and now discovered to his horror that in his own excitement he had edged out until he was almost on top of them. When they looked up at the stars, as surely they would in such a room, they would see his silhouette, as he had seen theirs.

He froze, afraid to breathe, waiting in terrible anticipation for them to gaze upward and open their eyes. He grew cold. He prayed they'd get up and find a drink or something. But they stayed where they were. They moved closer; slowly they touched and merged, blended, and embraced. Eddie Berger smiled again, his fear evaporating; he wished he could join them. And in a way, he thought, as he slithered off the glass, he would.

He scouted his prospects on the roof. Steel beams were stacked helter-skelter, and his mind conjured a vivid image of one of those twenty-foot, multi-ton monsters falling through Taggart's glass roof, through the room, and through the floor —racing their bodies to the street.

The steel-raising derricks projected dark, lopsided Vs against the sky. He approached the nearest derrick, which was poised temptingly close to Taggart's apartment. It was close enough to hook around a steel beam, lift the I-beam over the edge, and drop it through Christopher Taggart's glass house. But he had no partner to run the machinery on the ground, for the operating cable that raised and lowered the boom and its hook stretched the full height of the building and played off a drum at the bottom of the hole. He would have to improvise.

The vast boom was slanting east and Taggart's living room was to the south. A huge iron bullwheel circled the base of the derrick. Eddie Berger gripped the bullwheel, heaved his weight against it, and felt the finely balanced derrick begin to turn. There were rope falls attached to assist turning a heavy load, but the unburdened boom moved easily despite its many tons of weight.

He looked up. The shadowy form of the slanting boom was

swinging past the stars. It was much longer than the distance between the foot of the derrick and Taggart's apartment. He kept turning the bullwheel until the boom was leaning over the glass roof.

Then he went to the stairs to search for some sort of cable cutter. Three floors down he broke into a well-stocked toolshed and found a hacksaw. The blade looked pretty ground up, so he hunted some more until he found a new carbide blade still in its wrapper.

Somewhere in the silence, Taggart became aware of a grinding when Eddie Berger turned the bullwheel, less sound than feeling, and he did not consciously connect it with the derrick on the roof. He strained a moment, halfheartedly trying to make sense of it; then Helen touched him and the impression dissolved like perfume on a breeze.

"It's so quiet," she whispered. "I can hear our hearts."

Street noise did not penetrate the thick, air-locked glass. Nor did they hear the ordinarily half-noticed building sounds, because the apartment was serviced by temporary mains; the unfinished Spire was deathly still without the normal flow of air, gas, electricity, and water circulating through its ducts, lines, pipes, and wires.

Memory of the intrusion returned, and with it Taggart's vague feeling of disquiet. They were side by side now, touching fingers, returning slowly from far away. He raised his head and listened hard. But by then Eddie Berger had crept down to the toolshed, and Taggart heard only Helen's breathing. He lay back on the warm floor and lifted her onto him. She whispered, "Beautiful, beautiful," and then, with a luxurious smile in her voice, "Oh, look at us!"

Like magic, the barely perceptible light reflected their bodies in the nearby glass wall. Overhead their images glowed in the ceiling; Helen crouched among the stars. The shadow of a derrick nodded over her like a curious dragon.

The cable that supported the derrick boom was five-eighths-inch braided wire. Shortly after Eddie Berger started sawing, it occurred to him he had better stand clear in case the cable end whipped around when it snapped. Since the boom probably weighed five tons, all hell would break loose when he cut the final cable strands and the boom fell into Taggart's apartment. So he stood way back from the shaft through which the cable traveled up the mast, and he sawed at the end of his reach with short, jerky strokes. He had no real knowledge of the forces involved, but some instinct, keyed perhaps by enormous tension in the cable, made him raise his other hand to protect his face.

It was slow work. He stopped repeatedly to listen in case they heard the noise, but the fresh blade cut smoothly and made a lot less noise than sawing wood. After ten minutes of the difficult extended strokes, he felt the cut with his fingers and slashed his thumb on the jagged shavings. He cursed and sucked the blood. Despite the cold, he was perspiring, and the cut felt as if he hadn't done more than nick the outer strands.

What if the girl had left after all this time? He ran to the edge and looked down on the glass roof. They were still on the floor, still at it, he thought irritably. His thumb hurt, and their endless pleasure was making him angry. There was something unfair about their enjoying themselves while he was stuck out in the cold. He hurried back to the cable with new resolve, stepped a little closer, still guarding his face, and sawed with all his might.

Suddenly the tension felt different. He could feel the cable getting ready to part. He sawed harder, watching the top of the boom so he'd know to get out of the way the second it moved.

He heard a rifle-shot bang. The hacksaw blew out of his hand. The strands unfurled faster than the eye. Spinning like a gigantic Cuisinart blade, they lopped off the hand he had raised to protect his face and swiftly ground his head and shoulders into a fine, red mist.

The great boom crashed toward the roof, pivoting from the foot of the mast and gathering speed as it fell.

They were sitting face to face, Helen with her knees tucked up to her chin, Taggart holding her within his crossed legs and laughing. "What are you laughing about?" Helen demanded.

"I'm so damned happy, my bones feel happy."

"I never knew a guy who laughed."

"Hey, you know what I'm thinking? You want to sell everything we got, buy a castle in Europe? Make love till—"

She touched his mouth and murmured languidly, "You mean that, don't you? You mean, get out of the business."

Taggart kissed her fingers. "Maybe we should talk when this is over."

"What's that!"

The loud bang sounded like a gunshot. Taggart shoved her toward the furniture. She sprawled backward and screamed. An enormous shadow slashed across the stars and filled the sky. Taggart looked up and knew too late the meaning of the warnings he had ignored—the grinding he had felt and the sight of the derrick leaning where it hadn't been before.

A seventy-foot construction boom was plummeting down on the glass cube. The warnings might have gained him a vital fraction of a second. But his mind screamed empty questions: How had the derrick moved? Why was it falling?

He dragged Helen across the cantilevered room, toward the distant shelter of the hallway in the main building. The boom hit the outer wall first, thundering against the steel header. For an instant it was suspended between the Spire's roof and the outer wall of the glass cube. Then, screeching as welds tore and rivets sheared, the boom buckled and collapsed inward, shattering the ceiling.

Broken glass rained down around them. The collapsing boom plummeted like a spear and smashed the floor. Chairs, couches, and scattered clothing dropped into the night. Taggart and Helen Rizzolo were scrambling a few feet short of the safety of the entrance hall when the heater wires blew with a white flash. And then, like skaters falling through thin ice, they saw the glass floor disappear beneath their feet.

Chapter 21

TAGGART PITCHED FORWARD, pulling Helen with one hand and reaching toward the lighted hall with the other. She tried to jump, but the floor separated from the side of the building and fell away, growing small and glinting as it tumbled on its thousand-foot journey to the street. The hall appeared to rise as they fell. The cold city roared below.

Lengths of electrical cables, ripped from the falling glass, hung from the subfloor. Taggart clutched one and dangled from it as sections of broken glass hurtled past like guillotines, clanging against the side of the building and drifting into the dark.

They caught the hardwood floor with flailing hands. Taggart got his fingers around the doorjamb, rammed his other hand between Helen's legs, and heaved her up onto the floor. He lost his grip and felt himself falling backward, flailing in the dark for the cable. But she was on him in an instant, grabbing his arm with both hands even as his far greater weight started to drag her off.

Kicking the side of the building, he used his other hand to pull himself up to the solid floor beside her. They lay gasping for breath and staring in disbelief at the tangled steel draped over the naked headers of the living room.

"You okay?"

"I don't know."

"Are you cut?"

"I don't know."

Taggart felt her body in the near dark. They were naked, their clothes scattered to the wind. She started.

"Hurt?"

"No," she laughed, half in barely controlled hysterics, half giggling with sheer joy to be alive. "I don't believe it, but something's turning me on again."

Looking over the raw edge as Helen reached for him, he felt the same disbelief that he still had eyes to see and hands to feel. The high-pitched sounds of police and fire sirens rose on the wind. They sank to the cold floor.

"If I know Reggie, he's going to be here any minute."

"Tell him to come back when he finds out who did it."

Wrapped naked in her mink, which she had dropped in the foyer along with her heels, Helen waited in the car while Taggart dealt with the police. Reggie had spirited them down a freight elevator, and their story was that no one was in the apartment when the boom fell. Reggie had found a hacksaw beside a mutilated body on the top deck, which confirmed that the falling boom was no accident. By the simple expedient of removing the hacksaw, he had left the police with nothing more than speculation that an unknown person beheaded during the accident might have tampered with the cable that parted.

As soon as the cops confirmed that no one had been killed on the ground, and his own superintendents had reported to assess and deal with the damage, Taggart asked the senior officer, a one-time protégé of Uncle Eamon's, if he minded if he went home. When the officer said he didn't, Taggart walked to the Rolls and told his chauffeur to head for Canarsie. Reggie followed in a gypsy cab loaded with selected members of one of his street gangs.

"I'm still shaking," said Helen.

"Me, too." Holding her in one arm, he poured a brandy, which they shared.

"Want to hear something weird?" Helen asked.

"What?"

"I had a fabulous time tonight. I mean, I haven't been on a date like this ever."

"Want to go out again?"

"When?"

"Tonight?"

"Jeez, I wish I lived alone. I'd love to take you home and sleep all day with you."

"How about a hotel?"

"It wouldn't be the same. I'll see you tonight?"

"What would you like to do? Go to a fire? See a plane crash?"

"Boring," she said with an uncertain smile. "Maybe we should try something really dangerous. . . . "

"Like what?" He couldn't read her. Suddenly she seemed frightened.

"Like talking about that castle."

Taggart answered very carefully, "As soon as we finish the Cirillos."

Helen held his gaze a moment. "Before you came along, I thought about getting out. I was getting driven out. Now that we're strong, it's my choice, and it's getting harder. Tonight you're making me really happy."

"I'm glad."

"Do you know why?"

"Tell me."

"You're the first guy I ever went to bed with who didn't act like he was stealing something."

"Give me a list. I'll make my brother arrest them."

"They don't stick in my head."

It was a solid answer and banished his small thoughts of Tony and her together. She seemed poised to say more, and he waited in turmoil, fearing her mood would move her to say, Let's get out now. But to his relief—and confused disappointment, for that was what he wanted, but couldn't have—she turned her face instead to the bronzed window. Outside, the city streets were beginning to stir with the earliest joggers, janitors, and coffee-shop cooks, "Can they see in?"

"Nope."

She touched him. "Do you think you could—?"

Taggart reached inside her coat. "I would love to try. . . . "

"Cops," Taggart's driver said in the intercom, as the Rolls turned into Helen's block, and Reggie's car beeped a warning.

Helen pulled away from Taggart and pressed urgently against the glass. Half a dozen police cars were parked in front of her house, their lights revolving red and yellow reflections upon the two-story houses, their radios loud in the first silvery light of dawn. Riflemen patrolled the sidewalk. She spotted a couple of federal cars, too, unmarked but for winking red lights suction-cupped to their roofs. Uniformed officers stopped the Rolls-Royce and motioned for them to lower the windows, but Helen's attention was riveted to an ambulance, which was pulling out of the driveway, with its lights off and its siren quiet as death.

She fled out the door before Taggart could stop her, dodged the cops, and raced toward her house. Plainclothes agents grabbed her at her front walk.

"Hold it, miss."

"That's my house. Let me go!"

"Who are you?"

"I'm Helen Rizzolo. Let me go! What happened?"

Tony Taglione climbed out of an unmarked car.

"What happened?" she cried. "Let me go in."

Taglione put his hand on her shoulder and held her with his dark eyes. "They've killed your brother Frank."

She reeled as if he had hit her in the face.

She knew it couldn't be. It was a mistake—one of the bodyguards instead—and the cops had made a mistake. Then she saw Frank's van in the narrow driveway beside the house. The bulletproof windshield had been starred in a dozen places by armor-piercing shells, the passenger door was open, and dark blood had pooled beside a tire.

I betrayed him, she thought. *I betrayed my brother.*

"Eddie?" she asked, afraid to hear the answer.

"They shot Eddie, too. He's in surgery."

"How bad?"

"I don't know. Your aunts are with your mother."

She turned to the house.

Taglione took her arm. "Helen. Who did it?"

"What?"

"Who killed your brother?"

She went rigid. "You bastard."

"*I* didn't kill him," Tony shot back. "People *you* know killed him. *Who?*"

She observed him through a haze of tears. It was her fault.

She had manipulated Frank and Eddie to trust her; she had won their confidence; she had convinced them to serve her, so she could serve Christopher Taggart. Frank—her quiet and loyal panther—had been killed while she was at the Waldorf, falling in love with the man who had caused his murder.

"Who, Helen?" Taglione repeated harshly.

She turned her grief and confusion on him. "You animal! How could you talk to me like that?"

He lashed back savagely: "Frank's no innocent victim. Neither is Eddie. Neither are you. Your brothers did something to make the killers actually come to your *house*. They could have killed your mother, your relatives. Give me a lead, Helen. What's the war about?"

Taglione's coal-dark eyes mirrored the security lights. It was like looking into the face of a robot. Clearly, Tony Taglione shared his brother's capacity to hate, but not, she realized with aching sadness, Taggart's capacity to love.

She glanced down the street at Taggart, who was standing with the cops. He was straining to come to her. "I don't know," she said.

"It's because Eddie and Frank were expanding, isn't it? Because they were taking over Brooklyn? What ever gave them the idea the Cirillos would let them get away with it?"

"Fuck you!"

"Thank you, Helen. Let's talk again—after more people die."

Who's left? she wondered bleakly as the full horror of what she had done slashed through her mind. *I gave them the idea and they trusted me. . . .*

Taggart had tried to follow her, not caring who saw him, but the cops blocked the way. "Wait here, mister. That's a federal prosecutor talking to her."

"I'm Chris Taggart. He's my brother. I gotta see him."

One of the cops made the connection. "Hiya, Chris. Yeah, you probably don't remember me, but we met at a PAL supper. Okay. Let me just go ask." He approached Tony and Helen and waited close by for an opening. Taggart watched Tony raise a tentative hand to her shoulder, and for a second Helen drifted against him. Then she moved away, her body sagged, and she seemed to disappear within her coat. She suddenly screamed at him, and Tony yelled back. Then they were silent, like two actors caught in the spotlight with no lines to say. The cop caught Tony's attention. Tony glanced toward Taggart and nodded without expression. Taggart ran to her side.

"Helen."

Her face, trembling, and tear-streaked, turned to ice. She turned her back on Taggart and climbed unsteadily up the steps. Her mother opened the door and Helen fell into her arms. Crying, holding each other, the women moved inside. The door thudded shut.

"What did you do to her?"

"I told her some guys killed her brother."

"What?"

"In case you don't remember, Chris, your girlfriend's connected."

Taggart stared at Helen's house. Every window was lighted, as were the windows in the surrounding houses. Security lamps glared down on the vans parked in the driveway, the backyard garage, and the tiny square of front lawn, which had faded to winter straw. The lead van had its windshield shot out.

"Who did it?"

Tony shrugged. "They've been fucking with the Cirillo family. The Cirillos joined up with the Confortis and some other scum and hit their books and numbers all over Brooklyn. It was bound to happen."

Taggart was stunned. The derrick boom had been only part of the attack. The Cirillos had retaliated across the board. Reggie had warned him. He had been too sure of himself. And now Helen blamed him.

"I better go in and help her." Belatedly, he realized that Tony was as cold and angry as he had ever seen him.

"Chris, what in hell are you doing here?"

"Driving Helen home. She was at my table at the Waldorf."

"Alphonse's grandson's date?" Tony asked scornfully.

"You got guys following me?"

Tony reached into his car and held the bulldog edition of the *Daily News* to the streetlight. It was open to a photo on Suzy Knickerbocker's society page that showed Taggart shaking hands with the mayor. To his left were Helen and Alphonse's wide-eyed grandson.

"Her family's in a gang war," Tony said quietly, almost pleadingly. "If you don't care about your reputation—or mine—would you please remember that hanging around with her could get you killed?"

Which meant, Taggart realized with relief, the NYPD had not reported the fallen boom to the Strikeforce; the cops had bought the accident story. Now all he had to worry about was Helen. He said, "I'll take my chances. And the whole point of the beard was to protect your precious rep. . . . May I ask what *you* are doing here?"

Tony gave him a look and said only, "Doing my job."

"You're not a cop, you're a lawyer."

"Shut up, Chris. . . . Here, get in the car. I'm not having a family fight with you on the street." They closed the doors and Tony tore into him. "I can't believe you put that woman at the same table with Uncle Vinnie and Aunt Marie."

"She's a legitimate businesswoman."

"And it's just a coincidence that her bus line, wedding palaces, and nightclubs are cash businesses which just happen to lend themselves to laundering Mafia money? . . . You're forgetting Pop and everything decent he ever taught you."

"Oh, now Pop's decent? But not decent enough for you to work for him—you had to work for the fucking government."

"I didn't say Pop was decent. I said he *taught* us decent things."

"He did more than teach."

"He taught one thing and did another. Chris, I loved him too, but you gotta face that Pop rigged bids in the concrete business. And he paid off the Mafia."

"Shut up! *My father was not a crook.*"

"Neither was Nixon." Tony replied with bitter disgust.

Taggart balled his fist. An agent rapped on the window. Tony turned his face, revealing the angry white scar on his cheek. The sight stopped Taggart cold. He sagged against the door. He couldn't do that again, no matter what his brother said. Tony wound down the window, but his gaze burned hotly on Chris's face, daring him to lash out. "What?"

"Mr. Taglione, it just came over the radio. They got old man Rizzolo, too, in jail."

"Christ!" Tony shouted. "I told them to watch out for him." He banged the seat with his fist. "We could have pumped him like an oil well 'cause they killed his son."

Taggart jumped out of the car.

"Stop him!"

He got as far as Helen's front step. A telephone rang inside just as three marshals tackled him. He fought until Tony caught up. "Let me go in, Bro. Please. She adored him. It'll kill her."

"Go home, Chris."

"What are you going to do to her?"

"I'm hoping that maybe, just maybe, with her brother murdered and her father murdered, she'll be willing to talk about who did it. And why."

"But she doesn't know."

"Chris, I'm working. Get the fuck out of here."

Inside the house, women began to keen, an awful, cutting noise. The sound of Helen's rich, lovely voice rising to a shrill moan went through Taggart like a lance. He covered his ears; it was his fault. Her voice pursued him. She sounded as if her heart were clamped in cold iron. He couldn't abandon her.

"*Tony,* she needs me."

"Go home."

He struggled blindly toward the door. "I gotta help her."

"*Get him out of here!*"

The agents dragged Taggart to his limousine and ordered his driver away. As the car turned around, Taggart watched Tony mount the steps and bang hard on the door.

Book III

Death of a Racketeer
(The Present)

Chapter 22

*I*T LOOKS LIKE a giant broad dropped her stocking," said one of the ironworkers eyeing the wreckage atop the Taggart Spire. Taggart's supers were chewing Tums and debating cleanup techniques with the rigger and engineers. The boom was draped over the outside header. The midsection sagged into the shattered living room; the top dangled over Park Avenue.

Finally Ben, Taggart Construction's senior project manager, voiced the majority opinion. "Getting it down is easy. Getting it down without dropping it, that's the hard part."

"Get it down," Taggart ordered savagely. "Now!"

He had been up most of three nights, running on the ragged edge of sensibility. His face was lined and scruffy, with a yellow stubble. He was wearing jeans and an old Irish sweater, and he reeked of Canadian Club.

"There's a bow in that header."

"Can you straighten it?"

"I wouldn't in my house."

"Pull it."

"Yes, sir."

Seething, he directed the operation while the riggers and ironworkers cut the boom from the mast, repaired the bent bullwheel, and rigged the mast to haul a new boom up from the street. His crews eyed him nervously, thinking it was the damage that had caused his rage—but it was actually the wreckage of his plan that fueled it.

Down in the city, Reggie's people were searching for Don Richard to settle the score. For by now it was clear that Don Richard had persuaded the remnants of the Conforti, Imperiale, and Bono families to join the Cirillos' bloody citywide attack against the upstart Rizzolo clan. So clear, in fact, that Tony Taglione had convinced a grand jury to summon Don Richard to shed light on the affair. But Don Richard had disappeared.

His *consigliere* had been subpoenaed as well. Sal Ponte had turned in his usual skillful portrayal of an aggrieved Italian-American gentleman lawyer, confounding the best of Taglione's efforts to paint him as the mobster he was. No, he had not heard from his client for a week. Hardly unusual, he confided to the jury with a folksy smile; the elderly Mr. Cirillo was becoming a bit eccentric.

Taggart had found the Cirillos no less elusive than his brother had. Yesterday, Taggart had blown up at Reggie, who reminded him of reality. "The last time Don Richard dropped out of sight, no one—but no one—saw his face for five years. He ran Brooklyn from 1965 to 1970 like the invisible man."

"Find him."

"I'm using every means at our disposal. I've got Sicilians searching Sicily, New Yorkers searching New York, black gangs searching East Harlem where he was born, Ghost Shadows tossing Chinatown. Our bookmakers are nosing around Atlantic City, and every retired mobster on my payroll is searching the South. We're probably closer than the FBI, though not by a lot. There are more of them."

"What do you mean, the South? Florida?"

"Florida, South Carolina, the Caribbean. He's an old man, they get cold in winter."

"Ponte."

"Of course. We're watching Sal Ponte."

Taggart forced a plan out of his anger. "Contact Ponte. Remind him that Mikey owes us money. Tell him we understand it's a problem, but we want to be paid. Tell him we're willing to discuss a reasonable settlement."

Reggie sighed. "You haven't forgotten threatening Crazy Mikey about Helen?"

Finally, early in the morning of the third day since the Rizzolo massacre, Reggie's spies had learned that Salvatore Ponte had abruptly canceled all his meetings. Reggie had thrown a team around his Fifth Avenue office, and Taggart was waiting for the results.

Riley came up and said, "Those decorating broads are on the horn. I'm supposed to make changes in the lobby? They want enough juice to run a subway."

"Cancel it. Tell 'em I'll explain when I get the time."

Twenty minutes later, Chryl and Victoria appeared on the roof. They surveyed the damage with experienced eyes and joked with the ironworkers, comparing it to classic accidents they had all lived through on other jobs. Victoria waved. "The winner! Even Trump never had one like this, Chris."

"What do you want?"

"We thought you might be ready for a drink and a nap."

"I'm fine."

"Ben says you've been up here three days. Come, on we're taking a break." She reached under his sweater. "God, you smell. Make that a *bath,* a drink, and a nap."

"I'm busy."

"So are we. We want to move on the club. Come on, the Jacuzzi still works."

He turned on them, his mind boiling. *"We're not doing the club."*

Victoria grinned. "What, did you have a fight already?"

"Don't you read the fucking newspaper?"

"You know damned well we don't have time for newspapers," said Chryl. "When we're old we'll read books about what happened in the papers."

Victoria reached for him again. "Listen, fella, you're getting tired. Now come on."

Taggart whirled on them, the light so violent in his eyes that an ironworker moved to stop him. "Get off my job! Both of you."

Victoria backed away, blinking, and fled to the elevator. Chryl stood her ground, white with rage. Taggart said, "I'm sorry, what did I—?"

"Don't you *ever* treat her like that again." Chryl raced after her. She held Victoria as the elevator descended, stroked her hair, and kissed her tears. "Hey. He's under a ton of pressure. He didn't mean it."

"He never talked to us like that."

"Well . . ." Chryl touched her knuckles gently to Victoria's lips. "He had to find somebody someday. You knew. I knew. We had him on loan."

"It's not that! It's like he's getting scary."

Reggie returned at nightfall. He and Chris retreated from the mechanics who were stringing lights for the second shift and found a windswept perch on the north wall.

"What happened?"

"He got away. He somehow realized our meter maids were bogus and lit out the back door."

"Goddammit. Who fucked up?"

"Rather than allot blame," Reggie counseled, "I would give Don Richard credit."

"I want him dead. Now."

"He's gone to ground again, and I'm afraid that is that."

"How's he going to run things?"

"Don Richard will instruct Ponte. Ponte will pass it on to Mikey. And Mikey will carry through."

"We made Mikey. The bastard was a lousy bone breaker before we made him the biggest dope distributor in New York."

"What we did, just for the record, was reactivate Don Richard."

"I'm going to deactivate him permanently."

"In terms of your army," Reggie answered, "the Rizzolos are effectively destroyed. We haven't the means to attack Don Richard's whole network."

"Then attack the top again. Mobilize every foreign group you've got. Fly 'em in on the air ambulances. We'll attack the Staten Island house. Ponte's place in Alpine. Mikey's apartment in Whitestone. Fucking level them. Then—"

"No."

"What do you mean, no?"

"It's pointless. All the top people have gone to ground. They're not home."

"I don't care. I'm going to destroy—"

"Kill their wives and children?" Reggie looked at him coolly. "You don't want that."

Taggart fell silent. Of course he didn't, he told himself; he was just talking. But he had to do something.

"Get Ponte. Squeeze it out of him."

"At this moment Salvatore Ponte is better protected than the President of the United States. Besides, the Strikeforce is all over him because they know he'll be the go-between."

"Fucking wonderful." He watched the second shift of iron-workers trooping off the elevator and mused gloomily, "How do you suppose Helen would react if I knock off Don Richard?"

"She would sup on his entrails."

"But would she forgive me?"

"Good evening."

"What? Where you going?"

Reggie produced an Air France Concorde ticket from his Burberry pocket. "You suggested recently I take a vacation."

"Not when I need you."

"You need a plan, Chris. I can do nothing while you're besotted with that woman. You've lost sight of your revenge. You don't know what you want."

"I'm not besotted. I just feel I owe her something. Her brother and her father are dead because of me."

"They were racketeers."

"Tell her that. She blames me."

"Nothing happened that you did not initiate."

"None of this would have happened if they hadn't killed my father."

"That's more like it."

"I haven't forgotten."

Reggie rubbed his mustache and gazed out at the city. The winter sun was setting behind the Statue of Liberty, a red circle in a gray sky. "Do you recall the night on the boat Crazy Mikey's bodyguard broke my ribs?"

"I recall you pretending he hadn't until you started coughing blood."

"My first reaction was to hurt him back. But he would have killed me if I had merely caused pain. I had to concentrate fully on the job at hand, which was to immobilize him. Which I did. The same applies to you on a much larger scale. You've simply got to get ahold of yourself, forget revenge for this

attack, and stick to your original goal. You don't really care
what they did to the Rizzolos. It's your father. Either find a
meaningful way to attack the Cirillos or call the whole thing
off."

"What's your vote?"

Reggie gave him a long look.

"What's your vote? Come on, man, give it to me."

"Get out while you can. It's only a matter of time until
either the Mafia or the authorities stumble upon us."

"The authorities? That sounds like a euphemism for my
brother."

"Your brother is positioned to find out."

"I won't stop."

"Then what are you going to do?"

Taggart refused to meet Reggie's cold eye. "We shylocked
Mikey to smoke Don Richard out. I guess I sort of underesti-
mated how the old bastard would react."

"That's putting it mildly."

"Why didn't you stop me?"

"Let me remind you of something," Reggie shot back.
"Their attack on the Rizzolos was originally allowed for in
your plan. In fact, it was part of it. You created a Shadow
Mafia, remember, to attack and absorb attacks. A buffer between you and your chosen enemy. You weren't supposed to
fall in love with its boss."

"Take your vacation," Taggart answered coldly. "I'll figure
this out."

He had been too successful and the Mafia was the stronger
for it. The result of his provoking Don Richard to resume
command was that the powerfully led Cirillos were filling the
vacuum left by Taggart's devastation of the rival Mafia families.

At the same time, Taggart had made Crazy Mikey more
powerful than he would ever have become on his own. For in
the course of luring Crazy Mikey into a now uncollectable
debt, Taggart had created "The Man Who Can," as the black
heroin distributors had dubbed the younger Cirillo. Lost ship-
ments notwithstanding, independent smugglers eagerly sought

out Mikey's buyers, who now controlled more New York distribution than ever before.

Even worse, Taggart thought, was the long-term stability he had unwittingly helped the Cirillos establish. Having become such a money earner—and having his father's own *consigliere* as his ally—gave Crazy Mikey a power base from which he could seize control of the family the instant that old Don Richard died. Thus, even if Taggart managed to find and kill Don Richard, Mikey's immediate, orderly takeover would actually further strengthen the Cirillos.

Taggart concluded that he had only one hope of wreaking final revenge: destroy all three of the ruling triumvirate at once. Destroy Don Richard, Crazy Mikey, and *Consigliere* Ponte in swift and rapid sequence so that their surviving underlings tore themselves apart battling to take control. Tony's Strikeforce would finish the job.

Mikey and Ponte were the most visible targets. While they might be safe from ordinary rivals and law enforcement, Reggie Rand's assassins could eventually gun them down. But attacking Crazy Mikey and *Consigliere* Ponte would still leave Don Richard in firm control of the family. And he might easily live ten more years. It kept coming back to the old man. He had to find Don Richard.

Taggart turned to his law-enforcement contacts. He talked to cops, FBI men, DEA agents, a Strikeforce criminal investigator, and his friend Barney from the President's Commission. No one had the vaguest idea where Don Richard was hiding; even the rumors were halfhearted. Next he met Jack Warner. "Forget it, Mr. Taggart," Warner told him, nervously eyeing the city below the Spire. "The last time he went underground he was gone five years."

"Everyone keeps telling me that, Jack. I expect more from you."

"I wish I knew where he was. I could make my career; *and* a fortune from you at the same time."

"Find out and you can retire."

"I'm trying, Mr. Taggart. But I'll tell you honestly, it ain't gonna happen."

He tried a different tack. Perhaps Crazy Mikey and *Consigliere* Ponte had confided in someone they trusted as to Don

Richard's whereabouts; or maybe someone in their circle had overheard, or guessed. Taggart was prepared to pay any amount for the information. He tried tapping some of Reggie's spies who had access to Mikey and Ponte; three actually spent considerable time with Mikey—a bodyguard, a friend Mikey often had meals with, and a brothel manager who went whoring with him—but none was privy to Don Richard's hiding place. Reggie had been right; only Crazy Mikey and *Consigliere* Ponte knew where Don Richard was.

How could he penetrate the Cirillos at the very top—something neither Reggie nor the Strikeforce had ever managed to do? He considered the possibility of kidnapping Mikey or Ponte to force either to divulge Don Richard's hiding place. But kidnapping was much more difficult than killing. Both men moved in a war-alert entourage. Ponte seemed the more likely target, yet although he was not a fighter like Mikey, the *Consigliere* was rarely alone. Bodyguards drove him between his Alpine, New Jersey, estate and his Fifth Avenue office. He lunched with associates at Cristo's, a short, easily guarded ride to Lexington Avenue. Sundays he drove in convoy to the old neighborhood in Brooklyn to take his mother to church. The rest of the time he was indoors, his handsome tan apparently maintained under a sunlamp.

Frustrated two Sundays in a row at the church, Taggart drove his rented car aimlessly about Brooklyn until he found himself, as if by accident, in Canarsie. He turned down Helen's street, his pulse pounding.

Her house looked bleak. Dark shades and curtains veiled the windows and black ribbons had been tied to the fading Christmas wreath on the door. He sensed his car was being watched, and when he slowed, men stepped from the neighboring houses, each with a hand still in the door as if holding a weapon. A van followed him out of the neighborhood.

He went back an hour later. She was out on the front lawn warming up in a dark jogging suit, surrounded by bodyguards. Several cars were at the curb, engines running. Taggart kept going, a glimpse of her face seared in his mind. She had looked up when he passed; cold wind had whipped her silky black hair. Her eyes were sunken, her mouth sad and weary. He drove to Canarsie Park, walked to the shore, where Reggie had often met Helen. She appeared, running with long, beautiful strides, her breath sharp and white in the cold, her hair glinting in the sun. She was well ahead of her bodyguards and he could easily step into her path and fall in beside her. What could he say? What did he deserve to say? He turned away and hurried to his car.

A third fruitless week passed and suddenly, when he didn't know where to turn, an opportunity to force *Consigliere* Ponte to divulge Don Richard's hiding place came from a totally unexpected source. Uncle Vinnie showed up at the Taggart Spire office carrying a big waxed bakery bag and a thermos. "Thought I'd come over for coffee."

"Coffee" meant talk. Taggart was hardly in the mood, but he could never deny his father's favorite brother-in-law. "Hey, still working," Vinnie said cheerily, but his big, round face was tight and he kept twisting the bakery bag in his fat hands.

"Only way to get rich. How you doing?"

They embraced. Taggart helped him off with his coat.

"Great, great. Really good. . . . I brought some stuff from the bakery."

"What you got there?" Chris cleared his desk top.

Uncle Vinnie laid out Napoleons, cannoli, and plump Italian cheesecake bursting with colored citrons. From his thermos he poured pungent espresso into Styrofoam cups. "I thought since your place got messed up you wouldn't have coffee. How's it going?"

"Know anybody who needs an S-boom?"

"What about the guy they found?"

"Half a guy. Nobody knows."

"I hear sabotage."

"Was he gnawing the cable with his teeth?"

"Lucky nobody else was hurt."

"Middle of the night."

"God's on your shoulder." Uncle Vinnie popped a cannoli in his mouth and made a face. "I hate these places that fill 'em ahead of time. The shell's like macaroni."

Taggart bit into one and sipped the espresso. "So how you doing?"

"Well, I got a problem."

"Sit down."

Uncle Vinnie settled, flicked another pastry into his mouth, and studied Taggart's Chinese carpet. "It's about your brother."

"Oh, shit. Is he coming down on you?"

"No, no, nothing like that. I ain't done nothing."

"That's good, because there I can't help."

"Fix a case with Tony? You'd be in jail aheada me. No, Tony wants me to set up a sting."

"What kind of sting?"

"You know, where you set up a phony company to sucker some wiseguy into doing something."

"Yeah, I know what a sting is. I've helped him with a couple. What's Tony looking for?"

"He was over to supper and he sort of mentioned a sting while your Aunt Marie was in the kitchen. Then he looked at me—you know how he looks at you? Like he knows everything bad you ever done and the stuff you're thinking about doing?"

"He looked at me like that when I was born."

"He expects me to offer to help. Like I'd be a supplier getting hassled by other guys for bidding low. But it means pissing off a lot of people. If it wasn't Tony, I'd say, go fuck yourself. To him I don't know how to say no. Can you talk to him?"

Taggart stared. It was as if God had sent Vinnie, his father's favorite, when he needed help most. For unbeknownst to his uncle, Vinnie had just offered him Sal Ponte on a silver platter.

"Please, you talk to Tony?"

"I can get him off your back so he won't ask again," Taggart answered slowly, his mind racing with thoughts of how best to use this opportunity. If *he* couldn't kidnap Sal Ponte to make him divulge where Don Richard was, why not maneuver Tony's Strikeforce into doing it for him?

"Sure, I can get him off your back, but you know as well as me Tony won't excuse you for not helping."

"Shit, I know," Uncle Vinnie said miserably.

"No, the thing is to get out with respect. Right?"

"Right. But how the hell am I going to do that?"

Taggart took the plastic knife the bakery had supplied and

cut a wedge of cheesecake. Go slow, he told himself. Play this carefully. "Vinnie? You know who Sal Ponte is?"

"The rackets lawyer?"

"Old man Cirillo's *consigliere* is the way I hear it."

"What about him?"

"You ever hear of him messing around in our business?"

"Sure. You know that."

Taggart knew, of course, but he asked, "Doing what?"

Vinnie glanced around Taggart's empty office and lowered his voice. "You know. They got the Teamsters mobbed up from Jersey to Westchester. They took a big piece of my Newark runway job. So I wouldn't have driver trouble, I had to lease their mixers. Most of it went straight into Ponte's pocket."

Westchester fell within the Southern District—Tony's territory. Taggart cut another piece of cheesecake and passed it, balanced on the knife. "What you got going in Westchester?"

"A store in White Plains; a little office building over in Armonk."

"Anything bigger?"

"I'm bidding on a new parking garage at the county airport. What's Ponte got to do with Tony?"

"Tony would love to nail his ass to the wall."

"How's he going to do that?"

"How about extortion? How about bid rigging? How about featherbedding your drivers? How about false billing?"

"Yeah? I don't follow."

"What if I tell Tony you can't do a sting with him because you're already doing one with me?"

"What do you mean, with you?"

"I told you, I help Tony now and then. Couple of years ago I set the FBI up with a phony electrical contractor to get some wise guys in Chelsea. We'll tell Tony you didn't want to mention it without clearing it with me first."

"You think he'd believe you?"

"I'll say I was just getting it started and was going to tell him soon. But first, you and me will bid that airport garage to sucker Ponte into leaning on us. That'll make Tony happy. . . . What's wrong?"

"Hey, I don't need trouble with the Cirillos."

"Don't worry, I'll keep you out of it. Just make sure you bid low enough to get that job."

"You sure Tony'll go for it?"

Taggart wasn't sure, but Uncle Vinnie could make it sound a lot better than if he alone brought the sting to Tony's office. "Listen, just between us? Tony and me had it out a few weeks ago. Really bad stuff about Pop, and other stuff I don't even want to talk about. I've been looking for a way to make it up to him. This is perfect. I'm really grateful you came to me."

Vinnie still looked dubious. "So what happens when I get the bid?"

"Then you have lunch with Mr. Ponte. To pay respects and talk about making it a smooth job. Tony's agents will wire you and record Ponte demanding payoffs."

Vinnie got up, pushing the cakes aside. "No way! You expect me to testify against the *mob?*"

"No, no, not testify. Tony won't go to trial for just extortion against a guy as connected as Ponte. He'll use the evidence to force Ponte to build a bigger case against his bosses. Nobody will even know Ponte's been arrested. The whole idea is the agents arrest him secretly so nobody knows he's turned informant. They do it like a kidnapping."

"Ponte will know he's been arrested and he'll know why."

"I guarantee Ponte won't be in a position to do anything about it. Listen, we'll go partners. Who's the general contractor?"

Vinnie named Eastern Casting, a Westchester outfit.

"I'll buy the job."

"They won't sell the job. They're making out like bandits."

Taggart laughed. He was Chris Taggart of Taggart Construction, back on track and smokin'. "If Eastern won't sell the job, I'll buy *them.*"

After Uncle Vinnie left, he wired a Paris hotel that took Reggie Rand's messages: "Vacation's over."

Chapter 23

TWELVE WEEKS AFTER Don Richard vanished, Reggie Rand summoned Jack Warner to a Connecticut car-pool parking lot near Interstate 84 which offered a clear view in all directions. The spring night air was cool. At the edge of the blacktop was a little marsh, in which peepers were shrilling sharp invitations to mate. The men walked out of the light and patted each other for wires.

It was ten months since the Memorial Day weekend when Taggart had set his revenge in motion by simultaneously tipping the Strikeforce to Nicky Cirillo's crew leader's heroin deal and kidnapping Helen Rizzolo. Reggie imagined that he felt a gathering of forces; one way or another—he worried that he couldn't predict which—Taggart's revenge was about to explode.

"I want to give you something," he told Warner.

Warner chuckled. "You want to give *me* something? I'm supposed to give you the somethings. You give me the money."

The burly detective was the first agent to betray the Southern District in over eighty years, an achievement in which Reggie Rand, who admired that elite institution, took pride in engineering. Money was the key to this savvy product of New York's Lower East Side and the elite Stuyvesant High School. Reggie had already deposited one hundred and eighty thousand dollars in his Swiss bank account, but he had calculated Warner's magic number to be a half million, and he intended to keep him from that figure as long as he needed him. Warner was treacherous, but worth the risk. He knew the New York Mafia so intimately that he was regularly invited in on Strikeforce planning operations and had the confidence—to the extent that any human being could—of the Assistant U.S. Attorney and Strikeforce chief, Tony Taglione.

"Salvatore Ponte has a girlfriend."

Warner stopped laughing. "He does not."

"He's extremely careful about her. Nobody knows, not even Don Richard."

"How the hell did you find out?"

"Are you interested?"

"Fucking-A." This seemingly ordinary piece of information had enormous value because if Ponte sneaked off by himself he could be arrested secretly, without his friends knowing, and persuaded to cooperate. "What's her name?"

"Ask first why I'm telling you."

"You got it if I can give it. What do you want?"

"When and if you use this against Ponte, I want the results immediately, within the hour. Do we understand each other?"

"Do I get paid for those results?"

"Of course."

Warner looked around, scrutinized the highway ramps, the empty shoulders, the few cars still in the lot, each of which he had inspected minutely while waiting for the Brit. A BMW came down the exit ramp and parked beside a Saab. Warner waited until both commuters had left in opposite directions.

"I can see a problem. What if it works? We arrest him secretly when he's shacked up with his girlfriend and we break him down. What if he spills something big? If I tell you and you tell the wrong people, he's going to end up dead. When that happens, Taglione starts screaming, 'Who leaked?'"

"He won't be hurt. You have my word."

"Not good enough. I don't like it."

"Forgive me," Reggie said softly, "but I can't take no this time. It must be yes."

"Sorry, fella."

"So am I," Reggie replied, crouching and drawing his gun from his ankle in a single smooth action. He backed up, sheltering the gun against his side, because a New York cop who had survived eighteen years on the street ought reasonably to be considered a dangerous man.

Warner grinned. "I really don't believe you're going to

shoot. I'm not trying to take a gun away from a guy who has no reason to shoot me."

"Stand still."

"Sorry." Warner grinned again, patiently trying to puzzle out where Reggie was heading. Reggie reached into his pocket and tossed him a small metal container. "Do you recognize that?"

Warner turned it to the parking lot lights. "Sure. Magazine for your little ankle gun."

"Have another look."

Warner tried to remove a slug. "What is this?"

"Tape recorder."

Warner felt the blood rush from his head. *"What?"*

"I carry it in the gun whenever I'm more interested in recording—which I have been doing whenever we've met—than in shooting."

Warner lunged.

"But not tonight," Reggie replied, swiftly stepping back and cocking the slide.

"What the fuck are you doing to me?"

"When you report to me what Ponte has told Tony Taglione, I'll pay you three hundred and fifty thousand dollars."

"Slick, Reggie. Very slick. What are you doing this to me for? I never hurt you."

"I'm making you rich."

"There's a big chance I'll get fucked. To get in on the flip, I'm going to have to push to make the arrest."

"I'll look out for you, Jack. Remember, Mr. Taggart still regards you as a most valuable asset."

Warner ran his hand through his hair and looked at the mud on his handmade shoes. "Okay. What's her name?"

"Mrs. Hugel. She's married and lives in Great Neck. Ponte seems deeply in love with her."

"How in hell did you find this out?"

Reggie smiled. "As my friends in the rag trade say, 'Does Macy's tell Gimbel's?' Now listen. Tell Taglione you can arrest Ponte secretly when they tryst. You might suggest he can use the girlfriend as additional leverage to break him down."

"I think he'll figure that out himself."

"Walk to your car. Don't look back."

Warner started to walk away, but a thought struck him. "Hey, what makes you think that Taglione has something to arrest Ponte for?"

"I can feel it in my bones."

On the drive back to the city Warner concluded that the Brit had made a mistake telling him about the tape recorder. The existence of evidence that he had sold information meant that if Taggart were ever caught, Warner had to immediately offer to testify against Taggart in order to plea bargain his way out of going to jail himself. But, he reflected unhappily, he would still be finished on the Force. He comforted himself with the thought that Taggart was too careful to get nailed. And despite the spot Reggie had put him in, Warner found himself wondering how in hell Taggart's scam fit the weird stuff going down with the mob.

First, Taggart was dating the Rizzolo girl while the Rizzolos were romping over Brooklyn. Then the Cirillos hit the Rizzolos and, all of a sudden, Taggart was interested in Sal Ponte—Crazy Mikey's and old Don Richard's *consigliere*. Why? Suddenly, he remembered that last year, when Taggart had hung him off the building, Taggart had engineered the arrest of Nicky Cirillo. Warner smiled to himself, he was about to spend a long night with his files.

Reggie drove country roads until he was sure that Warner hadn't been followed, then headed down to Auberge Maxime in North Salem. It was late on a weekday night and the customers were finishing dessert. The exceptions were a company of fat men eating duck at a long table—chefs from the other country inns of Westchester, Putnam, and Fairfield counties—and Christopher Taggart, alone in a corner, sipping Bordeaux and reading the menu.

"Wine?"

"Whiskey, please."

A waiter was dispatched.

"How'd you do?"

Reggie covered his face and rubbed his eyes. "Splendidly, I suppose."

"What's wrong?"

He shrugged and thought about his answer. "I hope you

know what you're doing. Warner is naturally treacherous. Now we've threatened him, which makes him dangerous." His scotch arrived. "Cheers."

"Cheers. And cheer up. The next thing, Reg, we gotta get Mikey back on the tit."

"How do you propose to do that?"

"Tell his people we're considering rolling his debt so he can pay it off in new deals."

"Even if they'll listen, we don't have the heroin."

"We've got twenty or thirty keys."

"That's not enough for Mikey."

"More than enough." Taggart smiled. "More than enough. Just get him interested."

"You want to thank me?" Uncle Vinnie asked when Tony Taglione telephoned. "You have dinner with me and your brother."

"I'm really tied up."

"He helped, too. Come on, kid. You owe me. Abatelli's. Ten o'clock. You can work late. You gotta eat anyhow. Then around the corner to sleep."

Taggart sat across from them, warily. Tony—razor-slim to Vinnie's beachball-round—was remote at first, but his dark eyes warmed with affection as he said, "Uncle Vinnie, you really started something with Sal Ponte. I can't go into it, but you opened a whole can of worms."

"Hey, it wasn't just me," Vinnie protested. "It was Chris, too."

"Sure. Both of you. Don't expect to read it in the papers, but you've done a service."

"Anytime," said Taggart.

Helen Rizzolo was doing warm-up stretches in front of the house. Eddie stood by, instructing her bodyguards. "If you fuck up, you'll be guarding my uncle in Westport. No bars, no broads, no movies. Just trees."

"I'd rather do time."

Eddie forced a laugh, as he was forcing bad jokes, working hard to keep up morale, while his soldiers were going nuts waiting for the Cirillos' next surprise. Helen shot him a worried look.

Physically, Eddie still seemed indestructible; the only reminder of three Cirillo bullet holes was a slight limp and an occasional headache. But he seemed lost without Frank, quicker than ever to fly off the handle, and, she feared, even more inclined to take wild chances. Frank in his quiet way had been a calming influence.

Eddie had taken their father's death hard, too, harder than she would have guessed. Suddenly, in his thirties he found himself apparent head of the family—which was young for an Italian man with a strong father. He seemed to resent her, as if angry that they had survived while Frank and their father had not. Worse, he seemed determined to prove that he could stand alone. Her mother had suggested that he was afraid of losing her, too, which had the ring of simple truth; but her mother, of course, did not know how dangerous Eddie could be on his own.

Helen motioned him close. "What are you doing when I'm gone?"

"Digging a hole in the ground."

"Eddie. No dope deals."

"Sure."

"I mean it. I don't want to see any more of these so-called importers coming by the house. All I need is you busted."

"Don't worry about it."

"I do worry. You're all I have left."

She jumped the low hedge and hit the sidewalk running.

Eddie whirled angrily on the bodyguards. "What are you clowns waiting for? She's halfway down the block."

Three Rizzolo soldiers bolted after her. Cars followed.

She ran for miles. At last her stomach stopped churning and her exertions dissipated the adrenaline which had seared through her body like fiery knives. She circled Canarsie Park, slowing to study the canvases of the painters who were taking advantage of the day's uncommon warmth to stalk the shore like long-legged water birds. Down the sea wall one painter worked alone. Heart soaring, she walked toward him, tucked her arms under her breasts, and studied his canvas. It was the same gulls over the same barren islands in Jamaica Bay, but this painter had a gift for light, depicting the sun's angle so precisely as to date its swelling rays forever in early spring.

"You buy this or are you doing it for real?"

Reggie Rand indented a gull with his thumbnail and wiped his thumb on a handkerchief which extended from the sleeve of his neatly ironed smock. They had met this way often, up until the Christmas massacre, but this time he was actually painting. "I took up oils to mend once when I was convalescing. Food for the harried soul."

"Yeah, I know what you mean. I'm learning how to play the violin."

"Face the water when you speak in case they're using a gun-mike."

"Yeah, what if they're out there in a submarine? Listen. What's Taggart doing? Does he know what's happening to us?"

"Mr. Taggart indicated the risks at the beginning."

"We're getting killed."

"Can you hold out a little while longer?"

"How much longer?"

"I can assure you that Mr. Taggart has a plan in motion."

Helen stood silent as long as she could. She hated to ask, but had to. "Reggie?"

He looked at her. "What is it?" he asked, not unkindly.

"Why won't he talk to me himself?"

Reggie picked up his brush. She wished she hadn't asked. He must think she was a fool.

"Between us?"

"If you say so."

"He's embarrassed to face you."

"Embarrassed?"

"He won't until he makes it up. He blames himself. He can't apologize without doing something to set it right."

"So he sends you."

"We *are* in business."

Angry at herself for admitting she cared, embarrassed in front of Reggie, and enraged at Taggart for ducking her, she flared, "So he puts you up front just like me, and you take the heat just like me. While he's clear."

Reggie twirled the brush in gray paint and worked a moment on the western edge of the island, where the waves had molded a shallow beach. "People make a serious error thinking gray is a color between black and white. Gray is gray, my dear. It doesn't want to be black or white. It *likes* being gray, as I like being Mr. Taggart's servant. His youth and exuberance are stimulating. And as I grow older I crave more than the excitement of simply killing for killing's sake." He showed his even teeth. "Though I haven't lost the taste. Are we in understanding?"

"Don't threaten me."

"I'm not. Mr. Taggart has 'complex' feelings for you. That is all that matters to me. Therefore, you and I are not enemies. And you may take what you dubbed my threat as friendly advice never to try to drive a wedge between Mr. Taggart and me."

Helen looked into the flat pools of the Englishman's eyes and saw herself reflected. "Do you have any Italian blood?"

Reggie returned a smile as cold and mirthless as hers.

She burst into motion. Her bodyguards streamed after her, and when she looked back she saw Reggie dabbing thoughtfully with a long brush. Would the Englishman be as surprised as she was at how Christopher Taggart filled her thoughts?

Complex feelings? That was putting her own feelings quite mildly. Her father was gone and Frank was gone—reasons enough to hate Taggart. She had tried, but failed miserably, for she could not forget the earlier events of the night her father and Frank were murdered: Chris's pride at the Waldorf ball; the way she had poured her life out to him in front of Saks; making love like molton gold; and his sure, animal reactions when he nearly killed himself saving her on the Spire. Far from hating him, she felt a guilty longing to take him in her arms and curl up in his, share the blame, and start anew.

Jack Warner discovered that Sal Ponte's girlfriend, Mrs. Hugel, was a very pretty strawberry blonde of forty-five or so. Her husband owned a Volvo dealership, and neither had mob connections. Armed with arrest warrants written by Tony Taglione himself, Warner and a partner followed her for a week. On the eighth day she drove from her Great Neck home to the Boxtree Inn in Purdys, New York, an hour's drive north of the city. She entered the white clapboard inn with a timid flourish, and who should drive up in a rented Caddy and swagger in after her, but handsome Sal Ponte.

"Alone," sang Warner. "The prick's alone."

The agents hunkered down to watch from the Metro North train station across the highway. The afternoon darkened and grew cold. They smoked and talked and imagined the couple making love in the near-empty inn. For Warner she was all the rich women he saw in the department stores, stripped of their fancy clothes and makeup, perspiring freely, gasping their pleasure. His partner's imaginings, relayed in a monotone, were irritating him.

"Think her husband's got something on the side, too?"

"If he does he's an idiot."

"Think she knows Ponte's a hood?"

"No," Warner said firmly. He put away thoughts of the woman in bed and reviewed the Taggart situation, which was equally frustrating. It was as if Taggart had joined the Rizzolo family, but that was impossible; no family took in an outsider at the top level, especially not an old-fashioned clan like the Rizzolos. And why was Taggart on Ponte's case? Could he be looking for old Don Richard?

Warner's partner tried to guess what time she had to be home.

"Six."

"Her kids are in college."

"Seven."

At five, as the northbound traffic thickened, they moved closer, in front of the country grocery. Minutes later the couple came out and got into their cars, Ponte in the rental, Mrs. Hugel in her husband's Volvo. They drove in tandem down Route 684 to the Hutchinson River Parkway, which she took to the Whitestone Bridge and home to Long Island, while Ponte veered onto the Cross County Parkway, tooting his horn and blinking his lights goodbye.

Warner's partner made his move where the Thruway South exit of the Cross County emptied onto a service road in the path of cars attempting to enter the parkway. He tore ahead of Ponte, who had slowed to see if the road was clear, and cut across the Caddy's nose, forcing it into the Howard Johnson's parking lot.

Warner shoved his badge against the windshield.

Ponte took a long moment to hide his relief that they were not hit men. He pulled a red silk handkerchief from his pocket and dabbed his upper lip.

"Warrant?"

"Four of them. One for your office. One for your house. One for you and one for the car. Open the door."

Warner handed him the warrants and shoved behind the wheel. "More over!"

He handcuffed Ponte's wrist to the frame of the passenger seat to emphasize he was in deep trouble, and headed for New York, allowing the *consigliere* time to read the charges. He waited until he turned off the FDR Drive into lower Manhattan before he spoke.

"It's RICO, Sal. You're looking at twenty-plus."

Ponte leaned into the cuff, folded up the warrants, and passed them back coolly.

Warner said, "You want me to call the Strikeforce chief? See if he's willing to talk things over?"

Ponte smiled mirthlessly and shook his head.

"Nobody knows you've been arrested."

Ponte looked away. Warner hammered at him. "I can take you straight to prison. Or we can meet the chief. You don't lose anything talking. . . . Want me to try?"

"Want you to *try?*" Ponte mimicked. "Who do you think you're shitting? I know why you picked me up in the middle of nowhere. Tony Taglione wants to deal."

Jack Warner smiled back. "Mr. Taglione's offering twenty years. You got something worth twenty years?"

Warner parked behind the Metropolitan Correctional Center.

"That's the jail. It's connected to the U.S. Attorney's building and the Federal Courthouse. And there's a little church."

"What are you, a tour guide?"

Warner went on casually, "I like how they're clustered. Always reminds me of a medieval castle. You know? The king's chambers—his court, chapel, and dungeon. All of law and civilization right in one spot. Where the king is, so is God, law, and punishment."

"Fuck you."

"Of course, times change. Goddamned Supreme Court abolished trial by fire. So now the king's only a federal prosecutor. He has to convince a jury to order the judge to chuck you in the dungeon. . . . We got you cold, Sal. Why don't you talk to the king?"

Ponte shrugged. "I'll listen to anybody."

Warner signaled his partner, who cleared a side entrance. The mobster swaggered across the covered walkway into the U.S. Attorney's building, strutted the empty halls, and lounged insolently in the elevator. Upstairs, he cocked an ironic brow at the big "Strikeforce" sign.

One thing, Warner noticed, gave Ponte pause—a bold color photograph of a dozen Secret Service agents guarding the President's limousine. It shimmered with a kind of power that Ponte seemed to understand, though he sneered the next moment at the work-beaten furnishings. "Somebody oughta tell the king he's living like a peasant."

"Tell him yourself."

He led Ponte to a cluttered office ablaze in the fiery light of the setting sun. Papers buried the desk, extra chairs; and deep windowsills. Filing cabinets heaped with briefs and transcripts lined the walls. Evidence boxes overflowed a wire supermarket shopping cart parked behind the door. Snake nests of cables slithered from a row of battered telephones.

Tony Taglione sat behind his desk in a white shirt and navy tie. His sleeves were rolled up his slim forearms and his tie was loose at the neck. He stared at the mob lawyer like an angry priest, sickened and unforgiving.

"Taps on your secret phone line," Taglione said, handing Ponte a bound transcript. "The one in the office down the hall."

Ponte tried to meet his forbidding gaze, failed, and looked down at the transcript.

"We overheard the number on this bug we installed in Cristo's where you ate steaks with contractors you were ripping off."

Taglione watched him skim the phone taps. When Ponte

turned to the bug transcriptions, he said, "Your busboy was moonlighting," and turned on his cassette player, a big silvery ghetto blaster with a sharp treble tone. The mobster's voice filled the room, loud and clear against a background of silver clinking and an oceanlike murmur of conversations at other tables. Ponte stared at the player. Taglione stoped the tape in mid-sentence. "You were in good voice, Sal. The jury won't even need headsets."

"That's bullshit. That guy won't testify against me."

"He doesn't have to. In fact, we're not even going to ask him. But the busboy will." Taglione allowed himself a chilly smile. "Profitable investigation, Sal. Extortion led us to narcotics. You did a lot of business at the same table. Richie Cirillo's in the clear on this one, but *you* are fucked."

"You can't use this crap in court."

"Title Three warrants, Sal. Approved in Washington by the Attorney General himself. Scrupulously minimized—when you called your little girl about her sweet sixteen party, the agent turned his tap off. When your godson Mikey Cirillo telephoned about the heroin that gets pushed in the Bed-Stuy schools, the agent turned it back on. One hundred percent admissible evidence."

"My lawyers—"

"RICO, Sal—Racketeer Influenced Corrupt Organizations. It's like your confirmation name."

"My lawyers—"

"It's a federal crime to organize to commit crime. Every *consigliere* in town knows that's how we got the council. You and little Richie are the last."

"My lawyers—"

"Your lawyers are going to advise plea bargaining. I'm advising you to bargain now."

"You think you can send me to jail?" Ponte blustered. "Go ahead, send me to jail."

"That's easy. But I have a better idea. I've persuaded the U.S. Attorney to let me offer immunity—"

"You can shove your Witness Protection Program up your ass."

"I don't want your testimony."

"No?" Ponte asked warily, eyes darting toward Warner, who

stared back blankly. "What do you mean, you don't want me to testify?"

"I want an informant."

"Informer? You're nuts. I've been on the other side too long to turn on my people. I'll do the time."

"Twenty years for the Cirillos? They're not your blood. You're going to tell your wife and children that *twenty* years is okay?"

"I'd rather my kids know I'm a standup guy."

"Jack, see if Mr. Koestler and Ms. Gallagher are working late. I want some attorneys to witness our conversation with this gentleman."

"Here it comes," said Ponte, when Warner closed the door and they were alone.

"Here what comes?"

"The third choice. If I don't talk, you tell people I talked, anyway. So they kill me."

"Not in this office."

"Tell me another."

"We don't do business that way, Sal. We nail you fair and square in court."

Taglione studied Ponte. He *was* a standup guy. But he was also a fifty-one-year-old man who had fallen happily and un-expectedly in love, which made the woman the key to flipping him because suddenly he had more to lose than he had ever had in his life. It was a rare lapse by such a criminal, one to be exploited to the hilt. And Ponte knew damned well that Jack Warner hadn't caught him at the Thruway interchange by accident.

"For a man your age, prison is tantamount to life. Even if you gain parole, you'll be in your sixties."

Ponte pulled a face, but he was suffering. "What do you do this shit for? You get kicks locking up people you think are crooks?"

Taglione answered civilly to make it easier for Ponte to surrender. "If you believe in public service, which I do, you naturally believe people have a right to order in their lives. You guys take away that right."

"Come on. You want criminals, arrest Wall Street."

Taglione shrugged, though it was getting harder to play the

part of an understanding and respectful opponent. "Democracy's too fragile to survive guys like you."

"We protect democracy," Ponte retorted, rising to an avid defense. "We're like revolutionaries. We protect poor people, protect them from the rich people's rules. You call them crimes, but smuggling's been an American necessity since the Revolution. Jack Kennedy's father was a bootlegger, you know. Union organizing? Where would labor be without our muscle? You got a problem with shylocking? Tell it to the banks, who won't talk to the little guy."

"*Robin Hood bullshit!* You prey on the weak. You play by your own rules. And then you steal the game. When your victim protests, you murder him."

"Hey, if we weren't needed, we wouldn't be in business."

"You're in business, as you put it, by force."

"We provide services people want."

Taglione felt his blood rising. "Stop dicking with me. The mob says: '*We're* here! And *you're* there! *We* take what *we* want.' You're the enemy, Sal, a second, brutal society engulfing the first. Maybe I hate you for it, maybe I don't, but I'm sure as hell not going to let you get away with it."

"*Maybe?*" Ponte sneered. "Maybe? Everybody knows you hate us, Taglione. The prosecutor's so fucking high and mighty till it gets personal. Then you want revenge. What could be more Sicilian?"

"If I wanted revenge I'd do what you thought before." He closed the affidavits in his fist. "I'd use murder, extortion, dope as my excuse to tell the street you squealed. Let your friends take care of you."

"So what's stopping you?"

"We're not all greaseball hoods, Sal, no matter what you've made people think."

Ponte turned very cold. "There's an expression I haven't heard in a long time."

"My pop used it for wise guys like you. Behind that fancy so-called law office you're a greaseball hood."

"Your old man got his ass kicked, so you're going to get back at the whole Mafia?"

Tony Taglione heard the blood start roaring in his head. He pressed his long, tapered fingers to his ears and walked to the window and stared at his reflection. The sun was down, the window glass nearly black. Ponte started to get out of the chair. "Sit down!"

"I don't understand you," said Ponte. "Why can't you just accept things like your brother?"

"Careful, Sal."

"Chris Taggart lets bygones be bygones. He moves ahead. He takes responsibility for his family's business. There's a son your father would have been proud of."

Taglione jammed his hands in his pockets before Ponte could see them shaking. "Have you ever seen a man hurt so bad he cried?"

Ponte shrugged. "I'm a lawyer. I don't know about that shit."

"There was nothing left of him but the pain to cry. You say you don't know? Let me tell you, Robin Hood, the tears make streaks through the blood, but the sound is worse. . . . My pop finally got the guts to tell some hood to go fuck himself. So some guy like you in your goddamned Fifth Avenue office gave the order and hurt him so bad he died crying."

"Didn't they make a movie about that?"

"Jack, get in here! Let's get this creep down to arraignment." As Warner returned, Tony locked eyes with Ponte, forced him to look at the floor. Then he went back to the window and stared at the blocks of light the cleaning ladies had scattered around the Wall Street towers. He had blown it and lost his famous temper by letting Ponte get to him.

Ponte looked up when the door opened again and a young woman entered. "Put away your steno pad, sweetheart. I got nothing to say."

Taglione gave her a stiff nod of gratitude and she lighted like a candle. "Ms. Gallagher's not a stenographer, Sal. She's a prosecutor. In fact, she was on the team that prosecuted Pauly Conforti. Now she's bugging me to let her try *your* case if we can't come to an agreement which meets the approval of the United States Attorney. Ms. Gallagher, Salvatore Ponte, or to his intimates, 'Sally Smarts.'"

Sarah extended her hand, allowed Ponte to run appreciative eyes over her white-blonde hair, and asked, "What's it going to be, Counselor? Twenty years in prison? Or a little public service, undercover?"

"Pauly's gonna appeal."

"Not out on bail he isn't." Sarah smiled. "And I don't lose appeals."

Taglione nodded to her to join him at the window. Ponte looked a little shaken by the "cookie-cutter blitz," the threat that the Southern District could field endless ranks of assistant United States attorneys, elite, mean, and infuriatingly young. Having just made an ass of the Strikeforce chief by goading Taglione into losing his temper, he found himself confronted by a twenty-eight-year-old woman anxious to dedicate long hours to putting him behind bars.

"You're doing all right," Tony told her. "Where's Ron?"

"His wife's having a baby."

"Fuck. I really need him. What are you doing now?"

"I have to write warrants for the FBI bust."

"They can wait. Come on. Let's hit this turkey again."

"Do you want me to be nice?"

"Not yet." He whirled around and leveled the full force of his penetrating gaze at Ponte. "Who's your girlfriend, Sal?"

Ponte looked alarmed. "Her husband's a Volvo dealer. Take my word, they're straight."

"Your word?" Taglione picked up the affidavits. "Sal, I look at murder, I look at dope, I look at extortion. And I find it very hard to accept your honorable word."

"I'm telling you the truth. She—"

"You've lied and cheated your whole fucking life, you ass-hole. You want to finish it in jail or you want things moving almost as good as before we nailed you?"

"What do you mean?"

Taglione drew up a chair and sat down to face him. Perspiration dotted the mobster's tan skin. "In exchange for immunity from prosecution on these charges—and only these—I want regular reports on Cirillo operations."

"I can't turn in my friends."

"You better believe when I find Old Man Richie, he'll turn *you* in."

"Don Richard has been my friend for—"

"He'd do it to save his kid. . . . The line forms outside that door. We're busting left and right. Tonight's your last chance. That's it, Sal. After tonight, you're on your own."

He nodded to Sarah. She leaned close, stroking aside the hair that fell across her cheek, and whispered, as if all three were conspiring, which, of course, they were, "The Cirillos are a big family, Mr. Ponte. And they're not all your friends."

Craft and greed warred with the fear in Ponte's eyes. Suddenly Taglione gave Ponte what his assistants had dubbed "the Smile." Wry and fleeting, it hinted that there but for the grace of God go I, that maybe next time the luck of the draw would find the *consigliere* the prosecutor and Taglione his prisoner. He didn't believe it for a second, but it was very effective with lowlifes who liked to think they were really decent fellows underneath it all.

"Sarah's right. You can save your own life."

Ponte looked from him to Sarah and back. Taglione held his breath. The noises that made silence in an office, the whisper of forced air, the buzz of the fluorescent lighting, the hum of traffic beyond thick glass, gathered deeply. Taglione listened to his heart, watched the blood pulse through a blue vein in Sarah's temple, watched Ponte's lips grow tighter and tighter. He glanced longingly at the door.

"You're going to get me knocked off."

"No way. We're going to be very, very careful. You're worth too much alive. Jack will set up a safe house."

Ponte still hesitated.

Taglione said, "You just may get out of this mess relatively intact, Sal. You're young enough to retire, start something straight, and maybe make a new life for yourself. We won't stand in your way if you serve us." He reached into his desk and flashed a Polaroid shot Jack Warner had pulled down with a telephoto lens.

"I'll bet *she* thinks you're straight already."

Ponte nodded.

Taglione handed him the immunity agreement. "Contingent upon the United States Attorney's approval."

Ponte gave him a sour smile. "Pretty sure of yourself. Had it ready to go."

"Let's just say I was sure you weren't stupid."

Ponte opened a gold pen and signed. Taglione witnessed his signature, as did Sarah.

Taglione said, "You have my word. You play fair with me, I'll play fair with you. But if you ever go back on our agreement, you're finished." He stuck out his hand to seal the bargain.

"Fuck you. I'm not shaking your hand." He threw his pen at Taglione's brimming waste paper basket. Taglione watched it land on top, nestled on scrap. It looked to be solid gold and surely cost more than any single item in his office.

"You think it's all over when you get us?" Ponte shouted. "You think you win?"

"We are winning, Sal. We're going to beat you. We're going to break the rackets."

"You win shit." Ponte laughed savagely. "You're digging holes in sand. Guys'll fill our place."

"Not guys with thirty years' experience, *Consigliere* Ponte. Not pros like you."

"Maybe guys worse." He lunged blindly toward the door, and Warner followed.

"Sal? Before you go?"

"What now?"

"Where's Don Richard?"

Jack Warner made sure Sal Ponte returned his rental car without incident. Then, as they waited for a cab on East Forty-eighth Street so Ponte could return to his office, his bodyguards, and his real life, Warner said, "Sal, if you ever blow my cover I'll put it on the street about tonight."

"Fuck you. I made my deal with Taglione. You have to protect me."

"You made your deal with a lawyer. I'm a cop. You never saw me in your life." Smiling, he took Ponte's hand—one businessman bidding another good night—and ground the *consigliere's* rings until he winced.

A gyspy cab approached. Ponte hailed it, but Warner stopped him and put him in a yellow cab instead. Then he started walking toward Second Avenue. When Ponte's cab had rounded the corner the gypsy caught up and Warner got in.

Reggie Rand was at the wheel, wearing a cap and doper

glasses so dark that Warner wondered how he saw in the night. "What did he say?"

Warner sighed. He hadn't intended to report so soon to Reggie, hoping the FBI would find Don Richard quickly. But when Reggie stopped for a red light, removed his glasses, and turned his empty eyes on him, Warner could not risk lying. "Little Richie's in Miami."

"Anything else?"

"Anything else? It's the biggest secret in town."

Reggie shrugged and returned his attention to the traffic. "I'm interested in whatever Ponte reports next."

He was so casual that Warner got alarmed. "You gonna pay me?"

Reggie glanced in the rearview mirror. "Of course, Jack. We always pay you. Where can I drop you?"

"Foley Square."

Reggie let him off a hundred yards from the U.S. Attorney's building and drove blithely into the night. Warner went upstairs, more puzzled than ever about Christopher Taggart's dance with the Mafia. He had assumed that they were going to hit Don Richard and worried that he might get burned in the resultant heat. Reggie might be jerking him around, but he had seemed genuinely unimpressed by the news of the Cirillo boss's whereabouts. Tony Taglione was still at his desk, though it was nearly nine o'clock.

"Home free?"

"Ponte's fine."

"Good. Jack, sit down a minute. Stick that on the floor."

Warner removed the pile of papers and sat down warily. Tony Taglione never asked you to sit down before he got to the point.

"I have a problem. I think you can help."

Had he screwed up? Had the Brit turned on him? Taglione clasped his hands together and eyed Warner over his fingertips.

"I want to know something."

"Yeah?"

"Who my brother Chris hangs out with."

Warner had to stifle a smile of relief. Taglione's *brother*— the freelance racketeer—and he thought the Strikeforce chief was on to him. He said, "I'm not sure I know what you mean."

"Just what I said. But I want it done quietly."

"Any idea what I'm looking for?"

Taglione sighed, clearly upset. "I don't know. The Rizzolos, maybe. You know about his thing with Eddie the Cop's sister?"

Warner nodded carefully. "I hear the rumors."

"Rumors! Try the newspaper."

"I thought that had cooled down."

"I'm hoping so, but I want to know about her and whoever else he's involved with."

Warner hesitated, trying to figure how best to work what could be a very nice opportunity. He said, "Okay if I talk out of turn?"

"What?"

"Listen, Mr. Taglione. It's tough having your brother date a Mafia girl, but when you get down to it, so what? There's no law against fucking a good-looking broad whose brother happens to be a hood."

Taglione flushed.

"Or are we talking about something more than dating?"

"I don't know. I just don't like what I'm feeling."

"Can you—?"

"No! Just find out who he hangs out with."

Warner stood up. "Okay."

Taglione forced a smile. "Hey, you did a good job with Ponte. Thanks, Jack."

"You want I should get down to Miami?"

"No. The FBI's put Don Richard on the ten most wanted list. They'll find him. You just check out what I told you."

Taglione returned to his work, dismissing him. Warner put the papers on the chair and backed out. The funny thing was that he was already checking out Taggart on his own. He walked into Chinatown to a pay phone, called Reggie Rand's answering machine, and waited a few minutes for a return call.

"This is worth fifty grand."

"I'll be the judge of that."

"The boss asked me for postage on his brother's pals."

He listened to a short silence. Then Reggie said, "Your money will be deposited tomorrow."

"What should I do?"

"Stall him. We need a little more time."

Reggie hung up and turned to Taggart, who was avidly studying a silenced pistol. "That was Jack Warner. Your brother is getting curious about your friends."

"He'll waste six months on Helen. I was right to go public with her."

Reggie thought that was overly optimistic. "Perhaps, but—"

Taggart cut him off with a gesture. He was deeply absorbed in the weapon; the silencer screwed on and off the barrel like the finest machine tool, and the bullet-packed magazine was as heavy as a surf-casting weight. "Guaranteed they use this gun, right?"

He extended it to Reggie, who put it in a briefcase where it nested in a green velvet cradle. "Guaranteed."

"How do I know for sure?" Taggart demanded.

"Hit men never lie."

Don Richard Cirillo was sunning in a sand chair on an empty stretch of private beach situated slightly north of Miami. The house behind him was owned by a guy nobody knew. The ocean sparkled in ribbons of pale green and robin's-egg blue. Beside him sat Frankie DeLuca. Their acquaintance went back fifty years to Don Richard's apprenticeship breaking welshers' fingers at the Glen Island Casino.

The warm wind drove a brightly colored beach ball toward them. Some distance behind the ball came a girl chasing it. Don Richard saw she was pretty and was wearing a tiny bathing suit. He tried to stop the ball, but it skipped on a footprint in the sand, took flight for a short hop over his sandal, and rolled on, blurring red, white, and blue like a barber pole. The girl glanced over her shoulder. Way down the beach a child was toddling after her. It was too far away for him to hear if the child was crying, but Don Richard presumed it was.

"A grand on the ball."

Frankie DeLuca looked up from the racing form. He rubbed

his rheumy eyes, adjusted his sunglasses, and eyed the ball, which had rolled well past them. Then he gauged the girl, who broke into a determined run.

"You're covered," Frankie said, betting that the girl would catch the ball.

He had failed to notice the child, as Don Richard had assumed he would, because Frankie was closer to the umbrella they'd set up against the wind and it blocked his view; besides, his eyes were going bad.

The girl looked back at the kid and ran even harder, pumping her firm legs in the sand, shaking her breasts. Frankie gestured toward the water, where a catamaran with an orange sail was skimming onto the beach.

"Run on the hard sand! On the hard sand! By the waves! . . . What does she think, she's a mudder?"

She looked over her shoulder again, stopped abruptly, and jogged back to collect her baby. The ball rolled on, a bright dot receding in the distance where a cluster of high-rise condos gleamed like crumpled tinfoil.

Frankie smacked his forehead with his palm and picked up his paper. "That's why they use jockeys."

"You owe me a grand."

"Can you wait till lunch?"

Don Richard noticed his bodyguards, local boys who were edging nearer as the catamaran skidded onto the beach. The orange sail flapped in the stiff wind, crackling like pistol shots. Four guys jumped off—two rough-looking blacks with twists of dreadlocks swinging from their brows, and two whites carrying towels. The blacks were handling the boat. They looked like natives who had sailed straight from Jamaica. They quickly dragged the front of the catamaran around, heaved the twin hulls back into the low surf, and made the sail stop flapping. The whites trotted toward Don Richard, but his bodyguards intercepted them, twenty feet away.

"What's that?" asked Frankie, looking up again at a pair of muffled sounds, like somebody spitting. The noise was fainter than that of the sail, but the bodyguards dropped on the sand.

The tourists stepped over them and crouched in front of the old men. They had pistols with long, fat silencers under the towels.

"Mr. Cirillo?"

Don Richard jerked a thumb at his old friend Frankie. "Him."

Chapter 24

CHRISTOPHER TAGGART STOOD with his back to the door of a dark LaGuardia Airport hotel room. The wood vibrated against his spine as jets rumbled over. A thin, fuzzy gray line marked where the curtains touched, and a red dot glowed on the cigarette the coked-up gunman was smoking. Neither could see the other's face, and for double his usual fee, Don Richard's killer was describing the job. He was a New Zealander who traveled the world as foredeckman on a maxi ocean-racing yacht; his accent was mild, as if Reggie's crisp English had been slightly diluted by Ronnie Wald's Southern California accent. Swiftly he reported sailing into the beach and shooting the bodyguards.

"Down they go like stones, and we're over them and up to the old geezers in their chairs. I say 'Mr. Cirillo?' like I'm paging him for a phone call in the next coconut tree, and do you know what he does? He tells me his friend is him.

"Shit. Two old geezers side by side, no hair, no teeth, chests like spars with ribs, hair in their noses, how the fuck am I to sort them out? Strike me lucky, 'cause when the Pommy gave me the job, he slipped me Cirillo's picture. So I whip out the picture and, sure thing, Cirillo's sending his mate down the river. His mate looks like he's going to cry; really fixed him, doing him in to save his own neck.

"What else do you want to know? Right. I say, 'This is for Mike and Helen.' Just like the Pommy told me. . . . His mate's just sitting there and sort of smiles when it's over, like he won a race by living longer. I look at him and I know for sure that when the cops come, this old geezer will swear he was fast asleep. So I say ta-ta and he says ta-ta. I give him a little salute and we back down the beach, board the boat, and breeze out."

"Did Cirillo know what you meant?"

"He knew he was going to die."

"But did he know *why?*"

"Do you mean, 'Say, who are Mike and Helen?' Mate, if he didn't know then, he's got eight billion years in heaven to think it over."

"Heaven?"

The killer laughed. "Bastards like him phone ahead. They'll comp him right through the Pearly Gates."

Taggart walked through a long hall, down the stairs, and into the elevator. The deed was almost done, nearly eleven years since they had killed his father. Sometimes in the night he had wondered whether the long years' wait for vengeance might blunt his satisfaction; it had not.

Two uniformed state troopers intercepted him in the lobby. "We were about to come looking for you, Mr. Taggart. The governor's plane just landed. He wants to ride in your car."

"We're running late. I'll need an escort."

"Lights and sirens?" The trooper grinned, knowing what a cop buff Taggart was, and reached to slap him on the back. But Taggart was already striding toward the door, and his cold look told the young trooper that the governor's friend would not welcome being touched today.

They hurried from the hotel across the highway and into a side entrance to the airport. Taggart's driver maneuvered the Rolls onto the private docking apron as Costanza's New York State Gulfstream trundled in from the runway. The governor bounded athletically down the ramp and climbed in beside him.

"Welcome home," Taggart greeted him, waving a split of Moët that he was struggling to open with shaking hands.

"What's the occasion?"

"Pulled off a big one."

He tore the wire, but he couldn't get his fingers around the cork.

"Let me," said Costanza.

Taggart stabbed the partition button and thrust it at the driver. "Open this. Don't shake it up."

The driver fumbled.

"Hold the cork and twist the bottle, for crissake!"

The cork popped out at last and Taggart snatched the foaming bottle. He filled two glasses, handed one to Costanza, who was eyeing him curiously.

"Let's drink to my pop."

"Anytime." The governor raised his glass and touched Taggart's. "Mike Taglione."

"Mike Taglione."

Taggart drank deep. The car lurched into motion, and they raced out the airport, bracketed by howling state cruisers. The governor settled back. "Oh, that's delicious. What did you do this time, co-op Gracie Mansion?"

"Don't tempt me. The first sporting event in the Super-Spire Stadium, if I have my way, will be a fundraiser for Friends of the Zoo—throw that bald son of a bitch to a lion. So how we doing?"

They discussed the stadium project on the way into Manhattan. The governor was returning from Washington, where he'd had some luck with the DOT about the subway spur, but the reality, he reminded Chris, was that the mayor was still lukewarm. When Taggart dropped the governor at the World Trade Center, Costanza repeated what he had been saying for some time: "You're golden if you get the mayor's support. Without him we're in a nasty fight. I'll back you like I promised, Chris. And I'll lean on the UDC, but you know damned well I don't carry the weight in Manhattan that he does."

"I'm going to get him, one of these days, for jerking me around."

Costanza gave him a hard look. "You seem to be forgetting that politics isn't war, Chris. You don't win by destroying a guy you'll want on your side next time. Ease up. . . . Say hello to your brother."

Taggart ordered his driver to head back to Queens.

At Visions, Helen's club, the bartenders were setting up and vacuum cleaners were whining on the carpets. He pushed through the front door, wrote a note, and told three tough Sicilians guarding the hall to her office to deliver it.

Helen was at her desk, icily beautiful in a white silk blouse and black velvet suit. She seemed older, he thought, tempered, and dark with knowledge. She had changed her red nail polish to pink, and her lipstick, too, was paler. She was wearing large diamond stud earrings. Reggie's people had kept a close eye on her and there was no word that she had been going out, but he wondered with a stab of jealousy if the jewels were a gift.

She touched his note with her long fingernails. "Good news?"

"You know it was Don Richard who attacked your family."

"I know that," she said coldly. "And I know why."

"He's dead."

"When?"

"Today. In Florida. Shot. The papers will have it soon."

She studied his triumphant expression before saying, "My father would have been pleased."

"How about you?"

"Part of me cheers and says the old men are canceling each other out. The other part asks what difference any of it makes."

"I'm bringing the news to the part that cheers."

"And how do you feel?"

"What do you mean?"

"Didn't you blame him for killing your father, too?"

"I told you I didn't."

"I never believed that."

Taggart nodded; of course, he hadn't fooled her. "It's good news for me, too. Very, very good news. A big debt's been paid."

"And now what?"

"I've paid you a debt, too. Crazy Mikey's next."

"And then?"

Taggart wanted to say, *We're getting out,* but this was not the moment. There was still Crazy Mikey. He said only, "We'll talk about castles after Mikey."

"Castles?" Helen picked up a pencil and drew *A*'s into stars across the top of a letter. "In the meantime, we've lost territory and momentum. Eddie and I are holding on by our fingernails."

"I'm aware of that."

"You are? Has anyone taken your buildings? Has anyone

firebombed your plant, your trucks?" She drew the stars harder, gouging lines in the paper. Suddenly she turned the letter toward Taggart. "See this?"

Taggart's pulse quickened.

The Justice Department seal. And under the text, the razor strokes of his brother's signature. "It's a 'request' to come in for a little talk."

"He can't make you. Your lawyer can take care of it."

"I already went."

"What for?"

"Curiosity. Besides, as my father used to say, 'There's answers in questions.'"

"What is Tony investigating?"

Helen gave him a strange smile. "Everything . . . and nothing."

"What did he ask about?"

"He didn't ask. He told me to keep my 'filthy' hands off you."

"Tony called you into his office just to say that?"

She raised her eyes and gave him a shy smile. "You know what? I hate to say this. I feel like a fool, but I missed you these three months."

"Three months, two weeks, and one day. I couldn't call until I gave you Don Richard."

She nodded. "I think that's one of the things I like about you. . . . How are your women?"

"I haven't seen them except for business."

She stood up, rounded her desk, circled her arms around Taggart's neck, and kissed him. "I'm glad. Thank you for coming back."

"What did you tell Tony?"

"I told him he was abusing his office. I told him he was taking advantage of his power. I told him I ought to sue the government."

"You don't know how hard it was for him to do it."

"I do. He couldn't hide how much he cares for you. For a second I thought he would kill me right there at his desk."

"He's only trying to save me from myself."

"It's way too late."

She said it with a smile, and kissed his mouth again, and

even allowed him to carry her urgently to the couch for a sort of primitive victory feast. But inside she felt chilled by the matter-of-fact way he had reported the murder, and frightened by the icy look that turned his blue eyes gray when he promised Mikey was next. The Cirillos were her mortal enemies, yes, deserving to die if anyone did; but Chris seemed unable to see that the time was hurtling near when it would be too late to pretend he was different from them. And too late to pretend that their game of castles was more than a fantasy.

What did she care? she asked herself. And her answer, ironically, was that she had fallen in love—a dangerous state of the heart and mind that revealed beauty in places she had never seen it, and horrors that her father had raised her to ignore.

Sal Ponte was driving to meet Mrs. Hugel when he heard the news on the radio. He turned around and got on the Hutchinson Parkway south over the bridge to Long Island. Crazy Mikey's bodyguards had apartments around his in the townhouse condo. When Ponte arrived, two of them were watching Mikey's front door and three more waited in a car.

Mikey was drinking coffee alone at the kitchen table. It was a modern kitchen with a breakfast nook, all clean and shiny. There was a red-checked oilcloth on the table. The windows overlooked the broad, blue East River and the points spanned by the silvery Whitestone Bridge. Mikey had on a V-neck cashmere pullover, his gold chain and spoon, and tight shorts. Ponte smelled perfume, but the girl was gone.

"I got bad news, kid."

"I just heard. Sit down."

"Who told you?"

"The fucking radio. Sit down, Sal."

Ponte sank to the kitchen chair. "You got any more coffee?"

"*I* knew where he was. And *you* knew where he was. I didn't tell anybody. That leaves you."

"Wait a minute."

"Wha'd they give you?"

"Who?"

He saw the coffee mug coming, clenched in Mikey's hand, but couldn't move fast enough. It shattered against his forehead. Hot coffee burned his eyes. The force of it knocked him off the chair and he hit his head against the refrigerator as he went down. Mikey snatched the coffeepot off the stove and held the spout over his face. "What did the Rizzolos give you to tell 'em where my father was?"

"I didn't tell the Rizzolos!"

He said it with such utter conviction—after all, it was the truth—that Mikey hesitated long enough for Ponte to talk. "I didn't tell the Rizzolos. What the hell would I tell 'em for? You think I'm going to leave you and your father for a bunch of South Brooklyn *cafone?* What am I, crazy?"

Mikey didn't move. "Somebody told 'em."

Ponte had prepared an answer in his car. It was thin but he reasoned that if he himself didn't know that he had betrayed Don Richard to the Strikeforce and that someone on the Strikeforce blew it, he would have made a similar guess. "Probably somebody spotted him. Lousy luck."

Mikey shook his head. "I can't believe that. I can't do business believing in lousy luck. You know what I think? Maybe you didn't tell the Rizzolos."

"I didn't."

"So who *did* you tell?"

Ponte died inside. Mikey tipped the coffeepot and half a cup splashed in his face. Ponte yelled and covered his face. His heart started going in his chest like he was going to blow up.

"Sal. I'm not as dumb as you think. Who'd you tell where my father was?"

Ponte knew his only chance was to keep clearly stating his case. "Will you do me one thing for all the years I served your old man?"

"What?"

"Will you listen why?"

It was tantamount to an admission of betrayal and Mikey went rigid.

"Get up!"

Mikey wiped the shards of broken mug off the table and found a new one in the cabinet. He filled it for Ponte, topped off his own cup, and put the pot back on the stove. "Why?"

"For you."

"For me." Mikey looked out the window, looked back at Ponte. "You killed my father for me? I didn't like the bastard, but you know goddamned well I didn't hate him enough to kill him."

"I also did it for him."

"Don't jerk me around."

"I didn't tell the Rizzolos. I told Tony Taglione."

"Taglione?"

"He had me by the balls. I had to give him something."

"What do you mean you had to give him something?" Mikey screamed. "What do you mean *'something'*? Guys take their lumps. Since when is it okay to squeal?"

"I did it for a lot of reasons, not just for myself."

"You better name a few good ones fast."

"First of all, to guide you when you take over. I'm no good to you in jail. We've got eight hundred soldiers, Mikey. We'd be in the Fortune Five Hundred if they counted people like us. Half your *capos* think they should have the job. The older guys who've been around, they think you're a kid."

"I wouldn't have to take over if my father wasn't dead."

"I didn't mean for him to get killed. I did it to save his life. The Rizzolos would have hit your father sooner or later. How was I to know they had somebody inside the Strikeforce?"

"The Rizzolos couldn't put somebody inside the Strikeforce if he was invisible."

"Are you saying the Feds shot your father?"

Mikey slammed his fist on the table. "Don't you understand yet? There's somebody *else* doing this. Somebody *else* inside the Feds. Somebody *else* got my father."

"Who?"

"How the fuck should I know?" Mikey glared at Ponte and calmly returned to the first subject. "There's another reason you ratted on my father, you know? With him you were only his adviser. With me, you're older and smarter, and you think you can run me. With my father out of the way, you figure you're almost boss." He smiled. "Admit it, Sal, you must have thought that a little."

With nothing to lose, Salvatore Ponte took a chance on honesty. "A little."

Crazy Mikey looked out the window. His silence stretched

to a minute, then two. Ponte watched the second hand creep a third time around the kitchen clock. When he couldn't bear it any longer he asked, "What are you going to do?"

"Call up Eddie Rizzolo and stop this fucking war."

"Eddie Rizzolo?"

"Why not? I know he didn't kill my father. He's been trying to get in touch for some time. Wants to do some dope. Why not? We're both young guys. There's plenty in New York for the two of us. And if there is somebody else, we'll get him. What do you think, *Consigliere?* Let's stop the war before the Strikeforce blows us away."

"Your father thought his sister's running things."

"Nobody told me that."

"That's what he thought."

"What do you think?"

"Maybe. She has the brains."

"Fuck Eddie." Mikey laughed. "I'd rather do it with her."

"I don't advise that."

"I was joking. But why not, *Consigliere?*"

"Your father had me get a guy to take care of her."

"Jesus Christ. Was that your idea?"

"No."

"Does Eddie know?"

"The guy missed. I don't know what Eddie knows. I don't know if she told him."

"She probably didn't. He wouldn't be offering peace." He laughed softly. "Guy like Eddie, killing his father and brother is one thing, but if you even *look* like you wanna hit on his sister, he'll challenge you to a fucking duel."

"So now you know."

"Thanks for the warning," Mikey said, and fell silent again.

Ponte inched his eyes to the window, fixed on a sailboat beating across the water. The day looked so beautiful. He hoped—

"You know all the stuff I can do to you, Sal?"

"I know."

"To your girlfriend?"

"I know," Ponte said, wondering how Mikey knew about her; but by now he was beyond surprise.

"Even your family, if I have to."

"My *family?*"

"Sal. You killed my father."

"I didn't mean to."

Mikey stood up and stretched, rippling muscle through the arms of his cashmere pullover. Ponte saw him suddenly as the new man events had made him, the warrior prince turned king.

Ponte couldn't stand the silence. Hating the fear in his voice he asked. "What are you going to do?"

"I'm gonna get in touch with Eddie Rizzolo."

"What about me?"

Crazy Mikey stepped close to his godfather and Ponte thought he was going to kiss him. Instead, he took his coke spoon, extended it the length of the chain, and gently placed the miniature barrels of the replica sawed-off shotgun between Ponte's lips.

"Add it up, Sal. The best thing for you and me and your wife and your girlfriend is for you to jump in front of a subway."

Weary, fed up with himself, Jack Warner lay on his bed, staring at the ceiling and waiting for Tony Taglione to figure out who leaked that Don Richard was hiding in Miami. The *New York Post* lay unopened on the rug. The front page had a picture of an E train for those readers who hadn't seen one, and another of Sal Ponte, described as "Murdered Mob Kingpin's Adviser, Sally Smarts."

Once the Strikeforce chief eliminated himself and the new assistant, Sarah Gallagher, and maybe his senior assistant, Ron Koestler—all of which would take about five minutes— he might hit on one of the FBI agents assigned to search for Don Richard. Establishing that an FBI agent hadn't blown it deliberately or just plain screwed up might buy a few days. But in the end, Warner was screwed; or, more accurately, he thought with disgust, he had screwed himself, allowing himself to get suckered by Taggart and Reggie Rand. Of course, they were hunting Don Richard. Why else would they have paid him three hundred and fifty thousand bucks? At least, they had paid. He had checked his Swiss account. A lot of good it did him, with him lying on the bed in the fifth-floor studio apartment on East Ninth Street, a block from the tenement where he had grown up. Every time the stairs creaked he looked at the door, expecting his partners to break it down, waving guns and warrants—in that order. He had locked his own gun in his gun safe, a two-hundred-pound steel cube under his bed. Goddamned if he was going to kill one of the guys.

When they came he was dozing; it wasn't through the door and it wasn't anyone he knew. A guy swung through the window on a rope, like Tarzan. He was wearing leather, head to toe, which protected him from the broken glass. His eyes gleamed through slits in the mask. He held a gun on Warner, while he unlocked the bars on the fire-escape window, opened the sash, and offered a hand to the Englishman. Reggie Rand dropped lithely from the sill and told Tarzan to leave by the door.

"No," he told Warner, when they were alone. "I didn't come to kill you."

"You dropped in to apologize?"

"I gave you my word," Reggie replied. "Events moved out of my control. I'll do what I can to make it up."

"How about a Presidential pardon?" Warner hadn't moved an inch, nor did he intend to. He lay there, hands behind his head, wondering why the Brit was going to so much trouble to kill him when Tarzan could have done it for him.

"Tonight, I'll get you to Europe. You're a fairly wealthy man abroad. You'll want a plastic surgeon. It could be worse."

"Jail would be worse," Warner admitted. "Death would be worse, too."

"You speak Russian, don't you?"

"*Da.* I picked it up in the neighborhood."

"Not to worry," the Brit said, and Warner began to think maybe he was telling the truth. "If you get bored with your money, there'll be plenty of interesting work."

"Let me get this straight. You're saving my ass because you broke your word about that prick Ponte getting killed. And I don't have to do anything."

"One small service."

Here it came. "What's that? Hijack the plane?"

"When you land at Orly a lady will point out an American who keeps track of comings and goings for the CIA. You will let him intercept you and, before you vanish, you will volunteer the information that Crazy Mikey Cirillo has a narcotics deal going down on the Hudson River."

"What does the CIA care?"

"You will make it sound like an apology to your former colleagues."

"What if this guy doesn't let me vanish?"

"The lady will deal with him."

Warner swung his feet off the bed and regarded Reggie with interest. Now he knew why Reggie wasn't going to kill him. And at last he had an inkling of what Taggart was up to—though still no clue why—but he had run out of time and was in too much trouble himself to use his theory against Taggart.

"It sounds to me like Taggart's setting up Mikey."

"Can you think of a more deserving soul?"

Tony Taglione passed a glossy black-and-white photograph around a gang of agent supervisors who had crowded into his office. Papers had been removed from tables, chairs, and windowsills and restacked in the hall. Cigarette smoke loomed in the fluorescent lights. He didn't allow his attorneys to smoke around him, but cops and investigators had different needs.

"What's wrong with this one?" he asked.

Four mobsters were getting out of a limousine. In the background others were standing around the baroque iron gates of a New Jersey cemetery where family and associates had gathered to bury Don Richard.

"Come on, guys. Four hoods getting out of a car."

"Well, for starters," a woman answered, "Eddie 'the Cop' Rizzolo and Crazy Mikey are not shooting at each other."

"Good. What else?" he asked, and the others joined in.

"Eddie's hand is healed."

"What's left of it."

"He looks like a punch-press operator ordering four beers."

"Knock it off! Since last summer, when the New York families went to war, the body count includes five chiefs dead: Imperiale, Conforti, Bono, Rizzolo, and Cirillo. Between us destroying the council and them killing each other, the whole New York mob's been turned inside out."

"In fact," a police detective interrupted, "the guys we indicted turned out to be the lucky ones."

That got a laugh, and a wit from the DEA got another by calling, "With the possible exception of Eddie Rizzolo, Senior."

Taglione cut it off savagely. "None of us can be proud of a jailhouse murder. It reflects as badly on the Strikeforce as goddamned Jack Warner. So let's not pat ourselves on the back." He iced the room with his piercing eyes. "But that's water over the dam. The thing is now to capitalize on this bloodletting by continuing to go after the successors while they're still off balance—hopefully before citizens get caught in the crossfire. But we've got to know who the new leaders will be. Who's taking over?"

"Look at that grin on Eddie the Cop's face, an agent ventured. "Pretty happy for a guy whose father and brother got killed."

"The Rizzolos are really throwing their weight around."

"I hear Eddie's looking for dope again."

"So do I."

"Right, right."

Taglione asked, "What do you say we shift a ton of people onto Eddie Rizzolo? Let's find out who he's connecting with."

They went out gung-ho, but he still wondered. When in trouble, as he feared he was now, Tony Taglione turned to his boss and mentor, the patrician United States Attorney, Arthur Finch. He left telephone messages. Arthur dropped by the Strikeforce floor, winced as always at the chaos, and asked, "Time for a drink?"

"No way. Look at these transcripts from taps starting last summer."

"It's customary in the real world to say, 'Not this evening, thank you, Arthur.'"

"Look at this." Taglione shoved him a transcript at random. "Pay phone outside a Rego Park pizza joint."

Arthur donned half-moon glasses and read in Harvard tones the line highlighted with yellow Magic Marker. "'Pay the fucks what they want. They're connected with the Rizzolos.'"

Taglione handed him another. Arthur read, "'I got some postage on Frankie Rizzolo.'" He handed it back. "I'm always astonished how *lazy* racketeers are. Why won't they simply get in their car and drive half a mile to a safe phone?"

"Arrogance. Here's another."

"'We're doing good. We got to the Rizzolos.'"

"And . . ."

"'You know any Rizzolos? So ask them.'"

"Rizzolos, Rizzolos, Rizzolos. Suddenly, in less than a year—while we're chasing Cirillos—Rizzolos are big time, number two in New York."

Arthur cleared the edge of a chair and sat down. "Back up. Are you saying the Rizzolos killed Tommy Lucia's boss and Vito Imperiale and Joey Reina and Harry Bono and Al Conforti and Richard Cirillo?"

"The Rizzolos benefited."

"Until Edward Senior and his son Frank were murdered."

Taglione held up the cemetery shot. "But here's Eddie 'the Cop,' big as life at the funeral, as much as saying, Let's make peace."

"Statesmanlike."

"Eddie's a hood. The FBI expected him to be across the street with a rifle."

"So," said Arthur, folding his glasses and straightening his lions-rampant necktie, "we ask, how did a hood get so smart?"

Taglione found another picture. "His little sister."

Arthur read Helen Rizzolo's dossier, which covered major events in her life: marriage, annulment, college, visits to her father in prison, and the rumored kidnapping. Then he looked up with a kind smile. "I presume you haven't tried this theory on your staff."

"You heard about Chris?"

"I saw them at the Governor's Ball. Quite the striking couple, his Adonis to her dark Persephone. . . . 'Woe, woe to Adonis.'"

"What about my theory?"

"I like it. She starts out as her father's messenger. She's intelligent, has some education and a head for business, and she lets her bloodthirsty brothers do the dirty work."

"Except for one thing. Jack Warner lands at Orly Airport, pulls a James Bond, and disappears. Right? By the time Interpol gets on it, some thirty-nine-year-old burly Irish-American guys who look like New York cops are reported crossing Swiss, Italian, and Spanish borders, shipping out of Channel ports, and cruising the Mediterranean. How the hell did the *Rizzolos* get Jack out of the country?"

"And why did they take the chance?"

"They have their claws into freight forwarding at Kennedy, so maybe they could get him aboard a plane—maybe."

"But off in Paris? That's what I can't understand. What do they know of the French?"

"And who got Jack papers? The State Department swears there's no way he can flounce around Europe without topnotch forgeries."

"Actually," Arthur replied mildly, "these are questions the Attorney General's been asking me. How, as he put it, did a bunch of Brooklyn 'wops' turn into international spymasters? He thinks the Rizzolos have established international contacts."

"Brilliant. But with whom?"

"Someone she might have met in Europe. Did you know she'd been to Italy for earthquake relief?"

"Years ago."

"Still, the AG thinks it's worth investigating a Sicilian link."

"Bullshit. That's the first thing I thought of, but this is much classier."

Arthur raised an eyebrow.

"Look at the murders," Taglione retorted. "Joe Reina killed by a radio-controlled car bomb like in the Mideast. Imperiale shot by Berettas in the Israeli two-shot pattern. The agents told me Imperiale looked like he'd been bitten by a bunch of snakes. Something about how the Israelis teach their killers to shoot."

"But weren't they black?"

"Then they were trained by Israelis, who're all over Africa. And what happened to Joey Cirillo's goon squad in the Bronx with a rocket launcher? Doesn't this sound way too sophisticated for Brooklyn 'wops' or even for Sicilians?"

"Yes."

"Here's something else the AG doesn't know. A woman I worked with in Washington, who's since moved to the CIA, told me Jack Warner sent a message. Kind of a parting gift— or shot—I'm not sure which."

"What?"

"Before he disappeared, Warner sought out the CIA agent at Orly to tell him he heard that Mikey Cirillo buys most of his heroin right here in New York, from a guy he meets once a week on a boat in the Hudson."

Chapter 25

T WO OCEAN RACERS floated side by side in Taggart's Tarrytown boathouse, the stealthy black doper boat Taggart used for his meetings with Crazy Mikey Cirillo, and a bright-red luxury model. The newcomer, stolen the night before from the Hawk Racing Yard in Mamaroneck, was built on similar lines, though its hull was made of aluminum—which made it a radar beacon.

Reggie had pulled the head off one of the black boat's V-8s, while Taggart was busy stowing kilos of heroin under the floorboards of the red boat. The Englishman was wearing a white shirt and his Drumnadrochit Piping Society tie, and though he was adjusting the valves with socket wrench and calipers, his cuffs were as white as the heroin.

"I'm going to miss you, Reggie," Chris said.

"Why don't you simply *kill* Mikey?"

"Because someday—probably not when he's arrested, but maybe on the way to court, during the trial, or even on the way to jail—he'll start talking. He knows enough to destroy the whole Cirillo organization and what's left of the Confortis and Imperiales."

"Why would he talk?"

"Mikey's all that's left of his own blood. His brother's in jail, his father's dead, and Ponte's dead. The rest of the bosses and *capos* are his enemies. And if he doesn't talk, he rots in jail for the rest of his life. So me and my pop come out even, either way."

Reggie bolted the head back in place and inspected the wiring to the explosives in the bilge of the black boat. Then he climbed out of the compartment, started the engines, and closed the box. Turning to Taggart, he submerged him in the flat pools of his eyes.

"*Then* you will walk away?"

"You asked me that ten years ago."

"You have a long memory."

"Always."

"What about Miss Rizzolo? What if she won't walk away?"

Taggart smiled. "I'll reform her."

"And if she resists reformation?"

"I'll kidnap her back to Europe."

"She can destroy you, you know."

"She'd destroy herself in the process. But she has no reason. In fact, she might even be in love with me. Want to be my best man?"

"And we'll all live happily ever after."

"Except for Crazy Mikey."

"And the redoubtable Eddie Rizzolo?"

"Eddie's another reason to reform Helen. I want Helen clear before the dumb fuck finally gets himself indicted for something."

"Do it quickly. He's sniffing around for a drug deal."

Reggie cast off the lines and backed the red boat into the river, which approaching night had turned deep purple.

At the hour Taggart watched Reggie disappear down the Hudson, Tony Taglione got a call from the Strikeforce's FBI agent director. An agent planted as an instructor in a Manhattan health club where Crazy Mikey had agreed to meet Eddie Rizzolo had just recorded an incredible tape. Twenty minutes later the agent ran in, flinging open his raincoat. A skintight red Spandex T-shirt with East Side Ironworks stretched across his bulging chest drew whistles from the agents and attorneys that Taglione had hurriedly assembled to hear the evidence. Taglione shoved the cassette into his ghetto blaster. It started with a heavy grinding noise, punctuated by sharp hisses.

"Sounds like he's fucking a snake."

"The heavy sound is the chain pull," the agent explained. "The microphone's in the weight machine."

"What's the hiss?"

"That's the prick breathing. They start talking in a minute.

Mikey's on the machine, doing like bench presses. Eddie 'the Cop' comes up and stands over him. All around are their hoods, trying to outpump each other, which is kind of funny 'cause a lot of them are spaghetti bellies. It's a legit club, so regular guys and girls are passing through and using the other machines. You can hear 'em talking in the background. I'm next to Mikey, instructing my partner, Zell, how to exercise her lungs. . . . Okay. It starts in a second. Mikey pretends he's surprised to see Eddie, like they haven't set this thing up for a week."

Cirillo's voice rasped out of the machine. *"What the fuck?"*

The agents laughed. "Knock it off," said Taglione.

"Yes, sir. This is Eddie talking now. Mr. Subtlety."

Eddie Rizzolo's voice vibrated with the hearty tones of a radio announcer. *"I hear you owe a guy."*

"Where'd you pick that up?"

"The street says, 'The Man Who Can' owes a ton."

"You put out word about a deal."

"You put out word about peace. Business is the best way to make peace, my father always said. Buyers and sellers don't have to be friends, but they can't be enemies."

"I don't need your business."

"The more you sell, the faster you pay off."

"I don't need your business."

"Brooklyn."

"What about it?"

"If you don't supply me, I'm going to start a heroin detox program in Brooklyn."

"What?"

"Yeah. It's a new method. Instead of methadone and counseling and all that shit, we set the kiddie gangs on your pushers."

The weight chain ground. Mikey's breath hissed as he pumped. The agent said, "Get this. Mikey is really being nice. I mean this is not the Crazy Mikey we know and love. He smiles, like Eddie's joking."

"How will you know who are mine?"

"Anybody who's not mine. So be my Man Who Can, then we're both happy."

"Since when do you deal in product?"

"I been waiting for the right supplier. That's you. Hey, listen, I'm offering you the world on a platter. A steady street market from a guy you can trust."

Another silence was underscored by the sound of the weight machine. Taglione asked, "There are people around?"

"Yeah, but they're not close. And they're doing their own thing. Besides, what's he said so far?"

"Arrogant bastards."

"What does your sister say?"

"My sister's got nothing to do with this."

Taglione stared at the tape machine, aware the others were afraid to look at him.

"Relax. Just asking."

"Sure you are," said the agent.

"Shut up!" Taglione leaned over the tape player, but Mikey Cirillo abruptly changed the subject. *"Like I told you. We've fucked each other over. Your father and brother are dead. My brother's in jail. My father's dead. His* consigliere—*my god-father—killed himself."*

"From grief," said Sarah Gallagher.

"Who's left?" Mikey continued. *"You and me. Hey, like you said, we're two young guys. We're on our own. We can work it out."*

"So when do I meet your man?"

"That's going to be a problem. He said no partners."

"Who is this guy?" asked Taglione. "Why can't we get a line on this guy?"

"So we lean on him," said Eddie. *"Like I was kidding with you. He can figure out he'll have no customers."*

"This guy is independent."

"Come on, he's a businessman. He's not going to fight two families. If he does, we blow him away and then you don't owe nobody anything. So what do you got to lose?"

"A goddamned good source is what I got to lose."

"Sorry, Mikey. If we're going to trust each other, I gotta meet him."

The chain ground again.

"Get this," said the agent. "Remember, they're standing there in shorts."

"Eddie? You mind if I pat you for a wire?"

359

"So Mikey gets off the bench and pats Eddie for a wire and the whole gym stops. I mean, here's these two guys in shorts inspecting each other's asses like—"

"Where are they meeting this supplier?"

"I don't know, Tony. They went into the sauna. I hung close, but couldn't catch much."

"Did they say anything about a boat?"

The agent looked surprised. "You kidding?"

"I'm not kidding. What did they say?"

"Mikey told Eddie, 'I hope you don't get seasick.'"

Taglione looked around his office. Somebody said, "It sounds like they're meeting a mother ship offshore."

"Catch those two together with a load of dope?"

"No way."

"It can't be. Even Eddie's too smart to get near the stuff."

"Can you blanket Eddie Rizzolo?" Taglione asked the DEA agent director.

"Take a lot of guys."

"I don't care if it takes a hundred. I want to know every second where he is. And goddammit, anybody who gets made might as well join Jack in Europe."

Taggart's plan was simple—strand Mikey on the red boat, in which the heroin was hidden, turn the boat in to the Feds, and let the law-enforcement agents draw their own conclusions. He left Tarrytown at midnight and steered downriver on a cool breeze. At half-speed—an effortless thirty-five miles per hour—the engines were quiet, and he could hear the wake falling back on itself in the dark. He passed beneath the Tappan Zee Bridge, spotted the George Washington, and opened the throttles. In half an hour the George Washington's catenary lights draped the horizon, and on each sweep of the radar screen a massive target blossomed in the lower right quadrant like a huge white flower.

Taggart pulled his ski mask over his face and steered for it. He found Reggie anchored in the red boat, two miles up from the bridge and an eighth of a mile off the Palisades, which loomed darkly on the Jersey shore. Crazy Mikey was lounging in the stern beside a huge man whom Taggart assumed at first was a bodyguard. But as he eased the black boat alongside the red and handed Reggie a line to raft them by their midships cleats, he saw the Reggie had made the same mistake.

Eddie Rizzolo, with arms folded to conceal his missing fingers, was grinning.

"What the hell is he doing here?" Taggart whispered over the joined gunnels.

"He was aboard before I realized he wasn't the bodyguard. I decided best to play it through."

"Did you sweep them?"

"Oh, yes. And they swept me. Eddie brought cash."

"How much time do we have?"

"Time is not our problem. The phone dialer will send the Feds a recorded message with this location when I radio. Rizzolo's the problem. How do we separate him from Mikey?"

Taggart looked out in the dark. The bridge lights would reveal river traffic from the south. But they were sitting ducks from the dark water to the north. "Get on the radar. I don't like this at all."

"I don't trust it with the aluminium boat so near," Reggie warned, swinging aboard the black boat.

Taggart climbed onto the red boat. "I told you no partners."

"You want to get paid, you gotta ease up."

"I don't 'gotta' anything. You want to buy from me, you know the rules."

"All we're doing tonight is talking about changing the rules. No risk to you. I don't want to hear a word about product. Just meet my partner and see if you want to do business with us both."

"If I'm paying," Eddie Rizzolo interjected, "I want to know where my bread is going."

Taggart had to get Eddie away from the red boat. "Okay, Mikey, I'm taking Eddie for a ride. You wait here."

"No way," Mikey said.

"It's okay with me," said Eddie. "I don't mind."

"I mind," said Mikey. "This is my supplier. If you get on that boat with him, you can kiss the street goodbye."

Eddie grinned, his teeth flashing in the bridge lights. "Maybe I ought to throw you overboard." He looked ready to do it, Taggart thought, and he wondered, Why not? But Mikey was worth so much more alive than dead.

"Kill each other elsewhere. You coming, Eddie?"

Mikey moved faster, seizing his bug-sweeping briefcase and vaulting over the gunnels into the black boat. "Okay. Me and the Brit'll take a ride. You two talk."

Taggart looked at Reggie, who cocked an eye from the radar screen. Did Mikey suspect something or was it animal instinct to retreat from danger? Whichever, Taggart and Eddie were on the wrong boat. Not only was the red boat a radar target; it contained the heroin.

Powerful engines droned on the dark water in the north.

"One of you was followed," Reggie said calmly as a dozen white dots began to sizzle on his radar screen.

"Cops," Eddie Rizzolo shouted.

And, to the south, a helicopter buzzed under the bridge, flickering yellow and blue in the catenary lights. Taggart saw Mikey shift his attention from the helicopter to the loud drone of the boats, then to the radar screen fairly white with targets, and finally to Reggie at the controls.

"This boat!" Taggart yelled. "It's faster."

He cranked the red boat's engines and they started roaring. Reggie scrambled aboard as if his life were in the balance. Mikey seized the wheel of the black boat.

"Jump," Taggart yelled again. "This one's faster."

Mikey hesitated, frantically fingering his shotgun coke spoon.

"Hurry up."

"Wait for him," Eddie yelled.

Mikey dropped his coke spoon, snatched up a real sawed-off shotgun he had secreted in his electronics briefcase, jumped into the red boat, and leveled the yawning barrels at Taggart and Reggie. "Get off! Get on the other boat. I'm not getting caught on a conspiracy thing with you guys."

Taggart and Reggie retreated.

"If you make it we'll talk again. If they catch me and Eddie, we're just a couple of guys going for a ride. Right, Eddie?"

"Right," said Eddie. Although he looked bewildered, he

flung off the rafting line as Taggart and Reggie climbed over the gunnels into the black boat. Taggart had left the engines running and Reggie engaged them.

"I hope he remembers his anchor."

But they had cut it too close. A searchlight tore the dark like a grasping hand; then another, and a third from the side, a blinding white circle, dead on target. A bullhorn boomed, *"Freeze, you fuckers!"*

Chapter 26

CHASE BOATS LOOMED out of the dark, a dozen sturdy cutters and sleek new racers, whose decks were lined with rifle- and shotgun-toting agents in flack vests. Bullhorns boomed a warning that no one was to move. Taggart dived for the locker that held their night goggles as Reggie slammed the black boat's engines to full throttle and put the helm hard over. He saw the red boat pinned in the lights of the raiding fleet, frothing at the stern as propellers fought the drag of the anchor. Crazy Mikey Cirillo and Eddie Rizzolo struggled in the cockpit, fighting for the wheel.

The black boat lifted, stood up on its stern, spun a half circle like a cutting horse. Reggie reversed his helm and drove for a dwindling gap in their line. A police boat darted to fill it, but when the fifty-foot black hull slammed down at the space, the little boat fled. The turbochargers cut in with a liquid roar and Reggie ripped through the line, building up speed. Taggart thought they had made it. Then, overhead, a searchlight lunged out of the sky—a helicopter stabbing the dark.

Bullhorns boomed again, their warnings drowned by thundering engines and seconds later by the sharp, rapid notes of a machine gun. The air seemed to explode inches overhead. The helicopter's searchlight leaped at them; the spot swept the cockpit and whipped back, but the doper boat's flat black paint merged with the night, her soft materials and nonreflective surfaces forming a radar sieve. At seventy miles per hour they raced down the river as the helicopter searched water, far behind. Seconds later they were under the George Washington Bridge, and then out of its lights, deep in darkness.

Taggart heard a new sound—a high-pitched drone. "What

the hell is that?" He looked back at the Strikeforce armada circling the red boat in their wake. Reggie pointed at the radar screen where a pair of blips were closing swiftly from the Jersey side. Taggart slipped night goggles over Reggie's head and put his on. Scanning the now bright riverscape, he saw two small pursuit boats trailing enormous wakes like spearheads on creamy white shafts. "I thought we're not a radar target."

"We're not," Reggie yelled back. "They're using bloody night glasses just like us. And they're going to radio that damned helicopter."

He steered for the Manhattan side, angling toward the lights of the Seventy-ninth Street boat basin four miles downriver. The black boat poured across two miles in less than two minutes. "They're gaining," said Taggart.

Reggie steered within yards of the rocky shoreline, where cars were traveling the West Side Highway. The pursuit boats followed, closing until Taggart could distinguish their crews, one man driving, the other holding a long-barreled weapon. Reggie glanced back and eased his throttles.

"What are you doing?"

"Look ahead! Find the ice aprons."

A bullhorn crackled close behind. Taggart searched the water that lay ahead between their boat and the lighted docks. "There!" Two hundred yards upriver from the ranks of yachts and chunky houseboats was a row of wedge-shaped barriers rising out of the water. Fashioned of bent railroad track to protect the marina from river ice, they emerged at an angle.

Reggie looked back again and, when the lead pursuit boat was practically on their stern, pushed his throttles wide open and steered straight at the ice aprons. Taggart gripped the dashboard; the slots between the aprons were narrow and they were approaching at seventy miles per hour. When they were so close that Taggart could distinguish the individual rails, Reggie flicked his helm to starboard, wove between two aprons, and careened the black boat toward the middle of the river. Taggart, thrown across the cockpit by the force of the turn, looked back. The lead pursuit boat crashed against an ice apron, skidded up the steep incline, crossed a hundred yards of water airborne, and splashed down on its side.

The second boat clipped an apron, rose a few feet on screaming propellers, and landed upright. "Bloody hell," said Reggie. "Are they stopping to help?"

"Yes, he's circling . . . no! There's people on the dock pulling the men out. Here he comes!"

The pursuit boat tore downriver after them, gaining again, though not quite as quickly. The bullhorn boomed, angrily punctuated by a hail of gunfire. "He's damaged," Reggie said. A bullet slammed him to the deck.

"Reg!"

Taggart dropped beside him.

"Get the helm!"

"You okay?"

"No. But we're dead if you don't steer! Keep your head down."

Taggart hunched into the seat and steered, casting anxious glances astern and at Reggie, who was holding his left arm with bloody fingers. "Head for Twenty-third Street before they get that helicopter. World Yacht club."

Two miles. Taggart was competent on the boat, but no-where near as good as Reggie, and he knew he never could have pulled the stunt with the ice apron. They thundered abreast of midtown Manhattan, racing top speed down the center of the river, the pursuit boat gaining. Taggart saw the golden top of his Spire riding the rim of the skyline, and wondered if he would ever see it again.

"Are you okay?"

Reggie sat up, his right arm limp at his side. "Not entirely." He crawled toward the wet bar on the other side of the cockpit, packed ice against the wound, and hurriedly wrapped it with towels. "Here comes the helicopter."

Taggart saw the piers Reggie had indicated coming up fast. He said, "We can't just get off. We have to send the boat away and blow it up."

"My thought exactly." Reggie fumbled a red key from his pocket, inserted it in a panel under the wheel, and moved a series of switches. Each caused a red alarm to blink.

He looked back again. "We'll round the pier flat out and throttle back. You go over the side. Swim under the pier.

We've a motor yacht—*Popeye*—in the yacht basin. Climb aboard on the stern step."

"What about you?"

"I'll be right behind you as soon as I set the boat on her way."

"You've got one arm, Reg. I'll set the boat."

"Don't argue. I'll steer. Pull the throttles when I tell you."

He took the wheel. The black boat tore past the yacht basin and around the pier that formed its downriver boundary. "Now!"

The black boat slowed as if they'd hit a wall. Reggie turned the bow back to the river. "Go! *What are you doing?*"

"Sorry, old chap. I've already lost a father. I'm not going to lose a father figure." Taggart picked Reggie up, astonished how light he was, and swung him over the gunnel. Reggie fought with his good arm. "This is what you pay me for."

"This one's on me."

He threw Reggie overboard, steered around him, hit the throttles, set the black boat thundering for the river. The pursuit boat rounded the pier and the helicopter flew over it with a spotlight blazing. Taggart rolled off the far gunnel. The black boat ripped past him like a trailer truck. The hull smacked his head and he sank half-conscious into the bitter cold water. He heard a roar, saw the dark shape of the pursuit boat coming straight at him, and tried to dive. It clipped his back and drove him farther under. It sounded like a subway train going overhead. He surfaced, thrashing in the froth of its wake as it tore after the black boat.

The double roaring of the two boats moved swiftly across the river, trailed by the buzzing and thudding of the helicopter. Suddenly the middle of the Hudson was lit by a white flash. Flame and thunder split the night. Seconds later, all was silence, but for the frustrated growl of the Strikeforce craft hunting for survivors to arrest.

Taggart swam under the pier and found Reggie clinging to the teak stern step of *Popeye*, an enormous luxury trawler which was moored out of the light. Taggart helped him up. "Where'd you get this?"

Reggie stood up uncertainly. He had lost his night goggles and Taggart saw him try to smile. "We never gave second chances, but we always kept a backup. Leave your glasses on; my people shouldn't see your face."

A tough-looking charter captain greeted them in the salon. Reggie issued swift commands. "Our doctor, hot baths, dry clothes, and a car to the air ambulance."

An hour later, Taggart rode out of the marina with him. The car stopped at Park and Twenty-third, and Reggie extended his hand. He looked gray with pain and fatigue, but his eyes were fathomless flat pools. "You're done. It's been interesting."

"Well, let's—if your arm doesn't hurt too much—let's go have dinner or something. Tina's is right around the corner."

"I really ought to press on. I'll drop you here if you don't mind. I'm just a wee bit knackered."

Taggart embraced him suddenly, catching Reggie by surprise. He wanted to say something, but all he got out was "Where are you going?"

"Europe."

"Tonight?"

"Tonight. When your brother and his Strikeforce finish interrogating Crazy Mikey, they'll likely be looking for an Englishman."

Taggart stood in the street and watched his car drive away. He looked up Park Avenue where the lighted top of his Spire stood like a beacon. Mike Taglione would have loved it, and for a brief second he felt his father's presence, as if Mike's heart were beating in his own body. Then he hurried to a pay phone and tried to call Helen to see how he could help with her brother, but all her lines were busy.

Tony Taglione let a United States marshal drive him home, something he rarely did. Rather than be tempted to abuse the service, he took taxis or drove his own car. But tonight—or rather, morning, as a high white disk of sun burned through the fog—he had earned it.

Crazy Mikey Cirillo and Eddie "the Cop" Rizzolo were caught on a doper boat, thanks to Strikeforce agents sticking to Eddie Rizzolo and bugging the right weight machine. Eddie had thrown a briefcase overboard—somebody should have told him that cash floated. Eight million dollars. And under the boat's floor were fifty kilos of pure heroin.

Each swore he was framed, which had, Taglione recalled with a weary smile, some of the toughest DEA men in New York in giggles. Now the lawyer's job started. Fifty keys meant no bail. So while some of Taglione's attorneys prepared the drug case, they had time and opportunity to persuade one of the two to flip—not Eddie, but maybe Crazy Mikey, if he was handled properly. It was as good a day as he had ever had on the Strikeforce.

"Here you go, Mr. Taglione. You want I should wait?"

"I'm going to crash for a few hours. Can somebody pick me up at one?"

He staggered up the front walk, picked up two days of newspapers off the porch, and let himself in. Tired as he was, he knew he was miles from sleep. He poured three fingers of Canadian Club and sipped it straight. His eye fell on the piano, which he used to play, and on the model of his father's building.

"Hey, Pop. How you doing?"

The little derrick, which Chris had broken the night of Mike's funeral, still lay on its side on the top deck. Taglione swore, as he did each time he noticed it, that he was going to fix the model as soon as he had time. He looked around the room, glad he had stayed in this house. His mother and father were alive here. He had left the living room unchanged. Vicky and Chryl, in one of their attempts to befriend him, had recommended special East Side cleaners and upholsterers who took care of it.

He had to get out of here, someday. It was almost a sin to waste so much space on one person in such a crowded city. But it fitted his needs. Every now and then, when Arthur insisted he submit to an interview, the interviewer always asked, Was he lonely not being married? He had given up on the truth and said his work was everything. It *was* everything, but here he was connected. The house, and the mark his parents had put on it, and the neighborhood. Neighbors and aunts kept slipping in the back door to stash casseroles and cheesecakes in the refrigerator. And time went fast. Kids on bicycles grew into earnest teenagers who asked which was the best law school. The paper boy had just graduated from the Police Academy, and the little girl who weeded his mother's flowers was interning next summer at his office.

He started upstairs, where he had taken over his parents' bedroom. It was big and comfortable, had its own bath and a king-sized bed, convenient when he brought a date home. He used his father's desk in one corner and had a comfortable armchair for reading in the other. Heavy drapes blocked the daylight completely.

Either the booze was working or he was blind tired, but he was sitting on the bed, trying to get his shoes off, before he realized he wasn't alone. He smelled perfume and looked up sharply. A lamp flared, and there, in his armchair, with her feet tucked under her and her dark eyes luminous, was Helen Rizzolo.

Chapter 27

W HERE'S YOUR GEEPS, in the closet?"

He was afraid, and that made him angry. Prosecutors talked about this kind of thing happening. The office employed basic defenses—unlisted phone numbers, marshal protection when threatened, even transferring convicts who made threats to harsher prisons to remind them it was not the individual prosecutor but the government that meted out justice.

"I came alone," she said.

"Then leave alone. What the fuck are you doing in my house?"

"My brother was arrested."

"I know."

"You charged him with dope."

"Miss Rizzolo, I want you out of here."

"He doesn't deal dope."

"Out!"

"I don't *let* him deal dope."

"Miss, you are talking to an officer of the court. I have to advise you that anything you say can be used against you. Do you wish to continue informing me about what you allow and don't allow your brother to do?"

"My father is dead. My brother Frank is dead. Eddie is all I have left."

"I can't help you with that."

He got off the bed, but a sea of grief and weariness in her eyes made him extend his hand to help her out of the chair. "You're beat," he said. "Go home and sleep. Let your lawyers do their job."

"My family is dying."

"What are you saying to me, sweetheart? It's not me. It's them. They hurt people. They take, they subvert. And they got caught. We're going to put them away like the rest of the Cirillos. And like your father."

She looked up, her eyes liquid, wondering, Would she be afraid if she had nothing to sell? Would Tony Taglione terrify her if she were defenseless? Would she resign herself to her brother's being lost forever? But such questions dodged the issue. She had not entered the prosecutor's house empty-handed. She had plenty to trade, if she must; more to sell than Taglione could imagine, if she could bear to do so.

She prayed there was another way. "My father . . ." She wet her lips with her tongue. "You never once looked at me during his trial."

"I was busy. It was the biggest case I ever argued."

"His lawyers kept saying how good you were."

"They had to blame somebody."

"My father didn't blame his lawyers."

Taglione smiled coldly. "I forgot. Colombian hoods shoot their lawyers, but Italian hoods understand the power of the court, so they shoot witnesses."

"Why wouldn't you look at me?"

"Getting kicked and bitten by mobsters' female relatives is not my idea of courtroom demeanor."

"You know better than anybody I wouldn't do that."

Taglione shrugged. He had been unfair. "Of course I saw you. You came prim and proper to the courtroom every day. Little Miss Bus Line Executive in those linen suits and the lavender scarf and the Gucci briefcase. And that gold logging chain around your neck so no one on your side would forget exactly how rich and powerful you really are."

Helen smiled at him, relieved that somewhere behind his priestly gaze he still had feelings. Taglione felt himself drifting into her eyes . . . floating into the past, ten years back, nearly eleven, in a shimmering memory, a moment, spontaneous, wonderful, and never-ending . . . a crazy moment of his life that started the night Chris got beaten up at Abatelli's. It was frightening how well she knew what he was thinking.

"Did you ever tell him?" she whispered.

"Tell who what?" he asked, an involuntary smile making a lie of his question.

"Tell your brother how we met in the phone booth?"

"Just last fall, when you two started hanging out. He was my little brother; he saw you first and flipped. I couldn't do it to him."

Helen looked away from the bed; Chris had told her the truth. He *had* fallen for her at first sight.

"You never told him before that we went out?"

". . . I didn't want to. It was mine."

"Not just yours."

"But not his. And not my father's. The last crazy thing I did in my life."

"You opened the phone booth door," she said. "And you smiled. You'd already smiled when you went by my table. I thought, What the hell? They can marry me off, but this is my secret."

"You came out of the ladies' room, stoned to the ends of your beautiful hair. God, you were such a beautiful girl."

"Every time I see an old Lincoln I think of the front seat of your father's car. . . . I never asked you who was on the phone."

"A criminal investigator with the U.S. Attorney's office. He put me on hold while he checked out your father for me."

"I always wondered if you were dating me to investigate my family. Am I right?"

"They didn't teach that in law school."

"How come you stopped calling?"

"Somehow, back at Harvard, when I could finally think straight, it didn't seem like a relationship with a future. Besides, you were engaged."

"I thought it was because I wouldn't go to bed with you."

Tony smiled. "To tell the truth, Helen, making out with you in the front seat of my old man's car was better than sleeping with most women."

"Thanks."

"Why wouldn't you?"

She laughed. "You were a turning point in my life, Tony Taglione. It was the first time I was ever smart about a guy. I owe you one. You helped me settle down. I married. And even though that didn't work out, I became a real woman, so I was ready when my family needed me. Maybe my whole family owes you."

Tony stiffened and the humor went out of his eyes.

"Did you think of me when you persecuted my father?"

"The word is *prosecute*."

"Sorry."

"Of course I did. I think of it often. I'm in your debt for a memory that pops into my head at the oddest times. It's a moment I still cherish."

"You never mentioned it when you warned me off your brother."

"It happened years ago. It's not my life anymore. Nor yours."

He met her eyes and they stared at each other for a long time in silence.

"I'm in love with him," she said. "It's for real, with both of us."

"That's what you came here to tell me?"

"I didn't ask for it."

"I'll tell you right now I can't come to the wedding."

"We're not quite there—yet."

"I'm told you haven't seen him since your father was killed."

Helen nodded, although he could be lying; agents could have seen Chris come to her club after he killed Don Richard. She said, "It's been a terrible time."

"Yeah."

"So where are we?" she asked.

"Where we've always been. Across the street from each other."

"Tony, can't we work something out?"

"Because we were going out ten years ago?"

"It makes it easier to talk. I didn't bring a lawyer."

"Even your lawyers wouldn't break into my house."

"The back door was open."

"What did you have in mind?"

"My brother."

"What are you offering? Testimony?"

"I'll testify against Mikey Cirillo."

"Pertaining to what?"

"Whatever you need."

"You mean you'll lie on the stand?"

"What do you want?"

"You'll make something up?"

"Tell me what you want."

"I already have what I want—both those sons of bitches in jail."

"You still have to convict Mikey. He's the biggest boss in New York. My brother's just a dumb guy."

"Do you really believe I would let you lie on the stand to make a case? Helen, you are farther away than I thought."

She faltered, realizing she had mishandled him badly. "Give Eddie back to me. Please."

"Have you talked to your lawyers? Have you seen the charges?"

"He got suckered, Tony. Crazy Mikey set him up."

"How do you explain that Mikey's in the next cell?"

"One of Mikey's enemies double-crossed him."

"Your brother was arrested on a boat in the middle of the river with fifty kilos of pure heroin."

"He was tricked."

"I've been speculating about your brother's enterprises for a long time. Mikey's, too. But I'm done speculating. I've got them both. At least six investigators will swear they saw him heave a briefcase full of money into the water."

"They're lying."

"Here, you want to see?" Tony reached down for the briefcase he had dropped beside the bed. He pulled out a glossy black-and-white photograph and thrust it at Helen. The paper was still soft from the chemicals.

She screwed her eyes shut, but not before the image seared itself in her mind: Eddie swinging a briefcase over the side of a boat, his face frantic in the glare of searchlights, like a frightened little boy caught with a girlie magazine by the priest.

"Forget it, Helen. He made a dumb mistake and he got caught. Even your five-hundred-dollar-an-hour junk lawyers had nothing to say when they saw this."

She opened her eyes. "What can I do?"

"You want my advice?"

"I'll do anything."

"If you're in, get out. We're rolling up the Mafia. We got the old ones and we'll get the new ones."

"I'm not in," she retorted automatically.

Taglione took back the picture and closed his briefcase. "I'll give you one thing, Helen. Not for old times, but for my brother. Fair warning. You see, I think you're Eddie's *consigliere*. Maybe even more since your father died. Get out of it! Because when I find the evidence that you're running the Rizzolos, you're next. I'll get you like I got the Cirillos and the Bonos and the Confortis—and your father. When I can prove it, you're going to jail, too."

She wondered if Taglione would accept her own confession, right now, in trade for Eddie. The question was on her lips, but reality stifled it. Who would protect the family if she went to prison? She couldn't trust Eddie alone. Without her to watch over him, he would get caught again, and her mother, the old people, the businesses would all be cast into the world.

"Get out," said Taglione. "Get straight. And go away."

"Where?" she asked bleakly.

"You could try your uncle in Westport. He's a decent guy."

"It's kind of nice how you keep track of me."

"I keep track of every hood in this town."

"You missed one."

"What is that supposed to mean?"

Helen Rizzolo returned a cold smile, but she felt her mouth begin to tremble, as if her body knew before her mind that there was no way out, no other way to save her family. "I came here for my brother. I want Eddie home."

"You can't have Eddie home."

"I want him free, the charges dropped. I'm willing to pay."

"Hold it!"

"I'm willing to pay."

"Pay? You're going to pay *me?* That's a bribe. Helen, surely you don't mean—"

Her eyes filled with tears. *"I'll pay."*

"There's nothing for sale in this house."

"Yes, there is."

"Nothing."

"There is always something. Even when a guy thinks he's God."

"You are warned. I'll charge you with attempted bribery if you say another word." He stood up and took her roughly by the arm. "Get out of my house."

Helen tore away. "I'm here to bargain, you bastard! I've got something to bargain with."

"What?" he asked scornfully.

"Chris."

Taglione felt the blood rush from his face, leaving his cheeks prickling with cold and his heart afire. Of the thoughts racing through his head, he blurted the first he could accept: "You're lying!"

"About what?" she asked. "I haven't told you yet."

"You're *lying!*"

"Your brother for my brother."

"My brother isn't a criminal."

She saw by Taglione's agonized expression that she had won. Her heart withered, but it was the only way. "Shall I start with the day his people kidnapped me? Or the day your father was killed."

Chapter 28

"CHRIS? IT'S HELEN."

Sylvia had reached for his private line. Taggart beat her to it, and when he heard Helen's voice, he shooed her out of his office.

Sylvia mouthed, "What about the mayor saying no?"

"Excuse me." He covered the phone. "Fuck him," he said savagely. "Fuck his whole City Council. I've had it. Let him build his own stadium."

"Chris, listen a second. Henry Bunker's on the other line. Kenny Adler called him to smooth things over."

"I don't need his garbage."

"It's *Henry*. Talk to him, please."

"Goddammit. Okay, I'll talk to him—Helen, hold another second." He stabbed the button. "Henry?"

"Chris. Look, I'm as angry as you are. But Kenny called. His Honor thinks maybe things got out of hand between you."

"We agree at last."

"That's a big concession for him; don't forget he's a hot-tempered guy who happens to own a twenty-percent plurality in this town. He'd like you to know he's sorry. Maybe we can get the project going next year."

"I got to wait a year?"

"Years go fast when you're paying interest."

"Would you give him a message, Henry?"

"Sure."

"The message is: 'Fuck you, Your Honor.'"

"Chris, let's not be crazy."

"I'll have Sylvia send a confirming letter." He banged down the phone. "No more calls, Sylvia. And send that letter by messenger." Sylvia backed out, dismayed. Taggart composed himself and returned to the phone.

"Hi. I miss you a lot."

"Yeah, well, I've been hassled."

"How's your brother doing?"

"Not great. He's getting into fights with the guards. How's yours?"

"The darling of the *New York Post*—'Battlin' Tony.' Too bad he hates publicity."

"I want to see you."

"Is half an hour too soon?"

"Could we go away for the weekend?"

"That's like the original Helen asking a Greek shipbuilder if he's got anything that floats. Let's go up to the country. Cold as hell, still, but we'll build a fire and—"

"Take me to Atlantic City. I want to go to a casino."

"Casino? I'll take you to Monte Carlo."

"No. AC's fine."

"Hey, I'll charter a Concorde. Hit Monte Carlo, Macao, and AC on the way back."

She laughed. "The only traveling I want to do is between bed and the blackjack table. I want to beat the house and blow it all on dinner and presents."

"Okay. I'll call Trump and get his top floor."

"One big bed in a private suite will be perfect. I'll drive."

"No way I'm getting my hand caught in your gearshift. I'll pick you up with the Rolls. And wear something loose. It's a nice long ride."

Helen cradled the phone, her head resounding with the trust in his voice. "You heard."

Tony Taglione, Marty, the broad-chested agent of the East Side Ironworks FBI bug, and Zell, his platinum-blonde partner, removed their headsets.

"That means we have to wire her," said Marty. "I was hoping we could do the car."

"Wire me? Didn't you hear his voice? The guy loves me. Am I supposed to slap his hand?"

Tony Taglione had refused to believe her. He demanded proof she hadn't concocted a story about Taggart's scam to get her brother's charges reduced. He wanted his brother's guilt in his own words. So the price to free Eddie Rizzolo had gone up: Helen had to trick Taggart into admitting—on tape—how he had seized control of the New York Mafia.

"Zell?"

"Yeah, we have something new she can wear. It's soft and it's kind of pretty. Goes with your coloring. . . . You *are* a natural brunette?"

Taglione said, "They're intimate. A wire's too dangerous. What if he finds it?"

"He won't hurt me."

"I wouldn't bank on that," said Marty, and Zell nodded firm agreement.

Helen turned on Tony. "Let's get something straight. You know damned well he wouldn't hurt me."

The act was easy. She had to pretend she wanted to be with him, which she did, and pretend she wanted to sleep with him, which she did, and behave as if she adored him as he adored her. The hard part was concealing the secret knowledge of how it would end. Harder still was hiding the sorrow.

They made out like kids in the back seat of the Rolls on the drive down. Their suite had a pool table, on which she beat him twice, a hot tub they abandoned for the cool sheets on the mirrored bed, and a white piano that Chris said he wished he knew how to play. He took her out to dinner, but still, Friday night turned to disaster; she spent it crying in his arms. He comforted her, thinking she was crying only for Eddie.

Saturday morning they made up for it, in bed till lunch, then back for more. By Saturday evening, Taggart was sprawled happily on the sheets enjoying the sight of her as she chose a dress for dinner. "I never knew a girl who wore a garter belt."

"Just on special dates."

"Need help?"

"You stay there."

"Aren't you cold?"

"Back. Back."

"Exhibitionist."

She glanced over her shoulder. "That's a fancy word for tease."

"I told Reggie I want to marry you."

His words went through her like ice. She teased him, to hide her agony. "What is it with Italian boys? As soon as they pass thirty they have to get married?"

"I would have asked you when I was ten."

"What did Reggie say?"

"He agreed to be best man."

"First, we'd have to find him. Where is he?" Tony Taglione and his eager assistants had agreed that the existence of Reggie Rand would do a lot for her story. But Taggart, she knew, would never knowingly betray the Englishman.

"Will you?"

"Will I what?"

"Marry me."

"No."

"Why not?"

It killed her that he was making it easy, setting himself up in his innocence. She forced her mind to an image of Eddie bloodied on a concrete floor in a battle with the guards. It gave her the strength to seize the opening. "Because there's stuff going down you don't know about."

"Like what?"

"Like I have to see people."

"Who?"

"Philadelphia people."

"Hang on a minute." Taggart got off the rumpled bed and pulled a briefcase out of his two-suiter. "Certain habits don't go 'way."

"What are you doing?"

"Sweeping the room."

"We took it at the last minute with phony names. Who's going to bug us?"

"I didn't know we were doing business," Taggart replied, unlocking the case.

"We're not." Helen picked up her dress, sauntered around the bed, and wrapped his naked body with hers. "We came to play. I'm just going to check them out. Can you fix this damned zipper?"

"If I can do it without letting go. When did you connect with Philadelphia people?"

"Are you kidding? They connected with me. They came right up to me at the blackjack table the second you went for a walk."

"What if they're cops?"

"Oh, no. I recognized them. I'd seen them in Vegas and once in New York."

"What did they say?"

"You should hear them. They're like from another country. They talk out of the side of their mouths." She mimicked, "'We hear you're doing real good in New York. Maybe you want to come in with us down here.'"

"How do they know about you?"

"You can't fool the street, Chris. Everybody knows the Rizzolos are tops. Philly and New England have to connect in New York. Inviting me to take a shot at AC is like a peace offering. Of course, I'd have to fight to keep it, but we're talking gold, man. This place is making Vegas a ghost town. The only problem is, the connected people can't get their act together. The Philly *cafone* are killing each other off, messing up the image and wasting a great shot. Anyhow, that's why I'm getting dressed. I'm meeting a guy for dinner."

"What guy?"

"One of these guys."

"Mind if I come?"

"Relax, he's with his girl."

"I'll come along anyhow. Sounds interesting."

Their hosts were waiting in an Italian restaurant a block from the Boardwalk. Marty had a broad chest and a hearty conspiratorial laugh. He reminded Taggart of a young version of his Uncle Vinnie, the way he said, "It don't look like much, but it's nice and private and the food's good."

Marty's girlfriend, Zell, looked loud, but said little. She got flustered when Taggart grinned at her for staring at the love bites Helen had left on his neck.

"I know you," said Marty. "You're the builder."

"What do you do?" Taggart asked.

"I'm a builder, too. You wouldn't a heard a me, yet. I'm not as big."

"Around here?"

"Pennsylvania. This is just fun down here, but I was talking with Helen earlier about what a future this place has."

"I'm a builder, too," said Zell.

"What?"

"Honey . . . She's got a plumbing outfit. You know, affirmative action."

"But I really run it," said Zell.

"Honey, pipe down. Do you do that up in New York, Chris? Front companies for the civil rights quotas?"

"I don't." Taggart looked at Helen, who hadn't said a word since they sat down. She lifted her shoulder in a minute shrug.

"They kept trying to steer the conversation," Taggart said on the ride back to their hotel. "Like they were looking for quotes."

"I didn't like them, either."

"Too busy establishing credentials," he said in the room. "I think they're phonies."

"What do you mean?"

"Small-time hoods trying to get a free ride off you."

He went out on the terrace and stared at the dark ocean awhile.

She came out and stood with him, shivering until he wrapped his arms around her. "You're not really interested in Atlantic City, are you? We could go to Europe and—"

She turned her face. She wanted to scream, *Yes*. Let's go. Now! Run!

"It's a gold mine, Chris."

"But—"

"I could set up here and get the hell out of New York. Less heat."

"You really think so?"

"I could really take control. End the fighting here. And no one would ever try to take it away. It's like a gift for the right family."

They went in and had a drink. Taggart was quiet. He went to look at the ocean again. She watched him, her heart pounding. He leaned over the terrace railing so he could see the bright lights marching along the beach. He looked at New

York that way, she knew, hunting dark spots to fill with new buildings.

She had done it. She had wedged the idea into his head that the prize was worth taking. And, best of all, she thought bitterly, she supposedly came with it. A poisonous pot sweetener. She thought of her brother and her family. Had she not, she would have walked out on the terrace and thrown herself into the night.

Taggart stayed outside a long while, thinking. When he came back, she was hanging up her dress. He came up behind her, cupped her breast and her belly, and touched his lips to her ear.

"I'm going to make you an offer."

She turned swiftly in his hands and covered his mouth. "We'll sleep on it."

"It's wild. You'll love it."

She drew him to the bed. "Not another word till morning."

"I'm serious."

"Shut up. Everytime you open your mouth, I'm going to put part of me into it. Shhh."

"Listen—"

"I warned you. . . ."

In the morning, she awakened early and phoned quietly for coffee. Chris stirred sleepily when the waiter arrived. She pillowed his head on her thighs and sipped the coffee and stroked his hair, wishing they could sleep forever.

"Can I talk yet?"

"Tell me at breakfast."

"It'll be brunch by then."

Finally, at brunch in a hotel dining room with a gold-vaulted ceiling, huge chandeliers, and the flashing casino lights visible through many doors, Helen Rizzolo spread a pink linen napkin on her lap, clinked her mimosa glass against his, and listened to Taggart with somber eyes.

"If you want Atlantic City—"

"I don't know," she whispered. "Maybe you should—"

"You got me thinking. I've been thinking about how Las Vegas was years ago. With your support, I could be like the Howard Hughes of Atlantic City. We could own this town. It's a great place to build hotels, especially when the woman I love is in a position to help me with zoning. The town's got more class already than Vegas ever did, and it's near our stuff in New York. We'll run this place exactly the way we want it. We'll own it. No government bullshit."

"Chris, are you sure?"

"Consider it a wedding gift. If you want to take over Atlantic City, you've got Atlantic City."

She looked away, because if she looked into his eyes she would cry. But so far, nothing she had coaxed him to say would make a case for Tony Taglione. It was now or never.

"What do you say?" he prompted.

"How would we do it?"

"Exactly like New York. The hell with those clowns last night. We don't need them. We'll do it our way. Find a nice, tight family like yours to front the street for us. If we can't find one, organize one or bring in our own people. Then I'll talk Reggie into supplying the dope and the muscle to bust them up on top. We'll take this town in a month—if you're sure you want to do this again."

"I don't know," she whispered. She took his hand and pressed it between her thighs, covering the bug, but it was too late. She saw them coming from the doors.

"I'm sure," said Taggart. "I could build for ten years here if we controlled the government. It's a dynamite opportunity. And the best part is we'll do it together."

Helen leaned across the table and took the back of his head in both hands. She stared into his eyes. Taggart was astonished to see tears fill hers.

"What?" he asked. "What's wrong?"

She crushed his mouth with hers. When he opened his lips she pulled him harder. Her body shook with the strain. He felt her teeth and tasted blood. With a convulsive shudder she let him go. When they parted he thought he would die.

"*Jesus*. Come upstairs."

"I'm sorry," she said. There was blood on her lip, bright red, his or hers—he would never know. "I wish it never happened."

"Why?"

She turned her face. He looked up, his heart still pounding,

385

and broke into a startled smile. "Tony! There's Tony! Hey, Tony! What are you, on a junket? Sit down, man. Grab a chair. Waiter!"

The waiters had retreated to the wall. They were watching for something to happen. Taggart looked at Helen. Her face was white, her mouth a rough line crumbling at the edges. He turned back to his brother, saw the agents spreading out behind him, and thought, They got to Jack Warner. There were four big guys with Tony and agents at every door.

"What's going on, Tony? Who's the heavies?"

"They're going to arrest you, Chris."

"What?"

"I came to read you your rights. You have the right to remain silent. You have the right to legal counsel. You have the right—"

"What the hell for?"

"Heroin trafficking."

"Hey, I'm just a businessman." Taggart laughed. No way they could ever prove that.

"Racketeering."

"Forget it."

"And murder," Tony finished coldly. "I didn't believe her . . . I didn't *want* to believe her. So I needed this to start a case." He pulled a Sony out of his pocket and turned it on.

"Exactly like New York. The hell with those clowns last night. We don't need them. We'll do it our way. Find a nice, tight family like yours to front the street for us. If we can't find one, organize one or bring in our own people. Then I'll talk Reggie into supplying the dope and the muscle to bust them up on top."

Tony turned it off. "Who's Reggie?"

Taggart felt a sickening sensation that the casino lights were whirling around him. He looked at Helen. A tear skated down her cheek. She pulled back when he reached for her hand.

"Where'd you hide the wire?"

"Garter belt."

"I'd like to hear the rest of the tape, if we didn't melt it. Want to tell me why?"

"Don't say anything. They'll use it against you."

"I want to know why."

"Eddie. It's a trade for my brother."

"But we—"

"We are *stranieri*," she whispered. "'A wife is one thing, a sister something more.'"

Chapter 29

A PAIR OF AGENTS stepped toward the table. "Stand up, please."

Taggart pointed a big, blunt, manicured finger at his brother. "*You* know and *I* know, they owed us."

"They owed the law. And so do you. Make it easy for me and I'll do what I can to make it easy for you. Who's Reggie?"

"Reggie?" The whole room was spinning. Helen in the center, tears splashing the hands she held to her lips. He wanted to make her smile. "Reggie? Isn't that the rich kid in the Archie comics?"

Helen felt as if an earthquake had cleaved the gaudy room. With that joke he had forgiven her betrayal and the betrayals to come at his trial. It made it even more terrible that she could never see him again. Except, like her father, behind faraway prison walls.

They locked his handcuffs to a chain around his waist when they boarded the chartered plane. The NYPD escorted them with lights and sirens from LaGuardia Airport to Foley Square. Cops with shotguns lined the steps of the Federal Court House shouting, "*Get back! Back!*"

Barred, ethically, from participating in his brother's case, Tony Taglione observed Taggart's arraignment from the public area of the magistrate's courtroom. He maintained a scrupulous silence as the Strikeforce agents swore their complaints, but his gaze, alternately angry and stricken, flashed like high beams on ice.

Taggart pleaded not guilty. He was still deeply shaken by

the arrest. He was awed by the finality of the handcuffs; every few minutes he had to struggle with himself not to tear at the metal.

Taggart's lawyers—"graduates" themselves of the U.S. Attorney's office, Criminal Division—moved to seek bail.

Tony's assistants acted swiftly to dominate the bail hearing. They characterized Taggart as an international criminal with means to escape the court's jurisdiction before the government could finish investigating the scope of Taggart's conspiracy.

The head of Taggart's defense team rebutted: "To characterize the government's case as thinner than the thinnest ceramic wafer on the smallest chip in the tiniest component of a microscopic electronic element would be to overstate its validity manyfold. We will not dignify this entrapment by a woman scorned—a woman whose racketeering brother is in the slammer, a woman herself on the brink—by ever mentioning it again. Your Honor, Mr. Taggart seeks bail solely on the grounds that his roots are deep in the community." He sat down whispering, "If this ever goes to trial, we will eat their 'accomplice witness' for breakfast."

"Just keep me out of jail."

Tony's assistants offered their second argument. The accused was a danger to the community.

Taggart's lawyer rose again, chuckling. "A *danger* to the community? Perhaps the prosecutor has confused the breast-beating of a disappointed Landmarks Commission with reality, but I really can't accept that Mr. Christopher Taggart, developer of some four Manhattan skyscrapers this year alone, a Queens high school, and several thousand units of Bronx low-income housing, is a danger to the community. Good lord, Your Honor, Mr. Taggart *is* the community."

The magistrate, an ordinary-looking, round-faced woman of middle age, replied: "Obviously, the charges are extremely serious. And just as obviously, what the accused characterizes as roots in the community could also be construed as the wealth and power to escape the jurisdiction. Therefore, the accused will surrender his passport to the U.S. Attorney. And bail is set at eight hundred thousand dollars."

Taggart held up his hands. "Could Your Honor have these removed so I could write a check?"

Chapter 30

"AND OF COURSE," said the barfly, "you've heard of the Eton boy who ran away from school? Disguised himself by closing the bottom button on his waistcoat."

Jack Warner felt his vest—the goddamned thing was buttoned—finished his flat beer in the dreary pub near Charing Cross train station, and wandered unhappily into the cold, damp streets of London. He hated not knowing the rules. And he didn't really want to learn new ones. Loathing his weeks in continental Europe, he had retreated to England, and liked it even less. It was all, in a word, bush. Or, in three words, not New York. He missed Puerto Ricans, blacks, and Chinese. He missed fast, dirty streets and Italian guys on the make. He missed knowing who was good and who was bad. But most of all, he missed being a cop.

Heading for a newstand to buy a map of Ireland, he was amazed to find Christopher Taggart's picture plastered on the front pages. How in hell had they nailed the slick bastard? Warner started to read the story in the *International Herald Tribune*, but halfway down the first column he bolted into the street, hailing a cab with the paper.

"Heathrow Airport!"

"What's in the news, Guv?"

"My ticket home."

U.S. Customs didn't even blink at the forged passport Reggie Rand had supplied him when he had fled New York. Warner ducked the Immigration guys working Kennedy and caught a cab to his Lower East Side apartment. Slipping in unnoticed, he wedged himself into his kitchen closet and opened a tiny wooden door in the back, behind which sat the ancient fuse box. Helen Rizzolo might have told Tony Taglione *what* his brother had done, but knowing and *proving* were different matters, as any cop could tell you.

Five malevolent-looking glass fuses studded a metal frame. He disengaged the main switch; the lights went out and the refrigerator stopped with a shudder that shook the floor. Working by flashlight, he unscrewed the face of the fuse box, reached into the hole, and removed a long mailing tube. Then he stuffed the cardboard tube into the inside pocket of his raincoat, and headed for St. Andrew's Square.

The Strikeforce receptionist regarded him uncertainly.

"Tell Taglione it's Detective Jack Warner, NYPD, and I guarantee he'll drop everything."

As a cop, he had broken many a prisoner down; the coin of the realm was *I will send you to jail*, and there was only one winner in the race to cooperate. An FBI agent he knew came out and frisked him warily. He even peered inside the mailing tube.

"I'm not here to shoot him, asshole."

"I wish you were so I'd have an excuse to shoot you. Here's a warrant for your arrest."

"Save us both some trouble and wait till I've seen the boss."

Taglione was on the phone. Some exhausted-looking assistants were waiting with papers. Agents were pacing the halls, smoking too much. Warner smiled. Just as he had suspected when he had read the first news story—all the trappings of a big case turned sour.

Taglione covered the mouthpiece and drilled him with his piercing eyes. "Are you turning yourself in?"

"Alone."

Taglione studied him with dark contempt, muttered something into the phone, hung up, and asked his assistant attorneys to come back in five minutes.

Warner closed the door and leaned against it. "All I want is my badge."

"Your *badge?* You'll be lucky to pull ten years. Why should I give you your badge?"

"Because without me, you got shit on Taggart."

"We have an accomplice witness. I don't call that a weak case."

"You have no corroboration."

Taglione stared.

"Hey, I worked for your brother. I know how careful he was. He didn't give the broad anything she could use on him. All she's got is a story. No proof."

"Jack, you betrayed the most prestigious office in America. You sold out and ran for it. I can't give you your badge."

Warner shrugged. "So your brother walks."

"And you go to prison."

"Great. The big guy gets away and the little guy gets the slammer. Maybe the U.S. Attorney for Kansas plays that way. But the Southern District of New York? . . ."

Taglione reddened and Warner knew he had him. Taglione said, "Even if Arthur Finch goes along, the cops won't. Everybody knows you ran."

"I didn't run," Warner smirked. "Where'd you get that idea? It was a setup. I was working a deep-cover sting for you."

"You were not."

"But if you and Finch tell 'em we had to make it look like I ran, then I'm home free and you make your case."

Taglione glared, ready to kill, but he was stuck, and knew it. "You'd have to do a hell of a lot to get us to go along with that."

Warner laughed. "Hey, nobody knows more about the Maf than Jack Warner."

He pulled the mailer from his new trenchcoat, pried off the cap, and spilled the contents across Taglione's desk—notes, Xeroxes, recording transcripts, phone records, names and dates.

Taglione sifted through them with both hands. "What does this mean?"

"It means if I keep my badge, I can use my files to steer your investigation in seventeen directions your brother went. Helen Rizzolo don't know the half of it."

* * *

U.S. Attorney Arthur Finch invited Taggart and his lawyer to meet in his office. Tony Taglione was there when they arrived, sitting on a couch, his dark eyes burning. Taggart's lawyer walked around, sniffing the wind while he rolled a cigar pugnaciously between his fingers. Taggart stood quietly by the window gazing out at the Brooklyn Bridge, waiting to hear what had gone badly wrong. Arthur took the seat behind his desk.

"I'm going to let your client cop a plea."

"We're not copping any plea."

"You'll be begging to when you hear what we've got."

"You've got shit, Arthur. This is a charade to scare my client. You've got an asshole case and you're going to look like assholes in front of the grand jury. I'm moving to get this whole trumped-up mess dropped tomorrow morning."

Finch's eyes turned steely gray, and for the first time in the years he had known him, Taggart understood how earlier Finch generations had acquired railroads. "Are you quite through, Counselor?"

He held Taggart's lawyer's eye until the man looked away.

"Up until now, we knew your client did it. Now, we can prove how."

"If you're that sure, Arthur, how come you're talking plea?"

"Because I would much prefer a full list of all the government people your client corrupted and the Mafiosi he elevated and the dope networks he spawned, as well as your client himself under immediate lock and key."

"Should we throw in a cure for cancer?"

"We've cut a cooperation agreement with one of your client's helpers. He's steering us in every direction we need. The conspiracy is much bigger than we thought."

"Come off it. What 'helper'?" He glanced at Taggart, who shrugged and thought, *Jack Warner.*

"I'm willing to consolidate all the charges—those made and those to be made—into two RICOs on heroin trafficking, twenty years apiece, to be served concurrently. The *full*

393

twenty. I don't want to see your man on the street before he's fifty years old."

"I don't believe you guys. What 'helper'? Who is this 'helper'?"

The room was stuffy. Taggart unlatched the window and swung it open a crack. He held his face to the cool breeze, then turned to study the men debating his fate. Arthur glared back, and Taggart realized that even as he tried to put him in jail, the U.S. Attorney was hoping to save Tony's career. His own lawyer's mouth was a tight, worried line. And Tony's mask was slipping; a tic that Chris remembered from childhood was tugging at his brother's cheek.

"Sid, would you please leave the room?" he said to his attorney.

"Mr. Taggart—"

"Out! Please."

"I really strongly advise—"

Taggart glanced at Tony and Tony stood up. "Arthur? Why don't Chris and I take a walk?"

"Fine with me. Counsel and I can pass the time recalling the good old days before he left public service to get rich."

"Some of us weren't born with a silver suppository up our ass," Sid shot back. "Mr. Taggart, what you're doing is dangerous. I strongly advise—"

"I'm just going for a walk with my brother."

While riding the elevator and walking through the lobby and onto the pavestone plaza, Taggart could feel Tony assessing him, as if he was hunting the best approach to get him to open up. "No escort?" he asked.

"You're still out on bail, for the moment, Mr. Community. What do you want? Walk? Drink?" He nodded toward Police Headquarters, behind which nestled a cop bar. "Hamburger at the Mick's?"

Taggart raised his eyes to the building tops. "Let's go to the Spire."

"You gonna talk to me?"

"Yeah. We'll work something out. I want to see the job."

They hurried to Center Street and got into a cab. "Okay," Tony said, shutting the driver's shield. "Just us. It's all true, isn't it?"

"What do you think?"

"But *why?* Why'd you do it?"

"For Pop."

Tony stared. "Revenge?"

"I told you over ten years ago. They owed us."

"All for Pop?"

"All."

"What about the money?"

"What money? I spent more than I ever made."

They sat silently until the cab reached Union Square. Tony said, "You don't understand what you've done wrong, do you? You still don't understand the crimes. You sold dope."

"Bait."

"You killed people."

"Greaseball hoods."

"You corrupted—"

"I got caught."

"But don't you understand what you've done?"

"Yes. I destroyed the biggest Mafia family in New York."

"You can't do that!"

"I did it. The Cirillos are broken, man. Pick up the pieces."

"It's the wrong way."

"It *worked.*"

"You undermine everything. Why have a government if you can just run out and blow people away to satisfy your revenge? Why have law?"

"You tell me."

"Because a guy can always be wrong. And the rest of us have to be protected from a guy who can be wrong."

"But I was right. And you know it. We fought on this from the beginning. You're still trying to force theories on truth. But you know I was right."

"Not quite. You're going to jail."

"We'll see."

"Oh, you're going all right. You belong to the law now."

"The same law that did nothing when they killed Pop."

"Pop!" Tony yelled. "Blame it on Pop!"

"They killed Pop!"

"Pop! What about *me?*"

"What?"

"You used me. You used my office. You ripped me off, Chris. You tricked me into doing your dirty work."

"I gave you real leads."

"Thanks a lot. You two. You and Pop. Remember joking about me? Big joke. Tony's honest? Tony's straight? He's like a priest? Got it from Mom? And then in the next breath, Pop going, 'Tony's gonna be my lawyer.'"

"What's wrong with that? He loved you. You were his first-born son."

"Pop knew I couldn't have been his lawyer in a million years. Didn't you ever wonder? Who did he appoint executor of his will? You. I was studying law, and he put you in charge of the money."

"I was in the business," Taggart protested, but he too had wondered at the time, and despite the pride of being chosen, he had felt for Tony. Now he wished he had said something then, when it had mattered.

"And straight Tony was too honest," Tony said bitterly.

"*I* wanted you to be my lawyer. I asked you fourteen times."

"You didn't want a lawyer, you wanted a manipulator. You wanted to find the ways around the law like it's a game, and if you're smart you win. Well, that's bullshit. The law is supposed to protect helpless people from people who are so strong they think they can do what they please—people like you, Bro. Scary people. . . . Admit it, man. You wanted me off the Strikeforce because you knew I'd nail your ass in the end."

"All Pop or I ever wanted was you to be part of the family."

"You used me. You lied. You talked about family, but you treated me like I was one of your fucking women."

"Hey. Don't talk to me about women. You don't know them."

"You *do?*" Tony exploded. "You arrogant bastard! Do whatever you feel, whenever you feel. That's how you live. If you get mad, kill somebody—right, Bro? It's obvious you killed Rendini, or had him killed. You meet a Mafia girl, bingo, fall in love. Your brother, who you say you love, gets established in something he loves, so you use the dummy. You have no standards. You have no restraint. No *character*. Look what you've done. You've blown it all. The company. Us. Even Pop. I loved him too, you know. I didn't have to agree with him to love him. Do you think Pop would back you on this shit? Don't you see how far wrong you've gone? Do you think Pop would *approve?*"

"The only thing I regret is making you trouble," Taggart retorted angrily. "I am really sorry. You wouldn't have been hurt if I didn't get caught, and believe me, Tony, I did not intend to get caught."

"What are you, God? Of course you got caught."

Taggart flushed darkly. "Only because Eddie Rizzolo horned in on that phony dope deal. When you investigate you'll see I had Crazy Mikey set up. He was the last. I got Don Richard. I got Sal Ponte. I blew that whole stinking family apart. Then I was home free. Out and done. With my father's murder avenged . . . our father. *I don't apologize for avenging Pop.*"

"But you couldn't let it go," Tony shouted. "You love the power it took to beat them. *The Howard Hughes of Atlantic City!*"

"I—"

"How about the Al Capone of Chicago? Why not the Mussolini of Italy?"

Taggart stared back as long as he could. What could he say? For Helen? Partly. But as much for himself, he had to admit. A castle in Europe was a fantasy. He had to work. He had to build buildings. And what a temptation to build them without restraint.

"Do you deny it?"

"You've got it on tape," he admitted. For a long moment the only sounds he heard were the taxi's tires pounding asphalt and a bubbling murmur from its rusty muffler.

"Maybe that's the crime of revenge," Tony said softly. "It feels too good to stop."

Turning away, Taggart suddenly thought he saw his father standing at the bars of a prison cell. The image was so real— Mike Taglione had his coat over his arm and his eyes were dismayed, even as he tried to offer an encouraging smile.

"Chris? . . . Chris!"

The hallucination dispersed, and Tony was there again, beside him in the cab. Taggart's hands began to shake with a violence that frightened him. He looked at the plastic shield and the windshield beyond. His Spire was growing tall in the distance.

"What is it?" he asked dully.

"We've got you cold," Tony whispered. "It's just a matter of time. If you don't cooperate, Arthur will put you away a lot more than twenty years. He'll put you inside forever. And my outfit will have to help him."

Tony's whisper faded, like the voice of a child on the verge of tears. Taggart abruptly realized he would never get out of this. Fight as he would, the Strikeforce would put him in prison. There was no way to win. His hands were still shaking.

Tony noticed. "We gotta talk," he said. "Make the best deal for you. Chris, it's all I can do."

Quickly, as the cab snaked through the Helmsley Building and up Park Avenue, Tony described in detail the range of information that Arthur Finch would require to cut a cooperation agreement.

"There's a lot of stuff I don't know. I didn't walk around with a gun in my hand."

"Okay, who does know?"

Taggart shrugged. "Talk to Jack Warner."

"We already have. Who's Reggie Rand?"

"Forget it."

"Chris, this is your life."

"Sorry. I don't turn in my friends."

"Do Chryl and Vicky have anything to do with it?"

"Christ, no."

"Sylvia? Your supers?"

"No. The business is legit."

"It turns on Rand, doesn't it?"

"Forget it."

"You have to make a deal. You'll go away forever if Arthur takes you to trial."

The cab slowed in heavy traffic and Taggart sank into a deep silence that lasted, despite Tony's exhortations, until they finally arrived at the construction gate. There he surprised Tony, exploding back to life, tossing money at the cab driver, springing onto the sidewalk with all eyes for the job. Like their father, Tony thought; the boss—just like Mike Taglione.

Already Chris was charging through the gate. Tony scrambled after him, as he used to try to keep pace with the two of them. He caught up when Chris beckoned a foreman. "Charley, it's your ass if that dumpster catches fire. Get it out of here!"

"Sorry, Chris, the truck's on its way."

"Fuckin' better be. How's the kids?"

"They're trying out for Little League."

"Talk to Sylvia about uniforms. Hey, this is my brother, Tony. Maybe you can get the U.S. Attorney to sponsor a team, too."

The foreman, who read the newspapers, stared. Tony grabbed two hardhats and followed Chris into the site and aboard an outside hoist which had already started rising. As it clanked up the nearly completed building—ten, twenty, forty, eighty floors—Taggart grew pensive again as the city thrust crisp edges into the deepening afternoon light.

"I'll miss this," he said softly. "This time of day the sunlight makes the buildings better than the guy who built them. For a second, each stands alone." He smiled at Tony as the elevator stopped. "And that's when the whole thing looks best."

The roof was deep in fresh, white pea gravel. They crossed to the edge and climbed onto the only bare steel remaining, the new beams replacing those damaged in the attack on Taggart's cantilevered penthouse. He walked a narrow header to the far edge and rested against a column that stood alone. Tony caught up, swung gracefully around him, and leaned on the other side. The wind plucked at their jackets, tugged their hair. Tony slapped the steel. "What's this?"

"I had to pull a header that got creamed in the accident—which it wasn't, by the way; Don Richard sent a guy to kill Helen—so I figured what the hell, while I'm making repairs I'll add a room." He started to make a joke about slipping an unauthorized floor past the mayor, but suddenly the grief he had felt since Atlantic City swelled and rolled over him like a wave. He could only manage to say, "It was supposed to be a surprise—a little music room in the clouds."

Tony gathered his resolve and forced himself to look at Chris's face. He leaned around the column and saw what he had feared for days. There were guys who made it through prison and guys who couldn't. His brother would waste away like a tethered eagle.

"How could you be so stupid as to trust Helen Rizzolo?"

Taggart looked at him, puzzled, as the words sank in. "You're not talking about right and wrong, now. You're talking about getting caught."

"You heard me." Tony was trembling. "How could you be so stupid? She handed me your ass on a silver platter."

"I'm not sorry I fell in love."

Sweat glazed Tony's palms. They were suddenly so wet that his grip began to slide on the steel. He dried them on his trousers and grabbed hold again. He was the only force on earth that could save Chris, but it would cost him everything he believed in. He tried again to make something work.

"Listen. If I could maybe persuade Arthur to come down a few years, would you give him what he needs? You know, maybe you'd get out on parole in a few years."

"I can't give him Reggie Rand."

Tony wiped his palms again. "I didn't think so, " he whispered.

Chris felt his brother's hand, and looked down as Tony pressed a slim blue booklet into his palm.

"Take it!"

Taggart stared, utterly astonished. It was his passport.

"I'll give you three hours." Tony's lean face was working, his dark gaze opaque. "Three hours. Get on a plane. Go away. *Don't ever come back.*"

"What happens to you?"

"It's a little late to start worrying about that. Go! From what I know already, you can disappear in style."

Taggart thumbed the stiff pages. The wind seized them, flipping them like a slick-fingered dealer; the entry stamps of two dozen nations were a blueprint of all he had done to avenge his father. Now it was he who leaned around the column to see his brother's face. The tic was leaping in Tony's cheek, and the fire in his eyes was going out.

"What about the law?"

"I can't make it fit you."

"What about your office? What about the Strikeforce?"

"I can handle it."

"No, you can't. The law is your family, like Pop was my family. You can't betray it."

"Only for you."

Tony's need to sacrifice hit Taggart like a sledgehammer. "That's how I felt about Pop! *That's why I did it.*"

"Go!"

"No. I can't let you pay my dues." He tried to wedge the passport between the steel and Tony's fingers. Tony jerked his hand away.

"Don't be crazy, Bro. You'll spend the best part of your life in jail."

Taggart shuddered. Helen would make a loyal visit once a week, forever. For in a terrible, relentless way he would become part of her family and she would serve him. But he could no sooner ask that of her than let Tony betray himself.

"If I run, you'll be finished with the law. And dead in your heart."

Taggart retreated to his side of the pillar and gazed at the city. His eye fell on beauty wherever it roved—the exultant skyline, the sunlit forms, their shiny-colored glass skins, new concrete racing upward. He leaned out to see the ground. A quarter-mile down, Park Avenue was a broad river between shores of glass. Long beds of daffodils drifted down the middle of the avenue like a string of yellow barges. So much to remember.

"But you'll die in prison," Tony pleaded. "Let me do this for you."

Taggart knelt on the header and tucked the passport within the flange of the pillar where it was safe from the wind. He arose lightly, cupped his brother's face in his big hand. "I think it's more than I deserve."

"Chris!"

Tony reached for him, but it was too late.

"I love you," Taggart said, stepping into the sky.

Epilogue

Saints Avenged, Angels Seduced
(Two Months Later)

A WHITE ROLLS-ROYCE drifted slowly down Mott Street.

Jack Warner was out of breath, having toiled up the Mosco Street hill on his regular route from Police Plaza to Hunam House. His mind was on a stiff drink and a cold Chinese beer, so he didn't notice the limousine until they met in front of the restaurant.

"Jack!"

Warner flinched. Reggie Rand was sitting in the limousine.

Caught flatfooted, Warner knew he couldn't run, so he did the only thing possible. He charged, hurled himself into the passenger compartment, and rammed his gun into Reggie's belly.

"*Jack!* Easy."

Instead of a pistol, Reggie was holding an old-fashioned glass, and he looked and smelled like he had had a few. Warner frisked him thoroughly, nonetheless, but his ankle gun was gone, as were the holster and a throwing knife he sometimes carried in the back of his belt. "Would you like a drink?"

Warner closed the door and holstered his weapon. The partition was up, the driver invisible, and the air-conditioning made the car comfortably cool. "What are you doing in New York? Half the feds in America are looking for you."

"Tying up some loose ends. I saw you on the street and thought—"

"Where'd you get the car? I thought the Feds confiscated it."

"We maintained several in the event we were followed. In

fact," Reggie added dryly, "I recall we lost *you* a couple of times that way. Whiskey?"

Warner nodded, debating whether to arrest the Brit himself. Tough decision. He was valuable either way. Unless he was over the hill, in which case he was worth more in jail. He studied him as Reggie opened the bar, refilled his own glass first with a shaky hand, and poured another for him, neat.

"What shall we drink to?" Reggie asked with an ironic glance, tossing his whiskey back. "Survivors?"

"Okay. Survivors."

"Have the other half," Reggie said, pouring again. "Ice this time?"

"Yeah."

"Pardon my fingers. Someone pinched the bloody tongs."

Warner took a long sip and sat back to let the stuff do its work. Better . . . much better. No denying Reggie had scared the hell out of him—nice reflexes, though. Even if it had been a rubout, he might have saved himself by his quick action.

"What are you going to do?" he asked. "Got anything lined up?"

"I'm not really sure," Reggie replied. "This has all been rather a sudden shock."

"Well, if you get something, stay in touch. You know?"

Reggie swirled his glass and stared owlishly into the liquor. He drank some more, refilled, and added a splash to Warner's.

"Funny thing," Warner said, breaking the silence.

"Funny?"

"The wise guys always say, 'Never trust a woman.'"

"Helen? Oh, I don't know about that. Her family came first. That was her code and one has to respect the fact that she adhered to it."

"Italian women never forget. Screw them once and they make you pay. He musta done something to her."

Reggie put down his glass. "Whatever there was between Helen Rizzolo and Mr. Taggart, Helen *sacrificed* to save her brother. One must respect her strength as well as her . . . honesty?"

"She turned the guy in."

"She honored the greater whole. That is far different from treachery for one's own sake. Different from squealing on Mr. Taggart purely for your own advantage."

"What?"

"Jack, Mr. Taggart would have beaten the charge if his brother had not received additional evidence. Evidence which only you or I could have supplied. . . . I didn't."

The car started moving.

Warner reached in his jacket and touched his gun. "You got some crazy idea of doing something about it? Hey, fellow, you're talking to a cop. I'll blow your head off and deliver the carcass to the nearest station house."

"You betrayed your badge. You betrayed your fellow officers. And you betrayed Mr. Taggart. All for Jack and only for Jack. You serve no one. . . . I might feel sorry for you if your selfish treachery hadn't destroyed my friend."

"What are you going to do about it?"

Reggie raised his arm, wincing as if it had been hurt recently, and slid the French cuff off his wristwatch. A sweep timing hand was whirling around the face. He pressed a stud and the hand stopped, quivering. "It's already done."

Warner blinked. Reggie seemed suddenly very sober. The car slowed for a red light. Chinese people and tourists wandered by, gazing blankly at the mirrored windows.

Warner's throat felt tight. He looked at the drink. "Tastes funny."

"It's the poison," Reggie said gravely.

Warner reached for the door. It was four or five miles away. Reggie appeared to be falling down a deep hole, getting smaller and smaller. When Warner tried to speak, his voice was a whisper, and it hurt terribly. He pried a question like a claw from his throat. "How come you didn't just shoot me?"

In answer, Reggie lowered the chauffeur's partition, and Warner saw to his astonishment that the Englishman had a new boss. Helen Rizzolo turned from the wheel, her silky black hair cascading from a chauffeur's cap.

"That wasn't a choice I could live with," she said. "Mr.

Taggart would have wanted you to know that he had been avenged."

"You won it all" were Warner's dying words.

And perhaps, thought Reggie, Helen had—what little Taggart had left of it—but her somber eyes were dark with a thousand years of sorrow, her voice as lonely as the stars.

Income Tax I

BY MICHAEL R. ASIMOW
University of California, Los Angeles

Twentieth Edition

THE **barbri** GROUP
A THOMSON COMPANY

EDITORIAL OFFICES: 111 W. Jackson Blvd., 7th Floor, Chicago, IL 60604
REGIONAL OFFICES: Chicago, Dallas, Los Angeles, New York, Washington, D.C.

SERIES EDITOR
Elizabeth L. Snyder, B.A., J.D.
Attorney At Law

PROJECT EDITOR
Paul T. Phillips, B.A., J.D.
Attorney At Law

QUALITY CONTROL EDITOR
Sanetta M. Hister

Summary of Contents

Text Correlation Chart

Gilbert Law Summary INCOME TAX I	Freeland, Lathrope, Lind, Stephens *Fundamentals of Federal Income Taxation* 2002 (12th ed.)	Graetz, Schenk *Federal Income Taxation* 2001 (4th ed.)	Gunn, Ward *Federal Income Taxation* 2002 (5th ed.)	Klein, Bankman, Shaviro *Federal Income Taxation* 2000 (12th ed.) 2002 Supp.
I. IS IT INCOME?				
A. Constitutional Background	Page 14-21	Page 53-57	Page 1-4	Page 4-5, 157, 236-247
B. Definition of "Gross Income"	48-68	20, 85-87	45-50	9-27, 49-52, 82-87, 90-93
C. Exclusions from Gross Income	69-129, 155-164, 182-194, 227-240	92-119, 122-135, 162-167, 203-213	73-91, 113-115, 118-123, 124-128, 131-163, 172-200, 228	51-118, 124-147, 173-179, 182-191, 226-231; Supp. 5-7
D. Inclusions in Gross Income	48-68, 88-90, 92-96, 107-109, 113-114, 165-181, 195-208, 212-220	87-92, 104-106, 118-122, 130-131, 167-185, 470-478	51-62, 91-107, 123-139, 149, 222-224, 233-241	52-81, 117-118, 127-130, 147-155, 179-199, 371-375; Supp. 5
E. Tax-Exempt Organizations	807-809, 815	444-447	206-225	329, 426-446; Supp. 25-31
II. TO WHOM IS THE INCOME TAXABLE?				
A. Income Splitting by Gifts	242-282, 295-311, 377-385	475-515	186-187, 423, 435-451, 455-469, 473-482	250, 659-663, 671-695, 705-735
B. Statutory Divisions of Income	242-244, 929-936, 938-939, 940	456-475	423-424, 451-455, 469-471	663-671, 680
C. Below-Market Interest on Loans	478-506	107, 357-358, 738-746	415-422, 786-787	330-333
D. Taxation of Trusts	282-295	515-527	471-473	695-707, 735-744
III. IS IT DEDUCTIBLE OR IS IT A CREDIT?				
A. Introduction	314-316, 942-943	21-23, 214-215		28-29, 405-408, 459-460, 551
B. Business and Investment Deductions	314-475, 511-545, 785-799	215-343, 364-416	247-395, 532-538, 583-601, 644-654	459-651; Supp. 35-83
C. Personal Deductions	198-203, 212-220, 496-510, 520-525, 546-584, 785-832	21, 343-364, 376-381, 415-454, 474-475, 763-765	39-44, 63-71, 200-241, 293-299, 397, 401-424, 585-592, 644-656	15-16, 338-343, 371-376, 405-455; Supp. 9, 11-31
D. Tax Rates	928-941	29-38	7-14, 39-44, 231-232, 241, 451-455	16-20; Supp. 2
E. Credits	942-954	23, 252-253, 420-425, 427	241-246	29, 455-457, 509-513; Supp. 31-33
IV. GAIN OR LOSS ON SALE OR EXCHANGE OF PROPERTY				
A. Computation of Basis, Gain, or Loss	116-133	135-142, 185-203	60-61, 97-98, 247, 269-270, 499-502, 517-528, 538-539, 545-565	35-38, 119-126, 132-135, 194-204, Supp. 6-7
B. The Requirement of Realization	133-154, 852-858	142-160	99-107, 483-499, 503-519	34-35, 49-50, 201-220, 250-271, 299-303, 333-338; Supp. 3
C. Nonrecognition of Gain or Loss	129-130, 209-212, 221-226, 474-475, 891-926	472-475, 631-645	539-545, 567-584	231-233, 272-287, 360-366; Supp. 9
V. WHAT KIND OF INCOME IS IT? CAPITAL GAINS AND LOSSES AND TAX PREFERENCES				
A. Introductory Material	681-700	21-22, 528-542	603-614	31, 745-752
B. Is It a Capital Asset?	700-730, 741-750, 757-775	542-613	619-644, 656-673	752-834; Supp. 95

Gilbert Law Summary INCOME TAX I	Freeland, Lathrope, Lind, Stephens *Fundamentals of Federal Income Taxation* 2002 (12th ed.)	Graetz, Schenk *Federal Income Taxation* 2001 (4th ed.)	Gunn, Ward *Federal Income Taxation* 2002 (5th ed.)	Klein, Bankman, Shaviro *Federal Income Taxation* 2000 (12th ed.) 2002 Supp.
C. Was There a "Sale or Exchange"?	730-794	613-630	614-619, 644-656	835-839
D. Was There a Sufficient "Holding Period"?	750-756	630-631	604	745
E. Gains on Small Business Stock	693-694	575	607-610	746-747, 750
F. Special Computations	775-784, 861-869	331-340, 441-442, 738-746	398-399, 605-609, 639-643, 677	296-303, 612-613, 748, 796-801
G. Alternative Minimum Tax	954-966	24, 454, 785-797	300-302, 425-433	30, 651-658; Supp. 72-94
VI. TAX ACCOUNTING PROBLEMS				
A. Accounting Method— When Is an Item Taxable or Deductible?	586-647, 661-674, 834-852, 876-880	646-649, 670-784	63-72, 290-293, 675-686, 726-788	31-33, 297-359, 384-399, 558, 580-583; Supp. 9
B. The Annual Accounting Period	590, 648-660, 675-677	646-670	63-72	33-34, 155-173

Capsule Summary

loan, return of invested capital), from borrowing money, or from receiving money as a trustee.

b. **"Income" that is not cash** §19
Income need not be received in cash; it can be property or services.

c. **Windfalls** §20
Windfalls (*e.g.*, winning the lottery or finding money) are taxable.

d. **Unsolicited property** §21
Unsolicited property might not be taxable until the taxpayer indicates an intent to retain it (*e.g.*, by donating and claiming a charitable deduction).

e. **All-inclusive definition** §22
Any increment in net worth is presumed income unless specifically excluded by the Code or within a nonrecognition provision. Note that taxation depends on *realization*.

4. **Imputed Income** §23
Imputed income arises when a taxpayer **works for himself or uses his own property** (*e.g.*, housekeeping services done for one's own family). This type of income has never been taxed.

a. **Working for oneself** §24
If one renders services to himself and an **employment relationship is also involved**, that benefit is held to be gross income. And **interest income** often must be imputed.

b. **Exchange of services** §26
If two taxpayers exchange goods or services, **both** have gross income, unless an exclusion applies.

C. **EXCLUSIONS FROM GROSS INCOME**

1. **Gifts and Inheritances** §28
Gross income does not include the value of property received by gift, devise, bequest, or inheritance.

a. **What constitutes a "gift"** §29
The donor's **motive** must have been one of **"detached and disinterested generosity."** If there are mixed motives, the "primary" motive controls. The concept of a "gift" is narrowly construed for income tax purposes.

b. **Gift vs. compensation** §31
A problem arises when a payment is made without a legal obligation to one who has rendered services to the payor. The donor's primary motivation will determine the taxability. Payments by employer to employee are not gifts.

(1) **Deduction by donor** §35
An attempted deduction does not rule out a gift.

        (2)   Death benefits   **§36**

        Death benefits to a surviving spouse are not gifts if they are motivated by the deceased having been undercompensated.

        (3)   Gratuities   **§38**

        Tips and gratuities are **not gifts,** nor in most cases are **strike benefits** paid by a union.

        (4)   Bargain purchases   **§41**

        When a property is sold for less than fair value, the excess value may be a gift depending on the seller's motive. However, bargain purchases by an employee from an employer generally produce income.

    c.   What constitutes an "inheritance"   **§43**

    Any payment "referable" to an inheritance is excluded (*e.g.,* money received in settlement of a will contest), except that a bequest to an **employee** is taxable.

    d.   Income derived from gifts   **§47**

    Although the property transferred is a gift, all income derived from the gift is taxable to the donee. And all money received from a gift of future income is taxable to the donee.

2. Awards and Scholarships

    a.   Prizes and awards   **§49**

    Prizes and awards are **included in gross income**.

    b.   Scholarships and fellowships   **§53**

    A scholarship or fellowship is taxable unless it must be applied to tuition or books ("qualified scholarship").

3. Contributions to Capital   **§56**

Amounts received by partnerships and corporations as capital contributions are not taxable. Government inducements and amounts contributed by customers, however, are taxable.

4. Life Insurance   **§58**

Amounts paid by reason of **insured's death** are excluded.

    a.   Definition   **§59**

    A "life insurance" contract **shifts the risk** of premature death to the insurance company.

        (1)   Employer-paid benefits   **§60**

        Death benefits paid by an employer are taxable.

        (2)   Insurance by creditor   **§61**

        When a creditor takes out insurance on a debtor, the amount received by the creditor is **not excludible** life insurance. This money is treated as a payment of a debt.

        (3)   Accelerated death benefits   **§62**

        Life insurance amounts payable before death to a terminally ill or chronically ill individual are treated as if paid by reason of death.

b. Premium payments   §63

An exclusion is generally available to a recipient of insurance proceeds, *regardless of who paid* the premiums.

c. Purchasers of existing policies   §65

Purchasers of existing policies do *not* qualify for the life insurance exclusion, unless the purchaser is the insured, his partnership, or a corporation in which the insured is a shareholder or officer.

d. Installment benefits   §67

Benefits payable in installments are taxed to the extent that they represent *interest* on the unpaid balance.

5. Annuities   §68

The portion of an annuity payment that represents the *taxpayer's investment* in the policy is exempt as a return of capital. The portion excluded is
computed by dividing the consideration paid for the policy by the period
over which the payment is to be made.

a. Employee's annuity plans   §72

Annuity rules apply to amounts received from employee pension plans.
If the employee has a nonforfeitable right to the policy, she is taxed
on the purchase price when the employer purchases it. However, tax
on *qualified pension or profit-sharing plans* is *deferred* until payments are made.

6. Interest on State and Local Bonds   §75

Interest on state and local bonds is *excluded* from the income tax; however, interest received on *federal* obligations (*e.g.*, treasury bonds or notes)
is *included*.

7. Government Benefits

a. Social Security benefits   §78

A portion of Social Security benefits (old age and disability) is included in income if the taxpayer's *modified* adjusted gross income plus
50% of his Social Security benefits exceed $25,000 ($32,000 on joint
return). A greater portion is included in income if this sum exceeds
$32,000 ($44,000 on a joint return). However, Supplemental Security Income ("SSI") payments are nontaxable.

b. Welfare benefits   §82

Government benefits based on need (*e.g.*, welfare) are *excluded* from
income—even payments for government work required of welfare re-
cipients.

c. Unemployment compensation   §83

These payments are taxable.

8. Medical Insurance and Private Disability Payments

a. Medical insurance—employee pays premiums   §84

When the employee paid for medical or disability insurance, any benefit payments received under the policy are excluded from income.
However, if the employee *deducted* the medical expenses and then
was *reimbursed* for them, these reimbursements must be included in
income.

b. Employer-carried plans §86

If the employer pays for health and accident insurance for employees, the employees are **not** taxed on the premiums. Nor are they taxed on direct payments of medical expenses by the employer if the payments are made pursuant to a nondiscriminatory plan. All other **disability** payments are included in income.

9. Damage Payments

a. Personal injuries §89

Damages received, in lump sum or periodic payments, as a result of a judgment or settlement on account of physical personal injuries or physical sickness are **excluded**. Punitive damages are not excluded.

(1) Scope of exclusion §90

Damages for **emotional distress alone** are income unless a physical injury was also involved. Damages for **illegal discrimination** are also taxable.

(2) Attorneys' fees and costs §97

Since the taxpayer owns the tort claim, the majority of courts hold that costs and fees must be included in the recovery amount and then deducted.

b. Damages for business injuries §101

(1) **The recovery for damage to goodwill** was originally held excludible, but it was later held taxable to the extent that it exceeds the basis of the goodwill.

(2) **Damages for lost profits** are income.

(3) **The Code excludes damages for** patent infringement, breach of contract, breach of fiduciary duty, or antitrust violations. The amount excludible is the compensatory amount or the unrecovered losses, whichever is less. (The effect is an exclusion if there was no benefit from the prior losses.)

10. Miscellaneous Exclusions

a. Foreign earned income §109

Taxpayers working abroad may exclude up to $80,000 of their service income from a foreign source.

b. Group term life insurance premiums §110

Insurance premiums up to $50,000 per employee paid by the employer are not included in the employee's income. However, benefits must be provided to all employees on a nondiscriminatory basis.

c. Meals and lodging §111

The value of meals and lodging furnished by the employer to the employee and his family for the **convenience of the employer** is excluded if it is furnished on the employer's **business premises**.

(1) "Convenience of employer" §114

Under the Regulations, the "convenience of the employer" requires a *"substantial noncompensatory business reason."* However, a recent Supreme Court case indicates a narrower *"business necessity" test*.

(2) Cash reimbursements §118
Only meals and lodging furnished *in kind* are excluded; reimbursements in cash must be included in income.

d. Lessee's improvements §120
Lessee's improvements on leased property are *not* income to the landlord unless they are intended as *substitutes for rent*.

e. Insurance reimbursements for above-normal living expenses §122
Expenses resulting from fire, storm, or other casualty losses to a *taxpayer's home* are excludible.

f. Investment interest—higher education §123
Income from redemption of savings bonds, purchased after 1989 by a taxpayer at least 24 years old, that is used for higher education purposes is excluded. The exclusion is phased out as AGI exceeds $60,000 ($40,000 for singles).

g. Compensation for Holocaust victims §124
Excluded compensation includes direct payments, returned assets, and certain interest payments from funds arising from Holocaust litigation.

h. Other items §125
A minister's rental allowance, payments to foster parents, and combat and mustering-out pay to those in the service are excluded.

D. INCLUSIONS IN GROSS INCOME

1. Compensation for Services Rendered §127
Irrespective of the form of the payments, compensation for services rendered is includible in gross income.

a. Payment of employee's income taxes §128
The payment of an employee's income taxes or debts by an employer increases the employee's taxable income.

b. Reimbursements in connection with employment §129
Reimbursement for *travel, meals, and entertainment* costs is not income if the employee is primarily engaged in the employer's business.

(1) Frequent flier miles §134
It is unclear whether frequent flier miles credited by an airline to an employee for trips taken on an employer's business should be taxed to the employee. The IRS, due to the practical difficulties in taxing those miles, has never sought to tax those miles *unless* they are turned into cash by the employee.

c. Fringe benefits §135
Fringe benefits are generally taxable, but employees may exclude "no

additional cost" services, qualified employee discounts, working condition fringes (*e.g.,* car provided for business use), qualified transportation fringes (*e.g.,* vanpool), de minimis fringes (*e.g.,* on-premises gym), qualified moving expense reimbursement (*e.g.,* expenses employee would have been allowed to deduct if paid herself), and qualified retirement advice (if the employer has a qualified retirement plan). "Employee" includes an employee's spouse and dependent children, and also a retired or disabled former employee.

2. **Income from Cancellation of Indebtedness** §144

Unless within an exception (below), or unless the taxpayer had no net economic benefit, cancellation of debts is treated as income.

   a. **Exception as to insolvent taxpayers** §145

   No income exists to the extent that a debtor is insolvent before the debt cancellation (including discharge in bankruptcy). Note that other tax benefits are correspondingly reduced.

   b. **Exception for qualified real property business indebtedness** §148

   A taxpayer can elect to exclude debt cancellation from income where the debt is secured by real property used in a trade or business.

   c. **Exception for deductible payments** §149

   Income is not recognized to the extent that payment of the debt would have been deducted.

   d. **Cancellation as a "gift"** §150

   If the cancellation is a gift to the debtor, there is no income. There is rarely a gift motive unless there is a personal or family relationship.

   e. **Student loans** §151

   A student loan made by the government, a charitable hospital, or an educational institution that has been forgiven because the borrower has met certain conditions (*e.g.,* worked in certain areas or for certain employers), does not give rise to income.

   f. **Shareholder debt forgiveness** §153

   If a shareholder cancels a debt owed her by the corporation (either in exchange for stock or as a contribution to capital), the cancellation is treated as giving cash to the shareholder, and the corporation will also have debt cancellation income.

   g. **Reduction in purchase money debt** §157

   A reduction in purchase money debt by the *seller* is treated as a reduction in the basis, not as debt cancellation income.

   h. **Compromised claim** §158

   A compromise of a disputed claim does *not* produce income.

3. **Illegal Increases in Net Worth** §160

Money or property received through illegal activities is *included* in gross income irrespective of a promise to repay (*e.g.,* extortion money or embezzled money is included).

4. Spousal and Child Support Payments §162

Generally, payments by a separated or divorced spouse to the other spouse are *taxable to the recipient* and *deductible by the payor*. *But note:* Child support payments are *not deductible* to payor *nor are they taxable* to recipient.

E. TAX-EXEMPT ORGANIZATIONS

1. Charitable Organizations §173

To qualify, an organization must be organized and operated for religious, charitable, scientific, educational, etc., purposes; it must be nonprofit; no substantial part of its activities can include attempts to influence legislation. Contributions to such organizations are deductible.

a. Other tax-exempt organizations §176

Organizations such as unions, fraternities, civic leagues, etc., are exempt but contributions to them are *not* deductible.

b. Racial discrimination §177

Organizations engaging in racial discrimination are not tax-exempt.

2. Unrelated Business Income §178

Income from an activity substantially different from the nonprofit, charitable purpose is *not exempt*.

a. Rental income §179

Rental income from *real property* is exempt; however, rental income from personal property is not.

b. Debt-financed property §180

Investment income is taxed if the property involved was acquired with borrowed funds (unless the property is used solely for the purposes substantially related to the organization's charitable purposes).

3. Private Foundations §181

Foundations are subject to special restrictions; in any event, a blanket 2% tax is imposed on net investment income.

4. Political Organizations §184

These organizations are taxed like corporations on *investment* income, but they are not taxed on *"exempt function income."*

II. TO WHOM IS THE INCOME TAXABLE?

A. INCOME SPLITTING BY GIFTS

1. Gifts of Income vs. Gifts of Income-Producing Property §185

Income remains taxable to the *donor* if she retains ownership of the property to which she has transferred income.

a. Transfers of property §186

When the donor transfers income-producing property, income from the property is taxed to the donee. However, income accrued prior to the transfer is taxed to the donor. (Transfers of income-producing property are subject to gift tax.)

b. Sham transfers §192

A transfer lacking donative intent, delivery, and acceptance does *not* shift the income to the donee; nor will a transfer be effective if the donor retains *excessive controls*.

c. Transferring income while retaining property §193

Generally, if a donor transfers income from property while retaining the property itself, the income is taxed to the *donor* at the time the donee collects it.

(1) Rental income §195

Rental income is taxable to the *owner* of the reversion even though he has gratuitously assigned his right to another.

(2) Assignments of trust income §196

A trust beneficiary can shift trust income by assigning the *entire beneficial interest* (or an *undivided portion* thereof) to the donee. But no shift occurs if the interest transferred is considered insignificant (*e.g.*, shift for only one year).

(3) Distinguish—assignments for consideration §197

The tax burden on income *always shifts* when the transfer of the income right is supported by bona fide consideration.

d. No realization of income to donor making gift §198

Even if the donor receives an immediate tax benefit (*e.g.*, a charitable deduction), he realizes no gain or loss.

(1) Exception §201

A taxpayer will recognize gain, but not loss, from a transfer of property to a *political organization*.

(2) Exception §202

Realization can also occur from gifts of *mortgaged property* or gifts upon which the donee *pays gift tax*.

2. Personal Service Income §203

Generally, personal service income is taxed to the person who earned it, even if an agreement exists splitting it.

a. Obligatory assignments §205

Results are unclear when the employer is willing to make payments only to someone *other than the employee.* The decision may turn on whether the employment relation was a regular one, or whether the payment is pursuant to a "one-shot situation" wherein services do not resemble normal employment services (*e.g.*, father enters contest, but prize is paid to child). *Note:* I.R.C. section 83(a) requires that the service provider be taxed on compensation, regardless of who receives the payment, making even the exception for one-shot situations unclear.

b. Working for charity §206

A taxpayer can work for free without being taxed on the value of her services. But, if she promotes an event and pays the proceeds to the charity, she is taxed thereon.

c. Working for oneself §207

If the taxpayer creates something and then gives it away, this is treated as a *transfer of property* and the income shifts to the donee.

d.	**Commonly controlled businesses**	§208

To clearly reflect the income of two or more businesses where there is common control, the IRS can allocate income, deductions, or credits.

3. Excessive Controls §211

Generally, the retention of excessive controls over transferred property causes income to be taxed to the transferor. (For example, in *Helvering v. Clifford*, the grantor remained subject to the tax on the income from the trust property because he retained a reversion and broad managerial powers, including the right to control when the wife-beneficiary would receive the income). The law is now codified in "grantor trust rules" (*infra*).

a. Transfers of patents §213

A taxpayer who licenses his patent to a manufacturer *that he controls* is taxed on the royalty income; but the income shifts if the taxpayer does not control the donee-manufacturer.

b. Gift and leaseback §215

A taxpayer can give away a business asset and *lease it back,* and then deduct the rental as a business expense only if there is a transfer considered effective for tax purposes.

c. Family partnerships §216

When a parent seeks to make her children her partners, the income will shift as long as the capital is a *"material income-producing factor"* in the partnership; if not, the income shifts only if the donee contributes capital or services.

B. STATUTORY DIVISIONS OF INCOME

1. Income Earned by Children §222

Income earned by a child is taxable to the child even though it is paid to the parent. It is the parent's responsibility to file a tax return for the child. *Unearned* income of a child under age 14 is taxed in the parents' bracket.

2. Income of Husbands and Wives

a. Right to file joint return §229

Husbands and wives can *elect* to file a joint return, the effect of which is to tax the income one-half to each spouse, irrespective of which spouse earned it.

b. Marriage penalty and single penalty §233

The tax rate is structured so that single people are taxed more than a joint return for the same income. However, where married people have substantial income, they could pay less combined tax if they were single.

(1) Gradual elimination of marriage penalty §234

Beginning in 2005, the standard deduction and the size of the 15% tax bracket will be gradually increased so that the resulting amounts will be the same for each joint taxpayer as it would be for a single taxpayer.

or income. The result is contra only if the power can be exercised with the consent of an adverse party.

(1) Exceptions §256

The grantor of a trust is not taxed on the income in the following situations:

(a) *An independent trustee has the power to apportion the income or principal* among the beneficiaries. The grantor may not be a trustee and not more than half of the trustees may be relatives or subordinates subservient to the grantor's wishes;

(b) *The power of the trustee is limited by a reasonably definite external standard,* and neither the grantor nor a "nonadverse" spouse is trustee; or

(c) *The reasonable alterations of beneficial enjoyment* (e.g., the power to postpone income payments to beneficiaries under age 21 or under a legal disability) can be retained.

c. Power to revoke §260

If the power to revoke the trust is *retained by the grantor,* grantor's spouse, or a nonadverse party, the grantor is taxed on the income.

d. Income for benefit of the grantor or spouse §261

Income is *taxable to the grantor if,* in the discretion of the grantor or a nonadverse party, it is or may be:

(1) *Distributable to the grantor or spouse* (even if the income is not in fact distributed);

(2) *Accumulated for future distribution to the grantor or spouse;*

(3) *Used to pay premiums on life insurance policies* of the grantor or spouse; or

(4) *Used to support dependents* whom the grantor is legally obligated to support, but only to the extent that the income is so applied. (*Note:* Alimony trusts do shift the tax burden to the beneficiary.)

e. Administrative powers that may benefit grantor §269

Where administrative control is or may be exercised for the grantor's benefit, the income is taxed to the grantor (*e.g.,* where the grantor or a nonadverse party, or both, have the power to deal with trust property or income for less than adequate consideration, without the approval of an adverse party in interest).

f. Trust income taxable to person other than grantor §277

If a person other than the grantor has a general power of appointment, the trust income is taxed to her, whether or not she takes it, subject to the following limitations:

(1) *If the power is for the support of dependents* of the third party, the income is taxed to her only to the extent it is so applied;

(2) **If the income is taxed to the grantor** under the grantor trust rules, it is not taxed to the third party. Nor is a taxpayer taxed when she disclaims a power within a reasonable time after becoming aware of its existence.

2. Trusts Recognized for Tax Purposes §278
A trust is the recognized taxable entity where the grantor has **not** retained any substantial "strings."

a. Taxability of income §279
The income is taxed to the beneficiaries where it is distributed to them, and to the trust when it is retained by it. The beneficiaries are not taxed on distributions of the **corpus**.

b. Distributable net income ("DNI") §280
To prevent trust income from being taxed twice, a special deduction is allowed for distributions. (Distributions out of income or principal may be included in the deductible amount to the extent the deductible amount does not exceed DNI.) DNI is the maximum amount includible in a beneficiary's income and deductible by the trust. DNI for the trust is the trust's **taxable income** before the deductions for the distributions to the beneficiaries, the trust's personal exemption, or the undistributed capital gains or losses allocated to the corpus.

c. "Simple trusts" §281
Simple trusts are trusts that **must distribute all the current income** to the beneficiaries, but cannot distribute the corpus or deduct charitable contributions. The beneficiaries are taxed on the amounts distributed, or required to be distributed, and a corresponding deduction is given to the trust. Note that the deduction cannot exceed DNI. The trust is taxed on capital gains allocated to the corpus.

d. "Complex trusts" and estates

(1) First tier §284
All the income **required** to be distributed is taxed to the beneficiaries who are entitled to receive it, to the extent of DNI.

(2) Second tier §285
If DNI exceeds the amount required to be distributed, then **additional payments** (e.g., discretionary income payments) to the beneficiaries become taxable. Note that the includible amount **cannot exceed DNI less the amount taxed to first tier beneficiaries**.

(3) Tax to trust §287
The trust may deduct the amounts includible in the income of the first and second tier beneficiaries; however, if taxable income remains, the trust is taxed thereon.

(a) Exemptions §288
Simple trusts have a $300 personal exemption, complex trusts have a $100 personal exemption, and estates have a $600 personal exemption.

e. **Throwback rule** §289
A distribution in excess of the current DNI is "thrown back" into the accumulated income of the preceding years. It is treated as if it had been distributed in those years to the extent of the undistributed income of those years.

(1) **Taxing beneficiaries** §291
The beneficiary is taxed on the accumulated distribution in the year made, but the tax is determined by the amount the beneficiary would have paid had a distribution been made in prior years. A credit is given for taxes previously paid by the trust.

III. IS IT DEDUCTIBLE OR IS IT A CREDIT?

A. INTRODUCTION

1. **Deductions and Credits Defined** §292
A *"deduction"* is subtracted *from gross income* or adjusted gross income to arrive at *taxable income*. *"Credits"* are subtracted *from taxes* due.

2. **Business vs. Personal Deductions** §293
Generally, business costs are deductible, while personal costs are not.

3. **No Shifting of Deductions** §294
Payment of *another's liabilities* is not deductible, unless it serves an independent business purpose (*e.g.*, protecting taxpayer's job).

B. BUSINESS AND INVESTMENT DEDUCTIONS

1. **Business Expenses** §296
All "*ordinary and necessary expenses* paid or incurred during the taxable year in carrying on any trade or business" are deductible.

a. **"Trade or business"** §297
The Code does not define a "trade or business," but it generally requires an expectation of profit, regular and continuous operation, and the active pursuit thereof.

(1) **Legality of business** §299
The legality of the business is not per se relevant, but certain illegal expenses are not deductible.

(2) **Nature of taxpayer** §300
Expenses incurred in connection with a trade or business are deductible by any kind of taxpayer—corporation, trust, or individual. However, a stockholder is not in business merely because his corporation is in business.

(3) **Tax shelters** §301
Activities involving flagrant tax shelters do not meet the "trade or business" requirement; therefore expenses arising from these activities are not deductible.

b. **Business vs. personal expenses** §302
Individual taxpayers must prove that the particular expense was incurred

in connection with the taxpayer's trade or business. Corporate taxpayers have the benefit of a *presumption*.

(1) Requirement of proximate relationship to trade or business §303
If several purposes are involved, the *predominant* one controls.

(2) Travel expenses §304
Travel expenses incurred while *away from home in pursuit of a trade or business* are deductible.

(a) Pursuit of trade or business

1) Commuting to and from work §306
Costs for commuting to and from work are *not* deductible.

2) Combined business and pleasure trips §311
Combined business and pleasure trip costs are deductible on an *apportioned* basis. The entire cost of the transportation is deductible if the *primary* purpose of the trip was business.

3) Foreign meetings §312
Certain limitations are placed on expense deductions for attendance at foreign conventions.

4) Presence of spouse §313
A spouse's expenses are deductible only if there is a sufficient business connection.

(b) "Away from home" §314
There has been considerable controversy over whether this phrase means away from *business headquarters* or away from the *residence*.

1) "Homeless" taxpayers §315
If no business headquarters exist, the taxpayer's permanent residence can be "home." However, if the taxpayer has neither, there are no deductions for travel expenses.

2) Taxpayers with several offices §316
If the taxpayer has several business headquarters, he can deduct expenses of traveling between them.

3) Deductibility of meals §317
Only *50%* of meal costs are deductible, and that deduction is available only if the taxpayer is away from home for a time requiring *"sleep or rest."*

4) "Temporary" vs. "indefinite" rule §318
Deductions are not allowed where the taxpayer is away on an assignment of an *indefinite* duration, but are allowed for temporary assignments.

(3) Expenses of "businesses" operated for pleasure—hobby farm problem §319

Expenses are generally not deductible unless a **significant purpose** of the business is to earn a profit. However, interest and property taxes are deductible since they do not require profit-seeking, and if income exceeds this amount, expenses up to this balance can be deducted.

(4) Moving expenses §325

Employees or self-employed persons can deduct the costs of moving family and furniture to a new home, subject to certain limitations: The new job site must be more than **50 miles** farther from the old home than the old home was from the old job site; the taxpayer must work full-time; and the new place of work must be permanent.

(5) Entertainment expenses §331

Entertainment expenses are deductible only if they are **directly related** to the active conduct of the taxpayer's business. Only 50% of entertainment is deductible.

(6) Business gifts §336

Business gifts are generally deductible up to $25.

(7) Litigation expenses §337

Whether legal fees or other costs incurred in a lawsuit are deductible depends on the nature of the dispute. If the **origin of the dispute is related to a trade or business** and the expenses are **"ordinary and necessary,"** they are deductible. Litigation expenses incurred for the **production of income** are deductible, but only as miscellaneous itemized deductions. Special provisions allow a deduction for costs in connection with tax matters.

(8) Educational expenses §341

Educational expenses that qualify the taxpayer for a **new** trade or business, or constitute the **minimum education requirement** for qualification in her job, are **not** deductible. However, costs to **maintain or improve** skills required in a taxpayer's job are deductible.

(a) Higher-education costs §343

Regardless of the purpose of the education, a dependent's higher-education costs can be deducted by a taxpayer with certain limitations (*e.g.*, $3,000 is deductible in 2002 and 2003). No amount is **deductible** if one of the higher-education **credits** is claimed.

(9) Insurance premiums §344

The cost of insurance on business **property** is an ordinary and necessary business expense. **Life** insurance premiums for a "key person" (*i.e.*, officer or employee) are deductible only if the taxpayer is not the beneficiary.

(10) Offices at home §347

Generally, *no* deductions are given for a taxpayer's residence. There is a special exception for *certain business uses* if a portion of the home is used *exclusively* for business (*e.g.*, principal place of business, certain storage use, or if the residence is used as a day care facility). The deductible amount is limited to the gross income from such use, less the nonbusiness deductions.

(11) Vacation homes §356

Generally, no deduction is allowed in excess of the income if the dwelling unit is used *as a "residence"* (*i.e.*, if used for personal purposes for more than 14 days or 10% of the days rented, whichever is greater). Also, expenses must be prorated between rental and personal use.

(a) Limited rental use §363

If the dwelling unit is rented fewer than 15 days, no deduction is allowed, and the rental income is excluded from gross income.

(12) Clothing §364

Clothing is *not* deductible unless it cannot appropriately be worn for nonbusiness purposes (*e.g.*, firefighter's uniform).

c. Current expense vs. capital outlay §365

To be deductible as a business expense, an item must be an *expense*, rather than a *capital outlay*.

(1) Test §366

An expense is considered a "capital outlay" if it brings about the *acquisition of an asset or some advantage* to the taxpayer having a *useful life in excess of one year*.

(a) "Capitalization" distinguished §367

A *capital asset*, when sold, qualifies for capital gain or loss treatment (*infra*). However, expenditures must be *capitalized* if they create an asset or advantage lasting beyond the taxable year, whether or not a capital asset is produced (*i.e.*, match up income with costs of earning that income).

(b) Future benefit §369

An outlay must be capitalized if it produces significant long-term benefits (*INDOPCO* case). Thus, the costs of arranging a friendly corporate takeover must be capitalized because the benefits will inure into the future, but the costs of resisting a hostile takeover can be deducted currently because there is no long-term benefit created by the expenses.

(c) Ramifications §374

The *INDOPCO* case has cast doubt on many decisions that

allowed expensing, rather than capitalization, of business expansion costs because no distinct asset resulted, although a long-term benefit was produced.

(2) Repairs §376

Maintenance and repairs are current expenses and are deductible in the year paid **unless they improve** the value of the original property, make it suitable for a different purpose, or extend its original useful life. Certain **environmental cleanup costs** also may be deducted instead of capitalized.

(3) Property produced or sold §380

Taxpayers must capitalize the direct and indirect costs of producing property, including materials, labor, rent or depreciation on equipment, etc. **Interest** allocable to produced property must be capitalized only if the property has a long useful life or production period.

(a) Resale property §384

Costs associated with property acquired for resale (*e.g.,* inventory storage costs) are capitalized if the taxpayer has average gross receipts of at least $10 million.

(b) Exception for authors §385

Mandatory capitalization rules are inapplicable to the "qualified creative expense" of authors, artists, or photographers (*i.e.,* costs are deductible).

(4) Rent payments §386

Rental payments for the use of another's property are deductible. But **prepayments** of rent are **not** currently deductible, nor are **leases** that are actually payments towards the **purchase price** of the property.

(5) Acquisition costs §391

Amounts paid to **purchase** a business or an asset are capital outlays, as are "start-up" costs. However, costs of expanding an existing business are deductible. To equalize this situation between new and existing businesses, **section 195** was enacted to allow **amortization over a five-year period** of the costs of investigating and starting up a new business. However, the purchase price must still be capitalized.

(a) Employment agency fees §398

Employment agency fees are deductible (except the costs of seeking a **first** job).

1) Distinguish—running for office §399

Costs of running for office are **nondeductible**.

(b) Corporate organization and reorganization §400

Legal fees connected with the organizing or reorganizing of a business are capital outlays but can usually be amortized over a five-year period.

(c) Patents, copyrights, and trademarks §401
The purchase of patents, copyrights, and trademarks are *capital outlays*; but costs in creating them are currently deductible.

(d) Bar exam §402
Bar exam costs must be capitalized.

(e) Selling costs §403
Commissions paid on the sale of property are *not* deductible as expenses, but they do decrease the amount realized on the sale.

(f) Acquiring goodwill §404
The costs of acquiring goodwill in a new business are nondeductible. But amounts paid for the *protection or improvement* of the goodwill may be deductible. Purchased goodwill can be amortized over a 15-year period.

(g) Short-term prepayments §407
Routine and recurring payments lasting into the following year may be entirely deducted in the year in which they are made.

d. "Ordinary and necessary" expense §408
An expense must be: (i) of a type encountered by other businesses in the community, and (ii) appropriate or helpful to the business.

(1) Determinative factors §410
The following are the chief factors in determining if an expense is in fact "ordinary and necessary": the *voluntariness* of the payment, the *customariness* of the payment, and whether it is *"reprehensible"* (e.g., legal kickback).

(2) Compensation §415
"Reasonable" compensation costs for services rendered are deductible. A court considers the value of the service to the business and what similar businesses would pay for like services.

(a) Tests for reasonableness §418
Salary based on a *percentage of income* may be suspicious. Some courts consider what an *independent investor* would pay for the services. A salary *unrelated to the value* of the services may be disallowed on the basis that it is a "constructive dividend." A few cases have disallowed a reasonable salary to the extent the employee-shareholder has not received a reasonable return on her investment.

(b) Salaries in excess of $1 million §423
A publicly held corporation cannot deduct remuneration in excess of $1 million per year to certain top executives unless payments are commissions actually earned or are based on achievement of performance goals.

c. **Who is entitled to depreciation deduction** §459
Generally, the person suffering the economic loss due to the decreased value of the property from depreciation can claim the deduction.

(1) **Landlord-tenant** §460
The landlord gets the deduction where he improves the land and leases it to the tenant except when the **tenant is required to maintain** the land so that when it is returned it will be of equivalent value. If the tenant erects a building or constructs improvements in a leased building, the tenant gets the deduction.

(2) **Purchaser** §462
The purchaser under an executory sale contract gets the deduction on the property after the ownership burdens and benefits pass to him.

(3) **Future interest holder** §463
A life tenant is entitled to the deduction.

(4) **Trustee-beneficiary** §464
In trusts, the deduction is apportioned among income beneficiaries and the trustee.

d. **Computation of depreciation**

(1) **Recovery periods** §465
The accelerated cost recovery system ("ACRS") provides "recovery periods" of certain assets. These recovery periods are: for residential buildings—27.5 years; for nonresidential buildings—39 years; for tangible personal property—3, 5, 7, 10, 15, or 20 years.

(2) **Salvage value** §466
ACRS ignores salvage value and makes no distinction between new and used property.

(3) **Methods of depreciation** §467
ACRS provides two types of depreciation: straight-line and accelerated. **Straight-line depreciation** is computed by dividing the cost (or other basis) by the useful life. This method results in the same deduction for every year during the recovery period. **Accelerated depreciation** provides for a greater deduction in the early years and a lower deduction in later years.

(4) **Personal property—accelerated depreciation** §468
Double-declining balance is permitted for most personal property.

(a) **Half-year convention** §470
Regardless of when personal property is purchased, it is treated as if it were purchased halfway through the year. If more than 40% of assets are bought during the last

quarter of the year, **all** assets acquired during the year are considered purchased in the middle of the **quarter** in which they are purchased.

(b) Elections under ACRS §471

A taxpayer may elect to use *straight-line depreciation*.

(5) Stimulus bill §472

To stimulate the economy, 2002 legislation provided additional first-year depreciation for tangible personal property (and for certain leasehold improvements on nonresidential property) acquired between September 11, 2001 and September 11, 2004.

(6) Amortization of intangibles §473

Under section 197, many intangibles (*e.g.*, purchased goodwill, licenses, covenants not to compete, and franchises) are amortized over a 15-year period. Intangibles not covered by section 197 (*e.g.*, interests in companies, land, software, sports franchises, films) can be amortized only according to their proved useful lives.

(7) Real property §476

Depreciation is calculated on a monthly basis in the year in which the buildings are purchased or constructed (purchase is deemed to occur at mid-month in year of purchase). Only straight-line depreciation is permitted.

e. Election to expense purchase price §477

A small business taxpayer may elect to "expense" (*i.e.*, to deduct immediately) a certain amount of the purchase price of tangible personal property. The election maximum phases out for purchases over $200,000.

f. Limitations on consumer items §478

Limitations on depreciation and rental expense deductions apply to "listed property" (*e.g.*, cars, cellular telephones, home computers used for business). Only straight-line depreciation can be used for listed property used less than 50% for business.

g. Caution—ultimate effect of deduction §482

A depreciation deduction **reduces basis;** hence, the more depreciation taken, the greater the taxable gain (or less loss) is when the property is sold.

4. Depletion §483

The owner of the **economic interest** in a wasting asset (*e.g.*, oil, gas, or minerals) is entitled to a reasonable annual allowance to compensate for the diminution of the asset.

a. Methods of computing depletion

(1) Cost method §486

The cost or other basis of the wasting asset is allocated to each unit of the mineral deposit. Then, the depletion allowable for each year is computed by multiplying this amount by the number of units actually sold or withdrawn during the year.

(2) Percentage method §487
Under this more popular method, the deduction is a fixed percentage of the property's gross income during the taxable year. *Note:* With respect to **oil and gas**, the percentage depletion cannot exceed 50% of the taxpayer's net income from the property. *And note:* Percentage depletion is especially attractive because greater income results in a greater deduction and the deduction goes on **indefinitely**.

b. Drilling costs §490
The costs of production are deductible as **expenses.** Intangible drilling and development expenses (*i.e.*, wages, supplies, etc., in locating sites and preparing for production) in connection with oil and gas wells may be deducted as current expenses or capitalized and recovered through subsequent depletion and depreciation deductions.

5. Losses §493
A loss occurs when a transaction ends and the taxpayer has not recovered her basis for the assets involved. Corporate losses are generally deductible as business losses. Individuals can deduct only limited losses.

a. Types of losses allowed to individuals

(1) Losses incurred in a trade or business §496
Any loss incurred in a trade or business is deductible.

(2) Losses incurred in transactions entered into for profit §497
These are generally deductible. For example, losses from the sale of securities or other investments are deductible (as capital losses—the deductibility of which is limited); however, losses suffered on the sale of a **personal residence** are **not** deductible.

b. When loss allowable—"realization" §504
Generally, a loss must be realized (evidenced by a closed and completed transaction in the current tax year) to be deductible. A mere decline in value is **not** enough.

(1) Time of realization §506
The realization on a tangible asset usually occurs in the year of the intention to abandon **and** the affirmative act of abandonment. The remote possibility of recoupment is irrelevant.

(2) Exchanges §509
For loss to be realized on an exchange of property, the property received must differ materially either in kind or in extent from the property transferred.

(3) Exceptions §510
Theft losses are deductible the year in which the taxpayer discovers the loss. Casualty losses from natural disasters are deducted

either in the year of occurrence or on the return for the prior year. Declines in value in inventory may be deducted in the year they occur. The year they become worthless is the year of loss for stocks and securities.

c. Disallowed losses

(1) Losses between related taxpayers §511

Losses arising from a sale or exchange *directly or indirectly* of property between related taxpayers are not allowed. However, *gain* upon such transactions is taxable.

(2) Losses from "wash sales" of securities §517

When a taxpayer sells stocks or securities and *buys* substantially identical assets within 30 days before or after the sale, the transaction is ignored, and losses are not deductible.

(3) Sham transactions §518

If, in reality, there was no real interruption of the taxpayer's beneficial ownership, despite the appearance of a sale, losses from this "sham transaction" are disallowed.

(4) Public policy §519

Loss deductions violative of public policy are disallowed.

6. Bad Debts

a. Bad debt defined §520

A "bad debt" arises when an obligation owed to the taxpayer becomes uncollectible.

b. Requirements for deductibility §521

There must be a *valid debt* owing that arose from a *debtor-creditor relationship,* and the debt must have become unenforceable or uncollectible *during the tax year* for which the deduction is claimed.

c. Business and nonbusiness bad debts §528

Business bad debts are fully deductible, and a deduction is allowed for "partial worthlessness." Nonbusiness bad debts are deductible as *short-term capital losses* (e.g., a loan to a friend or family, or most shareholder loans to corporations (*Whipple* rule)).

d. Amount deductible §533

The amount deductible is *limited to the basis* of the debt. Uncollectible *accounts receivable* are deductible only if the taxpayer is on the accrual basis.

e. Recovery of bad debts §536

If a bad debt is deducted and then recovered, it must be included in the *gross income* in the year it is received. But to the extent that the previous bad debt deduction failed to effect a *tax benefit,* the income can be excluded.

7. "At Risk" Limitation on Tax Shelter Deductions §538

Deductions from operating losses for all investments *except real estate* are limited to the amount "at risk," *i.e.*, the amount of investment in the property excluding nonpersonal liability money loans. Operating losses are the excess of deductions from the activity over income from the activity during the year.

8. Passive Losses §543

Taxpayers who do not ***materially participate*** in a business cannot deduct losses from such "passive" activities except against income from such activities. Deductions are deferred until future years when there is passive income or the activity is disposed of.

a. Exceptions §549

A taxpayer may deduct up to $25,000 in losses from real estate ***rental activity*** if he ***actively participates***. The deduction is phased out when adjusted gross income ("AGI") exceeds $100,000. A taxpayer who is a ***real estate professional*** can deduct all losses if the taxpayer spends more than 750 hours a year materially participating in the business.

C. PERSONAL DEDUCTIONS

1. Introduction §552

Personal deductions are allowed for certain items even though there is no connection to a business or investment.

2. Definitions §553

A deduction is taken either from gross income or adjusted gross income.

a. Adjusted gross income §554

Adjusted gross income is gross income less certain deductions (*e.g.*, nonemployee trade or business or real estate investment deductions, and deductions for alimony). The remaining deductions are taken from AGI in computing taxable income.

b. Two-percent floor §561

Many miscellaneous itemized deductions are allowable only to the extent they exceed 2% of AGI. This category includes employee business expenses and many other items. Deductions ***not*** subject to the floor include interest, taxes, casualty losses, charitable contributions, and medical expenses.

c. Three-percent rule §565

Except for medical expenses, investment interest, or casualty losses, all itemized deductions are reduced by 3% of the excess of AGI over the applicable amount, but no more than 80% of the deductions are wiped out.

d. Standard deduction §566

In lieu of itemizing deductions, taxpayers can deduct the "standard deduction," which is an amount adjusted annually for inflation. In 2002, the standard deductions are $7,850 on a joint return and $4,700 for single taxpayers.

(1) Marriage penalty §568

Beginning in 2005, the standard deduction for married taxpayers will be increased (over five years) to twice the standard deduction for a single person.

(2) Elderly and blind taxpayers §569
An additional standard deduction is provided for taxpayers who turn 65 years of age during the tax year or who are blind.

3. Interest §572
Personal interest (except on a residence and some student loans) is *not* deductible. Business or investment interest is deductible, but there are numerous limitations.

a. Requirements §573
To be deductible, the interest must be incurred with respect to *bona fide debt* owed by the *taxpayer*. Interest is not deductible if the debt is a sham, there is no definite possibility of gain or loss, or if the taxpayer's sole motive was tax saving.

(1) Identifying interest §583
Payments for the *use* of borrowed money are interest and deductible (*e.g.*, "points"), while payments for a lender's *services* are *not* interest. Interest may be *imputed* in some situations when interest charged is less than the applicable federal rate.

b. Nondeductible interest

(1) Personal interest §591
Personal interest (*e.g.*, on credit cards) is not deductible. *Exception:* Interest on certain educational loans or on acquisition debt (cannot exceed $1 million), and home equity debt (cannot exceed $100,000) is deductible if *secured* by a principal residence (or a second residence).

(a) Interest on education loans §596
A taxpayer can deduct *from gross income* interest on educational loans (up to $2,500) incurred to pay higher education expenses for the taxpayer, her spouse, or a dependent. The deduction begins phasing out when AGI exceeds $50,000 on a single return or $100,000 on a joint return.

(2) Expense allocable to exempt income §601
Interest expenses attributable to the production of tax-exempt income are disallowed.

(3) Tax-exempt interest §602
Interest on debts incurred to purchase or carry tax-exempt state and municipal bonds is not deductible.

(4) Loans to purchase insurance §603
No interest deduction is allowed on a debt incurred to buy "single premium" life insurance, endowment, or annuity contracts, or on loans made as part of a systematic plan of financing insurance premiums. *Exception:* The disallowance rule is inapplicable

where: (i) no part of four of the first seven premiums is borrowed; (ii) the amount disallowed would be less than $100, if borrowing occurred because of unforeseen financial problems, or (iii) the borrowing was incurred in connection with a trade or business.

(5) Prepaid interest §605

Prepaid interest must be capitalized and deducted in the years the underlying loan is outstanding (except that *points* paid on a loan secured by a principal residence are immediately deductible).

(6) Excess investment interest §607

If the interest deductions on investments exceed the net investment income, the excess is *disallowed*, but may be *carried forward* and deducted against investment income in future years.

4. Taxes

a. Taxes deductible as such §611

Real or personal property taxes, and *state or local* income taxes (including payroll tax used to finance a disability income fund) are deductible as such.

b. Taxes deductible only as business or investment expense §615

Taxpayers engaged in a trade or business, or holding property for the production of income, can deduct taxes incurred *in connection with that business or property*.

c. Nondeductible taxes §616

Federal income taxes, Social Security tax imposed on employees, excess profit taxes, federal estate and gift taxes, and state and local inheritance taxes are *not* deductible.

5. Charitable Contributions §617

Taxpayers are entitled to a deduction for contributions to *recognized* charities. *Individuals* cannot deduct more than 50% of their AGI; *corporations* are limited to 10% of net income; and *estates and trusts* have no limitation.

a. Gifts in kind §623

Certain limitations apply when property, rather than cash, is given.

(1) Fractional and future interests §624

Gifts of a fractional or future interest in a donor's *personal residence or farm* are deductible in the amount of the value of the interest at the time of the gift. Gifts of *remainder* interests in *other real property* or gifts to a *trust* are deductible only if made in the form of a "fixed trust," or "unitrust," or "pooled income fund."

(a) Tangible personal property §626

Gifts of a *future* interest in tangible personal property are deductible only when the charity's interest becomes *possessory*.

(b) Income trusts
Gifts of an *income interest* in a trust are not deductible unless the income remains taxable to the *donor* and the interest is in the form of a fixed annuity or percentage of value of the property.

§627

(2) Gifts of appreciated property
Formerly, a taxpayer could deduct the present *fair market value* of property without realizing a gain or loss. This is still true if the donated property would (if sold) produce *long-term capital gain* and is donated to a *public charity.* However, the amount of the deduction is limited to 30% of the donor's AGI.

§628

(a) Amount limitations
The amount deductible is reduced by the capital gain if the gift is to a *private foundation* (unless an *"operating"* foundation) or the gift is of *tangible personal property unrelated* to the charity's charitable purpose.

§630

(b) Gift that would not produce long-term capital gain
If the property would produce short-term capital gain or *ordinary income,* then only the donor's basis, in effect, is deductible. However, if the gift is of inventory to a public charity to be used solely for the care of the ill, needy, or infants (and the charity does not resell the property), an amount in excess of basis is deductible.

§633

(3) Appraisals
For non-cash gifts, an appraisal is required if the claimed value of the property exceeds $5,000 ($10,000 for nonpublicly traded securities).

§636

b. Bargain sales
When property is *sold* to a charity *below* the fair market value, the difference between the fair market value and purchase price is deductible, but the basis must be *apportioned* between the gift and sale elements.

§637

c. Contribution of services or use of property
The value of *personal services* donated to a charity is nondeductible; *out-of-pocket expenses* (*e.g.*, automobile expenses) can be deducted.

§639

d. No deduction if taxpayer benefits
Contributions made with the anticipation of future economic benefit are not deductible.

§645

6. Medical Expenses
Amounts paid for the "*diagnosis, cure, mitigation, treatment or prevention of disease,* or for the purpose of affecting any structure or function of the body" are specifically deductible, as is the cost of prescription drugs. *Transportation* costs for essential medical care and the amounts paid for *medical insurance* (not disability insurance) are also deductible.

§650

$100 but **only if the damage is to taxpayer's own property.** And the **total** of casualty and theft losses is deductible only if it is **in excess of 10% of AGI**.

a. Amount deductible §679

Taxpayer can deduct the **lesser** of:

(1) **The adjusted basis** of property; or

(2) **The difference between the value** of the property before and after the casualty.

9. Other Personal Deductions §684

Nonbusiness bad debts, alimony payments, and certain contributions to retirement plans are allowed.

a. Contributions to retirement plans §686

A taxpayer may establish an individual retirement account ("IRA") and contribute and deduct up to $3,000 per year ($3,500 for taxpayers over age 50). Investment gains are not currently taxed, but are taxed when withdrawn. The deduction begins phasing out for single taxpayers when AGI reaches $34,000 ($54,000 for married taxpayers) **if** the taxpayer is covered by an employer-maintained retirement plan, but there is no phaseout for taxpayer not covered by such a plan.

(1) Roth IRAs §688

Contributions to Roth IRAs are not currently deductible, but like regular IRAs, investment gains are not taxed. Moreover, **none of the distributions** are taxed if made after the taxpayer reaches age 59½ and more than five years after the first contribution.

(2) Education IRAs §689

A taxpayer can contribute up to $2,000 per year to an education IRA for a beneficiary under age 18. The contributions are not deductible but investment income and distributions are not taxable.

D. TAX RATES §690

The tax rates depend on marital status. Married taxpayers may file joint or separate returns. Singles may qualify for the head of household rate. There are six tax brackets: 10%, 15%, 27%, 30%, 35%, and 38.6% for the year 2002.

E. CREDITS §692

Credits reduce the tax payable dollar for dollar.

1. Credit for Taxes Withheld and Prepaid §693

The taxpayer is entitled to a credit against taxes payable for all sums withheld from wages and for all amounts prepaid in connection with declarations of estimated tax.

2. Foreign Tax Credit §694

The taxpayer may elect to take as a credit in lieu of a deduction from income, the amount of income, excess profits, and similar taxes paid or accrued during the year to foreign countries, or possessions of the United States.

3. **Credit for the Elderly** §695

Taxpayers who are age **65 or over** (or retired on total or permanent disability) receive a credit of 15% of their "section 22 amount" ($5,000 for singles, $7,500 on a joint return if both spouses are eligible, or $3,750 for a married person filing separately). However, the "section 22 amount" must be reduced by excludible Social Security or other amounts excluded from gross income. And if gross income exceeds $7,500 ($10,000 on joint return, $5,000 for a married person filing separately), there is a further reduction of one-half the excess.

4. **Work Incentive Credit** §699

The Code allows a credit of 50% of the salaries paid to disadvantaged employees (*e.g.,* welfare recipient).

5. **Child Care Credit** §700

A credit is given for 20% (35%—effective in 2003—for lower income taxpayers) of expenses for household services and care of a "qualifying individual" (dependent under age 13 or unable to care for himself or herself). But the expenses must be incurred to enable the taxpayer to be gainfully employed.

   a. **Dollar limit** §705

   Expenses for which the credit is allowed cannot exceed earned income (if married, income of lower earning spouse used) or $3,000 (effective in 2003) for one qualifying individual or $6,000 (effective in 2003) for two or more.

   b. **Divorced parents included** §707

   Even though the parent is not entitled to claim the exemption, she can take the child care credit.

6. **Child Tax Credit** §708

A taxpayer who claims a **child under age 17 as a dependent** is entitled to a child tax credit of $600 per child for 2002-2004, after which the credit will increase gradually to $1,000 in 2010. The credit is gradually phased out when AGI exceeds $110,000 on a joint return and $75,000 on a single return.

7. **Earned Income Credit** §713

A credit of 34% of earned income up to a threshold amount (adjusted for inflation) is available to lower income taxpayers. The credit is less for taxpayers without children and is phased out above certain income levels.

8. **Adoption Tax Credit** §716

A taxpayer can claim a credit for adoption expenses up to $10,000 per child, although the credit phases out when AGI exceeds $150,000.

9. **Education Credits** §717

The HOPE credit is available for the first $1,500 of expenses for the first two years of post-secondary education (100% of the first $1,000 and 50% of the next $1,000 in tuition expenses). The lifetime learning credit, which applies in years when the HOPE credit is not claimed, is equal to 20% of the first $5,000 of tuition paid by the taxpayer (20% of $10,000 after

2003). These credits begin to phase out when AGI reaches $40,000 on a single return and $80,000 on a joint return.

IV. GAIN OR LOSS ON SALE OR EXCHANGE OF PROPERTY

A. COMPUTATION OF BASIS, GAIN, OR LOSS

1. Formula §721

a. *Unadjusted basis + additions - reductions = adjusted basis*

b. *Gain = amount realized - adjusted basis*

c. *Loss = adjusted basis - amount realized*

2. Basis

a. Unadjusted basis §723
This is usually cost. However, there are special rules for *gifts, inheritances,* and *tax-free exchanges*.

(1) Cost basis §724
Generally, the basis of property is the cost thereof. It includes cash, mortgages, or other property paid to obtain the asset. Income charged to the taxpayer in acquiring the property also is added to the basis.

(2) Inter vivos gifts §732
For the purpose of computing *gain,* the donee takes the *donor's basis;* but for *loss* purposes, the donee's basis is the *fair market value* at the time of the gift or the donor's basis, whichever is less.

(a) Increase by gift tax paid §733
The basis is increased by the gift tax the donor paid, which is attributable to an appreciation in property, but not in excess of the fair market value at the time of the gift.

(3) Tax-free exchanges §734
The basis of property in a tax-free exchange is that of the property transferred—adjusted upward for gain recognized and downward for money received on the exchange.

(4) Inherited property §735
The basis of inherited property in the hands of decedent's estate or the person inheriting it is the property's value at the date of death of decedent (or six months later if the alternate valuation date is elected).

(a) Form in which property is held

1) Community property §738
If decedent and her surviving spouse owned the property as community property, both halves receive a new basis.

(5) Exchanges between related persons §793

If a relation with whom taxpayer exchanged property disposes of the property *within two years* (or vice versa), the taxpayer must recognize gain or loss on the original exchange.

(a) Exceptions §794

Dispositions after the death of either the taxpayer or related person, involuntary conversion of the property, or a transaction that satisfies the IRS that tax avoidance is not a principal purpose do not trigger recognition of gain or loss.

b. Involuntary conversions §795

If the converted property is replaced with "similar or related in service or use" property *within two years* after the close of the tax year in which the insurance proceeds were received, gain is recognized only to the extent the realized amount exceeds the replacement cost. Nonrecognition under this section is *elective*.

(1) Special rules for condemnation §801

Condemnations (or threat of) causing sale of *business real property* results in no gain if the proceeds are reinvested in like kind property, whether or not it is similar or related in service or use. The replacement period is three years.

c. Nonrecognition of gain on sale of principal residence §802

No loss can be recognized on the sale of a personal residence. Gain from the sale of a principal residence generally is not recognized unless in excess of $250,000 (or $500,000 on a joint return), which excess is taxable as capital gain. To qualify for the exclusion, the taxpayer must have *owned and used* the dwelling as a *principal residence* for periods aggregating *two years or more in the five-year period* ending on the date of the sale or exchange.

(1) Married couples §805

To qualify for the $500,000 exclusion, a married couple must file a joint return for the year in which the sale or exchange occurs and must still be married on the last day of the taxable year. Either spouse can be the record owner of the house, but *both* spouses must meet the two-year use and two-year prior sale requirement.

d. Sales between spouses §808

If the sale is between spouses (or former spouses incident to a divorce), no gain or loss is recognized.

e. Mortgage repossessions §812

Gain is not recognized where the taxpayer forecloses on property he sold and financed with a mortgage.

V. WHAT KIND OF INCOME IS IT? CAPITAL GAINS AND LOSSES AND TAX PREFERENCES

A. INTRODUCTION

1. Capital Gains §813

The tax on an individual's net capital gain is 20%. (For an individual in the 15% bracket, the tax on net capital gain is only 10%.) Net capital gain means the excess of net long-term capital gain over net short-term capital loss. For this purpose, long-term means a holding period of **more than 12 months**. Lower rates apply to the appreciation of assets occurring after January 1, 2001, if held for more than five years (18%, or 8% for individuals in the 15% tax bracket).

2. Capital Loss §818

Capital loss can be deducted against capital gain for the year plus $3,000. Any excess can be carried forward to future years and offset against capital gain in that year plus $3,000.

3. Approach §820

In classifying the transaction, the following factors are considered: whether the property is a **capital asset**; was there a **sale or exchange**; was there a sufficient **holding period**; and is the gain or loss **long-term or short-term**; apply the rules for limitation of **capital loss deductions** and **capital loss carryforwards**.

B. IS IT A CAPITAL ASSET?

1. General Rule §821

All property held by a taxpayer is a capital asset with certain exceptions. However, courts have interpreted "all property . . . except" to mean that the statutory exceptions are **not** exclusive.

2. Statutory Exceptions

a. Property held for sale §823

Inventory and property held for sale **to customers** in the **ordinary course of business** are not capital assets. Problems arise in determining whether **real estate** is sold by an investor (making the land a capital asset) or by a dealer (one who holds the property for sale to customers).

b. Receivables §836

Accounts receivable **or notes** acquired in the ordinary course of business in **payment for services rendered** by taxpayer, or on a sale of an **inventory item** are not capital assets.

c. Depreciable personal property and realty §837

Depreciable property and any **real property used in a trade or business** are not capital assets. However, most of these assets are treated as **"quasi-capital assets"** and are accorded favorable tax treatment.

d. Copyrights and patents §838

Copyrights and other literary, artistic, or musical property are **not** capital assets in the hands of the creator (or any donee). **Patents** are **capital assets** in the hands of the **inventor** or the one who **financed** the invention.

  e. **Options**   §842

    If the optioned property would be, if acquired, a capital asset, then the option itself is a capital asset.

3. **Exceptions Developed in Case Law**   §845

  Courts have created other exceptions to provide a form of **income averaging** for long-term gains and to **remove disincentives** against sale of appreciated property. Courts generally try to distinguish **investments** from mere **substitutes for ordinary income**.

  a. **Sale of rights to income**   §847

    If a taxpayer sells the right to future income from her property while retaining the property, the sale proceeds are taxable to her as ordinary income, not capital gains.

    (1) **Sale of life estates**   §849

      A sale of a life estate by a trust beneficiary is taxed as a capital gain.

  b. **Contract rights**

    (1) **Is it "protectable in equity"?**   §851

      If the contract right is property "protectable in equity," it will be taxed as a capital gain (*Ferrer* case).

    (2) **Leases**   §852

      Amounts paid to a **lessee** for the **assignment** of a lease are given capital gains treatment. However, amounts paid for a **release** or **sublease** are not capital gains.

    (3) **Personal services**   §856

      Proceeds from the sale of a personal service contract are ordinary income.

    (4) **Insurance policies**   §858

      Amounts received for assignments of beneficial interests are capital gains but a sale of an **annuity or endowment** may be ordinary income.

  c. **"Personal rights"**   §860

    Personal rights are not "property"; therefore, income from the sale therefrom is given **ordinary income treatment** (*e.g.*, compensation paid for the sale of one's right of privacy).

  d. **Classification through correlation with related transaction** §861

    A transaction may be classed as ordinary or capital because it is part of a related transaction.

    (1) **Tax benefit rule**   §862

      If taxpayer deducts certain notes as bad debts and later recovers on the notes, the recovery produces ordinary income. Thus, if taxpayer sells these notes, it would result in ordinary income, not capital gain.

4. Sale of Business Interests

a. Sole proprietorships §865

In determining capital gain vs. ordinary income on the sale of a proprietorship (or the sale of assets by a partnership or corporation), each asset is examined separately to determine if it qualifies as a capital asset (*fragmentation theory*). The parties can make a *reasonable allocation* of price to each asset.

(1) Goodwill §867

Goodwill is a capital asset and is depreciable by the buyer over a 15-year period.

(2) Covenant not to compete §868

Payment for a covenant not to compete is ordinary income to the seller. The amount paid is an asset to the buyer, which can be amortized over a 15-year period.

b. Partnerships and corporations §870

A partnership *interest* or corporate stock is generally a capital asset. *Sale of assets* is treated the same as in a proprietorship.

5. Assets Used in Trade or Business—Quasi-Capital Assets §873

Section 1231 provides that real property and depreciable personal property *used in a trade or business* are not capital assets; however, if *held more than one year*, such property may be entitled to "quasi-capital assets" treatment (more favorable than for other kinds of assets).

a. Other assets §876

Quasi-capital assets also include *unharvested crops* sold with the land, *livestock herds* held at least 24 months, and in certain cases, *coal, timber, and minerals*.

b. Computation §878

If the gains exceed the losses, all the transactions are *long-term capital transactions.* If the losses exceed the gains, all the transactions are *ordinary*. Losses within the preceding five years will result in treating current gain as ordinary income to the extent of previously unrecaptured losses (*recapture of losses*).

c. Special rules for casualties and condemnation §880

If the taxpayer has recognized gains and losses from business or investment casualties and gains exceed losses, all such casualties are swept under section 1231. Gains and losses from condemnations of business or investment assets are included in the section 1231 calculation.

d. Limitation §884

Recapture of depreciation provisions *supersede* section 1231, turning capital gain into ordinary income. However, capital gains treatment for *any depreciable property* (not just section 1231 assets) is *not* allowed in sales or exchanges **between "related" taxpayers**, and **losses** are **not** deductible (*supra*).

C. WAS THERE A "SALE OR EXCHANGE"?

1. In General   §888
Usually, there must be a "sale or exchange" of a capital asset for the transaction to be taxed as a capital gain or loss.

a. Aborted sales   §889
If a "sale" occurred and the seller repossessed the property because of failure to pay the entire price, the amount that the seller keeps is capital gain.

b. Transfer of mineral interest   §890
A mineral interest is a capital asset, but if the seller retains an **economic interest,** she is treated as not having sold the minerals (she can deduct depletion).

c. Transfers of franchises, trademarks, and trade names   §891
Capital gains treatment is available on the transfer of a franchise, trademark, or trade name **only if** the transferor retains **no significant interest or power** therein. *Note:* **Sport franchises** are always entitled to capital gains treatment.

d. Contract rights   §893
Generally, the transfer of contract rights between contracting parties is considered a "sale" and is given capital gains treatment. However, a minority of jurisdictions hold that this transfer does not constitute a "sale or exchange."

e. Foreclosure   §895
Foreclosure is treated as a sale or exchange by the debtor; consequently it is given capital gain or loss treatment. But the **abandonment** of worthless property is **not** a sale or exchange and thus is an ordinary loss.

2. Special Situations in Which "Sale or Exchange" Deemed to Occur

a. Worthless debts and securities   §898
Nonbusiness bad debts and worthless securities are deductible as capital losses.

b. Payments to creditors   §899
Ordinarily, amounts paid by a debtor to a creditor are a return of capital and **not** a "sale or exchange." This general rule has been partially superseded by statute in that collection of a debt instrument (*e.g.,* bond, promissory note) is treated as a sale or exchange by the creditor.

c. Involuntary conversion   §902
This is deemed equivalent to a "sale or exchange."

3. Validity of "Sale or Exchange" Not Affected by Seller's Retention of Control §903
If there is a complete transfer of title for a fair consideration, there is a sale. Note that the grantor trust rules do not apply.

D. WAS THERE A SUFFICIENT "HOLDING PERIOD"?

1. In General §907
A capital asset must be held *more than 12 months* prior to a "sale or exchange" to qualify for a *long-term* capital gain; if held 12 months or less, it is a short-term gain.

2. "Tacking" of Holding Period Where Substituted Basis §909
A holding period commences only on a *change of basis* on the property. If there is no change, the taxpayer acquires the holding period of transferor and can "tack" it to the time he holds the property.

E. GAINS ON SMALL BUSINESS STOCK

1. General Rule §910
A taxpayer (other than a corporation) can exclude from income 50% of the gain on the sale of qualified small business stock that has been held for at least five years.

2. Limit §911
The amount of gain subject to the 50% exclusion cannot exceed the greater of $10 million or 10 times the adjusted basis of the stock.

3. Qualified Stock §912
The stock must have been *issued after August 1993*, taxpayer must be the *original purchaser*, and the corporation must conduct an *active business* (excluding most service and real estate businesses) with *assets* after stock issuance *not exceeding $50 million*.

F. SPECIAL COMPUTATIONS

1. In General §914
Special rules may turn capital gain into ordinary income or require the deferral of certain losses.

2. "Imputed Interest" §915
Interest is imputed on sales wherein the payments are *deferred* and interest is charged at less than the prescribed rate. Interest produces ordinary income.

a. Exceptions §921
Total and partial exceptions to imputed interest rules include a selling price of $3,000 or less (*de minimus rule*) and *intrafamily real estate deals* (imputed interest cannot exceed 7%). The rules also are inapplicable to *buyers of personal use property*.

3. Recapture of Depreciation §925
Long-term or short-term gain attributable to prior depreciation may have to be reported as *ordinary income* if subject to special provisions.

itemized deductions (*supra*), state and local taxes, standard deductions and personal exemptions, and home equity loan interest. Medical deductions are allowed but only if in excess of 10% of AGI, and depreciation is deductible only under a 150% declining balance formula.

3. Tax Preferences §948

The most important preferences are the bargain element of an incentive stock option, the excess of percentage depletion, intangible drilling costs, and interest on private purpose municipal bonds.

VI. TAX ACCOUNTING PROBLEMS

A. ACCOUNTING METHOD—WHEN IS AN ITEM TAXABLE OR DEDUCTIBLE?

1. Introduction §950

The Code authorizes the taxpayer to use whatever method she uses in keeping her books. However, a taxpayer may not change the method used, even if it is wrong, without prior government approval. The Commissioner may change a taxpayer's method if it does not clearly reflect income.

2. Cash Receipts and Disbursements Method §951

Items of income are includible in the year in which **cash** (or a cash equivalent) is received. Deductions are taken in the year the **payment is made**.

a. Constructive receipt doctrine §955

If a cash basis taxpayer has an **unqualified** right to a sum of money or property, plus the power to obtain it, this is equivalent to actual receipt and it is currently income.

(1) Deferred compensation §961

The doctrine often arises in connection with deferred compensation. If the compensation is placed in a trust, the employee is taxed immediately unless her interest is subject to a substantial risk of forfeiture. If the employee receives a **present economic benefit** (*e.g.*, annuity contracts), compensation is not deferred.

b. Qualified pension and profit-sharing plans §969

The Code allows deferral of an employer's contributions to qualified plans for employees. The employer is entitled to an **immediate deduction;** however, the employee is taxed only upon distribution.

(1) Tax treatment on retirement §971

Upon retirement, the employee's **own** contributions are returned (tax free) and the amount of the employer's contributions are generally taxed as **ordinary income**.

(2) Limits on contributions and benefits §972

There are limitations on the amount of contributions in any one year. Also, the plans must be nondiscriminatory.

c. Property transferred in connection with performance of services—"timing rule" §975

I.R.C. section 83 gives rules for the "timing" of an employee's income when the employer uses property (including stock) as compensation.

As a general rule, where the property is subject to **both** a substantial risk of forfeiture **and** is nontransferable, the employee is not taxed (and the employer does not claim a deduction) until the first year in which the property is either nonforfeitable or transferable. The amount includible is the value of the property at the later date.

(1) Nonlapse restrictions §978

If the property is subject to a restriction that will never lapse, the includible amount is the formula price.

(2) Other restrictions §979

Restrictions on property not amounting to a substantial risk of forfeiture or a nonlapse restriction are ignored in valuing the property.

(3) Employee election §982

In any event, the taxpayer can elect to include value in income when the property is received.

d. Employee's stock options §984

Generally, stock or an option to buy stock issued by an employer is taxed as **ordinary income** to the employee. The **exercise** of the option is usually the taxable event unless it has an ascertainable value, in which case it can be included in income when received.

(1) Employer's deduction §989

The employer gets a deduction when the employee has income.

(2) Incentive stock options §990

If a stock option qualifies based on certain requirements, there is no tax on either the grant or exercise of the option. The employer receives no deduction at any time.

e. Claim of right doctrine §991

If a taxpayer receives money or property and claims she is entitled to it and can freely dispose of it, she is immediately taxable, despite the fact that she might have to give it back.

(1) Repayment §993

If repayment is made, the taxpayer receives a deduction in the year of repayment.

f. Prepaid income §994

Prepayments are income when received.

(1) Deposits §995

An advance payment for goods or services is currently taxable to the seller even if the goods or services are to be furnished in a later year. A security deposit, however, is not currently taxable.

g. Prepaid expenses §997

Amounts prepaid for goods or services to be received in later tax years must be **capitalized** and deducted ratably in future tax years.

h. Credit card payments §1005

Payment for any deductible item by a credit card gives rise to a deduction when the item is charged, not when the bill is paid.

3. Accrual Method §1006

The taxpayer reports income in whatever year it is *earned* (not necessarily paid) and deducts expenses in the year *incurred.* This method is required in all cases where *inventories* are a material factor affecting income, and for corporations, partnerships with a corporate partner, and tax shelters.

a. Exceptions §1009

Important exceptions to the accrual method requirement include S corporations, corporations or partnerships with *average annual gross receipts of less than $5 million*, *qualified personal service corporations*, and *farming businesses*.

b. Special problems with income under accrual method

(1) Deferred income §1010

The test applied is whether *all events have occurred* that establish a right to income and the amount is reasonably determined.

(2) Prepaid income §1015

Supreme Court cases hold that prepaid income is taxable *when received;* the IRS permits deferral of advance payments from sale of goods and limited deferral for advance payments for services.

(3) Dividends §1021

Taxpayer is treated as having no income until dividends are actually received.

(4) Increasing rents §1022

When a lease calls for increasing payments with total rent payments in excess of $250,000, both lessor and lessee must account for the rent on an accrual basis.

c. Deductions under accrual method §1025

The criteria for deductibility are whether: (i) all events have occurred that establish an *unconditional duty to pay*; (ii) *economic performance* has occurred; and (iii) the amount is *reasonably ascertainable*.

(1) Fixed duty to pay §1026

It must be established that there is an unconditional duty to pay a reasonably determinable amount. Contingent liabilities and reserves are therefore not deductible.

(2) Economic performance rule §1030

The all events test is not met until economic performance occurs. Economic performance occurs when services or property are actually provided to the party obligated to pay for them.

(3) Disallowance of deduction for amount owed to related taxpayer §1036

The Code *disallows* the accrual of such a deduction *until paid*.

Note: No deduction is allowed until "economic performance" has occurred.

d. Inventories   §1039

When inventories are an income-producing factor, the taxpayer *must* account for purchases by using an *inventory.* The effect is that the taxpayer cannot deduct the cost of goods or materials in the year of the purchase *unless he sells them that year.* There are two methods by which the taxpayer may take his inventory:

(1) First-in, first-out ("FIFO")   §1041

The theory is that the goods first acquired were those that were first sold. The "cost" of the goods on hand at the close of the tax year is the cost of the goods last purchased.

(2) Last-in, first-out ("LIFO")   §1044

The last items placed in inventory are assumed to be the first sold. LIFO can be used for tax purposes only if also used for financial purposes.

4. Installment Method   §1047

This method is intended to allow sellers of *property* (other than "dealers") who are receiving payments on a deferred basis to include their gain only as they receive cash from the sale. The mechanics involve a fraction of the "gross profit" over "total contract price" being applied to each installment payment to determine how much of the payment is income (but interest payments are entirely includible). The installment method can be used only for sales of non-dealer property, not services, and only if the transaction produces a gain.

a. Restrictions   §1053

The installment method cannot be used for *debts payable on demand* (or readily transferable), *sales to related persons*, *dealer property*, or *sale of assets of an accrual method business*.

b. Interest on deferred income   §1056

When the installment sale price *exceeds $150,000*, the taxpayer must pay interest to the government on the deferred tax liability if the face amount of *all* such obligations held by the taxpayer and that arose during, and are still outstanding at the close of, the taxable year, exceeds *$5 million*.

c. Mortgaged property   §1060

When a buyer takes subject to a mortgage, the mortgage is not considered in determining the seller's total contract price or payments received in the year of the sale, unless the seller's basis is less than the mortgage.

d. Disposition of installment obligations   §1062

If the taxpayer has been using the installment method and sells or otherwise disposes of the obligation, the gain that was not previously taken into income is immediately recognized. *Exceptions* from the disposition rule occur upon the **death of a taxpayer** and **transfers between spouses**.

B. THE ANNUAL ACCOUNTING PERIOD

1. Introduction   §1065
The taxpayer ordinarily must pay the tax each year based on the income that year, even though taxpayer is engaged in transactions stretching over several years.

2. Selection of Tax Year   §1066
Generally, taxpayers must report on a calendar year.

3. Repayment of Income Reported in Prior Year   §1067
Payments made to the taxpayer during the tax year that he receives under a "claim of right" are taxed as income to him during that year. The repayment in the later year does not "reopen" the prior tax computation, but a **deduction is allowed in the year of repayment.** The taxpayer can choose to use the bracket of the earlier year or the current year if the amount repaid is at least $3,000.

4. Tax Benefit Rule   §1071
A recovery of an item deducted in a prior year is included in income in the year received if the deduction in a prior year gave the taxpayer a tax benefit in that earlier year. Any event inconsistent with that earlier deduction can trigger income in a later year even if there is no "recovery" in the later year.

5. Net Operating Loss ("NOL") Deduction   §1077
If all of the business deductions exceed his income, the taxpayer has a "net operating loss."

   a. Use of NOL   §1079
The NOL can be **carried back** and used as a deduction for the two years preceding the loss year. The taxes are refigured and taxpayer gets a refund. If some NOL is not used up by the carryback, it is **carried forward** into the next 20 years after a loss year and used as a deduction. **Stimulus legislation** allows NOL incurred in 2001 or 2002 to be carried back for five, rather than two, years.

   b. Amount of NOL   §1080
The amount of an NOL that may be carried forward or back is equal to a negative taxable income adjusted as follows:

      (1) **No deduction for capital losses in excess of capital gains** is allowed;

      (2) **Personal exemptions** are disallowed; and

      (3) **Deductions not attributable to trade or business** are allowed only to the extent of the income not attributable to that trade or business.

Approach to Exams

In spite of the great complexity in the income tax field, you will find that tax issues can be broken down into a relatively small number of areas. In resolving tax problems on your exam, it may be helpful to focus on each issue within the following analytical framework:

I. IS IT INCOME?

A. Does the particular item fall within the *definition* of income used under I.R.C. section 61?

B. Does it fall within any of the statutory *exclusions* from income?

II. TO WHOM IS THE INCOME TAXABLE?

If a gift has been made, is income shifted to the donee? Consider the following:

A. Was the gift of *property or* of the *income from property*?

B. Was the gift of income from *services*?

C. Did the donor retain *excessive controls*?

D. If the gift was in *trust*, is income taxed to the grantor, the beneficiary, or the trust?

III. IS IT DEDUCTIBLE?

A. Does it qualify as a *business or investment* deduction?

    1. Is the item *business or personal*?

    2. Is it a *current expense or a capital outlay*?

    3. Is it *ordinary and necessary*?

    4. Is it *barred by public policy*?

    5. If it is not an expense, can it be deducted as *depreciation, depletion, a loss, or a bad debt*?

    6. Is the deduction *above the line or below the line*, and is it limited by the restriction on "*miscellaneous itemized deductions*"?

B. Does it qualify as a *personal deduction*? If so, it must fit within the statutory provisions for interest, charitable contributions, etc.

IV. DOES A SALE OF PROPERTY PRODUCE GAIN OR LOSS?

A. How much was the *gain or loss*?

 1. What was the *basis*? Are there any adjustments to basis?

 2. Was there a *realization*? If so, what was the amount realized?

 3. Does the transaction qualify for *nonrecognition*?

B. Is the asset a *capital asset*? If so, was there a *"sale or exchange"*?

V. DOES THE ALTERNATIVE MINIMUM TAX ("AMT") APPLY?

A. What is the taxpayer's "alternative minimum taxable income"?

B. What is the taxpayer's exemption under the AMT?

C. What is the taxpayer's AMT?

D. Is the AMT greater than the taxpayer's "regular" tax?

VI. WHEN IS THE ITEM INCOME OR DEDUCTIBLE?

A. Does the taxpayer use the *cash* method, the *accrual* method, or the *installment* method?

B. If the transaction spans *several years*, should *each* year be taken separately, or can the *entire* period be considered?

STEPS FOR DETERMINING TAX LIABILITY

gilbert

STEP 1: **Gross Income (All includible income)**

STEP 2: − **"Above the Line" Deductions**

ADJUSTED GROSS INCOME

STEP 3: − **Personal Exemptions +** *either* **Standard Deduction**
or **Itemized ("Below the Line") Deductions**

TAXABLE INCOME

STEP 4: × **Applicable Tax Rate**

TAX LIABILITY

STEP 5: − **Tax Credits**

TAX DUE

STEP 6: ? **Calculate AMT. If AMT is greater than "TAX DUE," AMT becomes the amount due.**

Chapter One:
Is It Income?

CONTENTS

Chapter Approach

One of the most basic questions in a tax situation is whether an item is income. Therefore, you will almost certainly see a question that requires you to make such a determination. In considering whether an item is income, use the following checklist:

1. Is an item *income under I.R.C. section 61*? To decide, ask:

   a. Did the item increase the taxpayer's *net worth*?

   b. Or did it merely involve a *change of form*, like borrowing money or recovering basis?

2. Does the item fall under a *statutory exclusion* from gross income? Is it:

   a. *Gift or inheritance* (as opposed to compensation for services)?

   b. *Contribution to capital*?

   c. *Life insurance recovery*?

   d. *Recovery of the cost of an annuity contract*?

   e. *Interest on state or local bonds*?

   f. *Government benefits* (*but note:* some benefits, *e.g.*, unemployment compensation and a part of Social Security, are taxed)?

   g. *Medical insurance recovery*?

   h. *Damages for personal injuries*?

   i. *Meals and lodging for the convenience of the employer*?

3. Is it a taxable *form of compensation* for services? Most compensation (whether paid in cash or property) is taxable, including employer payment of employee expenses, but some forms of compensation are specially treated. Thus, is the item:

   a. A tax-free *fringe benefit*?

   b. *Employer-paid health insurance* or medical reimbursement?

   c. *Group term life insurance*?

4. Is the item *debt cancellation income* and, if so, does it qualify for exclusion? Remember:

a. *Insolvent and bankrupt taxpayers* can avoid debt cancellation income but must reduce tax attributes.

b. *Shareholder debt forgiveness* has special rules.

5. Is the item *spousal or child support*? Keep in mind that:

a. *Alimony* is taxable to the recipient, deductible by the payor.

b. *Recapture* is possible if the amount declines during the first three years.

c. *Child support* is neither taxable nor deductible.

A. Constitutional Background

1. Constitutional Provisions [§1]

The Constitution provides that Congress "shall have power to lay and collect taxes . . . ." [Art. I, §8, cl. 1] However, "[n]o capitation, *or other direct*, tax shall be laid unless in proportion to the census . . . ." [Art. I, §9, cl. 4; Art. I, §2, cl. 3] The meaning of the second provision is that a "direct" tax has to be apportioned among the states so that a state with 1% of the population will bear 1% of the tax.

a. Income tax held unconstitutional [§2]

An income tax statute was struck down in 1895 as an unapportioned direct tax. [**Pollock v. Farmers Loan & Trust Co.**, 157 U.S. 429 (1895)] The idea was that a tax on rents, interest, or dividends was equivalent to a tax on the underlying real or personal property and thus was a "direct" tax. In the same case, the Court also held unconstitutional a federal tax on the interest from state or municipal bonds. For this and other reasons, such interest is still not subject to federal taxation.

2. Sixteenth Amendment [§3]

The requirement of apportionment among the states made a federal income tax completely impractical. However, this problem was solved by the adoption in 1913 of the Sixteenth Amendment, which states: "The Congress shall have power to lay and collect taxes *on incomes, from whatever source derived,* without apportionment among the several states, and without regard to any census of enumeration."

3. *Eisner v. Macomber* [§4]

In only one case since 1913 has the Supreme Court held an income tax provision unconstitutional. Congress had attempted to tax a dividend of common stock distributed to existing holders of common stock. The Court held that the Sixteenth

Amendment requires a *realization*, an element lacking in a stock dividend. [**Eisner v. Macomber,** 252 U.S. 189 (1920); *see infra,* §§757 *et seq.*] Many but not all stock dividends are excluded from tax by the present statute. (*See* Income Tax II Summary.)

4. **Remaining Constitutional Issues [§5]**
    Since the adoption of the Sixteenth Amendment, constitutional issues have been of much less importance. However, certain constitutional issues can still be raised:

    a. **Due process violation [§6]**
        A tax imposing unreasonable or arbitrary distinctions could be a violation of the Due Process Clause of the Fifth Amendment. Thus, a now repealed provision on child care deductions was held unconstitutional because of arbitrary distinctions between men and women. [**Moritz v. Commissioner,** 469 F.2d 466 (10th Cir. 1972), *cert. denied,* 412 U.S. 906 (1973)]

    b. **Tax not on income [§7]**
        If a particular tax is not "on income," it is not legitimated by the Sixteenth Amendment. However, in that case it would probably be valid as an *indirect* tax under Article I, Section 8, Clause 1, as to which there was never an apportionment requirement. [**Penn Mutual Indemnity Co. v. Commissioner,** 277 F.2d 16 (3d Cir. 1960)]

    c. **Tax procedures invalid [§8]**
        Constitutional issues frequently arise in connection with tax procedures. These can include unlawful search and seizure, right to counsel, and the like.

B. Definition of "Gross Income"

1. **I.R.C. Definition [§9]**
    The definition of "gross income" set forth in Internal Revenue Code ("I.R.C.") section 61 echoes the language of the Sixteenth Amendment. Some cases have said that this section is intended to reach every transaction that it constitutionally could. It provides: "Gross income means *all income from whatever source derived* . . . ."

    a. **Specific items included**
        Section 61 lists many specific items that are gross income: interest, rents, dividends, business profits, salaries, gain on sale of property, alimony, etc.

    b. **Not exclusive list**
        However, as section 61 makes clear, this list is *not exclusive*. Many other transactions produce gross income although not mentioned in I.R.C. section 61.

2. **Early Attempts to Define Income [§10]**

   In **Eisner v. Macomber**, *supra,* the Court held that gross income (in both the constitutional and statutory senses) meant a gain "derived from capital, from labor, or from both combined . . . ." However, this definition proved far too narrow; it was difficult to stretch it to cover debt cancellation income or windfalls (both discussed *infra*). Consequently, it has now been abandoned.

3. **Net Worth Concept [§11]**

   The prevailing definition of income is that any item that increases a taxpayer's *net worth* is gross income. [*See* **Commissioner v. Glenshaw Glass Co.**, 348 U.S. 426 (1955)—punitive damages taxable as income] One's net worth (or *wealth*) is the difference between *assets and liabilities*. Anything that increases that difference is potentially income. Anything that decreases it is potentially deductible. (However, deductions must be specifically provided for by statute.)

   a. **Change in form [§12]**

      There is no income from a receipt that does not increase net worth.

      (1) **Loan repayment [§13]**

         The *repayment of a loan* does not produce income to the lender, because it does not increase her net worth. There is simply a change in the form of her property—from a loan receivable to cash.

         (a) **Interest is income [§14]**

            Interest paid to the lender for the use of her money is income.

            Example: Donny Debtor repays a note for $500 plus $50 interest to Larry Lender. Larry Lender must report $50 as taxable income (the interest), but he does not have to report the $500 repayment.

         (b) **Repayment when note purchased for less than face value [§15]**

            If the creditor bought the debt for *less than its face value,* its repayment by the debtor would produce a profit, which would be income.

            Example: Before repayment, Larry Lender sells the $500 note to Tom Transferee for $300. Tom collects full repayment ($500) from Donny Debtor, plus $50 in interest. Tom must report $200 (the difference between the face value of the note and the amount he paid for the note) and the $50 interest as taxable income.

      (2) **Return of capital [§16]**

         Similarly, a *return of invested capital* is not income; the taxpayer has merely recovered his cost, not increased his net worth. [**Doyle v. Mitchell Bros.**, 247 U.S. 179 (1918)]

Example: If Warren buys a share of stock for $30 and sells it for $32, his income is only $2; he is entitled to get back the $30 without tax.

b. Borrowing [§17]

There is no income from borrowing money. Borrowing increases assets and liabilities by the same amount and thus does not create net worth. However, monies obtained by *embezzlement or extortion* are treated as income. (*See infra,* §§160-161.)

c. Trust income [§18]

Amounts received by a taxpayer as a trustee do not increase the trustee's wealth since the trustee must use the amounts for a particular purpose that does not primarily benefit the trustee. Thus, these amounts are not income to the trustee. But note that a trust itself may be a taxable entity. (*See infra,* §§278 *et seq.; and see* Income Tax II Summary.)

Example: A political candidate is not taxed on political contributions since they must be expended for campaign purposes. However, if the candidate diverts the contribution to his personal use, it becomes taxable. [Rev. Rul. 74-22, 1974-1 C.B. 16; Rev. Rul. 74-23, 1974-1 C.B. 17]

d. "Income" need not be received in cash [§19]

The receipt of property or services is frequently treated as income. Thus, for example, noncash benefits and services received by an *employee* (*e.g.,* company car or free housing) may be taxable (*see infra,* §§127-143). Debt cancellation income is another example of noncash income (*see infra,* §§144-156).

e. Windfalls [§20]

Under authority of *Glenshaw Glass, supra,* "found money" or windfalls (*e.g.,* winning the lottery or finding money in a piano bought at a garage sale) are taxable. [**Cesarini v. United States,** 296 F. Supp. 3 (N.D. Ohio 1969), *aff'd,* 428 F.2d 812 (6th Cir. 1970)]

EXAM TIP   **gilbert**

For exam purposes, remember that *all* income from *whatever source* must be declared as income, even if, as a practical matter, the Internal Revenue Service would probably not be aware of the income, as in the piano windfall case above.

---

f. Unsolicited property [§21]

An item received involuntarily is not taxable until the taxpayer indicates that he intends to retain it.

 Example: A school principal received unsolicited books from publishers and then donated them to charity. He claimed that the books were not includible in income but took a charitable deduction for their value. The court disagreed; the books must be included in income. Possession of them increased the taxpayer's wealth, and his donation of the books, when coupled with the act of claiming a charitable deduction, indicated that he intended to accept them. [**Haverly v. United States**, 513 F.2d 224 (7th Cir.), *cert. denied,* 423 U.S. 912 (1975)]

(1) Note

The court in *Haverly, supra,* commented that the result might be different if the taxpayer did not accept the books but merely held them for the publishers. Indeed, the court did not decide whether the books would be income had the taxpayer *not claimed a charitable deduction.* Failure to claim the deduction could suggest that he failed to exercise "complete dominion" over the books—something that might be required by the realization requirement.

(2) And note

In *Haverly, supra,* the Internal Revenue Service ("IRS") conceded that it made no effort to tax unsolicited samples unless the taxpayer sought a double deduction (*e.g.,* by giving them to charity and claiming a deduction after excluding them from income). The court said that the IRS's decisions concerning allocation of enforcement resources were none of its concern.

g. All-inclusive definition [§22]

Any increment in net worth is presumed to be income unless specifically excluded (*see infra,* §§27 *et seq.*) or unless a nonrecognition section applies (*see infra,* §§779 *et seq.*). In other words, Congress is presumed to have fully used its constitutional power to tax income. However, a *realization* (*see infra,* §§757 *et seq.*) must occur before an increase in net worth becomes taxable. This means that some event must occur so that it is appropriate to tax the increase in wealth *now.*

Example: In 2000, Paul buys an "Elvis on Black Velvet" painting for $1 at a garage sale. In 2002, he has it appraised and discovers its value is $1,000. In 2003, he sells the painting for $1,000. Paul has $999 of income *in 2003* because that is when he realized his gain.

(1) Note

Eisner v. Macomber (*supra,* §4) held that a realization was a *constitutional* requirement. The courts today would probably permit Congress to dispense with the requirement of realization, but Congress has not done so.

4. Imputed Income [§23]

According to many economists, imputed income should be treated as gross income.

Imputed income is created when the taxpayer *works for himself or uses his own property*—for example, lives in his own house. Conceptually, this could be said to create rental income (and other countries have treated it as such). The point can be illustrated this way: If two taxpayers each own a house and rent it to the other, each one will have rental income. Why should it be any different if each lives in his own house? However, with the exception noted below, Congress has never sought to tax imputed income. Thus, for example, the value of housekeeping services to one's own family are not taxed.

a. Working for oneself [§24]

However, if one renders services to himself *and an employment relationship is also involved*, the courts have held that the benefit produced is income. [**Commissioner v. Minzer,** 279 F.2d 338 (5th Cir. 1960)]

Example: If a real estate *broker* buys a house for himself and splits the commission with the broker for the seller, the reduction in purchase price is not income. But if a real estate *salesperson* employed by a broker does the same thing, he does have income. The bargain purchase is seen as part of the employment relationship and thus produces taxable income.

b. Exception—interest income may be imputed [§25]

I.R.C. sections 483, 1274, and 7872 *require that interest income be imputed* in certain situations (*see infra,* §915).

c. Exchange of services [§26]

If two taxpayers exchange goods or services, both will have income unless some exclusion applies. Such a transaction is treated as though each taxpayer had charged an appropriate fee (thus receiving income) and then used the money to pay the other one. [Treas. Reg. §1.61-2(d)(1)]

Example: If a lawyer and a plumber each work for the other for five hours without any cash changing hands, each will have income in the value of services provided to him. [Rev. Rul. 79-24, 1979-1 C.B. 60]

C. Exclusions from Gross Income

1. In General [§27]

The scope of the Sixteenth Amendment and I.R.C. section 61 has been sharply limited by a long list of *exclusions*—items that would be income except that Congress has chosen to exclude them.

2. Gifts and Inheritances [§28]

Gross income does not include the value of property received by a gift, devise, bequest, or inheritance. [I.R.C. §102(a)]

a. **What is a "gift" [§29]**

The *motive of the donor* determines whether the transaction results in a tax-free "gift" to the donee. If the donor had mixed motives, his primary motive controls. There must be a showing of *"detached and disinterested generosity."* The transfer must be made "out of affection, respect, admiration, charity or like impulses." [**Commissioner v. Duberstein,** 363 U.S. 278 (1960)]

(1) Rule of construction [§30]

The concept of "gift" is *narrowly* applied by the courts, so as to limit the scope of the exclusion.

(a) Distinguish—gift tax construction

For *federal gift tax* purposes, the opposite is true: A broad construction of "gift" is adopted in order to reach as many transactions as possible.

(b) Note—different results

Hence, a particular transaction could be a taxable gift for gift tax purposes, but not a gift for income tax purposes. In such event, the donor would have to pay a gift tax and the recipient would have to pay income tax! [*See* **Farid-Es-Sultaneh v. Commissioner,** 160 F.2d 812 (2d Cir. 1947)]

(2) Gift vs. compensation [§31]

Amounts transferred by an employer to, or for the benefit of, an *employee* cannot be excluded as gifts. [I.R.C. §102(c)] Such transfers are taxable regardless of whether the employer intended to compensate the employee or whether the employer made the transfer solely out of affection or other disinterested generosity. However, a transfer to an employee who is also a relative can be treated as a gift if "the purpose of the transfer can be substantially attributed to the familial relation of the parties and not to the circumstances of their employment." [Prop. Regs. §1.102-1(f)(2)] *But note:* Many transfers to persons who are *not* employees involve mixed motivations by the transferor. It is often difficult to decide whether such transfers should be classified as gifts.

(a) Background—leading cases

1) *Commissioner v. Duberstein* [§32]

The *Duberstein* case, *supra,* presented this problem. Duberstein had frequently told Berman of potential customers for Berman's products. Berman sent Duberstein a Cadillac. Obviously, this represented both recognition of Duberstein's past services to Berman and also was designed to encourage future referrals. The Supreme Court held that it was not a gift. As to the past referrals, Berman owed Duberstein a moral obligation (although not a legal obligation) for the valuable favors. As to the future referrals, Berman was actuated by self-interest. In both cases, Berman's primary motivation was not "detached and disinterested generosity" or "affection, respect, admiration, charity or like impulses."

2) ***Stanton v. United States* [§33]**
Yet in **Stanton v. United States,** 287 F.2d 876 (2d Cir. 1961) (which was decided with *Duberstein*), the Court declined to rule as a matter of law that a gift can never arise from an employment relationship. Stanton was a church treasurer who was given a bonus by the church when he retired. The Court held that it was for the trier of fact to decide the church's primary motivation; it was possible that the church could meet the "detached and disinterested generosity" test. In fact, it was subsequently held that the payments were gifts.

a) **Note**
Under section 102(c) (above), which was enacted in 1986, the transfer to Stanton would be treated as income regardless of the church's motivation, because a transfer to an employee cannot be excluded as a gift.

3) **Effect [§34]**
When a transfer falls outside the terms of section 102(c), because it does not arise out of employment, the law is very unclear. The result of *Duberstein* and *Stanton* is to leave great discretion with the trier of fact. Inconsistent and unpredictable results are inevitable.

---

e.g. **Example:** A man made large transfers of cash and property to his mistress, who did not include them in income. The mistress was convicted of criminal tax evasion. The conviction was reversed; the court held that she could not have had the requisite willfulness to be guilty of tax evasion since she could not know whether the man made the transfers out of affection or to compensate her. Yet this distinction, based on the transferor's intention, is critical in deciding whether the transfers were taxable under section 102. In dictum, the court suggested that such payments should generally be treated as gifts under section 102. [**United States v. Harris,** 942 F.2d 1125 (7th Cir. 1991)]

(b) **Deduction by donor [§35]**
Ordinarily, if a transfer is a "gift," it could not also be deductible as

a business expense to the transferor since it would lack sufficiently close connections to business. (*See infra,* §303.) However, the income issue and deduction issue are not inseparably connected and it is possible that an item could be *both* a gift and deductible, especially if the issues are considered by different courts. If the transferor deducts the payment to the transferee, this fact is relevant, but not conclusive, in ascertaining the transferor's motive. The transferor's action in taking the deduction suggests that there was a business reason for making the transfer, which would negate its being treated as a gift to the transferee. [**Commissioner v. Duberstein,** *supra,* §32]

1) Note

If the recipient is entitled to exclude the payment as a gift, the payor's deduction is limited to $25. [I.R.C. §274; *see infra,* §336]

(c) Death benefits [§36]

Many cases have considered whether a payment by an employer to an employee's surviving spouse (or other beneficiary) can be treated as a gift. It might be argued that the payment is motivated by sympathy rather than by a desire to provide additional compensation for the decedent's services. [*See* **Estate of Carter v. Commissioner,** 453 F.2d 61 (2d Cir. 1971); **Poyner v. Commissioner,** 301 F.2d 287 (4th Cir. 1962)] Section 102(c) might render all such payments *taxable* to the recipient, regardless of the employer's motivation. Section 102(c) provides that a payment cannot be treated as a gift if paid by an employer "on behalf of" an employee; it could be argued that a payment to a surviving spouse is such a payment. The point has not yet been settled.

1) Deductibility by employer [§37]

If found to be taxable to the surviving spouse, the payment is probably deductible as a business expense. However, if the payment is found to have been a gift to the recipient, the payment is probably nondeductible to the employer. If the payment were found to be a gift to the recipient but also deductible to the employer, the deduction is limited to $25. [*See* I.R.C. §274(b)(1); *infra,* §336]

(d) Gratuities [§38]

Tips and gratuities, such as those received by waiters or taxi drivers, are compensation for services rather than gifts, and hence taxable to the recipient. [**Roberts v. Commissioner,** 176 F.2d 221 (9th Cir. 1949)]

Example: "Tokes" received by gambling dealers are not gifts. Since gamblers pay them out of a superstitious belief that they produce good luck, they are not paid from detached or disinterested generosity. They are taxable even though they are not payment for any special service and there is no social compulsion to pay them. [**Olk v. United States,** 536 F.2d 876 (9th Cir. 1976)]

(e) Strike benefits [§39]

Benefits paid to striking union members by their union are ordinarily taxable income. Such benefits are paid to further the union's objectives and to induce persons to join the union; they are not "gifts" from the union. [**Hagar v. Commissioner,** 43 T.C. 468 (1965)]

1) Distinguish—benefits paid to nonmembers [§40]

In one case the Supreme Court upheld a jury's finding that strike benefits paid by a union to *nonmembers* were "gifts" from the union, ". . . proceeding primarily from generosity rather than from the incentive of anticipated economic benefit." [**United States v. Kaiser,** 363 U.S. 299 (1960)]

(3) Bargain purchases [§41]

When a person "sells" property to another for less than the property's value, an issue arises whether the difference between the value and the amount paid should be treated as a gift to the "buyer," as income to the "buyer," or as an ordinary purchase transaction that is neither a gift nor income to the "buyer." This issue depends on the "seller's" motives and the circumstances of the parties.

(a) Application

1) *If the "seller" is misinformed as to the value,* or knows the value but must make a *distress sale,* there is no income or gift. The "buyer" has merely made an advantageous purchase.

Example: To pay off a note that is about to come due, Sam sells an antique that he had appraised at $5,000 to Bart for $3,500. Sam had earlier purchased the antique for $300. Sam and Bart are not related and do not know each other, and the sale to Bart occurs on an Internet auction site. The difference between market value and sales price ($1,500) is neither income nor a gift to Bart. However, Sam has a gain of $3,200 on the sale to Bart.

2) *If the "seller's" motives proceed from disinterested generosity,* the "bargain" element is an excludible gift. Also, if the "buyer"

is a recognized charity, the "bargain" element may be ***deductible*** by the seller as a ***charitable contribution*** (*see infra*, §637).

---

e.g. **Example:** Mary sells her car (actually worth $2,000) to her granddaughter, April, for $800. April has probably received a gift of $1,200.

(b) Distinguish—compensation cases [§42]
Bargain purchases that are compensation for services produce income to the person who rendered the services. [I.R.C. §83(a), discussed *infra*, §§975-983] However, certain bargain purchases are excluded fringe benefits. [I.R.C. §132(c), discussed *infra*, §137]

---

e.g. **Example:** As part of his employment, Eastco grants Paul a nontransferable ***option*** to purchase shares of Eastco's stock at $5 per share. Because the option is difficult to value, the receipt of the option is not a taxable event. [I.R.C. §83(e)(3)] Paul exercises the option, purchasing 100 shares for $500. The stock is then worth $2,000. Paul has received income of $1,500. [**Commissioner v. LoBue,** 351 U.S. 243 (1956)] In *LoBue,* the Court held it immaterial that the employer's purpose was to give its employee a proprietary interest in the business. *Note:* Certain stock options that meet precisely defined criteria do not produce income when exercised (*see infra,* §§ 984-990).

---

b. What is "inheritance" [§43]
The exclusion applies not only to property received under a will or through intestate succession, but also to any other payment that is "referable" to such a gift or inheritance.

(1) Will contest settlement [§44]
Money received by an heir in settlement of a will contest has been held tantamount to receiving an inheritance and, therefore, excluded from income. [**Lyeth v. Hoey,** 305 U.S. 188 (1938)]

(2) Compensation for past services [§45]
But a bequest from an employer to an employee is taxable. [I.R.C. §102(c)]

EXAM TIP	gilbert

On your exam, be sure to remember that ***all*** "gifts" or "bequests" ***from employers to employees are taxable*** under section 102(c), no matter how much the facts of the problem try to point you in the other direction. Thus, if Faithful Butler has worked for Testator for 20 years, tending to Testator's every need, while Testator's children could not be bothered to visit Testator during the past 10 years, and as a result, Testator leaves all of his estate to faithful Butler, the "bequest" is taxable income to Butler.

(3) Payment for services to estate [§46]

Similarly, a *"bequest" made to an executor* is not exempt if intended as a *substitute* for the fees payable for his services to the estate. The test is whether the beneficiary was required to perform the services as an executor to obtain the gift. [*See* **United States v. Merriam,** 263 U.S. 179 (1923)]

(a) Note

An executor who *waives* the commissions due him for his services to the estate will not be taxed on the value of his services, even though he is also a legatee, provided the waiver is "within a reasonable time after entering upon his duties." [Rev. Rul. 66-167, 1966-1 C.B. 20]

c. Income derived from gifts [§47]

Even though property is transferred as a tax-free gift, any *income subsequently derived* by the donee from the property is taxable. [I.R.C. §102(b)(1)]

Example: Father conveys to son (by inter vivos or testamentary gift) an apartment building worth $500,000. Son is not required to include the value in his gross income. However, the rentals thereafter received from the apartment building are income to son.

---

(1) Distinguish—gift of future income [§48]

If the gift involved is *solely of future income,* then *all* money received is taxable to the donee. [I.R.C. §102(b)(2)—codifies **Irwin v. Gavit,** 268 U.S. 161 (1925)] However, if a donor gives the donee income from the property but retains the property for herself, the donor is taxed on the income (*see infra,* §193). (*See also* the discussion of the taxation of trusts, *infra,* §§249 *et seq.,* as to dividing the income from the gift between the trust and beneficiaries.)

Example: If Andy bequeaths to Betty the income for life from certain stocks, remainder to Clyde, the dividend income thereafter received by Betty is taxable to her, even though she received it as a gift.

---

3. Awards and Scholarships [§49]

Under present law, most awards and scholarships do *not* qualify for exclusion and thus are taxable.

a. Awards and prizes [§50]

Awards and prizes are taxable to the recipient. [I.R.C. §74(a)] Thus, for example, the Nobel Prize is taxable. (It was excludible prior to 1987.)

(1) Exception—charitable transfer [§51]

A prize is not taxable to the recipient if: (i) it was received for scientific, educational, or similar achievements, and (ii) the recipient orders that it be transferred to a charity. [I.R.C. §74(b)]

> **e.g.** **Example:** If the winner of the Nobel Prize orders the Nobel committee to transfer her award to the American Cancer Society, the recipient would not include the award in income (but also would not be entitled to a charitable deduction for the transfer).

(2) Exception—employee achievement awards [§52]

An award to an employee for length of service or safety achievement is not taxable unless it cost the employer more than $400. [I.R.C. §§74(c), 274(j)]

b. Scholarships and fellowships [§53]

With certain exceptions, scholarships and fellowships are taxable to the recipient. [I.R.C. §117]

(1) Exception—qualified scholarship [§54]

An amount received as a "qualified scholarship" is excluded from income. A qualified scholarship is an amount that can be used only to pay *tuition and fees* or for *required books or supplies*. Only degree candidates at tax-exempt educational organizations are entitled to this exclusion. [I.R.C. §117(b)] An amount received in payment for teaching, research, or other services, required as a condition for receiving the grant, does not qualify. [I.R.C. §117(c)]

> **e.g.** **Example:** Sandra receives a scholarship of $8,000 per year to attend law school. The school requires that $6,500 of this grant be applied to tuition and books. Of the $8,000, $6,500 is excludible, but the remaining $1,500 of the grant (which defrays Sandra's living expenses) is taxable.

(2) Exception—tuition reduction [§55]

With some qualifications, a tuition reduction plan does not result in taxable income. Generally, such plans must not discriminate in favor of highly compensated employees. Also, the tax benefit applies only with respect to undergraduate, not graduate, education. [I.R.C. §117(d)]

> **e.g.** **Example:** The child of Tina, a Princeton professor, is an undergraduate at Stanford. There is a plan by which the children of full-time employees of either school can attend the other school free of tuition. The tuition reduction at Stanford is not taxable to Tina.

4. Contributions to Capital [§56]

If an investor contributes capital to a corporation or partnership, the amount received is *not* taxable to the recipient (whether or not the investor receives stock or a partnership interest in exchange). [I.R.C. §§118(a), 1032]

a. Distinguish—contributions by government or customers [§57]

Amounts received from a government to induce business construction in a particular area are taxable. Similarly, any amount contributed to a business by a customer or potential customer is taxable. [I.R.C. §118(b)]

 Example: Wisconsin gives $2.5 million to Cheesy, Inc. to locate one of its plants in the state. The amount is taxable.

---

5. Life Insurance—Amounts Paid by Reason of Insured's Death [§58]

Benefits paid under an insurance contract, by reason of the death of the insured, are *excluded* from gross income. [I.R.C. §101(a)]

a. "Life insurance" defined [§59]

Neither the Code nor the Regulations defines what constitutes "life insurance" as used in section 101(a). However, the Supreme Court has indicated that "life insurance historically and commonly *involves risk-shifting and risk-distributing*." [**Helvering v. Le Gierse**, 312 U.S. 531 (1941)] Therefore, if the particular contract does not shift any risk of premature death to the insurance company, it is not life insurance. [Rev. Rul. 65-57, 1965-1 C.B. 56]

(1) Distinguish—employer-paid benefits [§60]

Death benefits paid by an employer, whether voluntarily or under a plan, are taxable (*see supra*, §36).

(2) Debtor's insurance [§61]

Creditors often take out life insurance on the life of the debtor. If the debtor dies, the insurance is applied to pay off the debt. The amount thus received by the creditor is treated as payment of the debt (which might be taxable if it exceeds the basis of the debt), *not* as excludible life insurance. [Rev. Rul. 70-54, 1970-1 C.B. 218]

(3) Accelerated death benefits [§62]

Life insurance amounts payable before death to a terminally or chronically ill individual are treated as if paid by reason of death. For this purpose, a terminally ill individual is one certified by a physician as having less than 24 months to live. A chronically ill individual is one unable to perform at least two of the activities of daily living without assistance. Similarly, amounts received by reason of the sale of a life insurance policy to a "viatical settlement provider" is treated as if paid by reason of death. A "viatical settlement provider" is in the business of purchasing life insurance policies from terminally or chronically ill insured persons. [I.R.C. §§101(g), 7702B(c)]

EXAM TIP	gilbert

Remember that although life insurance death benefits, inheritance, and gifts are *excluded* from income *for income tax purposes*, they may be subject to *estate or gift taxes*.

b. Premium payments [§63]

Life insurance proceeds are excluded regardless of *who* paid the premiums on the policy. And it does not matter that the proceeds are paid to the insured's estate, to her family or creditors (except as discussed *supra,* §61), or to the partnership or corporation of which she was a member. [Treas. Reg. §1.101(a)]

(1) Policy owned by corporation [§64]

If a corporation owns and pays the premiums on an insurance policy on the life of its controlling shareholder, the proceeds are subject to *estate tax* in the shareholder's estate. [Treas. Reg. §20.2042-l(c)(6); *and see* Estate and Gift Tax Summary] But payment of the proceeds will *not* be taxed as a *dividend* to the beneficiary, even if he is himself a shareholder. [**Ducros v. Commissioner,** 272 F.2d 49 (6th Cir. 1959); **Estate of Horne v. Commissioner,** 64 T.C. 1020 (1975)]

c. Purchasers of existing policies [§65]

The exclusion for life insurance does *not* apply to a taxpayer who has *purchased* an existing policy for consideration.

Example: The owner of an existing policy sells it to Tammy for consideration. Tammy pays additional premiums. The insured dies. The proceeds are taxed to Tammy, except, of course, she can recover her basis—purchase price plus subsequent premiums. [I.R.C. §101(a)(2)]

---

(1) Exception [§66]

The "purchaser" rule does not apply if the purchaser is the insured himself, his partner or partnership, or a corporation in which he is a shareholder or officer. It also does not apply if the person acquiring the policy has a carryover basis from the transferor (as could occur, for example, if the policy was purchased by one spouse from the other; *see infra,* §§808 *et seq.,* discussing I.R.C. section 1041). In these situations, the entire proceeds are excludible, not just the transferee's basis.

d. Installment payments [§67]

If the death benefits are payable by the insurer in installments, and the unpaid balance bears *interest*, that portion of the installment payments that represents interest is taxable, although the balance is exempt. If the insurer simply holds the proceeds and pays interest thereon, the interest is taxable. [I.R.C. §101(c), (d)] If the installment payments are computed without a separate allocation of interest in each payment, the amount treated as interest is determined in the same manner as for annuities (below).

6. Annuities [§68]

An annuity contract is one in which the taxpayer invests a fixed sum, which is later paid back, with interest, in installments for a set period or for life. That part of each annuity payment that represents the taxpayer's *investment* in the policy is exempt as a return of capital. The interest portion, however, is income. [I.R.C. §72]

a. Computation of excluded portion [§69]

The excludible portion of an annuity contract payment can be calculated by multiplying the payment by a fraction, the numerator of which is the amount that the taxpayer invested in the annuity contract and the denominator of which is the taxpayer's total expected return from the annuity contract. Mathematically:

$$\text{excludible amount} = \text{annuity payment} \times \frac{\text{investment}}{\text{total expected return}}$$

Example: Thurston purchases an annuity contract for $9,000 (investment). The contract provides that Thurston will receive $1,200 annually for 10 years (a total expected return of $12,000). The excludible amount of each annual payment is $900 ($1,200 × ($9,000 ÷ $12,000)). Thus, only $300 of each annual payment is includible in Thurston's income each year.

(1) Payments "for life" [§70]

Often, annuity contracts provide that payments will be made to the taxpayer "for life." In such cases, the taxable portion of each payment is calculated exactly as explained above, but the total expected return must be calculated by referring to a life expectancy table.

Example: Thurston purchases an annuity contract for $9,000. The contract provides that Thurston will receive $600 annually for life, beginning on his 50th birthday. If tables provide that Thurston can be expected to live 25 more years, his total expected return is $15,000 ($600 × 25). The annual exclusion would be: $600 × ($9,000 ÷ $15,000) = $360.

(2) Limits on proration [§71]

If the recipient outlives his life expectancy, all amounts received thereafter are income. If the recipient fails to reach his life expectancy, however, the unrecovered amount would be *deductible* in the year the recipient dies. [I.R.C. §72(b)(3)]

> **Example:** In the scenario set forth in the example above, assume that Thurston lives more than another 25 years; in that case, Thurston would have recovered his entire $9,000 investment, and the entire annual payment of $600 would be taxable (beginning in year 26).

> **Example:** Assume now that Thurston only lives to age 56. In that case, he would only have recovered $3,600 of his investment ($600 × 6 years); thus, $5,400 could be deducted from his income in the year of his death.

b. Employees' annuity plans [§72]

The annuity rules apply to the taxation of amounts received under pension plans provided by employers for employees.

(1) Nonforfeitable rights [§73]

If the employer purchases an annuity policy for the employee, and the employee has a nonforfeitable right to the policy, he is taxed on its purchase price when the employer purchases it, even though payments will not begin until years later. [**United States v. Drescher,** 179 F.2d 863 (2d Cir. 1950); *and see infra, §§961 et seq.*] In such a case, the employee's basis, which he can recover tax-free when the payments finally begin, will include the amount previously taxed to him when the employer bought the policy.

(2) Qualified plan [§74]

However, if the annuity is part of a *qualified pension or profit-sharing plan,* no tax is payable in the year in which the employer makes the contribution to the plan. The tax on the employer's contribution is *deferred* until the year in which the annuity becomes payable to the employee, at which time the employee will presumably be in a lower tax bracket. [I.R.C. §402(a)(1); *see infra, §§969-974*]

7. Interest on State and Local Bonds [§75]

Interest earned on bonds and other obligations of state and local governments is *excluded* from federal income taxation. [I.R.C. §103] However, if the proceeds of the bond issue are used for private purposes (*e.g.,* construction of factories), the interest is taxable in most cases. [I.R.C. §§103(b)(1), 141]

a. Background [§76]

This exemption was originally of constitutional origin, required under the doctrine of intergovernment tax immunity (*see supra, §1, and see* Constitutional Law Summary). Although no longer constitutionally required [**South Carolina v. Baker,** 485 U.S. 505 (1988)], the exemption now serves the function of encouraging investment by high-bracket taxpayers in state and municipal bonds, thereby allowing these governments to borrow at a reduced rate of interest.

b. Distinguish—federal obligations [§77]

Interest on *federal* bonds, notes, postal savings, etc., is wholly taxable. [I.R.C. §103(b)]

8. Government Benefits [§78]

Certain amounts received from the government as benefits under social programs are *wholly or partially tax-free*.

a. Social Security benefits [§79]

Social Security benefits (both old age and disability benefits) are partially taxable. [I.R.C. §86] Supplemental Security Income ("SSI") payments, which are based on need, are nontaxable. [I.R.C. §86(d)(1)(A)]

(1) Taxable amount at lower levels of modified AGI [§80]

Social Security benefits may be taxable in an amount equal to *the lesser* of (i) one-half of the benefits received during the year *or* (ii) one-half of the amount by which the sum of 50% of Social Security benefits plus taxpayer's *modified* adjusted gross income ("AGI") exceeds a statutory floor. (Modified AGI means AGI increased by tax-exempt interest received during the year.) The floor is $32,000 on a joint return or $25,000 on a single person return. The formula for calculating the excess is:

Excess = (50% of Social Security benefits + Modified AGI) - Floor Amount

The lesser of 50% of excess or 50% of Social Security benefits is taxable.

Example: Tammy Taxpayer files a single person return, and she received Social Security benefits of $7,200. Assume that her modified AGI is $22,000. The sum of modified AGI and 50% of Social Security benefits is $25,600. This exceeds the statutory floor by $600. The amount taxable is the lesser of 50% of benefits ($3,600) or 50% of the excess ($300). Thus, Tammy must include $300 in income.

---

(2) Taxable amount at higher levels of modified AGI [§81]

At higher income levels, up to 85% of Social Security benefits received during the year are taxable. The income levels (the "adjusted base amount") are $44,000 on a joint return and $34,000 on the return of a single taxpayer. The calculation of the amount taxable at higher levels involves a complex phase-in as modified AGI rises above the base amount or the adjusted base amount.

b. Welfare benefits [§82]

Governmental payments based on *need*, such as welfare benefits, are excluded from income—even if a welfare recipient must work for the government to get the payments. [Rev. Rul. 71-425, 1971-2 C.B. 26]

c. **Unemployment compensation [§83]**
Unemployment compensation payments are taxable. [I.R.C. §85]

9. **Medical Insurance and Private Disability Payments**

a. **Medical insurance—employee pays premiums [§84]**
Benefit payments received under a medical or disability insurance policy purchased *by the taxpayer* are *excluded*, whether or not the taxpayer deducted the premiums paid to purchase the insurance. [I.R.C. §104(a)(3)]

(1) **Exception—no double exclusion [§85]**
If medical expenses were deducted (*see infra*, §§650-662), the insurance reimbursements for these expenses must be included in income.

b. **Employer-carried plans [§86]**
If the employer pays for health and accident insurance for its employees, the employees are not taxed on the premiums or on benefits received. [I.R.C. §106] Similarly, if the employer directly pays for medical expenses of employees or their dependents, the employees are not taxed on these payments (except to the extent they also deducted the same costs). [I.R.C. §105(d)] Finally, a medical reimbursement plan may not discriminate in favor of "highly compensated individuals"; it must cover a broad range of employees or the amounts received will not be excludible. [*See* I.R.C. §105(g)]

(1) **Permanent injuries [§87]**
An employee may exclude amounts received from the employer (or from insurance paid for by the employer) that are payment for the permanent loss of a member or function of the body or a permanent disfigurement. To be excludible, payments must be based on the nature of the injury without regard to the period the employee is absent from work (*e.g.,* loss of big toe pays $2,000 whether the employee returns to work after a week or after a month). [I.R.C. §105(c)]

(2) **Other disability payments [§88]**
With the above exceptions, payments received under disability insurance policies paid for by the employer must be *included* in income. [I.R.C. §105(a)]

10. **Damage Payments**

a. **Payments for personal injuries [§89]**
Damages received, whether in a lump sum or as periodic payments and whether by judgment or settlement, on account of *personal physical injuries* or *physical sickness*, are excluded. However, punitive damages are not excluded [I.R.C. §104(a)(2)]; similarly, amounts received by a plaintiff in a physical injury case for prejudgment interest on damages are not excluded. [**Rozpad v. Commissioner,** 154 F.3d 1 (1st Cir. 1998)]

(1) Scope of exclusion [§90]

As long as an action has its origin in physical injury or sickness, all damages received (except punitive damages) are excluded.

(a) Damages for emotional distress [§91]

Damages for emotional distress *alone* (*e.g.,* in a suit for intentional infliction of emotional distress) are not the result of a "physical injury" or "sickness," even if the emotional distress is accompanied by a physical manifestation (such as headaches). However, if the tort giving rise to the emotional distress *also involved* a physical injury, damages for emotional distress may be excluded (*e.g.,* in a car accident). [I.R.C. §104(a)]

(b) Damages for illegal discrimination [§92]

Damages arising out of illegal discrimination (race, sex, age, or disability) are taxable because they do not result from a physical injury.

(2) Prior law [§93]

Under the prior version of section 104(a)(2), taxpayers could also exclude damages received by reason of intangible injuries, such as injury to reputation or privacy or certain violations of civil rights, if compensated for by tort-type remedies. [*See* **Commissioner v. Burke,** 504 U.S. 229 (1992)] However, punitive damages were taxable even in personal injury cases. [**O'Gilvie v. Commissioner,** 519 U.S. 79 (1996)]

(3) Common law background [§94]

Before and after enactment of section 104(a)(2), personal injury recoveries were held not to be income under section 61 by rulings and judicial decisions on the rationale that they did not represent any accretion in net worth; *i.e.,* they "roughly correspond to a return of invested capital." [**Commissioner v. Glenshaw Glass Co.,** *supra,* §11]

(a) Scope of common law exclusion [§95]

The early rulings and case law exempted damages recovered for any interference with personal or family rights—*e.g.,* recoveries for alienation of affections or breach of contract to marry, as well as libel and slander. [*See* Sol. Op. 132, I-1 C.B. 92 (1922); Rev. Rul. 74-77, 1974-1 C.B. 33; **McDonald v. Commissioner,** 9 B.T.A. 1340 (1928)]

(b) Probably not excludible now [§96]

Since the sort of damage claims involved in the older cases are not damages for personal physical injuries or sickness, they would not qualify for exclusion under the present version of section 104(a)(2). Probably these cases, which are based on early definitions of income, would no longer be followed because they would be considered preempted by section 104(a)(2).

(4) Attorneys' fees, costs, and taxable tort recoveries [§97]

By the majority rule, a taxpayer cannot exclude attorneys' fees related to taxable tort recoveries. Under normal assignment of income rules, the taxpayer owns the tort claim and must include the entire amount recovered in income. Then she deducts the costs of obtaining the income. [**Kenseth v. Commissioner**, 259 F.3d 881 (7th Cir. 2001); *but see* **Srivastava v. Commissioner**, 220 F.3d 353 (5th Cir. 2000)—indicating that the attorney, rather than the client, owned the contingent fee and thus the client should not be taxed on it]

---

e.g. **Example:** Assume Travis wins an award of $900,000 in a civil rights case, and that he has a one-third contingent fee arrangement with his attorney. Assume further that $100,000 of court costs were incurred. The entire award of $900,000 is taxable to Travis under section 104(a)(2). The fee of $300,000 and the costs of $100,000 may be deducted, *but not excluded*, under section 212(1). (*See infra,* §§437 *et seq.*)

(a) Reasons taxpayer prefers exclusion [§98]

There are several reasons why a taxpayer would prefer to exclude attorneys' fees from income rather than deduct them.

1) Below-the-line deduction

First, the deduction is treated as a below-the-line deduction, meaning that it does not reduce adjusted gross income and cannot be taken if taxpayer takes the standard deduction. (*See infra,* §§556 *et seq.*)

2) Miscellaneous itemized deduction

Second, the deduction is treated as a "miscellaneous itemized deduction," and is deductible only to the extent that it exceeds 2% of adjusted gross income. [I.R.C. §67; *see infra,* §§562-564]

3) Alternative minimum tax

Third, and most important, the item is not deductible for purposes of the alternative minimum tax ("AMT"). Thus, it can trigger a very large AMT. (*See infra,* §§937-949.)

(5) Reimbursed medical expenses [§99]

If the damages compensate the taxpayer for medical expenses that were previously deducted (*see infra,* §§650-662), the damage payment must be included in income.

(6) Periodic payments [§100]

The exclusion under section 104(a)(2) for personal physical injury damages applies to both lump sum and periodic payments. [Rev. Rul. 79-220,

1979-2 C.B. 74—monthly payments to compensate for personal injury, to be paid over a period of 20 years or taxpayer's life, whichever is longer, are fully excluded, including the portion representing interest] Note, however, that the payor of periodic damage payments cannot deduct them until they are actually paid, even though the payor uses the accrual method. [I.R.C. §461(h)(2)(C); *see infra*, §§1030-1034]

b. Damages for business injuries

(1) Damage to goodwill [§101]

Case law also excluded damages for injuries to business goodwill under the "return of capital" theory. [**Farmers & Merchants Bank v. Commissioner,** 59 F.2d 912 (6th Cir. 1932)] But in a later case, this theory was questioned; if the destroyed goodwill had a tax basis of zero (*i.e.,* no money was paid to acquire it), the amount received as damages for its destruction should be treated as income. [**Raytheon Production Corp. v. Commissioner,** 144 F.2d 110 (1st Cir.), *cert. denied,* 323 U.S. 779 (1944)] Also, damages attributable to *lost profits* (as well as punitive damages) are treated as income.

(a) Note

Sometimes it is necessary to fragment a damage award to ascertain the tax treatment accorded to different elements.

(2) Statutory provision [§102]

A special statute confers a partial exclusion on certain recoveries of damages for business injuries. [I.R.C. §186]

(a) Injuries covered [§103]

The statute covers damages for patent infringement, breach of contract, breach of fiduciary duty, and antitrust violations.

(b) Amount excludible [§104]

The amount that can be excluded is the compensatory amount or the unrecovered losses, whichever is less.

1) "Compensatory amount" [§105]

The "compensatory amount" is the damages recovered minus the amounts paid in securing the judgment or settlement.

2) "Unrecovered losses" [§106]

The "unrecovered losses" are the amount of net operating loss carryovers attributable to the injury that have not been carried to other taxable years. (For explanation of net operating loss carryovers, *see infra,* §1077.)

3) Effect [§107]

The effect of this provision is to allow exclusion of damage recoveries only if the taxpayer had no tax benefit from the prior losses for which he now obtains a recovery. (*See infra,* §§1071-1076, for discussion of the "tax benefit rule.")

---

e.g. Example: As a consequence of violations of the antitrust law, Tammy Taxpayer lost $1 million because she had to pay excessive prices for drugs sold at her drugstore. The excessive amounts paid were part of the basis for the drugs that had been sold. However, in each year during which the injury occurred, Tammy Taxpayer had taxable income and therefore received a tax benefit by deducting the cost of the drugs. She cannot exclude any part of the damage recovery.

---

cf. Compare: Suppose in the previous example that Tammy Taxpayer did not have taxable income in the years of the injury but instead had deductions in excess of income. Furthermore, this went on a long time so she could never carry those losses to other years and use them as deductions, and the carryovers have now expired. She can exclude the damage recovery because she received no tax benefit from the losses that she is now recovering.

---

11. Miscellaneous Exclusions [§108]
A variety of other exclusions are scattered throughout the Code.

a. Foreign earned income [§109]
Taxpayers working abroad can exclude up to $80,000 per year of their service income from foreign sources. To qualify, the taxpayer must be either a bona fide foreign resident for an uninterrupted period that includes an entire taxable year or present for 330 days in a foreign country during a period of 12 consecutive months. [I.R.C. §911] In addition, such taxpayers can exclude substantial amounts of housing reimbursements (or deduct a substantial part of their housing costs). [I.R.C. §911(c)]

b. Group term life insurance premiums [§110]
The cost of group term life insurance (up to a maximum coverage of $50,000 per employee) purchased by an employer for employees is not includible in the employee's income as compensation, even though the employer receives a deduction for the premiums. However, benefits must be provided to all employees on a nondiscriminatory basis. [I.R.C. §79]

c. Meals and lodging furnished for convenience of employer [§111]
The value of meals and lodging furnished by or on behalf of an employer to an employee, his spouse, or dependents *for the convenience of the employer* is excluded from gross income. [I.R.C. §119(a)] This section codifies prior case law that allowed employees to exclude meals and lodging furnished for the convenience of the employer. [**Benaglia v. Commissioner,** 36 B.T.A. 838 (1937)]

(1) Business premises requirement [§112]

The meals or lodging must be furnished *on the business premises of the employer.* In the case of lodging, it must be accepted as a condition of employment, *e.g.,* meals and quarters furnished firefighters at the station house.

---

e.g. Example: A house provided for a hotel manager located across the street from the hotel and next to an overflow parking lot was held to be on the business premises. [**Lindeman v. Commissioner,** 60 T.C. 609 (1973)]

---

(2) "Meals and lodging" [§113]

The terms "meals" and "lodging" are also broadly construed. Thus, groceries supplied to an employee, including nonfood items such as soap and toilet paper supplied to an employee residing on the employer's premises, can be treated as "meals" or "lodging." [**Jacob v. United States,** 493 F.2d 1294 (3d Cir. 1974)]

(3) Convenience of employer [§114]

The "convenience of the employer" provision requires a *"substantial noncompensatory business reason"* for providing meals and lodging. [Treas. Reg. §1.119-l(a)(2)]

(a) "Substantial noncompensatory business reasons" [§115]

Substantial noncompensatory business reasons for providing meals include situations in which employees must be present to deal with emergencies or in which employees must take short lunch breaks because that time of day is the busiest for the employer. [**Boyd Gaming Corp. v. Commissioner,** 177 F.3d 1096 (9th Cir. 1999)—casino's requirement that all employees stay on premises during their entire shift provided substantial noncompensatory business reason for free meals in employee cafeteria even though there was sufficient time for most of them to leave the casino and eat elsewhere] Substantial noncompensatory business reasons for supplying lodging include situations in which no accommodations are available in the vicinity or in which an employee must be on call 24 hours a day. [Treas. Reg. §1.119-1(a)(2), (b)]

1) Note

In the case of meals, if more than half of the employees receiving meals qualify for exclusion, meals provided to the rest of the employees will qualify as well (even if those employees could not meet the convenience of the employer test on their own). [I.R.C. §119(b)(4)]

(b) But note—"business necessity" test [§116]

The Supreme Court has suggested that convenience of the employer means "business necessity"—*i.e.,* that the job could not be performed unless meals or lodging were supplied. [**Commissioner v. Kowalski,** 434 U.S. 77 (1977)] This is seemingly a much narrower test than the "substantial noncompensatory business reason" test of the regulations.

(4) Campus lodging [§117]

An employee of an educational institution (and her family) can exclude the value of "qualified campus lodging" provided on or near the campus. Because of the conditions placed on this exclusion, it is best to think of it as a type of tax-free employee discount. The exclusion applies if the lodging is on or near the employer's campus and the employee pays "adequate rent." Rent is deemed adequate if it is equal to the lesser of: (i) 5% of the appraised value of the lodging or (ii) the average rent paid by individuals other than employees or students for similar housing owned by the educational institution. If rent is inadequate (*i.e.,* the employee pays less than the lesser of (i) or (ii) above), the taxpayer must treat the difference between what he pays and adequate rent as income. Note that the exclusion does not require the lodging to be furnished for the convenience of the employer and that the lodging does not have to be on the employer's premises; it need only be nearby.

Example: Faber College owns an apartment building near its campus. The college rents apartments in the building to its faculty members and students for $500 per month ($6,000 per year), while it charges the general public $1,000 per month ($12,000 per year) for similar apartments. The appraised value of each apartment is $120,000 (5% of which would be $6,000). Bluto Blutarsky, a distinguished history professor at Faber College, rents one of the apartments for $500 per month. Bluto does not owe any tax on account of the $6,000 annual discount in rent because the rent that he pays is (at least) equal to 5% of the appraised value of the housing.

Compare: Same facts as above, but in order to convince Bluto to teach at Faber, the college agreed to rent him an apartment for $1 per year. Bluto will be taxed on $5,999, the difference between the rent that he pays and 5% of the appraised value of the apartment.

---

(5) Cash reimbursements [§118]

Amounts paid *in cash* to compensate an employee for meals or lodging must be included in income. They cannot be excluded under section 119, since that section covers only meals and lodging furnished *in kind*. Nor can the payments be excluded by applying a nonstatutory convenience of the employer test. [**Commissioner v. Kowalski,** *supra*]

e.g. **Example:** In *Kowalski,* state police troopers were reimbursed for meals taken during midshift breaks. The Court held that section 119 does not cover cash payments of any kind. Even assuming the payments were made for the convenience of the employer (so as to be excludible under the law in effect prior to adoption of section 119), that section was intended to *narrow the circumstances* in which meals could be excluded, and hence to *replace* prior law. Therefore, the payments were includible as gross income and not excludible under section 119 or otherwise.

(a) Note

The troopers in *Kowalski* could not *deduct* the payments they made for meals because they could not meet the "overnight" rule of section 162(a)(2). (*See infra,* §317.)

EXAM TIP **gilbert**

On your exam, be sure to remember the difference between employer-provided meals and lodging *furnished for the convenience of the employer* for (at least) a *substantial noncompensatory business reason* and employer reimbursement for expenses incurred on *business trips* (*see infra,* §§314 et seq). The former implies a more permanent arrangement (*e.g.,* hotel manager lives at the hotel) and *must* be furnished *in kind* to be *excluded* from gross income. The latter implies a more temporary arrangement (*e.g.,* the traveling salesperson), and generally may be *excluded* from gross income.

---

(6) Fixed charges for meals [§119]

Fixed charges for meals furnished for the convenience of the employer are excluded from the employee's gross income, provided the employee is required to make the payment whether or not he accepts the meals. This rule applies whether the employee pays the charge out of his compensation or out of his own funds. [I.R.C. §119(b)(3)]

d. Lessee's improvements [§120]

The value of a lessee's improvements on leased property is *not* income to the landlord, either at the time of the improvement or on termination of the lease, even though the improvement increases the value of the property. [I.R.C. §109] And the lessor makes no adjustments to the tax basis of the property. [I.R.C. §1019]

(1) Exception—disguised rent [§121]

A contrary result is reached, however, if the landlord and tenant intend the improvements as a substitute for rent. [Treas. Reg. §1.109-1(a)]

e. Insurance reimbursements for above-normal living expenses [§122]

Insurance reimbursements for above-normal living expenses, resulting from fire, storm, or other casualty loss to the *taxpayer's home,* are excludible. [I.R.C. §123]

f. Investment interest—higher education [§123]

The Code excludes the income resulting from the redemption of United States savings bonds if a taxpayer spends an amount equal to the redemption proceeds for "qualified higher education expenses." The bonds must be purchased after 1989 and the taxpayer must be at least 24 years old when the bonds are purchased. The exclusion is phased out as AGI exceeds $60,000 ($40,000 for singles). This exclusion is designed to give a tax break to middle-class parents for higher education expenses of their children; it will seldom apply to bonds purchased by the students themselves (since to take advantage of the exclusion a taxpayer must be at least 24 years old when the bonds are issued, as opposed to when they are redeemed). [I.R.C. §135] Note the assumption made by section 135: The rising redemption value of the savings bonds is deferred until the bonds are cashed in; the Code allows this deferral (unless the taxpayer elects to include the interest in income during the year). [I.R.C. §454]

g. Compensation for Holocaust victims [§124]

In addition, certain forms of reparation received by persons persecuted by Nazi Germany (or other Nazi-allied countries) on the basis of race, religion, physical, or mental disability, or sexual orientation, are excluded from income. The exclusion covers direct payments as well as the assets (or their value) stolen from victims of Nazi persecution and returned to the victim. In addition, certain interest payments on funds arising out of Holocaust litigation are excluded. [Economic Growth and Tax Relief Reconciliation Act of 2001, Pub. L. No. 107-136, §803, 115 Stat. 38 (2001)]

h. Others [§125]

A rental allowance or the rental value of a home furnished to a minister as part of compensation is excludible from gross income [I.R.C. §107; **Toavs v. Commissioner,** 67 T.C. 897 (1977)], as are combat pay and mustering-out pay to those in the service [I.R.C. §§112, 113], and payments to foster parents for caring for foster children [I.R.C. §131].

D. Inclusions in Gross Income

1. In General [§126]

As discussed in the initial definition of "gross income" (*supra,* §11), it is generally held that any increase in net worth is income. Certain includible items, however, merit special consideration.

2. Compensation for Services Rendered [§127]

As previously noted, cash or property received as compensation for services rendered is includible in the gross income of the recipient, irrespective of the form such payments take.

a. Payment of employee's income taxes [§128]

If an employer (whether or not pursuant to contract) pays an employee's income taxes (or any other debts of the employee), the amount of the tax payment is considered additional compensation to the employee. [**Old Colony Trust Co. v. Commissioner,** 279 U.S. 716 (1929)]

b. Reimbursements or expense payments by employer [§129]

Employers often pay travel or entertainment expenses of employees (or prospective employees), or reimburse them for such expenses. Whether such reimbursements and expense payments are income depends on the employer's motive. If the motive was to award additional compensation to the employee, the reimbursement or expense payment is taxable to the employee. But if the payment was designed to serve the employer's business (or was for the convenience of the employer), it is not taxable to the employee.

e.g. **Example:** A free trip to a company convention in New York was taxable because the purpose was to reward an insurance salesman for a job well done. [**Rudolph v. United States,** 291 F.2d 841 (5th Cir. 1961), *aff'd,* 370 U.S. 269 (1962)]

cf. **Compare:** A free trip to Germany provided by Volkswagen to a potential dealer was not taxable because it was provided for Volkswagen's business purposes. [**United States v. Gotcher,** 401 F.2d 118 (5th Cir. 1968)—note that the value of spouse's trip was taxable because there was no business reason for her to go]

(1) Reimbursed and nonreimbursed expenses [§130]

Reimbursements of employees for travel, meal, and entertainment expenses incurred in pursuit of the employer's business are not taxable. [Treas. Reg. §162-2(c)(4)]

(a) Accountable plans [§131]

The most common practice is for the employer to reimburse the employee for expenses and not include the reimbursement amount on the employee's W-2 form. This practice is authorized if: (i) the expense is related to business; (ii) the employee substantiates, or is deemed to have substantiated, the claim; and (iii) the employee returns payments in excess of the amount substantiated. This type of arrangement is called an "accountable plan." Additionally, the 50% limit on these deductions (*see infra,* §331) applies to the employer.

(b) Note—nonaccountable plans and unreimbursed expenses [§132]

If the employee cannot meet the criteria listed above, the reimbursement is deemed to be made under a "nonaccountable plan." If reimbursement is deemed made under a nonaccountable plan, the employer must include the amount of reimbursement as income on the employee's W-2 form. The employee may take a deduction for the business-related expenses, provided she can substantiate them. Unreimbursed expenses are treated in the same manner—the employee may take a deduction for them if she can substantiate them. *Note:* A 50% limit and a 2% floor applies to these types of deductions. (*See infra,* §§331 *et seq.*).

---

e.g. **Example:** Tom Taypayer travels from his office in Chicago to New York to attend company meetings. He stays one night at a hotel (cost $200) and orders three meals (cost $100). After returning to Chicago, Tom submits receipts to his employer for reimbursement, and his employer reimburses him with a check for $300 from an accountable plan. The reimbursement is not taxable.

EXAM TIP **gilbert**

On your exam, be sure to remember that an employee may have reimbursed expenses under an accountable plan, reimbursed expenses under a nonaccountable plan, and unreimbursed expenses from the same trip. ***Each type of expense is treated separately*** and is subject to the rules and limits stated above.

(2) Meals and lodging [§133]

Meals and lodging provided *in kind* are excludible if they meet the standards of I.R.C. section 119 (*see supra,* §§111-116). Cash reimbursements of *routine* meals and lodging costs are taxable (*see supra,* §118).

(a) Note

Cash reimbursement for expenses incurred *while traveling* are treated differently. (*See supra,* §130-132; *see infra,* §§314 *et seq.*)

(3) Frequent flier miles [§134]

It is unclear whether frequent flier miles credited by an airline to an employee, that arose out of a trip paid for by the employer, should be taxed to the employee. If the miles are taxable, it is unclear whether they should be taxed when credited to the employee's account or when they are actually used for personal purposes. Although logically the miles should be taxable at some point, there would be many practical difficulties in doing so. As a result, the IRS has never sought to include their value in income.

(a) Exception

If frequent flier miles are turned into cash, the cash is taxed to the employee. [**Charley v. Commissioner,** 91 F.3d 72 (9th Cir. 1996)]

---

e.g. **Example:** In *Charley*, taxpayer frequently flew on business. His employer would bill its clients for the cost of taxpayer's first class tickets, but taxpayer had instructed his travel agent to purchase coach tickets, upgrade taxpayer with the frequent flier mileage taxpayer earned on previous business trips, and forward the difference in ticket prices to him. In effect, taxpayer had exchanged his miles for cash. These amounts were taxable to the employee/taxpayer on either of two theories: (i) he had sold zero basis miles for cash, or (ii) he received additional compensation from his employer because the employer allowed him to cash in his miles—miles that were both earned and used in traveling on business.

---

c. Fringe benefits [§135]

Some "fringe benefits" furnished by employers are specifically excludible, *e.g.*, group term life insurance coverage up to $50,000 per year and employer-paid accident and health insurance. (*See supra,* §§86, 110.) Congress has set forth the following rules for determining whether other fringe benefits should be excludible. [I.R.C. §132]

(1) "No additional cost" service [§136]

A "no additional cost" service is excludible from income. This term refers to a service provided to the employee if the same service is routinely offered for sale to customers and the employer incurs no substantial additional cost (and forgoes no revenue) in providing the service to the employee (*e.g.*, allowing a flight attendant to fly free if she goes on standby). [I.R.C. §132(b)]

(2) Qualified employee discount [§137]

A qualified employee discount is excludible from income. This term refers to allowing an employee to purchase a good or service routinely sold by the employer at a price at least equal to cost (in the case of products) or at not more than a 20% discount (in the case of services). In the case of this and the preceding paragraph, the fringe benefit must be offered on a nondiscriminatory basis to the employees—not just to highly compensated ones. [I.R.C. §132(c), (h)(1)]

---

e.g. **Example:** Big-Mart allows employees to buy goods at a 10% discount (so that the price received exceeds Big-Mart's cost). The employee is not taxed on the discount.

---

(3) Working condition fringe [§138]

A working condition fringe is excludible from income. This term refers to any property or services provided to an employee which, if the employee had paid for the item herself, would have been deductible to the employee (or depreciable by the employee). [I.R.C. §132(d)]

> **e.g. Example:** If an employer furnishes an employee salesperson with a car that she uses *exclusively* for business, the value of the car is not taxable to the employee.

(4) Transportation fringes [§139]

The cost of commuting to work is not deductible (*see infra*, §306), but a qualified transportation fringe benefit is not taxable. A qualified transportation fringe benefit includes an employer-provided vanpool (in a vehicle holding at least six persons), a transit pass, and free parking. The amount that can be excluded, however, cannot exceed $100 per month (in the case of vanpool and transit pass) and $185 per month (in the case of free parking). [I.R.C. §132(f)] These figures are adjusted for inflation. In the case of parking, an employer may offer the employee a choice of free parking or additional compensation in lieu of free parking. An employee who chooses the free parking is not taxed on the forgone extra compensation. [I.R.C. §132(f)(4)]

(5) De minimis fringe [§140]

A de minimis fringe is excludible from income. This term refers to a fringe that is so small as to make accounting for it unreasonable or administratively impracticable. [I.R.C. §132(e), (h)(5)]

> **e.g. Example:** A company cafeteria open to all employees sells lunch for a price that is less than those of comparable eating facilities, but still high enough for the cafeteria to break even. The value of the reduced lunch price is not taxable. Similarly, an employee is not taxed on the value of an on-premises gym.

> **cf. Compare:** Airline distributed American Express vouchers to its employees entitling them to $50 worth of restaurant meals. Employees used 97% of the vouchers. This was not a de minimis fringe because it was administratively practical for Airline to account for and value each voucher. [**American Airlines, Inc. v. United States,** 204 F.3d 1103 (Fed. Cir. 2000)]

(6) Qualified moving expense reimbursement [§141]

To the extent that the employee would have been entitled to a moving expense deduction had she paid for the moving expenses herself (*see infra*, §325), she will have no tax if the employer pays or reimburses her moving expenses. [I.R.C. §132(g)] Employer reimbursements of moving expenses that are *not* deductible under section 217 are taxable. [I.R.C. §82]

(7) Qualified retirement advice [§142]

A taxpayer can exclude the value of qualified retirement planning services provided by the employer, provided that the employer also maintains a qualified retirement plan for its employees. [I.R.C. §132(m); *see infra*, §969, for treatment of qualified retirement plans]

(8) Definition of "employee" [§143]

For purposes of I.R.C. section 132, the term "employee" includes an employee's spouse or dependent child. It also includes a former employee who has retired or is disabled. [I.R.C. §132(h)(2)]

NONTAXABLE FRINGE BENEFITS	**gilbert**
EXCLUDED BY I.R.C.	• *Group term life insurance* up to $50,000 • Employer-paid *accident and health insurance*
EXCLUDED IF CONDITIONS MET	• *"No additional cost" services—if* the employer (i) routinely offers the services for sale and (ii) does not incur any substantial additional cost • *Qualified employee discount—if* discount does not (i) reduce sale price to below cost of products or (ii) exceed 20% of the normal price for services • *Working condition fringe—if* item or service would have been deductible or depreciable to the employee had the employee paid • *Qualified transportation expenses—if* the amount does not exceed (i) $100 per month for vanpools or transit passes or (ii) $185 for parking expenses • *De minimis fringes—if* fringe is too small to track • *Qualified retirement advice—if* employer maintains a qualified retirement plan for its employees • *Qualified moving expenses—if* the amount does not exceed the employee's actual expenses and employee would have been able to deduct the expense if employee paid

3. Income from Cancellation of Indebtedness [§144]

The reduction or cancellation of a person's debts increases his net worth. Therefore, it is treated as income, unless it falls within several possible exemptions.

Example: A corporate taxpayer issues bonds (evidence of indebtedness) having a face value of $12 million. Later, it is able to purchase a number of bonds on the open market at a discount from face value, totaling $137,000. Thus, its assets went down but its liabilities went down more—creating an increase in net worth and hence income. [**United States v. Kirby Lumber Co.**, 284 U.S. 1 (1931)]

EXAM TIP	gilbert

On your exam, be alert to *cancellation of debt* that results in an *increase of the taxpayer's net worth*. The cancellation may be a taxable event, subject to exceptions (*see* chart, *infra*).

a. Exception as to insolvent taxpayers [§145]

To avoid hardship, a cancellation of debt is not taxable if the taxpayer is insolvent immediately before the cancellation (*i.e.,* liabilities exceed the value of taxpayer's assets). However, the exclusion cannot exceed the amount by which the taxpayer is insolvent. [I.R.C. §108(a), (d)(3)] In addition, a taxpayer whose debts are discharged in a statutory bankruptcy proceeding is not subject to debt cancellation income.

(1) Definition of assets [§146]

For purposes of the insolvency exception, the term "assets" includes assets that are exempt from execution under state law. [**Carlson v. Commissioner**, 116 T.C. 87 (2001)—taxpayers had to include their valuable fishing license in calculating their assets for purposes of determining whether they were insolvent, even though such licenses are exempt from execution by creditors under state law]

(2) Price tag [§147]

In both insolvency and bankruptcy cases, the Code exacts a price: The taxpayer must *reduce certain tax benefits* by the amount of the debt cancellation income not recognized. These benefits include: net operating loss carryovers (*see infra,* §1079), disallowed passive loss carryovers (*see infra,* §547), and capital loss carryforwards (*see infra,* §818). In the event these are insufficient to absorb the entire amount of untaxed income, the basis of assets must be reduced in accordance with section 1017. [I.R.C. §108(b)]

Example: Before a debt cancellation, Teri Taxpayer's assets are worth $1,000 and her liabilities total $1,600. One of her debts, in the amount of $900, is canceled upon payment of $100. Ordinarily this would result in debt cancellation income of $800. However, Teri is insolvent to the extent of $600, and so $600 of the income is not taxed. Consequently, her income on the transaction is only $200. Teri must reduce tax benefits (such as loss carryforwards) by the remaining $600.

b. Exception for qualified real property business indebtedness [§148]

A taxpayer can elect to exclude debt cancellation from income when the debt is secured by real property used in a trade or business. If the debt arose after 1993, to qualify for this election it must have been incurred in connection with the acquisition or improvement of the real property. The basis of all real property owned by the taxpayer is reduced by the amount of debt cancellation income that was excluded by the election. A taxpayer cannot exclude more than the difference between the debt (before reduction) and the value of the property (reduced by the amount of any other debt to which it is subject). [I.R.C. §108(a)(1)(D), (c)]

Example: Teri Taxpayer is solvent and owns an apartment building worth $12 million that is subject to a debt owed to Bank of $17 million. The debt was incurred in connection with acquisition of the apartment building. Rather than foreclose, Bank reduces the debt to $11 million. Teri can exclude $5 million from income, but she must reduce the basis of all of her realty by $5 million. The remaining $1 million is taxable as debt cancellation income.

c. Exception for deductible payments [§149]

Income is not recognized on cancellation of a debt to the extent that payment of the debt would have given rise to a deduction. [I.R.C. §108(e)(2)]

d. Cancellation as a "gift" [§150]

A creditor's reduction or cancellation of indebtedness may be a gift to the debtor, in which case the resulting increase in net worth would be excluded. However, unless the creditor and debtor have a personal or family relationship, the creditor's intent would seldom be the "detached generosity" required to establish a gift (*see supra*, §29). Rather, the creditor usually intends either to keep the debtor in business so that he may remain as a customer in the future or to get as much as possible out of a debtor in precarious financial circumstances. [**Commissioner v. Jacobson,** 336 U.S. 28 (1949)]

e. Student loans [§151]

Some student loans are discharged if the borrower works for a certain time for certain employers. For example, a government loan might provide that if the student graduates and teaches in the inner city, the loan will be forgiven. Such loan discharges do *not* give rise to income. [I.R.C. §108(f)(1)] The lender must be the government, a charitable hospital, or an educational institution. In the case of an educational institution, the forgiveness must be pursuant to a program designed to encourage its students to serve in occupations or geographic areas with unmet needs. [I.R.C. §108(f)(2)]

f. Net benefit [§152]

If a taxpayer does *not* benefit economically from the debt cancellation, he has no income.

Example: Taxpayer Corp. issued preferred stock in exchange for $100. When the stock was worth $165, it exchanged the stock for a bond that was also worth $165. Later it bought back the bond for $118. The issue was whether the $118 should be compared to the $100 that the company originally received or the $165 that the stock was worth when the bond was exchanged for it. The court held that the company had no debt cancellation income because the $118 should be compared to the $100 originally received. When the entire transaction is viewed together, the taxpayer had no net economic benefit. [**United States Steel Corp. v. United States,** 848 F.2d 1232 (Fed. Cir. 1988)]

g. **Shareholder debt forgiveness [§153]**

Special rules govern a discharge of corporate debt by a shareholder. Such transactions may produce income to the corporation and gain or loss to the shareholder.

(1) **Income of corporation [§154]**

If a corporation transfers stock in discharge of its debt, it is treated as having satisfied the debt with money equal to the value of the stock.

Example: Car Corp. owes Kirk $1,000. Kirk cancels the debt in exchange for stock worth $600. The company has debt cancellation income of $400. The usual exceptions to debt cancellation income (*see supra,* §145 relating to insolvency or bankruptcy) can apply in this situation where stock is substituted for debt.

(2) **Treatment of shareholder [§155]**

If a shareholder receives stock in exchange for a corporate debt, the shareholder will recognize gain or loss, unless a nonrecognition section is applicable.

Example: Assume in the previous example that Kirk's basis for the Car Corp. debt was $860. Kirk would have a bad debt of $260. (*See infra,* §531, for discussion of bad debt deductions.) [I.R.C. §351(d)] However, such loss might be nondeductible if the exchange was part of a corporate recapitalization. (*See* Income Tax II Summary for discussion of corporate recapitalization and other reorganizations.)

(3) **Contribution to capital [§156]**

Suppose a shareholder forgives a corporate debt as a "contribution to capital" (*i.e.,* gets nothing in exchange). In this situation, the corporation is treated as having satisfied the debt with an amount of money equal to the shareholder's basis in the debt.

e.g. **Example:** In the previous example, in which Kirk has an $860 basis for a $1,000 debt of Car Corp., assume Kirk simply cancels the debt. Kirk already owns most of the stock of Car Corp. The company is treated as having satisfied the $1,000 debt for $860. Car Corp. has debt cancellation income of $140. [I.R.C. §108(e)(6)] Kirk adds $860 to the basis of his Car Corp. stock.

h. Reduction in purchase money debt [§157]

Suppose Bill buys a house from Sally, giving Sally a $20,000 mortgage. Bill claims that the purchase was fraudulently induced. As a compromise, Sally reduces the purchase money debt $5,000. This is treated as a reduction of basis, not as debt cancellation income. The theory is that the purchase price has been retroactively adjusted downward. [I.R.C. §108(e)(5)] The debt reduction must, however, come from the *seller,* not from a third-party lender. [**Preslar v. Commissioner,** 167 F.3d 1323 (10th Cir. 1996); Rev. Rul. 92-99, 92-2 C.B. 35]

i. Compromise of disputed claim [§158]

There is *no* income where the cancellation or reduction was in reality a compromise of a disputed claim, rather than a fixed indebtedness.

e.g. **Example:** Plaintiff sues Taxpayer for $10,000 for personal injuries. Taxpayer obtains a dismissal of Plaintiff's claim for $1,000. Since Taxpayer never acknowledged a fixed indebtedness of $10,000 to Plaintiff, the compromise of Plaintiff's claim for $1,000 does *not* result in $9,000 income to her.

e.g. **Example:** Taxpayer incurred debts to a gambling casino of $3.4 million. The debt was unenforceable under state law. Nevertheless, Taxpayer and the casino settled for $500,000. *Held:* Taxpayer does not have debt cancellation income because the debt was disputed. [**Zarin v. Commissioner,** 916 F.2d 110 (3d Cir. 1990)] This holding is remarkable since taxpayer actually received $3.4 million in chips, which he gambled away; when he was not required to pay for the chips, he should have income. (Alternatively, he should have had income when he received the chips in exchange for a nonenforceable promise to pay for them.) In most cases involving disputed debts, like the personal injury claim in the first example, the taxpayer never actually received cash or a cash equivalent.

(1) *Zarin* disapproved [§159]

Another court has disapproved of *Zarin.* It held that the disputed debt doctrine should apply only when the *amount* of the original debt is *unliquidated,* meaning uncertain or disputed in amount, as in the personal injury case in the first example. If the amount is liquidated, but the liability to pay it is disputed, as in *Zarin*, the normal debt cancellation rules should apply. [**Preslar v. Commissioner**, *supra*—taxpayer has debt cancellation income when he pays less than the amount of a $1 million debt that was subject to a liability dispute]

EXCEPTIONS—CANCELLATION OF DEBT AS INCOME

WHEN A TAXPAYER'S DEBT IS CANCELED, HER NET WORTH INCREASES, AND THE INCREASE IS USUALLY TAXABLE. HOWEVER, THERE ARE SEVERAL EXCEPTIONS:

☑ *Insolvent taxpayers* are not taxed to the extent that the amount of the exclusion does not exceed the amount of the insolvency

☑ Amounts discharged in **statutory bankruptcy proceedings**

☑ Debt cancellations when the debt is **secured by real property used in trade or business**, but the taxpayer may not exclude any amount greater than the difference of the debt (before reduction) and the value of the property (minus other debts relating to the property)

☑ To the extent that repayment of the canceled debt **would have been deductible**

☑ When cancellation is intended to be a **gift**

☑ When **student loans** are canceled as part of student's agreement to work in a high-need area

☑ To the extent the **taxpayer does not benefit economically** from the cancellation

☑ To the extent a **corporation substitutes stock** for debt

☑ For **reduction in purchase money debt**

☑ When cancellation was in reality a **settlement of a disputed claim**

---

4. Illegal Increases in Net Worth [§160]

Money or property the taxpayer obtains through illegal activities is includible in gross income. *Rationale:* Such property is taxable because, as a practical matter, the criminal derives readily realizable *economic value* from it. The fact that the money really belongs to another is immaterial.

> **Example:** *An embezzler* is taxable on the amount of money embezzled. [**James v. United States,** 366 U.S. 213 (1961)]

> **e.g.** **Example:** *A swindler who "borrows" money* from his victims, *never intending to repay*, has immediate income. [**United States v. Rochelle**, 384 F.2d 748 (5th Cir. 1967), *cert. denied*, 390 U.S. 946 (1968)] *But note*: A loan that was illegal under corporate law, but which the taxpayer intends to repay and expects he can repay, is not treated as income. [**Gilbert v. Commissioner**, 552 F.2d 478 (2d Cir. 1977)]

> **e.g.** **Example:** *Gambling winnings* are includible in the gross income of the gambler to the extent they exceed gambling losses. This is true whether or not the gambling is illegal. However, gambling losses are not deductible to the extent they *exceed gambling gains*. [I.R.C. §165(d)]

a. Promise to pay irrelevant [§161]

It is immaterial that the criminal is under an obligation to restore the money on which he is taxed. Even the taxpayer's promise to repay the money, made in the same year as his embezzlement, is unavailing to avoid tax. [**Buff v. Commissioner**, 469 F.2d 847 (2d Cir. 1974)] However, if in fact he does make restitution, he can deduct the amount in the year in which restitution is made. [*See* **James v. United States**, *supra*]

5. Spousal and Child Support Payments [§162]

Payments of spousal support (sometimes called "alimony" or "maintenance") and child support are treated consistently with respect to the spouses. If the payor can deduct the payment, it is taxable to the payee, but if the payor cannot deduct the payment, it is not taxable to the payee.

a. Spousal support—general rule [§163]

A cash payment by a separated or divorced spouse to the other spouse is *generally taxable to the recipient* and *deductible to the payor*. [I.R.C. §§71(a), 215] The payor deducts the payment in computing adjusted gross income. [I.R.C. §62(a)(10)]

(1) Instrument requirement [§164]

To be deductible by the payor (and thus taxable to the payee), the payment must be required by a "divorce or separation instrument." An "instrument" is a judicial decree of divorce or separate maintenance or a decree for temporary support. An instrument also includes a written agreement incident to a divorce or written separation agreement. [I.R.C. §71(b)(2)]

(2) Designated payment [§165]

The instrument can designate that otherwise taxable and deductible payments will not be taxable and deductible. [I.R.C. §71(b)(1)(B)] This provision gives the spouses flexibility in negotiating the treatment of support payments.

Have the parties executed a **separation agreement**, or is there a **court order** requiring support?

— NO →

Does the **agreement or order state that the payments are taxable** to payor?

— YES →

Payor may **not deduct** the support payments from income.

— NO ↓

Do the parties still **live together**?

— YES →

— NO ↓

Do the payments **stop if the payee dies**?

— NO →

— YES ↓

Do the payments **stop when** the couple's **children reach certain life events**?

— YES →

Payments are deemed **child support** payments—thus, they are **not deductible** by the payor and not includible by the payee.

— NO ↓

Does the **first-year payment** exceed the average of second- and third-year payments **by more than $15,000**?

— YES →

Recapture rules apply.

— NO ↓

Does the **second-year payment** exceed the third-year payment **by more than $15,000**?

— YES →

— NO ↓

Payor may deduct support payments; payee must include payments in income.

(3) Cohabitation [§166]

A payment is not deductible to the payor nor taxable to the payee if the parties are living in the same household after being legally divorced. [I.R.C. §71(b)(1)(C)]

(4) Cessation at death [§167]

Payments will not be deductible and taxable unless payments cease on the recipient's death. Moreover, there cannot be any liability to make payments after the recipient's death as a substitute for payments cut off because of her death. [I.R.C. §71(b)(1)(D); *see* Treas. Regs. §1.71-1T, A-13, A-14]

(5) Recapture of spousal support [§168]

When the amount paid in the first year exceeds average second- and third-year payments by more than $15,000, the excess is recaptured in the third year. Similarly, if second-year payments exceed third-year payments by more than $15,000, the excess is recaptured in the third year. The term "recapture" means that the amount is ordinary income to the payor and a deduction to the payee.

---

e.g. **Example:** An instrument calls for Husband to make payments to Wife of $24,000 in Year 1 and $1 per year in Years 2 and 3. Payments in Year 1 exceed average payments in Years 2 and 3 by $23,999. The excess over $15,000 ($8,999) is recaptured as income in Year 3. Thus, Husband has $8,999 of income in Year 3, and Wife has an $8,999 deduction.

---

(6) Identification numbers [§169]

The recipient of spousal support is required to furnish her social security number to the payor of alimony. Failure to furnish the number, or to disclose it on the return, will trigger a $50 penalty. The requirement of furnishing identification numbers helps the IRS cross-check these support deductions and income. [I.R.C. §§215(c), 6676(c)]

(7) Alimony trusts [§170]

When a trust is used to pay spousal support, the recipient's only income is limited to the taxable income of the trust. The payor gets no alimony deduction. Child support payments from the trust are not taxable to the recipient but are taxable to the grantor of the trust. [I.R.C. §682]

b. Child support [§171]

Basically child support is any amount that the instrument *designates* as for the support of a child. Child support is *not taxable to the recipient* or the child, and is *not deductible by the payor*. [I.R.C. §71(c)(1)]

(1) Contingencies [§172]

Any amount that is reduced on the happening of a contingency related to the child or at a time associated with such a contingency is deemed child support. Thus, if payments decline around the time a child reaches majority or gets married, they are treated as child support no matter how the instrument describes them. [I.R.C. §71(c)(2)] This provision changes prior law. [**Commissioner v. Lester**, 366 U.S. 299 (1961)—overruled]

EXAM TIP   **gilbert**

On your exam, be sure to remember that *alimony* is included as income to the payee and excluded from income by the payor; *but* this treatment *can* be changed by an instrument. *Child support* is not deductible by the payor spouse and is excluded from income by the payee spouse; *and* this treatment *cannot* be changed by the instrument.

INCLUDIBLE VS. EXCLUDIBLE INCOME ITEMS   **gilbert**

THE FOLLOWING SHOWS WHETHER CERTAIN ITEMS ARE INCLUDIBLE OR EXCLUDIBLE AS INCOME TO THE RECIPIENT:

INCLUDIBLE	EXCLUDIBLE
• Compensation for services	• Meals and lodging for employer's convenience
• Gratuities and tips	• Gifts and inheritance
• Most interest payments	• Interest on state and local bonds
• Punitive damages	• Damages for personal physical injury
• Alimony and maintenance	• Child support
• Cancellation of indebtedness	• Repayment of indebtedness
• Prizes	• Contribution to capital
• Gambling winnings	• Life and medical insurance recovery
• "Earnings" from illegal activities	• Recovery of cost of annuity contract

E. Tax-Exempt Organizations

1. Charitable Organizations [§173]

Certain types of organizations are *exempt* from income tax. To be exempt under

I.R.C. section 501(c)(3), an organization must be organized and operated for religious, charitable, scientific, educational, etc., purposes. The organization's status must also be determined by the IRS. [I.R.C. §501] No part of the net earnings can inure to a private shareholder, and no substantial part of the organization's activities can include carrying on propaganda or otherwise attempting to influence legislation.

a. **Charitable purposes [§174]**

Tax exemption is not available if the organization is primarily dedicated to providing social or recreational opportunities for its members. [**Wayne Baseball, Inc. v. Commissioner,** T. C. Memo. 1999-304—organization devoted to sponsoring particular amateur baseball team is not exempt; *but see* **Hutchinson Baseball Enterprises, Inc. v. Commissioner,** 73 T.C. 144 (1979), *aff'd,* 696 F.2d 757 (10th Cir. 1982)—exemption granted to an organization that sponsors a team but that also showed dedication to promoting amateur baseball in the area in other ways, such as by operating a field for and coaching the local little league team]

b. **Other effects of status [§175]**

Exemption from tax is not the only benefit of a section 501(c)(3) organization. Contributions to such organizations are also deductible for income, estate, and gift tax purposes. (*See infra,* §617; *and see* Estate and Gift Tax Summary.)

c. **Other tax-exempt organizations [§176]**

Many other kinds of organizations are also exempt from tax, such as unions, fraternities, civic leagues, chambers of commerce, etc. [*See* I.R.C. §501(c)(4) - (6)] However, contributions to them are *not* deductible.

d. **Discrimination disqualifies organization [§177]**

Organizations that practice racial discrimination cannot qualify as tax-exempt organizations. [**Bob Jones University v. United States,** 461 U.S. 574 (1983)—college that banned interracial dating not exempt]

2. **Unrelated Business Income [§178]**

The exemption from tax is limited to the income derived by eligible organizations from their nonprofit, charitable activities or their investments (interests, rents, dividends, etc.). It does *not* extend to "unrelated business income"—*i.e.,* income from an activity substantially different in purpose from the organization's nonprofit, charitable purpose. [I.R.C. §511]

---

e.g. **Example:** The American Bar Association ("ABA") sells life insurance to its members. Because it keeps the "dividends" refunded by the life insurance companies, the ABA makes a large profit on its insurance programs. Because this profitable business is unrelated to its charitable activity, it gives rise to unrelated business income. [**United States v. American Bar Endowment,** 477 U.S. 105 (1986)]

---

a. **Rental income [§179]**

Rentals from a tax-exempt organization's *real property* are generally treated as investment income and therefore exempt from tax. But rental income from a tax-exempt organization's *personal property* is treated as unrelated business income.

b. **Debt-financed property [§180]**

Investment income is also taxable as unrelated business income if the property involved was acquired with *borrowed funds,* unless it is used solely for purposes "substantially related" to the organization's charitable purposes. [I.R.C. §514] Only that portion of the income that results from investment of borrowed funds is taxed. *Gain* on the sale of any such property is also taxed. (This section was designed to prevent the tax avoidance scheme involved in the *Brown* case; *see infra,* §§903-905.)

3. **Private Foundations [§181]**

Nonpublic charitable organizations (other than churches) are subject to special restrictions. Generally speaking, if the organization receives more than one-third of its support from the general public, it is not a private foundation. [I.R.C. §509] The charter of a private foundation must require the prompt distribution of all income for charitable purposes. It must also prohibit "self-dealing" between the foundation and any substantial contributor, and further prohibit "excess" business holdings and certain types of expenditures (*e.g.,* lobbying). [*See* I.R.C. §508(e)]

a. **Note**

Even if the organization otherwise qualifies, a blanket 2% tax is imposed on its net investment income. [I.R.C. §4940]

b. **And note**

Violation of any of the above charter restrictions results in stiff penalty taxes against the foundation and (in certain cases) its management. [*See* I.R.C. §§4941-4945]

4. **Political Organizations [§182]**

To clear up much confusion, Congress passed I.R.C. section 527, detailing the taxation of political organizations. They are taxed like corporations on investment income, but they are not taxed on *"exempt function income."*

a. **"Exempt function income" [§183]**

"Exempt function income" is contributions of money or property, membership dues, or proceeds from political fundraising or entertainment events, or from sale of political campaign materials (as long as such sales are not in the ordinary course of trade or business). To be excludible, this income must be segregated for an *"exempt function."*

b. **"Exempt function" [§184]**

An "exempt function" is one that attempts to influence the nomination, election, or appointment of individuals to public office.

Chapter Two:
To Whom Is the Income Taxable?

CONTENTS

Chapter Approach

Chapter Approach

Assuming that a particular item is income, the question then becomes to whom is it taxable? In general, income is taxed to the person who earned it, to the owner of the property that produced it, or to the person who controls it. Problems arise when taxpayers spread income by making gifts among several persons or entities, so as to minimize the tax rates. Exam questions on income splitting are common. Some key things to remember for exam purposes are discussed below.

1. **Income from Property**

   Income is shifted in the case of a gift of the income-producing *property*, but does not shift with a gift of the *income* from the property. If a question involves income from property, ask:

   (i) Does the donor actually *give up control* over the property, or is the transfer a sham? Remember that even if the transfer is effective under state law, the income may be taxed to the donor if he retains *excessive controls* over the management of the property and over who receives the income.

   (ii) Has the income already *accrued or matured*? If so, it may be too late to shift the income.

   Keep in mind that the donor does *not* realize income on a gift of appreciated property.

2. **Income from Services**

   If the question concerns income from personal services, remember that generally this income *cannot be shifted by gift* either before or after services are rendered. Note that it is possible to work for free, without imputed income, but if payment is made to anyone, it is taxable to the *earner*.

3. **Statutory Divisions of Income**

   Watch for the following income-splitting situations that are specifically addressed by the Internal Revenue Code:

   a. **Commonly controlled businesses**

      Code section 482 allows the IRS to reallocate income among businesses controlled by the same people.

   b. **Children's income**

      All of a child's income is taxed to the child [I.R.C. §73], and under what is known as the *"kiddie tax,"* the child's *unearned* income is taxed to her at her parents' top marginal rate [I.R.C. §1(i)].

   c. **Income of husbands and wives**

      The *joint return* privilege allows income splitting between spouses.

d. Gift or compensation loans

Imputed interest rules require fictitious interest payments on gift or compensation loans bearing below-market interest rates.

4. Trust Income

Although the regular trust taxation rules are not often tested in Tax I courses, you should remember the basic rule that a trust is taxed on its income except to the extent the income is distributable to a beneficiary, in which case the beneficiary is taxed. Also, *grantor trust rules* are more frequently tested. When faced with a question involving a trust, remember that the grantor is taxed on trust income if:

(i) Nonindependent parties have *excessive control over distributions* of income or corpus;

(ii) The trust *can be revoked* by the grantor or a nonadverse party;

(iii) The income can be paid for the *benefit of the grantor* or the grantor's spouse;

(iv) The income is actually paid to *discharge the grantor's support obligation*; or

(v) The general powers of administration are exercisable by a person in a *nonfiduciary capacity*.

Be aware that the same principles can be applied to third parties with control of a trust. Thus, if a third party has a *general power of appointment* over a trust, the third party is taxed on the trust income.

A. Income Splitting by Gifts

1. Gifts of Income vs. Gifts of Income-Producing Property [§185]

If a taxpayer makes a gift of the *income* from property, but retains ownership of the property, the income remains taxable to the taxpayer/donor. But an effective transfer of the *property itself* shifts the tax burden on the income to the donee, except for income that has already accrued. (Note the special rule for unearned income of a child under age 14, *infra*, §§226-228.)

a. Transfers of property [§186]

As stated, a transfer of income-producing property shifts the income to the donee. Similarly, a transfer of an *undivided interest* in the property shifts the appropriate *fraction of income* to the donee.

> **e.g. Example:** Dad gives Son an undivided one-quarter interest in an apartment house. One-quarter of the rental income is taxed to Son from that time onward. If the building is sold, Son is taxed on one-quarter of the gain (or deducts one-quarter of the loss).

(1) Right to receive income [§187]

Even if the donor owns only a right to receive income, the donor can shift part or all of that income to the donee by giving away that right. [**Blair v. Commissioner,** 300 U.S. 5 (1937)]

---

e.g. **Example:** Donor owned the right to receive income from a trust for his life. He gave his daughter the right to $9,000 per year of this income. *Held:* The $9,000 is taxable to the daughter because the donor parted with ownership of an undivided interest in his property. [**Blair v. Commissioner,** *supra*]

EXAM TIP	gilbert

On your exam, be sure to remember that if the income is *derived from property*, the taxpayer *must give away the property* itself to avoid the tax consequences of the income—transfer of the income alone would be ineffective in this situation. However, if the taxpayer "merely" has the *right to receive income*, a gift of that income would be effective to avoid the tax consequences of that income, assuming that the income has not yet accrued (*see infra,* §§189 *et seq.*).

(2) Other consequences of transfer [§188]

These transfers of income-producing property are subject to gift tax. (*See* Estate and Gift Tax Summary.) The donee will usually have the same basis for the property as the donor had (*see infra*, §732). The donee does not treat the receipt of the property as income, since it will generally be an excludible gift under I.R.C. section 102 (*see supra*, §28). However, section 102 does not protect the donee from taxation on the income subsequently produced by the gifted property (*see supra*, §47).

CONSEQUENCES OF GIFT OF PROPERTY	gilbert
TO DONOR	**TO DONEE**
• Will not be taxed on income produced after the transfer.	• Will be liable for income tax on the income the property produces after the transfer.
• Transfers tax liability for any capital gain, or benefit of any capital loss, to the donee.	• Usually has the same basis in the property as the donor had.
• May be liable for gift tax on the transfer.	• Excludes the value of the property from income since it will be treated as a gift under I.R.C. section 102.

(3) Accrued income [§189]

A gift of property does not shift income that has already accrued on the date of the gift. When the donee ultimately collects the accrued income, it will be taxed to the *donor* and treated as an additional gift to the donee.

Example: Alice gives a corporate bond to Bob on June 1. Interest accrues on the bond on a daily basis and is actually paid on January 1 and July 1. When Bob collects interest on July 1, Alice is taxed on the interest that accrued from January 1 to June 1; Bob is taxed on the interest that accrued from June 2 to June 30. Note that this result occurs whether Alice uses the cash or the accrual methods of taxation (which are discussed *infra,* §§950 *et seq.*).

(a) Shift of dividend income [§190]

There are conflicting decisions about whether a transferor can shift dividend income on stock after the dividend is declared but before the "record date." (The "record date" is the date on which a person must be a registered holder of the security in order to, among other things, collect the dividend.)

Example: Wiley owns preferred stock in Acme Corp. worth $100. On January 5, Acme Corp. declared a $50 dividend on the stock, payable to holders of record on January 15. On January 10, Wiley gave the stock to a qualified charity. The charity then collected the dividend.

---

1) Better view—dividend cannot be shifted

The better view is that the dividend income cannot be shifted. The declaration creates a fixed obligation to pay the dividend and, at that point, it becomes too late to transfer the income to a donee. [**Estate of Smith v. Commissioner,** 292 F.2d 478 (3d Cir. 1961), *cert. denied,* 368 U.S. 967 (1962)]

2) Contrary view

The contrary view is that the dividend income can be shifted because the transfer occurred before the record date. Under state corporate law, the holder on the record date is entitled to a dividend. Moreover, for tax purposes, even an accrual method taxpayer is not required to accrue a dividend on the declaration date, only on the due date (*see infra,* §1021). [**Caruth v. United States,** 865 F.2d 644 (5th Cir. 1989)]

EXAM TIP

On your exam, be sure to remember the two conflicting theories of whether a taxpayer can shift dividend income by means of a transfer of the stock. Under one theory (the better view), the tax on a dividend may not be transferred because the dividend becomes *accrued income* when it is *declared by the company*. Under an alternative theory, because collecting the dividend is *contingent* on actually owning the stock on the record date (*i.e.,* the dividend *accrues on that date*), a taxpayer may avoid tax liability on the dividend by transferring ownership of the stock (whether by sale or gift of the stock) before the record date.

(b) Gift of contingent contracts [§191]

A similar problem arises when the taxpayer gives a contingent contract that has not yet been paid off. Whether income is shifted to the donee depends on just how certain it was that the contingency would occur and the income would be realized. These cases are difficult to predict.

Example: A gift of an endowment insurance contract that would certainly mature later that year does not shift income to the donee. [**Friedman v. Commissioner,** 41 T.C. 428 (1964)]

Example: Johnson had a contract to sell British pounds at $2.80 each. After devaluation of the pound, this contract had great value, and Johnson donated the contract to a charity. *Held:* Johnson had accrued no income on the contract when he gave the contract away—so Johnson cannot be taxed on any gain from the sale of the contract by the charity—because Johnson did not yet have a "fixed legal right" to the profit when Johnson gave away the contract. For example, the pound could have been revalued upward or the dollar devalued before the contract was sold, which would have wiped out the profit. Thus the case is no different from a gift of appreciated stock, which successfully shifts income to the donee. [**Johnson & Son, Inc. v. Commissioner,** 63 T.C. 778 (1975)]

b. Sham transfers [§192]

Frequently, the courts hold that a purported gift to the donee does not shift income because there has been no real transfer. The transfer must be actually effective from a *state law* point of view. This means that there must be donative intent, delivery, and acceptance by the donee—the usual property law requirements.

(1) But note

Even if the transfer is actually effective from the point of view of state law, it will not be effective for income tax purposes if the donor retained *excessive controls.* (*See infra*, §211.)

c. **Transferring income while retaining the property**

(1) General rule [§193]

If the donor transfers the income from property to the donee *while retaining the income-producing property*, the income is taxed to the donor at the time the donee collects it. For tax purposes, income is to be taxed to the person who bears the risks of *gain or loss* from the investment that produces the income.

Example: In the leading case, Father owned a coupon bond. He removed the coupons (*i.e.*, the rights to collect interest) from the bond and gave them to Son. Father was taxed on the income when Son collected the interest. [**Helvering v. Horst,** 311 U.S. 112 (1940)] If Father had given Son both the bond and coupons, the income would have been shifted to Son, except that if any interest had *accrued* at the date of the gift, that would be taxed to Father (*see supra*, §189).

(a) Note—coupon bonds [§194]

The Code has changed the outcome of *Horst*. It now requires the donor of coupons stripped from a bond to take into income on a daily basis the increase in value of the bond and the donee to take into income on a daily basis the increase in value of the coupons. [I.R.C. §1286]

(2) Rental income [§195]

Rental income remains taxable to the *owner* of the reversion who has given away the right to the income. [**Galt v. Commissioner,** 216 F.2d 41 (7th Cir. 1954)]

(3) Assignments of trust income [§196]

The beneficiary of a trust can shift the income from the trust to a donee if he assigns his *entire* beneficial interest to the donee. Similarly, he can shift a portion of the income if he assigns an *undivided portion* of the *entire interest*.

Example: The owner of a life estate in trust transferred $9,000 per year of income to his daughter. The gift was effective for the life tenant's *entire life*. The court held that $9,000 per year of income was shifted to the daughter. [**Blair v. Commissioner,** *supra*, §187]

Compare: Where the owner of a life estate in trust transferred the income for only *one year*, the income was held not to have shifted—because the interest transferred was too insubstantial. [**Harrison v. Schaffner,** 312 U.S. 579 (1941)]

---

(4) Note—assignments for consideration [§197]

The rules above apply only to *gifts* of income. If a transfer of an income right is supported by bona fide consideration received from the transferee, the tax burden on income thereafter received is shifted to the transferee. [**Commissioner v. P.G. Lake,** 356 U.S. 260 (1958)]

(a) But note

The seller's profit will be ordinary income, not capital gain. (*See infra,* §847.)

d. No realization of income to donor making gift [§198]

The donor does not realize *gain or loss* when she makes a gift of property.

Example: Mother owns stock for which she has paid $5,000, but which is now worth $2,000. Mother makes a gift of the stock to Daughter. Mother cannot deduct the capital loss; she should have sold the stock and given the proceeds to Daughter. Daughter's basis for the stock is $5,000 for purposes of computing gain but only $2,000 for computing loss. (*See infra,* §732.)

---

(1) Charitable contributions [§199]

Gain or loss is not realized when a taxpayer gives an asset to a charity even though the making of the gift results in immediate tax benefits to the donor-taxpayer.

Example: Trent purchased a residence for $100,000. Years later, when the house was worth $1 million, Trent gave it to Charity (a recognized charitable organization). On the same day Charity received the residence, Charity sold the residence to a third party for $1 million. Trent is entitled to a $1 million charitable contribution deduction. Trent does not realize the $900,000 gain on the house, and Charity does not pay tax on the gain because it is a tax-exempt organization (*see supra,* §173).

(a) "Ripened" gifts [§200]

In a transaction such as the one described in the above example, the IRS may contend that the taxpayer made the sale before making the charitable gift and merely transferred the proceeds of the sale to the charity. This is a distinct possibility if the donor prearranged the sale or if the charity was required by the terms of the gift to sell the property. It is also a possibility if the donor's business premises are used for the purposes of making the sale. [*See* **Kinsey v. Commissioner,** 477 F.2d 1058 (2d Cir. 1973)]

> **Example:** Wally owns stock of Acme Corp., a publicly traded corporation. On August 3, Eddie makes an offer to purchase in cash (a "tender offer") all shares of Acme. The tender offer was contingent on Eddie being able to purchase at least 50% of Acme's shares. On August 31, more than 50% of the shares are tendered, although numerous corporate formalities have not yet been performed. On September 8, Wally transfers his shares of Acme to a charity. The charitable gift is too late, and Wally will be taxed on his capital gain. The stock "ripened" into a right to receive cash on August 31. [*See* **Ferguson v. Commissioner**, 174 F.3d 997 (9th Cir. 1999)]

(2) Exception for gifts to political organizations [§201]

A gain is recognized when a taxpayer transfers property to a political organization—although a loss is not recognized. The political organization receives a basis equal to the transferor's basis, plus gain recognized to the transferor. [I.R.C. §84]

(3) Exception for certain gifts [§202]

Realization can occur by reason of gifts of *mortgaged* property or gifts for which the donee *pays gift tax*. (*See infra*, §§760-761.)

2. Personal Service Income

a. General rule [§203]

The income from personal services is taxed to the person who earns it.

> **Example:** In the leading case, an attorney and his wife agreed that income from their future services would be owned by them as joint tenants. (This case arose before the joint return privilege made it pointless to split income with a spouse.) The Court held that Congress had intended to tax personal service income to the person who had performed the work. Consequently, it was taxed to the husband; the transfer of half of the money to the wife was treated as a gift to her. [**Lucas v. Earl**, 281 U.S. 111 (1930)]

(1) Time agreement made immaterial [§204]

The same rule applies if the income-splitting agreement is made *after the work is done*: It is still taxed to the person who did the work. [**Helvering v. Eubank**, 311 U.S. 122 (1940)]

EXAM TIP   **gilbert**

On your exam, be sure to remember that *income from services* generally *cannot* be shifted by gift.

---

b. Obligatory assignments [§205]

If an employer is willing to make payments only to someone *other than the employee*, the result is not clear under present law.

> **e.g. Example:** An employer made payments to an educational benefit trust. Payments from the trust could be made only for the college expenses of an employee's child. *Held:* These payments were simply substitutes for salary and were taxable to the employee at the time payments were made to the employee's child. [**Armantrout v. Commissioner,** 67 T.C. 996 (1977), *aff'd,* 570 F.2d 210 (7th Cir. 1978)]

> **cf. Compare:** In an earlier case, a father entered a contest, the terms of which were that the prize could be paid only to a child. The court held the prize taxable to the child and not the father. [**Teschner v. Commissioner,** 38 T.C. 1003 (1962)]

(1) Distinction between *Armantrout* and *Teschner*

Armantrout dealt with a regular employment relation, and it seems reasonable that all of an employee's earnings be taxed to him, whether or not he receives them. The employee probably perceived the educational benefit payments as a substitute for salary and conceivably could have bargained to receive the payments himself. *Teschner,* on the other hand, dealt with a one-shot situation in which payment to the child was not perceived as a substitute for anything. Moreover, the services rendered in *Teschner* (submitting a jingle) did not resemble normal employment services and no bargaining was possible. Note also that the explicit language of I.R.C. section 83(a) (adopted after *Teschner*) requires that the service provider be taxed on compensation, regardless of who receives the payment. As a result, it is unclear whether *Teschner* would be followed under existing law.

c. Working for charity [§206]

A taxpayer can work for free without being taxed on the value of services rendered. However, income from employment cannot be diverted to charity. [Treas. Reg. §1.61-2(c)]

> **e.g. Example:** Tonya, a rock star, volunteers to entertain at a benefit for a political candidate. The candidate is the promoter of the concert. Tonya is not taxed on the value of her services.

> **e.g. Example:** Vicky, a concert promoter, promotes a benefit concert for a candidate, collects the money, and pays it to the candidate. Vicky is taxed on the proceeds. She cannot deduct the payment to the candidate. [G.C.M. 27026, 1951-2 C.B. 7]

> **Example:** Theresa, a nun who is under a vow of poverty, is a nurse at a public hospital. Her entire salary is paid to her order. Theresa is taxable on the salary, since she is an agent of the hospital, not of the order. The salary is treated as if paid to her, then contributed to the order. She can deduct the payment to the order, but is subject to the percentage limitations on charitable contributions (*see infra*, §§618-620). [**Schuster v. Commissioner,** 800 F.2d 672 (7th Cir. 1986); **Fogarty v. United States,** 780 F.2d 1005 (Fed. Cir. 1986)]

d. Working for oneself [§207]

Suppose a taxpayer invents something or constructs a building for himself and then gives the invention or building to his child. The child derives income from the property. This is treated as a transfer of *property*, thus shifting income to the child. It is not treated as an assignment of rights to personal service income since the *services* involved were *rendered to the taxpayer himself*, not to another. [**Heim v. Fitzpatrick,** 262 F.2d 887 (2d Cir. 1959)] However, in an earlier case, a taxpayer rendered *personal services* to a group of inventors. Later he became entitled to a share of the royalties, which he sought to shift to other family members. It was held that this income stream derived from personal services rendered *to others*; consequently, the resulting income could not be shifted. [**Strauss v. Commissioner,** 168 F.2d 441 (2d Cir.), *cert. denied*, 335 U.S. 858 (1948)]

e. Commonly controlled businesses [§208]

I.R.C. section 482 applies to situations in which there is common control of two businesses (whether or not incorporated). To clearly reflect the income of the businesses, the IRS can allocate income, deductions, or credits among them. This section provides the IRS with a potent weapon to challenge income-splitting schemes.

(1) Intercorporate transactions [§209]

When two companies are controlled by the same people and deal with each other, section 482 is frequently employed. For example, if one company is profitable but the other is not, the profitable company might sell goods to the unprofitable company at an unrealistically low price. Alternatively, the profitable company might loan money interest-free to the unprofitable company. Both have the effect of shifting income. Using section 482, the IRS is permitted to allocate income to the profitable company from the unprofitable one by requiring that the bargain between the companies be at arm's length. [**Latham Park Manor, Inc. v. Commissioner,** 69 T.C. 199 (1977)—interest-free loan between related corporations; IRS can require interest to be charged]

(2) Services [§210]

I.R.C. section 482 has frequently been employed in situations in which an individual seeks to shift income to her corporation.

(a) Illustration

Tina is a management consultant. She forms a corporation, Consult Corp. Consult Corp. arranges to supply Tina to Acme Co., a business that needs her help. Acme Co. pays Consult Corp. for Tina's services, but Consult Corp. does not pay Tina any salary.

(b) IRS position

The IRS contends in this situation that Consult Corp. should be ignored entirely and the money paid by Acme Co. should be directly taxed to Tina. However, the courts say that section 482 offers a more discriminating approach to the problem. When the arrangement between Tina and Consult Corp. is analyzed under this approach, Tina is charged with the income that an unrelated management consultant would have required as a salary, and this same amount is then allowed to Consult Corp. as a deduction. [**Rubin v. Commissioner,** 429 F.2d 650 (2d Cir. 1970)] However, there is a split in authority as to whether section 482 applies. [*See* **Fogelsong v. Commissioner,** 691 F.2d 848 (7th Cir. 1982)—section 482 not applicable to employee who works exclusively for controlled corporation; **Haag v. Commissioner,** 88 T.C. 604 (1987), *aff'd*, 855 F.2d 855 (8th Cir. 1988)—section 482 applies in this situation]

(c) Rationale

According to the decisions applying section 482 in this situation, Tina's work as a consultant and Consult Corp.'s activity in lending Tina out are considered two separate businesses—both controlled by Tina. Consequently, I.R.C. section 482 applies. Since the arrangement between Tina and Consult Corp. does not clearly reflect income, the IRS can require an allocation that does clearly reflect income, which, in this situation, means requiring payment of compensation for Tina's services.

3. Excessive Controls [§211]

In general, if a taxpayer makes a legally valid transfer of property, but retains "excessive" controls over how the property is managed and who gets the income from it, the taxpayer will be taxed on the income.

Example: In **Helvering v. Clifford,** 309 U.S. 331 (1940), the grantor made a transfer *in trust*, giving income to his wife but retaining a *reversion* after five years. The wife was entitled to the income, but the grantor retained control over *when* she would get it. In addition, he retained broad managerial powers over the trust. Tax avoidance was concededly involved. The Court held that the grantor remained subject to tax on the income. *Rationale:* On the facts, this transfer did not appreciably change the way in which grantor had always held this property. Consequently, in substance he was still the owner and should be taxed as such.

---

a. **Statutory codification [§212]**

Clifford has now been codified by an elaborate body of statutes that leave it intact in some respects and change it in others. These statutes—the grantor trust rules, discussed *infra*, §§253 *et seq.*—are the exclusive source of law concerning whether a transfer to trust shifts income. However, the *Clifford* rationale is still applicable to transfers not in trust in which controls have been retained.

b. **Transfers of patents [§213]**

When a taxpayer licenses his patent to a manufacturer, and then gives away all his retained rights, he can shift the royalty income to the donee. However, if the taxpayer controls the manufacturer, he has power to decide how to use the patent and thus can control the stream of royalties to the donee. This retained control causes the royalties to be taxed to the donor. [**Commissioner v. Sunnen,** 333 U.S. 591 (1948)]

(1) **Distinguish—effect if no controlling interest [§214]**

If the donor owns stock in the manufacturing corporation but does *not control it*, he is not treated as having retained excessive control. Thus, the transfer of the patent *does* shift the income to the donee. [**Heim v. Fitzpatrick,** *supra*, §207]

c. **Gift and leaseback [§215]**

In many cases, taxpayers (particularly doctors and dentists) have given business assets to their children (or trusts for their children) and *leased them back*. They have sought to deduct the rentals as business expenses. This plan will work if the gift and leaseback are upheld as valid business transactions—if, in other words, it is not a sham. One of the factors that courts have looked to is whether an independent trustee for the children is used; hypothetically, at least, such an independent trustee will force the grantor-lessee to pay the rent if he defaults. [**Van Zandt v. Commissioner,** 341 F.2d 440 (5th Cir. 1965), *cert. denied*, 382 U.S. 814 (1966)]

d. **Family partnerships [§216]**

Many of the ingredients of the foregoing cases are involved when a parent seeks to make her children into her *partners*, hopefully causing partnership distributive shares to be taxed to the children instead of the parent.

(1) **Judicial response [§217]**

The Supreme Court held that this device would work if the taxpayers had an "intention" to be partners together. In general this would require some significant contribution by the donee of either services or capital to the partnership. [**Commissioner v. Culbertson,** 337 U.S. 733 (1949)]

(2) **Statutory change [§218]**

Congress has substantially relaxed the requirements of *Culbertson*. When capital is a *"material income-producing factor"* in the partnership, the gift will effectively shift income, even though the donee contributes neither capital nor services. [I.R.C. §704(e)]

(a) Reasonable compensation [§219]

The Commissioner can require that the donor receive reasonable compensation for her services before anything is left to be divided with the children. [I.R.C. §704(e)(2)] This is to insure that personal service income is taxed to the one doing the work; only the return from capital supposedly can be divided with the children.

(b) Sham transfers [§220]

However, the Commissioner frequently attempts to circumvent section 704(e) by arguing that there has been *no real transfer* of partnership interests to the children—thus the transfer is a sham and the parent still owns the business. The regulations supply the standards for determining whether the transfer is a sham. [Treas. Reg. §1.704-1(e)(2)]

(3) Materiality of capital [§221]

If capital is not a "material income-producing factor," section 704(e) is not applicable and the *Culbertson* standards apply.

EXAM TIP   **gilbert**

Watch for fact patterns in which a parent makes his child a partner. This is an effective way to shift income if **capital** is used **to produce income**. If partnership income is generated by fees, commissions, or personal services, the income is taxable **only to the service provider/parent**, even if large amounts of capital are otherwise employed. (Thus, for example, the doctor or dentist in §215, *supra*, could not form a family partnership with her children.)

B. Statutory Divisions of Income

1. Income Earned by Children [§222]

Income earned by a child is taxable to the child. [I.R.C. §73] This is true even though the income is paid to the parent rather than the child, and even though under state law such income may be the property of the parent rather than the child. However, if a parent agrees to do a job, and puts his child to work on the job but does not pay the child a salary, the income is taxed to the parent, not to the child. The rationale is that the third party contracted with the parent, not the child, to do the work. [**Fritschle v. Commissioner**, 79 T.C. 152 (1982)]

a. Filing of return [§223]

The *parent* has the responsibility to see that an income tax return is filed on behalf of the child. [I.R.C. §6201(c)]

b. Expenditures [§224]

Expenditures made by the parent in connection with the business or activity from which the child's income is derived are treated as if made by the child and are deductible on the child's tax return. [I.R.C. §73(b)]

c. Dependency [§225]

As to the effect of a child's earnings on the parent's right to a dependency exemption, *see infra*, §664.

2. Kiddie Tax [§226]

All *unearned* income of a child under age 14 in excess of $500 is taxed to the child at the top marginal rate *of her parents*. The $500 figure is *indexed for inflation* (*e.g.,* in 2002, the figure was adjusted to $750). This provision is often referred to as the "kiddie tax." [I.R.C. §1(g)]

a. Unearned income [§227]

Unearned income refers to rent, dividends, interest, and similar items that are not produced by rendering personal services. [I.R.C. §911]

b. Allocable parental tax [§228]

If a child's parents are not married, the tax bracket of the *custodial* parent is used. If the parents are married but file separately, the bracket of the parent with the greater income is used.

---

e.g. Example: Claudia is 12 years old. Last year, Claudia's grandfather gave her bonds that produce interest income of $5,000. Claudia's parents are divorced; she lives with her mother. Her mother's top tax bracket is 28%. Claudia must pay an income tax of 28% of $4,250 ($5,000 minus $750).

---

3. Income of Husbands and Wives

a. Right to file joint return [§229]

A husband and wife may elect to file a joint income tax return. [I.R.C. §§2, 6013] The effect of such a return is to tax income one-half to each spouse, irrespective of which spouse actually earned it. This generally reduces the overall tax liability of the spouses, since it has the effect of using the lower brackets twice.

(1) Background [§230]

The joint return privilege was enacted in 1948 to eliminate the special tax advantage that had theretofore existed for spouses in community property states. Because husbands and wives in a community property state had a vested, equal interest in each other's earnings, the Supreme Court held that one-half of the earnings of one spouse were taxable to the other spouse. [**Poe v. Seaborn,** 282 U.S. 101 (1930)] However, spouses in non-community property states were *not* permitted to split personal service income. [**Lucas v. Earl**, *supra*, §203—husband taxable on his earnings although he had assigned one-half to wife]

(2) Elective community property [§231]

Later, other states enacted statutes under which spouses could "elect" to make their earnings community property, but the Court held that such local statutes were not binding for tax purposes, so that the income would remain taxable to the one who earned it. [**Commissioner v. Harmon**, 323 U.S. 44 (1944)]

(3) Effect of joint return [§232]

A joint return treats the spouses as if their incomes were equal. Thus, it achieves the same result as if all of their income were community property.

b. Marriage penalty and single penalty [§233]

The rate structure can penalize both married and single people. Single people are penalized because the tax on a given income is always lower on a joint return than on a separate return. But married people can also be penalized when each of them has substantial income. In that situation, they would pay less combined tax if they were single rather than married.

(1) "Quickie" divorce

To avoid the marriage penalty, some taxpayers get divorced at the end of the year (thus allowing them to file as singles), then remarry. This technique is in considerable doubt—either because the "quickie" divorce may be invalid under state law or because the divorce and remarriage will be ignored as a sham for tax purposes. [*See* **Boyter v. Commissioner**, 668 F.2d 1382 (4th Cir. 1982)]

(2) Gradual elimination of the marriage penalty [§234]

Beginning in 2005, the standard deduction for married taxpayers will be increased over five years to twice the basic standard deduction for an unmarried person. This provision is designed to reduce the marriage penalty. [I.R.C. §63(c)(7); *see infra*, §§566-569] Also beginning in 2005, the marriage penalty will be reduced by gradually increasing the size of the 15% tax bracket for joint filers until it reaches twice the size of the 15% bracket applicable to single taxpayers.

c. Liability for tax due on joint return [§235]

If spouses file jointly, each is jointly and severally liable for the payment of income tax on *all* income reported. Thus, the husband becomes liable for payment of tax on his wife's earnings, and vice versa. [I.R.C. §6013(d)] Both spouses are liable for penalties if the return is fraudulent.

(1) Exception—innocent spouse rule [§236]

Under the "innocent spouse" rule, a spouse who signs a joint return is relieved of liability for tax, interest, and penalty if she establishes that in signing the return she did not know, or have reason to know, of the understatement. The "innocent spouse" is entitled to this relief only if it would be inequitable to hold her liable. [I.R.C. §6015(b)] In addition, a spouse who is divorced or has been living apart from the other spouse for 12 months can file an election to be taxed only on that portion of a deficiency attributable to items on the joint return that are attributable to the electing spouse. [I.R.C. §6015(c), (d)]

d. Joint return not mandatory [§237]

Spouses do not have to file joint returns. However, it is almost always advantageous for them to do so because a special table of higher rates applies to married persons filing separately. [I.R.C. §1(d)]

4. Income Earned by Head of Household [§238]

A "head of household" is an unmarried individual who maintains for more than one-half of the year a household for qualified relatives (such as children). "Maintaining a household" means supplying over one-half of the cost of running the household. By filing a "head of household" return, special tax rates are provided that in effect split 25% of taxpayer's income with the relatives (as contrasted with the 50% split allowed between spouses filing joint returns, above). [I.R.C. §2(b)] Even if a taxpayer is married at the close of the year, she can be treated as a head of household if she files separately and her spouse was not a member of the household during the last six months of the taxable year. [I.R.C. §§2(c), 7703(b)]

C. Below-Market Interest on Loans

1. In General [§239]

Loans that carry no interest (or interest below prevailing rates) were once a useful income-splitting device (as well as a valuable way to compensate employees or reward corporate shareholders). However, the Code now requires that interest be *imputed* to the lender, thus wiping out the income tax advantage of the plan. It also subjects below-market interest loans to the gift tax. [I.R.C. §7872]

---

e.g. Example: Suppose that on January 1, Mother loans Daughter $150,000 interest free. Daughter puts the money in the bank and earns interest of $12,000 on it. She uses the $12,000 to pay her college expenses. Formerly, the interest would be taxed to Daughter in her low tax bracket, rather than to Mother. When Daughter finishes college, she repays the loan. Now, however, Daughter is treated as if she had paid interest to Mother at the applicable federal rate (*infra,* §242) minus the interest Daughter actually pays (if any). Additionally, Mother is subject to gift tax for the value of the interest-free loan.

---

gilbert

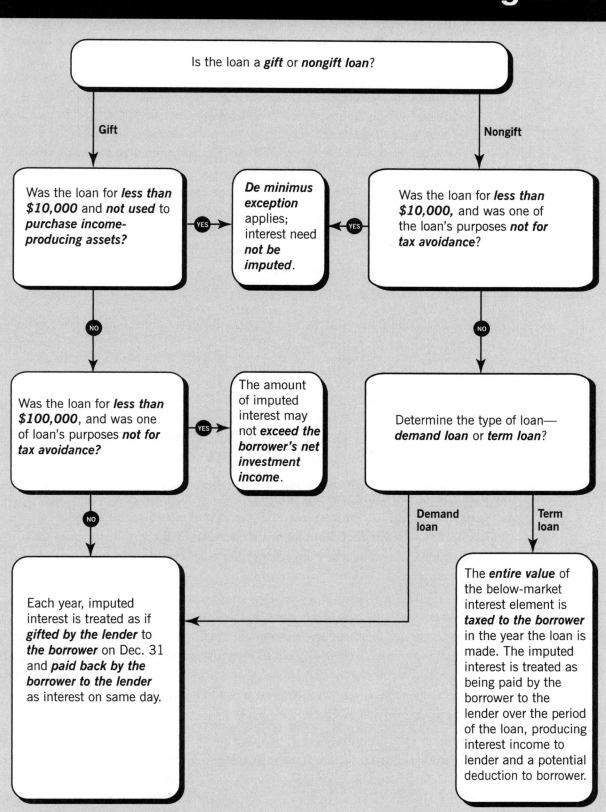

Is the loan a **gift** or **nongift loan**?

Gift

Nongift

Was the loan for **less than $10,000** and **not used** to **purchase income-producing assets?**

De minimus exception applies; interest need **not be imputed**.

Was the loan for **less than $10,000,** and was one of the loan's purposes **not for tax avoidance?**

NO

NO

Was the loan for **less than $100,000**, and was one of loan's purposes **not for tax avoidance?**

The amount of imputed interest may not **exceed the borrower's net investment income**.

Determine the type of loan— **demand loan** or **term loan**?

Demand loan

Term loan

NO

Each year, imputed interest is treated as if **gifted by the lender** to **the borrower** on Dec. 31 and **paid back by the borrower to the lender** as interest on same day.

The **entire value** of the below-market interest element is **taxed to the borrower** in the year the loan is made. The imputed interest is treated as being paid by the borrower to the lender over the period of the loan, producing interest income to lender and a potential deduction to borrower.

2. Coverage [§240]

The imputed interest rule of section 7872 applies to gift loans (as in the above example). It also applies to compensation loans, to corporation-shareholder loans, to any loan that has tax avoidance as one of its principal purposes, or to any other loan that has a significant effect on the tax liability of the lender or borrower. [I.R.C. §7872(c)]

a. De minimis exception [§241]

Section 7872 will not apply to gift loans on any day when the loan balance does *not exceed $10,000—unless* the loan is used to purchase or carry income-producing assets. Of course, that is exactly what the loan is used for in the above example (*supra*, §239). Also, if a gift loan is $100,000 or less, the amount of imputed income may not exceed the borrower's net investment income ($12,000 in the example)—*unless* tax avoidance was one of the principal purposes. Finally, the section will not apply to compensation or corporate loans that do not exceed $10,000—*unless* one of the principal purposes for the arrangement is tax avoidance.

(1) Note

In all these cases, if there are several outstanding loans between the parties, they must be added together to see whether the taxpayer exceeds the ceilings. [I.R.C. §7872(c)(2) - (3), (d)]

3. Measurement of Market Interest [§242]

Section 7872 is triggered if an interest rate is below the "applicable federal rate." These rates, which differ depending on the maturity of the loan, are set periodically by the IRS. The rates require semi-annual compounding.

4. Mechanism for Imputing Interest [§243]

If section 7872 applies, interest must be imputed. This will require the lender to include imputed interest income. However, because of the prohibition on deducting personal interest (except some mortgage interest), the borrower will probably be denied a deduction.

a. Gift loans [§244]

When interest is set below market as a gift (as in the mother-daughter example above), each year's forgone interest is treated as if it were transferred on December 31 by the lender to the borrower (as a gift), *then retransferred as an interest payment* by the borrower to the lender. [I.R.C. §7872(a)]

---

e.g. **Example:** Assume an applicable rate of 6% compounded semi-annually and the above example about the mother and daughter (*supra*, §239). Mother is treated as having made a $9,135 transfer to Daughter on December 31 (this is $150,000 at 6% interest compounded semi-annually). Then Daughter is treated as having paid back $9,135 to Mother as interest. Mother has

$9,135 in interest income. Daughter is denied interest deduction because the interest is personal. [I.R.C. §163(h); *see infra*, §591]

---

(1) Term of loan [§245]

The same rules apply to all *gift loans* whether they are "demand loans" (*i.e.*, repayable on the lender's demand) or "term loans" (*i.e.*, repayable at a fixed date). However, in the case of the other kinds of loans covered by section 7872 (such as compensation, corporate, or tax-avoidance loans), there are different rules depending on whether the loan is a demand loan or a term loan.

b. Nongift demand loans [§246]

Nongift *demand* loans are treated much like gift loans. The forgone interest each year is treated as if it were paid by the lender to the borrower, then re-transferred from the borrower to the lender. [I.R.C. §7872(a)]

Example: John works for Kap Co. On January 1, Kap Co. loans John $80,000 at 2% interest, repayable when Kap Co. demands it. Assume the applicable federal rate is 6%. On December 31, Kap Co. is treated as having transferred $3,264 to John (*i.e.*, the difference between 6% and 2% of $80,000 compounded semi-annually). This is treated as compensation income to John and a compensation deduction to Kap Co. Then John is treated as having paid the $3,264 back to Kap Co. This payment is interest income to Kap Co. Whether John is entitled to an interest deduction depends on his use of the borrowed funds. If the interest is personal, it is not deductible.

Example: Suppose in the previous example that John was a stockholder of Kap Co. In that case, $3,264 would be considered a dividend to John (nondeductible to Kap Co. but taxable to John). John would then be treated as having retransferred the $3,264 to Kap Co. as interest.

---

c. Nongift term loans [§247]

Different rules apply to nongift loans for a *fixed term*. In that case, the *entire value* of the below-market interest element is treated as transferred from the lender to the borrower as soon as the loan is made. The value of the below-market feature is equal to the difference between the amount of the loan and the present value of the interest and principal payments the borrower is to make. [I.R.C. §7872(b)]

Example: John is an employee of Kap Co. On January 1, Kap Co. loans John $80,000 at an interest rate of 3% for five years. Assume that the applicable federal rate is 6%, and that the present value of the principal and interest payments John will make over the term of the loan (using present value tables) is only $69,000. Kap Co. is treated as having transferred $11,000 to John on January 1 ($80,000 minus $69,000). John has compensation income of $11,000 (bunched in the first year of the loan), and Kap Co. has a compensation deduction of $11,000 (assuming that the deduction is not disallowed as unreasonable compensation). John is then treated as paying interest on the loan over the five-year period the loan is outstanding. The amount of interest is computed according to a formula that produces an ascending amount each year. For example, in the first year, the interest would be 3% (*i.e.*, 6% less 3%) of $69,000 compounded semi-annually or about $2,085. In the second year, the interest would be 3% of $71,085 compounded semi-annually, or about $2,148. These amounts would be interest income to Kap Co. and an interest deduction (if otherwise allowable) to John.

---

5. Imputed Interest Under Other Code Sections [§248]

I.R.C. sections 483 and 1274 also provide for imputed interest (*see infra*, §§915 *et seq.*). These sections come into play in cases of *sales* of property in exchange for deferred payments if an obligation fails to call for interest at the applicable federal rate. When the rules of section 483 or 1274 are applicable, section 7872 is not applicable.

D. Taxation of Trusts

1. Introduction [§249]

A brief summary of the taxation of trusts is provided here. (A considerably more detailed treatment is given in the Income Tax II Summary.) There are two different schemes for trust taxation: the *grantor trust rules* (which provide for taxing the trust's income to the grantor) and the rules for *dividing trust income between the trust and the beneficiaries.*

2. Grantor Trust Rules—In General [§250]

The *Clifford* case (*see supra*, §211) established a rather vague principle under which the grantor of property to a trust would be taxed on the trust's income if he retained excessive controls. The IRS adopted regulations spelling out the *Clifford* principle, and these later became the statutory grantor trust rules. They are now the *exclusive* criteria for deciding whether the income of a trust should be taxed to the grantor. [I.R.C. §671] However, the vague *Clifford* rule is still applicable to gifts that are not in trust.

a. Tax effect [§251]

When the grantor is treated as the "owner" of a trust, he is taxed in the same way as if the trust did not exist: The grantor must include all the "trust" income in his gross income but is allowed whatever deductions and credits are attributable to that income. The trust and beneficiaries are not taxed on the income and cannot take the deductions or credits. [I.R.C. §671]

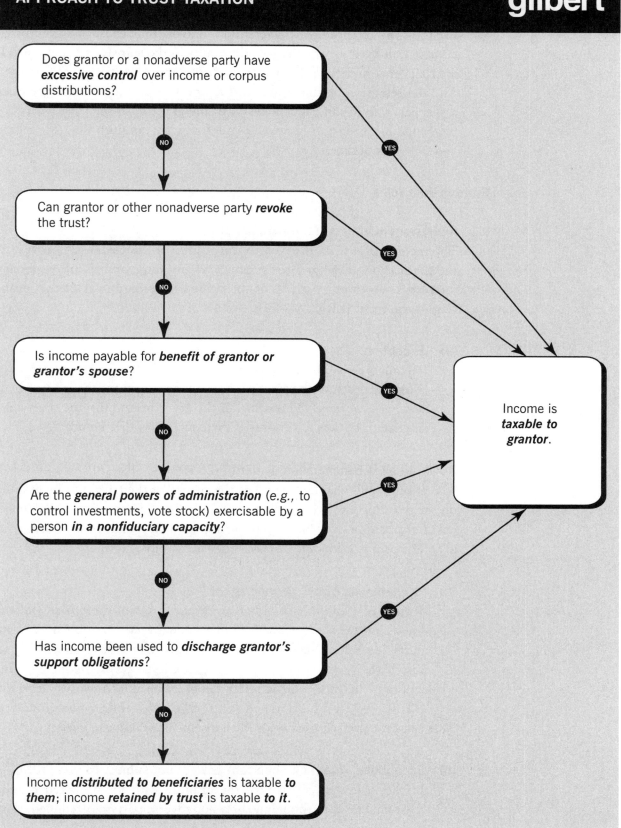

Does grantor or a nonadverse party have **excessive control** over income or corpus distributions?

NO

Can grantor or other nonadverse party **revoke** the trust?

NO

Is income payable for **benefit of grantor or grantor's spouse**?

NO

Are the **general powers of administration** (e.g., to control investments, vote stock) exercisable by a person **in a nonfiduciary capacity**?

NO

Has income been used to **discharge grantor's support obligations**?

NO

Income **distributed to beneficiaries** is taxable **to them**; income **retained by trust** is taxable **to it**.

YES

YES

YES

YES

YES

Income is **taxable to grantor**.

(1) Correlation with estate and gift taxes [§252]

There is a substantial (but by no means complete) correlation between the income tax rules and the estate and gift tax rules applicable to trusts. Broadly, the retention of powers and controls that cause the grantor to be taxed on trust income frequently results in the transfer's being considered an "incomplete" gift so that it is *not* subject to the federal gift tax. And the retention by the trustor of such powers and interests in the trust assets generally results, on the death of the grantor, in the trust assets being includible as part of his gross estate for estate tax purposes. (*See* Estate and Gift Tax Summary.)

b. Grantor trust rules

(1) Reversionary interest retained [§253]

The income of a trust is taxed to the grantor if the corpus will revert to the grantor or to the grantor's spouse at any time, and the reversionary interest is worth at least 5% of the value of the corpus as of the inception of the trust. [I.R.C. §§672(e), 673]

(a) Exception

The income is not taxed to the grantor if: (i) the corpus reverts only after the death of the trust's income beneficiary; (ii) the income beneficiary is a *lineal descendant* of the grantor; and (iii) the reversionary interest takes effect only if the beneficiary dies *before age 21*.

(2) Power to alter beneficial enjoyment [§254]

The grantor will also be treated as the owner of the trust and be taxable on the trust income if he or his spouse or a "nonadverse party" has *powers of disposition* over the corpus or income. This means control over *who* gets the corpus or income or *when* they get it. [I.R.C. §674]

(a) "Nonadverse party" defined [§255]

Section 674 applies not only if the grantor retains the power himself, but also if the control is lodged in a "nonadverse" party. An "adverse party" is a beneficiary of the trust who would have something to lose if the power were exercised. [I.R.C. §672(a)] Anyone else (including a trustee who is not a beneficiary) is a nonadverse party. [I.R.C. §672(b)] Section 674 is *not applicable* if the power involved can be exercised *only* with the consent of *an adverse party*.

(b) Exception—retention of certain powers not subject to rule [§256]

In the following situations, the grantor will not be taxed on the trust income even though he or a nonadverse party has retained powers of disposition:

1) **Certain powers of independent trustees [§257]**

Where *independent trustees* have the power to *apportion income or pay out principal* among the beneficiaries, the income will not be taxed to the grantor. However, the grantor cannot be a trustee, and not more than half the trustees can be his relatives or subordinates *subservient* to his wishes. [I.R.C. §674(c)]

2) **Power limited by standard [§258]**

If a reasonably definite external *standard* for apportionment of trust income (or accumulation of trust income) is spelled out in the trust instrument, the grantor will not be treated as owner of the trust even if the trustees are relatives or subordinates subservient to him. However, none of the trustees can be the grantor or the grantor's spouse living with him. [I.R.C. §674(d)]

> **Example:** A trust that allows a trustee to distribute the corpus for the medical bills of the beneficiaries is one subject to *reasonably definite external standards.*

3) **Reasonable alterations of beneficial enjoyment [§259]**

The following powers are deemed reasonable controls and will not cause the trust income to be taxed to the grantor—even if retained by the grantor himself [I.R.C. §674(b)]:

a) *Power to invade corpus* for the benefit of a designated beneficiary, if limited by a *reasonably definite standard* [I.R.C. §674(b)(5)];

b) *Power to postpone payments* of income to a beneficiary who is under 21 years old or under a legal disability [I.R.C. §674(b)(7)];

c) *Power to change the distribution* of income by will [I.R.C. §674(b)(3)];

d) *Power to either distribute or accumulate income*, provided that the accumulated income is certain eventually to be paid to the person who would have received it currently (or to his estate or appointees) [I.R.C. §674(b)(6)].

(3) Power to revoke [§260]

The grantor is taxable on the income of a trust if either he, his spouse, or a nonadverse party (*see* definition, above) has the power to *revoke* the trust and revest all or part of the *corpus* in the grantor. [I.R.C. §676; **Corliss v. Bowers,** 281 U.S. 376 (1930)]

(4) Income for benefit of grantor or spouse [§261]

The grantor is also taxable on the trust income if it is, or *may be* in the *discretion* of the grantor or any nonadverse party, applied to any of the following purposes [I.R.C. §677]:

(a) Distributable to grantor or spouse [§262]

If any part of the income *may* be distributed to the grantor or his spouse (without the consent of the beneficiary), such income is taxable to him, even though none of it is in fact so distributed.

1) Note

Income is considered distributable to the grantor if it can be used to pay his debts. [**Morrill v. United States**, 228 F. Supp. 734 (D. Me. 1964)]

(b) Accumulated for future distribution to grantor or spouse [§263]

If income is accumulated for future distribution to the grantor or his spouse, it is taxable to the grantor.

(c) To pay premiums or insurance policies on life of grantor or spouse [§264]

If trust income is used to pay for insurance policies on the life of the grantor or his spouse, it is taxable to the grantor even if the policy was taken out by the trustee and belongs to the trust.

1) Distinguish—charity as beneficiary [§265]

If a recognized *charity* is the beneficiary of the policy, then the trust income is not taxed to the grantor. [I.R.C. §677(a)(3)]

(d) To support other dependents [§266]

Trust income is also taxable to the grantor if it may be used for the support of any beneficiary whom the grantor is legally obligated to support—*but only to the extent that the income is actually so applied.*

1) Distinguish—support of spouse [§267]

The mere fact that income *may* be used to support the grantor's *spouse* renders trust income taxable to the grantor (*see* above). But as to other dependents, the income is taxed to the grantor only to the extent that it is *actually so used.*

2) Distinguish—alimony trusts [§268]

The grantor trust rules are superseded in divorce cases. For example, assume Husband creates a trust whose income is payable to Wife. After Husband and Wife are divorced, the income is taxable to Wife, not to Husband. [I.R.C. §682—overrides I.R.C. §677(a)(1)] Similarly, if Husband sets up a trust for Wife as part of their divorce agreement, the income is taxed to Wife under the usual trust rules, not to Husband. However, child support paid through such a trust is taxable to Husband, not to Wife. [I.R.C. §682—overrides the rules of I.R.C. §71]

EXAM TIP   **gilbert**

For your exam, remember that a trust that was initially set up to support the grantor's spouse may "morph" into an alimony trust after divorce. Thus, trust income that was initially taxable to the grantor because it was used to support the grantor's spouse *may become taxable to the spouse* after the parties divorce.

---

(5) Administrative powers that may benefit grantor [§269]

The grantor is taxable on the income of a trust where the administrative control of the trust is, or may be, exercisable primarily for the benefit of the grantor or his spouse instead of the beneficiaries. [I.R.C. §675] The following are the kinds of administrative powers that will cause the trust income to be taxed to the grantor:

(a) Dealing not at arm's length [§270]

The trust income will be taxed to the grantor if the grantor or a nonadverse party, or both, have the power to *deal* with the trust property or income for *less than an adequate consideration* without the approval of an adverse party. [I.R.C. §675(1)]

(b) Borrowing not at arm's length [§271]

The grantor will also be taxed on trust income if the grantor or a nonadverse party, or both, have the power to *borrow* the corpus or income, directly or indirectly, *without adequate interest or security*. [I.R.C. §675(2)]

(c) Borrowing part of corpus or income [§272]

If the grantor directly or indirectly borrows any part of the income or corpus and does not repay the loan *before the beginning of the year*, he will be taxed on the appropriate portion of the trust income (*e.g.,* if he borrows half the corpus, he is taxed on half the income). This rule applies even though the grantor has given *adequate security* and is paying *adequate interest*. [I.R.C. §675(3)]

1) Exception [§273]

This rule does not apply if the loan was made by a trustee other than the grantor or a related or subordinate trustee subservient to him, and the loan provides for adequate interest and security.

2) Tax to grantor [§274]

If the grantor borrows a portion of trust *income*, he is taxed on the appropriate portion of the income until the year following the year in which the loan is repaid. In each year, the appropriate percentage is the amount of the loan divided by the sum of the trust's total income for all the years that the loan was outstanding. [*See* **Bennett v. Commissioner,** 79 T.C. 470 (1982)]

---

e.g. **Example:** Gina Grantor established a trust. She borrowed $10,000 from the trust for three years—Year 1, Year 2, and Year 3. In each year that the loan was outstanding, the trust made $20,000 in income. Gina would be taxed on 50% of the Year 1 income, 25% of the Year 2 income, and 16.67% of the Year 3 income.

---

3) "Borrowing" from trust [§275]
A grantor is treated as borrowing from a trust if a loan is made to the grantor's partnership, but *not* if the loan is made to a corporation of which the grantor is the majority stockholder. [**Bennett v. Commissioner,** *supra*]

(d) Powers exercised by nonfiduciary [§276]
Trust income will be taxed to the grantor if general powers of administration are exercisable by anyone in a *nonfiduciary capacity*. These include powers to control investments, vote stock in the trust, or reacquire assets in the trust. However, if these powers can be exercised by someone only in a *fiduciary capacity*, they will not cause the income to be taxed. [I.R.C. §675(4)]

c. Trust income taxable to person other than grantor [§277]
The *Clifford* principle is also applied when a person *other than the grantor* has a *general power of appointment*. In other words, if a grantor sets up a trust for a beneficiary, but gives a third party the power to *vest in herself the trust income or corpus*, the third party is taxed on the income whether or not she takes it. [I.R.C. §678]

(1) Rationale
This statute is derived from the *Mallinckrodt* doctrine—the third party's power to control the flow of income is tantamount to ownership of the income for tax purposes. [**Mallinckrodt v. Nunan,** 146 F.2d 1 (8th Cir.), *cert. denied,* 324 U.S. 871 (1945)]

(2) Note
If the third party has the power only to apply the trust income for the *support of her dependents*, the income is not taxable to her except to the extent that she actually applies the income to their support. [I.R.C. §678(c)]

(3) And note

Section 678 is not applicable to powers over income if the *other grantor trust rules* would *cause the income to be taxed to the grantor*. It is also inapplicable if the third party *renounces or disclaims* the power within a reasonable time after becoming aware of its existence. [I.R.C. §678(b), (d)]

3. Trusts Recognized for Tax Purposes [§278]

If the grantor has not retained substantial "strings" on the trust, the trust itself will be recognized as a separate taxable entity. Trust income will be taxable to the trust itself or to the beneficiaries, rather than to the grantor. A decedent's estate computes its taxable income in the same manner as a trust. The following is an abbreviated treatment of the taxation of trusts and estates (often called "fiduciaries"). A more complete discussion appears in the Income Tax II Summary.

a. Taxability of income [§279]

In general, either the trust or the beneficiaries will pay tax on the income earned by the trust. If the income is distributed to the beneficiaries, it is includible in their income and deductible by the trust. If the trust retains the income, it pays tax thereon.

(1) Note

Distributions of *corpus* by the trust are not taxed to the beneficiaries. However, the precise rules for distinguishing income from corpus are quite complex.

b. Distributable net income [§280]

The concept of distributable net income ("DNI") is an essential element of the taxation of trusts and estates. DNI is the "measuring rod" to determine the maximum amount that can be included in the beneficiary's income and be deducted as a distribution by the trust. It is defined as the trust's *taxable income*, with the following special adjustments (among others) [I.R.C. §643(a)]:

(1) *No deduction for distributions to beneficiaries*;

(2) *No deduction for the trust's personal exemption* (*see* below); and

(3) *No deduction for undistributed capital gains or losses allocated to corpus*.

c. "Simple trusts" [§281]

A simple trust is basically a conduit for moving current trust income to the beneficiaries. A trust will be treated as a simple trust if it is *required to distribute* all of its current income to the beneficiaries, makes no distribution of corpus, and claims no deduction for charitable contributions. [I.R.C. §651(a)]

(1) Taxation of simple trusts [§282]

The beneficiaries of a simple trust are taxed on the income of the trust that is distributed or (if not actually distributed) *required to be distributed*. The amount taxed to the beneficiaries is deducted by the trust. However, the amount included in income cannot exceed the trust's DNI. The trust will be taxed on capital gains allocated to corpus. [I.R.C. §652(a)]

d. "Complex trusts" and estates [§283]

A complex trust is any trust that does not fall within the definition of a simple trust (above). Decedent's estates are treated as complex trusts, as are all trusts that accumulate income, trusts that distribute corpus, or trusts in which the trustee has discretion in distributing income. Taxation of complex trusts is as follows:

(1) First tier [§284]

All of the income *required* to be distributed is included in the income of the beneficiaries entitled to it, whether or not distributed. However, the amount taxed can never exceed DNI. [I.R.C. §662(a)(1)]

(2) Second tier [§285]

If DNI exceeds the amount *required* to be distributed, then *additional payments to beneficiaries become taxable*. These would include discretionary income payments or distributions from corpus or accumulated income. Again, however, the amount includible *cannot exceed DNI less the amount that was taxed to first tier beneficiaries*. DNI is allocated among the second tier beneficiaries in proportion to the amounts they receive. [I.R.C. §662(a)(2)]

(3) Nonperiodic payments [§286]

Even if there is available DNI, certain nonperiodic distributions are not taxed to second tier beneficiaries: If the governing instrument requires payment of a lump sum (or payments of a set amount in not more than three installments), this payment is treated as a tax-exempt gift, even if there is DNI available. [I.R.C. §663(a)]

(4) Tax to trust [§287]

To the extent that amounts are includible in income of first and second tier beneficiaries, the trust deducts these amounts from its own income. If these deductions leave taxable income above zero, the trust pays tax on these amounts.

(a) Exemptions [§288]

A simple trust has a $300 personal exemption, a complex trust has a $100 personal exemption, and an estate has a $600 personal exemption. Trust and estate exemptions are not indexed for inflation (in contrast to individuals, who have an indexed $1,000 personal exemption). [I.R.C. §642(b)]

e. Throwback rule

(1) The problem—tax avoidance through delay [§289]

If the trust is in a low bracket and the beneficiaries are in a high bracket, considerable tax savings could be obtained by delaying distributions. For example, assume that in 2000 and 2001, DNI of the trust is $20,000. The trust makes no distribution in 2000 (and therefore has taxable income of $20,000 less a $100 personal exemption). But in 2001, it distributes $40,000. Since DNI is only $20,000 in 2001, the beneficiary would have to include only $20,000 in income.

(2) Taxing the trust—throwback rule [§290]

The throwback rule is designed to prevent such avoidance. It provides that a distribution in excess of current DNI is "thrown back" to the accumulated income of any preceding years. It is treated as though it had been distributed in those years, to the extent of the undistributed income in those years. The tax that the trust previously paid on the income is also treated as though it had been distributed in the prior years. [I.R.C. §§665-669]

(3) Taxing beneficiaries [§291]

The beneficiary is taxed on the accumulation distribution in the year in which it is made. The procedure involves a shortcut method so that the tax of each prior year in which there was undistributed net income does not have to be recomputed. Instead, the accumulation distribution (plus the taxes previously paid by the trust), divided by the number of years to which it is being thrown back, is added to taxable income of three of the preceding five taxable years. (Of the five preceding taxable years, the highest and lowest are disregarded and the remaining three are used.) The average increase in tax for each of those three years is then multiplied by the total number of years to which the distribution is thrown back. [*See* I.R.C. §667, described in much greater detail in the Income Tax II Summary]

(a) Note

The amount distributed includes the tax paid by the trust during the years in which there was undistributed net income. However, the beneficiary is given a *credit* for the amount of those taxes.

Chapter Three:
Is It Deductible or Is It a Credit?

CONTENTS

Chapter Approach

The income tax is a tax on *net* income, not on gross income. Therefore, after gross income is determined (Chapter I, *supra*) and after it is assigned to the proper taxpayer (Chapter II, *supra*), the next set of questions relates to deductions from income and credits against the tax. Deductions are a favorite exam topic.

1. **Business and Investment Deductions**

   When a potentially deductible item appears on your exam, you should first determine whether it qualifies as a business or investment deduction—*i.e.*, as expense, depreciation, depletion, loss, or bad debt.

   a. **Expense**

      If the item might be a business or investment expense, ask whether it was incurred: (i) in connection with a *trade or business* [I.R.C. §162], (ii) for the *production of income* [I.R.C. §212(1)], or (iii) for the management or maintenance of *income-producing property* [I.R.C. §212(2)].

      (1) The next issue to address is whether the item is *business or personal*. Ask yourself:

         (a) Was it deductible *traveling expense* or personal commuting? If a meal, does it satisfy the "overnight" test or meet the test for entertainment? (Note that only 50% of meal and entertainment costs are deductible.) If a meals and lodging expense, is the taxpayer "away from home"?

         (b) If expenses arise from a business that might be a hobby, does it meet the test of *intention to make a profit* under section 183?

         (c) If it is an *educational expense*, does it qualify the taxpayer for a new trade or business?

         (d) If it involves a *home office* or a rented *vacation home*, does it meet all the requirements of section 280A?

         (e) If it involves *attorneys' fees*, what was the origin of the dispute? If the origin was personal (*e.g.*, divorce), the fees are not deductible.

      (2) To determine whether an item is an *expense* or must be *capitalized*, ask:

         (a) Is it a *repair* or a *permanent improvement*?

(b) Is it a *cost* of purchasing or producing property? Watch here for the strict requirements of section 263A for capitalization of *interest and overhead*.

(c) If the item involves *rent with an option* to purchase, analyze whether it is a concealed purchase.

(d) Is it a *start-up cost* or a cost of searching for a new business? Apply section 195.

(e) Is it a *selling cost*? If so, it reduces the amount realized on the sale.

(f) Is it a cost of *acquiring goodwill*? Distinguish from the cost of maintaining existing goodwill, which may be deductible.

(g) If it is an *attorneys' fee* incurred in litigation relating to property, distinguish disputes over title (not deductible) from disputes concerning income (deductible).

(3) The item must be *ordinary and necessary* to qualify as a deductible expense. Ask yourself whether the expense helps the business and whether other businesses in the community would, under similar circumstances, incur this expense. If the item involves compensation, it must be reasonable.

(4) Certain expense items are disallowed if a deduction would be contrary to *public policy*, so watch for: bribes to government officials and any other type of illegal payment; fines or similar penalties paid to the government; certain punitive antitrust damages; and ballot initiatives or political campaigns (but distinguish lobbying expenses, which are deductible at the local level).

b. **Depreciation and amortization**
If the item might be deductible as depreciation or amortization, consider:

(1) The item's *useful life*. An arbitrary 15-year useful life is provided for many intangibles.

(2) Who is seeking the deduction; *i.e.*, is the taxpayer the *owner* of the property? Generally only one who has a capital investment in the property is entitled to claim a deduction.

(3) Whether the item is *"listed property"* (*e.g.*, cars, home computers). If so, the deduction is limited.

(4) Which depreciation *method* (accelerated or straight-line) should be used, and whether the election to deduct up to $17,500 in the year of purchase can be used.

c. Depletion

If the taxpayer owns an asset subject to depletion, important issues will be whether he can use *percentage* depletion, and whether he can deduct *intangible drilling costs.*

d. Loss

If the item might be deductible under I.R.C. section 165 as a loss, you will want to ask:

(1) If the taxpayer is an individual, is it a *business or investment loss*? Personal losses are not deductible except for casualty losses.

(2) Was the loss *realized*?

(3) Was the loss *ordinary or capital*? The deduction of capital losses is restricted.

(4) What is the *amount* of the loss? It is limited to a taxpayer's basis in the asset.

(5) Will the deduction be *disallowed* because of sale to a *related party*? Because the transaction was motivated by *tax avoidance*? Because of *public policy*?

e. Bad debt

If you suspect the item might qualify for a bad debt deduction, ask:

(1) Was there a *bona fide debt*? Intrafamily debts are suspect.

(2) Did it become *worthless in the taxable year*? Remember, however, that a deduction for partial worthlessness is permitted for business debts.

(3) What was the *basis* of the debt? No bad debt deduction is allowed if the debt had no basis, as in the case of the account receivable of a cash-basis taxpayer.

(4) Is the deduction *ordinary or capital*? Nonbusiness bad debts produce capital loss.

f. Limitations on deductibility

Finally, you will want to determine whether there are any rules that limit the deductibility of the item in question. You must consider:

(1) *The at risk rules:* Operating losses cannot be deducted beyond the amount at risk in the activity.

(2) *The passive loss rules:* Loss from passive activity can be deducted only against passive income. There are, however, exceptions to this rule for

certain real property rentals by moderate income taxpayers and for real estate professionals.

(3) The limitations on *excess investment interest*.

(4) The rule that the cost of earning *tax-exempt interest* is not deductible.

2. Personal Deductions

Certain items are deductible even though they have no connection to business or investment. These items fall into two categories: "above-the-line" deductions, which are deducted from gross income; and "below-the-line" deductions, which are deducted from adjusted gross income ("AGI"). *Below-the-line deductions must exceed the standard deduction*. Be aware that certain below-the-line deductions (such as employee business expenses and most expenses deductible under section 212) are subject to a 2% floor; *i.e.*, they are deductible only to the extent they exceed 2% of AGI. Note also that itemized deductions are further reduced by 3% of AGI in excess of the $100,000 threshold. The following are personal deductions that are popular exam subjects:

a. Qualified residence interest

Most personal interest is not deductible. When you encounter the issue of whether the interest on a debt secured by a residence is deductible, the important issues will be:

(1) Whether the debt is secured by a *personal* residence or a designated second residence.

(2) Whether it is *acquisition* debt or *home equity* debt.

(3) Whether it is *within the monetary limits* ($1 million on acquisition debt, $100,000 on home equity debt).

b. Taxes

When the item in question is taxes, remember that *state and local taxes* on income, real property, and personal property are deductible.

c. Charitable contributions

When the item in issue is a gift to charity, ask:

(1) Is it within the applicable *percentage limits*? Taxpayers may deduct up to 50% of their AGI for gifts to most charities.

(2) If a gift of *appreciated property*, does it encounter any of the limits on deducting fair market value? To deduct the fair market value, the property must have been a long-term capital asset and donated to a public charity. Also, the deduction for gifts of property is limited to 30% of AGI.

(3) Does the taxpayer receive any *benefit* from the transfer that *exceeds* that of the general public? If so, it is not deductible.

d. Medical expenses

Most medical expenses are deductible to the extent they exceed 7.5% of AGI. However, expenses compensated by insurance are not deductible.

e. Casualty loss

If an exam question concerns an item that might be a casualty loss, remember that the loss must be over $100 and exceed 10% of AGI. In addition, consider whether the requisite element of suddenness is present. Finally, note that the amount deductible is the lesser of the adjusted basis and the difference in the value of the property.

f. Personal and dependency exemptions

A taxpayer is entitled to a personal exemption for himself (and another for a spouse on a joint return). The question most likely to arise on an exam in this area is whether the taxpayer can claim an exemption for a dependent. If you encounter this situation ask:

(i) Is the person in question a *close relative* of the taxpayer or does he have his principal place of abode with the taxpayer?

(ii) Is the "dependent" person's *income less than the exemption* amount? (Note that there are important exceptions to this requirement.)

(iii) Does the taxpayer supply *over one-half of the person's support*?

(iv) If the exemption is for a *child of divorced parents*, which parent is entitled to the exemption? Absent a waiver of the exemption, the custodial parent is entitled to the exemption.

Watch out for the phaseout of exemptions when AGI exceeds various thresholds.

3. Personal Credits

Taxpayers are entitled to a number of *credits*—meaning that the item reduces the tax due *dollar for dollar*. Important personal credits include (i) credits for low-income elderly persons, (ii) the child care credit, (iii) the child tax credit, (iv) the earned income credit, and (v) educational credits.

A. Introduction

1. Deductions and Credits Defined [§292]

A *deduction* is subtracted either from gross income or from adjusted gross income (*see infra*, §§552 *et seq.*). In either case, the deduction reduces **taxable income**. A **credit**, on the other hand, reduces the **tax** that is payable dollar for dollar.

---

e.g. **Example:** What is the difference between a $1,000 deduction and a $1,000 credit? Assume that Tom's taxable income is $25,000 and the tax is $5,000 (in both cases, before taking the $1,000 into account). Assume further that Tom is in the 28% tax bracket. If the $1,000 is a **deduction**, it will reduce his taxable income to $24,000 and reduce his tax by $280 (*i.e.*, 28% of $1,000) to $4,720. However, if the $1,000 is a **credit**, it will reduce his tax from $5,000 to $4,000.

---

2. Business vs. Personal Deductions [§293]

As a broad general principle, the costs of doing business (or of otherwise making money through investments) are deductible. The costs of a taxpayer's personal life are not deductible, but for various reasons the Code makes a few personal costs (such as medical expenses or charitable contributions) deductible.

3. No Shifting of Deductions [§294]

In general, payment of **another's liabilities** (*e.g.*, paying interest on someone else's loans) will not create a valid deduction for the taxpayer. [*See* **United States v. Davis**, 370 U.S. 65 (1962)]

a. Exception—separate business purpose [§295]

Payment of another's debt may be deductible if it serves **independent business purposes** of the taxpayer.

---

e.g. **Example:** Taxpayer Gould owned all of the stock of insolvent Gould Plumbing & Heating, Inc. and was an employee of Industrial Mechanical Contractors, Inc. Unless the debts of Gould Plumbing & Heating, Inc. were cleared up, he was in danger of losing his job with Industrial Mechanical Contractors, Inc. He paid Gould Plumbing & Heating's debts. Ordinarily, a stockholder cannot deduct the payment of any corporate debts or expenses, but here the deduction was allowed because the payment was related closely enough to protecting taxpayer's job with Industrial Mechanical Contractors. [**Gould v. Commissioner**, 64 T.C. 132 (1975)]

B. Business and Investment Deductions

---

1. Business Expenses [§296]

The most important provision for deducting the costs of doing business is set forth in I.R.C. section 162, which provides that all "ordinary and necessary **expenses** paid or incurred during the taxable year in carrying on any trade or business" are deductible. Thus, to be deductible under this section, an expense must meet several criteria. It must:

(i)   Be paid or incurred during the year in connection with a *trade or business*;

(ii) Be a *trade or business*, rather than a *personal*, expense;

(iii) Be a *current expense*, as opposed to capital outlay;

(iv) Be *"ordinary and necessary"*; and

(v)   *Not violate public policy*.

a.   **Trade or business [§297]**
     Characterization of an activity as a *trade or business* is important for many tax provisions. For example, a taxpayer in a trade or business can deduct depreciation on business property, business expenses, and business losses. [I.R.C. §§167(a)(1), 162, 165(c)(1)] Alternatively, depreciation, expenses, and losses can be deducted with respect to transactions entered into for profit, even though the activity does not rise to the level of trade or business. [I.R.C. §§167(a)(2), 212(1) - (2), 165(c)(2); *see infra*, §§437-440] However, for various reasons, the treatment of a "transaction entered into for profit" is not as favorable as the treatment of a "trade or business." For example, net operating losses arising out of nontrade or nonbusiness activity cannot be carried forward or back [I.R.C. §172(d)(4); *and see infra*, §1079], and some of the deductions arising from such activity are "below the line" and subject to the restriction on "miscellaneous itemized deductions" [*see* I.R.C. §§62, 67; *and see infra*, §§555, 562-564]. Similarly, the costs of a home office devoted to nontrade or nonbusiness activity cannot be deducted. (*See infra*, §§347-348.)

     (1) "Trade or business" defined [§298]
          The I.R.C. never defines "trade or business," but the most important factors are:

          (i)   The activity must be entered into with the *expectation of making a profit*;

          (ii) There must be some *regularity and continuity* in its operation; and

          (iii) The taxpayer must be *actively* engaged in pursuing it (either herself or through agents).

          ---

          e.g. **Example:** A full-time gambler is in a trade or business, even though he provides no goods or services to others. Note, however, that gambling losses in excess of gains are not deductible. [**Commissioner v. Groetzinger,** 480 U.S. 23 (1987); I.R.C. §165(d)—*see infra*, §501]

          ---

(2) Legality of business [§299]

An illegal business (*e.g.*, bookmaking) is entitled to deduct its operating expenses, like any legitimate business enterprise. [**Commissioner v. Sullivan,** 356 U.S. 27 (1958)] However, certain *illegal expenses* (violative of public policy) are *not* deductible (*see infra*, §§424-435).

EXAM TIP　　　　　　　　　　　　　　　　　　　　　**gilbert**

For your exam, remember it is the *legality of the expense*, *not* the legality of the *business*, that governs whether the expense is deductible. Thus, the operating expenses of an illegal business are deductible.

---

(3) Nature of taxpayer [§300]

Expenses incurred in connection with a trade or business are deductible by any kind of a taxpayer—individual, trust, or corporation. *Employees* are in a "trade or business" and can deduct the costs incurred in connection with their jobs. Thus, union dues or the costs of uniforms are deductible as business expenses—usually from adjusted gross income (*see infra*, §554) and only in excess of 2% of adjusted gross income (*see infra*, §§562-564). However, a *stockholder* is not treated as being in business merely because his corporation is in business. [**Whipple v. Commissioner,** 373 U.S. 193 (1963)] The costs of *investment*, such as holding stock, are deductible under I.R.C. section 212 (*see infra*, §§437-440).

(4) Tax shelters [§301]

The courts have frequently characterized activities involving flagrant tax shelters as not meeting the "trade or business" requirement. Thus, deductions arising out of such activities are denied. [**Rose v. Commissioner,** 88 T.C. 386 (1988), *aff'd*, 868 F.2d 851 (6th Cir. 1989); *see infra*, §322]

b. Business vs. personal expenses [§302]

Expenses incurred by a *corporate* taxpayer are *presumed* to have been incurred "in connection with" its trade or business—since a corporation normally exists only for business purposes. However, corporate outlays for the personal benefit of the shareholders are treated as nondeductible dividends (*e.g.*, paying for shareholder's house). *Individual* taxpayers must prove that the particular expenditure was incurred *in connection with* the taxpayer's trade or business—rather than as a personal, family, or living expense, which is expressly *not* deductible. [I.R.C. §262]

EXAM TIP　　　　　　　　　　　　　　　　　　　　　**gilbert**

For your exam, remember that an *individual must be able to prove* that an expense was incurred "in connection with" his trade or business in order to deduct the expense, but that *a corporation's expenses are presumed* to be incurred in connection with its trade or business.

---

(1) Requirement of proximate relationship to trade or business [§303]

A remote connection to business is not enough. There must be a direct, *proximate* relationship between the business and the purpose of the expenditure. If the expenditure is for several purposes, and is not susceptible to proration, the *predominant* purpose determines deductibility.

Example: Taxpayer is sued for *personal injuries* resulting from an auto accident that occurred while he was driving between two jobs. Although the driving cost is deductible in this situation (*see infra*, §316), the costs of settling the lawsuit were held not proximately connected to either of the jobs and thus nondeductible. [**Freedman v. Commissioner**, 301 F.2d 359 (5th Cir. 1962)]

Compare: On the other hand, expenses incurred in defending an action brought by a former business partner *have* been held to be "trade and business" expenses. Although the partnership was dissolved, and the taxpayer was no longer in business at the time of the suit, the Court declared that the expenses bore a "proximate relationship" to a *former* business and were deductible. [**Kornhauser v. United States**, 276 U.S. 145 (1928)]

---

(2) Travel expenses [§304]

I.R.C. section 162(a)(2) allows deduction of "traveling expenses (including amounts expended for meals and lodging if not lavish and extravagant under the circumstances) while *away from home* in the *pursuit of a trade or business*." In the case of food or beverages, however, only 50% of their cost is deductible. [I.R.C. §274(n)]

(a) "Pursuit of trade or business" [§305]

The expenses must have been incurred primarily in furtherance of business rather than personal objectives.

1) Commuting to and from work [§306]

Expenses incurred in traveling to or from the taxpayer's place of business or employment are *not* deductible. Commuting represents a *personal* choice to live far from work. [**Commissioner v. Flowers**, 326 U.S. 425 (1946)—lawyer lived 250 miles from employer's office; expenses in traveling to and from office held not deductible]

a) Involuntary commuting [§307]

The same rule applies even if there is not a place closer to work for taxpayer to live. Commuting, even from the closest possible dwelling place, is still nondeductible. [**Sanders v. Commissioner**, 439 F.2d 296 (9th Cir. 1971)]

b) Transportation between businesses [§308]

If a taxpayer has several business locations, the costs of traveling between them are deductible, regardless of distance. For example, an attorney can deduct the cost of traveling from her office to a courthouse or a doctor can deduct the cost of traveling from his office to a hospital.

1/ Home-to-business commutes [§309]

The rules are not clear when a taxpayer travels from home to business and the trip does not meet the normal pattern of commuting. According to the IRS, the cost of a home-to-business commute is generally non-deductible, except in the following situations: [Rev. Rul. 99-7, 1999-1 C.B. 361]

a/ A taxpayer *may deduct* the cost of travel from home to a temporary work location *if the commute is outside of the metropolitan area* in which the taxpayer normally lives and works. A temporary work location means a location where the work is realistically expected to last for less than one year (*see infra*, §318). However, unless the taxpayer falls under b/ or c/, below, he *may not deduct* the cost of travel from home to a temporary work location *if the commute is within the same metropolitan area* in which the taxpayer normally lives and works.

b/ If a taxpayer has at least *one regular workplace away from home*, he *may deduct* the cost of a commute *from home to a temporary work location that is in the same trade or business.*

Example: An attorney who travels from home to the courthouse without stopping first at the office may deduct the cost of the trip.

---

c/ If a taxpayer's home is also his *principal place of business* as defined by I.R.C. section 280A(c)(1) (*see infra,* §351), his home becomes a "business location." Thus, he may deduct the cost of travel from home to a secondary place of business—regular or temporary workplace without regard to distance—as a *cost of traveling between several business locations* (*see supra*, §308).

WHEN THE TAXPAYER'S HOME IS ALSO A PLACE OF BUSINESS, CONSIDER THE FOLLOWING:

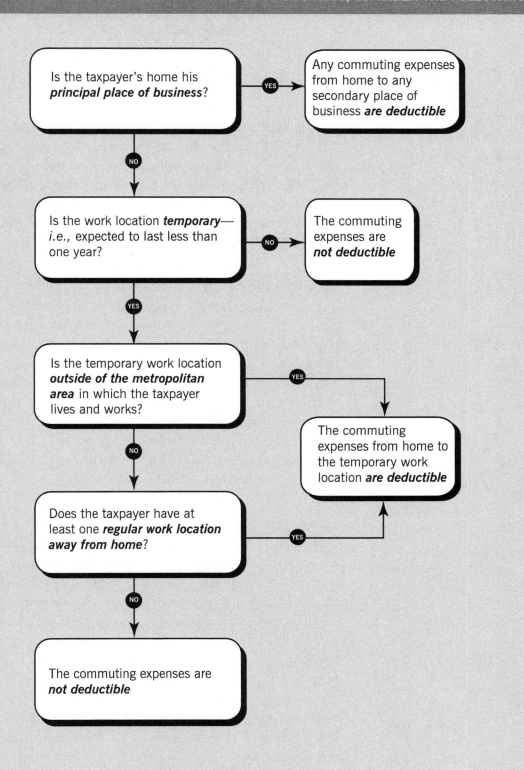

Is the taxpayer's home his *principal place of business*?

YES → Any commuting expenses from home to any secondary place of business *are deductible*

NO ↓

Is the work location *temporary— i.e.,* expected to last less than one year?

NO → The commuting expenses are *not deductible*

YES ↓

Is the temporary work location *outside of the metropolitan area* in which the taxpayer lives and works?

YES → The commuting expenses from home to the temporary work location *are deductible*

NO ↓

Does the taxpayer have at least one *regular work location away from home*?

YES → The commuting expenses from home to the temporary work location *are deductible*

NO ↓

The commuting expenses are *not deductible*

c) Transporting equipment [§310]

Even if a taxpayer has to transport heavy tools to work, he still cannot deduct the cost of commuting by car. However, if he can show that he incurred additional costs (like trailer rental) for the purpose of transporting the tools, the additional costs are deductible. [**Fausner v. Commissioner,** 413 U.S. 838 (1973); Rev. Rul. 75-380, 1975-2 C.B. 59]

2) Combined business and pleasure trips [§311]

Transportation expenses incurred on a combined business-pleasure trip are entirely deductible if the *primary purpose* of a trip was business, *but lodging and meals* must be fairly allocated between business and pleasure. If the primary purpose was pleasure, then no part of the transportation expense is deductible (although any meals or lodging attributable to business would be). [Treas. Reg. §1.162-2] Note that travel costs are nondeductible if the travel is engaged in as a form of professional education (*e.g.*, high school French teacher visits France in the summer). [I.R.C. §274(m)(2)]

3) Foreign meetings [§312]

Section 274(h) imposes special limitations on the deduction of expenses of attending foreign conventions, seminars, or other meetings. If the meeting is outside North America, the taxpayer must establish that the meeting is *directly related* to the active conduct of trade or business or investment and that it is as reasonable for the meeting to be held outside North America as inside it. In deciding the reasonableness question, consider the purpose of the meeting and activities taking place at the meeting, the purposes and activities of the sponsors, the residences of active members of sponsoring organizations, and the places where other meetings have been held. No deduction is allowed for meetings on cruise ships, except for American registered ships sailing between American ports.

4) Presence of spouse [§313]

No deduction is allowed for the travel expenses of a person (such as a spouse) accompanying the taxpayer (or an officer or employee of the taxpayer), unless that person is an employee of the taxpayer, the person's travel had a bona fide business purpose, and the expenses would otherwise be deductible by that person. [I.R.C. §274(m)(3)] Prior law allowed deduction of a spouse's expenses if there was a valid reason for the spouse to come along, such as assisting with entertainment of clients. [**United States v. Disney,** 413 F.2d 783 (9th Cir. 1969)]

EXAM TIP   **gilbert**

On your exam, if you encounter a question that has a married couple traveling together, be sure to check if *each has an independent basis* for claiming a deduction for a business trip. Only if each spouse has an independent basis will each be able to claim a deduction.

(b) "Away from home" [§314]

The meaning of the phrase "away from home" is the subject of considerable controversy. The Commissioner and the Tax Court hold that it means away from the taxpayer's *business headquarters*. [Rev. Rul. 75-432, 1975-2 C.B. 60] However, some courts of appeal have held that it means away from the taxpayer's *residence*. [**Rosenspan v. United States,** 438 F.2d 905 (2d Cir. 1971)—taxpayer without permanent residence cannot be "away from home"] The Supreme Court has not squarely ruled on this point, except in the case of military personnel, as to whom "home" means the duty station to which the taxpayer is assigned. [**Commissioner v. Stidger,** 386 U.S. 287 (1967)]

1) "Homeless" taxpayers [§315]

If the taxpayer has no business headquarters, the Commissioner will permit the taxpayer's residence to be treated as his "home," provided it is a "regular abode in a real and substantial sense." [Rev. Rul. 73-529, 1973-2 C.B. 37]

a) Note

A taxpayer who does not have a "business headquarters" or a permanent "residence" (such as a transient worker) is not entitled to deduct travel expenses because he does not have duplicated living expenses. [**Henderson v. Commissioner,** 143 F.3d 497 (9th Cir. 1998)]

2) Taxpayers with several offices [§316]

Conversely, if the taxpayer has *several* "business headquarters" (*e.g.*, several offices or several different businesses), the expenses of traveling *between them* are deductible. Moreover, it is necessary to decide which of them is his principal business, since meals and lodging would be deductible only when he is away from the principal business. This should be done by an "objective" test—the business that produces the most money and consumes the most time is usually considered the principal business. [**Markey v. Commissioner,** 490 F.2d 1249 (6th Cir. 1974)]

3) Deductibility of meals—the "sleep or rest" rule [§317]

To limit claims for deduction of every meal taken by the taxpayer while away from home (business headquarters *or* residence), the Commissioner ruled that the cost of meals may be deducted only when the taxpayer is away from home on an *overnight trip*—or if not actually overnight, at least for such a period of time as requires "*sleep or rest*." The validity of this rule was upheld by the Supreme Court. [**United States v. Correll,** 389 U.S. 299 (1967)] Recall that only 50% of the cost of meals or beverages is deductible. [I.R.C. §274(n)]

4) "Temporary" vs. "indefinite" rule [§318]

Suppose the taxpayer is sent to work at a distant job site. Instead of commuting to and from his residence, he chooses to live at the job site. Are his *food and lodging* there deductible? In other words, is he "away from home" or does his "home" shift to the job site where he is living?

a) Rule

A taxpayer is entitled to deduct his transportation, food, and lodging if the job assignment is *temporary*, but not if the assignment is of *indefinite* duration. [**Peurifoy v. Commissioner,** 358 U.S. 59 (1958)] The theory is that when the work is temporary in nature, it is unrealistic to expect the taxpayer to uproot his family and home and take them with him, as he might do when the work is indefinite. In no event is an assignment temporary if it exceeds one year. [I.R.C. §162(a)]

b) Application of one-year rule

If the taxpayer expects that the job assignment will last more than one year, the living expenses at the job site are not deductible, even if, in fact, the job lasts less than one year. On the other hand, if the taxpayer expects the job to last less than one year, but, in fact, it lasts more than one year, the living expenses are deductible up until the time the taxpayer learns that she will be away more than a year. [Rev. Rul. 93-86, 1993-2 C.B. 71]

c) Business reason for maintaining home

To deduct expenses at the temporary job location, there must be a *business* reason for maintaining a home at the permanent location. [**Henderson v. Commissioner**, *supra,* §315—lighting technician, who is usually on the road but sometimes stays rent-free in his parents' home in Boise, had no duplicated living expenses and no business reason to maintain Boise home and was thus not "away from home"; **Hantzis v. Commissioner**, 638 F.2d 248 (1st Cir. 1981), *cert. denied,* 452 U.S. 962 (1981)—law student who takes summer job in New York cannot deduct costs there because she had no *business* reason for maintaining permanent home in Boston, where her husband remained and where she attended law school]

TRAVEL-RELATED EXPENSES — gilbert

DEDUCTIBLE EXPENSES	NONDEDUCTIBLE EXPENSES
• Home-to-business commute *if*: (i) "Home" is principal place of business and "work" is second place of business; (ii) "Work" is temporary location *outside* the metropolitan area in which the taxpayer lives; or (iii) If the taxpayer has a regular workplace away from home and the taxpayer travels to a temporary work location.	• "Normal" home-to-work commute.
• Commute *between* business locations.	
• Meals falling under *sleep or rest* rule.	• Meals and lodging that are allocated to "pleasure" in a mixed-purpose trip.
• Lodging for a *temporary* (less than one year) job assignment.	
• Travel to out-of-town locations for business purposes where an overnight stay is necessary.	• Travel expenses of person accompanying taxpayer (*e.g.,* spouse) *unless* that person has an independent basis for a deduction.
• Transportation to a foreign meeting if *directly related* to the active conduct of trade or business.	

(3) Expenses of "businesses" operated for pleasure—hobby farm problem [§319]

A frequent problem is the deductibility of the expenses of a hobby farm or other business that produces some income but consistently operates at a loss because expenses exceed income. [I.R.C. §183] To deduct the annual loss, the taxpayer must demonstrate that at least a *significant* purpose of the venture was to earn a profit. Some cases hold that profit must be the *primary* purpose. [**Nickerson v. Commissioner,** 700 F.2d 402 (7th Cir. 1983)] The intended profit need not be reasonable or immediate; long-run profitability is sufficient. [**Nickerson v. Commissioner,** *supra*] Note that the deduction of expenses incurred on hobby farms or similar businesses may well be disallowed under the provisions restricting deduction of passive losses. (*See infra*, §§543-551.)

EXAM TIP   **gilbert**

On your exam, don't be fooled by facts indicating that the business run by the taxpayer is also a hobby. A hobby *could* be a business, so long as profit was a *significant* (some courts say *primary*) *purpose* of the venture.

(a) Determinative factors [§320]

The taxpayer's purpose is determined by the particular facts. If the taxpayer hired professional help to operate his farm, made marketing surveys, purchased the best available machinery, and personally involved himself in the details of the farm's operation, these factors would indicate a purpose to make a profit. But if he built a lavish home on the property in which he lived on weekends and took little interest in financial details, this would show a purpose of operating the farm for pleasure rather than profit. Horse breeding and racing are particularly apt to be treated as a personal rather than business venture. [*See* Treas. Reg. §1.183-2]

1) Actual profit-and-loss history

The actual profit-and-loss history of the enterprise is an important factor in determining its purpose. If the activity occasionally produces a profit, this tends to show that the taxpayer did have a reasonable expectation of profit. By statute, if the activity produced a profit (*i.e.*, income exceeded expenses) in three or more of the five years ending with the taxable year, there is a rebuttable presumption that the activity was engaged in for profit. [I.R.C. §183(d)]

Example: A middle-income taxpayer lost money for several years running a pet store. His recordkeeping was very sloppy and the store was run incompetently. In overturning a Tax Court decision treating the business as a hobby, the appellate court stressed (i) the store had once been profitable; (ii) the taxpayer had previously changed locations to cut costs; (iii) the poor recordkeeping and failure to improve business methods could be explained by time constraints—the taxpayer had several other jobs; (iv) the taxpayer had real out-of-pocket loss—not just depreciation; (v) the taxpayer was not wealthy; (vi) the taxpayer had no other obvious purpose in mind such as pleasure; (vii) a retail business run by the taxpayer and his family is hard work and very different from a pleasurable activity like weekend farming or horse breeding. In short, a businessperson's incompetence does not turn his business into a hobby. [**Ranciato v. Commissioner,** 52 F.2d 23 (2d Cir. 1995)]

(b) Amounts deductible [§321]

If it is found that the activity was **not** for profit, the taxpayer can still deduct items, such as property taxes, that are deductible regardless of whether the activity was profit-seeking. However, as to expenses without an independent basis for deduction, the expenses of an activity not engaged in for profit can be used to offset the income it produces, but no more. [I.R.C. §183(b)] The deduction for hobby expenses up to hobby income is a miscellaneous itemized deduction, and miscellaneous itemized deductions in total must exceed 2% of adjusted gross income to be deductible (*see infra*, §§562 *et seq.*) [I.R.C. §67]

e.g. Example: Steve raises race horses as a hobby. Last year, he had no income from horse racing. However, he incurred property taxes of $5,000, groomer fees of $7,000, and feed expenses of $10,000. The property taxes are deductible (*see infra*, §§612-613). However, none of the other costs are deductible.

cf. Compare: Same facts as above, except that one of Steve's horses earns $6,800 in prize money. Steve can deduct the property tax and $1,800 of his other costs (to offset his winnings). The $1,800 is a miscellaneous itemized deduction.

(c) Tax shelters [§322]

The courts have decided numerous cases in which taxpayers claimed deductions for flagrant "tax shelters"; *i.e.*, gimmicky transactions that give rise to deductions far in excess of cash investment and which are heavily motivated by tax avoidance. The Tax Court has characterized such deals as "generic tax shelters" and disallowed all deductions in excess of income. [**Rose v. Commissioner,** 88 T.C. 386 (1987)]

1) *Rose* decision [§323]

In *Rose, supra*, taxpayers claimed large deductions and credits arising out of the purchase of rights to make reproductions (prints, posters, etc.) from works of art. Finding that the tax savings were the focus of the deal, that the investors accepted the deal without investigation or price negotiation, that the assets were substantially overvalued, and that the bulk of the consideration was paid through nonrecourse notes, the Tax Court simply disallowed all deductions. This approach seems not only to be based partly on section 183, but also on a holding that the activity is not a "trade or business" (*see supra*, §§298-301) and a holding that the activity is so lacking in economic substance that it should be ignored for tax purposes. *Rose* was affirmed by the court of appeals on the latter ground, finding that the deal had no practicable economic effect (and no purpose) other than the creation of tax deductions. [**Rose v. Commissioner,** 868 F.2d 851 (6th Cir. 1989)] Note that deductions based on such deals would now be disallowed under the passive loss rules. (*See infra*, §§543-551.)

2) Economic substance rule [§324]

Be wary of any transaction that generates tax benefits but is motivated only by tax avoidance and lacks nontax economic consequences. The transaction will probably be ignored and the tax benefits denied. [*See, e.g.*, **Yosha v. Commissioner,** 861 F.2d 494 (7th Cir. 1988)—commodity transactions arranged so that taxpayer could not make or lose money but could get tax benefits]

(4) Moving expenses [§325]

Ordinarily, moving costs are personal expenditures. However, a limited exception exists for employees (existing or newly hired) *or* self-employed individuals. They are permitted to deduct expenses of moving their family and furniture to their new home. [I.R.C. §217]

(a) Distance limitation [§326]

However, the new job site must be more than *50 miles* farther from the old home than the old home was from the old job site. [I.R.C. §217(c)]

Example: Courtney commutes 55 miles per day to her job at a downtown Chicago law firm. If she finds another position with a rival firm in Los Angeles, her moving expenses from Chicago to Los Angeles are deductible. However, if she finds a job with a rival firm across the street and moves downtown in order to devote more time to her new job, her moving expenses would not be deductible.

(b) Full-time employee [§327]

In addition, the taxpayer must be a full-time employee during at least *39 weeks* of the 12-month period following the move. If self-employed, the taxpayer must perform services during 78 weeks of the succeeding 24-month period. [I.R.C. §217(c)(2), (d); *and see* **Muse v. Commissioner,** 76 T.C. 574 (1981)]

(c) Allowable deductions [§328]

A taxpayer may deduct any amount for moving her household goods and for traveling (including lodging) from the former residence to the new residence. However, meals consumed during travel cannot be deducted. The moving expenses of individuals other than the taxpayer can be deducted only if the individuals had both the former residence and the new residence as their principal place of abode. Other costs relating to the move, such as costs of searching for a new residence, living in temporary quarters before finding a new residence, or selling the old house and buying or renting a new one, are not deductible. [I.R.C. §217(b)]

JOB-RELATED MOVING EXPENSES	
MOVING EXPENSES ARE DEDUCTIBLE FOR EMPLOYEES OR SELF-EMPLOYED PERSONS IF 50-MILE DISTANCE LIMITATION MET (*see supra*, §326). *EXAMPLES:*	
DEDUCTIBLE EXPENSES	**NONDEDUCTIBLE EXPENSES**
• Cost of moving household goods from old residence to new residence • Traveling expenses (including lodging but ***not*** meals) incurred during move from old residence to new residence.	• Meals taken during travel from old residence to new residence • Costs of searching for a new residence • Temporary lodging while searching for a new residence • Costs of selling, buying, or renting a new or old residence

(d) Reimbursement by employer [§329]

Employer reimbursement of deductible moving expenses is not taxed to the employee, but employer reimbursement of ***nondeductible*** moving expenses is taxable to the employee. [I.R.C. §§82, 132(g)]

(e) Permanent place of work [§330]

A taxpayer cannot deduct moving expenses when she is away from home "temporarily" on business; such expenses are deductible only if the taxpayer moves to a new *permanent* place of work. [Treas. Reg. §1.217-1(c)(3)(iii); **Goldman v. Commissioner**, 497 F.2d 832 (6th Cir.), *cert. denied*, 419 U.S. 1021 (1974)]

(5) Entertainment expenses [§331]

Expenses incurred with respect to entertainment, amusement, or recreation are deductible only if the taxpayer can establish that the expenses were *directly related* to the active conduct of her business. The costs of socializing (*e.g.*, by attending sports events or nightclubs) are deductible only if it immediately precedes or follows a *substantial and bona fide business discussion*. [I.R.C. §274(a)] Only 50% of the cost of entertainment expense (or of any food or beverage) is deductible. [I.R.C. §274(n)]

(a) Entertainment facilities [§332]

No deduction is allowed for costs relating to entertainment "facilities," such as yachts or hunting lodges, or for amounts paid for membership in any club organized for business, pleasure, recreation, or other social purpose. [I.R.C. §274(a)(1)(B), (2)(A), (3)]

(b) Burden of proof [§333]

The Code imposes a special requirement that travel and entertainment expenses be substantiated either by adequate records or by sufficient evidence corroborating a taxpayer's own statement. The evidence must substantiate the amount of the expense, the time and place, the business purpose, and the business relationship to the taxpayer of the persons entertained or using the facility. [I.R.C. §274(d)]

(c) Business meals [§334]

To deduct the cost of a meal as an entertainment expense, the taxpayer must meet the general standards set forth for entertainment expenses: The taxpayer must be present, and the meal must be related to the active conduct of a trade or business (or precede or follow a substantial and bona fide business discussion). Note that only 50% of meal and beverage costs are deductible. [I.R.C. §274(k), (n)]

(d) Caution—taxpayer's own meal [§335]

The cost of a taxpayer's own meal is generally not deductible, even if business is discussed, because the taxpayer would have eaten the meal anyway. The cost is deductible only if the business aspects somehow increase the cost of the meal, as when the taxpayer pays for a client's meal at the same time. [**Moss v. Commissioner**, 758 F.2d 211 (7th Cir. 1985)—lawyer cannot deduct cost of daily lunches with his partners even though business is discussed]

(6) Business gifts [§336]

Logically, it is not likely that an item could be both a deductible business expense and also excludible as a gift to the recipient, because the "disinterested generosity" necessary under I.R.C. section 102 is inconsistent with the business motivation necessary to deduct an item under I.R.C. section 162. In the event that this unlikely combination emerges, however, I.R.C. section 274(b) limits the deduction to $25.

(7) Litigation expenses [§337]

Whether legal fees or other costs incurred in a lawsuit (including payments made by way of judgment or settlement) are deductible depends on the nature of the dispute.

(a) Business expense [§338]

If litigation costs are related to the taxpayer's trade or business, they may be deductible if *"ordinary and necessary"* (*see infra*, §408).

(b) Personal litigation [§339]

Costs of *personal litigation* are *not deductible*. Costs of litigation incurred as part of the taxpayer's trade or business are deductible under section 162. Costs of litigation incurred for the *production of taxable income* (but not as part of a trade or business) are deductible under section 212, but only as miscellaneous itemized deductions. The test for distinguishing between personal litigation and business (or income production) litigation is the origin of the dispute. For example, the costs of divorce litigation are *generally* not deductible as a business expense since the origin of the dispute lies in the personal life of the taxpayer. This is true even if the taxpayer's sole reason for contesting the divorce is to protect his business from the community property claims of his wife. [**United States v. Gilmore**, 372 U.S. 39 (1963); *and see infra*, §§446-449]

(c) Distinguish—tax matters [§340]

I.R.C. section 212(3) specifically allows a deduction for expenses "in connection with the determination, collection or refund of any tax" *whether or not* related to a trade or business. This covers costs of tax litigation and having tax returns prepared. It also permits deduction for legal fees and related expenses in connection with *tax planning*. However, costs of estate planning (other than the tax aspects) are personal, nondeductible items. [**Merians v. Commissioner**, 60 T.C. 187 (1973)] Note that this deduction is a "miscellaneous itemized deduction." Such deductions are subject to a floor; *i.e.*, they can be deducted only to the extent that they exceed 2% of adjusted gross income. [I.R.C. §67, *see infra*, §§564-565; Rev. Rul. 89-68,

1989-1 C.B. 82—cost of obtaining IRS ruling is deductible subject to 2% floor]

EXAM TIP **gilbert**

For your exam, be sure to remember the rules of deductibility for litigation costs. If the litigation relates to the taxpayer's *business*, the costs could possibly be *deducted* as an "ordinary and necessary" business expense under I.R.C. section 162. If the litigation relates to *the production of income* or to a *tax matter*, the costs could possibly be *deducted* under I.R.C. section 212. Otherwise, the litigation is most likely *personal* in nature, and the costs *may not be deducted*.

---

(8) Educational expenses

(a) General rule [§341]

Educational costs that either qualify the taxpayer for a *new* trade or business or that constitute the *minimum educational requirement* for qualification in her job are not deductible. [Treas. Regs. §1.162-5(b)(2), (3)]

Example: The costs of going to law school are not deductible. Similarly, the cost of a bar review course is not deductible, even if the taxpayer is already admitted to practice in another state, since practicing in a new state is considered a new business. [**Sharon v. Commissioner,** 66 T.C. 515 (1976), *aff'd*, 591 F.2d 1293 (9th Cir. 1978)]

Compare: The cost of taking the bar exam is not considered an educational expense; it produces an economic benefit that lasts for more than a year, and hence may be capitalized and amortized and deducted over its useful life—the taxpayer's life expectancy. (*See infra*, §§402, 450.) [**Sharon v. Commissioner,** *supra*]

(b) Deductible educational costs [§342]

Certain kinds of educational costs are deductible, *as long as they do not qualify the taxpayer for a new trade or business* or constitute the *minimum educational requirement* for her job. These include:

(i) *Education that maintains or improves* skills required by the individual in her job or other trade or business; or

(ii) *Education that meets the express requirements* of the individual's employer, or the requirements of law, as a condition to *retention* of a job or an increase in the rate of compensation.

Example: Continuing education courses for lawyers and summer courses for teachers are deductible under this provision.

Compare: An IRS agent who goes to law school cannot deduct the costs on the argument that law school improves her skill as an accountant. Since it is also the minimum educational requirement for a *new* profession, the costs are automatically nondeductible.

(c) Exception—higher-education costs [§343]

A taxpayer can deduct his or his dependent's higher-education costs (tuition and fees) regardless of the purpose of the education. [I.R.C. §222] The deduction is *above the line*, meaning that it can be deducted even if the taxpayer claims the standard deduction. [I.R.C. §62(a)(18); *see infra*, §§553-561] The total costs deductible in 2002 and 2003 are $3,000. No amount is deductible if the taxpayer's AGI exceeds $65,000, or $130,000 on a joint return. In 2004 and 2005, $4,000 is deductible, with the same AGI limits as those in 2002 and 2003. Additionally, $2,000 is deductible if the taxpayer's AGI exceeds $80,000, or $160,000 on a joint return. No amount is deductible if it is claimed under one of the higher-education credits. (*See infra*, §§717-720.) Finally, the deduction for higher-education costs is scheduled to be repealed after 2005. [I.R.C. §222(e)]

(9) Insurance premiums

(a) Property insurance [§344]

The cost of insurance on business *property* is an ordinary and necessary business expense.

(b) Life insurance [§345]

Premiums for insurance on the *life* of an officer or employee are deductible *provided* the taxpayer-employer is *not* the direct or indirect beneficiary of the policy. [I.R.C. §264(a)(1)] If the taxpayer-employer is the beneficiary, the proceeds of the policy are tax-exempt income to the taxpayer-employer, and the expenses allocable to the production of tax-exempt income are not deductible.

1) Note

If the taxpayer-employer is not the beneficiary, so that the premiums may be deductible, the amount of the premium payments will then probably constitute taxable income to the insured (*e.g.*, as additional compensation to the employee-insured; as a dividend to the shareholder-insured, etc.; *see supra*, §135). However, if the insurance is group term life insurance, the employer can deduct premiums and the employees can exclude them to the extent of $50,000 worth of insurance. (*See supra*, §110.)

---

e.g. **Example:** Corporation hires Perry Taxpayer as its president and agrees to pay him $1 million per year and to pay for a $10 million life insurance policy that names Perry's wife as the beneficiary. The life insurance premiums are deductible by the corporation and probably constitute income to Perry (except to the extent they constitute $50,000 of group term life insurance). If the corporation purchased a similar policy naming itself as the beneficiary (to cover potential losses that will arise from changes in leadership after Perry's death), the premiums will not be deductible by the corporation and will not constitute income to Perry.

---

2) Split dollar life insurance [§346]

In split dollar life insurance, the employer pays part of the annual premium of a whole life policy covering the life of the employee, and the employee pays the balance. When the employee dies, the employer receives the cash surrender value of the policy and the employee's beneficiary receives the balance of the payout. Under this arrangement, the employer cannot deduct its premium payments as compensation because it is a partial beneficiary of the policy. Assuming the employee pays the correct proportion of the annual premium, the employee has no income from the arrangement. If the employee pays less than the cost of the insurance protection received during the year, the employee has income in an amount equal to the difference. [Rev. Rul. 64-328, 1964-2 C.B. 11]

(10) Offices at home [§347]

Generally, no business deductions are allowable for part or all of the costs relating to a taxpayer's personal residence. [I.R.C. §280A] (Of course, this does not preclude deduction of qualified residence interest, real estate taxes, or casualty losses, which need not be connected to business or investment.)

(a) Exception for certain business use [§348]

However, costs of a portion of a taxpayer's residence can be deducted if that portion is used *exclusively* [I.R.C. §280A(c)(1)]:

Is the taxpayer considered **an employee**?

YES →

NO ↓

Does the employee maintain a portion of his residence as a "home office" **for the convenience of her employer**?

YES →

NO ↓

Is a portion of the taxpayer's residence used **exclusively** as the taxpayer's **principal place of business**?

YES →

NO ↓

Is a portion of the taxpayer's residence used **exclusively** as a place where the taxpayer **sees clients, patients, etc.,** in the normal course of business?

YES →

NO ↓

Is the "home office" located in a **separate structure** that is used **exclusively** for the taxpayer's **trade or business**?

YES →

NO ↓

Is the portion of the taxpayer's residence used to **store inventory**, and is the residence the **sole fixed location of the business**?

YES →

NO ↓

Is the portion of the taxpayer's residence used as a **daycare facility**?

YES →

NO ↓

No part of the cost of the taxpayer's residence may be deductible as a business expense.

Part of the cost of the taxpayer's residence **may be deductible** as a "business expense."

1) **As the taxpayer's principal place of business** (if the taxpayer has several businesses, the residence qualifies for deductions if it is the principal location of any of the businesses); or

2) **As a place of business used by patients, clients, or customers,** when visiting the taxpayer in the normal course of business; or

3) **In the case of a separate structure not attached to the dwelling,** in connection with the trade or business.

(b) Principal place of business [§349]

The test set forth in section 280A requires a taxpayer with several business locations to establish that her home is the "principal" location.

1) Factors considered [§350]

Two factors are significant when determining whether the taxpayer's at-home office qualifies as her principal place of business: (i) the relative importance of the activities performed at home and elsewhere and (ii) the amount of time spent working at home and elsewhere. [**Commissioner v. Soliman**, 506 U.S. 168 (1993)]

---

e.g. **Example:** A musician spends five hours per day practicing in her home studio (used exclusively for business) and much less time actually performing at different concert halls or movie studios. The court thought that the relative importance of practice and performance were about equal. Thus, the time factor was determinative, and the studio was treated as the principal place of business. [**Popov v. Commissioner**, 246 F.3d 1190 (9th Cir. 2001)]

---

2) Management at home [§351]

A home office qualifies as a principal place of business if it is used to conduct administrative or management activities of the taxpayer's trade or business and there is no other fixed location where such administrative or management activities can be performed. [I.R.C. §280A(c)(1)]

---

e.g. **Example:** An anesthesiologist renders services to patients at a hospital, but performs all of the managerial tasks (such as billing insurance companies) in his home office because the hospital provides no office space. The home office is used exclusively for this purpose. The home office is treated as the taxpayer's principal place of business. [I.R.C. §280A(c)(1)— *superseding* **Commissioner v. Soliman**, *supra*]

(c) Exception for certain other uses [§352]

A taxpayer can deduct the costs of a portion of his residence if that portion is used for storage of an inventory held for sale in his business—but only if the dwelling is the sole fixed location of the business. Also, a portion of the costs can be deducted if the residence is used as a daycare facility. [I.R.C. §280A(c)(2), (4)]

(d) Employees [§353]

If a taxpayer is an employee, there is an *additional* requirement: The exclusive use of the residence must be for the *convenience of the employer*. [I.R.C. §280A(c)(1); *and see supra*, §§113-116] For example, if no space is provided at work for necessary tasks, the home office would serve the convenience of the employer. [**Drucker v. Commissioner**, 715 F.2d 69 (2d Cir. 1983)—concert violinist's home practice studio deductible because no practice space available at concert hall]

(e) Investors [§354]

The management of investments is not a trade or business. Therefore, a taxpayer cannot deduct any portion of a home office used exclusively to manage an investment portfolio—even though he does it 40 hours per week. [**Moller v. United States**, 721 F.2d 810 (Fed. Cir. 1983), *cert. denied*, 467 U.S. 1251 (1984)] Most of the costs of investing, such as subscriptions to business periodicals, are deductible under I.R.C. section 212 (*infra*, §§437-445) but not the costs of a home office. *Moller* distinguished the case of a *trader* in securities, who might be in a trade or business. The difference between an "investor" and a "trader" is that a trader looks to quick turnover and short-term profits rather than to long-term profits or to earning dividends and interest. [*See* **Estate of Yaeger v. Commissioner**, 889 F.2d 29 (2d Cir. 1989)]

(f) Limitation on the amount deductible [§355]

Even if the taxpayer falls within one of the exceptions, he cannot deduct any more than the gross income from such use, less the deductions (*e.g.*, qualified residence interest or property tax) allowed without regard to business. [I.R.C. §280A(c)(5)]

(11) Vacation homes [§356]

Section 280A imposes limitations on deductions with regard to dwellings that are rented out. There are two rules: (i) deductions must be *prorated between personal and rental use*, and (ii) if the dwelling is "*used as a residence*," business and investment deductions are *limited to income generated by the property*.

(a) Caution—some items may be otherwise deductible [§357]

Deductions that need not be connected to profit-making activities—*e.g.*, qualified residence interest, property tax, or casualty losses—are deductible in full.

(b) "Used as a residence" defined [§358]

A dwelling is used *as a residence* if it is used for *personal purposes* by any of its owners, or their relatives, for more than 14 days *or* more than 10% of the days it was rented at a fair rental, whichever figure is greater. [I.R.C. §280A(d)]

Example: Bob lived in his ski condominium seven days last year. He rented it (at a fair rental) to nonfamily members for 40 days. Since he did not use it for the greater of 14 days or 10% of the rented days (four days), he did not use it "as a residence."

Compare: Alice and Sally own a beach house as tenants in common. Alice used it one day, Sally eight days, and Sally's daughter six days. It was rented to others (at a fair rental) for 85 days. Since personal use for 15 days exceeds the greater of 14 or 8.5 days (10% of 85), the house was "used as a residence."

1) Exception [§359]

If the dwelling is rented for at least one year, the taxpayer's personal use before or after the rental period is ignored. Similarly, if the dwelling is sold at the end of the rental period, personal use before the rental period is disregarded. [I.R.C. §280A(d)(3)]

2) Exception [§360]

A dwelling is not "used as a residence" if rented at a fair rental to a relative of the owner as the occupant's principal residence. [I.R.C. §280A(d)(3)]

(c) Proration [§361]

If the dwelling was used at all for personal purposes (*whether or not* it was "used as a residence," *supra*, §358), the various expenses (other than qualified residence interest on a second home or property taxes) must be *prorated*. Only the portion allocable to rental use is deductible. [I.R.C. §280A(e)]

Example: Thus in Bob's case above, 40/47th of the expenses (other than qualified residence interest or taxes) is deductible as that is the amount attributable to rental use.

Example: In the case of Alice and Sally (*supra*), 85/100th of the expenses (other than qualified residence interest or taxes) would be deductible, but in their case, there is an additional limitation (*see* below).

(d) Limitation on amount [§362]

The expenses prorated to rental use are deductible only in part if the dwelling was "used as a residence." In that case, the owners cannot deduct more than the gross rental income less a prorated share of the qualified residence interest and taxes.

Example: This limitation does not apply to Bob (*supra*), since the ski condominium was not "used as a residence."

Compare: This limitation does apply to Alice (*supra*). Assume that her share of the qualified residence interest and taxes for the year is $1,200 and 85/100th of her share of the other expenses (such as depreciation and repairs) is $2,000. Her share of gross rentals is $2,800. She can deduct all of the qualified residence interest and taxes. In addition, she can deduct only $1,600 of the remaining expenses (*i.e.*, $2,800 less $1,200). [I.R.C. §280A(c)(5)]

(e) Special rule for limited rental use [§363]

If a dwelling unit is rented fewer than 15 days during the year, no deductions are allowed and the income from rental is not included in gross income. [I.R.C. §280A(g)]

> **EXAM TIP**   **gilbert**
>
> Remember that if the vacation home is rented out for *fewer than 15 days* per year, *neither income nor expenses* are taken into account.

(12) Clothing [§364]

Most clothing costs are not deductible because clothing bought for business use (like a three-piece suit) can be used for nonwork purposes. However, if the clothing *cannot appropriately be worn for nonbusiness purposes* (*e.g.*, a firefighter's uniform), its cost is deductible. [*See* **Pevsner v. Commissioner**, 628 F.2d 467 (5th Cir. 1980)—designer clothes not deductible since they could be worn on the street even though taxpayer's lifestyle precluded such use]

c. Current expense vs. capital outlay [§365]

To be deductible as a business expense, the item must be an *expense*, as distinguished from a *capital outlay*. A capital outlay is expressly not deductible. [I.R.C. §263]

(1) Test [§366]

The distinction between an "expense" and a "capital outlay" is often difficult to draw. Generally, an expenditure should be treated as of a *capital* nature if it brings about the *acquisition of an asset or some advantage to the taxpayer having a useful life in excess of one year*. [Treas. Reg. §1.263(a)] In that situation, the taxpayer has purchased an *asset*, not incurred an expense. The business cost can be deducted through depreciation, loss, depletion, or bad debt (all discussed *infra*) but not as a business expense.

(a) Caution—distinguish "capitalization" from "capital assets" [§367]

Do not confuse "capitalization" with "capital assets." A capital asset is one which, when sold, qualifies for capital gain or loss treatment. (*See infra*, §§821 *et seq.*) But expenditures must be "capitalized" if they create an asset or advantage lasting beyond the taxable year—whether or not they produce a "capital asset." [**Georator Corp. v. United States**, 485 F.2d 283 (4th Cir. 1973), *cert. denied*, 417 U.S. 945 (1974)]

(2) Purpose of rule [§368]

The idea of capitalization is to match up income with the costs of earning that income. Outlays that produce long-term benefits must be capitalized, not deducted, in order to match the costs with future income that they will produce. [**Encyclopedia Britannica v. Commissioner**, 685 F.2d 212 (7th Cir. 1982)—publisher must capitalize cost of acquiring manuscript] A factor to be considered in a close case is whether the item is recurring as opposed to extraordinary; recurring items are more likely to be expenses. Another factor is whether the administrative burden of allocating costs to particular assets outweighs the benefit of improved matching. [**Encyclopedia Britannica v. Commissioner**, *supra*]

(3) Future benefit [§369]

An outlay must be capitalized if it produces significant long-term benefits. [**INDOPCO, Inc. v. Commissioner**, 503 U.S. 79 (1992)]

(a) "Long-term benefit" does not have to be an asset [§370]

In *INDOPCO*, a corporation incurred substantial costs in arranging to be taken over in a friendly corporate acquisition. This takeover was expected to produce important long-term benefits for the corporation because of the superior financial strength of the acquiring corporation. Additionally, the takeover reduced the number of public shareholders by 3,500, saving the corporation substantial expenses in dealing with the shareholders by 3,500. The Supreme Court rejected the idea that an outlay had to produce some specific, identifiable asset in order to be capitalized rather than deducted. The costs of arranging the takeover did not produce any specific asset, but they did produce long-term benefits for the corporation that were more than "incidental." That was sufficient to require the costs to be capitalized.

(b) Distinguishing *INDOPCO* [§371]

The exact scope of *INDOPCO* is very uncertain. Several cases have distinguished *INDOPCO* and did not require the taxpayer to capitalize certain expenses.

1) *Wells Fargo* case [§372]

In **Wells Fargo & Co. v. Commissioner,** 224 F.3d 874 (8th Cir. 2000), officers of the company spent time evaluating and negotiating a friendly takeover. The IRS required the acquired company to capitalize the salaries that it paid to its officers while they worked on the acquisition, but the court held that the salaries were deductible, and it distinguished *INDOPCO.* The court observed that the officers' salaries were regular and recurring costs that would have been paid notwithstanding the acquisition. The salaries were "merely incidental" to the future benefit to be obtained through the acquisition. Moreover, the salaries would have been difficult to allocate between work on the acquisition and other work. The court also held that legal expenses for the proposed transaction were deductible up to the time that the companies entered into a definitive agreement; and that legal fees incurred after that date must be capitalized.

2) *PNC Bancorp* case [§373]

In **PNC Bancorp, Inc. v. Commissioner,** 212 F.3d 822 (3d Cir. 2000), a bank incurred various costs (*e.g.,* investigating borrowers) in making loans. Some of the costs included payments to outsiders for such items as property reports and appraisals, while other costs included such items as the regular salaries of employees. For financial reporting purposes, the bank must capitalize these costs as part of the acquisition cost of valuable assets (the loans made by the bank). However, the court held these costs were deductible for tax purposes because they were ordinary, recurring expenses in operating the bank.

(c) Ramifications [§374]

The *INDOPCO* case casts doubt on many lower court decisions in which the courts allowed expensing, rather than capitalization, of business expansion costs because the costs did not yield a separate and distinct asset (despite the fact that they produced a long-term benefit). [*See, e.g.,* **Briarcliff Candy Corp. v. Commissioner,** 475 F.2d 775 (2d Cir. 1973)] On the other hand, *Wells Fargo* and *PNC*

Bancorp suggest that cases such as *Briarcliff* were correctly decided. The Supreme Court may have to reconsider this area in order to make clear how far *INDOPCO* was intended to reach.

(d) Resisting a hostile takeover [§375]

The costs of unsuccessfully resisting a hostile takeover are deductible because these costs do not produce a long-term benefit and cannot be defined as the costs associated with facilitating a capital transaction. Instead, such costs are incurred in defending the business against attack, which makes them currently deductible. [**A.E. Staley Manufacturing Co. v. Commissioner,** 119 F.3d 482 (7th Cir. 1997)]

(4) Repairs of property vs. capital improvement to property [§376]

Maintenance and repair costs are "current expenses," and hence entirely deductible in the year paid. [Treas. Reg. §1.162-4] This rule was not altered by the *INDOPCO* case, *supra*. [Rev. Rul. 94-12, 1994-1 C.B. 36] However, what is a "repair" and what is an "improvement" could be at issue.

(a) Capital improvements [§377]

If the "repairs" actually make the property more valuable than it was originally, or make it suitable for a different use, or extend its useful life beyond what it was originally, the cost is regarded as a capital improvement, not an expense. [Treas. Reg. §1.162-4]

(b) Environmental remediation costs [§378]

Taxpayers may deduct certain environmental cleanup costs that would otherwise have to be capitalized. [I.R.C. §198] These are expenditures incurred in connection with the abatement or control of hazardous substances at a qualified contaminated site. A qualified site is one that a state environmental official has certified as located in an area where there has been a release (or threatened release) of a hazardous substance on the site. Additionally, the site must be in a targeted area, meaning one with a poverty rate of at least 20%, an empowerment zone, or a site announced as being included in a brownfields pilot project of the Environmental Protection Agency.

(c) Nonstatutory authority for deduction of environmental remediation costs [§379]

Section 198 apparently does not erase a series of rulings and cases that allowed deductions for certain environmental cleanup costs. Under this authority, cleanup costs which do not meet the precise definitions of section 198 may still be deductible because the cleanup restores the property to the value it had before the problem arose (but does not otherwise significantly enhance the value of the property).

[**Midland Empire Packing Co. v. Commissioner,** 14 T.C. 635 (1950)—cost of installing concrete basement to stop oil seepage is currently deductible repair; Rev. Rul. 94-38, 1994-1 C.B. 35—costs of removing toxic substances from land and groundwater are deductible]

(5) Property produced or sold by taxpayer [§380]

A taxpayer must capitalize all of the direct or indirect costs of producing property. [I.R.C. §263A]

(a) Direct cost [§381]

The direct cost of producing property is the materials and labor consumed in producing it.

(b) Interest [§382]

A taxpayer is required to capitalize any interest incurred during the production period that is allocable to produced property. [I.R.C. §263A(f)—applies only to property with a long useful life or a long production period]

(c) Overhead [§383]

Section 263A requires capitalization of various items of "overhead," such as the rent or depreciation on buildings and equipment used to produce property. [*See* **Commissioner v. Idaho Power Co.,** 418 U.S. 1 (1974)—depreciation on construction machinery cannot be deducted but must be added to the basis of produced property]

Example: The costs of designing a package for a new product must be capitalized under section 263A. Since these costs will benefit sales for both the current and future years, the IRS will allow amortization of the costs over an arbitrary five-year period. [Rev. Rul. 89-23, 1989-1 C.B. 85; Rev. Proc. 89-17, 1989-1 C.B. 827]

(d) Property acquired for resale [§384]

The rules of section 263A also apply to property acquired for resale, but only if the taxpayer has average annual gross receipts of at least $10 million. [I.R.C. §263A(b)(2)] For example, if the taxpayer has gross receipts above $10 million, he would have to add to the basis of his inventory (rather than deduct) the cost of guards or storage of the inventory.

(e) Exception for authors [§385]

The mandatory capitalization rules of section 263A do not apply to the "qualified creative expense" of individual authors, artists, and photographers. Thus, for example, research costs for an uncompleted book can be deducted rather than capitalized. [I.R.C. §263A(h)]

(6) Capitalization of rental payments [§386]

Rental payments for the use of property belonging to another are a deductible business expense unless they must be capitalized as part of the cost of production. [I.R.C. §§162(a)(3), 263A—*see supra*, §§380 *et seq*.] However, deductions for lease payments for automobiles used in business, or for home computers, are limited in amount. They cannot exceed the amounts that would be deductible as depreciation if the car or computer were purchased rather than rented. [I.R.C. §280F(c); *see infra*, §§478 *et seq*.]

(a) Prepayments [§387]

Prepayments of rent in excess of one year *cannot* be deducted currently. They must be capitalized because they create an asset having a useful life extending into future years. [**University Properties, Inc. v. Commissioner,** 45 T.C. 416 (1966); *and see infra*, §999]

(b) Lease vs. sale [§388]

"Rental" payments that are in reality payments on the *purchase price* of the asset are treated similarly; *i.e.,* when the form of the transaction is a lease but its substance is a *purchase*, no "expense" deduction is allowed.

1) Determinative factors [§389]

While not conclusive, the courts are apt to treat the lease *as a sale* if:

(i) The payments are *higher than normal rent* for the property involved;

(ii) The amount of "rental" payments over the term of the lease *equals the value of the property plus financing charges*; or

(iii) The "lessee" has the *option to acquire title* at the end of the "lease" for *only a nominal payment*.

[**Starr's Estate v. Commissioner,** 274 F.2d 294 (9th Cir. 1959)]

2) Tax consequences [§390]

In such cases, the "rental" payments are not deductible. However, the taxpayer may capitalize his investment and recover the cost through depreciation over the useful life of the property involved (*see infra*, §§455-460). He might also be able to show that part of the payments were deductible interest.

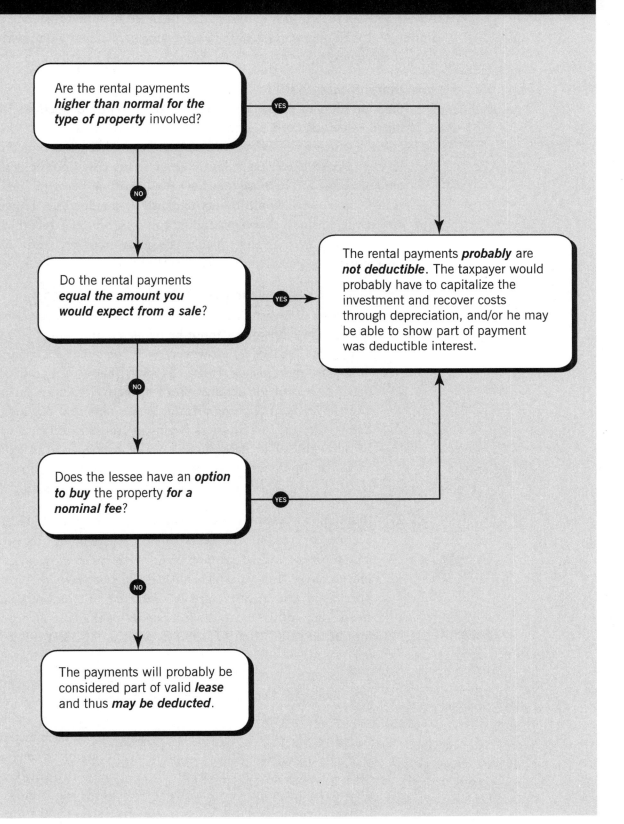

(7) Capitalization of acquisition costs [§391]

Amounts paid to *purchase* a business or asset (tangible or intangible) are clearly capital outlays and not deductible. [**Woodward v. Commissioner,** 397 U.S. 572 (1970)—costs of litigation incurred in acquiring stock from minority stockholders under state law must be capitalized along with the cost of the stock]

(a) Start-up costs [§392]

Start-up costs of a new business are not currently deductible. [**Richmond Television Corp. v. United States,** 345 F.2d 901 (4th Cir. 1965)—costs of starting new television business before license obtained must be capitalized] Under prior law, start-up costs could not be depreciated or amortized because they have no determinable useful life. As a result, these costs would be permanently nondeductible. However, an existing business that is expanding could currently deduct the costs of expansion. To partially equalize the situation of new and existing businesses, Congress enacted section 195.

1) Scope of I.R.C. section 195 [§393]

The costs of investigating a new business and the costs of starting up a new business cannot be deducted and must be capitalized. [I.R.C. §195(a)] However, such costs may be *amortized over a five-year period*. [I.R.C. §195(b)] The costs of investigating the creation or acquisition of an active trade or business, and the costs of creating a trade or business that are incurred before the trade or business begins operations and that would be allowable as a current deduction if incurred by an existing trade or business, may be amortized under section 195. [I.R.C.§195(c)]

2) Distinction between investigation and purchase costs [§394]

Section 195 covers the costs of deciding whether to enter a new business and which new business to enter. However, once the taxpayer decides which business to purchase, the costs of purchasing the business are not covered by section 195. Instead, they must be capitalized as part of the cost of purchasing the assets of that business. [Rev. Rul. 99-23, 1999-1 C.B. 998]

---

e.g. Example: U Corp. hired an investment banker to evaluate the purchase of a new business. The banker considered various industries and zeroed in on one of them. He then evaluated several businesses within that industry. So far, these investigatory costs are covered by section 195—the costs must be capitalized, but they may be amortized over a five-year period. The banker then decided that V Corp. was the best bet and appraised

V Corp.'s assets to determine the purchase price. Ultimately, U purchased V. The costs that were incurred after the investment banker had decided that V Corp. was the best bet are not covered by section 195 and must be capitalized as part of the cost of purchasing V Corp. [Rev. Rul. 99-23, *supra*]

---

3) Exceptions [§395]

The ban on deducting start-up costs does not apply to business interest, deductible taxes (such as property or state income taxes), or research and experimentation expenditures. [I.R.C. §195(c)(1); for discussion of research and experimentation expenditures, *see infra*, §401]

(b) Unsuccessful searches [§396]

The cost of investigating a business opportunity by one not yet in business is not deductible if the deal falls through. [**Frank v. Commissioner,** 20 T.C. 511 (1953)] Moreover, the IRS takes the position that the costs of unsuccessfully trying to buy a business cannot even be added to the basis of a different business that the taxpayer successfully locates later on. [Rev. Rul. 57-418, 1957-2 C.B. 143]

1) Effect of I.R.C. section 195 [§397]

It is not clear what effect I.R.C. section 195 will have on the cost of unsuccessful business investigation. If the taxpayer never finds a business, no amortization would be permitted. However, arguably, if the taxpayer ultimately finds a business, he could capitalize and amortize all the costs of investigation, including the deals that fell through. Clearly, he can amortize the cost of investigating and acquiring the business he actually buys.

(c) Finding employment [§398]

Fees paid to employment agencies are deductible, whether or not a job was actually found. However, the costs of looking for one's *first* job in his trade or business are not deductible—only the costs connected with subsequent jobs. The IRS has also cautioned that expenses are not deductible "where there is a substantial lack of continuity" between the time of a previous job and the beginning of a new job search. [Rev. Rul. 75-120, 1975-1 C.B. 55; **Cremona v. Commissioner,** 58 T.C. 219 (1972)]

1) Distinguish—running for office [§399]

The costs of running for office, even for reelection, are not deductible on the theory that they are costs of obtaining a new position. Neither can such expenses be amortized over the term of office. This rule seems to be based on the notion that the tax system should not subsidize the expenses of wealthy people in running for office. [**McDonald v. Commissioner**, 323 U.S. 57 (1944)]

2) Criticism

This position seems inconsistent with the rule that fees paid to employment agencies are deductible, but the Fifth Circuit felt it must adhere to the *McDonald* rule until the Supreme Court changes it. [**Nichols v. Commissioner**, 511 F.2d 618 (5th Cir. 1975)—en banc decision with five dissenters]

(d) Corporate organization and reorganization [§400]

Legal fees in connection with the *organization* of a business (*e.g.*, incorporation and stock issuance) are deemed capital outlays, which cannot be deducted currently. Legal expenses in corporate reorganizations [**Bush Terminal v. Commissioner**, 7 T.C. 793 (1946)] and the costs of facilitating a corporate takeover [**INDOPCO, Inc. v. Commissioner**, *supra*, §369] are also capital outlays. However, corporate organization expenses can be amortized over an arbitrary five-year period [I.R.C. §248], as can the costs of organizing an unincorporated business [I.R.C. §195; *and see supra*, §393].

(e) Patents, copyrights, trademarks [§401]

Although the cost of *purchasing* patents, copyrights, and trademarks is clearly a capital outlay [Treas. Reg. §1.263(a)], research and experimental expenditures incurred by the taxpayer in creating his own patents, copyrights, etc., may be deducted currently [I.R.C. §174].

EXAM TIP   gilbert

On your exam, note that the election to deduct research and experimentation costs is an **exception** to the "current expense" vs. "capital outlay" rule, since the costs of research and experimentation often result in acquisition of an asset having a useful life longer than one year.

---

1) Note

The benefit of I.R.C. section 174 is available even to a taxpayer with a new invention that has not yet produced any income and thus is not yet a trade or business. [**Snow v. Commissioner**, 416 U.S. 500 (1974)]

2) And note

In addition to the deduction under I.R.C. section 174, there is a *credit* for increased research and experimentation. To compute the credit, take the current year's research expense and compare it to the average for the three preceding years. The credit is 25% of the excess. [I.R.C. §44F]

(f) Bar exam [§402]

The cost of taking the bar exam must be capitalized rather than deducted. It can be amortized over the lawyer's estimated life. [**Sharon v. Commissioner,** *supra,* §341]

(g) Selling costs [§403]

Commissions paid on the sale of property are not deductible as expenses. However, they decrease the amount realized on the sale and thus decrease the gain (or increase the loss) on the sale of the asset.

(h) Acquiring goodwill [§404]

The cost of acquiring goodwill in a new business is a nondeductible capital expenditure. [Treas. Reg. §1.263(a)]

Example: Taxpayer took over a defunct business and paid off the debts of the prior owners for the purpose of acquiring the goodwill of customers. It was held that these expenditures were capital, not expense, because they were in effect the purchase of goodwill. It was also held that they were not "ordinary" (*see infra,* §409). [**Welch v. Helvering,** 290 U.S. 111 (1933)]

---

1) Tax treatment [§405]

Purchased goodwill can be amortized over a 15-year period. [I.R.C. §197; *see infra,* §456]

2) Distinguish—preserving goodwill [§406]

But amounts paid for the *protection or improvement* of the goodwill of a going business (*e.g.,* advertising expenses or public relations) are deductible. [**Dunn & McCarthy, Inc. v. Commissioner,** 139 F.2d 242 (2d Cir. 1943)]

(i) Short-term prepayments [§407]

Frequently, taxpayers pay for items in one year that last until sometime during the following year. If a payment is routine and recurring, it does not have to be capitalized, and it may be entirely deducted in the year in which it is made. [*See,* **U.S. Freightways Corp. v. Commissioner,** 270 F.3d 1137 (7th Cir. 2001)—licenses and insurance payments beginning in one year and lasting into the following year are currently deductible; *see infra,* §§998-1001, for further discussion of prepayments]

CAPITALIZATION VS. DEDUCTION

COST	RULE
REPAIR TO PROPERTY	If property's *useful life or value is increased*, the associated cost must be capitalized. Otherwise, cost is deductible as a current expense.
ENVIRONMENTAL CLEANUP	*Specifically deductible* under section 198 (if conditions met). If conditions not met, could still be deductible *as repair*.
PROPERTY PRODUCED OR SOLD BY TAXPAYER	Direct costs (cost of producing property—*e.g.,* materials and labor) and indirect costs (*e.g.,* overhead) must be *capitalized*.
PROPERTY ACQUIRED FOR RESALE	If the taxpayer has gross receipts of more than $10 million, the cost of maintaining the property is *added to the property's basis*.
RENTAL PAYMENTS	Rental payments are generally *deductible*.
ACQUISITION OF BUSINESS, START-UP OF BUSINESS; SEARCHING FOR NEW BUSINESS	"Investigating" a new business *must be capitalized* and may be amortized over a five-year period. Once decision is made to pursue business, costs must be capitalized.
FINDING EMPLOYMENT	Costs of finding *first job* are *not deductible*. Thereafter, they *may be deductible*—assuming there isn't a long break in employment.
CORPORATE ORGANIZATION, REORGANIZATION	Capital outlay *amortized* over a five-year period.
PATENTS, COPYRIGHTS, AND TRADEMARKS	Costs of *buying* these items are *capitalized*. Costs of *developing* them are *deducted*.
GOODWILL	Capital outlay that is *amortized* over a 15-year period.
SHORT-TERM PREPAYMENT	May be deducted entirely in year it was paid, assuming prepayment is *routine and recurring* and covers no more than one year.

d. "Ordinary and necessary" expense [§408]

Even if the expense is of a business (rather than personal) nature, and is a current (rather than a capital) item, to be deductible it must be both "ordinary and necessary" in the taxpayer's business.

(1) "Ordinary and necessary" defined [§409]

The terms "ordinary" and "necessary" are given a broad but vague interpretation. An expense is "ordinary" if other businesses in the community, confronted with the same problem, would incur the same type of expense. "Necessary" means that the expense is appropriate or helpful to the business. [**Welch v. Helvering,** *supra,* §404]

EXAM TIP   **gilbert**

On your exam, be sure to remember that an "ordinary and necessary" expense is one (i) that *other businesses would incur* if confronted with a similar problem and (ii) that is *appropriate or helpful* to the taxpayer's business.

(a) Note

The standard of what is "ordinary and necessary" is "not a rule of law; it is rather a way of life. Life in all its fullness must supply the answer to the riddle." [**Welch v. Helvering,** *supra*]

(2) Determinative factors [§410]

The following are the chief factors relied on by the courts in determining whether a claimed expense is in fact "ordinary and necessary."

(a) Voluntariness of payment [§411]

People in business ordinarily make only those payments they are required to make. Hence, a payment made without legal obligation may not be "ordinary and necessary."

---

e.g. **Example:** Taxpayer, an attorney, represented that his client would deposit certain funds in court; when the client failed to come up with the funds, the attorney made the deposit on his client's behalf. Since this was a voluntary payment, it was not "ordinary," and hence could not be deducted as a business expense. [**Friedman v. Delaney,** 171 F.2d 269 (1st Cir. 1948), *cert. denied,* 336 U.S. 936 (1949)]

---

1) Voluntary payments could be deductible [§412]

However, voluntariness does not always disqualify a payment as a deductible business expense—as when an obvious business advantage was gained thereby (*e.g.,* corporate-taxpayer pays off debts of one of its officers in order to preserve corporate goodwill). [**Pepper v. Commissioner,** 36 T.C. 886 (1961), *and see supra,* §295]

(b) Customariness of payment [§413]

The more common the payment in the trade, the more likely it will be deductible. However, an expense may be unusual and nonrecurring, but still be "ordinary and necessary"— *e.g.,* heavy counsel fees and litigation expenses are customary in the business world, even though the taxpayer may encounter them only once in a lifetime. [**Commissioner v. Tellier,** 383 U.S. 687 (1966)]

(c) Unsavoriness [§414]

Occasionally, courts seem to hold that an expense is not "ordinary" or "necessary" because they find it reprehensible, even though it does not fall within the public policy rules (*see infra,* §424). [**Car-Ron Asphalt Paving Co. v. Commissioner,** 758 F.2d 1132 (6th Cir. 1985)—legal kickbacks not "necessary"; *but see* **Raymond Bertolini Trucking Co. v. Commissioner,** 736 F.2d 1120 (6th Cir. 1984)—different panel holds legal kickbacks "ordinary"; IRS had conceded they were "necessary"]

(3) Compensation [§415]

Compensation costs for services rendered are deductible, but only if "reasonable." [I.R.C. §162(a)(1)]

(a) Reasonableness of compensation—in general [§416]

The reasonableness of salaries or other compensation to executives is often a matter of litigation. For example, corporate taxpayers (particularly closely held corporations) frequently attempt to deduct as business expenses huge salaries paid to executives who are also shareholders of the corporation. The issue in such cases is whether the salary payments are compensation for services or are really nondeductible *constructive dividends*. [**Nor-Cal Adjusters v. Commissioner,** 503 F.2d 359 (9th Cir. 1974)]

1) Note

On rare occasions, the IRS attacks as unreasonable the compensation of an employee other than a stockholder or a relative of a stockholder. These attacks have been upheld by the courts, even though the compensation in such cases could not be a constructive dividend. [**Harold's Club v. Commissioner,** 340 F.2d 861 (9th Cir. 1965); **Patton v. Commissioner,** 168 F.2d 28 (6th Cir. 1948)]

(b) **Determining "reasonableness" [§417]**

The main questions in such cases are the *value* of the services rendered to the business and what *similar businesses are paying* for like services. [Treas. Reg. §1.162-7]

1) **Salary based on percentage of income [§418]**

The fact that a salary is based on a percentage of income (or net profits) is suspicious, because of the resemblance to a dividend. However, in some cases, a percentage contract has been found *reasonable when entered into*; consequently, the salary payments were deductible even though in later years the percentage resulted in payment of more than the replacement value of the services. [**Rogers v. United States**, 340 F.2d 861 (9th Cir. 1965); Treas. Reg. §1.162-7(b)(2)] However, if the percentage contract was not the result of a "free bargain," it cannot be used to validate the reasonableness of large salary payments in later years. [**Harold's Club v. Commissioner**, *supra*—agreement between sons and their father, who was the "brains of the operation"]

2) **Independent investor test [§419]**

Several courts have employed an "independent investor" test rather than the vague multifactor balancing test. Under the "independent investor" approach, the amount of reasonable compensation is the amount that a hypothetical independent investor would choose to pay for the services, given the return on equity enjoyed by that investor after paying for the services. [**Exacto Spring Corp. v. Commissioner**, 196 F.3d 833 (7th Cir. 1999); **Dexsil Corp. v. Commissioner**, 147 F.3d 96 (2d Cir. 1998)] Thus, if the hypothetical independent investor is earning a very high rate of return on equity even after he pays very high salaries, the salaries are presumptively reasonable.

3) **Salary unrelated to value of services [§420]**

"Salary" payments that bear *no real relationship to value* of services have been disallowed. For example, an end-of-year discretionary bonus paid to a doctor-shareholder of a professional service association was held a "constructive dividend" where the total "salary" exceeded the *gross billings* for his services. [**Klamath Medical Service Bureau v. Commissioner**, 261 F.2d 842 (9th Cir. 1959)]

4) **Agreement to return unreasonable salary [§421]**

An agreement that the salary will be returned to the corporation if found to be unreasonable may suggest that the salary actually is unreasonable. [**Saia Electric Inc. v. Commissioner,** T.C.M. 1974-390] Under such an agreement, the employee is allowed to deduct salary repayments, if the agreement to return the salaries was made at or before the time the salary was paid. [**Oswald v. Commissioner,** 49 T.C. 645 (1968)] (*See infra,* §1068, for application of I.R.C. section 1341 to this situation.)

(c) Effect where salary represents distribution of profits [§422]

A few cases indicate that even though a salary is reasonable, a deduction will still be disallowed to the extent that the employee-shareholder *has not received a reasonable return* on his investment in stock of the corporation [**McCandless Tire Service v. United States,** 422 F.2d 1336 (Ct. Cl. 1970)], or that the payment otherwise resembles a dividend [**Nor-Cal Adjusters v. Commissioner,** *supra*].

(d) Salaries in excess of $1 million per year [§423]

A publicly held corporation cannot deduct remuneration (including most noncash compensation) in excess of $1 million per year to its chief executive officer or to one of its four most highly compensated executives. *Exception:* The employer can deduct such payments if they are payable on a commission basis on account of income generated by the employee or in certain other cases in which compensation is based on attainment of performance goals. [I.R.C. §162(m)]

e. Public policy limitation [§424]

Although formerly a matter of case law, I.R.C. section 162 now specifically disallows the deduction of certain expense items because the deduction would be contrary to public policy. These are the *only categories* of expenses that are disallowed; the courts cannot create new ones.

(1) Bribes to government employees [§425]

No deduction is allowed for any *illegal* bribe or kickback to any official or employee of *any government*. [I.R.C. §162(c)(1)] Additionally, no deduction is allowed for payments to a foreign official if the payment violates the Foreign Corrupt Practices Act of 1977. [15 U.S.C. §78]

(2) Other illegal payments [§426]

No deduction is allowed for any other *illegal* bribe, kickback, or other payment to anyone. The illegality can be established by a federal, state, or local *criminal law* or by a statute or rule that would subject the payor to *loss of license or privilege of doing business*. However, if a state statute or regulation (rather than a federal provision) is in issue, the IRS must prove by clear and convincing evidence that it is *generally enforced* before the deduction can be disallowed. [I.R.C. §162(c)(2); *see* **Boucher v. Commissioner,** 77 T.C. 214 (1981)—state law against insurance premium discounting was "generally enforced" even though there had been no prosecutions because of lack of aggressive law enforcement]

Example: An employment agency advertised for jobs and indicated sex preferences. Although this violated the Civil Rights Act of 1964, the cost was deductible because the statute does not provide for criminal penalties or the loss of license to engage in a trade or business for making payment to the newspaper. [Rev. Rul. 74-323, 1974-2 C.B. 66] (This point might have been decided differently under prior law (below), since the payments might have been viewed as frustrating sharply defined public policies.)

(a) Medical kickbacks [§427]

The Code provides for automatic nondeductibility of kickbacks or bribes by providers of services paid for under Medicare or Medicaid—whether or not they violate state law. [I.R.C. §162(c)(3)]

(b) Drug dealers [§428]

The Code also bars deductions or credits for any amount paid by illegal drug dealers. [I.R.C. §280E]

(c) Exception—reduction in sales price of goods [§429]

The disallowance of deductions for illegal payments does *not* apply to illegal rebates. As a result, a seller of goods or services who illegally rebates part of the purchase price back to the buyer can reduce gross income by the amount of the rebate. [**Sobel Liquors, Inc. v. Commissioner,** 628 F.2d 670 (9th Cir. 1980); Rev. Rul. 82-149, 1982-2 C.B. 56]

(d) Prior law [§430]

The prior law on illegal payments was confusing. Unethical kickbacks were allowed as deductions, even though contrary to good medical practice. [**Lilly v. Commissioner,** 343 U.S. 90 (1952)] Illegal rent payments by a bookie were also allowed. [**Commissioner v. Sullivan,** 356 U.S. 27 (1958)] But more unsavory payments, such as bribes or kickbacks, were not allowed if they violated state law. [**Boyle, Flagg & Seaman, Inc. v. Commissioner,** 25 T.C. 43 (1955)]

(3) Fines [§431]

No deduction is allowed for any fine or similar penalty (criminal or civil) paid to a government for the violation of any law. [I.R.C. §162(f)] Note that this provision does not disallow deduction of a payment to a victim of crime rather than to the government. [*See* **Stephens v. Commissioner,**

905 F.2d 667 (2d Cir. 1990)—restitution payment to an embezzlement victim imposed as condition of probation deductible under section 162 since not paid to government] Note also that attorneys' fees incurred in resisting criminal sanctions related to an illegal business are deductible. [**Commissioner v. Tellier,** *supra*, §413]

(a) Prior law [§432]

The rule concerning fines was the same under prior law—it did not matter whether the violation was intentional or negligent, or whether the taxpayer had to commit the crime to stay in business. [**Tank Truck Rentals, Inc. v. Commissioner,** 356 U.S. 30 (1958)]

(4) Appearance with respect to legislation [§433]

In general, no deduction is allowed for any payments relating to the political campaign of a candidate for public office or to any attempt to influence the general public about legislative matters, elections, or referendums. [I.R.C. §162(e)(2); **Southern Pacific Transportation Co. v. Commissioner,** 90 T.C. 771 (1988)—no deduction for costs of seeking to influence voters on ballot propositions]

(a) Lobbying [§434]

Similarly, no deduction is allowed for any amount incurred to influence legislation, including the cost of direct communication with high officials of the federal executive branch intended to influence the official position of the officials. The ban on deducting lobbying expenses does not apply to attempts to influence local legislation (such as city or county government ordinances), but it does apply to attempts to influence state and federal legislation. The same ban applies to the deduction of an appropriate portion of dues paid to organizations engaged in lobbying. There is a de minimis provision for in-house expenditures up to $2,000 (in-house expenditures do not include payments to lobbyists or dues to lobbying organizations). [I.R.C. §162(e)]

(5) Damage payments [§435]

Civil penalties (such as double damage wage payments for violation of the Fair Labor Standards Act) paid to persons *other* than a government generally are deductible.

(a) Distinguish—antitrust violations [§436]

If a taxpayer is convicted of a criminal *antitrust violation* (or pleads nolo contendere), and later makes damage payments to the persons harmed by the antitrust violation, two-thirds of those payments are not deductible. [I.R.C. §162(g)]

Is the activity a *"trade or business"*? Look for: (i) expectation of profit; (ii) regularity of operation; and (iii) taxpayer actively pursuing activity.

NO →

The expense may *not be deducted as a "business expense."*

↓ **YES**

Is it a *business*, not personal, expense?

NO →

↓ **YES**

Does the expense relate to an *acquisition of an asset* or bring some *advantage to the taxpayer having a useful life of more than one year*?

YES →

The expense is a *"capital outlay,"* and may not be deducted as a "business expense" but could possibly be deducted as depreciation, loss, depletion, or bad debt.

↓ **NO**

Is the expense *"ordinary and necessary"*— *i.e.,* do other businesses in the community incur the same type of expense *and* is the expense appropriate or helpful to the business?

NO →

↓ **YES**

Does a *public policy limitation* apply?

YES →

↓ **NO**

The expense *may be deducted as a "business expense."*

2. "Nonbusiness" Expenses—Expenses for Production of Income

a. General rule [§437]

An *individual* taxpayer is entitled to deduct expenses paid or incurred [I.R.C. §212]:

(1) *For the production* or collection of income;

(2) *For the management, conservation, or maintenance of property* held for the production of income; or

(3) *In connection with the determination, collection, or refund of any tax.*

b. Effect of I.R.C. section 212 [§438]

This section makes available to the individual *investor* the same type of expense deduction available to business. Expenses deductible under section 212 are commonly referred to as "nonbusiness" or *investor expenses*. Thus, the costs of investing in stocks, bonds, and commodities are generally deductible under section 212 rather than section 162. [*See* **Moller v. United States**, *supra*, §354—person holding stocks for dividend income and long-term capital gains is not in trade or business] Similarly, certain real estate investments may fall under section 212 rather than 162 if very little work is required (*e.g.*, a factory leased out to a tenant under a long-term net lease).

(1) Limited to individuals [§439]

This section authorizes deductions only by individual taxpayers—not by trusts or corporations. Trusts or corporations can deduct this type of expense under section 162 (trade or business expense) since they are automatically treated as being in business.

c. Similarity to I.R.C. section 162 [§440]

The scope of expenses deductible under section 212 is substantially the same as under section 162 (business expense). For example, the expense must be:

(i) *A "current" item*, as opposed to a capital outlay;

(ii) *"Ordinary and necessary"*;

(iii) *Not violative of public policy*; and

(iv) Incurred for *the production of income*, or *the management of income-producing property*, rather than for personal reasons.

However, for a variety of tax purposes, deductions under section 212 are less favorably treated than those under section 162. (*See supra*, §297.) In particular, section 212 expenses (other than those relating to the production of rent or royalties) are deductions from adjusted gross income ("below the line") and are subject to the rule that allows deduction of miscellaneous itemized deductions only in excess of 2% of adjusted gross income. [I.R.C. §§62(a)(4), 67; *see infra*, §§555-557, 562-564]

EXAM TIP	gilbert

For your exam, you should be careful to point out that deductions for "business expenses" and deductions for "expenses related to the production of income" fall *under separate I.R.C. provisions*, even though the requirements for taking the deductions are very similar. A *"business expense" falls under I.R.C. section 162*, while an *"expense related to the production of income" falls under I.R.C. section 212*.

---

d. Illustrations

(1) Proxy fight [§441]
Expenses incurred by a shareholder in connection with a proxy fight to obtain control of a corporation are deductible under I.R.C. section 212. Deduction of such expenses is allowed even to a minority shareholder who was not himself attempting to become a director, but who wished to replace management simply in hope of making a greater profit on his shares. [**Surasky v. United States**, 325 F.2d 191 (5th Cir. 1963)]

(2) Stockholder's travel [§442]
A stockholder could possibly deduct travel costs incurred in attending stockholder meetings or visiting the factories of his companies, but he would have to establish that the trip was rationally planned and the costs incurred were reasonable in relation to the amount of his investment and the value of information to be obtained. [**Kinney v. Commissioner**, 66 T.C. 122 (1976)] Note that no section 212 deduction is allowed for expenses allocable to a convention, seminar, or similar meeting. [I.R.C. §274(h)(7)]

(3) Litigation expenses related to property matters [§443]
The problem with litigation expenses is determining whether they were incurred for the "production or collection of income" (and hence deductible), or for the *acquisition* or *defense of title* to property (in which case they are capital items and not deductible).

(a) "Primary purpose" test [§444]
The key in these cases is the primary purpose of the litigation.

1) *If the primary purpose* of the litigation is to *establish or defend title or ownership* of some particular asset, the fees are nondeductible capital expenditures. [Treas. Regs. §§1.263(a)-2(c); **Lark Sales Co. v. Commissioner**, 437 F.2d 1067 (7th Cir. 1971)—disallowing litigation costs relating to establishment of title to trademark "Dairy Queen"]

2) *If the primary purpose* of the litigation is to *recover profits or damages*, the legal fees and litigation expenses are deductible, even if issues as to title are incidentally involved.

Example: Taxpayer, a corporate director, was sued in a derivative suit for having usurped a corporate opportunity. Plaintiffs alleged that taxpayer's participation in another venture violated his fiduciary duties, and they sought to assert the corporation's title to the venture. The court held that the primary purpose of the litigation was defense of taxpayer's conduct as a fiduciary—and thus a business expense—not defense of title. [**Hochschild v. Commissioner,** 161 F.2d 817 (2d Cir. 1947); *but see* **Larchfield Corp. v. United States,** 373 F.2d 159 (2d Cir. 1967)—seems to be contrary]

(b) Acquisition costs [§445]

The Supreme Court declined to apply the primary purpose test to expenses relating to the *acquisition* of property. Under state law, majority shareholders had to buy out dissenting shareholders to prevent a corporate dissolution. They incurred litigation expenses in determining the value of the shares and argued that the primary purpose was to fix the price of the stock, not to determine title. The Court held that this was irrelevant; all costs were referable to acquisition of the shares of the minority and hence not deductible. [**Woodward v. Commissioner,** 397 U.S. 572 (1970)]

(4) Divorce and property settlement expenses [§446]

Attorneys' fees incurred in connection with divorce litigation are generally treated as nondeductible *personal* expenses arising from a family relationship, rather than any profitmaking activity.

(a) Property settlements [§447]

This is true even as to fees incurred (by either spouse) in connection with property settlements. The courts have consistently rejected the argument that the fees should be deductible as expenses for the "preservation of income-producing property." The *origin* of the dispute—*i.e.*, marital problems—controls. [**United States v. Gilmore,** *supra*, §339]

(b) Alimony [§448]

However, a spouse may, under section 212(1), deduct legal fees attributable to the production or collection of *alimony income*. [**Wild v. Commissioner,** 42 T.C. 706 (1965)]

(c) Tax consequences of divorce [§449]

Legal fees paid for advice on the *tax consequences* of divorce are deductible under I.R.C. section 212(3), which authorizes the deduction of "expenses incurred in connection with the determination, collection or refund of any tax." [**Carpenter v. United States**, 338 F.2d 366 (1964); *see supra*, §340] But to be deductible, the tax advice must pertain to the *taxpayer's own tax problems*, not the spouse's. [**United States v. Davis**, *supra*, §294]

3. Depreciation [§450]

To measure the wearing out of an asset used in business or for investment, a taxpayer owning the asset deducts annually an arbitrary percentage of the cost of the asset. This deduction is known as *depreciation* (if the asset is an intangible such as a copyright, the deduction is known as *amortization*). For this purpose, "cost" is the unadjusted basis of the asset plus subsequent expenditures that were "capitalized." (*See supra*, §§365 et seq.) The depreciation rules are set forth in section 168, which for tangible assets replaces the previous rules in section 167. The system of depreciation under section 168 is called the "accelerated cost recovery system" ("ACRS").

a. Rationale

The traditional theory of depreciation required a taxpayer to allocate an asset's decline in value to the appropriate tax year, thereby matching the asset's decline in value against the income that it produces in any given year. However, the depreciation allowances under ACRS are much larger in the early years than in later years. Thus, *ACRS departs from the traditional theory* and is, in effect, a subsidy to business that encourages greater investment in plants and equipment.

b. Limitations on depreciation

(1) Passive loss rules [§451]

Deductions relating to passive activities cannot exceed income from those activities. [I.R.C. §469, *see infra*, §§543 et seq.] In many cases, the deductions disallowed by this provision consist largely of real estate depreciation.

(2) "At risk" limitation [§452]

The "at risk" limitation on deductions from certain investments is a significant limitation on depreciation (*see infra*, §538). Depreciation is based on cost, which frequently includes a nonpersonal liability obligation (*see infra*, §§725-727). But under section 465, depreciation (and other deductions) cannot exceed the amount of the taxpayer's actual investment and his personal liability obligations. Special at-risk rules apply to real estate (*see infra*, §539).

(3) Property worth less than debt [§453]

If the property is worth less than the amount of the nonpersonal liability mortgage to which it is subject at the time of purchase, it has been held that the taxpayer *cannot* deduct depreciation on the property. [**Estate of Franklin v. Commissioner**, 544 F.2d 1045 (9th Cir. 1976); **Waddell v. Commissioner**, 86 T.C. 848 (1986), *aff'd*, 841 F.2d 264 (9th Cir. 1988)— no basis because loan unlikely to be paid]

(4) Generic tax shelters [§454]

Many deals that give rise to large depreciation deductions are now treated as "generic tax shelters," and all deductions are disallowed under authority of section 183 or because the transaction lacked economic substance. [**Rose v. Commissioner**, *supra*, §323]

c. What property can be depreciated [§455]

All physical property (except land) that is used in a trade or business or held for production of income, and that has a *limited useful life*, may be depreciated.

(1) Intangibles [§456]

Intangible assets, including goodwill, that have a basis can be amortized over an arbitrary 15-year life. Contract rights, such as covenants not to compete, are also amortized over a 15-year life, regardless of the actual term of the covenant. [I.R.C. §197, *see infra*, §473]

(a) Prior law

Under prior law, goodwill could not be amortized. There was a large amount of case law struggling with the question of whether particular purchased intangibles had a determinable useful life so that they could be amortized. If a taxpayer could establish a determinable useful life for such intangibles, they could be amortized over that useful life. [**Newark Morning Ledger Co. v. United States**, 507 U.S. 546 (1993)] These cases are superseded, however, by I.R.C. section 197, which imposes a 15-year amortization period on such "customer-based" intangibles regardless of whether the taxpayer can establish a determinable useful life and regardless of the length of that life.

e.g. **Example:** Taxpayer purchased a newspaper, allocating $67 million to an intangible asset entitled "paid subscribers." The taxpayer amortized this asset, claiming that the list was a wasting asset because the subscribers would cancel their subscriptions over a determinable period. (The taxpayer presented strong expert testimony at the trial to this effect.) The Court held the asset was distinguishable from goodwill and could be amortized. [**Newark Morning Ledger Co. v. United States**, *supra*] Present law allows a 15-year amortization period regardless of whether the asset is goodwill.

(b) Books, films, sound recordings, software [§457]

The production costs of books, films, recordings, or other copyrighted items produced by the taxpayer are amortized over the period during which they are expected to produce income. Computer software produced by the taxpayer is depreciated over a 36-month period using the straight-line method, *i.e.*, one-third of the total depreciation is taken each year (*see infra*, §467). [I.R.C. §167(f)] If copyrights or software are purchased as part of the assets of an acquired trade or business, their cost is amortized over a 15-year period. [I.R.C. §197, *see infra*, §474]

---

e.g. **Example:** Suppose a film costs $1 million to produce and is expected to return $4 million in income. In the first tax year, it produces $800,000 in income (20% of the total expected). The taxpayer claims amortization of $200,000 (20% of the total cost). [*See* I.R.C. §167(g)—giving detailed rules and requiring that taxpayer estimate revenue from all markets for 10 years]

---

(2) Property having unlimited useful life [§458]

Assets other than intangibles that do not wear out (*e.g.*, works of art and land) cannot be depreciated. Thus, when a building is purchased, it is necessary to **allocate the cost between the building and the land** on which it is built, since only the building is depreciable.

(a) But note

The courts have allowed musicians to depreciate rare musical instruments, even though such instruments generally increase in value and last for hundreds of years, because they do suffer wear and tear with use. [**Liddle v. Commissioner,** 65 F.3d 329 (3d Cir. 1995)—17th century bass viol]

d. Who is entitled to depreciation deduction [§459]

The general rule is that the person who suffers the economic loss as a result of the decrease in value of the property due to depreciation is the one entitled to claim the deduction. Ordinarily, this is the person who owns, or at least has a capital investment in, the property. [**Helvering v. Lazarus,** 308 U.S. 252 (1939)]

(1) Landlord-tenant [§460]

When a lessor improves her land and then leases the property to a tenant, the lessor is entitled to the depreciation deductions.

(a) *However, if the tenant is required to maintain the property* so that when the property is returned, it will be of equivalent value, the lessor is not entitled to depreciation. [**Kem v. Commissioner,** 432 F.2d 961 (9th Cir. 1970)]

(b) **When the tenant leases unimproved land** and then constructs a building on the land, or constructs leasehold improvements in a leased building, the tenant is entitled to the depreciation deduction. However, the building or the improvement is depreciated over its normal recovery period (27.5 years or 39 years for the building) regardless of whether the term of the lease is shorter than the recovery period. If the lease terminates before the building or improvement is fully depreciated, the lessee would take a loss deduction at the time the lease terminates. [I.R.C. §168(i)(6)]

(c) **If the taxpayer purchases the lessor's interest** in leased property that has been improved by the tenant, the purchaser is entitled to depreciate the portion of his cost allocable to the improvements over their useful life. However, the purchaser is not entitled to allocate any amount of his purchase price to the lease, even if it calls for rentals above market value. [I.R.C. §167(c)(2)]

(2) Sale-leaseback [§461]

When the owner of a building "sells" it to an investor and then "leases" it back, the investor can claim depreciation only if he is treated as the **owner** of the building. If the investor is regarded as a mere **lender**, rather than a purchaser, he is not entitled to the depreciation deduction. [*See* **Frank Lyon Co. v. United States**, 435 U.S. 561 (1978)]

(a) Illustration

In *Frank Lyon Co.*, a bank constructed a building and sold it to Lyon. Lyon leased the building back to the bank, giving the bank the option to purchase. A third party ("NYLIC") had loaned Lyon the money to buy the building. The Court held that Lyon could depreciate the building because he was a true purchaser, not just a lender to the bank. The following factors were relevant:

(i) NYLIC loaned money to Lyon, not to the bank, and Lyon was primarily liable to repay this loan, no matter what happened to the bank or the building.

(ii) If the bank never exercised its option to buy the building, Lyon would own the building after 25 years.

Note: A factor that pointed toward treating Lyon's "purchase" as a mere loan was that the bank's payments to Lyon (both rental and on its option to purchase) exactly matched Lyon's obligations to NYLIC. Unless something unusual occurred, Lyon would simply make a 6% profit on its investment. For at least 25 years, Lyon's position was precisely the same economically as if it had merely loaned money to the bank.

(3) Purchaser [§462]

The purchaser under an executory sale contract may claim the depreciation deduction on the property after the burdens and benefits of ownership pass to him, even though the seller retains title for the purpose of securing the loan.

(4) Future interest holder [§463]

A life tenant is entitled to the deduction as if he were the absolute owner of the property. After the life tenant's death, the deduction is allowed to the remainderman or reversioner. [I.R.C. §167(h)]

(5) Trustee-beneficiary [§464]

In the case of property held in trust, the allowable deduction is apportioned between the income beneficiaries and the trustee on the basis of the percentage of trust income allocable to each (in the absence of anything to the contrary in the trust instrument). [I.R.C. §167(h)] Similar rules govern in the case of a decedent's estate.

e. Computation of depreciation

(1) Recovery periods [§465]

All assets are classified into a few brackets (which are generally intended to be considerably shorter than their actual economic lives). These "recovery periods" are:

(a) *For residential real property,* 27.5 years;

(b) *For nonresidential real property,* 39 years; and

(c) *For tangible personal property,* there are six possibilities: 3, 5, 7, 10, 15, and 20 years. The applicable recovery period for a particular asset depends on its "class life" as previously determined by the IRS. The majority of machinery and equipment items fall into the five-year class (because those are assets that have economically useful lives of five to nine years). Longer-lived equipment usually falls into the seven-year class. Cars and light-duty trucks fall into the five-year category, even though that period is probably longer than their economically useful lives in most cases. Rent-to-own property (property such as furniture that consumers rent for relatively short periods, often with options to buy) qualifies for the three-year category. [I.R.C. §168(e)(3)(A), (i)(14)]

(2) Salvage value [§466]

Salvage value is the value that an asset is expected to have at the end of its useful life. Salvage value is ignored for ACRS depreciation.

(3) Methods of depreciation [§467]

ACRS provides for two kinds of depreciation: straight-line and accelerated. Straight-line depreciation provides for the same deduction every year during the recovery period. Accelerated depreciation provides for a greater deduction during the early years of ownership and a lower deduction in later years.

(4) Personal property—accelerated depreciation [§468]

A taxpayer may depreciate property in the three-year, five-year, and seven-year classes using the double-declining balance method of depreciation. In the 15-year and 20-year classes, 150%-declining balance depreciation may be used.

(a) Declining balance [§469]

To compute declining balance depreciation, first compute the straight-line rate. Then increase that rate by the appropriate factor (double or 150%). Apply that factor to the adjusted basis each year. Eventually, the basis will be reduced to the point that straight-line depreciation would provide a larger allowance. At that point, the taxpayer switches to straight line. [I.R.C. §168(b)]

(b) Half-year convention [§470]

Personal property is deemed to have been acquired and sold exactly halfway through the year, regardless of whether it was purchased or disposed of at the beginning or the end of the year. Therefore, the first year's depreciation will be half of a full-year's depreciation. [I.R.C. §168(d)]

Example: A delivery truck is five-year property. Assume that a taxpayer purchases a delivery truck in January of Year 1 for $15,000. The straight-line rate would be 20% (for five-year property, straight-line depreciation is one-fifth of the total cost each year, or 20%). Since the truck is five-year property, the taxpayer may use the double-declining balance depreciation. That means that the depreciation rate is 40% (double 20%). Applying 40% to the adjusted basis each year would produce depreciation of $6,000 in Year 1, except that under the half-year convention the taxpayer can deduct only $3,000. In Year 2, the basis of the truck is reduced to $12,000. Thus, the depreciation available in Year 2 is 40% of $12,000 ($4,800). In Year 3, the basis of the truck is reduced to $7,200. Thus, the depreciation available in Year 3 is 40% of $7,200 ($2,880).

---

1) Exception

If more than 40% of the assets are bought during the last three months of the year, *all* assets acquired during the year are deemed to have been purchased in the middle of the *quarter* when they were purchased. [I.R.C. §168(d)(3)]

(c) Straight-line election [§471]

A taxpayer can elect to use straight-line depreciation instead of accelerated depreciation. [I.R.C. §168(a)(3)(C), (a)(5)] Thus, in the previous example, if the taxpayer elected straight-line depreciation, he would simply deduct 20% of its original cost in each year (except for the first, in which it could take only half). Thus, in that example, the taxpayer would deduct $1,500 in Year 1, $3,000 in Year 2 to Year 5, and $1,500 in Year 6.

(5) Extra first-year depreciation—stimulus bill [§472]

Legislation adopted in 2002 was designed to stimulate the economy by providing additional first-year depreciation. The additional depreciation applies to tangible personal property acquired between September 11, 2001, and September 11, 2004. It also applies to certain leasehold improvements to nonresidential real property. [I.R.C. §168(k)] Under the provision, taxpayers may claim depreciation of 30% of the adjusted basis of the property in the year the property is placed in service. The adjusted basis is reduced by this bonus depreciation. The taxpayer then takes the normal depreciation for the year of acquisition, but computes it with regard to the reduced adjusted basis. (*See supra*, §470.)

---

e.g. Example: Acme Corp. purchases a $1 million punch press for its factory on October 1, 2001, and immediately places it in service. The press is seven-year property. Acme should claim bonus depreciation of $300,000, which reduces the adjusted basis to $700,000. Assume Acme uses accelerated depreciation. The straight-line rate is 1/7. That figure is doubled to 2/7 and multiplied by the adjusted basis ($700,000 times 2/7 equals $200,000). This result is cut in half under the first-year convention—so ordinary depreciation is $100,000. Acme deducts a total depreciation of $400,000 in 2001 (bonus depreciation of $300,000 plus ordinary depreciation of $100,000). In 2002, the adjusted basis is $600,000, and Acme deducts approximately $170,000 ($600,000 times 2/7).

---

(6) Amortization of intangibles [§473]

Historically, although a taxpayer was not permitted to amortize purchased goodwill because it had no determinable useful life, courts permitted amortization of contract rights or of other purchased intangibles if the taxpayer met the burden of proving that the asset had a determinable useful life. [*See* **Newark Morning Ledger Co. v. United States**, *supra*, §456—allowing amortization of purchased subscription list of newspaper] The resulting confusion led Congress to provide a uniform system for the amortization of intangibles (including goodwill) over a 15-year period. [I.R.C. §197] Under this provision, some assets (such as a purchased three-year covenant not to compete) will have a much longer amortization period than under prior law; but some assets (such as goodwill) will be amortizable that were not amortizable under prior law.

(a) Section 197 intangibles [§474]

The 15-year amortization period under section 197 applies to the following intangibles:

1) Any of the following *purchased* (but not self-created) intangibles:

   a) *Goodwill;*

   b) *Going-concern value*;

   c) *Workforce* in place;

   d) *Business books and records,* and other information bases;

   e) *Patents, copyrights, formulas, and know-how* (when these assets were purchased together with other assets of a trade or business);

   f) *Customer-based intangibles* (*e.g.,* the subscription lists in *Newark Morning Ledger*); and

   g) *Supplier-based intangibles*;

2) Licenses, permits, or other *rights granted by government*;

3) A *covenant not to compete* entered into in connection with the acquisition of a trade or business; and

4) *A franchise, trademark, or trade name.*

(b) Intangibles not covered by section 197 [§475]

Section 197 does not apply to certain intangibles. These items either cannot be amortized at all or can be amortized only according to their proved useful lives. Examples of these types of intangibles are:

1) An interest in a *corporation, partnership, trust, or estate* (not amortizable);

2) Any interest in *land* (not amortizable);

3) *Computer software* (amortizable over 36 months);

4) *Professional sports franchise* (not amortizable); and

5) An interest in a *film, sound recording, videotape, book, or similar property, or a patent or copyright that was self-created or purchased separately* (as opposed to being acquired as part of the assets of a trade or business). These intellectual-property-type assets are amortized under the income-forecast method described in §457, *supra*, when they are not covered under I.R.C. section 197.

(7) Real property [§476]

Buildings can be depreciated only on the straight-line method. Nonresidential real property (*i.e.*, a factory) is depreciated over a 39-year life. Residential real property (*i.e.*, apartments) is depreciated over a 27.5-year life.

(a) Convention

Real property is depreciated on a mid-month convention. That means that depreciation is calculated on a monthly basis in the year that the property is purchased or constructed and in the year that it is disposed of. The property is deemed to have been acquired or disposed of in the middle of the month. [I.R.C. §168(d)(2), (d)(4)(B)]

Example: Acme Co. purchases a factory in November of Year 1 for $1 million. The straight-line rate is .0256 per year (*i.e.*, 1/39). Thus, in Year 2, Acme can deduct $25,600 in depreciation ($1 million × .0256). However, in Year 1, Acme can deduct depreciation only for December and half of November. That produces a deduction of $3,200 in Year 1 (*i.e.*, 1/12 of a year for December, 1/24 of a year for November).

---

f. Election to expense purchase price [§477]

The Code allows taxpayers to expense (*i.e.*, deduct immediately) a maximum of $24,000 ($25,000 after 2003) of the purchase price of tangible personal property used in business. For every dollar of qualifying investment in excess of $200,000, the maximum figure is reduced by one dollar. [I.R.C. §179]

g. Limitations on deductions relating to consumer items [§478]

The Code imposes limitations on deductions (depreciation and rental expense) on "listed property." This category includes cars, cellular telephones, and home computers used for business. [I.R.C. §280F]

(1) ACRS depreciation [§479]

Unless the business use of listed property is more than 50% of its total use, only straight-line, not ACRS, depreciation can be used. [I.R.C. §280F(b)]

(a) Note

Of course, the percentage of business use determines the amount of depreciation available. For example, if the item is used 35% for business, only 35% of the depreciation is deductible.

(2) Limits on ACRS [§480]

During the first year after a car is purchased, no more than $2,560 can be claimed as depreciation (including the amount allowed under I.R.C. section 179—*see supra*, §477). No more than $4,100 can be claimed in the second year, $2,450 in the third year, and $1,475 for any succeeding year. These figures are indexed for inflation (starting from 1989). Thus, for example, it would take quite a few years to recover the full purchase price of a Mercedes acquired for business purposes. [I.R.C. §280F(a)]

(3) Employee use [§481]

No ACRS deductions, section 179 year-of-purchase deductions, or rental deductions are available to an employee for listed property purchased for use in her job unless the use is for the convenience of the employer and required as a condition of employment. [I.R.C. §280F(d)(3)] (For definitions of these terms, *see supra*, §§111 *et seq.*)

Example: Taxpayer, a law professor, buys a personal computer for working at home. Since her law school supplied a computer for her use at work, she cannot deduct depreciation. Nor could she deduct rental payments if she leased the computer. [*But see* **Cadwallader v. Commissioner,** 57 T.C.M. 1030 (1989)—allowing husband (a psychology professor) and wife (a state transportation planner) to deduct, under section 179, the cost of personal computers, which their employers did not require them to purchase but were necessary for them to do their jobs, because no computers were available for them at work]

---

h. Caution—ultimate effect of deduction [§482]

The depreciation deduction taken each year *reduces the taxpayer's basis*. The result is that the more depreciation taken, the more gain (or less loss) there is when the property is ultimately sold.

(1) Note

In many cases, a gain will result from the fact that the depreciation exceeded the decline in value. Because of the "depreciation recapture" provision, such gains are often ordinary income rather than capital gain. [I.R.C. §1245, *see infra*, §§925-930]

4. Depletion [§483]

The owner of a wasting asset (*e.g.*, oil or minerals) is entitled to a reasonable, annual allowance as compensation for the diminution of the asset. [I.R.C. §611] This depletion allowance thus provides to the owner of a wasting asset substantially what the depreciation deduction provides to the owner of a building.

a. Depletable property [§484]

Any "wasting asset" is depletable. This term covers not only oil, gas, and minerals, but also timber, gravel, certain deposits of ground water, etc. Basically, any natural deposit that is consumed by use or exploitation may qualify. [Treas. Reg. §1.611-1]

b. Who is entitled to depletion deduction [§485]

The holder of the *"economic interest"* in the oil or other mineral is entitled to the deduction. [**Palmer v. Bender,** 287 U.S. 551 (1933)] To have an economic interest, the taxpayer must (i) have acquired, by investment, an interest in the mineral in place; and (ii) be entitled, by legal relationship, to a share in the income to be derived from the extraction of the mineral. [**Commissioner v. Southwest Exploration,** 350 U.S. 308 (1956)—owner of adjacent lands had sufficient economic interest where driller used the lands for slant drilling onto property from which oil was extracted, paying a percentage of profits for such use]

c. Methods of computing depletion

(1) Cost method [§486]

The cost or other basis of the wasting asset is divided by the estimated number of recoverable units (tons of ore, barrels of oil, board feet of timber, etc.) to arrive at the "depletion unit." Then, the depletion allowable for each year is determined by multiplying the depletion unit by the number of units actually sold or withdrawn during the year. [I.R.C. §§611-612]

(2) Percentage method [§487]

Under this method (far more popular), the deduction is a fixed percentage of the *gross income* from the property during the taxable year. [I.R.C. §613] The percentage figure is set by Congress, and ranges from 5% (gravel deposits) to 15% (oil and gas) of gross receipts. [I.R.C. §613(b)]

(a) Limited application for oil and gas properties [§488]

Percentage depletion cannot be used for all oil and gas properties. It is available only to independent producers of gas and oil, and then only as to 1,000 barrels per day of oil or 6,000 cubic feet of gas per day. [I.R.C. §613A] The percentage depletion deduction cannot exceed 50% of the taxpayer's net income from the property.

> **e.g. Example:** If the gross income from an oil well in the tax year is $100,000 and the various operating expenses are $80,000, the taxpayer's net income therefore is $20,000. Assuming that the taxpayer qualifies for percentage depletion, it would be $15,000 (15% of gross), but here it must be limited to $10,000 (50% of net).

(b) Tax advantages [§489]

Percentage depletion (particularly in the oil and gas industry) is especially attractive because:

1) *The greater the income, the greater the depletion deduction.* (*Contrast:* Depreciation and cost depletion are based on cost, not income; they stay the same regardless of the income produced from the property.)

2) *The deduction goes on indefinitely.* The percentage depletion allowance continues at the same rate *even after the entire cost of the property has been recovered tax free. But note:* Any percentage depletion claimed in excess of the taxpayer's cost of the property is subject to the minimum tax on *tax preferences.* [*See* I.R.C. §57(a)(8), *and see infra,* §§937 *et seq.*]

d. Drilling costs [§490]

In addition to depletion, the costs of production are deductible as *expenses* under I.R.C. section 162 (*see supra,* §§296 *et seq.*) or I.R.C. section 212 (*see supra,* §§437 *et seq.*).

(1) Oil and gas wells [§491]

In the case of oil and gas wells, the Code recognizes a borderline class of expenditures known as *intangible drilling and development expenses* (wages, supplies, etc., in locating sites, preparing for production and drilling), which the taxpayer may *elect* to either deduct as current expenses, or capitalize and recover through subsequent depletion and depreciation deductions. [I.R.C. §263(c)]

(a) But note

If the property is sold at a gain, prior deductions for intangible expenses are *recaptured* as ordinary income. [I.R.C. §1254] And excess intangible drilling costs are a tax preference. [I.R.C. §57(a)(11)]

(2) Mineral deposits [§492]

Owners of other mineral deposits are afforded a similar option to expense, rather than capitalize, exploration and development costs. [I.R.C. §§615-616]

5. Losses [§493]

I.R.C. section 165 covers the deductibility of losses. To be deductible, a loss must qualify under section 165. As will be seen in the discussion below, deductibility depends on a number of factors, including the kind of taxpayer involved, the nature of the transaction out of which the claimed loss arose, and when the loss was sustained.

a. Definition of "loss" [§494]

A loss occurs when a transaction comes to an end and the taxpayer has not recovered her basis for the assets involved.

Example: Teri purchases a share of stock for $20. She could not deduct the $20—it is a capital outlay, not an expense. Therefore, she has a $20 basis for the asset. Later she sells the stock for $4. The transaction has come to an end and she has failed to recover her basis. She has a $16 loss. As will be discussed below, this loss is deductible since it arises in an investment activity, but only in the limited form of a "capital loss."

Compare: In the above example, suppose the stock had become *worthless* because the company was bankrupt. Again, the transaction has come to an end and the entire $20 will be a deductible loss. By statute, this is also treated as a capital loss. (*See infra*, §898.)

Example: Tina is an inventor and incurred $100,000 in costs developing a new bookbinding process. Under I.R.C. section 174, Tina has an option to either deduct these costs as expenses or capitalize them as part of the basis of the invention (*supra*, §401). If Tina deducts the costs, she will have a *zero basis* for the asset. If she then abandons work on the invention, *she would have no loss because she would have no basis*. If she elected to capitalize the costs, however, she would have a $100,000 basis; when she abandons the venture, she would have a $100,000 loss deduction. This would be deductible as a trade or business loss and would be an ordinary rather than a capital loss.

---

(1) Is there a "loss"? [§495]

The courts often scrutinize loss transactions closely to see whether a loss really occurred. *Illustration:* If a taxpayer sells a building at a substantial loss and then leases it back, it is possible that there would be no loss deduction if the rentals on the lease are below fair market rentals. If so, the taxpayer would have received not only cash for the building but also a discounted lease—and the sum of these items could be equal to or more than the taxpayer's basis. [*See* **Leslie Co. v. Commissioner**, 64 T.C. 247 (1975)] The loss could also be disallowed in this case if the transaction falls under I.R.C. section 1031 as a like kind exchange. (*See infra*, §§781 *et seq.*)

Has a loss *actually occurred*?

NO

YES

Has the loss been *realized* (e.g., by sale, exchange, theft, abandonment, etc.)?

NO

YES

Is there a basis for *disallowing* the loss? Consider whether the loss:

— Was the result of a *transaction between related parties*;

— Was a *"wash sale"* of securities;

— Was the result of a *sham transaction*; and

— Would result in a *deduction that would violate or frustrate public policy*.

YES

Taxpayer may *not take a loss deduction*.

NO

Taxpayer *may take a loss deduction*.

b. Types of losses allowed to individuals [§496]

A *corporate* taxpayer by its very nature is a business entity (and hence its losses are generally deductible as business losses). In the case of *individuals*, however, only certain types of losses are deductible.

(1) Losses incurred in trade or business [§497]

Any loss incurred in a trade or business is deductible. (*See supra*, §298, for definition of "trade or business.") [I.R.C. §165(c)(1)]

(2) Losses incurred in transactions entered into for profit [§498]

Losses incurred in transactions entered into for profit are deductible. This covers losses from the sale of securities or other *investments*. [I.R.C. §165(c)(2)]

(a) Personal residences [§499]

Since personal residences are not deemed held for profit, losses sustained on the sale of a personal residence are *not deductible*. [**Austin v. Commissioner**, 298 F.2d 583 (2d Cir. 1962)] *Note:* This is true even though a *gain* on sale or exchange of a residence is taxable unless it meets a statutory nonrecognition provision (*infra*, §§802-807).

1) Distinguish—conversion of residence to rental property [§500]

A taxpayer can convert her residence to an investment asset by renting it prior to sale. Then any decline in value that occurs after conversion to rental use would be deductible at the time of sale as a loss. [Treas. Reg. §1.165-9(b)] However, the conversion to rental use must be *bona fide*, and mere listing for rental is probably insufficient. [**Gevirtz v. Commissioner**, 123 F.2d 707 (2d Cir. 1941)]

(b) Wagering [§501]

Gambling is a profit-seeking activity, and hence wagering losses are deductible—but *only* to the extent of wagering gains. [I.R.C. §165(d)]

(c) Demolition losses [§502]

Loss is not allowed for demolition of a structure. The adjusted basis of the structure, and the cost of demolition, must be added to the basis of the underlying land. [I.R.C. §280B]

1) Exception—certain losses occurring before demolition [§503]

However, a loss may be deductible if incurred before the demolition occurs. For example, if a building is damaged by a casualty (such as a tornado), and then must be demolished, the casualty loss is deductible. It reduces the basis of the structure, and the remaining basis is then added to the basis of the land. [I.R.C. Notice 90-21, 1990-1 C.B. 332] Similarly, if the building is abandoned as the result of extraordinary obsolescence, then demolished, a loss deduction can be taken by reason of the abandonment. [**Cou v. Commissioner**, 103 T.C. 80 (1994)]

(3) Casualty losses

See infra, §§672-683.

DEERCTIBILITY OF LOSSES—EXAMPLES	gilbert
LOSSES DEDUCTIBLE BY AN INDIVIDUAL:	**LOSSES *NOT* DEDUCTIBLE BY AN INDIVIDUAL:**
• Losses incurred in a trade or business • Losses incurred in a for-profit transaction • Gambling losses (but only to offset gambling earnings) • Casualty and theft losses	• Losses on sale of home • Most demolition costs

c. When loss allowable—"realization" [§504]

A loss is generally deductible only if "realized." This means it must be evidenced by a "closed and completed transaction" (*e.g.*, sale, exchange, theft, destruction, worthlessness, abandonment, etc.) in the current tax year.

(1) Decline in value [§505]

A mere decline in value of property is not enough. [**Reporter Publishing v. Commissioner**, 201 F.2d 743 (10th Cir. 1953)—news service membership declining in value due to change in law not a deductible loss, since taxpayer continued to use news service in its business]

(2) Time of realization [§506]

Generally, the realization of loss on a *tangible asset* occurs in the year when there is *both* an intention to abandon the asset *and* an affirmative act of abandonment.

> (e.g.) **Example:** A loss on a gold mine was realized when the directors resolved to abandon the mine and a contract to salvage the machinery and equipment was executed. [**A.J. Industries v. United States,** 503 F.2d 660 (9th Cir. 1974)]

(a) Treatment as "sale or exchange" [§507]

Whether a loss that is triggered by abandonment or worthlessness will be treated as a "sale or exchange" for the purpose of determining whether it is a capital loss or an ordinary loss is a complex question. (*See infra,* §§888-902.)

(3) Finality of loss [§508]

If there is a closed and completed transaction, the fact that there is a remote possibility of recoupment does not prevent deductibility. [**United States v. White Dental,** 274 U.S. 398 (1927)—property seized during war; possibility of reparation after war immaterial to deductibility] However, a reasonable possibility of recoupment would delay deduction of the loss until the possibility is exhausted (*e.g.,* fire loss to building that might be covered by insurance; no deduction until the insurance dispute is finally resolved).

(4) Exchanges [§509]

For loss to be realized by reason of an exchange of property, the property received must "differ materially either in kind or in extent" from the property transferred. [Treas. Reg. §1.1001-1(a)] Thus an exchange of a pool of mortgages secured by land in City A for a pool of mortgages secured by land in City B is a realization because the two pools of mortgages "differ materially" despite the fact that they have the same total principal amount, interest rate, and fair market value. The rates of default, prepayments, etc., are bound to differ in the future. Thus, loss on the exchange can be deducted. [**Cottage Savings Association v. Commissioner,** 499 U.S. 554 (1991)—loss deductible despite tax avoidance motive for exchange]

(5) Exceptions [§510]

There are a few exceptions to the rule requiring realization:

(a) *Theft losses* are deductible in the year in which the taxpayer *discovers* the loss. [I.R.C. §165(e)]

(b) *Casualty losses* in a natural disaster (proclaimed by the President) can be deducted either in the year the disaster occurs or on the tax return for the prior year. If the return for the prior year has already been filed, the taxpayer can obtain a refund of the prior year's tax. [I.R.C. §165(h)]

(c) *Declines in value in inventory* may be deducted in the year they occur since the Code permits an annual valuation of inventory (when the FIFO method of inventory costing is used) (*see infra*, §§1039 *et seq.*). [**Thor Power Tool Co. v. Commissioner,** 429 U.S. 522 (1979)—inventories cannot be valued below market value even if they will ultimately be scrapped]

(d) *In the case of stock or securities*, the year of loss is the year in which they become worthless, which requires an analysis of all the facts and circumstances. [**Boehm v. Commissioner,** 326 U.S. 287 (1945)]

d. Disallowed losses

(1) Losses between related taxpayers [§511]
I.R.C. sections 1041 and 267 disallow loss deductions on certain sales between related taxpayers.

(a) Spouses [§512]
Under section 1041, neither gain nor loss can be recognized on a transfer between spouses or between former spouses incident to divorce. (*See infra*, §808.)

(b) Related parties [§513]
Under section 267, no loss deduction is allowed on a sale or exchange *"directly or indirectly"* between related taxpayers, even if the sale was at arm's length and the price was fair. Of course, *gain* on such sales is taxable.

(c) Who are relatives [§514]
Taxpayers within the following categories are deemed "related" within the meaning of section 267:

1) *Family members*—limited to taxpayer's siblings, ancestors, and lineal descendants. [I.R.C. §267(c)(4)]

2) *Individual and a corporation* in which the individual owns *50%* or more in value of the outstanding shares. [I.R.C. §267(b)(2)]

3) *Trustor and trustee* of same trust. [I.R.C. §267(b)(4)]

4) *Trustee and beneficiary* of same trust; or trustee of one trust and beneficiary of another trust having the same trustor. [I.R.C. §267(b)(6), (7)]

5) *Individual and tax-exempt entity* that the individual or his family controls. [I.R.C. §267(b)(9)]

(d) Indirect sales [§515]

The courts have broadly construed the phrase "directly or indirect-ly."

---

e.g. Example: A husband sold certain shares on one day, and claimed a loss from that sale. His wife purchased similar shares the same day. The Court held that the series of transactions were "indirectly" sales between related taxpayers, and the losses were disallowed. [**McWilliams v. Commissioner,** 331 U.S. 694 (1947); *and see* **Merritt v. Commissioner,** 400 F.2d 417 (5th Cir. 1968)—husband's assets sold at *forced sale* and wife was buyer]

(e) Relief provision for disallowed losses [§516]

If a loss has been disallowed under section 267, and the *transferee* later sells the property at a gain, she can offset against that gain whatever amount of loss was previously denied to the *transferor.* The effect is that the tax benefit of the loss deduction is shifted from the transferor to the transferee, and deferred until she can sell the property at a gain. [I.R.C. §267(d)]

---

e.g. Example: Doug sells his farm, in which he has a basis of $100,000, to his son Kevin for $75,000. Doug cannot claim a $25,000 loss—it is *disallowed*. A couple of years later, Kevin sells the farm to a real estate development company (in which he has no interest) for $115,000. Kevin's gain ordinarily would be $40,000 ($115,000 minus $75,000); however, Kevin can take advantage of the previously disallowed loss of $25,000—thus, his recognized gain is $15,000 ($40,000 minus $25,000).

---

(2) Losses from "wash sales" of securities [§517]

When a taxpayer sells stocks or securities and buys the same (or sub-stantially identical) assets within 30 days before or after the sale, the transaction is dubbed a "wash sale" and, in effect, ignored. I.R.C. sec-tion 1091 expressly provides that losses from wash sales are not deduct-ible. The basis of the repurchased stock is its cost plus the disallowed loss.

---

e.g. Example: Five years ago, Wiley purchased 1,000 shares of Acme, Inc. for $50 per share (or $50,000 in total). Recently, due to an ac-counting scandal, the price of Acme's shares declined to $5 per share. To offset other gains from the sale of stock, Wiley decided to sell all of his shares of Acme, thus tentatively realizing a loss of $45,000. Three days later, Wiley has a change of heart and buys 1,000 shares of Acme for $4 per share ($4,000 in total). Wiley does not realize any loss on the sale of stock, and the basis of the repurchased stock is adjusted to $49,000 ($4,000 plus the $45,000 disallowed loss).

(3) Sham transactions [§518]

Even if a transaction does not fall within sections 1041, 267, or 1091, it can still be disallowed if it was a "sham"; *i.e.*, despite the appearance that a sale occurred, in reality there was no real interruption of the taxpayer's beneficial ownership. [**Higgins v. Smith,** 308 U.S. 473 (1940)]

(4) Public policy [§519]

Although the *judicially created* public policy theory has been repudiated as to deductions of ordinary business expenses under I.R.C. section 162 (*see supra,* §424), deductions of losses under I.R.C. section 165 can be disallowed if the court finds that allowing the loss deduction would immediately and severely frustrate a clearly defined public policy. [**Mazzei v. Commissioner,** 61 T.C. 497 (1974)] Moreover, if allowing a deduction would violate a public policy as defined by I.R.C. section 162, the deduction probably would not be allowed under I.R.C. section 165. [**Stephens v. Commissioner,** 905 F.2d 667 (2d Cir. 1990)—restitution to embezzlement victim imposed as condition of probation would not be considered a fine under I.R.C. section 162(f); thus, allowing a deduction under I.R.C. section 165 would not frustrate a clearly defined public policy]

Example: Two men showed Taxpayer a black box that purportedly could copy money to produce counterfeit bills. They demonstrated the machine with a $10 bill, but explained to Taxpayer that they needed a number of $100 bills to make the process worthwhile. After several more demonstrations, Taxpayer provided the men with $20,000 in $100 bills and the men absconded with the money. On his tax return, Taxpayer claimed a loss deduction for the theft. The deduction was *not* allowed because allowing a deduction under these circumstances would frustrate the federal policy against counterfeiting. [**Mazzei v. Commissioner,** *supra*]

EXAM TIP   gilbert

For your exam, remember that although *judicially created* public policy exceptions no longer exist as to deductions of ordinary business expenses under I.R.C. section 162, there still are *statutory* public policy exceptions under I.R.C. section 162 that the deduction cannot violate.

6. Bad Debts

a. "Bad debt" defined [§520]

A "bad debt" arises when an obligation owed to the taxpayer becomes uncollectible. It is simply one kind of loss. Like a loss, a bad debt is the end of a transaction in which the taxpayer fails to recover his basis in an asset (the debt owing to him). However, the Code provides special rules concerning the deduction of bad debts.

b. Requirements for deductibility

(1) Bona fide debt [§521]

First of all, there must be a valid debt owing to the taxpayer arising from a *debtor-creditor relationship*. This requires a showing that the taxpayer (creditor) made a loan to the debtor with the expectation that it would be repaid.

(a) Family loans [§522]

Alleged "loans" to family members or relatives are always closely scrutinized to determine the bona fides of the indebtedness. [**Smyth v. Barneson**, 181 F.2d 143 (9th Cir. 1950)]

(b) Guaranty [§523]

The loss on a guaranty is treated as a bad debt, because the guarantor (through subrogation) becomes the creditor when he is forced to pay his principal's debt. If the principal is insolvent, the debt is "bad" and a deduction is available. [**Putnam v. Commissioner**, 352 U.S. 82 (1956)]

(2) Worthlessness [§524]

It must appear that the debt became unenforceable or uncollectible *during the tax year* for which the deduction is claimed.

(a) Proof of "worthlessness" [§525]

"Worthlessness" requires a showing that something has happened that puts an end to any realistic hope of repayment, *e.g.*, bankruptcy of debtor.

(b) Debt became worthless in prior year [§526]

When the taxpayer finds out in a subsequent year that the debt became worthless in a prior year, his remedy is to recompute his income for the prior year, taking the deduction, and file a *claim for refund*. He can do so up to seven years after the return is filed, rather than the usual three-year period. [I.R.C. §6511(d)(1)]

EXAM TIP   gilbert

For your exam, be sure to remember that in order for a bad debt to be deductible, the taxpayer must be able to show **both** that the debt was **bona fide** and that the debt became **worthless** (*i.e.*, unenforceable or uncollectible). Also note that if the debt became worthless in the prior year, the taxpayer must file an amended return for the prior year in order to benefit from the loss.

(c) Partially secured debt [§527]

A taxpayer holding a partially secured debt can postpone the "worth-lessness" of the unsecured part (if desired for greater tax saving in a later year) by putting off liquidating the collateral. Until the collateral is liquidated, the unpaid balance of the note cannot be determined. [**Loewi v. Ryan**, 229 F.2d 627 (2d Cir. 1956)]

c. Business and nonbusiness bad debts

(1) Business bad debts [§528]

Bad debts incurred in connection with the taxpayer's trade or business are fully deductible. [I.R.C. §166(a)]

(a) And note

In the case of business bad debts, a deduction may be taken for *"partial worthlessness"* in the year in which part, but not all, of the debt becomes uncollectible. [I.R.C. §166(a)(2)]

(2) Nonbusiness bad debts [§529]

Nonbusiness bad debts are deductible as *short-term capital losses*. [I.R.C. §166(d)] (*See infra*, §818.)

(a) Family and investment loans [§530]

A nonbusiness bad debt might arise from a loan to a friend or family member (assuming that it is shown to be a bona fide debt). It might also arise in connection with *investment activities* since these must be distinguished from an active trade or business.

(b) Loans to corporations [§531]

Shareholder loans to corporations are usually treated as nonbusiness bad debts. The reason is that the shareholder, in making the loan, is treated as an *investor* in the corporation; consequently, he is not in a trade or business and does not have a business bad debt. [**Whipple v. Commissioner**, *supra*, §300]

1) Exceptions [§532]

There are some exceptions to the above rule:

a) The *Whipple* rule does not apply when the lender to a corporation can show that he is really trying to *protect his job*. Serving as a corporate employee is a trade or business, while investing is not. However, to prevail on this point, the taxpayer must prove that his *primary purpose* in making the loan was to keep his job, rather than protecting his stock investment. [**United States v. Generes**, 405 U.S. 93 (1972)]

b) Another exception to *Whipple* is the situation in which the taxpayer's purpose in making the loan to the corporation was to **promote some other distinct business** in which the taxpayer was also engaged. [**Maloney v. Spencer**, 172 F.2d 638 (9th Cir. 1949)—loans from the taxpayer (who the court found was "engaged in the business of acquiring, owning, expanding, equipping, and leasing food processing plants") to three corporations (in which taxpayer was the sole shareholder and which leased their plants from taxpayer) were made to promote the corporations' food packing businesses]

c) Similarly, a taxpayer can circumvent *Whipple* by showing that he is **in the trade or business** of buying, reviving, and selling corporations at a profit. However, this would require more than proof of many stock trades; the taxpayer would have to establish that he is actually a "promoter" of business enterprises. [**United States v. Clark**, 358 F.2d 892 (1st Cir. 1966)]

d. Amount deductible

(1) Limited to basis [§533]

The basis of the debt in the taxpayer's hands is the amount deductible. If the taxpayer lends money, the amount loaned is the basis. If the taxpayer purchases the debt from a third party (*e.g.*, Dealer sells Buyer a car in exchange for a $3,000 promissory note; Taxpayer Bank purchases the note from Dealer for $2,750), the purchase price is the basis.

(2) Accounts receivable [§534]

Whether an uncollectible account receivable can be deducted as a bad debt depends on whether the taxpayer is on the cash or accrual basis. (*See infra*, §§950 *et seq.*) If the taxpayer is on the accrual basis, she has previously taken the debt into income; this gives it a basis in her hands. When it becomes uncollectible, she deducts the amount of the basis. But if she is on the cash basis, she did not take the receivable into income; consequently, it has a zero basis in her hands and its uncollectibility gives rise to no deduction. [**Alsop v. Commissioner**, 290 F.2d 726 (2d Cir. 1961)]

(3) Child support [§535]

Suppose Husband owes $10,000 in child support to Wife but fails to pay. The obligation is uncollectible and Wife gives up trying to collect it. Can Wife take a bad debt deduction? Answer: No, because the debt has no basis in her hands—not even to the extent that she has expended funds in support of the child. [**Diez-Arguelles v. Commissioner**, 48 T.C.M.

496 (1984)] This result is questionable because child support, when received, is tax free to the recipient. [I.R.C. §71(c), *and see supra*, §171] If, for example, Wife sold the $10,000 obligation (before it became uncollectible) to a third party for $7,000, the $7,000 should not be taxed to Wife (since it substitutes for a payment that would have been tax free). This result suggests that Wife indeed has a $10,000 basis in the debt and should receive a bad debt deduction. Similarly, Husband should have debt cancellation income when Wife fails to collect the $10,000 from him.

e. Recovery of bad debts [§536]

Bad debts taken as a deduction, but subsequently recovered, must be included in gross income in the year of recovery.

(1) Tax benefit rule [§537]

However, if all or any portion of the prior bad-debt deduction did not result in a *tax benefit* to the taxpayer (*i.e.*, it did not result in a reduction of taxes), then she may exclude a portion of the recovery to the extent the previous bad-debt deduction failed to effect a tax benefit. [I.R.C. §111] (*See infra*, §§1071-1076.)

7. "At Risk" Limitation on Tax Shelter Deductions [§538]

The Code sharply limits the current deduction of operating losses from certain investments to the amount that the taxpayer has "at risk" in the investment. [I.R.C. §465(a)]

a. Definition of "at risk" [§539]

The term "at risk" means the amount of the taxpayer's investment in the property, not counting loans the taxpayer has *no personal liability* to repay (a "nonrecourse" loan). Recourse loans from other investors in the activity or from relatives also do not count. [I.R.C. §465(b); *and see* **Waddell v. Commissioner,** 86 T.C. 848 (1986), *aff'd,* 841 F.2d 264 (9th Cir. 1988)—loan agreement was structured in a way as to make taxpayer/borrower liable for an interest payment of only $1,500 per year (and taxpayer/borrower could convert this liability to a nonrecourse liability after seven years for a fee of $1,000), with 50% of net profit greater than $1,500 used to reduce the principal; taxpayer/borrower was therefore only at risk in the amount of his original investment]

(1) Exception

In the case of *real estate investments* only, a taxpayer is at risk with respect to a nonrecourse loan from a *"qualified lender"*—meaning a lender such as a bank or thrift institution that is not the seller of the property or an investor in the property.

b. Activities covered [§540]

Section 465 applies to all business or investment activities. [I.R.C. §465(c)]

c. Definition of operating losses [§541]

"Losses" under section 465 are the excess of deductions from the activity over income from the activity during the year.

---

e.g. **Example:** Gina invests in producing a movie, using $50,000 of her own money and borrowing $550,000 from a studio. Gina has no personal liability to repay this loan and she is not personally involved in the actual production process. Gina uses the whole $600,000 to make the movie. In the first year of distribution, the movie brings in income of $160,000. However, the deductions allocable to the movie (mainly depreciation) are $400,000. Ordinarily, all of the $400,000 would be deductible. But, because of section 465, the excess of deductions over income ($240,000) can be deducted only to the extent Gina is "at risk"—$50,000. Consequently, she can deduct only $50,000. The remaining $190,000 is not deductible until some later year when the amount "at risk" rises above zero.

---

d. Relation to passive loss [§542]

Note that the "at risk" rules and the "passive loss" rules (below) can overlap. The movie deal just described would also produce a passive loss, so that the loss could be offset only against passive income. In such situations, the "at risk" rules should be applied first, limiting the amount of available loss to $50,000. Then that $50,000 could be deducted, but only against Gina's passive income, if any.

8. Passive Losses [§543]

A person engaged in a "passive activity" (individually or as a partner) cannot deduct the losses from such activities except against income from passive activities. [I.R.C. §469] This provision is intended to destroy tax shelters.

a. Definition [§544]

A passive activity is a business in which the taxpayer does not *"materially participate."* To materially participate, the taxpayer must be involved on a "regular, continuous, and substantial" basis. A limited partner never materially participates. A general partner may or may not materially participate.

(1) Objective tests [§545]

A taxpayer's participation in an activity is material if the taxpayer participates for more than 500 hours in the year. Even if the taxpayer cannot meet the 500-hour test, her participation will be deemed material if she participates in the activity for at least 100 hours and her participation is not less than that of any other individual (including nonowners). Married taxpayers can combine the work of both spouses to meet these tests. [Treas. Reg. §1.469-5T(a)(1), (a)(3), (f)(3)] The Regulations set forth a number of other mechanical tests based on hours worked.

(2) All facts and circumstances [§546]

Even if a taxpayer cannot meet the mechanical tests above, her participation is material if, "based on all of the facts and circumstances," the taxpayer "participates in the activity on a regular, continuous, and substantial basis" during the year. [Treas. Reg. §1.469-5T(a)(7)] An individual's management activities cannot be taken into account under the "facts and circumstances" test unless no person (other than the taxpayer) receives compensation for management services and no individual provides management services that exceed those of taxpayer. [Treas. Reg. §1.469-5T(b)(2)(ii)] This provision is designed to prevent passive investors in an activity from claiming that they were involved in management even though there is a paid manager.

EXAM TIP   **gilbert**

The passive activity rule is likely to show up on your exam. Be sure to remember that a taxpayer can deduct losses from passive activities **only against income from passive activities**. Remember also that what is "passive" is determined by three tests—(i) whether the taxpayer spent **500 hours in a year** on the activity; (ii) whether the taxpayer spent **100 hours in a year** on the activity, and the taxpayer's participation **was not less than that of any other individual;** or (iii) whether the taxpayer was involved in the activity **on a regular, continuous, and substantial basis.**

---

b. Disallowed loss [§547]

Passive loss can be deducted only against *passive income.* Disallowed passive loss is *carried forward* and can be used against passive income in future years. On a fully taxable disposition of an activity, all previously suspended passive losses from that activity are deductible.

Example: Todd is a general partner in F Partnership, which owns a money-losing farm. Todd occasionally visits the farm and discusses its management with Farmer Brown, the other partner who lives on the farm and manages it on a day-to-day basis. For Todd, the farm is a passive activity. For Farmer Brown, it is not a passive activity. Assume that Todd's share of the farm's loss is $20,000. Todd has income from his law practice and also has income of $30,000 from interest and dividends. Todd cannot currently deduct his share of the farm's loss. Neither income from an active business (law practice) nor income from investments (*e.g.*, interest and dividends) can be offset by passive losses. He can deduct the $20,000 only against future income from the farm (or other passive activity) or when the farm is sold in a taxable disposition. However, Farmer Brown can fully deduct his share of the farm's losses because it is not a passive activity for Farmer Brown.

---

c. Rentals [§548]

All rental activity is passive regardless of whether the taxpayer meets the material participation standard.

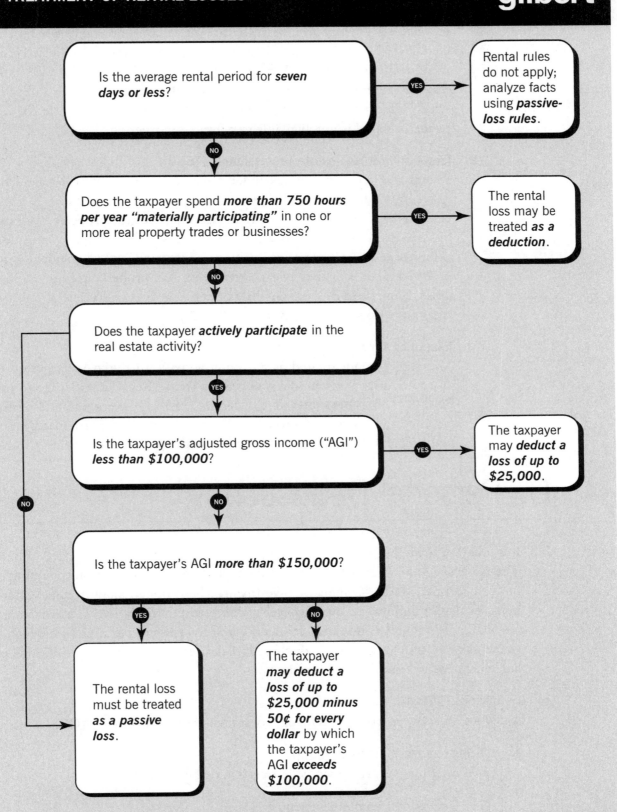

Is the average rental period for **seven days or less**?

YES → Rental rules do not apply; analyze facts using **passive-loss rules**.

NO ↓

Does the taxpayer spend **more than 750 hours per year "materially participating"** in one or more real property trades or businesses?

YES → The rental loss may be treated **as a deduction**.

NO ↓

Does the taxpayer **actively participate** in the real estate activity?

NO → The rental loss must be treated **as a passive loss**.

YES ↓

Is the taxpayer's adjusted gross income ("AGI") **less than $100,000**?

YES → The taxpayer may **deduct a loss of up to $25,000**.

NO ↓

Is the taxpayer's AGI **more than $150,000**?

YES → The rental loss must be treated **as a passive loss**.

NO → The taxpayer **may deduct a loss of up to $25,000 minus 50¢ for every dollar** by which the taxpayer's AGI **exceeds $100,000**.

(1) Exception for moderate income lessors [§549]

A taxpayer (as individual or general partner) is allowed to deduct currently up to $25,000 in losses from real estate rental activity if the taxpayer *"actively participates"* (*e.g.*, by finding tenants, arranging for repairs, etc.). However, this exception applies only to taxpayers with adjusted gross income under $100,000. If adjusted gross income exceeds $100,000, the $25,000 figure is phased out at the rate of 50 cents for each dollar by which adjusted gross income exceeds $100,000. The exception for real property rental is not available to a limited partner.

(2) Exception for real estate professionals [§550]

Rental real estate can be excluded from the passive loss rules (and the losses are deductible in full) if the taxpayer spends more than 750 hours per year materially participating in one or more real property trades or businesses. A real property trade or business includes real property development, construction, acquisition, conversion, rental, management, or brokerage. The taxpayer's services in real property trades or businesses must be more than one-half of her total personal services rendered during the taxable year. [I.R.C. §469(c)(7)]

(3) Exception for short-term rentals [§551]

An activity is not treated as a "rental activity" if the average period of customer use is seven days or less. [Treas. Reg. §1.469-1T(e)(3)(ii); **Pohoski v. Commissioner,** T.C. Memo. 1998-17—average rental period for condo was less than seven days; owners materially participated in its management, making losses deductible under passive-loss rules]

C. Personal Deductions

1. Introduction [§552]

The Code specifies a limited number of items that are deductible even though they have no connection to business or investment. The rationale may be that certain items probably diminished the taxpayer's ability to pay taxes (*e.g.*, extraordinary medical expense or casualty loss), it was difficult to separate business and personal elements (*e.g.*, moving expense), or there is a desire to encourage certain kinds of behavior (*e.g.*, charitable contributions).

2. Definitions [§553]

A deduction is *either* from gross income or adjusted gross income ("AGI").

a. "Adjusted gross income" [§554]

AGI is defined as gross income less certain deductions. [I.R.C. §62]

(1) Deductions from gross income [§555]

The following deductions are *from gross income* (sometimes called "above the line"). All other deductions are *from AGI* (sometimes called "below the line").

(a) ***Trade or business deductions*** (except trade or business deductions of employees). [I.R.C. §62(a)(1)]

(b) ***Reimbursed expenses of employees*** (*e.g.*, travel and transportation expenses, union dues, etc.). The reimbursement is included in income, and the expense is deducted from AGI. [I.R.C. §62(a)(2)(A)] If the employee is required to account precisely for her reimbursed expenditures, however, she is permitted to exclude both the reimbursement from income and the expenditures from deductions. The reimbursed expenditure is simply dropped from the tax return entirely.

  1) The expenses of certain ***"qualified performing artists"*** are deductible from AGI. A "qualified performing artist" is a person who performed services in the performing arts for at least two employers during the year, who did not have AGI in excess of $16,000, and whose deductions exceeded 10% of gross income attributable to performance of such services. [I.R.C. §62(a)(2)(B), (b)]

  2) Some expenses of teachers ***incurred in 2002 or 2003*** are deductible from adjusted gross income. Kindergarten, elementary, middle, and secondary school teachers may deduct expenses (not exceeding $250) related to books, supplies, computer equipment, software, and supplementary material for the classroom. [I.R.C. §62(a)(2)(D)] This provision was designed to benefit teachers (as well as counselors, principals, or aides) who pay for classroom material out of their own pockets. The provision was part of stimulus legislation enacted by Congress in 2002—whether it will be extended past 2003 remains to be seen.

(c) ***Deduction for capital losses or other losses from the sale and exchange of property.*** [I.R.C. §62(a)(3), (4)] Note that if such losses are capital, they may not be fully deductible. [I.R.C. §1211; *see infra*, §818]

(d) ***Expenses deductible under I.R.C. section 212*** applicable to rent and royalty income only. Other section 212 expenses (such as the cost of a safe deposit box to hold stock certificates) are deductible from AGI (*supra*, §437). [I.R.C. §62(a)(4)]

(e) ***Alimony.*** [I.R.C. §62(a)(10)]

(f) *Moving expenses* allowed by I.R.C. section 217 (*supra*, §325). [I.R.C. §62(a)(5)]

(g) *Interest on education loans* (*see infra* §§596-600). [I.R.C. §62(a)(17)]

(h) *Higher-education expenses* (*see supra*, §343). [I.R.C. §62(a)(18)]

(2) Significance of distinction [§556]

It is almost always preferable to have deductions from gross income ("above the line") than from AGI ("below the line") because:

(a) Below-the-line deductions must exceed standard deduction [§557]

If a taxpayer's below-the-line deductions are less than the standard deduction (*see infra*, §566), the taxpayer can use the standard deduction *and* claim above-the-line deductions. But to such a taxpayer, below-the-line deductions (except for personal exemptions—*see infra*, §§663 *et seq.*) are useless.

(b) Medical expenses [§558]

Medical expense deductions are reduced by 7.5% of AGI (*see infra*, §650). Therefore, the lower AGI is, the more medical expenses can be deducted.

(c) Child care credit [§559]

The child care credit is greater if AGI is lower (*see infra*, §§701-704).

(d) Distinguish—charitable contributions [§560]

Limitations on charitable contribution deductions are based on a percentage of AGI (*see infra*, §618). Thus, the higher AGI is, the more charitable contributions can be deducted. However, very few taxpayers encounter this limitation.

(e) Two percent floor and phaseout [§561]

As discussed in the next section, some below-the-line expenses are subject to a 2% floor. If an item is an above-the-line deduction, it cannot be subjected to the 2% floor. Moreover, some below-the-line deductions are phased out at the rate of 3% of the excess of AGI over a particular threshold (*infra*, §565). Thus, the higher the AGI, the greater the phaseout.

(3) Miscellaneous itemized deductions [§562]

Many, but not all, itemized deductions (*i.e.*, deductions from AGI) are subject to a 2% floor. Such items are deductible only to the extent that, in total, they exceed 2% of AGI. [I.R.C. §67]

(a) Deductions not subject to the floor [§563]

The more important itemized deductions that are *not* subject to the 2% floor are:

1) *Interest*;

2) *Taxes*;

3) *Casualty losses*;

4) *Charitable contributions*; and

5) *Medical expenses*.

(b) Deductions subject to the floor [§564]

This leaves many important below-the-line deductions subject to the 2% floor. For example, unreimbursed employee business expenses (*e.g.*, for union dues, transportation, travel, entertainment); the cost of preparing tax returns; and the costs of obtaining income from investments (other than rents or royalties).

Example: Tony's AGI is $100,000. His itemized deductions include qualified residence interest of $4,000, charitable contributions of $5,000, unreimbursed costs of working as an associate in a law firm (telephone, transportation, attending continuing education lectures) of $3,500, and the cost of $300 for having his tax return prepared. Tony can deduct his qualified residence interest and charitable contributions in full. However, the remaining $3,800 in itemized deductions are subject to the 2% floor. Two percent of his AGI is $2,000. Thus, only $1,800 of his unreimbursed employee business expenses and tax return preparation costs are deductible.

DEDUCTIONS—EXAMPLES　　　　　　　　　　**gilbert**

NOT SUBJECT TO THE 2% FLOOR:	SUBJECT TO THE 2% FLOOR:
• Interest	• Unreimbursed employee business expenses (for union dues, travel, entertainment, etc.)
• Taxes	
• Casualty losses	• Cost of preparing tax returns
• Charitable contributions	• Costs of obtaining income from investments (other than from rents or royalties)
• Medical expenses	

(4) Phaseout of itemized deductions [§565]

Itemized deductions are reduced by 3% of the excess of AGI over the applicable amount (adjusted for inflation to $137,700 in 2002). [I.R.C. §68] However, no more than 80% of itemized deductions are wiped out by this provision.

(a) Exceptions

This provision does not apply to *medical expenses, investment interest, or casualty losses*. But it does apply, for example, to charitable deductions and qualified residence interest.

(b) Effect of other provisions

This provision is applied *after* all other deduction-limitation provisions, such as the 2% rule (*supra*, §§562, 564).

Example: Ed's AGI is $237,700 in 2002. His itemized deductions (exclusive of medical deductions, investment interest expense, and casualty losses) total $28,000. His AGI is $100,000 in excess of the applicable amount ($137,700). Thus, Ed's itemized deductions are reduced by 3% of $100,000, or $3,000. He can deduct only $25,000 instead of $28,000.

(c) Future phaseout

The provision reducing personal itemized deductions is scheduled to be phased out between 2006 and 2009 and eliminated in 2010. [I.R.C. §68(f)(2)]

b. Standard deduction [§566]

The standard deduction is a substitute for deducting below-the-line deductions. If a taxpayer's itemized deductions are less than the standard deduction, he simply takes the standard deduction instead. [I.R.C. §63]

(1) Amount of deduction [§567]

The standard deduction is $5,000 on a joint return, $4,400 for head of household, $3,000 for singles, and $2,500 for married persons filing separately. These amounts are adjusted for inflation, so that in 2002, the standard deduction is $7,850 on a joint return, $6,900 for a head of household, $4,700 for a single person, and $3,925 for a married person filing separately.

(a) Gradual elimination of the marriage penalty [§568]

Beginning in 2005, the standard deduction for married taxpayers will be increased over five years to twice the basic standard deduction for an unmarried person. This provision is designed to reduce the so-called marriage penalty (*see supra*, §233). [I.R.C. §63(c)(7)]

(2) Additional standard deduction for elderly and blind taxpayers [§569]

The Code provides an "additional standard deduction" for taxpayers who turn 65 years of age before year-end or who are blind. This additional deduction is adjusted for inflation—in 2002, the additional standard deduction is $1,150 for an unmarried taxpayer and $900 *per taxpayer* for a married taxpayer. These deductions are also cumulative—*i.e.*, a taxpayer may claim an additional standard deduction for being over age 65 *and* for being blind. [I.R.C. §63(c)(3), (f)]

Example: Tom Taxpayer, who is 70 years old and blind, is married to Tina Taxpayer, who turned 65 during the tax year but who is not blind. The couple may claim an additional standard deduction of $2,700—$900 for Tom being over 65, $900 for Tom being blind, and $900 for Tina being over 65.

EXAM TIP gilbert

Note that there is a "marriage penalty" at work in the additional deductions for elderly and blind taxpayers. Two *unmarried* elderly taxpayers would be able to deduct $2,300, but two *married* elderly taxpayers would be able to deduct only $1,800.

---

(3) Dependents [§570]

If a taxpayer is claimed as a dependent on another's return, the dependent's standard deduction is limited to the *greater* of $750 or $250 plus the individual's earned income. The $750 figure will be adjusted for future inflation. [I.R.C. §63(c)(5)]

(4) Effect of standard deduction [§571]

If a taxpayer does not itemize deductions from AGI, he takes advantage of the standard deduction instead. He also receives the benefit of deductions *from gross income* and the deduction for personal exemptions. (*See infra*, §§663 *et seq.*)

3. Interest [§572]

Interest on personal debts (other than qualified residence interest and some student loan interest) is *not* deductible. Interest on investment or business debts is deductible, but with numerous limitations.

a. Requirements for deductibility

(1) Debt of taxpayer [§573]

The indebtedness must be owed by the taxpayer, not someone else. However, interest is deductible even though there is *no personal liability* on the loan. [Treas. Reg. §1.163-1(b)]

Example: Karen has a first and second mortgage on her house but has no personal liability on either one. She is in default in paying interest on the first mortgage. To prevent foreclosure of the first mortgage, Sam, the second mortgagee, pays the delinquent interest. The interest paid by Sam is probably deductible *by Karen* (on the theory that, in substance, Sam loaned the money to Karen and Karen paid it to the first mortgagee). Note that Karen receives this deduction even though she did not make the payment and was not personally liable to do so. [*See* Rev. Rul. 76-75, 1976-1 C.B. 14] Sam cannot deduct the payment, since he is not the debtor. Instead, he must add the payment to the basis for the debt owed to him by Karen.

(2) Bona fide debt [§574]

Courts disallow interest deductions in cases where the debt was a sham or the transaction lacked economic substance.

(a) Shams [§575]

If there was no real debt, interest payments are not deductible.

Example: Tess purports to purchase treasury notes with borrowed money. But the "lender" never had any money to loan and the notes are bought and resold the same day. Despite paperwork purporting to show a loan and an investment, the loan was nonexistent and the interest is not deductible. [**Goodstein v. Commissioner,** 267 F.2d 127 (1st Cir. 1959); Rev. Rul. 82-94, 1982-1 C.B. 31—purported loan from parent to child and immediate loan of same amount from child to parent]

(b) No economic substance [§576]

Even though the lender has money to loan, interest is not deductible if the transaction has no reasonable possibility of producing an economic gain or loss apart from the tax savings.

Example: Taxpayer buys a single-premium annuity policy from Insco (a reputable insurance company), but borrows both the premiums due on the policy and the increasing cash value of the policy from Insco each year. As a result, the annuity ultimately payable will be a mere pittance. Moreover, the interest rate on the loans from Insco is more than the interest rate at which the policy gains in value. Consequently, there is no "substance" to the transaction because it does not affect Taxpayer's "beneficial interest" (except taxwise), and the interest is not deductible. [**Knetsch v. United States,** 364 U.S. 361 (1960); **Winn-Dixie Stores, Inc. v. Commissioner,** 254 F.3d 1313 (11th Cir. 2001)]

1) Enactment of I.R.C. section 264 [§577]

Today, the interest deduction in the above example would be

barred by I.R.C. section 264 (*see infra*, §603). However, the Court refused to interpret the later enactment of I.R.C. section 264 as implied approval of single-premium annuity schemes entered into before its effective date. [**Knetsch v. United States**, *supra*]

2) Application when property worth less than debt [§578]

When property is purchased with a nonpersonal liability loan, and the property is worth less than the amount of the loan, the debtor probably cannot take an interest deduction on any part of the loan. However, some authority indicates that interest may be deductible on that portion of the loan that equals the value of the property. The theory for denial of any deduction is similar to that of *Knetsch; i.e.*, the transaction lacks economic substance. [**Estate of Franklin v. Commissioner**, 544 F.2d 1045 (9th Cir. 1976)—deduction disallowed; *compare* **Pleasant Summit Land Corp. v. Commissioner**, 863 F.2d 263 (3d Cir. 1988), *cert. denied sub nom.*, **C.I.R. v. Prussin**, 493 U.S. 901 (1989)—loan treated as valid to extent of value of property]

(c) Business purpose [§579]

Even if the debt is not a sham, and there is a definite possibility of gain or loss, interest is not deductible unless the taxpayer had *some purpose other than tax saving* in incurring it. Mixed motives (*i.e.*, tax saving plus some other economic purpose) would be sufficient. [**Goldstein v. Commissioner**, 364 F.2d 734 (2d Cir.), *cert. denied*, 385 U.S. 1005 (1966)]

1) Rationale

I.R.C. section 163 was intended to equalize the positions of people who borrow and people who use their own capital to enter into transactions having some economic purpose—not to induce transactions that lack any such purpose.

---

e.g. **Example:** Taxpayer won $140,000 in the Irish Sweepstakes. She then borrowed $1 million from a bank at 4% interest to purchase a like amount of Treasury notes bearing interest of 2%. Although gains or losses on this transaction were possible, because the price of the notes could fluctuate, Taxpayer was not concerned with anything but tax saving; hence, no deduction was allowed. [**Goldstein v. Commissioner**, *supra*]

---

2) Note—current rule

Both *Knetsch* and *Goldstein* involved attempts to write off large amounts of *prepaid* interest. As discussed *infra*, §605, immediate deduction is no longer allowed for prepaid interest, regardless of the bona fides of the indebtedness.

3) "Generic tax shelters" [§580]

The theories of *Knetsch* and *Goldstein* (*i.e.*, no economic substance and requirement of business purpose) were the basis for the concept of the "generic tax shelter" described in **Rose v. Commissioner** (*supra*, §301). *Rose* describes a class of heavily tax motivated "investments," lacking in any economic substance, that give rise to no tax deductions.

(d) Family loans [§581]

While interest on a debt owed to a family member or relative is not *per se* disallowed, courts scrutinize such transactions carefully to make sure there is a bona fide debt—*i.e.*, a contract backed by consideration and an expectation of repayment. [*See* **Brown v. Commissioner,** 241 F.2d 827 (8th Cir. 1957)]

(e) Loans to controlled corporation [§582]

A corporation can deduct interest paid, even where the lender is the controlling shareholder. But if the "loan" is reclassified as "equity," the "interest" payments are *constructive dividends* to the shareholder. (This problem is fully discussed in the Income Tax II Summary.)

b. Identifying interest [§583]

Payments for the *use* of borrowed money are interest and deductible as such. But payments for the lender's *services* are *not* interest.

(1) Service charges [§584]

Lenders frequently charge a fee for such services as appraisal of the collateral or investigation of the debtor's credit. Such charges are not deductible as interest. [Rev. Rul. 67-297, 1967-2 C.B. 87] However, a business or investment borrower could capitalize such charges as part of the cost of obtaining the loan and amortize them over the period the loan is outstanding. [**Lovejoy v. Commissioner,** 18 B.T.A. 1179 (1930)]

(2) "Points" [§585]

Many lenders charge "points"—*i.e.*, additional amounts paid when the loan is obtained. These are additional interest. [Rev. Rul. 69-188, 1969-1 C.B. 54] (*See infra*, §606, for discussion of timing of the deduction for "points.")

(3) Imputed interest [§586]

In several situations, interest income and deductions are "imputed." That means that the borrower is treated as having paid interest, and the lender has interest income even though the contract called for no interest or for a lesser rate of interest.

(a) Loans [§587]

If a loan agreement calls for interest below the "applicable federal rate" (as periodically established by the IRS), interest is imputed. [I.R.C. §7872—*see supra*, §§239 *et seq.*] This provision applies especially to gift loans, to employer-employee loans, and to corporate-shareholder loans.

(b) Sales of property [§588]

If there is a sale of property in exchange for deferred payments, and the agreement calls for interest that is less than the applicable federal rate, interest is imputed. [I.R.C. §§483, 1274—*see infra*, §§915 *et seq.*]

(4) Tracing [§589]

Because some types of interest (*e.g.*, trade or business interest) are deductible, some types are not deductible (*e.g.*, personal loans), and some types may or may not be deductible (*e.g.*, interest on a loan incurred to purchase a passive activity), it is necessary to trace borrowed money into its actual use. A taxpayer who borrows money and commingles it with other funds in a single bank account and then uses the loan proceeds for various purposes may encounter serious difficulty in meeting her burden of proof as to how the borrowed funds were used. Separate bank accounts for each different use of the borrowed funds would be a good idea. [*See* Treas. Reg. §1.163-8T—stating general rule that debt proceeds are spent before any unborrowed amounts and before any later deposits into the account]

c. Exceptions—interest disallowed [§590]

In several situations, interest deductions are disallowed by statute.

(1) Personal interest [§591]

No deduction is allowed for interest incurred on debts arising out of the taxpayer's personal life. This includes interest other than interest incurred on debt arising out of a trade or business, an investment, or a passive activity (*see supra*, §543). Thus interest payments on credit card loans or personal car loans are not deductible. However, interest on certain education loans and qualified residence interest are deductible even though these arise out of personal life.

(a) Exception—qualified residence loans [§592]

A taxpayer can deduct interest on a loan *secured* by a qualified residence if it is either acquisition indebtedness or home equity indebtedness. [I.R.C. §163(h)(3), (4)]

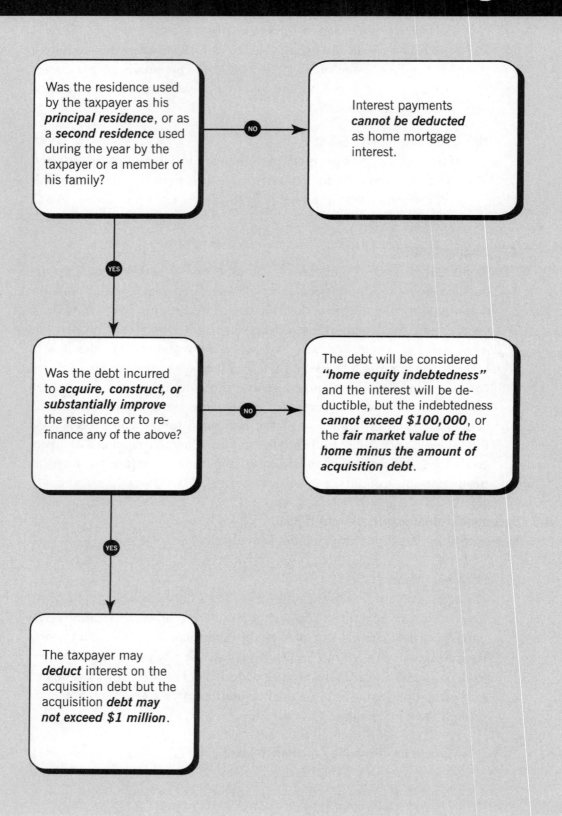

Was the residence used by the taxpayer as his *principal residence*, or as a *second residence* used during the year by the taxpayer or a member of his family?

NO → Interest payments *cannot be deducted* as home mortgage interest.

YES

Was the debt incurred to *acquire, construct, or substantially improve* the residence or to re-finance any of the above?

NO → The debt will be considered *"home equity indebtedness"* and the interest will be de-ductible, but the indebtedness *cannot exceed $100,000*, or the *fair market value of the home minus the amount of acquisition debt*.

YES

The taxpayer may *deduct* interest on the acquisition debt but the acquisition *debt may not exceed $1 million*.

1) **Acquisition indebtedness [§593]**

"Acquisition indebtedness" is debt incurred to acquire, construct, or substantially improve a qualified residence. However, the aggregate amount of acquisition debt cannot exceed $1 million. If a taxpayer refinances an acquisition debt, the refinanced debt remains acquisition debt—but only to the extent of the amount of the original acquisition debt. [I.R.C. §163(h)(3)(B)]

2) **Home equity indebtedness [§594]**

"Home equity indebtedness" means any debt (other than acquisition debt) secured by a qualified residence. However, home equity indebtedness cannot exceed $100,000. Also, it cannot exceed the fair market value of the residence reduced by the amount of acquisition debt on the residence. [I.R.C. §163(h)(4)(C)]

3) **Qualified residence [§595]**

A "qualified residence" is either the taxpayer's principal residence or a second residence used during the year by a taxpayer or a member of the taxpayer's family as a residence. [I.R.C. §§163(h)(4)(A), 280A(d)(1); *see supra*, §358]

(b) **Exception—interest on education loans [§596]**

A taxpayer can deduct interest on qualified education loans but the amount of interest that can be deducted is quite limited. In addition, the ability to deduct education loans is phased out as income rises. [I.R.C. §221]

1) **Amount deductible [§597]**

The amount of education interest that can be deducted is $2,500. This figure is *not* indexed for inflation.

2) **Income phaseout [§598]**

If AGI exceeds $50,000 ($100,000 on a joint return), the amount deductible is phased out. Interest becomes completely nondeductible if AGI equals or exceeds $65,000 ($115,000 on a joint return). These phaseout levels will be adjusted for inflation.

3) **Definitions [§599]**

A qualified education loan is a debt incurred to pay higher-education expenses incurred on behalf of the taxpayer, the taxpayer's spouse, or any dependent of the taxpayer. The student must be a degree candidate and carrying at least half the normal load. The taxpayer claiming the deduction may not be claimed as the dependent of another taxpayer. The creditor cannot be a party related to the borrower (*e.g.*, the student's grandmother).

4) Above the line [§600]

The deduction for interest on education loans is "above the line," meaning that it is a deduction from gross income. [I.R.C. §62(a)(17)] As a result, a student who pays interest on an education loan receives a tax benefit even if the student takes the standard deduction.

EXAM TIP   gilbert

For your exam, remember the only two instances where a taxpayer may deduct personal interest are *interest on a qualified residence* and *student loan interest*. *But note:* The interest on a qualified residence is *below the line*, while student loan interest is *above the line*.

---

(2) Expenses allocable to exempt income [§601]

The Code disallows any expense, including interest or attorneys' fees, attributable to producing income (other than interest income) that is tax-exempt. [I.R.C. §265(a)(1)] *Rationale:* Allowing such deductions would give an unwarranted double tax benefit.

Example: Personal injury damages are excludible from income. [I.R.C. §104(a)(2), discussed *supra*, §§89-100] Thus, the attorneys' fees incurred in recovering such damages cannot be deducted. However, if a lawsuit resulted in the recovery of damages that were partly taxable and partly nontaxable, a pro rata portion of the attorneys' fees would be deductible. [**Church v. Commissioner,** 80 T.C. 1104 (1983)]

---

(3) Tax-exempt interest [§602]

Interest on debts incurred to purchase or carry tax-exempt state and municipal bonds cannot be deducted. [I.R.C. §265(a)(2)]

(a) Note

It is not enough that the taxpayer simply borrows money at the same time he owns tax-exempt bonds—some "purposive connection" between the two is required. But the case law is quite strict in finding such connections. [**Wisconsin Cheeseman v. United States,** 388 F.2d 420 (7th Cir. 1968)]

(b) Connection

A "connection" between the debt and the tax-exempt bonds is obvious if the taxpayer either uses the proceeds to buy the bond or uses the bond as security for the debt. A borrowing in connection with an active business would not usually be connected to a tax-exempt bond that the taxpayer also owns (unless the borrowing was in excess of business needs). However, if a taxpayer borrows money, owns portfolio investments (*i.e.*, stock and taxable bonds), and also owns tax-exempt bonds, the IRS will disallow the interest because the taxpayer could have sold the portfolio investments to raise money to purchase or carry the tax-exempt bonds, rather than borrowing the money. [Rev. Proc. 72-18, 1972-1 C.B. 740]

(4) Loans to purchase insurance [§603]

No interest deduction is allowed on a debt incurred to buy "single-premium" life insurance, endowment, or annuity contracts (including those in which substantially all premiums are paid within four years). Similarly, the deduction is disallowed on loans made as part of a *systematic plan* of financing insurance premiums (generally by borrowing against increases in cash values under the policy). [I.R.C. §264(a)(2), (3)]

(a) Rationale

Since the interest element in life insurance is not taxed (*i.e.*, it becomes part of the tax-exempt life insurance proceeds payable at death), it is not fair for the interest incurred to purchase the insurance to be deductible.

(b) Exceptions

The disallowance rule of section 264(a)(3) does not apply if no part of four of the first seven premiums is borrowed. Also it does not apply if the amount disallowed would be less than $100, if the borrowing occurred because of unforeseen financial problems, or if the borrowing was incurred in connection with trade or business. [I.R.C. §264(c)]

(5) Accrued interest owed to "related" cash basis taxpayer [§604]

Also nondeductible until paid is unpaid interest (or any other deductible expense) owed by a debtor on the *accrual basis* to a creditor on the *cash basis* who is *related* to or *controlled* by the debtor (*see infra*, §§1036 *et seq.*).

(6) Prepaid interest [§605]

Prepaid interest is not immediately deductible. It must be capitalized and deducted in the years the underlying loan is outstanding. [*See* I.R.C. §461(g)]

(a) Exception—"points" [§606]

Payment of "points" incurred to purchase the taxpayer's *principal residence* is immediately deductible if the payment of points is an established business practice in the area and the amount does not exceed that generally charged. [I.R.C. §461(g)(2)] *But note:* Points paid on refinancing a home are not immediately deductible. They must be deducted over the years the loan is outstanding.

(7) Excess investment interest [§607]

To further discourage uneconomic, tax-motivated transactions, if interest deductions on investments exceed the net investment income, the excess is *disallowed*. [I.R.C. §163(d)] But disallowed interest can be *carried forward* and deducted against investment income in future years.

(a) "Net investment income" [§608]

"Net investment income" is gross income from the investment, less all expenses directly connected to the investment, including depreciation at *straight-line* rates (*see supra*, §467).

(b) Additional exception for corporations [§609]

A limitation, applicable to *corporate* taxpayers, disallows interest deductions in excess of $5 million on certain debts convertible into stock incurred in connection with corporate acquisitions. [I.R.C. §279]

(8) Passive activity [§610]

As noted above, losses on passive activities are not deductible in excess of income from such activities. [I.R.C. §469; *see supra*, §543] A large part of passive loss that is disallowed under this provision consists of interest incurred to purchase or to operate the passive activity.

4. Taxes [§611]

A tax may be either deductible as such, deductible only as a business or investment expense, or not deductible at all.

a. Taxes deductible as such [§612]

Every taxpayer is entitled to deduct *state and local* real or personal property taxes and state and local income taxes. [I.R.C. §164]

(1) Deduction of property taxes as between purchaser and seller [§613]

The portion of the property tax allocable to that part of the year *preceding* the date of the sale is considered imposed on the seller and she is entitled to a deduction in that amount. The balance is considered imposed on the buyer. [I.R.C. §164(d)]

(2) Disability insurance tax [§614]

A state payroll tax, used to finance a state disability insurance fund, is considered an income tax. Consequently, it is deductible as a tax. [**Trujillo v. Commissioner,** 68 T.C. 670 (1977)]

b. Taxes deductible only as business or investment expense [§615]

A taxpayer engaged in trade or business, or holding property for the production of income, is entitled to deduct, *in addition* to the taxes enumerated in the previous paragraph, all other taxes incurred *in connection with his business* or his property held for income production. [I.R.C. §§162(a), 212] For example, excise tax, federal import duties, federal social security tax on employers, state sales tax, and gasoline taxes may be deducted.

c. Taxes entirely nondeductible [§616]

Certain taxes are not deductible under any circumstances: federal income taxes, social security tax imposed on employees, excess profits taxes, federal estate and gift taxes, and state and local inheritance taxes. [*See* I.R.C. §§275, 164(b)]

5. Charitable Contributions [§617]

Taxpayers may deduct contributions to *recognized* charities—basically, to the *government* or any entity organized and operated *predominantly* for *charitable, religious, scientific, literary, or educational purposes.* [*See* I.R.C. §170(c)] No deductions are allowable for contributions to educational institutions practicing racial discrimination. [**Bob Jones University v. United States**, *supra*, §177]

a. Limitations

(1) Individuals [§618]

Individual taxpayers are entitled to deduct up to 50% of their *adjusted gross income* (*see supra*, §554) for gifts to most charities. [I.R.C. §170(b)(1)] Gifts to "nonoperating" private foundations and gifts of appreciated capital assets are subject to a 30% ceiling.

(a) Carryover

However, if an individual's contributions exceed the 50% or 30% ceiling, she can carryover and deduct the excess in the five succeeding taxable years. [I.R.C. §170(d)]

(2) Corporations [§619]

Corporations can deduct gifts only up to *10%* of their taxable income (although again contributions in excess of that amount can be carried over to the next five years). [I.R.C. §170(b)(2)]

(3) Estates and trusts [§620]

There is no limit on the amount an estate or trust may deduct for charitable contributions. [I.R.C. §642(c)]

(4) Recipient [§621]

The gift must be "to or for the use of" a recognized charity. The term "for the use of" means in trust for the charity. [**Davis v. United States**,

495 U.S. 472 (1990)—no deduction for parent's payment of child's expenses as a Mormon missionary since the transfer was not to the church or a trust for the church]

(5) Substantiation [§622]

All charitable gifts over $250 must be substantiated by a contemporaneous written acknowledgment from the donee organization. The donee organization must also state whether it provided any goods or services in consideration for any gift, and it must describe and value such goods or services. If the goods or services consist solely of intangible religious benefits, there must be a statement to that effect. [I.R.C. §170(f)(8); *and see infra,* §636—additional appraisal requirement]

b. Gifts in kind [§623]

A taxpayer may deduct the *fair market value* of contributions of property. [**Campbell v. Prothro,** 209 F.2d 331 (5th Cir. 1954)] Thus, for example, a taxpayer may deduct the value (not the basis) of stocks donated to a charity. However, there are several important *limitations* to consider where property, rather than cash, is donated.

(1) Fractional and future interests

(a) Residence or farm [§624]

Gifts of a fractional or future interest in the donor's *personal residence or farm* are deductible in the amount of the value of the interest at the time of the gift. [I.R.C. §170(f)(3)] In determining value, depreciation by reason of the donor's continued use must be taken into account.

---

e.g. **Example:** Martha conveys her farm to United Way, reserving a life estate for herself. Martha can deduct in the year of the gift the value of the remainder interest in her farm.

(b) Other real property and gifts to trusts [§625]

Gifts of *remainder* interests in *real property* (other than a personal residence or farm) or gifts to a *trust* (*e.g.,* "to B for life, remainder to Benevolent Charity") are deductible only if made in the form of a "*fixed annuity trust*" (which pays no more than a fixed dollar amount to the income beneficiary), a "*unitrust*" (which pays the beneficiary a fixed percentage of the value of the property), or a "*pooled income fund*" (a fund contributed to by many donors). (*See* detailed rules in I.R.C. section 170(f)(2) and discussion in the Estate and Gift Tax Summary.)

(c) Tangible personal property [§626]

A gift of a *future* interest in tangible personal property is *not* deductible at all when made. It becomes deductible only when the charity's interest becomes *possessory*. [I.R.C. §170(a)(3)]

---

e.g. **Example:** Paul has a valuable painting, an original "Dogs Playing Cards," which he gives to an art museum, reserving a life estate. He is allowed no current deduction. When Paul dies, either he (on his final return) or his estate will get the deduction.

(d) Income trusts [§627]

A deduction is also not allowed for a charitable gift of an *income* interest in a trust or other property, unless the income remains *taxable* to the donor (*see supra*, §§253-276), and the income interest is in the form of either a fixed annuity or a fixed percentage of the value of the property determined annually. [I.R.C. §170(f)(2)(B)]

(2) Gifts of appreciated property [§628]

Prior to 1969, a deduction was allowed for the *fair market value* of *any* property gifted to charity (rather than its cost to the taxpayer). This encouraged taxpayers to make gifts of appreciated property because they could *deduct* the present value of the property without realizing the gain or loss they would otherwise incur if they sold the property and donated the proceeds.

---

e.g. **Example:** Teri owns stock that cost her $2,000, but is now worth $10,000. If she gives it to charity, she can deduct the full $10,000—the $8,000 gain goes untaxed.

(a) Code provision limits former rule [§629]

This is still permitted when the donated property would (if sold) produce a *long-term capital gain*, *and* it is donated to a *public* charity. However, the amount of the deduction is limited to *30%* of the donor's AGI (instead of the regular 50%). [I.R.C. §170(b)(1)(D)]

(b) Deduction reduced further in two situations [§630]

Even if the property would have produced long-term capital gain, the amount deductible is reduced by *the amount of that gain* in the following cases:

1) Private foundation [§631]

When the gift is to a private foundation (*i.e.*, a charity supported by only one or a few donors), the amount deductible is reduced by the amount of appreciation. However, this limitation does not apply if the foundation is an *operating foundation*—

meaning it is directly engaged in doing charitable work as opposed to merely funneling money to other charities. [*See* I.R.C. §170(e)(1)(B)(i)] The limitation also does not apply to gifts of corporate stock for which market quotations are readily available. [I.R.C. §170(e)(5)]

2) Unrelated tangible personal property [§632]

When the gift is of tangible personal property unrelated to the charity's charitable purpose or function, the deduction is reduced by the amount of potential gain. [I.R.C. §170(e)(1)(B)(ii)]

> **Example:** Paul's valuable painting (worth $10,000 and having a basis of $7,000) is given to an art museum. The *entire* $10,000 could be deducted because the painting is *related* to the charitable function. But if the painting is given to a public charity that *operates a medical research clinic*, the amount deducted must be reduced by the amount by which the value exceeds Paul's basis (*i.e.*, the $10,000 is reduced by $3,000; only $7,000 is deductible).

(c) Gifts that would not produce long-term capital gain [§633]

If the donated property would, if sold, produce short-term capital gain or *ordinary income*, then the amount deductible is reduced by the amount that would not have been long-term capital gain if the property had been sold. The effect of this reduction is generally that only the *amount of the donor's basis* is deductible—and *not* its higher fair market value. [I.R.C. §170(e)(1)(A)] This rule applies regardless of whether the donee charity is public or private, and it applies both to individual and corporate donors.

1) Application

Thus, charitable gifts of all noncapital assets (*e.g.*, farm products or inventories), or capital assets held for one year or less, are deductible only at the donor's basis.

> **Example:** An artist donates her painting to a museum. Her basis is $100 and the value is $10,000. If the painting were sold, it would produce $9,900 ordinary income. Only $100 is deductible (*i.e.*, $10,000 less $9,900).

2) Recapture of depreciation [§634]

If depreciation would have been recaptured had the property been sold (*see infra*, §§925-930), the amount deductible must be reduced by the amount that would have been ordinary income because of recapture.

3) Exception—certain contributions of inventory or equipment [§635]

A deduction is allowed to corporate donors for an amount in excess of basis for gifts of inventory to a public charity to be used solely for the care of the ill, the needy, or infants; however, the charity cannot resell the property. The amount deductible is the value of the inventory, less 50% of the amount of ordinary income that would have been realized if it had been sold. In addition, the deduction cannot exceed twice the donor's basis. A similar provision allows deductions for gifts of scientific equipment to educational institutions. [I.R.C. §170(e)(3), (4)]

(3) Appraisals [§636]

Taxpayers must submit appraisals in support of the valuation of gifts other than cash to charity. An appraisal is required if the claimed value of the property (plus similar items donated to other donees) exceeds $5,000. In the case of nonpublicly traded securities, the value must be $10,000. [Tax Reform Act of 1984 §155(a)]

c. Bargain sales [§637]

When a taxpayer *sells* property to a charity for a price *below* fair market value, the difference (the bargain element) is deductible as a charitable contribution.

(1) Calculation of gain [§638]

The transaction is treated as part sale and part gift, and the bargain seller is required to *apportion his basis* between the gift part and the sale part. This will increase the gain recognized by the donor. [I.R.C. §170(e)(2)]

---

e.g. **Example:** Terri sells shares of stock (held for more than one year) to a public charity at her cost ($12,000) although the stock is presently worth $20,000. Terri is entitled to an $8,000 charitable contribution deduction. But her basis in the stock at time of sale is deemed to be only 12/20th of cost—*i.e.*, $7,200 instead of $12,000—so that she realizes a $4,800 gain.

---

d. Contribution of services or use of property [§639]

There is no deduction allowed for a contribution of the taxpayer's services or use of his property.

(1) Personal services [§640]

The value of personal services donated to a charity (*e.g.*, movie star entertains at a charity ball) is not deductible by the donor. [Treas. Reg. §1.170A-1(g)] Similarly, the IRS has ruled that a blood donation is not deductible because it is analogous to a transfer of services. [Rev. Rul. 53-162, 1953-2 C.B. 127]

(a) Distinguish—out-of-pocket expenses [§641]
The taxpayer-donor *can* deduct any out-of-pocket expenses incurred in rendering services (*e.g.*, transportation costs). [Treas. Reg. §1.170A-1(g)]

1) Automobile expenses [§642]
A taxpayer who uses her own car to render services to a charity can deduct 14 cents per mile. [I.R.C. §170(i)] In addition, the taxpayer can deduct out-of-pocket costs, such as parking, but not general repair expenses or depreciation on her car.

2) Only taxpayer's own expenses [§643]
A taxpayer can deduct the expenses only of *her own* service to charity, not the costs of a third party's service. [**Davis v. United States**, *supra*, §621—parent cannot deduct child's outlays while serving as Mormon missionary]

(2) Use of property [§644]
Likewise, a taxpayer who donates to a charity the use of his property (*e.g.*, free rent in his office building) cannot take a charitable deduction for the value of such use. [I.R.C. §170(f)(3)]

e. No deduction if taxpayer benefits [§645]
Contributions made with the anticipation of economic benefit rather than from "detached and disinterested generosity" are not deductible as charitable contributions. [**Winters v. Commissioner**, 468 F.2d 778 (2d Cir. 1972)]

Example: A church operated a school that charged no tuition. The parents of the students, however, were encouraged to contribute to the school, and realized that they had to in order to keep the school operating. Under these circumstances, no deduction was available; payments were treated as costs of education from which an economic benefit was anticipated. [**Winters v. Commissioner**, *supra*]

Example: The Church of Scientology requires payment of a fixed amount for "auditing" sessions. The Church regards auditing as a religious experience designed to promote spiritual awareness. Because the taxpayer was required to pay for an identifiable benefit, the payment is not deductible. Denial of a deduction did not violate either the Establishment Clause or Free Exercise Clause of the Constitution. [**Hernandez v. Commissioner**, 490 U.S. 680 (1989)]

---

e.g. **Example:** Corporation donates part of a large parcel of land to build a school. However, it expected that the school district would build a road that would make Corporation's remaining property much more valuable. The deduction was denied because the taxpayer will extract a benefit greater than that which would inure to the general public. [**Ottawa Silica Co. v. United States,** 699 F.2d 1124 (Fed. Cir. 1983)]

(1) Right to purchase season tickets with donation to college or university [§646]

If a taxpayer makes a contribution to a college or university, and the contribution entitles her to purchase season tickets to athletic events, 80% of the contribution is deductible. Of course, the actual cost of the tickets is not deductible. [I.R.C. §170(l)]

e.g. **Example:** Bluto Blutarksy contributes $1,000 to Faber College, which entitles Bluto to purchase season football and basketball tickets for $750. Bluto may deduct 80% of the $1,000 contribution ($800), but he may not deduct the season ticket costs of $750.

(2) Part gift, part purchase [§647]

If a taxpayer intentionally purchases property or services from a charity at a price in excess of value, the difference qualifies as a charitable contribution. [**United States v. American Bar Endowment,** *supra*, §178]

e.g. **Example:** The American Bar Association ("ABA") offers to sell life insurance to lawyers at a price exceeding the market value of the insurance. If the lawyer can prove (i) the difference between the amount she pays and the market value *and* (ii) that she knew about the difference and intended to make a gift to the ABA, she can deduct the difference as a charitable contribution. [**United States v. American Bar Endowment,** *supra*]

(a) Disclosure requirement [§648]

A payment made partly as a contribution and partly in consideration for goods or services provided by the charity to the donee is known as "a quid pro quo contribution." A charity that receives a quid pro quo contribution in excess of $75 must provide a written statement (at the time of solicitation or receipt of the contribution) that informs the donor that the charitable contribution is limited to the excess of the payment over the value of the goods or services received. The charity is subject to a penalty of $10 for every quid pro quo contribution it receives as to which it failed to make the required disclosure (with a limit of $5,000 for a particular fundraising event or mailing). [I.R.C. §§6115, 6714]

> **EXAM TIP**   **gilbert**
>
> Be alert for signs that a taxpayer in an exam question is *receiving consideration* in exchange for his charitable contribution. A taxpayer cannot receive value in return for a gift unless he can show that the value of what he contributed clearly exceeds the value of what he received (in which case, the *excess is deductible*).

(3) Travel [§649]

No outlay for traveling expenses (including meals and lodging) while away from home can be deducted as a charitable contribution unless there is no significant element of personal pleasure, recreation, or vacation in the travel. [I.R.C. §170(j)]

6. Medical Expenses [§650]

I.R.C. section 213 provides a limited deduction for medical expenses of the taxpayer and her dependents. In the case of divorced parents, a child will be considered the dependent of both parents for purposes of the medical expense deduction. Thus, if a father is entitled to claim the exemption for a child living with her mother (*see infra*, §§668-669), the mother can still deduct any medical expenses she pays for the child. [I.R.C. §213(d)(3)]

a. Items specifically deductible under the Code [§651]

Certain medical expenses are specifically listed in the Code as appropriate deductions. [I.R.C. §213] Taxpayers may deduct:

(1) *Any amount paid "for the diagnosis, cure, mitigation, treatment, or prevention of disease*, or for the purpose of affecting any structure or function of the body." [I.R.C. §213(d)(1)(A)] However, the cost of cosmetic surgery is not deductible unless necessary to ameliorate a deformity arising from a congenital abnormality, a personal injury, or a disfiguring disease. [I.R.C. §213(d)(9)]

(2) *Payments for transportation* that is essential to medical care. [I.R.C. §213(d)(1)(B)]

(3) *Amounts paid for medical insurance* (including Medicare insurance premiums) are deductible, but disability insurance premiums are not. The medical insurance premium must be separately stated. [I.R.C. §213(e)(1)(C), (e)(2)]

(4) *The cost of prescription drugs or insulin.* [I.R.C. §213(b), (d)(2)]

b. Borderline expenses [§652]

Many borderline expenses have required litigation to establish whether they are proximately related to health needs.

(1) Nonhospital living expenses [§653]

Amounts paid for lodging (although not in a hospital) are amounts paid for medical care if care is provided by a physician in a licensed hospital (or medical facility related to a hospital) and there is no significant element of personal pleasure, recreation, or vacation in the travel. The amount deductible cannot exceed $50 per individual per night, and the payments cannot be lavish or extravagant under the circumstances. [I.R.C. §213(d)(2); *and see* **Commissioner v. Bilder,** 369 U.S. 499 (1962)—disallowing hotel costs of heart patient recuperating in Florida (before enactment of §213(d)(2))]

(a) Distinguish—some special diet foods [§654]

Costs of special diet foods may be deducted as a medical expense when prescribed by a doctor as a *supplement* to, rather than a substitute for, the taxpayer's regular diet (which would be a nondeductible living expense). [**Harris v. Commissioner,** 46 T.C. 672 (1966)]

(2) Long-term care costs [§655]

Long-term care ("LTC") costs incurred by chronically ill individuals are deductible as medical expenses. [I.R.C. §§213(d)(1)(C), 7702B] "Chronically ill" means the taxpayer is certified by a licensed health care practitioner as unable to perform, without substantial assistance, at least two activities of daily living due to a loss of functional capacity. The activities of daily living are eating, toileting, transferring, bathing, dressing, and continence. The costs of care in a nursing home or other LTC facility, or of a caretaker in the taxpayer's home, are deductible LTC costs. Within limits, the costs of LTC insurance are deductible as medical expenses. If an employer pays for such insurance for employees, it is a tax-free fringe benefit subject to the same limits. Receipt of the proceeds of such insurance is not taxable up to certain limits.

(3) Child care expenses [§656]

Child care expenses incurred while a mother is ill are *not* deductible as medical expenses because they are not sufficiently related to the mother's health. [**Ochs v. Commissioner,** 195 F.2d 692 (2d Cir.), *cert. denied,* 344 U.S. 827 (1952)]

(4) Legal expenses [§657]

Expenses incurred in establishing a guardianship for the taxpayer's mentally ill wife have been held deductible as "medical" expenses—where she refused voluntary hospitalization and the guardianship was necessary to have her committed for treatment. [**Gerstacker v. Commissioner,** 414 F.2d 448 (6th Cir. 1969)]

(5) Cost of a capital improvement [§658]

A capital improvement prescribed by a physician for medical reasons (*e.g.*, air conditioner, elevator, etc., for heart patient) is *deductible* as a medical expense, but the deduction is limited in *amount* to the excess of the cost of the improvement over any increase in the value of the property by reason of the improvement. [**Riach v. Frank**, 302 F.2d 374 (9th Cir. 1962)]

(6) Depreciation [§659]

Depreciation on a car used for medical transportation is not deductible since it is not considered an "amount paid" for medical expenses. [**Weary v. Commissioner**, 510 F.2d 435 (10th Cir.), *cert. denied,* 423 U.S. 838 (1975); *but see* **Commissioner v. Idaho Power Co.**, *supra*, §383—depreciation on construction machinery had to be treated as a "payment," which added to the basis of the building constructed, a result not altogether consistent with *Weary*]

c. Effect of insurance [§660]

Medical expenses are not deductible if compensated by insurance or otherwise.

d. Limitations on deductible amount [§661]

A taxpayer may deduct medical expenses only in excess of 7.5% of AGI. [I.R.C. §213(a)]

e. Self-employed persons [§662]

Self-employed persons are entitled to deduct their medical insurance premiums (assuming they are not entitled to participate in any subsidized health plan maintained by an employer) as business expenses. The deduction is 70% of the premiums in 2002 and 100% in 2003 and later years. [I.R.C. §162(l)]

7. Personal and Dependency Exemptions and Child Tax Credits

a. Personal exemptions [§663]

A taxpayer is entitled to an exemption for himself. If spouses file a joint return, each claims an exemption. The exemption amount is $2,000. This amount is adjusted for inflation; so the exemption amount is $3,000 in 2002. Exemptions are below-the-line deductions (*i.e.*, deducted from AGI). However, they can be deducted in addition to the standard deduction (*see supra*, §557). Exemptions are not subject to the 2% floor on miscellaneous itemized deductions (*see supra*, §562) or the deduction phaseout (*see supra*, §565).

b. Exemptions for dependents [§664]

An additional exemption is also provided for each "dependent." However, an individual cannot claim a personal exemption for himself if he is eligible to be claimed as a dependent on another taxpayer's return. A person is a dependent if the following conditions are met:

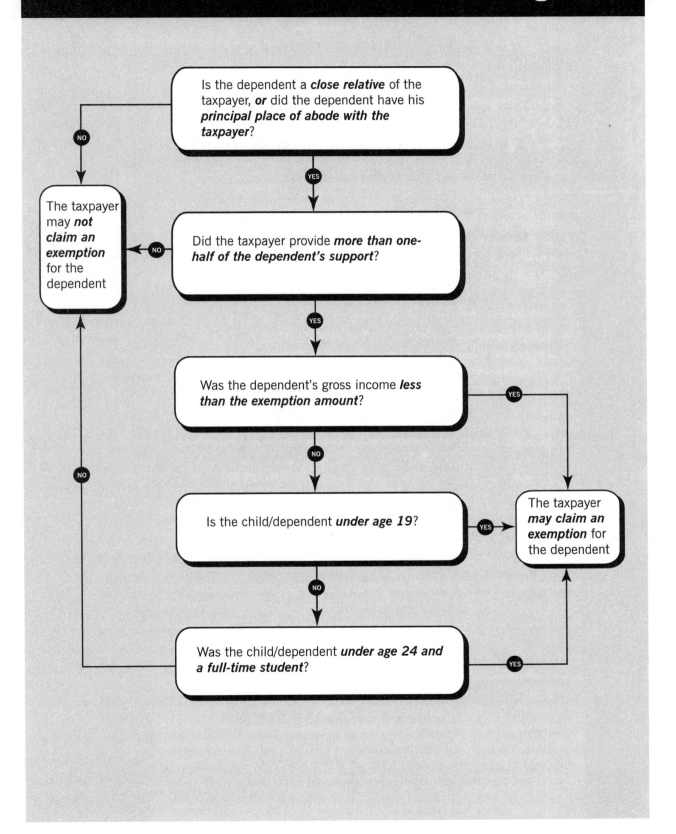

(1) *His gross income is less than the exemption amount.* However, if the individual is a *child of the taxpayer and is either under age 19 or a full-time student under age 24*, this rule is waived. It is also waived for gross income of disabled persons in sheltered workshops. [I.R.C. §151(c)]

(2) *The taxpayer supplies over one-half of the support* of the dependent. [I.R.C. §152(a)]

(3) *The dependent is either a close relative of the taxpayer or has his principal place of abode with the taxpayer.* [I.R.C. §152(a)] In the latter situation, their relationship must not violate local law. [I.R.C. §152(b)(5)]

c. Special rules concerning dependents

(1) Support in kind [§665]

In determining whether the taxpayer supplied over one-half of the dependent's support, items provided *in kind*, such as housing and food, are included—but not the value of services provided to the dependent.

(a) Note

Welfare payments for a child are treated as support provided by the *state*, not by the parent. Therefore, if state provides more than one-half of the total support costs, the parent cannot claim an exemption. [**Lutter v. Commissioner**, 61 T.C. 685 (1974)]

(2) Multiple support agreement [§666]

If several people all contribute to the dependent's support (*e.g.*, four children each contributing 25% of their mother's support), any one of them can claim the exemption pursuant to a *multiple support agreement*. Such an agreement will allocate the exemption to one of the contributors, often rotating it from year to year. [I.R.C. §152(c)]

(3) Scholarships [§667]

In determining whether a taxpayer supplied over one-half of the dependent's support, a scholarship received by a dependent is ignored.

(4) Divorced parents [§668]

A frequent problem is determining which of the divorced parents is entitled to exemptions for the children. As a general rule, the exemption is given to the parent who *has custody* for the larger part of the taxable year. [I.R.C. §152(e)(1)]

(a) Exception for release of claim [§669]

The noncustodial parent gets the exemption if the custodial parent signs a written release of her right to claim the exemption for the current year. [I.R.C. §152(e)(2)] The noncustodial parent must attach this declaration, executed by using IRS Form 8332, to his return. This provision permits the parents to negotiate over who gets the exemption and to compensate the parent who does not claim it. The custodial spouse can waive her right to the exemption for all future years or can waive the right one year at a time. However, the exemption cannot be shifted unless the custodial spouse actually signs the waiver. [*See* **Miller v. Commissioner**, 114 T.C. 184 (2000)—exemption not shifted when spouse attached a court order awarding him the exemption, and not a signed waiver by his ex-wife]

d. Phaseout of personal exemption [§670]

Personal exemptions are phased out at the rate of two percentage points for each $2,500 (or fraction thereof) by which the taxpayer's "AGI" exceeds the threshold amount. However, the personal exemption phaseouts themselves are scheduled to be phased out between 2006 and 2009. [I.R.C. §151(d)(3)]

(1) Threshold amount [§671]

The threshold amount is adjusted annually for inflation. In 2002, the threshold amounts are: $206,000 on a joint return, $171,650 on a head of household return, $137,700 on a single return, and $103,000 on the return of a married person filing separately. The exemption is completely phased out when AGI exceeds $328,500 on a joint return, $294,150 on head of household, $259,800 for singles, and $164,250 for married filing separately.

Example: Gloria, who is single, is entitled to three personal exemptions. Her 2002 AGI is $158,700, which is $21,000 more than the threshold amount. For each $2,500 over the threshold amount (or fraction thereof), Gloria's exemptions are reduced two percentage points. Therefore, her exemptions are reduced by 18% ($21,000 ÷ $2,500 = 8.4, which is treated as 9; 9 x 2 = 18). Because personal exemptions are $3,000 each in 2002 ($9,000 for Gloria's three personal exemptions), she must reduce her exemptions by 18% of $9,000, or $1,620. Thus, Gloria's exemptions are worth only $7,380 instead of $9,000.

---

8. Casualty and Theft Losses [§672]

Individuals can deduct losses arising from "fire, storm, shipwreck, or other casualty, or from theft" even though not connected to business or investment. [I.R.C. §165(c)(3)] However, each such loss is deductible only to the extent it *exceeds $100*, and the total of casualty and theft losses is deductible only to the extent it *exceeds 10% of AGI*. [I.R.C. §165(h)(1)] A business or investment casualty loss, however, is not limited either by the $100 or 10% provisions. [I.R.C. §165(c)(1), (2)]

a. Casualties [§673]

To be deductible as a casualty, there must be an element of *suddenness* about the event.

> **e.g. Example:** Damage to the taxpayer's own car from an auto accident is deductible even though the taxpayer was negligent. (But damage to the other car involved in the accident is not; *see infra*, §678.)

(1) Inclusion in statute not required [§674]

Other sorts of disasters beyond those specifically mentioned in the statute are deductible if sufficiently sudden and unusual.

> **e.g. Example:** A taxpayer was allowed to deduct the loss of a diamond when a car door was slammed on her finger and the diamond popped out of the ring and vanished. [**White v. Commissioner,** 48 T.C. 430 (1967)]

(2) Nonphysical causes [§675]

However, declines in value resulting from nonphysical causes are not deductible as casualty losses even though they may meet the requirement of suddenness. [**Chamales v. Commissioner,** T.C. Memo. 2000-33—property owner, whose property was besieged by media and tourists because it was located next to O.J. Simpson's home, could not claim a casualty loss]

(3) Anticipated physical losses [§676]

Mere decline in value of the property caused by apprehension of *future* disasters is not deductible as a casualty. [**Pulvers v. Commissioner,** 407 F.2d 838 (9th Cir. 1969)—decline in value due to nearby landslide that caused no physical damage to taxpayer's property not deductible; *but see* **Finkbohner v. United States,** 788 F.2d 723 (11th Cir. 1986)—allowing casualty loss deduction because of decline in the property's value due to the fact that it was adjacent to properties that were abandoned and torn down because of the threat of flooding]

b. Thefts [§677]

The taxpayer must prove actual criminal theft of property *as defined under local law,* not merely that the property was lost or that it mysteriously disappeared.

> **e.g. Example:** In **Paine v. Commissioner,** 63 T.C. 736 (1975), corporate officials engaged in various fraudulent acts that violated federal securities laws, eventually resulting in taxpayer's stock declining in value. The taxpayer was not allowed to deduct the loss in value as a theft loss. *Rationale:* Breaches of fiduciary duty by the corporate officials may have wiped out the value of stock, but this was not a theft loss to the taxpayer because the taxpayer failed to prove that the actions of the corporate officials were criminal under state law. Instead, when the stock became worthless, the stockholders could take a capital loss deduction.

(1) Note

Similarly, an act of a foreign state cannot be treated as a theft loss. [**Billman v. Commissioner**, 73 T.C. 139 (1979)—worthlessness of Vietnamese currency]

c. **Limited to taxpayer's property [§678]**

Taxpayer can deduct casualty losses only for damages to her *own* property.

Example: Taxpayer drove her car into someone else's house. She could not deduct the damages to the house as a casualty loss since such losses are limited to damages to one's own property. Note, however, that if the accident had occurred in connection with taxpayer's trade or business, the costs would have been deductible as business expenses under section 162. [**Dosher v. United States**, 730 F.2d 375 (5th Cir. 1984)]

d. **Amount deductible [§679]**

A taxpayer can deduct the *lesser* of:

(i) *The adjusted basis* of the property; *or*

(ii) *The difference between the value of the property before and after* the casualty.

Note: For *personal* casualty and theft losses, *each* must be reduced by $100, and the *total* of personal casualty and theft losses is deductible only to the extent it exceeds 10% of AGI.

(1) Cost of repair [§680]

Repair costs are considered good evidence of decline in value occurring by reason of the casualty if the property is restored to its original condition.

Example: Alice's car (not used for business) had a basis of $1,200 and a value of $800 when it was damaged in a collision. Repair costs were $250. After repair, the car was in the same shape it had been before the accident. Alice had no insurance. Assuming that repair costs fairly measure the decline in value from the collision, she can potentially deduct $150: the lesser of $1,200 or $250, less $100 (since it is a personal casualty loss). Alice's adjusted gross income is $8,200; she also has a $900 theft loss ($1,000 less $100). Her total casualties are $1,050. She can deduct only the excess over 10% of AGI or $230 ($1,050 less $820).

(2) Insurance [§681]

Any insurance recoveries reduce casualty losses. If a taxpayer fails to file a claim with her insurance company (fearing that the policy might be canceled), the loss deduction is wiped out. [I.R.C. §165(h)(4)]

> **e.g. Example:** Betty owned a valuable painting, which was held for investment and was stolen. Her basis was $8,000 but the value of the painting was $19,000. She recovered $5,000 of insurance. Her casualty loss is $3,000: the lesser of $8,000 or $19,000, reduced by the insurance recovery. Since the painting was held for investment, and not personal use, the casualty loss is *not reduced* by $100 and it is *not limited* to the excess over 10% of AGI.

e. Personal casualty gains and losses in the same year

(1) Gains exceed losses [§682]

If a taxpayer has both personal casualty or theft losses and gains in the same year, the gains and losses are netted. If the gains exceed the losses, all of the gains are treated as capital gains and all of the losses (in excess of $100 per loss) are deductible, but they are treated as capital losses. "Personal" means a loss of property that is used neither for business nor investment. (Casualty gains usually arise from insurance payments that exceed the basis of the damaged asset—note that these gains are unrecognized if the taxpayer appropriately reinvests the insurance proceeds.) [I.R.C. §165(h)(2)(B)—for discussion of nonrecognition of gain from involuntary conversions, *see infra*, §§795-799; for discussion of capital gains and losses, *see infra*, §§813 *et seq*.]

(2) Losses exceed gains [§683]

If personal casualty losses exceed casualty gains, the two figures are netted. Both gains and losses are ordinary rather than capital. The losses after subtracting $100 from each loss are deductible to the extent of the gains, but only so much of the excess over the gains as exceeds 10% of AGI is deductible. [I.R.C. §165(h)(2)(A)]

9. Other Personal Deductions

a. Nonbusiness bad debts [§684]

As discussed previously (*see supra*, §529), any debt not in connection with a trade or business is treated as a nonbusiness bad debt and is deductible only as a short-term capital loss.

b. Alimony payments [§685]

A payor-spouse is entitled to deduct alimony payments, which constitute taxable income to the payee-spouse. Conversely, payments such as child support, which do not constitute taxable income to the payee, are not deductible by the payor (*see supra*, §§162-172). [I.R.C. §§71, 215] Note that alimony is deductible from gross income ("above the line"). [I.R.C. §62(a)(10)]

c. Contributions to retirement plans [§686]

A taxpayer may establish an "individual retirement account" ("IRA") and contribute and deduct up to $3,000 per year ($3,500 for taxpayers who are over 50 years old). [I.R.C. §219(b)(5), (f)(1)] This deduction is "above the line" (*i.e.*, from gross income). [I.R.C. §62(a)(7)] Investment gains in the IRA are not currently taxed. Generally, the taxpayer *may* start distributing the funds in an IRA when he reaches age 59½ and *must* start distributing the funds at age 70½. ***Distributions from an IRA are taxable.***

(1) Limitation [§687]

An IRA contribution can be made only to the extent that the taxpayer has "earned income." Moreover, *no* deduction for IRA contributions may be taken if the taxpayer (or her spouse) is an active participant in an employer's qualified pension or profit-sharing plan [I.R.C. §219(g)], with the exception that the full $3,000 (or $3,500 for taxpayers who are over 50 years old) deduction is available if the taxpayer's 2002 adjusted gross income is $34,000 or less (for single taxpayers) or $54,000 (for married taxpayers). Both figures sharply increase after 2002. Part of the maximum $3,000 (or $3,500) deduction is available if taxpayer's adjusted gross income exceeds the applicable figure by less than $10,000. Note that if taxpayer or taxpayer's spouse is not covered by a qualified employer-maintained pension or profit-sharing plan, they can contribute and deduct $3,000 (or $3,500) per year to an IRA regardless of income.

(2) Roth IRAs [§688]

Contributions to Roth IRAs are not currently deductible. However, investment income is not taxable and ***none of the distributions from the Roth IRA are taxable*** if made after the taxpayer reaches age 59½ and more than five years after the first contribution to the Roth IRA. As a result, a very large amount of investment income can be sheltered from income tax since distributions need not begin by age 70½ and can be made to the taxpayer's heirs after death. Contributions to regular IRAs plus Roth IRAs cannot exceed $3,000 per year, but the income limitations on Roth IRAs are much higher than for regular IRAs. The amount is $150,000 for a taxpayer filing a joint return (with the total permitted contribution phasing out at $160,000) or $95,000 for a taxpayer filing a separate return (with the total permitted contribution phasing out at $110,000). These limitations apply whether or not the taxpayer is covered by an employer-maintained retirement plan. [I.R.C. §408A]

(3) Education IRAs [§689]

A taxpayer can contribute up to $2,000 per year to an education IRA for a beneficiary under 18. The contributions are not deductible, but investment income is not taxed and distributions are not taxable. The funds in an education IRA may be used to pay qualified post-secondary educational expenses—tuition, fees, books, supplies, and equipment at any educational institution—whether public, private, or religious. [I.R.C. §530] There are income limitations and phaseouts for education IRAs that are the same as for Roth IRAs (*supra*).

DEATIONS—ABOVE THE LINE VS. BELOW THE LINE	**gilbert**
FROM GROSS INCOME (*i.e.,* "ABOVE THE LINE")	**ADJUSTED GROSS INCOME** (*i.e.,* "BELOW THE LINE")
• Trade or business deductions	• Standard deduction
• Reimbursed expenses of employees	*or*
• Capital losses	• Medical expenses
• Deduction from sale or exchange of property	• Charitable contributions
• Deductible "nonbusiness" expenses related to rent or royalty income (*see supra,* §440)	• Casualty and theft losses
	• "Nonbusiness" expenses for property held for the production of income
• Alimony	• "Nonbusiness" expense—expenses of a tax-related matter
• Moving expenses	• Other "miscellaneous itemized deductions"
• Interest on educational loans	
• Contributions to IRAs (but not Roth IRAs)	• Home mortgage interest

D. Tax Rates

1. Return Category [§690]

Once taxable income is determined, the tax is computed. The rates are set forth in I.R.C. section 1 and depend on whether the taxpayer is married or single. Most married taxpayers file a joint return. Single persons may qualify as a head of household (with lower rates than for other single people). (*See supra,* §238.)

2. Tax Rates [§691]

There are six tax brackets for 2002: 10%, 15%, 27%, 30%, 35%, and 38.6%. [I.R.C. §1(a) - (d), (i)] These brackets will decline beginning in 2004. The levels at which the brackets change are adjusted for inflation. [I.R.C. §1(f)]

E. Credits

1. In General [§692]

After the amount of tax has been determined, the taxpayer may be entitled to certain *credits*. These reduce the actual tax payable on a *dollar-for-dollar* basis.

2. Credit for Taxes Withheld and Prepaid [§693]

The taxpayer is entitled to a credit against taxes payable for all sums withheld from wages for payment of taxes [I.R.C. §31]; and for all amounts prepaid in connection with declarations of estimated tax [I.R.C. §6315].

3. Foreign Tax Credit [§694]

In lieu of a deduction from income, the taxpayer may elect to take as a credit against tax the amount of income and similar taxes paid or accrued during the year to foreign countries or possessions of the United States. The amount of the credit is limited to that proportion of the tax that the taxable income from sources within the foreign country bears to the entire taxable income of the individual. [I.R.C. §§27, 901-905] Note that the taxpayer has the *option* to treat foreign taxes as a credit or a deduction from gross income, whichever is the most advantageous to the taxpayer.

4. Credit for the Elderly [§695]

Taxpayers who are age 65 or over receive a credit of 15% of their "section 22 amount." [I.R.C. §22]

a. "Section 22 amount" [§696]

The "section 22 amount" is $5,000 for a single individual, $7,500 in case of a joint return where both spouses are eligible, or $3,750 in the case of a married person filing a separate return.

b. Reductions from "section 22 amount" [§697]

The taxpayer must reduce the "section 22 amount" by Social Security received or other amounts excluded from gross income. (The "section 22 amount" does not have to be reduced by life insurance, annuities, compensation for personal injuries or sickness, or amounts received under accident or health plans.)

(1) And note

If AGI exceeds $7,500, the "section 22 amount" is further reduced by one-half of the excess over $7,500. (This figure is $10,000 in case of a joint return, $5,000 in case of a married person filing a separate return.)

c. Disabled persons [§698]

The credit also applies to disability income received by a taxpayer under age 65 who is retired due to a permanent and total disability.

5. Welfare Employees and Work Incentive Credit [§699]

The Code allows for a credit of 50% of the wages paid to a person who is a member of a disadvantaged class (such as a welfare recipient or economically disadvantaged youth). The 50% credit applies to the first $6,000 of wages during the employee's first year; during the second year, the credit is 25% of the employee's wages. [I.R.C. §§38(b), 51]

6. **Child or Dependent Care Credit [§700]**

To enable themselves to work, many parents incur child care costs. Traditionally, the courts did not permit taxpayers to take such costs as a business expense deduction. [**Smith v. Commissioner,** 40 B.T.A. 1038 (1939), *aff'd*, 113 F.2d 114 (2d Cir. 1940)] Eventually, however, Congress provided a limited deduction, then broadened the deduction, and finally switched to a credit. [I.R.C. §21]

a. **Who is entitled to the credit [§701]**

The child care credit is available to a taxpayer who incurs "employment-related expenses" in order to be gainfully employed. "Employment-related expenses" are those for household services and for care of a qualifying individual. A "qualifying individual" is a dependent under age 13 for whom the taxpayer is entitled to claim the exemption, or a dependent of taxpayer (or taxpayer's spouse) who is unable to care for himself. [I.R.C. §21(b)]

(1) **Transportation costs excluded [§702]**

The cost of transporting a child to a day-care center does not qualify for the credit even though the cost of the center itself does qualify. [**Warner v. Commissioner,** 69 T.C. 995 (1978)] The cost of summer camp likewise does not qualify for the credit.

(2) **Taxpayer identification numbers required [§703]**

The name, address, and social security number of the care provider must be provided on the return (unless the care provider is a tax-exempt organization, in which case only the name and address must be provided). [I.R.C. §21(e)(9)]

b. **Amount of credit [§704]**

The amount of the credit is equal to a percentage of the child care costs that the taxpayer incurs. The percentage varies depending on income. The percentage is 30% if taxpayer's AGI is $10,000 or less. The applicable percentage is decreased by one percentage point (but not below 20%) for each $2,000 (or fraction thereof) by which AGI exceeds $10,000.

---

e.g. **Example:** Alice and Bob, a married couple, have AGI of $17,200 in 2002. Their applicable percentage is 26%. Their AGI exceeds $10,000 by $7,200—which is three whole $2,000 units and a fraction of a fourth. Thus, the applicable percentage (30%) must be reduced by four percentage points.

---

(1) **Credit to increase in 2003**

Beginning in 2003, the credit will be 35% of employment-related expenses. The income threshold for the phaseout will be increased to $15,000 from $10,000. If adjusted gross income exceeds $43,000, the applicable percentage will be 20%.

Example: Assume that Alice and Bob in the previous example have AGI of $17,200 in 2003. Their applicable percentage is 33%. Their AGI exceeds $15,000 by $2,200, which is one whole $2,000 unit plus a fraction of a second. Therefore, the applicable percentage is reduced by 2% from 35% to 33%.

c. **Dollar limit [§705]**

The amount of expenses for which a credit can be taken cannot exceed $2,400 for one qualifying individual and $4,800 for two or more qualifying individuals. [I.R.C. §21(c)] Beginning in 2003, the maximum amount of eligible expenses will be increased to $3,000 from $2,400 for one dependent child and to $6,000 from $4,800 for two or more dependent children.

(1) **Earned income limitation [§706]**

Nor can such expenses exceed earned income. In the case of a married couple, the expenses cannot exceed the earned income of the spouse with the *lower* earned income. (There is a special rule for spouses who are students or disabled; they are treated as if they had monthly income of $200 if there is one qualifying individual or $400 if there is more than one.) [I.R.C. §21(d)(2)]

Example: In 2003, Alice and Bob, whose applicable percentage is 33%, have one child, nine-year-old Chuck. Assume that child care costs for Chuck are $3,200, that Alice's earned income is $18,000, and that Bob's earned income is $1,200. Ordinarily, $3,000 could be taken into account (since they have one child and the limit in 2003 is $3,000). However, this limit is capped by the lower-earning spouse's earned income (Bob's earned income of $1,200). Thus, the child care credit is 33% of $1,200, or $396.

d. **Divorced parents included [§707]**

Even if a custodial parent is not entitled to claim an exemption, she can take the child care credit. [I.R.C. §21(e)(5)]

7. **Child Tax Credit [§708]**

If a taxpayer is entitled to claim a ***child under age 17 as a dependent***, the taxpayer is also entitled to a child tax *credit* of $600 per child for 2001 - 2004. The child tax credit will be gradually increased to $1,000 in 2010. [I.R.C. §24] The child cannot have attained the age of 17 by the end of the calendar year. *Note:* A credit reduces tax dollar for dollar—so a $600 credit reduces tax liability by $600.

a. **Phaseouts [§709]**

The child tax credit is reduced by $50 for each $1,000 (or fraction thereof) by which the taxpayer's AGI exceeds the threshold amount. For this purpose, the threshold amount is $110,000 on a joint return, $75,000 on a single return, and $55,000 for a married individual filing a separate return. [I.R.C. §24(b)] Neither the amount of the credit nor the threshold amounts are indexed for inflation.

b. Definition of child [§710]

For purposes of the credit, a "child" includes a son or daughter of the taxpayer (including adopted children) or a descendant of either, a stepson or stepdaughter of the taxpayer, or an eligible foster child of the taxpayer. [I.R.C. §§24(c)(1)(C), 32(c)(3)(B)] The child must be a United States citizen or resident.

c. Refundability [§711]

The child tax credit is usually *refundable*, meaning that it can produce a refund even though it exceeds an individual's tax liability for the year. For 2001-2004, the credit is refundable to the extent of 10% of earned income in excess of $10,000. The credit is capped at $1,200. For 2005, the percentage is increased to 15%. [*See* I.R.C. §24(d)]

---

e.g. **Example:** In 2003, Tony Taxpayer has two children who qualify as dependents, and he has earned income of $23,000. Further assume that Tony does not have any tax liability. Tony is entitled to a refund of $1,200, because 10% of Tony's earned income is $1,300 ([$23,000 - $10,000] x 10% = $1,300) and the credit is capped at $1,200. (Note that if this credit were not refundable, Tony could not have taken advantage of it.)

---

d. Divorced parents [§712]

The rules for shifting child tax credits between divorced parents are the same as the rules for shifting dependency exemptions. (*See supra*, §668.) Thus, as a general rule, a custodial parent is entitled to the child tax credit as well as the exemption, but the credit can be shifted to the noncustodial parent if the custodial parent signs a written release of the right to claim the credit.

8. Earned Income Credit [§713]

The Code provides a credit against tax for lower income taxpayers. This credit is quite valuable because it is refundable—if the credit exceeds the tax due, the taxpayer gets a refund. [I.R.C. §32] The earned income credit is an important anti-poverty device that has been significantly expanded in recent years.

a. Amount of credit for taxpayers with qualifying children [§714]

For 2002, a taxpayer with one child under age 19 (or under age 24 and a full-time student) may claim a credit of 34% of earned income up to $7,370 (or a maximum of $2,506). If the taxpayer has two or more children, the credit is 34% of earned income up to $10,350 (or a maximum of $4,140). The credit is reduced by 15.98% of earned income in excess of $13,520 ($14,520 on a joint return). Thus, for a taxpayer with one child, the earned income credit is completely phased out when the taxpayer has earned income of $29,201 (single taxpayer) or $30,201 (joint return). For a taxpayer with two or more children, the earned income credit is completely phased out when the taxpayer has earned income of $33,178 (single taxpayer) or $34,178 (joint return). For future tax years, these amounts will be adjusted for inflation.

b. Amount of credit for taxpayers without qualifying children [§715]

If the taxpayer does not have qualifying children, the earned income credit is 7.65% of earned income up to $4,910 (or a maximum of $376). The credit is phased out at the rate of 7.65% for earned income in excess of $6,150 ($7,150 on a joint return). Thus, the earned income credit is completely phased out at $11,060 (single return) or $12,060 (joint return). For future tax years, these amounts will be adjusted for inflation.

9. Adoption Tax Credit [§716]

A taxpayer can claim a credit for adoption expenses up to $10,000 per child. If the taxpayer's AGI exceeds $150,000, the amount allowable is phased out. It is completely phased out at AGI of $190,000. The expenses for which a credit can be claimed are for the legal adoption of a child under age 18 (or a person over age 18 who is physically or mentally incapable of caring for herself). The expenses cannot be incurred in carrying out a surrogate parenting arrangement. [I.R.C. §23]

10. Education Credits [§717]

Several tax credits are provided for the higher education costs of low- or moderate-income taxpayers. These credits are nonrefundable. They apply to tuition payments for the taxpayer, the taxpayer's spouse, or the taxpayer's dependent. [I.R.C. §25A]

a. HOPE scholarship credit [§718]

The HOPE credit provides a maximum allowable credit of $1,500 per year for each of the first two years of post-secondary education. This consists of 100% of the first $1,000 of tuition and 50% of the second $1,000 of tuition. This credit is allowed per student; thus a parent with several children in college could claim several HOPE credits.

b. Lifetime learning credit [§719]

The lifetime learning credit provides a credit for 20% of qualified tuition expenses in any year when the HOPE credit is not claimed. The credit is 20% of tuition paid on the first $5,000 of tuition ($10,000 after the year 2003). These limits are per taxpayer; thus they do not increase if the taxpayer is paying for several children.

c. Phaseouts [§720]

Both credits begin to be phased out if AGI exceeds $40,000 on a single return and $80,000 on a joint return. They are completely phased out when AGI reaches $50,000 on a single return and $100,000 on a joint return.

COMPARISON OF DEDUCTIONS, EXEMPTIONS, AND CREDITS

gilbert

	EFFECT	EXAMPLES
ABOVE-THE-LINE DEDUCTION	Deducted *from gross income* to arrive at adjusted gross income ("AGI")	Ordinary and necessary business expenses (except of employees); alimony payments; some IRA contributions; capital losses
BELOW-THE-LINE DEDUCTION	Deducted *from AGI only if exceeds the standard deduction*; some subject to a floor	Qualified interest on residence; state and local income and property taxes; charitable contributions (up to 50% of AGI); medical expenses exceeding 7.5% of AGI; ordinary and necessary business expenses of employees
PERSONAL AND DEPENDENCY EXEMPTIONS	Deducted *from AGI to determine taxable income even if standard deduction is used*; phases out at high income levels	Exemption for taxpayer; exemption for dependents
CREDITS	*Reduces tax due dollar for dollar*	Child tax credit; credit for the elderly; welfare employees and work incentive credit; child care credit; earned income credit; adoption tax credit; education credits

Chapter Four:
Gain or Loss on Sale or Exchange of Property

CONTENTS

Chapter Approach

Chapter Approach

This chapter considers the tax consequences of transfers of property. An exam question concerning a property transfer will usually require *computation of the amount of gain or loss* and will often involve issues of *realization and recognition.*

1. **Basis**

   To calculate the gain or loss from the disposition of property, it is first necessary to *ascertain the basis* of the property. In most cases, that basis must be "adjusted" for various items (such as depreciation). Analyze basis issues as follows:

   a. If basis is *cost*, what was the cost? Be sure to include purchase-money debt.

   b. If the property was received by *gift*, apply the carryover basis rules.

   c. If the property was *inherited*, use the date of death value (unless it was income in respect of a decedent).

   d. If the property was received as *compensation*, use the amount included in income.

   e. If the property was received as a result of a *nonrecognition provision*, use the carryover basis with appropriate adjustments.

   f. Then *adjust basis* by *depreciation* (including depreciation that could have been but was not claimed), *capitalized expenditures, casualty losses, etc.*

2. **Amount Realized**

   The transaction in which the property is disposed of must be analyzed. To tax the gain (or deduct the loss) on disposition, the transaction must be treated as a *"realization."* It is necessary to compute the amount realized in the transaction in order to compute the gain or loss and to properly apply any nonrecognition provision (below). When discussing realization on an exam, keep in mind the following points:

   a. The amount realized includes all *debts* from which the transferor is relieved (even if property is worth less than a nonrecourse debt).

   b. If the amount is *not ascertainable*, you should argue both the open and closed transaction methods.

   c. If the property received is of *indeterminate value*, it is presumed equal in value to the property given up.

d.   Gifts are not ordinarily realizations, but watch for a *discharge of debt coupled with a gift*.

3.   **Nonrecognition of Gain or Loss**

The taxation of gain (or deduction of loss) may be deferred if a *"nonrecognition"* section of the Code is applicable. The nonrecognition issue should be analyzed as follows:

a.   Determine whether there was an *exchange* qualifying under section 1031 by asking:

   (1)   Does the property received meet the *"like kind"* test?

   (2)   Was there a *triangle* exchange or *deferred* exchange?

   (3)   Was *boot* received? If so, figure recognized gain and adjust basis. Note that if boot was transferred, gain or loss is recognized on the transferred boot and it also increases the taxpayer's basis in the new property. Watch for related party rules, which require recognition if the related party disposes of the property within two years.

b.   Determine whether there was an *involuntary conversion* qualifying under section 1033 by asking:

   (1)   Was the property involuntarily converted by *condemnation or casualty*?

   (2)   Was it *replaced by similar property* within two years?

   (3)   Was there an *election* not to recognize gain?

   (4)   Was the full amount received *reinvested*? If not, adjust basis.

c.   Determine whether there was a gain on the *sale of a principal residence* qualifying for exclusion by asking:

   (1)   Was the dwelling the taxpayer's *principal residence* for *two* or more of the *five years* preceding the sale?

   (2)   Has the taxpayer excluded gain on the sale of a principal residence within the past *two years*?

   (3)   The taxpayer may exclude up to $250,000 of gain; a married couple, each of whom meets the two- and five-year qualifications, may exclude up to a $500,000 gain if they file a joint return.

d.   Determine whether there was a *transfer between spouses* or former spouses incident to divorce. Gain or loss is not recognized and basis stays the same.

4. Character of Gain or Loss

After all of the above is done, the character of the gain or loss must be analyzed to see whether it is *capital or ordinary*. (This material is discussed in the next chapter, along with the alternative minimum tax on tax preferences.)

A. Computation of Basis, Gain, or Loss

1. Computation Formula [§721]

To determine gain or loss on the disposition of property, adjusted basis must first be calculated using the following formula:

adjusted basis = unadjusted basis + additions - reductions

If the amount realized on disposition of the property is greater than the adjusted basis, the difference is a gain, but if the amount realized is less than the adjusted basis, the difference is a loss, or mathematically:

gain = amount realized - adjusted basis

loss = adjusted basis - amount realized

2. Basis [§722]

Basis must be known both for computation of gain or loss and also for computing depreciation (*see supra*, §§465 *et seq.*).

a. Unadjusted basis [§723]

Unadjusted basis is usually cost. However, there are special rules for *gifts, inherited property, and tax-free exchanges*. [I.R.C. §§1012-1015]

(1) Cost basis [§724]

Generally the basis of property is the cost of the property. [I.R.C. §1012] Cost includes the cash or other property paid to obtain the asset.

(a) Mortgages [§725]

Cost also includes any purchase-money mortgage or trust deed on the property, regardless of whether the taxpayer is personally liable on the mortgage or assumes or takes subject to existing mortgages. [*See* **Commissioner v. Tufts**, 461 U.S. 300 (1983)]

####### 1) Depreciation [§726]

Because the basis of property includes purchase-money debt, a taxpayer frequently will have a high basis for purchased property even though she has not expended much cash of her own. This means that the property will generate high depreciation deductions (if it is held in a trade or business or for the production of income). Note, however, that the ability to deduct losses on such property may be sharply limited by the "at risk" rules (*see supra,* §§538-542) if the debt is nonrecourse, and by the passive activity loss rules (*see supra,* §§543-550) if the property is held for rental or other passive activity.

(b) Contingent liabilities [§727]

If the liability is contingent and might never have to be paid, the basis of the property does *not* include the debt. [**Albany Car Wheel Co. v. Commissioner,** 40 T.C. 831 (1963), *aff'd,* 333 F.2d 653 (2d Cir. 1964)] Similarly, if the property is worth significantly less than the amount of a nonrecourse liability, it is likely that no part of the debt is included in basis. [**Estate of Franklin v. Commissioner,** 544 F.2d 1045 (9th Cir. 1976)] However, it is possible that part of the debt will be included in basis to the extent of the fair market value of the property. [**Pleasant Summit Land Corp. v. Commissioner,** *supra,* §578] This issue remains unresolved.

(c) Long term obligations [§728]

A court will examine all the realities of a transaction to determine whether the property is actually worth more than the debt and whether the debtor is really the owner of the property. If the risks of gain or loss are on the lender, rather than on the borrower, the lender is treated as the real investor, and the borrower cannot treat the loan as part of her basis. [**Carnegie Productions, Inc. v. Commissioner,** 59 T.C. 642 (1973)]

---

e.g. **Example:** In **Mayerson v. Commissioner,** 47 T.C. 340 (1966), although a building's purchase price of $332,500 was financed with $5,000 down, $5,000 payable in one year, and $322,500 payable in 99 years ("interest only" payments were required to that time), the Tax Court allowed a purchaser to include in basis the entire debt. The building in question was old, and it needed a number of repairs—both to attract tenants and to correct numerous building code violations. As a result of the building's age and condition, a traditional mortgage was unavailable. The parties agreed that the buyer would renovate the building and correct any building code violations. The parties also contemplated that traditional mortgage financing would be procured as soon as practicable, which would enable the taxpayer to retire the note before the end of the 99-year term. This in fact occurred. Furthermore, it was the taxpayer's responsibility to determine the most profitable use of the building and to find tenants. Finally, the parties had no prior contact with each other prior to the transaction in question. Thus, the debt was treated as realistic and not a sham.

(d) Purchase expense [§729]

Expenses of acquisition, such as broker's or attorneys' fees, are added to basis.

(e) Option cost [§730]

If the property was purchased through exercise of an option, any amount paid for the option (if not already credited to the purchase price) is added to the purchaser's cost basis.

(f) "Tax-detriment" rule [§731]

"Cost" also includes any income charged to the taxpayer in acquiring the property. For example, if Taxpayer pays $10 for stock in her employer's corporation that is really worth $30, the "bargain purchase" being a form of additional compensation to Taxpayer, Taxpayer has $20 worth of income (*see supra*, §41). This $20 becomes part of Taxpayer's "cost basis" on the stock; *i.e.*, her basis is $30, not merely $10.

EXAM TIP **gilbert**

In exam questions, be on the lookout for noncash sources of basis. Cost basis of property *includes more than the cash that was exchanged* between the parties. Cost also includes *debts incurred* to purchase the property (*e.g.*, a purchase-money mortgage), *purchase expenses* (*e.g.*, a broker's fee), amounts paid for *options* (if the amount is not credited to the purchase price), and *any income charged* to the taxpayer *as a result of the transaction*.

---

(2) Inter vivos gifts [§732]

For purposes of computing *gain* (as well as for depreciation purposes), the donee takes the donor's basis on property acquired as a gift. However, for purposes of computing *loss*, the donee's basis is the *fair market value* at the time of gift, *or* the donor's basis, whichever is *lower*. [I.R.C. §1015]

Example: Alex gives Becky land that originally cost $10,000, but is worth $12,000 at the time of gift. Becky's basis for the land is $10,000 for all purposes.

Example: If, however, the land in the example above was only worth $8,000 at the time of the gift, and Becky later sold it for

$7,500, Becky's basis for determining *loss* would be $8,000 (not $10,000), and Becky's loss would be only $500.

Example: If the land in the example above was worth $8,000 at the time of the gift and Becky sold it for $9,000, there would be *neither gain nor loss:* no gain, because basis for determining gain is $10,000, and no loss, because basis for determining loss is $8,000. [Treas. Reg. §1.1015-1(a)(2)]

(a) Increase by gift tax paid [§733]

The donee can increase her basis by a portion of the gift tax paid by the donor. The portion of the gift tax that can be used to increase basis is the amount determined by a fraction—the net appreciation in value of the gift over the amount of the gift—multiplied by the total gift tax paid. In other words, "increase in basis" is to "gift tax paid" as "appreciation" is to "amount of gift." [I.R.C. §1015(d)(6)]

Example: On Alice's gift of stock to Trudy, she pays a gift tax of $10,600. Alice's basis for the stock was $40,000, and the stock was worth $50,000 at time of transfer to Trudy. Therefore, the net appreciation is $10,000. The net appreciation ($10,000) over the amount of the gift ($50,000) is 20%. Twenty percent of the gift tax ($10,600) is $2,120. Thus, Trudy's basis is $42,120 ($40,000 + $2,120).

1) Limitation—ceiling on increase

Gift taxes paid can never increase basis to an amount in excess of the property's value at the date of the gift. Thus, there would be no increase for gift tax in the second and third examples above (*supra,* §732).

(3) Tax-free exchanges [§734]

The basis of property acquired in a tax-free exchange is that of the property transferred. However, it must be adjusted for any nonqualifying consideration paid or received (*see infra,* §§779 *et seq.*).

(4) Inherited property [§735]

The basis of inherited property in the hands of a decedent's estate or in the hands of the person inheriting it is its value at the date of decedent's death. [I.R.C. §1014] If the estate elected to use the "alternate valuation date" for the estate tax purposes, the income tax basis of the property would be its value six months after the date of death.

(a)   **Note—carryover basis after 2010 [§736]**

Under legislation passed in 2001, the treatment of inherited property is scheduled to change in 2010. Taxpayers who die in or after 2010 will not receive the "stepped up" basis provided for in the present version of section 1014. Instead, after 2010, the basis of inherited property will be *the lesser* of the decedent's basis or the fair market value of the property on the date of death. [I.R.C. §1022] However, executors will be able to increase the basis of property in the estate in aggregate by up to $1.3 million (or $3 million for property passing to a surviving spouse). This new provision is extremely complex and will, in all likelihood, be amended before it goes into effect.

---

e.g. Example: Alice bought stock for $2,000 in 1947. It was worth $100,000 when Alice died in 2002. Alice leaves it to Bob. Bob's basis is $100,000; the $98,000 appreciation in the stock is *never* subjected to income tax.

(b)   **Form in which property is held [§737]**

When property is owned by more than one person, the basis may be affected on the death of one owner. The effect depends on the form in which the property was held.

1)   **Community property [§738]**

If a decedent and her surviving spouse owned the property as community property, both halves receive a new basis. [I.R.C. §1014(b)(6)]

---

e.g. Example: Harold and Wanda owned real estate as community property. Its basis was $150,000 and it was worth $600,000 when Wanda died. Wanda left her community interest to Sally. Sally's basis is $300,000. Harold's basis for his retained half is also increased to $300,000.

---

2)   **Tenants in common [§739]**

When a married couple owns property as tenants in common rather than as community property, the surviving spouse's half interest does not receive a new basis, but the deceased spouse's half does.

---

e.g. Example: Harold and Wanda owned a home as tenants in common. The property's basis is $150,000. The property was worth $600,000 when Wanda died. Wanda left her interest in the property to Sally. Sally's basis would be $300,000, but Harold's basis would still be $75,000.

3) Joint tenancy [§740]

If two people owned the property as joint tenants, the portion of the property that was includible in the decedent's gross estate for estate tax purposes under I.R.C. section 2040 receives a new basis and the balance of the property retains its basis. In the case of married joint tenants, half of the value of the property is subject to estate tax on the death of the first tenant; consequently, the result would be the same as that described for tenancy in common in the preceding paragraph. [I.R.C. §1014(b)(9)]

Example: Fred and Wilma own Blackrock as joint tenants. Blackrock's basis is $100,000. The property was worth $1 million when Fred died. Wilma's basis would be $550,000— $500,000 for Fred's interest and $50,000 for Wilma's interest. If Fred and Wilma were married, the value of half of Blackrock would be subject to estate tax.

(c) Term interests [§741]

Special rules apply to "term interests" received by gift or bequest. "Term interests" include a life estate, a term for years, or an income interest in a trust. In such cases, the recipient of the term interest has a basis for her interest but, in most situations, is not allowed to make any use of it.

Example: Homer gives property to Marge for life, remainder to Bart. Assume that, considering Homer's basis and actuarial tables for Marge's life, the life estate has a basis of $7,500 in Marge's hands. Marge cannot amortize this basis. As a result the entire amount of income that Marge receives annually is taxed, without any reduction to measure the decline in value of her interest as she gets older.

1) Sale of term interest [§742]

The seller of a term interest is treated as if her basis was zero. [I.R.C. §1001(e)(2)] *Rationale:* The term interest is treated as a capital asset under **McAllister v. Commissioner** (*see infra,* §849). The Code denies the seller a basis in order to make such sales less attractive to the seller.

> **Example:** Same facts as above, except now Marge decides to sell her life estate to Montgomery for $12,000. She cannot offset the sale price with any of her $7,500 basis—the entire $12,000 is taxed as a capital gain. Note that this result would *not* change even if Marge were to sell her life estate to Bart.

2) Exception [§743]

If both the holder of the remainder and the holder of the term interest sell their interests to a third party, each of them is entitled to use his basis. [I.R.C. §1001(e)(3)]

> **Example:** Same facts as in the example at §741, *supra*, except now both Marge and Bart agree to sell their respective interests to Montgomery. Now, Marge *is allowed* a basis recovery. Assuming that she receives $12,000 for her interest, her capital gain would be only $4,500.

3) Amortization [§744]

The holder of a term interest cannot reduce the income received by a deduction for the decline in value of her interest that occurs with time (*e.g.*, a 10-year term is worth more in the first year than in the last year). [I.R.C. §§102(b)(2), 273]

4) Not always applicable [§745]

These rules denying the use of basis to holders of term interests apply only to interests received by gift or bequest—not to purchased interests.

(d) Income in respect of a decedent [§746]

Certain items inherited from a decedent do not receive a basis adjustment to fair market value by reason of I.R.C. section 1014. These items are known as "income in respect of a decedent." They involve situations in which income was not taxed to the decedent even though most of the events leading to the realization of income occurred before the decedent's death. [I.R.C. §§1014(c), 691]

> **Example:** Decedent, a salesperson, negotiated a sale for which she was entitled to receive a commission. However, the money was not paid until after her death. Because she used the cash basis of accounting, the $10,000 was not taxed to her while she was alive. This is income in respect of a decedent.

METHOD OF TRANSFER	RESULT
INTER VIVOS GIFT	*Gain:* Donee's basis is **donor's basis** plus a portion of any gift tax that the donor paid. *Loss:* Donee's basis is the **lower** of the property's **fair market value** at the time of the gift **or** the **donor's basis** plus a portion of the gift tax paid.
TAX-FREE EXCHANGE	The basis in the new property is the **basis of the transferred property** plus adjustments for any nonqualifying consideration paid or received.
INHERITANCE	*In General:* Legatee's basis is the property's **value at the time of decedent's death** (or alternatively six months thereafter). *Community property:* Legatee's and/or surviving spouse's basis in property is its **value at the time of decedent's death**; both halves receive a new basis. *Tenancy in common or joint tenancy:* Legatee's basis in property is its **value at the time of decedent's death**, but **surviving spouse's basis** in property **does not change**.
GIFT OR BEQUEST OF TERM INTEREST (*e.g.,* **life estate, income interest in trust**)	The holder of the term interest has a **basis of zero**. If the holder and remainderman combine their interests and sell to a third party, the basis of the term interest would be calculated by using the donor's basis and actuarial tables.

e.g. **Example:** A bonus was paid after the decedent's death attributable to services rendered before death. However, the exact amount was not determined until after death and, consequently, it could not have been income to the decedent before death even under the accrual method of accounting. Still, it was held income in respect of a decedent since it was traceable to pre-death services. [**O'Daniel's Estate v. Commissioner,** 173 F.2d 966 (2d Cir. 1949)]

e.g. **Example:** Decedent was a farmer who turned over grapes to a marketing co-op, but the price had not been fixed at that time and payment was not made until after decedent's death. It was held immaterial whether decedent had sold the grapes to the co-op or merely entrusted the grapes. In either case, the proceeds were attributable to a transaction entered into during life and thus were income in respect of a decedent. [**Commissioner v. Linde,** 213 F.2d 1 (9th Cir. 1954)]

1) **Distinguish—services not completed at time of death [§747]**
If significant services remained to be rendered at the time of death and before payment was due, the item would *not* be income in respect of a decedent. [**Commissioner v. Peterson,** 667 F.2d 675 (8th Cir. 1981)—decedent made contract for future sale of calves that had to be cared for before payment was due; gain is not income in respect of decedent]

2) **Taxed to recipient [§748]**
Whoever receives income in respect of a decedent (decedent's estate or legatee) is taxed on it to the same extent the decedent would have been taxed. If the item would have been capital gain to the decedent, the recipient can treat it as such.

3) **Deduction for estate tax [§749]**
If the item of income in respect of a decedent was also subject to estate tax in the decedent's estate, the recipient is allowed to treat the estate tax as a deduction from income. [I.R.C. §691(c)]

b. **Adjusted basis [§750]**
Adjusted basis is determined by *adding* to the unadjusted basis all subsequent expenditures chargeable to the asset that were not deductible as current expenses, *i.e.,* items properly capitalized (*see supra,* §§365-406). From this sum is subtracted (i) receipts, losses, or other items properly chargeable to the capital account; and (ii) depreciation, depletion, amortization, or obsolescence allowed (or allowable) on the capital asset. [I.R.C. §1016]

HOW TO CALCULATE BASIS AND ADJUSTED BASIS

gilbert

STEP ONE: UNADJUSTED BASIS	
	Cost of property
	+ Debt to purchase property
	+ Purchase expenses
	+ Amounts paid for options
	+ Any income to taxpayer as a result of transaction
	= **UNADJUSTED BASIS**

STEP TWO: ADJUSTED BASIS	
	Unadjusted basis
	+ Items properly capitalized
	− Receipts, losses, or other items properly chargeable to the capital account
	− Depreciation, depletion, amortization, or obsolescence allowed or allowable
	= **ADJUSTED BASIS**

(1) Treatment of depreciation [§751]

If a taxpayer failed to claim as much depreciation as was "allowable," the full amount *allowable* reduces the basis anyway. However, if the taxpayer deducted and was allowed more than the amount that was legally allowable (*e.g.*, due to mistake, aggressive tax practices, etc.), the full amount *actually allowed* reduces the basis.

Example: Taxpayer bought a building for $100,000 and deducted depreciation of $40,000 on it. However, $45,000 was the amount legally allowable. He built interior walls to create office space; this cost $8,000. One room was rendered unusable by an explosion; Taxpayer deducted a loss of $16,000 and did not repair this part of the building. His basis is now $47,000. This figure is computed by starting with $100,000 and adding the capitalized improvement ($8,000) and deducting depreciation allowable ($45,000) and the casualty loss ($16,000).

(a) Tax benefit limitation [§752]

If the taxpayer claimed more than the legally allowable amount, but did not receive any tax benefit from the excess, he does not reduce the basis by the excess. [I.R.C. §1016(a)(2)(B)]

(2) Tenant's improvements [§753]

A lessor has no income by reason of the lessee's construction of improvements on the leased property—either at the time of construction or at the termination of the lease. [I.R.C. §109; *and see supra*, §120] However, if the improvements are intended as a substitute for the payment of rent, they are taxable when built. The lessor is not entitled to increase the basis of the property for the tenant's improvements *unless they were in fact treated as rent* and taxed to him when built, in which case they would increase basis. [I.R.C. §1019]

c. Allocation of basis

(1) Partial sale [§754]

When the taxpayer sells or exchanges only a *part* of his asset, he must allocate basis between the part sold and the part retained "in some reasonable manner." [Treas. Reg. §1.61-6(a)]

(a) But note

If this cannot be done conveniently, then the amount received is simply applied against the basis of the part retained. For example, Taxpayer sold an easement to kill fish in a river that formed part of the property. Because the basis of the easement as compared to that of the remaining property was uncertain, the amount received by Taxpayer was held to reduce Taxpayer's basis on the retained property. [**Inaja Land Co. v. Commissioner,** 9 T.C. 727 (1947)]

(2) Lump sum purchase of several assets [§755]

Likewise, when a taxpayer purchases a number of different assets for a lump sum (*e.g.,* purchase of a going business), he must allocate the purchase price to the various assets involved in accordance with their relative values.

B. The Requirement of Realization

1. In General [§756]

Before any increase in net worth becomes taxable (or a decline in value can be deducted as a loss), a *realization* must occur. This means that a crystallizing event has taken place that makes it reasonable and convenient to compute gain or loss. [**Cottage Savings Association v. Commissioner,** 499 U.S. 554 (1991)]

EXAM TIP　　　　　　　　　　　　　　　　　　　　　　**gilbert**

For your exam, be sure to remember that a gain or loss must be *both realized and recognized* before it would be taxable. (*See infra,* §§779 *et seq.*)

---

a. Note

The requirement that income be realized has been held to be a *constitutional limitation* on the government's power to tax. [**Eisner v. Macomber,** *supra,* §4—however, few believe that this case would be followed today]

2. Realization in Property Transactions [§757]

The owner of property realizes gain or loss only on the *sale or other disposition* of property. [I.R.C. §1001] In other words, the disposition is deemed the most appropriate time for computing the owner's gain or loss.

a. Mortgages [§758]

Mortgaging is *not* a realizing transaction—even when the taxpayer-owner borrows more than the basis of the property. [**Woodsam Associates, Inc. v. Commissioner,** 198 F.2d 357 (2d Cir. 1952)]

b. Transfers as payments of debt [§759]

The transfer of appreciated property by a taxpayer in satisfaction of a claim against him is a realization—it is the equivalent of an *exchange.*

> **e.g.** **Example:** Taxpayer owes Lender $1,000. Taxpayer transfers to Lender property worth $1,000, but on which Taxpayer's basis is only $400. There is a realization of $600 gain to Taxpayer. [**United States v. Davis,** 370 U.S. 65 (1962)]

(1) Mortgage plus gift [§760]

A gift of property is not a realization (*see supra,* §198), just as mortgaging is not. However, if the two transactions are *combined*, the result may be a realization.

---

e.g. **Example:** Taxpayer had property with a basis of $100 and a value of $400. He mortgaged the property, borrowing $250; there was no personal liability. Then Taxpayer gave the property to a trust for his children subject to the mortgage. *Held:* Because the effect of the transaction was to relieve Taxpayer of the debt, he is deemed to realize the amount of the debt. Thus, Taxpayer realized a gain of $150 on the gift ($250 liability minus $100 basis). [Treas. Reg. §1.1001-2(a)(4)(iii); **Johnson v. Commissioner,** 495 F.2d 1079 (6th Cir. 1974)]

---

(2) Effect of donee's gift tax payment [§761]

If the donor makes the gift conditional on the donee's payment of gift tax, the donor realizes a gain if the gift tax liability exceeds his basis. According to the Supreme Court, the donee's payment of the donor's gift tax produces an immediate economic benefit to the donor equal to the excess of the gift tax over the donor's basis. [**Diedrich v. Commissioner,** 454 U.S. 813 (1982)]

(3) Mortgage foreclosure [§762]

Foreclosure of a mortgage is also a realization—it is treated as a sale by the debtor-mortgagor to the creditor-mortgagee. [*See* **Parker v. Delaney,** 186 F.2d 455 (1st Cir. 1950)]

c. Exchanges [§763]

An exchange is a realization of gain or loss if the property received "differs materially either in kind or in extent" from the property given up. [Treas. Reg. §1.1001-1(a)] Thus, a swap of a pool of mortgages secured by homes in City A for a pool of mortgages secured by land in City B is a realization. This is so even if the swap is done purely for tax avoidance reasons (to recognize a loss) and even if the mortgages in each pool have the same total principal amount, interest rate, and fair market value and are viewed by banking regulators as economically identical. For tax purposes, the mortgages are different because they are secured by different real property; thus, the rates of default or prepayment will vary in the future. The mortgages, therefore, "differ materially" under the regulation. [**Cottage Savings Association v. Commissioner,** *supra,* §756]

EXAM TIP   **gilbert**

On your exam, be sure to be able to identify *when a realization occurs*. Realization does not only occur by sale—it can take many forms, including by sale, by payment of debt, by mortgage foreclosure, and by exchange for property that is materially different.

3. **Amount Realized [§764]**

The amount realized is the sum of the money, plus the fair market value of any other property, received by the taxpayer in a realizing transaction—*i.e.,* on the sale or other disposition of the asset. [I.R.C. §1001(b)]

a. **Mortgaged property [§765]**

Upon disposing of mortgaged property, a taxpayer's "amount realized" is the sum of the cash received *plus* the amount of any debt secured by the property for which the taxpayer is no longer liable.

(1) *Crane* **rule [§766]**

In **Crane v. Commissioner,** 331 U.S. 1 (1947), a leading case in the area, a taxpayer inherited an apartment building from her husband. The building was appraised for federal estate tax purposes at $262,042.50, an amount that was exactly equal to an outstanding mortgage on the building ($255,000) plus the interest then in default ($7,042.50). The taxpayer agreed with the mortgagee to continue to operate the building—collecting rents, paying for operating expenses, etc.—and to pay the mortgagee any net rentals. This relationship continued for seven years, during which time the taxpayer reported the rents as gross income and claimed (and was allowed) deductions for taxes, operating expenses, interest, and depreciation. The interest in default, however, continued to increase. The taxpayer then sold the building to a third party for $3,000 and an agreement to assume the mortgage. The taxpayer claimed that her equity in the building when she acquired it was zero. The Court disagreed, holding that the seller realized the full amount of the outstanding note even though she had no personal obligation to pay it and received only a token amount of cash from the buyer.

(2) **Significance [§767]**

In many real estate deals, the buyer of property (such as an apartment house) acquires it with a small down payment and borrows the balance using a nonrecourse loan (*i.e.,* a loan for which the borrower has no personal liability). For purposes of claiming depreciation on the building, the taxpayer's basis includes not only the down payment but also the full amount of the nonrecourse loan (*see supra*, §725). However, when the property is disposed of—whether by sale or foreclosure—the taxpayer must treat as an amount realized not only the cash received, but also the full amount of the outstanding loan. Often, this treatment produces a substantial gain because the taxpayer claimed depreciation that exceeded the actual decline in value of the property.

Example: Taxpayer bought Blackacre in Year 1 for $20 down and $140 of nonrecourse debt, making his basis $160. During years 1 to 6, Taxpayer correctly claimed depreciation of $45, making Taxpayer's adjusted basis of the property $115. During year 6, Taxpayer sold

Blackacre for $135. Taxpayer's depreciation ($45) exceeded the decline in value of the property ($25). Therefore, Taxpayer has a gain on the sale of $20.

---

(3) Property worth less than nonrecourse loan [§768]

Suppose that property that secures a nonrecourse loan is worth less than the amount of the loan. The taxpayer might sell property subject to the loan or the loan may be foreclosed by the lender. Since the loan is nonrecourse, the lender cannot collect the deficiency. Nevertheless, the taxpayer still is treated as realizing the full amount of the mortgage then outstanding. Any other treatment would be inconsistent with allowing her to include the nonrecourse loan in her basis when she acquired the property. [**Commissioner v. Tufts**, 461 U.S. 300 (1983); I.R.C. §7701(g)]

(a) When transferor realizes amount of mortgage [§769]

Property is considered to be disposed of, so the transferor realizes the full amount of the mortgage, when the property is given away, when the mortgage is foreclosed, or when the property is held by a grantor trust and the trust is converted to a nongrantor trust. [Treas. Reg. §1.1001-2; *see supra*, §§760-762; on grantor trusts, *see supra*, §§249-276]

(4) Nonrecourse vs. recourse debt [§770]

The rules relating to recourse debts are not entirely the same as those relating to nonrecourse debts.

(a) Disposition of property under nonrecourse debt [§771]

In the case of a nonrecourse debt, a taxpayer realizes the full amount of the debt when he disposes of the property. The debt is simply treated as part of the sale price of the property. Consequently, if the property was a capital asset, the resulting gain is capital gain (except to the extent it is turned to ordinary income by the depreciation recapture rules). [**Commissioner v. Tufts**, *supra*]

(b) Recourse debt [§772]

Suppose that a creditor under a recourse debt forecloses his mortgage. Since the property is worth less than the mortgage, the creditor could collect a deficiency judgment from the borrower. However, the creditor fails to do so. The amount forgiven by the failure to collect the deficiency is treated as debt cancellation income to the borrower. Debt cancellation income is ordinary income, not capital gain, although there are a number of exceptions to the rule that such income is immediately taxable. [Treas. Reg. §1.1001-2; **Aizawa v. Commissioner**, 99 T.C. 197 (1992), *aff'd*, 29 F.3d 630 (9th Cir. 1994)—taxpayer realizes bid price at foreclosure sale, since bid was equal to value of property, *not* full amount of debt; **Frazier v. Commissioner,** 111 T.C. 243 (1998)—fair market value of property much less than bid price; Rev. Rul. 90-16, 1990-1 C.B. 12] For a discussion of debt cancellation income, *see supra*, §§144-159.

---

e.g. **Example:** Taxpayer owns Blackacre, which has a basis of $4,000. Blackacre is subject to a mortgage of $9,000, but it is only worth $8,100. Taxpayer transfers the property, either to the lender or to a third party. *If the debt is nonrecourse*, Taxpayer has a capital gain of $5,000 because she is treated as having realized the amount of the debt. *If the debt is recourse*, Taxpayer has a capital gain of $4,100 and debt cancellation income of $900 if the creditor does not collect the $900 deficiency. Debt cancellation income is ordinary, not capital. However, if Taxpayer were insolvent, Taxpayer could exclude the debt cancellation income. (*See supra*, §145.)

---

b. Sale for future payments [§773]

Property is frequently sold in exchange for a down payment plus additional payments in the future. (Note that the deferred payment obligation must call for interest at or above the applicable federal rate or interest will be imputed; *see infra*, §§915 et seq.)

(1) Installment method [§774]

Normally in this situation, the seller will use the installment method of taxation, under which the income will be recognized as payments are made. (*See infra*, §§1047 et seq.) If the seller elects not to use the installment method (or does not qualify for it), the amount realized on the sale and the timing of income recognition depends on several factors.

(2) Cash method [§775]

If the sale price is a fixed amount and the seller uses the cash method of taxation, the seller treats the fair market value of the consideration received (cash and installment obligation) as the amount realized. In no event will the value of the consideration received be less than the value of the property given up. [Treas. Reg. §15.453-1(d)(2)(ii); **Philadelphia Park Amusement Co. v. United States,** 126 F. Supp. 184 (Ct. Cl. 1954)—property received presumed equal in value to property given up] If the amount is a contingent payment obligation, the normal rule is that the obligation must be assigned a valuation; only in rare and extraordinary cases in which the market value of neither the property surrendered nor the obligation received can be determined can the open transaction method (*see* below) be used. [Treas. Reg. §15.453-1(d)(1)(2)(iii)]

(3) Accrual method [§776]

If the sale price is a fixed amount and the seller uses the accrual method of taxation, the seller treats the full sale price as the amount realized, regardless of the market value of the obligation. [Treas. Reg. §15.453-1(d)(2)(ii)] If the sale price is contingent, an accrual method taxpayer includes the market value of the obligation in income unless it cannot be valued. [Treas. Reg. §15.453-1(d)(1)(2)(iii)]

(4) Open transaction method [§777]

In rare and extraordinary cases in which neither the obligation received nor the property surrendered can be valued, taxpayers can use the open transaction method. Under this method, gain is reported only after the payments have exhausted the seller's basis; the buyer's obligation is treated as having no present value. [**Burnet v. Logan,** 283 U.S. 404 (1931)] Even in such cases, the installment method can be (and normally is) used. (*See infra,* §§1052 *et seq.*)

(a) IRS opposition [§778]

The IRS opposes the open transaction method because it defers the seller's income until after the entire basis has been recovered. Such deferral of tax is quite valuable. Moreover, once basis is exhausted, the gain is entirely capital gain. However, if the installment method is not used and the transaction is closed by valuing the obligation and including that value in income, any subsequent income (*i.e.,* amounts received in excess of the valuation) are taxed as ordinary income. [**Waring v. Commissioner,** 412 F.2d 800 (3d Cir. 1969)]

---

e.g. **Example:** Taxpayer owns Acme Co. stock, having a basis of $40. Taxpayer sells it to Byer for $15 down and an annual payment for the next five years of 20% of Acme Co.'s profits. Taxpayer elects out of the installment method. Under **Burnet v. Logan,** *supra,* this might well be considered an "open transaction." The $15 down payment would not be taxed but would reduce Taxpayer's basis to $25. The next $25 would also be tax-free and would reduce the basis to zero. All subsequent payments would be taxable as capital gain.

---

e.g. **Example:** Suppose in the preceding example that it is held that the stream of payments has a present value of $110. The transaction is "closed." Consequently, Taxpayer would realize a capital gain of $85 in the year of sale (amount realized of $110 plus $15, less basis of $40). The contract right would have a basis of $110 in Taxpayer's hands. Recovery on the contract right would be allocated between tax-free recovery of the $110 basis and profit. The profit would be ordinary income because there is no sale or exchange when a debt is collected (*see infra,* §899).

C. Nonrecognition of Gain or Loss

1. In General [§779]

I.R.C. section 1001(c) provides that the gain or loss realized on the sale or exchange of an asset is *recognized* (taxed) only to the extent provided in I.R.C. section 1002. Section 1002 states that all gain or loss is recognized subject to certain exceptions—the "nonrecognition" provisions discussed immediately below. Thus, the "nonrecognition" statutes are a second line of defense: Gain or loss must be both *realized* and *recognized*.

2. Nonrecognition Provisions [§780]

The Code provides many exceptions to the general rule that all gain or loss is recognized at the time of a sale or exchange. However, there is a price for nonrecognition: The basis of the property received by the taxpayer is the basis of the property transferred (a substituted basis; *see supra,* §734). Therefore, the gain or loss is simply *deferred* until the acquired property is ultimately sold.

a. Like kind exchanges [§781]

No *gain or loss* is recognized on an exchange where property held either for investment or for use in business is exchanged solely for property of *like kind*. [I.R.C. §1031(a)]

(1) Like kind defined [§782]

Like kind refers to the *general nature or character* of the property, not to its grade or quality. For example, real estate held for business use or investment is of like kind with any other business or investment real estate—and this is true even though one parcel is improved and the other is unimproved (*e.g.,* a ranch held for investment traded for a hotel used in business). However, property within the United States and property outside of the United States are not of like kind. [I.R.C. §1031(h)]

(a) Personal property [§783]

The definition of like kind is stricter for personal property. For example, coins that are valuable for collecting purposes are not of like kind with foreign currency. [**California Federal Life Insurance Co. v. Commissioner,** 680 F.2d 85 (9th Cir. 1982)] Indeed, the IRS asserts that gold bullion and silver bullion are not of like kind since silver is used primarily as an industrial commodity while gold is primarily an investment. [Rev. Rul. 82-166, 1982-2 C.B. 190]

(2) Coverage limited to tangible property other than inventory [§784]

I.R.C. section 1031 does *not* apply to stocks and bonds or partnership interests; neither does it apply to stock in trade, inventory, or other property held for *sale* to customers in the ordinary course of a trade or business.

(*See infra*, §§823 *et seq.*) It covers only real or tangible property held for investment or for use in business, *e.g.*, buildings, machinery, fixtures, etc.

EXAM TIP   **gilbert**

On your exam, it is very important to remember that the nonrecognition provision [I.R.C. §1031] for like kind exchanges is very narrow: It applies only to *real or tangible personal property* held for investment or for use in business. Don't be fooled by facts telling you, *e.g.*, that an insurance company exchanged 100,000 shares of Kohl's stock that it was holding as an investment for 100,000 shares of Sears stock; such an exchange does not qualify as a like kind exchange.

---

(3) "Triangle exchanges" [§785]

A three-way exchange may qualify under the statute. For example, suppose Taxpayer wants to sell his ranch property to Purch for $100,000, but wants to defer the tax. Taxpayer intends to reinvest the proceeds in an apartment house anyhow, so he has Purch buy the apartment house for $100,000 and then Purch and Taxpayer exchange properties. This qualifies as a like kind exchange for purposes of I.R.C. section 1031. [**Alderson v. Commissioner**, 317 F.2d 790 (9th Cir. 1963)—the fact that property is acquired solely for the purpose of making the exchange held immaterial]

(a) Deferred exchanges [§786]

Suppose that Taxpayer has not yet selected the apartment house that is to be exchanged for his ranch. It is possible to have a deferred exchange in which Taxpayer transfers his ranch to Purch, and Purch agrees to purchase an apartment house (when Taxpayer selects it) and transfer it to Taxpayer. If Taxpayer fails to select an apartment house within five years, Purch will pay Taxpayer cash for the ranch. An apartment house was selected within the five-year period, and the court held that Taxpayer was entitled to nonrecognition of gain. [**Starker v. United States**, 602 F.2d 1341 (9th Cir. 1979)]

(b) Statutory limit [§787]

The rule in *Starker* has been limited by a subsequent statute. Although a deferred exchange is still permitted, the replacement property must be "identified" within 45 days after the taxpayer transfers the property to the purchaser, and the replacement property must be actually received by the taxpayer within 180 days after he transfers his property (or, if earlier, the due date of the tax return for the year in which the taxpayer transferred the property). [*See* I.R.C. §1031(a)(3); Treas. Reg. §1.1031(k)—detailed definitions and examples of deferred exchanges]

(4) Sale and leaseback [§788]

Suppose Taxpayer sells his building to Purch for a price substantially less than his basis in the property and then leases it back from Purch on a long-term lease. Can Taxpayer claim a loss on the transaction, or is this an exchange of like kind properties within I.R.C. section 1031, so that no loss is recognized?

(a) IRS position

If the lease is for *more than 30 years*, the IRS deems it the equivalent of a fee interest [Treas. Reg. §1.1031(a)], so the "like kind" requirement is met, and the loss is not recognized.

(b) Judicial approach

Although an earlier case upheld the IRS position [**Century Electric Co. v. Commissioner**, 192 F.2d 155 (8th Cir. 1952)], the trend of judicial opinion is that a sale and leaseback cannot be treated as an "exchange"—so section 1031 is not applicable. [**Jordan Marsh Co. v. Commissioner**, 269 F.2d 453 (2d Cir. 1959); **Leslie Co. v. Commissioner**, 64 T.C. 247 (1975), *aff'd*, 539 F.2d 943 (3d Cir. 1976)]

(5) Effect of "boot" [§789]

If a taxpayer receives both like kind and non-like-kind property in a section 1031 exchange, the non-like-kind property is called "boot." *Realized gain is recognized* to the extent of the boot. [I.R.C. §1031(b)]

Example: Taxpayer owns a hotel with a basis of $30,000 and a value of $100,000. She exchanges it for an apartment building having a value of $85,000, together with $15,000 in cash. The cash is boot. Her realized gain is $70,000. The recognized gain is $15,000.

Example: Same as previous example except that Taxpayer's basis is $90,000. Her realized gain is $10,000. All of it is recognized. Although the boot was equal to $15,000, the taxpayer *never recognizes more than her realized gain.*

Example: Same as the first example except that Taxpayer's basis for the hotel was $110,000. She has a realized loss of $10,000. None of it is recognized. The presence of boot in a section 1031 exchange *does not permit recognition of loss.* [I.R.C. §1031(c)]

(a) Transfer of boot [§790]

A taxpayer does not recognize any gain on the *like kind* property if she *transfers* boot to the other party, rather than receiving it. However, if the boot transferred by the taxpayer consists of property other than money, and this property is worth more or less than its basis, the taxpayer *must recognize gain or loss on the boot.*

---

e.g. **Example:** Taxpayer exchanges land with a basis of $60,000 and a value of $180,000 for land worth $200,000, and to equalize the deal, also transfers IBM stock having a basis of $8,000 and a value of $20,000. Taxpayer does not recognize any of the gain on the land because he did not receive any boot. But Taxpayer must recognize the $12,000 gain on the stock.

(b) Adjustment to basis [§791]

The presence of boot requires adjustments to basis of the acquired property. The formula is:

New basis = old basis + gain recognized − money received.

Thus in the three examples above (§789), the basis of the new apartment house would be $30,000, $85,000, and $95,000. [*See* I.R.C. §1031(d), *and see* additional examples in Treas. Reg. §1.1031(d)-1]

1) If the boot received is in a form other than money, part of the basis must be allocated to the boot. Thus, in the first example (*supra,* §789) suppose that Taxpayer received stock worth $15,000 instead of $15,000 in cash. The basis of the apartment building plus the stock would be $45,000 (old basis + gain recognized − money received). Of the $45,000 basis, $15,000 is allocated to the stock (its fair market value). That leaves $30,000 for the apartment house.

2) If a taxpayer pays boot (rather than receives it), the basis of the new property is *increased* by the amount of cash paid, the basis of the property paid, and gain recognized on the boot; it is reduced by loss recognized on the boot. Recall the example above (§790) where Taxpayer exchanges land with a basis of $60,000 and a value of $180,000 for land worth $200,000 and Taxpayer also transfers IBM stock with a basis of $8,000 and a value of $20,000. Taxpayer's basis for the new land is $80,000: old basis ($60,000 + $8,000) + gain recognized ($12,000) = $80,000.

(6) Effect of mortgages [§792]

Most real property that is exchanged is subject to outstanding mortgages. Usually, the property will remain subject to the mortgage in the hands of the person acquiring it. For tax purposes, this is treated the same as if the acquiring party paid cash.

(a) Illustration

Alex owns land with a basis of $65,000 and value of $100,000. It is subject to a mortgage of $40,000. Alex exchanges it for Becky's land, which is worth $85,000 and is subject to a mortgage of $25,000.

(i) The effect of Alex and Becky's each taking subject to the other's mortgage is that each is treated as having paid cash to the other. Thus, Becky has paid Alex $40,000; Alex has paid Becky $25,000. These amounts are then netted out—so that the only boot payment is the difference—$15,000 to Alex.

(ii) Alex's realized gain is $35,000 (value of $100,000 less basis of $65,000). Of this amount, $15,000 is recognized—the boot received.

(iii) Alex's basis for the new land is $65,000: old basis ($65,000) + boot paid ($25,000) + gain recognized ($15,000) − cash received ($40,000) = $65,000.

[*See* Treas. Reg. §1.1031(d)-2—additional examples]

(7) Exchanges between related persons [§793]

If a taxpayer exchanges property under section 1031 with a related person, and the related person disposes of the property within two years of the exchange, the taxpayer must recognize gain or loss on the original exchange. The same thing happens if the taxpayer disposes of the property acquired in the exchange within two years of the exchange. [I.R.C. §1031(f)(1)] The gain or loss is recognized in the year the related party disposes of the property. The definition of related person is supplied by I.R.C. section 267(b) (*see supra*, §514).

(a) Exceptions [§794]

Certain dispositions by the related party will not trigger recognition of gain or loss. These include dispositions after the death of either the taxpayer or the related person, an involuntary conversion of the property (*see* below), or a transaction with respect to which the IRS is satisfied that neither the exchange nor the disposition had tax avoidance as one of its principal purposes. [I.R.C. §1031(f)(2)]

Example: In 2001, Stocker and Bigco engage in a swap. Stocker transfers Blackacre to Bigco, and Bigco transfers Whiteacre to Stocker. Bigco is a corporation, and Stocker owns 60% of Bigco's stock. Thus, Stocker and Bigco are related parties. [I.R.C. §267(b)(2)] In 2002, Bigco sells Blackacre. This sale requires Stocker to recognize in 2002 the gain on Blackacre that was not recognized in 2001, when the swap occurred. Moreover, Bigco's disposition of Blackacre requires Bigco to recognize in 2002 its gain on Whiteacre, which it did not recognize in 2001, when the swap occurred.

---

b. Involuntary conversion [§795]

Gain is frequently realized when a taxpayer's property is condemned and she receives an eminent domain award from the government. Similarly, gain is often realized when property is destroyed or stolen and the taxpayer recovers insurance proceeds. These transactions are called "involuntary conversions." Since by definition the realization was involuntary and probably undesired, the Code allows the taxpayer to elect not to recognize the gains.

(1) Code provision [§796]

I.R.C. section 1033 provides that if the taxpayer replaces the property "involuntarily converted" *within two years* after the close of the tax year in which she receives the proceeds from the conversion, with other property "*similar or related in service or use*" to the property converted, realized gain will be recognized only to the extent that the amount realized from the conversion exceeds the cost of replacement.

Example: Taxpayer's factory had a value of $100,000 and an adjusted basis of $60,000. It was totally destroyed by fire, and Taxpayer received $100,000 in insurance proceeds. She invested $86,000 in a new factory within two years and elected to take advantage of section 1033. Her realized gain was $40,000, and her recognized gain is $14,000 (the proceeds that were not reinvested).

(a) Method of replacement [§797]

The replacement may be made by actually purchasing property "similar or related in service or use" to the converted property, or by acquiring at least 80% of the voting stock of a corporation owning such property. [I.R.C. §1033(a)]

(b) Section is elective [§798]

Unlike the other nonrecognition provisions, nonrecognition under I.R.C. section 1033 is *elective*, not mandatory. A taxpayer can recognize the gain if she wishes to do so. Also, I.R.C. section 1033 applies only to nonrecognition of gain—not loss. Realized losses on involuntary conversion must be recognized.

(c) Moving expenses related to condemnation of property [§799]

Amounts received from the state for the expenses of moving to a new factory after the old one is condemned are eligible for nonrecognition under section 1033. Similarly, severance damages are eligible (they are damages paid by the state to reflect the decline in value of the retained portion of a condemnee's land). [**Graphic Press Inc. v. Commissioner,** 523 F.2d 585 (9th Cir. 1975)]

(2) Distinguish—section 1031 (like kind exchanges) [§800]

The "similar or related in service or use" test of section 1033 is considerably stricter than the "like kind" test of section 1031 (especially as applied to real property). Under the section 1033 test, the end uses of the property must be similar; *e.g.,* a drill press used by taxpayer in a factory would not be similar to equipment that the taxpayer leases to others. Nor would the fixtures in a retail grocery be similar to a drill press in a factory. However, if the taxpayer was the lessor of the original property and also of the replacement property, I.R.C. section 1033 applies even though the use by the tenants is different. [**Liant Record Inc. v. Commissioner,** 303 F.2d 326 (2d Cir. 1962)]

(a) Special rules for condemnation of business real property [§801]

A special rule applies to condemnations of business real property (or sales of such property under threat of condemnation). No gain is recognized if the proceeds are reinvested in like kind property, whether *or not* the property is "similar or related in service or use" to the property condemned. Thus, the more generous test of I.R.C. section 1031 is used rather than the stricter section 1033 test. Moreover, three years is allowed as the replacement period instead of the usual two. [I.R.C. §1033(g)]

COMPARISON OF LIKE KIND EXCHANGES, INVOLUNTARY CONVERSIONS, AND CONDEMNATIONS OF BUSINESS REAL PROPERTY			gilbert
	LIKE KIND EXCHANGES	**INVOLUNTARY CONVERSIONS**	**CONDEMNATIONS OF *BUSINESS REAL PROPERTY***
SITUATION	Voluntary exchange of property	Exchange due to casualty, loss, condemnation, or theft	Condemnation of business real property only
TYPE OF REPLACEMENT PROPERTY	Same general nature or character; stricter similarity requirement for personal property	Similar or related in service or use	Any real property used for business
ELECTIVE/NOT ELECTIVE	Not elective	Elective	Elective
REPLACEMENT PERIOD	Replacement property must be identified within 45 days of sale and must be transferred within 180 days	Two years	Three years

c. **Nonrecognition of gain on sale of principal residence [§802]**

No loss can be recognized on the sale of a personal residence (*see supra*, §499). In most cases, gain from the sale of a principal residence is not recognized. However, gains on the sale of a residence in excess of $250,000 (or $500,000 on a joint return) are taxable as capital gain. [I.R.C. §121] Prior law, which allowed nonrecognition of gain of any amount, but only if taxpayer reinvested the sales price in a new home, has been repealed. [Former I.R.C. §1034]

(1) **Requirements for section 121 [§803]**

To qualify for exclusion of gain ($250,000 or $500,000), the taxpayer must have *owned and used* the dwelling as a *principal residence* for periods aggregating *two years or more in the five-year period* ending on the date of the sale or exchange. [I.R.C. §121(a)]

(2) **Once every two years [§804]**

The exclusion is not available if during the two-year period ending on the date of the sale or exchange there was *any other sale or exchange to which section 121 applied.* [I.R.C. §121(b)(3)]

(3) **Married couples [§805]**

To qualify for the $500,000 exclusion, a married couple must file a joint return for the year in which the sale or exchange occurs. To file a joint return, the couple must still be married on the last day of the taxable year. Either spouse can be the record owner of the house, but *both* spouses must meet the two-year use and two-year prior sale requirements. [I.R.C. §121(b)(2)] The $250,000 exclusion is available on a joint return if *either* spouse (but not both spouses) meets the ownership, use, and prior-sale requirements. [I.R.C. §121(d)(1)]

---

e.g. **Example:** Jack owns a condominium, which he bought in 1995 and for which his basis is $150,000. In 2001, he marries Diane and has her added as a record owner of the condo. They live happily thereafter in Jack's condo. In early 2002, they decide to move into a larger house in the suburbs in order to start a family, and they sell Jack's condo for $500,000 in the same year. Only $250,000 of the $350,000 gain may be excluded because Diane has not lived in the condo for more than two years.

EXAM TIP   **gilbert**

A question regarding the sale of a taxpayer's residence may come up on your exam. Remember the test—if the taxpayer (i) owned and used the house as a *principal residence for two of the past five years* and (ii) has *not used the exclusion in the past two years*, he may exclude $250,000 of the gain ($500,000 for married couples, assuming *both* spouses meet the above test) from income.

(4) Marital dissolution rules

(a) Marital property divisions [§806]

If a spouse or former spouse receives a residence in a marital property division described in I.R.C. section 1041 (*see infra*, §808) the period that the spouse or former spouse owns the property *includes the period that the transferor owned the property*. [I.R.C. §121(d)(3)(A)]

(b) Out spouse rule [§807]

Frequently in marital dissolution situations, one spouse ("in spouse") is allowed to remain in the house but the house continues to be owned by both spouses. Later the house is sold and the proceeds are divided between the in spouse and the out spouse. The out spouse is treated as using the property as a principal residence during the period that the in spouse is granted use of the property *under a divorce or separation instrument*. [I.R.C. §121(d)(3)(B); *see supra*, §164, for discussion of the phrase "divorce or separation instrument"]

d. Sales between spouses [§808]

No gain or loss is recognized on *sales or other transfers* between spouses or between former spouses if the sale is *incident to a divorce*. [I.R.C. §1041]

(1) Prior law [§809]

Under prior law, property settlements in divorce frequently were taxable. [**United States v. Davis**, 370 U.S. 65 (1962)—Husband's transfer of appreciated stock to Wife in discharge of Wife's marital property rights produced gain to Husband] This created serious problems in negotiating property divisions and resulted in enactment of section 1041, which makes all such transfers nontaxable events.

(2) Recipient's basis [§810]

The recipient's basis remains the same as the transferor's basis—whether the property was appreciated or depreciated and regardless of whether the acquiring party paid for the property. [I.R.C. §1041(b)(2)]

(3) Incident to divorce [§811]

Even if a property division occurs after divorce, it still falls under the nonrecognition rule if it occurs within one year after the marriage ceases or (even if after one year) it is "related to the cessation of the marriage." [I.R.C. §1041(c); *see* Treas. Reg. §1.041-1T—transfer within six years of divorce and required by divorce instrument presumed to be related to cessation of marriage]

Example: Husband and Wife own property accumulated during their marriage worth $500,000. The property is in Husband's name. As part of a property division ordered by the family court, an asset worth $250,000 is conveyed to Wife. Husband's adjusted basis for this asset was $60,000. Under section 1041, Husband recognizes no gain on this transfer. Wife's basis for the asset is $60,000. Under prior law, the transfer would have produced $190,000 in gain to Husband, and Wife's basis would have been $250,000. The result is the same whether Husband and Wife live in a community property or noncommunity property state.

e. Mortgage repossessions [§812]

In the past, sellers of property who financed the purchase with a mortgage were taxed when they foreclosed on the property and took it back. Under the current rule, however, the gain is not recognized in this situation, and the seller does not get a bad debt deduction. [I.R.C. §1038]

NONRECOGNITION CHECKLIST · gilbert

GAINS FROM THE FOLLOWING EVENTS GENERALLY ARE NOT RECOGNIZED AND THEREFORE MAY NOT BE CURRENTLY TAXABLE

☑ *Like kind exchanges*—When *real property* held for investment or business purposes is replaced with other real property, no gain or loss is recognized. When *tangible personal property* held for investment or business purposes is replaced with other property having the same character, gain or loss is not recognized. If the taxpayer receives "*boot,*" gain but not loss is recognized. "Transfers" include replacement property identified within 45 days and actually transferred within 180 days of the original sale.

☑ *Involuntary conversion*—A gain on property that was involuntarily converted need not be recognized if replaced with property "*similar or related in service or use*" within two years of conversion.

☑ *Sale of principal residence*—*Gain* of up to $250,000 on the sale of a taxpayer's principal residence is not recognized, *provided* that the taxpayer (i) owned and used the "*principal residence*" for periods aggregating *two years or more during the past five years*; and (ii) the taxpayer has *not used this provision during the past two years*. *Losses* on a principal residence *cannot* be recognized.

☑ *Sales between spouses*—*No gain or loss* is recognized on sales or other transfers between spouses or former spouses *when the transfer is incident to divorce*.

☑ *Mortgage repossessions*—A seller who financed a sale with a mortgage does not recognize a gain if he forecloses on the property. Note, however, that he also does not receive a bad debt deduction.

Chapter Five:
What Kind of Income Is It? Capital Gains and Losses and Tax Preferences

CONTENTS

Chapter Approach

Chapter Approach

This section deals with items of income or deduction that are specially treated. Most of the chapter concerns capital gains and losses, which arise on the sale or exchange of certain kinds of property ("capital assets"). Capital gain is taxed at a lower rate than ordinary income, but the deduction of capital losses is restricted. The chapter also covers the alternative minimum tax on tax preferences, which imposes a special tax on certain deductions and items of income.

1. **Capital Gains and Losses**

   Long-term capital gain is taxed at a maximum rate of 20%, while ordinary income can be taxed at rates up to 35% (by the time the rate reductions are fully in place in 2005). Capital losses are fully deductible against capital gains, and deductible up to $3,000 against ordinary income. If a possible capital gain or loss issue arises on your exam, analyze it as follows:

   a. Determine whether the asset is a *capital asset*. All assets are capital unless they fall within a statutory exception (dealer property, taxpayer-produced copyrights, etc.) or within a case law exception (sales of rights to income, contract rights to render personal services, and certain personal rights).

      (1) Be sure to *fragment assets* if the question involves the sale of a business. This allows for a separate examination of each asset to determine gain or loss.

      (2) Real property and depreciable personal property held for one year or more and used in a trade or business are *quasi-capital assets* under I.R.C. section 1231. If there is a net gain, all transactions are capital. If there is a net loss, all transactions are ordinary.

   b. Determine whether there was a *sale or exchange*. Note that a foreclosure of mortgaged property is a sale or exchange. On the other hand, some cases hold that a transfer of contract rights to the other party to the contract is not a sale or exchange.

   c. Determine whether any *special restrictions* apply:

      (1) In a sale for deferred payments, where a contract fails to charge the applicable rate, *interest is imputed*. Thus, the buyer may have an unexpected interest deduction, and the seller may have interest income rather than capital gain.

      (2) All *depreciation* (up to the realized gain) on personal property is *recaptured* and thus treated as ordinary income. For buildings, the depreciation

is not recaptured as ordinary income, but it is taxable at a higher rate than the balance of the gain.

(3) Losses in *transactions between family members* or between an individual and a corporation that he controls are not deductible.

2. Alternative Minimum Tax

For any exam question that asks you to compute the amount of tax owed, consider whether the alternative minimum tax applies. The tax is arrived at by adding back certain tax preferences, making certain deductions, subtracting an exemption, and applying a 26% or 28% rate. If the result exceeds the taxpayer's regular tax, he *must pay* the alternative minimum tax instead.

A. Introductory Material

TAX ON CAPITAL GAINS		gilbert
LENGTH OF HOLDING	**TYPE OF GAIN**	**TAX RATE**
12 months or less	short-term capital gain	taxpayer's normal rate
more than 12 months	long-term capital gain	10% for taxpayer in 15% bracket 20% for other taxpayers
more than 5 years*	special long-term capital gain	8% for taxpayer in 15% bracket 18% for other taxpayers

* For appreciation occurring after January 1, 2001

1. Capital Gain [§813]

Long-term capital gain is taxed at a lower rate than ordinary income.

a. General rule [§814]

The tax on an individual's net capital gain is 20%. For an individual in the 15% bracket, the tax on net capital gain is only 10%. [I.R.C. §1(h)] Net capital gain means the excess of net long-term capital gain over net short-term capital loss. [I.R.C. §1222(11)] For this purpose, "long term" means a holding period of more than 12 months.

b. Sales of real estate [§815]

Gain on depreciable real estate is recaptured to the extent of depreciation on the property. The maximum tax on the recaptured portion of the gain is 25%. The maximum tax on additional gain, if any, is 20%. [I.R.C. §1(h)(6)]

c. Property held for more than five years [§816]

Lower rates apply to assets that have been held more than five years. The rate is 18% (or 8% for individuals in the 15% tax bracket). However, this lower rate applies only to appreciation occurring after January 1, 2001. [I.R.C. §1(h)(2)]

d. Collectibles [§817]

Collectibles, such as stamps, most coins, antiques, gems, etc., do not qualify for the low capital gain rates (20% or 10%). Such items are taxed at a maximum rate of 28%. [I.R.C. §§1(h)(4)(A), 408(m)]

2. Capital Loss [§818]

Capital loss can be deducted against capital gain for the year (long-term or short-term) plus $3,000. If capital loss exceeds capital gain plus $3,000, the excess can be carried forward to future years and offset against capital gains in that year plus $3,000. [I.R.C. §§1211(b), 1212]

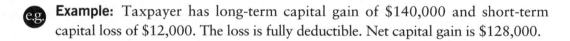 **Example:** Taxpayer has long-term capital gain of $140,000 and short-term capital loss of $12,000. The loss is fully deductible. Net capital gain is $128,000.

Example: Taxpayer has short-term capital gain of $60,000 and long-term capital loss of $220,000. Of this loss, $60,000 is deductible against the capital gain and an additional $3,000 is deductible against ordinary income. The balance of the loss ($157,000) is carried forward to future years.

EXAM TIP **gilbert**

On your exam, you may encounter a fact pattern in which the taxpayer will attempt to *treat a gain differently than is provided in the Code*. For example, such a fact pattern could arise when a taxpayer has a large ordinary loss in a given year, thereby providing the taxpayer with a motive to improperly treat a capital gain as an ordinary gain in order to take full advantage of his ordinary loss, even though the tax rate is higher for an ordinary gain. Don't be fooled by this type of fact pattern—just follow the approach *infra*, §820.

3. Other Implications of Capital Asset Treatment [§819]

The capital versus ordinary distinction must be drawn for numerous other purposes under the Code. For example, a charitable contribution deduction is reduced by the amount of gain that would have been either ordinary income or short-term capital gain had the asset been sold. [I.R.C. §170(e)(1)(A)]

gilbert

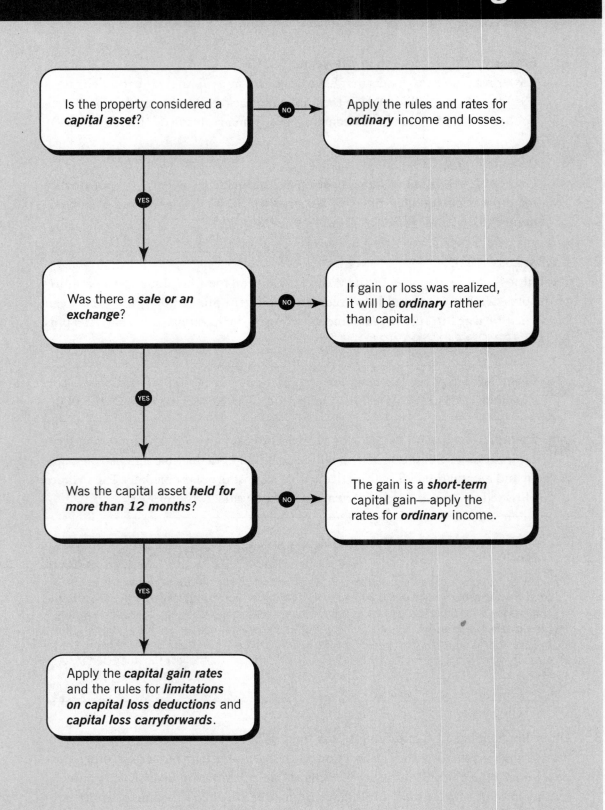

Is the property considered a *capital asset*?

NO → Apply the rules and rates for *ordinary* income and losses.

YES ↓

Was there a *sale or an exchange*?

NO → If gain or loss was realized, it will be *ordinary* rather than capital.

YES ↓

Was the capital asset *held for more than 12 months*?

NO → The gain is a *short-term* capital gain—apply the rates for *ordinary* income.

YES ↓

Apply the *capital gain rates* and the rules for *limitations on capital loss deductions* and *capital loss carryforwards*.

4. Approach [§820]

To classify a particular gain or loss arising from the disposition of property, use the following approach:

a.   Is the property involved a *"capital asset"*?

b.   Was there a *"sale* or *exchange"*?

c.   Is the gain or loss *long-term* or *short-term*?

d.   Apply the rules for limitation of *capital loss deductions* and *capital loss carry-forwards*.

B. Is It a Capital Asset?

1.   General Rule [§821]

I.R.C. section 1221 states that *all* property held by the taxpayer is a capital asset—except the specific types of property discussed in the following paragraphs.

a.   Note—judicial interpretation

In spite of the broad language of I.R.C. section 1221 ("all property . . . except"), the courts have held that the statute does not mean what it says; *i.e.,* the statutory exceptions below are *not* exclusive.

2.   Statutory Exceptions [§822]

I.R.C. section 1221 specifically states that the following types of property are *not* capital assets (and hence any gain or loss on disposition of the property is treated as "ordinary" income or loss):

a.   Property held for sale [§823]

Inventory and property held for *sale to customers in the ordinary course of business* are not capital assets. [I.R.C. §1221(1)]

 Example: Shoes in the hands of a shoe manufacturer or in the stockroom of a shoe store are inventory and thus are not capital assets.

---

(1)   Real estate [§824]

Most of the problems in applying this section arise in connection with real estate. Although land and buildings can be held for investment, this is frequently not the case. When a taxpayer buys a large parcel of land and splits it into smaller lots, which she then sells to individual customers, the lots generally will not be capital assets since the lots are held "primarily for sale to customers in the ordinary course of business." The same result follows if the taxpayer builds and sells many houses. The problem is in deciding whether the taxpayer is an investor or a "dealer" (someone who holds the property for sale to customers).

(a) Determinative factors [§825]

These cases are decided by considering all the particular circumstances. The most important factor is the number and continuity of the sales. If only isolated sales have been made, it is likely that the taxpayer is an investor. But if there is a steady flow of sales, the taxpayer will probably be considered a dealer. Another important factor is the extent to which the taxpayer improved or subdivided the property. If the taxpayer merely buys a parcel of land and sells it intact, the land is probably a capital asset. If the taxpayer subdivides it or builds on it, it is more likely held for sale. Other relevant factors are the purpose for which the property was purchased and used (*e.g.*, a farm field purchased for farming is probably a capital asset; a farm field purchased and subdivided for sale is probably not a capital asset) and the extent to which the taxpayer made efforts (through advertising, etc.) to sell the property. [*See* **Biedenharn Realty Co. v. United States**, 526 F.2d 409 (5th Cir.), *cert. denied*, 429 U.S. 819 (1976)]

(b) Liquidating investments [§826]

According to some cases, when property is purchased and held for investment or farming, and then is liquidated through many piecemeal sales, and the taxpayer does not reinvest the proceeds in real estate, the sales give rise to capital gain. [**Curtis Co. v. Commissioner**, 232 F.2d 167 (3d Cir. 1956)] The prevailing view, however, is that large-scale sales activity changes the taxpayer's purpose into holding for sale in the ordinary course of business—and thus the sales produce ordinary income, unless the change in purpose was induced by unanticipated, external factors such as acts of God. [**Biedenharn Realty Co. v. United States**, *supra*]

(c) Undecided or dual purpose [§827]

Sometimes property will be held for several purposes. In that case, the property is a capital asset unless sale to customers is the *most important purpose*. [**Malat v. Riddell,** 383 U.S. 569 (1966)—defining the word "primarily" in §1221(1)] Indeed, a taxpayer who is a real estate dealer as to some parcels can be an investor as to other parcels. [**Malat v. Riddell,** *supra*]

(d) Exception—real property subdivided for sale [§828]

One rather narrow statutory provision is sometimes of assistance in classifying these transactions. Under I.R.C. section 1237, a parcel of land will be treated as *not* being held primarily for sale to customers in the ordinary course of business if:

(i) *The taxpayer holds no other real estate for sale;*

(ii) *The taxpayer made no substantial improvement* in the land, such as installing sewers; and

(iii) *The land was held for five years.*

In addition, after *five or more lots from a single tract* are sold, the taxpayer must treat an amount equal to 5% of the selling price as ordinary income; the balance of the gain, if any, would be capital gain.

(2) Securities [§829]

Unlike real property, securities are generally treated as capital assets, regardless of the extent and continuity of the taxpayer's dealings with them. This was Congress's intent when it added "to customers" to I.R.C. section 1221(1). [**Bielfeldt v. Commissioner,** 231 F.3d 1035 (7th Cir. 2000); **Van Suetendael v. Commissioner,** 152 F.2d 654 (2d Cir. 1946)]

(a) "Dealers" and "traders" of securities [§830]

However, if a taxpayer is classified as a "dealer" in securities, the securities are not treated as capital assets. To be considered a dealer, the taxpayer must do more than buy and sell large amounts of securities in an attempt to make a profit on price fluctuations. Instead, the taxpayer must also render some form of service.

Example: A stockbroker who owns shares that he sells to his customers at market price plus a commission would be a "dealer," as would a floor specialist on one of the stock exchanges (a floor specialist is a person or entity that maintains an inventory in a particular stock, and that agrees to buy and sell that stock under certain conditions in order to ensure that there is always a market for the stock). [**Bielfeldt v. Commissioner,** *supra*—taxpayer who lost hundreds of millions of dollars speculating in government bonds is not a dealer and thus has a capital loss rather than an ordinary loss]

---

1) Mark-to-market accounting [§831]

Dealers in securities *must value securities they are holding at year-end* (called "mark to market"). This means that all gains and losses at year-end are taken into income even though the securities have not been sold. [I.R.C. §475(a)] This is an important exception to the realization requirement. (*See supra,* §§756 *et seq.* for discussion of the realization requirement.) All gains and losses on securities that are marked to market are *ordinary* and not capital. [I.R.C. §475(d)(3)]

2) Traders [§832]

Individuals who are "engaged in a trade or business as a trader in securities" can elect to use mark-to-market accounting and thus treat all transactions as ordinary rather than capital. [I.R.C. §475(f)] A trader (as opposed to an investor) engages in a *continued series of short-term speculations* rather than a person who holds securities for the long term or in order to make a profit on dividends or interest. [*See* **Moller v. United States,** *supra*, §354] Had section 475(f) been in effect at the time, the taxpayer in *Bielfeldt*, *supra*, probably could have claimed that he was "engaged in a trade or business as a trader" in government bonds, and he probably could have elected mark-to-market treatment and received an ordinary loss.

EXAM TIP   gilbert

These cases highlight why an individual would (or would not) want to treat a gain or loss as capital or ordinary—and they can be used to help you remember the effects of different treatment for your exam. A trader would prefer the mark-to-market accounting method when he has large amounts of *losses* in order to have the losses be *treated as "ordinary,"* which in turn could enable him to offset many other types of ordinary income. Equally as important, however, is the fact that mark-to-market accounting is often *disadvantageous* for a dealer, because that accounting method requires him to treat securities *gains as ordinary income*. If the stock market is performing well, he may have a large "gain" as ordinary income, which has a higher tax rate than a capital gain.

---

(3) Hedging transactions [§833]

Assets acquired in a "hedging transaction," which are so identified on the date acquired, are not capital assets. [I.R.C. §1221(7)] A hedging transaction is a transaction entered into in the normal course of trade or business to manage risk of price, currency, or interest rate fluctuations (*e.g.,* a breadmaker may purchase wheat "futures"—contracts calling for future delivery at a fixed price—in order to stabilize its manufacturing costs). [I.R.C. §1221(b)(2)]

(a) Prior law [§834]

Prior law relating to hedging transactions was very confused. Generally, gains and losses from the sale of commodity futures contracts that were an integral part of a business's inventory purchase system were ordinary, not capital. [**Corn Products Co. v. Commissioner,** 350 U.S. 46 (1955)]

1) *Corn Products* case

In the *Corn Products* case, a manufacturer of products made from corn bought corn "futures" to protect itself against a sharp increase in the price of corn. The Supreme Court held that the futures were an "integral part" of the taxpayer's business and therefore could not be capital assets.

(b) Current regulations [§835]

Corn Products was superseded by regulations. [Treas. Reg. §1.1221-2(a)] These regulations provide that the term "capital assets" does *not* include property that is "part of a hedging transaction." Thus, since the taxpayer's corn futures in *Corn Products* were purchased as an attempt to protect the taxpayer against a sudden price increase, the futures were "part of a hedging transaction" and would not be capital assets. The regulations have not yet been amended to take account of section 1221(7), *supra*.

1) Non-hedging transactions

Under the regulations, assets that are acquired for business (not investment) purposes, but that are not part of a hedging transaction, may be treated as capital assets if that treatment is not excluded for some other reason. The regulations provide: "gain or loss from the [non-hedging] transaction is not made ordinary on the grounds that the property involved in the transaction is a surrogate for a noncapital asset, that the transaction serves as insurance against a business risk, that the transaction serves a hedging function, or that the transaction serves a similar function or purpose." This regulation is consistent with a Supreme Court decision that limited *Corn Products* to its facts. Note that *Corn Products* does not cover investments in corporate stock, even if the "investments" were made to protect the taxpayer's business rather than for investment purposes. [**Arkansas Best Corp. v. Commissioner**, 485 U.S. 212 (1988)]

b. Receivables [§836]

An *account receivable or note* acquired in the ordinary course of business in *payment for services rendered* by the taxpayer, or on sale of an *inventory item*, is not a capital asset. [I.R.C. §1221(4)]

c. Depreciable property and realty [§837]

Depreciable property and any real property (depreciable or not) *used in a trade or business* are not capital assets.

(1) Note

Actually, such assets if held more than one year are treated as *"quasi-capital assets"* under I.R.C. section 1231 (*see infra*, §§873 *et seq*.) with *very favorable tax treatment*. Generally speaking, losses on sales of such assets are treated as ordinary losses (fully deductible), while gains are capital gains.

d. Copyrights [§838]

Copyrights (and other literary, musical, or artistic property) are *not* capital assets in the hands of the taxpayer whose *personal effort created them* (or any donee). [I.R.C. §1221(3)]

(1) Letters [§839]
Letters or memoranda are not capital assets in the hands of the creator or the person for whom they were produced.

(2) Purchasers distinguished [§840]
An investor who *purchases* artwork or other copyrightable works from the creator may be entitled to treat them as capital assets (unless he is a dealer and purchased them primarily for resale in the ordinary course of his business, in which case they would fall under section 1221(1)).

e. Patents [§841]
I.R.C. section 1235 provides that a patent is a *capital asset* in the hands of the *inventor* or anyone who *financed* the invention (other than a relative or employer of the inventor). Hence, monies derived from the sale or transfer of a patent are capital gains—even the monies that are payable to a person in the business of inventing or financing patents.

(1) Note
And this is true even where the royalty payments are made payable over a period coterminous with the transferee's use of the patent, or contingent on the productivity of the patent. [I.R.C. §1235(a)]

(2) But note
To qualify for the capital gains treatment, there must be a bona fide transfer of all *substantial* rights under the patent. And even so, transfers between related taxpayers or to a corporation in which the inventor owns 25% or more of the stock do *not* qualify. [I.R.C. §1235(d)]

STATUTORY TREATMENT OF CERTAIN ASSETS AS CAPITAL OR NONCAPITAL — gilbert

CAPITAL ASSETS	NONCAPITAL ASSETS
• Real estate not held for sale	• Real estate held for sale
• Securities in the hands of an "average" investor or in the hands of a "trader" when the trader does not elect mark-to-market accounting	• Securities in the hands of a "dealer" or in the hands of a "trader" when the trader elects mark-to-market accounting
• Copyrights held by purchaser	• Copyrights in the creator's hands
• Patents in the hands of its inventor or person who financed its invention	• Assets held in a "hedging transaction"

f. Options [§842]

If optioned property would be, if acquired, a capital asset in the hands of the option holder, then the option itself is a capital asset, and its sale will yield capital gain or loss. [I.R.C. §1234]

(1) Distinguish—ordinary income property [§843]

However, if the option relates to a *noncapital* asset (inventory, personal services, etc.), any gain or loss is ordinary income.

EXAM TIP | **gilbert**

For exam questions asking you whether the gain or loss on the sale of an option is capital or ordinary, you need only look *at the optioned property*. If the underlying property would be considered a *capital asset* in the hands of the purchaser (*e.g.,* option for a copyright), then a gain or a loss on the sale of that option would be considered capital. The converse is also true—if the asset on which the taxpayer holds an option would be considered a *noncapital asset* in the hands of a taxpayer (*e.g.,* option to buy inventory), the sale of that option would produce an ordinary gain or loss.

---

(2) Effect of failure to exercise [§844]

If the optionee fails to exercise the option, the amounts paid by him for the option are deductible only as a capital loss (assuming the option relates to a capital asset). [I.R.C. §1234]

(a) Distinguish

But such payments are *ordinary income to the optionor* since he has not sold or exchanged the underlying property. If the option had been exercised, any payments under the option attributable to the purchase price would be entitled to capital gains treatment if the underlying asset was a capital asset.

3. Exceptions Developed in Case Law [§845]

As noted above, the courts have developed additional categories of items that are not capital assets. Generally, they have done so when the property or the transaction seems to fall outside of the purposes for granting the favored capital gain treatment. These purposes are to provide a form of *income averaging* for gains that are likely to have occurred over a long period of time and to *remove the disincentives* against sale of appreciated property. Generally, the courts try to distinguish between items that are *investments* (which qualify for capital gain) and mere *substitutes for ordinary income* (which produce ordinary income).

a. Rights to income [§846]

As discussed in detail earlier in this summary (*see supra*, §§193, 203), income is chargeable to the person either rendering the services for which the income is paid or owning the property from which the income is earned.

(1) Sale of right to income [§847]

The above principles and cases are also relevant with respect to *sales* of the right to income. Thus, if the taxpayer sells (rather than gives away) the right to future income from her property, while retaining the underlying property, the sales proceeds—*being a "substitute" for the income*—are taxable to her as ordinary income, not capital gains. Moreover, none of the taxpayer's basis in the property is allocated to the income right.

---

e.g. Example: Taxpayer is entitled to future cash dividends of $122,820 from Champion Spark Plug Company. To offset a large deduction in the current tax year, Taxpayer needs to produce a large amount of current income. Taxpayer agrees to sell his right to receive the future dividends—some of which extend into the next tax year—to his son for $115,000 (representing the discounted present value of $122,820). Taxpayer retains ownership of the stock. The payment of $115,000 is ordinary income to Taxpayer. [**Stranahan's Estate v. Commissioner**, 472 F.2d 867 (6th Cir. 1973)]

---

e.g. Example: Taxpayer owns certain oil lands. She sells her rights to the next $10,500 of royalties to Bob Buyer for $10,000. Since Taxpayer retained the oil lands while merely anticipating some of the ordinary income, the $10,000 is ordinary income. None of the basis for the land is allocated to the income right. [**Commissioner v. P.G. Lake**, *supra*, §197]

---

(2) Distinguish—sale of source of income [§848]

The result would be different if the taxpayer had sold her *entire interest* in the *property* from which the right to income springs (*e.g.*, the shares of stock or the entire oil deposit). In such a case, the sales proceeds would be *capital gain*, rather than ordinary income. The same result would occur if the taxpayer sold an undivided fractional interest in the entire property (such as one-third interest in the stock or in all the oil).

(a) Sale of life estates [§849]

A close case occurs where the *life beneficiary of a trust* sells her interest in the trust (or a portion thereof lasting for her life). It could be argued that her "interest" is nothing more than the right to receive income during her life, and hence the proceeds of sale should be ordinary income. However, the courts have held the opposite, treating the sale as the sale of an *interest in property* (rather than merely as assignment of income), so that capital gains treatment can be obtained. The key point is that the seller disposes of the interest for the entire time it will exist (her life), as opposed to selling a few years of income but retaining the right to subsequent income. [**McAllister v. Commissioner**, 157 F.2d 235 (2d Cir. 1946)]

1) No basis recovery

Under present law, the seller of the income interest is denied any basis recovery on such a sale. [I.R.C. §1001(e); *see supra*, §741]

b. Contract rights [§850]

Classifying the proceeds from the sale of contract rights as capital gain or ordinary income has caused considerable difficulty.

(1) Is it "protectable in equity"? [§851]

According to one notable decision, a possible standard for analyzing whether a contract right is "property" for purposes of capital gains taxation is whether it is "protectable in equity." [**Commissioner v. Ferrer,** 304 F.2d 125 (2d Cir. 1962)]

Example: In *Ferrer,* the court held that the sale of an exclusive right to produce a particular play and a right to prevent a particular story from being made into a movie were both protectable in equity and thus capital assets. However, a right to a percentage of the proceeds from a particular movie was held not protectable in equity and thus its sale gave rise to ordinary income. (The latter determination is inconsistent with some other cases in the area.)

(a) Note

The *Ferrer* result requires an allocation of a lump-sum purchase price into its various component parts, some of which are capital gains and some of which are ordinary income.

(2) Leases [§852]

A lease is an interest in property and hence amounts paid *to the lessee* for an *assignment* of the lease is capital gain.

(a) Payment by lessor [§853]

Likewise, amounts paid *by the lessor* to the lessee for a *cancellation* or *change in terms* of the lease are treated as capital gains. [Rev. Rul. 56-531, 1956-2 C.B. 983]

(b) Distinguish—payment for release [§854]

But an amount paid *by the lessee* to the lessor for a *release* from the lease is not capital gain. *Rationale:* The lessor is not really selling a contract right; he is compromising a rent obligation while retaining the reversion. [**Hort v. Commissioner,** 313 U.S. 28 (1941)]

(c) Sublease distinguished [§855]

The above discussion applies to assignments of the entire leasehold (a complete transfer of the lessee's interest). If the transfer is only a sublease (a reversion of some sort is retained by the master tenant), the income received by the master tenant is ordinary income, like any other rents.

(3) Personal services [§856]

A sale of one's contractual rights to render personal services produces ordinary income.

---

e.g. **Examples:** Taxpayer, a noted celebrity, contracts to render future services for XYZ Corp., for which XYZ Corp. agrees to pay her a stipulated amount. Taxpayer then sells her rights to payment from XYZ Corp. to Bob Buyer. The sale proceeds received by Taxpayer are clearly ordinary income—just as the payments from XYZ Corp. would have been. [**McFall v. Commissioner,** 34 B.T.A. 108 (1936)] Similarly, amounts paid to a theatrical agent to transfer her contract for exclusive rights to represent a singer produced ordinary income. [**General Artists Corp. v. Commissioner,** 205 F.2d 360 (2d Cir. 1953)]

---

e.g. **Example:** As a result of rendering services, Taxpayer, a real estate broker, received the right to 25% of the profits when the buyer of land ultimately resold it. When Taxpayer finally received his interest in the profits, it was treated as ordinary income since it was originally referable to his services. [**Pounds v. United States,** 372 F.2d 342 (5th Cir. 1967)]

(a) Distinguish—consideration in property and services [§857]

But when, in addition to services, the seller transfers other consideration in the nature of "property" (*e.g.,* patent rights), there must be an *allocation* of any "package" compensation paid—*i.e.,* a value assigned to "each stick in the bundle," and the compensation treated as ordinary income and capital gain proportionately. [**Commissioner v. Ferrer,** *supra*, §851]

(4) Insurance policies [§858]

An insurance policy is basically a contract, and amounts received for assignments of beneficial interests in insurance policies are therefore usually capital gains.

(a) Distinguish—annuities and endowments [§859]

A group of cases has held that if a taxpayer who owns an *annuity or endowment* policy sells his contract to a third person shortly before it matures, the monies received from the buyer are taxable to the seller as ordinary income. These cases proceed on the rationale that the sale proceeds are merely substitutes for amounts receivable upon a maturity or surrender of the contract, which would be ordinary income. [**Commissioner v. Phillips**, 275 F.2d 33 (4th Cir. 1960)]

c. **"Personal rights" [§860]**

Although I.R.C. section 1221 states that "all property" held by the taxpayer (other than the enumerated exceptions) are capital assets, it appears that personal rights are *not* "property" within this definition. Hence, income from "personal rights" is ordinary income, not capital gain.

Example: Glenn Miller's widow sold the "right" to make a movie based on Glenn Miller's life. *Held:* The sale was not the sale of a capital asset. [**Miller v. Commissioner**, 299 F.2d 706 (2d Cir. 1962)—"not everything which commands a payment may be regarded as property"]

---

(1) Note

Similar holdings are encountered with regard to compensation paid for invasion of the "right" of privacy, sale of the "right" to use one's name or picture for commercial purposes, etc. [Rev. Rul. 65-261, 1965-2 C.B. 281]

d. **Classification through correlation with related transaction [§861]**

In a number of situations, transactions have been classified as capital or ordinary because they are deemed to be part of a related transaction.

(1) Illustration—tax benefit rule [§862]

Alex holds certain notes of Becky, which he deducts as bad debts. Later, the debts prove to have value. If Alex had collected the debts, he would have had ordinary income (*see* discussion of I.R.C. section 111, *supra*, §§536-537). If he sells the debts to others, he has ordinary income, not capital gain, because the prior bad debt deductions offset ordinary income. [**Merchants National Bank v. Commissioner**, 199 F.2d 657 (5th Cir. 1952)]

(2) Illustration—lookback rule [§863]

Taxpayer sells stock and treats it as capital gain. Later, the buyer claims there was fraud and Taxpayer returns part of the money, attempting to treat the repayment as producing an ordinary loss. However, it produces capital loss: The sale or exchange of a capital asset is present because of the prior sale of stock at a capital gain. [**Arrowsmith v. Commissioner**, 344 U.S. 6 (1952)]

(a) Application to insiders' profits [§864]

A corporate employee who is an "insider" makes a "short-swing" profit by selling his shares in the corporation then buying them back in a short time period when the share price falls. The "profit" must be returned to the corporation under section 16(b) of the Securities Exchange Act. Several decisions hold that this creates a capital loss under *Arrowsmith*. [**Commissioner v. Cummings**, 506 F.2d 449 (2d Cir. 1974)]

4. Sale of Business Interests

a. Sole proprietorships—fragmentation theory [§865]

A sole proprietorship business is not regarded as an entity. Rather, it is an aggregate of the various assets of the business. Therefore, in determining gain or loss, as well as in distinguishing capital gain from ordinary income, each asset must be examined separately. Then, the basis, gain, or loss on each capital asset must be computed separately. This is the so-called fragmentation theory. [**Williams v. McGowan**, 152 F.2d 570 (2d Cir. 1945)]

(1) Allocations [§866]

If the parties make a reasonable *allocation* of price to each asset, it will be respected. Otherwise, the IRS will make the allocation, which will be upheld by the courts unless shown to be arbitrary. Some courts have held that if the sale agreement makes an allocation, the parties are *bound* by it, but the IRS is not. [**Commissioner v. Danielson**, 378 F.2d 771 (3d Cir.), *cert. denied,* 389 U.S. 858 (1967)]

(2) Goodwill [§867]

Goodwill is treated as a capital asset. It is depreciable by the buyer over a 15-year period. [I.R.C. §197; *see supra,* §§473-474]

(a) Note

The practice of a single professional—*e.g.,* doctor, lawyer, or accountant—can contain goodwill. Thus when the professional sells all or a part of the practice, there may be a goodwill element entitled to capital gain. However, the facts will be closely scrutinized to make sure that there really is goodwill. [Rev. Rul. 70-45, 1970-1 C.B. 17]

(3) Covenant not to compete [§868]

On the other hand, money paid to the seller in consideration of his promise not to compete in the future is treated as ordinary income to the seller (a substitute for income). As a corollary, the amount paid is an asset to the buyer, which he can amortize over a 15-year period regardless of the actual term of the covenant. [**Hamlin's Trust v. Commissioner**, 209 F.2d 761 (10th Cir. 1954); I.R.C. §197]

(4) Allocations to assets, goodwill [§869]

Because goodwill is depreciable over a 15-year term, taxpayers often try to allocate the purchase price of a business to assets depreciable over shorter periods, leaving very little to be allocated to goodwill. However, the rule is that taxpayers can allocate to tangible assets not more than the value of those assets; all residual value must be allocated to goodwill. [I.R.C. §1060, Treas. Reg. §1.1060-1T(d), (e)]

b. Partnerships and corporations [§870]
The treatment of the sale of a partnership or a corporation differs from the treatment of the sale of a proprietorship.

(1) Sale of assets [§871]
If either a partnership or corporation *sells its assets*, the result is the same as in a proprietorship—*i.e.,* the consideration paid is fragmented between the various assets.

(2) Sale of interest [§872]
But if a partnership *interest* is sold, it is treated as a capital asset, except that the amount referable to "unrealized receivables" or "substantially appreciated inventory" is ordinary income. [I.R.C. §§741, 751] Similarly, corporate stock is treated as a single capital asset unless it is a "collapsible corporation." [I.R.C. §341] (The treatment of sales of partnerships and corporations is discussed in detail in the Income Tax II Summary.)

5. Assets Used in Trade or Business—Quasi-Capital Assets [§873]
I.R.C. section 1221(2) provides that certain assets *used in a trade or business* and *held for more than one year* are not capital assets. These assets are specifically provided for in I.R.C. section 1231. They are sometimes called "quasi-capital" assets and are treated more favorably than any other kind of asset. In addition, "supplies of a type regularly used or consumed by the taxpayer in the ordinary course of a trade or business of the taxpayer" are not capital assets. [I.R.C. §1221(8)]

a. Coverage [§874]
Quasi-capital assets described in section 1231 are those held more than one year and used in a trade or business.

(1) Property used in a trade or business [§875]
Quasi-capital assets are real property used in a trade or business (whether or not depreciable) and personal property used in a trade or business that is subject to depreciation under section 167 (*e.g.,* machines or trucks). Assets such as goodwill, which are amortized under section 197 (not section 167), are not treated as quasi-capital assets. (*See supra,* §§473-474.)

(2) Other section 1231 assets [§876]
Section 1231 assets also include the following:

(a) *Unharvested crops sold with the land*;

Are the assets in question considered "supplies of a type *regularly used or consumed by the taxpayer in the ordinary course of a trade or business* of a taxpayer"?

NO

YES

Were the assets held for *more than one year* and *used in the taxpayer's trade or business*?

NO

The assets are *not considered capital assets*.

YES

Section 1231 calculation: Do *gains exceed losses*? (Note that casualty gains are included in the section 1231 calculation if casualty gains exceed casualty losses.)

NO

All of the transactions are considered *ordinary gains and losses*.

YES

Has the taxpayer had *net section 1231 losses in the preceding five years*?

NO

YES

All of the transactions are considered *long-term capital gains*.

An amount equal to the past net section 1231 losses is considered an *ordinary gain*. The remainder, if any, is considered a *long-term capital gain*.

(b) *Herds of livestock* held at least 24 months for draft, breeding, sporting, or dairy purposes (but not poultry); and

(c) *Coal, timber, and minerals* in certain cases. [*See* I.R.C. §1231(b) for details]

(3) Exclusions [§877]

However, section 1231 does *not* include inventories, stock in trade, property *held primarily for sale* in the ordinary course of a taxpayer's trade or business, or *copyrights in the hands of the creator*. (*See supra*, §§822 *et seq.*)

---

e.g. **Example:** Machinery that a taxpayer generally leases to customers, but sells if the customer insists, is held primarily for sale. Consequently, the assets are not section 1231 assets and the gain is ordinary income—even though sales, as opposed to leasing, yield only about 2% of the taxpayer's income. The theory is that the sales are "accepted and predictable." [**International Shoe Machinery Co. v. United States**, 491 F.2d 157 (1st Cir.), *cert. denied,* 419 U.S. 834 (1974)]

---

b. Computation [§878]

All the gains and losses on section 1231 assets are grouped together. If the gains exceed the losses, all the transactions are *long-term capital transactions*. (Thus, the gains are long-term capital gains and the losses are long-term capital losses.) But if the losses exceed the gains, all the transactions are *ordinary* (*i.e.,* ordinary income and ordinary loss).

(1) Recapture of losses [§879]

If a taxpayer has a net gain on section 1231 assets (ordinarily long-term capital gain), but had net section 1231 losses within the preceding five years, the gain will be treated as ordinary income to the extent of previously unrecaptured losses. [I.R.C. §1231(c)]

c. Special rules for casualties [§880]

Taxpayers must aggregate all recognized gains and losses arising from casualties of assets used in the trade or business or for investment. If the gains exceed the losses, *all* transactions are included within the section 1231 calculation. If the losses exceed the gains, *none* of the gains or losses are included in the section 1231 calculation. [I.R.C. §1231(a)(4)(C)]

(1) Casualty gains [§881]

A casualty can produce a gain if the insurance proceeds exceed the taxpayer's basis. In many cases, however, gains from casualties or government condemnations are not recognized because the proceeds are *reinvested in qualifying property*. [*See* I.R.C. §1033; *and see supra*, §§795-801]

(a) Note

The reason for inclusion of casualties under section 1231 is that otherwise they would not be capital gains or losses because of the absence of a "sale or exchange." (*See infra,* §902.)

(2) Distinguish—personal casualty gains or losses [§882]

Gains or losses on personal assets (such as one's personal car or residence) are not included under section 1231. If personal casualty gains exceed personal casualty losses, both gains and losses are treated as capital. [I.R.C. §165(h)(2)(B)] If personal casualty losses exceed personal casualty gains, the losses are deductible to the extent of the gains, but the excess is not deductible except to the extent it exceeds 10% of AGI. [I.R.C. §165(h)(2)(A)] Recall that personal casualty losses are always first reduced by $100 (*see supra,* §672).

d. Limitation—recapture of depreciation [§883]

The provisions requiring recapture of depreciation *supersede* section 1231 and turn capital gain into ordinary income. Only the excess of gain over the amount of recaptured depreciation is treated as a section 1231 gain (*see infra,* §§925-930).

e. Illustration of section 1231 [§884]

Belle owns a health club and has many investments. Consider the following items of loss and gain:

(i) *Condemnations*

Gain on condemnation of Oregon land held as investment $ 4,000

(ii) *Casualties*

Loss on theft of painting held as investment − 9,000

(iii) *Sale of assets used in business (and held more than one year)*

Gain on sale of land used for parking lot	3,000
Loss on sale of gym equipment	−17,000

The casualty loss is not included in the section 1231 calculation (because casualty losses exceed casualty gains). The net of the other items (condemnation of investment property, sale or exchange of business property) shows a $10,000 loss. Therefore, the condemnation and the gain and loss on sale of business assets are all *ordinary* items.

f. Exception as to sales between "related" taxpayers (I.R.C. section 1239) [§885]

The preferential tax treatment accorded to depreciable property used in a trade or business is subject to a limitation—capital gains treatment is *not* allowed if the sale or exchange is between the taxpayer and a *controlled corporation*, or two controlled corporations. In such a case, any gain is ordinary income. [I.R.C. §1239]

(1) Treatment of losses [§886]

Loss in such a transaction is *not* deductible at all (*see* discussion of "losses among related taxpayers"; *see supra*, §§511-514).

(2) Coverage [§887]

I.R.C. section 1239 applies to gain on *any depreciable property*, which means that it is not limited to section 1231 assets (used in a trade or business), but also covers "nonbusiness" assets (used for production of income). It is *not* applicable to certain important types of property, *e.g.*, securities and land.

C. Was There a "Sale or Exchange"?

1. In General [§888]

Ordinarily, there must be a "sale or exchange" of a capital asset for the transaction to be taxed as a capital gain or loss. Case law and statutes have clarified some borderline situations.

a. Aborted sales [§889]

Difficult problems often arise when a sale of property falls through and the seller retains the buyer's money. If a "sale" occurred and the seller repossessed the property because of failure to pay the entire price, the amount that the seller keeps is entitled to capital gain. But if the sale never occurred (*i.e.*, the seller retained the benefits and burdens of ownership), the amount the seller keeps is viewed as liquidated damages and taxed as ordinary income. [**Handelman v. Commissioner**, 509 F.2d 1067 (2d Cir. 1975)]

b. Transfer of mineral interest [§890]

A mineral interest is a capital asset, and therefore an outright sale or assignment thereof will ordinarily produce capital gains. However, if the seller retains an *economic interest*, he is treated as not having sold the minerals. His receipts are ordinary income (but he can deduct *depletion*; *see supra*, §§483-485). [**Wood v. United States**, 377 F.2d 300 (5th Cir. 1967)]

c. Transfers of franchises, trademarks, and trade names [§891]

Capital gains treatment is possible for transfers of franchises, trademarks, and trade names, but *only if* the transferor did *not* retain "any significant power, right, or continuing interest" with respect to the subject matter of the franchise, trademark, or trade name. [I.R.C. §1253(a)]

(1) Application

Thus, in the usual commercial franchise (in which the franchisor imposes strict controls on operation by franchisee, reserves the right of termination, etc.), payments received from a franchisee are ordinary income to the franchisor.

(2) Exception—sports franchises [§892]

Franchises to engage in professional sports do not fall within the above rule and hence are entitled to capital gains treatment in spite of "strings" or "controls" retained by the transferor. [I.R.C. §1253(e)]

d. Contract rights [§893]

As discussed previously (*see supra*, §§850-859), the courts have classified many contract rights as capital assets. However, according to a minority view, when the contract right is transferred from *one party to the contract to the other*, there is no sale or exchange. [**Commissioner v. Pittston Co.**, 252 F.2d 344 (2d Cir. 1958)] Under that view, the contract right would have to be transferred to some *third party* to produce capital gain. However, the better view is that a sale or exchange occurs even in a transfer to the other contracting party. [**Commissioner v. Ferrer**, *supra*, §851]

(1) Legislative clarification [§894]

To some extent, this problem has been clarified by legislation:

(a) Amounts received by a lessee for cancellation of a lease, or by a distributor of goods for the cancellation of a distributor's agreement (if the distributor has a substantial capital investment) are treated as received in exchange for the lease or agreement. [I.R.C. §1241]

(b) The amount lost on expiration of an option contract is treated as if the option were sold for zero dollars; thus the expiration produces a capital loss if the option was to acquire a capital asset. [I.R.C. §1234; *see supra*, §§842-844]

(c) Gains or losses on the cancellation, lapse, expiration, or other termination of any right or obligation, including securities futures, are treated as capital rather than ordinary. [I.R.C. §1234A]

e. Foreclosure [§895]

When a creditor forecloses and takes back property that secured a debt, this is treated as a sale or exchange by the debtor. Consequently, his gain or loss is capital. [**Helvering v. Hammel**, 311 U.S. 504 (1941)]

f. Abandonment [§896]

If property becomes worthless or is abandoned, there is no sale or exchange, and the taxpayer has an ordinary (vs. capital) loss. [**Matz v. Commissioner**, T.C. Memo. 1998-334—abandonment of worthless mineral rights; **Citron v. Commissioner**, 97 T.C. 200 (1991)—worthless partnership interest; *see infra*,

§898, for discussion involving a special rule for worthless bad debts or securities]

2. Special Situations in Which "Sale or Exchange" Deemed to Occur [§897]

There are certain transactions that do not fall within the ordinary meaning of "sale or exchange," but are nevertheless considered to be such for tax purposes.

a. Worthless debts and securities [§898]

Nonbusiness *bad debts* (*see supra*, §529) and *worthless securities*, although not actually sold or exchanged, are deductible only as capital losses in the year they become "worthless." [I.R.C. §§182-183]

b. Payments to creditors

(1) General rule [§899]

Ordinarily, a creditor who collects a debt has neither a gain nor a loss on collection (except for interest) because he has a basis equal to the amount of the debt. However, if a creditor has a gain or loss on the collection of a debt, an issue arises whether the collection can be treated as a "sale or exchange." The courts have held that collection of a debt is not a sale or exchange. [**Fairbanks v. United States,** 306 U.S. 436 (1939); **Nahey v. Commissioner,** 196 F.3d 866 (7th Cir. 1999)—no sale or exchange where taxpayer acquired rights to a lawsuit and settled the case for $6 million]

(a) Note

A statutory change has partially superseded the rule that collection of a debt is not a sale or exchange. By statute, the collection of a "debt instrument," such as a bond or a promissory note, is treated as a sale or exchange by the creditor. [I.R.C. §1271(a)(1), (b)(1)]

(b) Legislative change [§900]

The rule of *Fairbanks* has been changed by legislation described above. Since the debt involved was a "debt instrument," its sale by the creditor would be treated as a sale or exchange. However, the result in *Nahey, supra,* is not changed by section 1271—the right to collect money from a lawsuit for breach of contract is not a "debt instrument."

---

e.g. **Example:** In Year 1, Acme Corp. borrowed $5,000 from George in exchange for a promissory note bearing 6% interest due in Year 4. The interest is payable each year and it is currently paid in Years 1 to 4. (The interest is ignored in this example.) In Year 2, George sells this note to Dick for $3,700. George has a $1,300 capital loss on this sale. In Year 4, Acme Corp. pays Dick $5,000.

The note is a "debt instrument," and Dick has a capital gain of $1,300.

(2) Exception—original issue discount [§901]

The Code requires imputation of interest on discount debts (such as bonds or other obligations). For example, X Corp. might borrow $10,000 in year 1 from Taxpayer and promise to repay $12,000 in year 6. The debt might carry interest at only 3%, even though the prevailing market rate of interest is 7%. The $2,000 discount on the debt occurred because the bond pays a low interest rate. The $2,000 discount is called "original issue discount" and it is taxed to the creditor as ordinary income during the period the debt is outstanding. Thus, Taxpayer cannot claim the $2,000 profit he makes in year 6 as a capital gain because it has already been taxed to him as ordinary income. X Corp. receives a corresponding deduction for interest during the period the debt is outstanding. [I.R.C. §§1272-1275] (For more information on imputed interest, see infra, §§915 et seq.)

c. Involuntary conversion [§902]

Involuntary conversion of property (e.g., receipt of insurance after a fire) and cutting of timber are treated as the equivalent of a "sale or exchange" and included within the section 1231 calculation (see supra, §880).

3. Validity of "Sale or Exchange" Not Affected by Seller's Retention of Control [§903]

If there is a complete transfer of title for a fair consideration, the "sale" will probably be upheld—even where the purchase price is made payable out of income to be earned from the assets transferred (so that buyer assumed no financial risk) and seller retains control of the business.

Example: Taxpayer sold his business to a charity on an installment purchase contract, with a nominal down payment. To avoid any taxable income to itself, the charity dissolved the business and leased the assets to an operating company (managed but not owned by Taxpayer) at a high rental (equal to substantially all of the profits from the business). The rental income was tax-exempt to the charity (under former law), and it used the tax-exempt income (i.e., the operating profits) to pay off the purchase price of the business. The "sale" was upheld, and Taxpayer was thus entitled to capital gain on the payments received from the charity, even though the charity had assumed no real risk and Taxpayer retained operating control of the business. The business profits that would otherwise have been taxable to Taxpayer as ordinary income were taxable to him only at capital gains rates, as payments on the "purchase price." [**Commissioner v. Brown**, 380 U.S. 563 (1965)]

a. Treatment of excess price [§904]

When the purchase price is more than the value of the assets sold, the excessive part is taxed as ordinary income, but the balance is taxed as capital gain. [**Berenson v. Commissioner,** 507 F.2d 262 (2d Cir. 1974)]

b. Effect of I.R.C. section 514 [§905]

The tax dodge sanctioned in *Brown* is no more. I.R.C. section 514 now provides that a charity, otherwise tax-exempt, is *taxable* on income from debt-financed property unrelated to its charitable purposes. However, the principle enunciated by the Court—that the validity of a "sale or exchange" is not affected by the seller's retention of control—seems unimpaired.

c. Distinguish—grantor trust rules [§906]

The *Clifford* rules (*see supra,* §§250 *et seq.*) apparently do not apply in determining the validity of a "sale or exchange" for capital gains purposes.

D. Was There a Sufficient "Holding Period"?

1. In General [§907]

To qualify as *long-term* capital gain, the capital asset must have been held by the taxpayer for *more than 12 months* before the "sale or exchange." (*See supra,* §§813-814.)

a. Calculating the holding period [§908]

The holding period is measured from the time the property is acquired until it is transferred. If an escrow is involved, the date the escrow closes is regarded as the acquisition (or transfer) date. However, if all conditions of sale have been satisfied, the transfer would be deemed to occur even if the escrow were kept open. [*See* **Dyke v. Commissioner,** 6 T.C. 1134 (1946)] Moreover, the day of acquisition is excluded and the date of disposition is included in measuring the one-year period. [Rev. Rul. 66-7, 1966-1 C.B. 188]

2. "Tacking" of Holding Period Where Substituted Basis [§909]

A holding period commences only on a *change of basis* on the property. If there is no change in basis (as in the so-called tax free exchanges; *see supra,* §§779 *et seq.*), there is no new holding period. In such cases, the taxpayer acquires the holding period of his transferor and can "tack" it to the time he holds the property.

Example: When Nicholas makes a *gift* of an asset to Tina, Tina's basis for the property is a "substituted basis" (*see supra,* §732), and hence there is no new holding period. Tina is allowed to "tack" Nicholas's holding period on to her own.

E. Gains on Small Business Stock

1. General Rule [§910]

A taxpayer (other than a corporation) can exclude from income 50% of the gain on the sale of qualified small business stock. The stock must have been held at least five years. [I.R.C. §1202(a)] This benefit is much more favorable than treating the gain as a long-term capital gain.

2. Limit [§911]

The amount of gain subject to the 50% exclusion may not exceed the *greater* of:

(i)   *$10 million* (in the taxable year and prior taxable years); or

(ii) *Ten times the adjusted basis* of the stock being disposed of.

[I.R.C. §1202(b)(1)]

Example: Taxpayer has a basis of $4 million in his Mom-and-Pop Co. stock. The stock is qualified small business stock. He sells the stock for $28 million. Taxpayer can exclude $12 million from income (50% of the total gain). Although the gain exceeded $10 million, it did not exceed 10 times the adjusted basis of the Mom-and-Pop Co. stock.

3. Qualified Small Business Stock [§912]

In addition to being held for at least five years, to constitute qualified small business stock: (i) the stock must have been *issued after August 1993*; (ii) the taxpayer must be the *original purchaser* of the stock from the corporation; and (iii) the corporation must conduct an *active business* (excluding most service and real estate businesses) and have *assets after the stock issuance not exceeding $50 million.* [I.R.C. §1202(c) - (e)]

4. Minimum Tax [§913]

Twenty-eight percent of the excluded gain from the sale of qualified small business stock acquired after December 31, 2000, is treated as a tax preference under the alternative minimum tax. [I.R.C. §57(a)(7); *see infra*, §§937 *et seq.*, for discussion of the alternative minimum tax]

F. Special Computations

1. In General [§914]

In addition to the normal computations above, special rules either turn capital gain into ordinary income or require deferral of certain losses.

2. Imputed Interest [§915]

Interest on deferred payments is ordinary income to the seller of property, deductible by the purchaser (unless the interest deduction is disallowed). However, sometimes taxpayers sell property for deferred payments without providing for any interest (or for interest at below market rate) and correspondingly increase the sales price. This converts the seller's ordinary income to capital gain on the sale of the property (but of course it also decreases the buyer's interest deduction and increases his basis for the property). To prevent this sort of manipulation, the Code provides for imputing interest—turning some of the payments labeled as "principal" into interest. This gives the seller ordinary income and gives the buyer an interest deduction (if the interest is the type that is deductible—*see supra,* §§572 *et seq.*). [I.R.C. §§483, 1274]

a. Imputed interest rate [§916]

Sections 483 and 1274 both require comparison of the interest rate in a transaction to the "applicable federal rate" ("AFR"). AFR is the rate the federal government pays on its debt of various maturities: up to three years (short-term), three to nine years (mid-term), and over nine years (long-term). These rates are periodically announced by the IRS.

b. Section 483 [§917]

Section 483 uses a different computation method from section 1274. Section 483 applies to sales of farms (if the sale price does not exceed $1 million), to sales of a principal residence, or to any sale for less than $250,000 in principal and interest payments. [I.R.C. §1274(c)(4)]

c. Computation [§918]

Assume the AFR is 7% but that a particular deal calls for only 3% interest. Figure the present value of the principal and interest payments due under the contract using the AFR and an actuarial table. This is called the "imputed principal" amount. The imputed principal amount is the buyer's basis and the seller's amount realized. The difference between the stated principal and the imputed principal is original issue discount ("OID"). OID is included in the seller's income (in addition to the 3% stated interest) and is treated as interest paid by the buyer (in addition to the 3% stated interest).

---

e.g. **Example:** In Year 1, Sue sells Blackacre for $1 million to Bob. Bob is to pay nothing down and $200,000 per year for five years plus interest at 3%. The AFR is 7%. The stated principal amount is $1 million, but the imputed principal is only $855,000. Thus, Bob's basis and Sue's amount realized are both $855,000. The difference between the two amounts ($145,000) is OID, which will be taxed as interest income to Sue and will be treated as an interest payment by Bob (deductible if Bob meets the various tests for deductibility).

---

d. Timing [§919]

Under section 483, interest imputation occurs as payments are made. Part of each principal payment will be treated as interest rather than principal. Under section 1274, an accrual method is used. Each year part of the OID is treated as interest regardless of whether any principal payments are made.

(1) OID accrual [§920]

Under section 1274, multiply the imputed principal amount plus OID taken into income in prior years times the difference between the AFR and the stated interest (4% in the example). Thus in Year 1, the interest payment is \$34,200 (\$855,000 × 4%). In Year 2, the interest payment is \$35,568 (\$855,000 + \$34,200 × 4%).

e. Exceptions [§921]

There are a number of total and partial exceptions to the imputed interest rules of I.R.C. section 483.

(1) De minimis rule [§922]

Section 483 does not apply if the selling price is \$3,000 or less. [I.R.C. §483(d)(2)]

(2) Intrafamily real estate deals [§923]

The imputed interest rate cannot exceed 7% with respect to land sales between family members (up to \$500,000 per sale). [I.R.C. §483(e)]

(3) Personal use property [§924]

Finally, in the case of "personal use property," the imputed interest rules do not apply to the buyer (thus giving him no deductions for imputed interest)—only to the seller. For this purpose, "personal use property" means property that the buyer will not use in business or for investment. [I.R.C. §1275(b)]

3. Recapture of Depreciation [§925]

Special provisions require taxpayers to report as *ordinary income* (rather than as capital gain) certain portions of any gain attributable to prior depreciation. In addition, recapture amounts do not qualify for deferral under the installment method of accounting. (*See infra,* §1051.) Recapture amounts also reduce charitable contribution deductions. (*See supra,* §634.)

a. Personal property [§926]

Recognized gain on depreciable personal property is treated as ordinary to the extent of all depreciation taken. It does not matter whether the depreciation was straight-line or accelerated.

(1) Application [§927]

This provision applies to all tangible personal property (such as machinery) and also to fixtures (*e.g.,* a furnace that is attached to a building). [I.R.C. §1245(a)]

(2) Statutory scheme [§928]

"Recomputed basis" means the adjusted basis plus all depreciation. Amounts deducted in the year of purchase under section 179 must also be added (*see supra*, §477). The amount by which the lower of recomputed basis or the amount realized exceeds adjusted basis is treated as ordinary income. [I.R.C. §1245(a)(1), (2)]

Example: Assume Tina buys a printing press in Year 1 for $25,000. From Year 1 to Year 3, she deducts straight-line depreciation of $18,000. Assume she sells the press in Year 3 for $11,000. Her adjusted basis is $7,000 (*i.e.*, $25,000 - $18,000). Her recomputed basis is $25,000 (*i.e.*, $7,000 + $18,000). Ordinary income is calculated by subtracting the adjusted basis ($7,000) from the lesser of the amount realized ($11,000) or recomputed basis ($25,000). Thus, the ordinary income is $4,000 (the entire realized gain).

Compare: However, if Tina sells the press for $28,000, her ordinary income is $18,000 (*i.e.*, $25,000 - $7,000). The remaining $3,000 is section 1231 gain.

Compare: Assume now that Tina sells the press for $4,000. Her loss is $3,000 (*i.e.*, $4,000 - $7,000), and it is a section 1231 loss. There is no recapture since section 1245 does not apply to losses.

(3) Summary

Section 1245 can be summarized as follows: The realized gain is turned into ordinary income to the extent of depreciation previously claimed.

b. Real property (buildings) [§929]

I.R.C. section 1250 recaptures "additional" depreciation deductions taken with respect to **buildings**. "Additional" depreciation is any depreciation in excess of the straight-line rate. Since only straight-line depreciation can now be deducted on buildings, section 1250 is of diminishing importance.

c. Certain transfers not subject to depreciation recapture [§930]

Depreciation is recaptured on any sale or other disposition of property except as specifically provided in I.R.C. sections 1245(b) and 1250(d). Among the more important exceptions are:

(1) *Transfers by reason of death or gifts.*

(2) *Nonrecognition transfers,* such as I.R.C. sections 1031 and 1033 (*see supra*, §§780-801). However, if those transfers become partially taxable because of the presence of boot, the gain will become ordinary income to the extent of the recapturable depreciation.

(3) **In case of a gift**, the donee keeps the donor's basis (*see supra, §732*) and, if he sells the property, depreciation recapture is applicable to him, as it would have been to the donor. **In case of a nonrecognition transfer**, the new property derives its basis from the old property, and on sale of the new property, depreciation would be recaptured.

4. Disallowed Losses [§931]

It is well to recall at this point that certain types of losses (be they "ordinary" or "capital") are disallowed entirely. These issues have been discussed previously and are mentioned here only for review.

a. Losses between related taxpayers [§932]

As discussed previously (*see supra, §§511-514*), losses in transactions between members of the same family, between an individual and a corporation he controls, etc., are **not** deductible. This is true irrespective of the bona fides of the transaction, and even though **gain** in transactions between related taxpayers is recognized and taxed. [I.R.C. §267]

b. Personal losses [§933]

As discussed previously (*see supra, §§496 et seq.*), personal expenses or losses not connected with a trade or business are generally not deductible. This covers losses on sales of personal residences. [I.R.C. §262]

 Compare: But casualty losses are deductible if they exceed 10% of AGI. [I.R.C. §165(c)]

c. Losses on "wash-sales" [§934]

Losses on "wash-sales" also are not recognized and cannot be deducted in computing tax liability. [I.R.C. §1091; *see supra, §517*]

d. Passive losses [§935]

Loss on a passive activity is deductible only to the extent of income from the activity. [I.R.C. §469; *and see supra, §547*]

e. "At risk" rules [§936]

For certain investments, annual operating losses are limited to amounts "at risk." [I.R.C. §465; *see supra, §538*]

G. Alternative Minimum Tax

1. Introduction [§937]

Once taxable income is calculated by reducing gross income and adjusted gross income by the deductions to which the taxpayer is entitled (including deductions arising from capital gains and losses), the percentage tax rates [I.R.C. §1] are applied to determine the tax payable. However, an "alternative minimum tax" may apply. [I.R.C. §55]

2. Computation [§938]

To compute alternative minimum tax ("AMT"), start by computing "alternative minimum taxable income" ("AMTI"). This consists of taxable income plus certain tax preferences and disallowed deductions. Then subtract an exemption. The exemption is $49,000 on a joint return and $35,750 on a single return. Then compute the AMT on the balance at the rate of 26% on AMTI up to $175,000 and 28% on AMTI in excess of $175,000. If the AMT exceeds the taxpayer's regular income tax, the taxpayer must pay the AMT instead of the regular tax.

a. Phaseout [§939]

The exemption amounts are phased out as AMTI rises over designated amounts. These amounts are $150,000 (joint return) and $112,500 (single return). The phaseout is at the rate of 25% of the excess over these levels.

---

e.g. **Example:** Suppose Taxpayer is single and has AMTI of $118,500. This is $6,000 over the phaseout amount for a single person. Therefore, Taxpayer's minimum tax exemption is only $34,250 instead of $35,750 (it was decreased by $1,500—an amount equal to 25% of the excess of AMTI over $112,500). [I.R.C. §55(d)(3)]

---

b. Capital gains [§940]

The AMT on net capital gain is computed separately from the AMT on ordinary income. The AMT on net capital gain is at the same rate as for regular tax purposes. Thus the reduced capital gain rates payable under the regular tax will not have the effect of triggering additional AMT. [I.R.C. §55(b)(3)]

3. Disallowed Deductions Under the AMT [§941]

Certain regular income tax deductions are not allowable under the AMT. The disallowed amounts must be added to taxable income to compute AMTI.

a. Medical deductions [§942]

The AMT allows deduction of medical expenses in excess of 10% of AGI (whereas the regular income tax allows deduction of medical expenses in excess of 7.5% of AGI). [I.R.C. §56(b)(1)(B)]

b. Depreciation [§943]

For AMT purposes, a taxpayer must use 150% declining balance depreciation instead of 200% on nonreal business property (such as trucks or machines). Thus depreciation on nonreal business property must be recomputed for AMT purposes. [I.R.C. §56(a)(1)]

c. Miscellaneous itemized deductions [§944]

Miscellaneous itemized deductions under the regular tax are not deductible for AMT purposes. [I.R.C. §56(b)(1)(A)(i); *see supra,* §§562 *et seq.,* for discussion of miscellaneous itemized deductions under I.R.C. §67(b)] Thus, taxpayers with large employee business expenses or expenses of earning income may find themselves subject to significant AMT liability. [**Prosman v. Commissioner,** T.C. Memo. 1999-87—employee business expenses; **Kenseth v. Commissioner,** 259 F.3d 881 (7th Cir. 2001)—attorneys' fees in bringing successful age discrimination suit]

d. State and local taxes [§945]

The deduction from AGI for state, local, and foreign taxes (such as income tax and real property tax) is not allowed for AMT purposes. [I.R.C. §56(b)(1)(A)(ii)]

e. Standard deduction and personal exemptions [§946]

These are not available under the AMT. [I.R.C. §56(b)(1)(E)] On the other hand, the overall limit on itemized deductions which applies on the regular tax does not apply to the AMT. [I.R.C. §56(b)(1)(F); *see supra,* §565, for a discussion of the limits on itemized deductions under I.R.C. §68]

f. Qualified residence interest [§947]

Only interest incurred in acquiring, constructing, or improving a qualified residence is deductible under the AMT. In other words, interest on a home equity loan is not deductible. [I.R.C. §56(b)(1)(C), (e); *see supra,* §§592-595 for discussion of qualified residence interest]

4. Tax Preferences [§948]

The tax preferences subject to the alternative minimum tax include [I.R.C. §57]:

a. *The bargain element of an incentive stock option when exercised* (*see infra,* §990);

b. *The excess of percentage depletion over adjusted basis of a mine or oil and gas well* (*see supra,* §487);

c. *Intangible drilling costs* on oil and gas wells (less the amount of such costs that would be recovered through straight-line depreciation) in excess of 65% of the net income from oil and gas (*see supra,* §490); and

d. *Interest on certain private activity municipal bonds* (*see supra,* §75).

e. *Twenty-eight percent of the excluded gain from the sale of qualified small business stock* acquired after December 31, 2000 (*see supra,* §§910-913).

5. Illustration [§949]

Tom Taxpayer is unmarried and has taxable income under the regular tax of $250,000. He deducted and paid state income and property taxes of $20,000 and interest on a home equity loan of $12,000. He exercised an incentive stock option, paying $4,000 for stock worth $84,000. Assume Tom's regular income tax was $80,000. Must Tom pay AMT?

Computation:

Taxable income		$250,000

Plus Adjustments:

State taxes	20,000	
Home equity loan	12,000	
Incentive stock option	<u>80,000</u>	
Total adjustments:		<u>112,000</u>
AMTI		362,000

Less Exemption: $35,750 minus 25% of the excess AMTI over $112,500. Since the excess AMTI here is $249,500 ($362,000 - 112,500), and 25% of $249,500 = $62,375, the exemption is reduced to zero   <0>

Subject to AMT (excess over exemption)		<u>$362,000</u>

AMT

26% on $175,000	45,500	
28% on excess over $175,000	<u>52,360</u>	
Total tax:		$ 97,860

Since the taxpayer's regular tax was $80,000, he must pay the AMT of $97,860 instead—an additional amount of $17,860.

EXAM TIP   **gilbert**

AMT was originally imposed to ensure that wealthy people and corporations do not use tax loopholes to avoid paying their "fair share" of taxes. However, unlike many other tax provisions, AMT is not adjusted for inflation and therefore it can now reach middle-class taxpayers as well as the wealthy. Thus, if an exam question involves a taxpayer with a *large amount of deductions* or *income over the AMTI exemption phaseout thresholds*, be sure to at least mention the possibility that the taxpayer might owe AMT.

Chapter Six:
Tax Accounting
Problems

CONTENTS

Chapter Approach

The problems to be covered in this chapter include the determination of *when* income becomes taxable (or a deductible item becomes deductible), and special rules governing how various items of income or deductions may be reported for best tax advantage. Accounting issues are frequently tested because timing questions are critical in tax law.

1. **Accounting Method**

   The primary accounting methods are cash and accrual, but you also need to know how to apply the installment method.

   a. **Cash method**

   Under the cash method of accounting, an item is income when cash (or its equivalent) is received. An item is deductible when cash (or its equivalent) is paid. When solving a problem with a cash method taxpayer, be prepared to confront the following issues:

   (1) **Constructive receipt**

   If the taxpayer has *both the right and the power* to receive the income, she has "constructively received" it; the income cannot be delayed.

   (2) **Timing rule**

   If an employer uses property as compensation and the property is subject to a *substantial risk of forfeiture* and is *nontransferable*, taxation is deferred until the property becomes nonforfeitable or transferable. If the property must be sold at a formula price, and the restriction never lapses, the formula determines the amount included in income.

   (3) **Claim of right doctrine**

   If a taxpayer receives money or property under a claim of right, it is *income* even though it may have to be returned.

   (4) **Prepaid income and expenses**

   Prepayments are generally income when received. Deposits are more like loans and thus are not income. Prepaid expenses are *not deductible*; they must be capitalized and amortized.

   b. **Accrual method**

   Under the accrual method of accounting, an item is income when earned and is deductible when the obligation to pay arises. In both cases the test is whether *all events* have occurred that establish a legal right to receive or make payment. The following issues may arise in connection with an accrual method taxpayer:

(1) Prepaid income

The Supreme Court has held that prepaid income is *taxable when received* even though it is unearned. Watch for statutory and regulatory exceptions to this rule (*e.g.,* automobile clubs, magazine publishers).

(2) Contingent liabilities

There is *no deduction* for contingent liabilities, estimates, or disputed items.

(3) Economic performance rule

Economic performance does not occur, and no deduction is allowed, until property or services are *received* by the taxpayer (or provided by the taxpayer), or in the case of tort liability, until payment is made. [I.R.C. §461(h)]

(4) Inventories

You should be familiar with the *FIFO* (first in, first out) and *LIFO* (last in, first out) methods of computing inventories.

c. Installment method

The installment method automatically applies when a seller receives payment on a deferred basis, unless the seller-taxpayer elects out of it. Under this method, income is recognized pro rata *as payments are received*. When dealing with a problem concerning an installment method taxpayer, the following rules are important:

(1) *Depreciation recapture* is taxed in the year of the sale.

(2) Special calculations are required when *mortgaged property* is sold.

(3) Under the *related party rule*, if a related buyer resells within two years, the seller must recognize income.

(4) *Dealers* cannot use this method.

(5) If *outstanding debt exceeds $5 million*, a special rule requires payment of interest.

2. Annual Accounting Period

Our system is primarily annual—the income and deductions of each year are reported separately, regardless of what happened in earlier or later years. However, there are important exceptions:

a. Repayment of amount previously received

When an amount previously received under a claim of right is repaid, the taxpayer may choose the brackets of the income or the repayment year.

b. Tax benefit rule

A taxpayer must include the recovery of an item previously deducted in income in the brackets of the recovery year.

c. Net operating loss deduction

If a taxpayer's business deductions exceed her income, she has a net operating loss. These losses can be carried back three years, forward 15 years.

A. Accounting Method—When Is an Item Taxable or Deductible?

1. Introduction [§950]

I.R.C. section 446 authorizes taxpayers to use whatever method of accounting that they ordinarily use in keeping their books. However, in practice, the methods expressly recognized in the Code [I.R.C. §446(c)], and discussed below, are the most frequently encountered. Taxpayers cannot change their accounting method without prior approval of the government, even from a wrong method to a correct method. [**Witte v. Commissioner**, 513 F.2d 391 (D.C. Cir. 1975)] The Commissioner, on the other hand, may change the taxpayer's method if the method being used does not "clearly reflect income." [I.R.C. §446(b)]

2. Cash Receipts and Disbursements Method [§951]

Under the cash receipts and disbursements method, items of income are includible in the year in which *cash* (or cash equivalent) is *received*. Deductions are taken in the year in which *payment is made*.

a. Cash equivalents [§952]

An item is income even if paid in a medium other than cash.

(1) Stock [§953]

If an employer pays an employee in corporate stock or other property, the fair market value of the property is income when received. However, if the property is forfeitable, special rules apply. (*See infra*, §§976 *et seq.*)

(2) Promissory notes [§954]

If a taxpayer receives a promissory note or other deferred payment obligation in exchange for property, the fair market value of the obligation is normally treated as the equivalent of cash. The obligation is normally valued at the value of the property surrendered (less any cash down payment). (*See supra*, §775.)

b. **Constructive receipt doctrine [§955]**

If a cash basis taxpayer has an *unqualified right* to a sum of money or property, plus the power to obtain it, she has "constructively received" it. Thus, it is income currently even though she has not actually received it. [Treas. Reg. §1.451-2(a)]

EXAM TIP   gilbert

Don't oversimplify the *cash receipt and disbursement method*. Although income is generally included in the year it is received, you must also remember that a taxpayer *must* include income once a taxpayer has an unqualified right to receive it. This is called the *constructive receipt doctrine*.

---

(1) Rationale

The main purpose of this doctrine is to prevent cash basis taxpayers from avoiding taxes by putting off actual receipt of income until their tax circumstances are more favorable.

(2) Illustrations of constructive receipt doctrine

(a) Uncashed checks [§956]

A taxpayer who receives a check in December of Year 1, but fails to cash it until January of Year 2, is in constructive receipt in Year 1 of the funds called for in the check. [*See* **Lavery v. Commissioner,** 158 F.2d 859 (7th Cir. 1946)]

(b) Interest not withdrawn [§957]

Interest on a savings account is taxable to the taxpayer in the year in which the account is credited, even though not actually withdrawn in that year. Similarly, maturing bond coupons are income to the bondholder in the year of maturity, even though not cashed until a later year. [Treas. Reg. §1.451-2(a), (b)]

(c) Unpaid corporate salaries [§958]

A taxpayer who has *voting control* of a corporation that *owes* him salaries or other taxable funds may be treated as in constructive receipt of such income—provided the corporation has authorized the payment and the funds are available. This is particularly true if the corporation has accrued an expense payment for the money owed. [**Benes v. Commissioner,** 355 F.2d 929 (5th Cir. 1966)]

1) But note

The taxpayer must have both *a right and a power* to receive payment to be in constructive receipt.

> **Example:** Assume Taxpayer owns all of the stock of Acme Corp., and that the corporation declares a dividend in Year 1 "payable January 1, Year 2." Taxpayer will **not** be taxed on this dividend until Year 2. She has no **right** to the money until that time, and it makes no difference that she had the **power** to declare it payable at an earlier date.

(d) Difficulty in obtaining check [§959]

In a questionable decision, a taxpayer was held not in constructive receipt of a check that he could have picked up on December 31 (a weekend day). He would have had to drive 40 miles to obtain it. Moreover, he could not have cashed it at a bank until January 2. The day, the distance, and the futility of the trip were "substantial barriers" to asserting control over the check. [**Baxter v. Commissioner,** 816 F.2d 493 (9th Cir. 1987)]

(3) Mandatory application [§960]

The constructive receipt doctrine must be applied even where it **aids the taxpayer**.

> **Example:** Suppose Taxpayer fails to report certain income in Year 1, although he constructively received it. He actually receives the income in Year 2, when his tax bracket is higher. The government can only assess a deficiency for the **earlier** tax year. [**Ross v. Commissioner,** 169 F.2d 483 (1st Cir. 1948)]

(4) Deferred compensation [§961]

If, before services are rendered, the employer and employee agree that payment will be deferred until a year after that in which the work is done (**e.g.**, at retirement), the money is not constructively received. It is not taxed until actually paid. [Rev. Rul. 60-31, 1960-1 C.B. 174; **Robinson v. Commissioner,** 44 T.C. 20 (1965)] It does not matter that the employer would have been willing to pay the employee currently; the terms of the contract are controlling. [**Amend v. Commissioner,** 13 T.C. 178 (1949)] However, the agreement can be evidenced only by the employer's **unsecured** promise to pay.

(a) When agreement made [§962]

The IRS says that a deferred compensation agreement must be made **before the services** are rendered. [Rev. Rul. 69-650, 1969-2 C.B. 106] However, case law indicates that if the agreement to defer is made after the work is done **but before payment is due**, deferral will still be permitted. [**Veit v. Commissioner,** 8 T.C.M. 919 (1949)]

For your exam, remember that if a cash basis taxpayer agrees to receive income for current services in later years, the payments will not be currently taxable *if* (i) the agreement to delay payment is made *before the services are rendered* (according to the IRS) or made *before payment is due* (according to case law) and (ii) the contract *does not confer an economic benefit* (e.g., does not provide security for payment) on the taxpayer.

(b) Employer's deduction [§963]

The timing of the employer's deduction is matched with the employee's income. The employer cannot deduct deferred compensation until it is actually paid, even if the employer uses the accrual method. [I.R.C. §404(a)(5)]

(c) Economic benefit [§964]

Even if deferred compensation is not constructively received, it is currently taxable to the employee if paid in a form that confers an "economic benefit" on the employee. Sometimes, the same idea is expressed by saying that the deferred compensation is "the equivalent of cash" ("equivalent of cash" and "economic benefit" mean the same thing).

1) Security [§965]

If the employer's promise is secured (*e.g.,* by a mortgage), the promise confers an economic benefit on the employee.

2) Payment to a trust [§966]

Deferred compensation that is paid to a trust for the employee's benefit is an economic benefit to the employee if the assets of the trust are beyond the reach of the employer's creditors. [**Minor v. United States,** 772 F.2d 1472 (9th Cir. 1985)] However, if the assets in the trust can be reached by the employer's creditors, the payment to the trust does not confer an economic benefit on the employee.

3) Forfeitability [§967]

If deferred compensation paid to a trust is subject to a *substantial risk of forfeiture* and is also nontransferable, it is not considered an economic benefit. [I.R.C. §402(b)(1)] The principles of I.R.C. section 83 (*see infra,* §§975-976) are followed in making this determination. For example, if an employee is required to render substantial future services in order to receive the deferred compensation in the trust, the benefit would probably be considered forfeitable. It would not be taxed to the employee until the forfeitability conditions were removed or until the interest became transferable. [**Minor v. United States,** *supra*]

---

e.g. **Example:** A medical partnership rendered services and received deferred compensation, which was placed into a trust. The interest of each doctor in the trust was forfeitable, but the interest of the *partnership as a whole was nonforfeitable*. The Court held that the partnership realized income in the year the payment was made to the trust. This meant that each partner was currently taxed on his pro rata share—even though his own interest in the plan was forfeitable. [**Basye v. United States,** 410 U.S. 441 (1973)]

---

cf. **Compare:** Attorneys settled a personal injury suit. In payment of their contingent fee, they received an annuity from the defendant's insurance company. The insurance company promised to pay them a certain amount per year for 12 years. The annuity was not treated as an economic benefit because it was a mere unsecured promise to pay and was not protected from claims of the insurance company's creditors. [**Childs v. Commissioner,** 103 T.C. 634 (1994), *aff'd*, 89 F.3d 356 (11th Cir. 1996)]

---

4) Annuity contracts [§968]

If the employer funds deferred compensation by purchasing a nonforfeitable annuity contract for the employee, the employee is currently taxed—even though he cannot collect under the annuity contract until retirement. [**United States v. Drescher,** 179 F.2d 863 (2d Cir. 1950)—employee received "present economic benefit"]

c. Qualified pension and profit-sharing plans [§969]

I.R.C. sections 401 through 407 permit the deferral of an employer's contributions to "qualified" pension and profit-sharing plans for its employees. The employer can immediately *deduct* the contributions. [I.R.C. §404] Even if employees' interests are nonforfeitable, they do not realize income until the funds are actually distributed to them—usually after retirement, when the employees are in a lower tax bracket. [I.R.C. §402(a)]

(1) Income not currently taxed [§970]

Another major tax advantage is that income earned by such plans (interest, dividends, etc.) is not currently taxable to the employee. It is taxed only at the time of distribution. Moreover, the trust that holds and invests the money is a tax-exempt entity, so it pays no tax.

(2) Tax treatment on retirement [§971]

At retirement, the employee gets back her *own* contributions paid into the plan as a return of capital (tax free, of course); the part equal to her *employer's* contributions is then taxed to the employee as ordinary income.

(3) Plan must be nondiscriminatory [§972]

To "qualify" for this favorable tax treatment, a plan must have broad employee coverage. This requirement is designed to head off plans that benefit only officers or key employees. [I.R.C. §§401(a)(4), (5), 410]

(4) Limits on contributions and benefits [§973]

There are limitations on the amount of contributions that can be made in any one year to a "defined contribution" plan such as a profit-sharing plan or money-purchase pension plan. The limit is not more than 15% of salary and not more than $30,000 per year (adjusted for inflation to $40,000 in 2002). Also, the benefits payable from a "defined benefit" plan such as a traditional pension plan cannot exceed $90,000 per year (adjusted for inflation to $160,000 per year in 2002). [I.R.C. §§404(a)(3), 415]

(5) Application to noncorporate employers ("Keogh plans") [§974]

Partnerships and proprietorships also can have qualified pension and profit-sharing plans. They can provide the same benefits as a corporate plan.

d. Property transferred in connection with performance of services—"timing rule" of section 83 [§975]

I.R.C. section 83 sets forth ground rules for the "timing" of an employee's income (and the employer's deduction) when the employer uses property (including stock) as compensation. As a general rule, the property is taxed to the employee when she receives it, at its fair market value, without taking into account any restrictions on the property.

(1) Effect of forfeitability [§976]

However, if the property is *both* subject to a substantial risk of forfeiture *and* is nontransferable, taxation is *deferred*. The employee is not taxed until the first year in which the property is *either* nonforfeitable or transferable. The amount includible in income is thus the value of the property in that later year.

Example: In Year 1, Erin Employee is allowed to purchase stock in her employer (Acme Corp.) for $6 per share. The stock is then worth $20 per share and is nontransferable. In addition, Erin is required to resell the stock to Acme Corp. for $6 per share if she resigns or is fired, but this restriction will terminate in Year 5. In Year 5, the stock is worth

$100 per share. Assuming Erin still works for Acme Corp. in Year 5, she is taxed for the first time that year on $94 per share ($100 per share value less $6 per share purchase price). Her basis is now $100 per share.

(a) Employer's deduction [§977]

As a general rule, the employer takes a deduction arising out of the transfer of property to an employee in the same year that the employee is required to include the transfer in income. [I.R.C. §83(h)] However, the employer loses the deduction unless the employee actually includes the value of the stock in income. [**Venture Funding Ltd. v. Commissioner,** 110 T.C. 236 (1998), *aff'd in unpublished opinion*, 198 F.3d 248 (6th Cir. 1999)] The employer can guard against losing the deduction by filing an information return that alerts the IRS that the employee has received compensation through a transfer of property. [Treas. Reg. §1.83-6(a)(2)]

> **Example:** Same facts as above. Assume also that Acme filed an information return indicating that Erin received compensation through a transfer of property, and that Erin correctly claimed the transaction as income. Acme should take a deduction of $94 per share in Year 5.

(2) Nonlapse restrictions [§978]

If the property is subject to a restriction that will never lapse, so that it must be resold at a formula price, the price set by the formula determines the amount to be included in income. [I.R.C. §83(d)]

> **Example:** In Year 1, Eric Employee purchases stock from his employer (Acme Corp.) for $6 per share when its book value (*i.e.,* value determined according to financial statements) is $9 per share. However, a restriction is imposed that if Eric ever wants to sell the stock, he must first offer it to Acme Corp., which will have the right to buy it at book value. The value of Acme stock on the stock exchange in Year 1 is $13 per share. Eric is taxed only on $3 per share (the $9 per share book value less the $6 per share purchase price), not $7 per share (market value less purchase price).

(3) Distinguish—other restrictions ignored [§979]

Restrictions on the property not amounting to substantial risks of forfeiture or formula-price limitations that will never lapse are ignored in valuing the property.

(a) Constitutionality [§980]

This rule has been upheld as constitutional, despite the fact that it requires taxpayers to pay tax on income they have not yet realized. [**Sakol v. Commissioner,** 574 F.2d 694 (2d Cir.), *cert. denied,* 439 U.S. 859 (1978)]

(b) Exception [§981]
If profit on the stock would be payable to the corporation under section 16(b) of the Securities Exchange Act of 1934 (*see supra,* §864), the stock is considered to be both forfeitable and nontransferable until the six-month period of section 16(b) expires. [I.R.C. §83(c)(3)]

(4) Employee election [§982]
A taxpayer may elect to include the value of the property in income when received, even though it is nontransferable and subject to a substantial risk of forfeiture. [I.R.C. §83(b)]

(5) Proper taxpayer [§983]
The Code makes it clear that the employee is taxed, even if the property is transferred to someone else (*e.g.,* his children). [I.R.C. §83(a)] Similarly, the person for whom the services were performed gets the deduction, even if the transfer is made by someone else (*e.g.,* stockholder of employer). [I.R.C. §83(h)]

e. Employee's stock options [§984]
An increasingly common form of compensation to employees is the issuance of stock or stock options by the employer company. Several issues arise from such transactions: Are the stock options taxable as income, or excludible? If taxable, at what value? When are they taxable? And, if the stock has increased in value, is the increase capital gain?

(1) General rule [§985]
Stock or an option to buy stock, issued by an employer to an employee, is in the nature of compensation for services rendered (or to be rendered). As such, the option or the stock is taxed as ***ordinary income*** to the employee, despite the argument that it was granted to give the employee a stake in the business rather than to compensate him. [**Commissioner v. LoBue,** 351 U.S. 423 (1956)]

(2) Timing of income [§986]
Generally, the *exercise* of the option is the taxable event.

(a) Grant not taxed [§987]
Since the option by itself usually lacks an ascertainable market value, the grant of the option is generally not the taxable event. However, if the option does have an ascertainable value (*i.e.,* there is an established market for it), it can be included in income when received.

(b) Tax treatment upon exercise [§988]

If an option was not taxed when it was granted, its exercise is the taxable event. The difference between the current market price and the option price is treated as ordinary income to the employee, and the basis of the stock will be the option price plus the amount included in income. Any subsequent gain would be capital gain.

---

e.g. **Example:** In Year 1, Acme Company issues an option with no ascertainable market value to Elmer Employee to purchase one share of its stock for $10 anytime for the next five years. Acme Company stock was selling for $11 when the option was issued. Assume further that Elmer exercises the option in Year 3 when the share is worth $19. Elmer has $9 of ordinary income in Year 3 and a basis of $19 for the share.

---

1) But note

If the stock is subject to a substantial risk of forfeiture and is nontransferable, the income would be deferred under I.R.C. section 83 (*see supra*, §§975-976) until either of those restrictions ceased to apply.

(3) Employer's deduction [§989]

The employer gets a deduction at the same time the employee has income. Thus, in the example above, Acme Company has a $9 deduction in Year 3.

(4) Incentive stock options [§990]

If a stock option qualifies as an "incentive stock option," there is no tax on either the grant or the exercise of the option. The employee is not taxed until he sells the stock, and then the sale is taxed as a capital gain or loss. The employer receives no deduction at any time. [I.R.C. §422A] Requirements for incentive stock options are that:

(i) *The employee may not dispose of the stock for a period* extending two years after the option was granted and one year after exercising the option. (These requirements are waived if employee dies.)

(ii) *The option price must equal or exceed the value of the stock* when the option is granted.

(iii) *The term of the option must not exceed 10 years*, and the option must be *nontransferable.*

(iv) *The employee cannot own more than 10% of the employer's stock* when the option is granted (although this requirement is waived if

gilbert

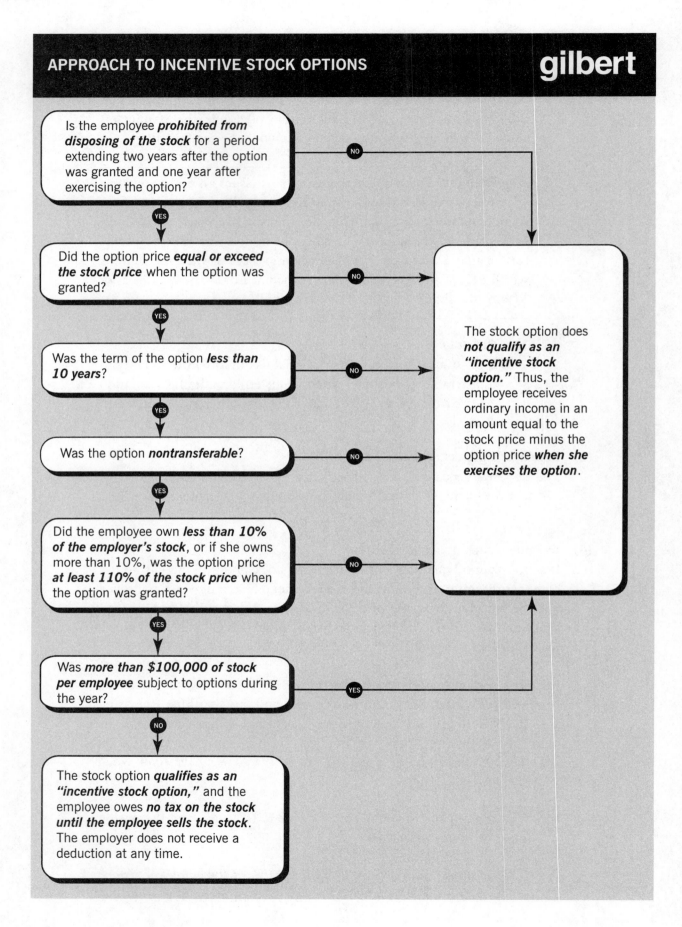

Is the employee **prohibited from disposing of the stock** for a period extending two years after the option was granted and one year after exercising the option?

— NO →

Did the option price **equal or exceed the stock price** when the option was granted?

— NO →

Was the term of the option **less than 10 years**?

— NO →

Was the option **nontransferable**?

— NO →

Did the employee own **less than 10% of the employer's stock**, or if she owns more than 10%, was the option price **at least 110% of the stock price** when the option was granted?

— NO →

Was **more than $100,000 of stock per employee** subject to options during the year?

— YES →

The stock option does **not qualify as an "incentive stock option."** Thus, the employee receives ordinary income in an amount equal to the stock price minus the option price **when she exercises the option**.

NO ↓

The stock option **qualifies as an "incentive stock option,"** and the employee owes **no tax on the stock until the employee sells the stock**. The employer does not receive a deduction at any time.

the option price is at least 110% of the value of the stock when granted).

(v) *Not more than $100,000 of stock per year per employee can be subject to options.*

(a) Note

The exercise value of an incentive stock option is a tax preference subject to the alternative minimum tax. (*See supra*, §§937 *et seq.*)

f. Claim of right doctrine [§991]

If a taxpayer receives money or property and claims he is entitled to it, and he can freely dispose of it, he is immediately taxable. The fact that he might have to give it back is disregarded. [**North American Oil Consolidated v. Burnet**, 286 U.S. 417 (1932)] This rule is equally applicable whether taxpayer is on the cash or the accrual basis.

(1) Rationale—"administrative convenience" [§992]

Although it would make sense to delay taxation until the taxpayer's entitlement to the money has been confirmed, this might not be administratively feasible. The taxpayer might "forget" to take the money into income in the later year. Besides, his power to use the money as he likes makes immediate taxation not unjust.

Example: *Amounts received by mistake* are taxable when received even though they may have to be repaid. [**United States v. Lewis**, 340 U.S. 590 (1951)—employee received $22,000 bonus in 1944 that was incorrectly calculated; state court order required him to pay back a portion of bonus in 1946]

Example: *Money received because of a favorable trial court judgment* is income when received, despite the possibility that it will have to be returned should an appeal be successful. [**North American Oil Consolidated v. Burnet**, *supra*—company won right to funds in receivership in 1917; final appeal dismissed in 1922]

Example: *Embezzled money* is immediately income to the embezzler, even though he is under duty to repay. [**James v. United States**, *supra*, §160]

---

(2) Treatment upon repayment [§993]

The taxpayer receives a deduction in the later year when he repays money received under a claim of right. As to some (but not all) such repayments, he is entitled to figure the deduction at the tax bracket of either the year of receipt or the year of repayment. [I.R.C. §1341; *see infra,* §1068]

g. Prepaid income [§994]

Since income under the cash method is tied to the receipt of cash, rather than the time the money is earned, prepayments are income when received (*e.g.,* prepaid interest or rent).

(1) Deposits [§995]

If a customer makes an advance payment for goods and services to the seller, the amount received is currently taxable to the seller, even though the goods or services are furnished in a later year. Similarly, an advance payment of rent is taxable to the lessor. However, a security deposit is not currently taxable to the seller or lessor because such a deposit is more like a loan than an advance payment. [**Commissioner v. Indianapolis Power & Light Co.,** 493 U.S. 203 (1990)—deposit by utility customer treated as loan]

(a) Explanation

In *Indianapolis Power,* the Supreme Court analogized the security deposits to loans which, of course, are not taxable to the borrower, rather than to advance payments. The utility paid interest to the customers on the deposits, which made them seem like loans. More important, however, was the fact that the customer controlled whether the deposit would be applied to utility bills or whether the deposit would be returned to the customer (after service was terminated or after the customer established that he was a reliable billpayer). Because the utility had no guarantee that it would be able to keep the funds, it was more like a borrower than the recipient of an advance payment. In the case of an advance payment, the recipient is entitled to keep the funds if it honors its contractual commitments. [**Commissioner v. Indianapolis Power & Light Co.,** *supra*]

h. Prepaid expenses [§996]

Ordinarily, a cash basis taxpayer is entitled to deduct expense items in the year paid. However, according to most cases, this rule does not apply to amounts prepaid for goods or services to be received in later tax years.

(1) Rationale—preventing tax avoidance [§997]

To allow a cash basis taxpayer to deduct prepaid expenses currently would allow her to **distort** her income and to reduce taxes in years of high income. Also, the prepayment can be considered the purchase of an asset—a future benefit—which must be **capitalized.** Thus, generally, no current deduction is allowed for amounts expended by a cash basis taxpayer during the year for rents, salaries, or other expenses attributable to future tax years.

(2) Effect—capitalization and amortization [§998]

The deduction is not lost. Rather, the prepaid expense must be *capitalized* (treated as the acquisition of an asset in the year of payment), and then deducted ratably (amortized) in the future tax year. (Amortization is discussed *supra*, §§456, 473-475.)

(a) Prepaid rent [§999]

Prepaid rent on business property must be capitalized in the *year paid*, and then *amortized* over the years to which the prepayment applies.

(b) Prepaid insurance [§1000]

Likewise, prepaid insurance on investment property is treated as an asset, to be deducted ratably over the period covered by the insurance. [**Commissioner v. Boylston Marketing Association**, 131 F.2d 966 (1st Cir. 1942); *but see* **Waldheim Realty v. Commissioner**, 245 F.2d 823 (8th Cir. 1957)]

(c) One-year prepayments [§1001]

A prepayment of an expense for a period that does not exceed one year need not be capitalized, even though the year extends beyond the end of the taxable period in which the payment is made. [**Zaninovich v. Commissioner**, 616 F.2d 429 (9th Cir. 1980); **U.S. Freightways Corp. v. Commissioner**, 270 F.3d 1137 (7th Cir. 2001)—same rule for accrual method taxpayer] However, a taxpayer cannot deduct a prepayment for less than one year if no payment was yet due under the taxpayer's contract with the payee. [**Bonaire Development Co. v. Commissioner**, 679 F.2d 159 (9th Cir. 1982)]

EXAM TIP   gilbert

On your exam, don't apply the general rule that a cash basis taxpayer must take a deduction for an expense in the year it was paid too liberally. Many types of *prepayments* require the expense to be *capitalized and amortized*.

---

(3) Application

(a) Prepaid interest [§1002]

Prepaid interest can be deducted only over the period of the underlying loan. [I.R.C. §461(g)]

1) Distinguish—"points"

"Points" paid on purchase money loans secured by a taxpayer's principal residence are currently deductible. [I.R.C. §461(g)(2)]

(b) Farming [§1003]

Traditionally, farmers could deduct planting costs and farming supplies immediately. However, there are now some limitations.

1) *"Farming syndicates"* cannot deduct feed, seed, or fertilizer until it is used. [I.R.C. §464]

2) *Farmers* cannot deduct planting costs of *fruit trees*. [I.R.C. §278]

3) *Corporations* must capitalize all pre-production expenses—although there are exceptions for small businesses and family farms. [I.R.C. §447]

(c) Property taxes [§1004]

Prepaid property taxes are deductible. [**Glassell v. Commissioner,** 12 T.C. 232 (1949)]

i. Payment with credit cards [§1005]

If any deductible item is paid by a credit card, the deduction is taken when the item is charged—not when the bill is later paid to the issuer of the credit card. [Rev. Rul. 78-38, 1978-1 C.B. 68; 78-39, 1978-1 C.B. 73]

3. Accrual Method [§1006]

Under the accrual method, the taxpayer reports income in whatever tax year it is *earned*—even though not paid or payable until a later year. Likewise, a taxpayer deducts expenses in the tax year in which the expenses are *incurred*, even though not yet actually paid out. Under this method, the *right to receive* income and the *duty to pay* the various items of deduction are the elements by which the tax is computed. This method is more complex than the cash method, but it is economically sounder.

a. Accrual method required [§1007]

In some circumstances, a taxpayer is required to adopt (or switch to) the accrual method rather than use the cash method.

(1) Income-producing inventories [§1008]

Generally, if inventories are a material income-producing factor for a taxpayer, the accrual method must be used. [Treas. Reg. §1.446-l(c)(2)] (For discussion of inventories, *see infra,* §§1039-1045.) However, the IRS has modified this principle by several administrative decisions. First, a taxpayer with average annual gross receipts of less than $1 million is not required to account for inventories (*see infra,* §§1039 *et seq.*) or use the accrual method. [Rev. Proc. 2001-10, 2001-2 C.B. 272] Second, the IRS will permit certain small service businesses with annual gross receipts of more than $1 million but less than $10 million to use the cash method, even though the business sells goods and would otherwise be required to account for inventories. This decision covers primarily service businesses that also sell goods (*e.g.*, plumbers, auto mechanics). It does not cover businesses engaged in manufacturing or wholesale or retail trade. [Rev. Proc. 2002-28, 2002-18 I.R.B. 875]

(2) Corporations, some partnerships, tax shelters [§1009]

Corporations, partnerships that have a corporate partner, and tax shelters must use the accrual method. [I.R.C. §448]

(a) Exceptions

There are some important exceptions to this rule:

1) An *S corporation* is one that has elected to be taxed in a manner similar to partnerships (*i.e.,* the corporation is not separately taxed; its profits and losses flow directly through to the returns of its shareholders). S corporations are not required to use the accrual method, nor are partnerships that have an S corporation as a partner.

2) A corporation or partnership (with a corporate partner) need not use the accrual method if its *annual gross receipts average less than $5 million*. [I.R.C. §448(b)(3), (c)]

3) A corporation or partnership need not use the accrual method if it is a "*qualified personal service corporation.*" This means that substantially all of its activities involve performance of services in the fields of health, law, engineering, architecture, accounting, actuarial science, performing arts, or consulting. In addition, substantially all of its stock must be held by employees performing the services (or retired employees or the estate of deceased employees or persons who inherited the stock within the previous two years). [I.R.C. §448(d)(2)]

4) *Farming businesses* need not use the accrual method. [I.R.C. §448(b)(1), (d)(l)]

(b) Note

Tax shelters are required to use the accrual method because much of the tax avoidance potential of such enterprises arises from use of the cash method. For this purpose, a tax shelter is any publicly offered partnership, any partnership where at least 35% of the losses are allocated to limited partners, or any other plan whose principal purpose is tax avoidance. [I.R.C. §§448(d)(3), 461(i)(3), 1256(b)(3)(B), 6661(b)(2)(C)(ii)]

b. Special problems with income under accrual method

(1) Deferred income [§1010]

As indicated, the income of an accrual basis taxpayer includes all amounts that the taxpayer has a *fixed* right to receive. The test is whether *all the events that establish a right to income have occurred* and whether the *amount of the income is reasonably determinable*.

(a) When income accrues [§1011]

A seller of goods accrues income when all events have occurred that establish the buyer's obligation to pay. However, sellers have some latitude about whether the critical event is the shipment of goods or the passage of title. Either approach clearly reflects income if used consistently. [**Hallmark Cards Inc. v. Commissioner,** 90 T.C. 26 (1988)—Valentine cards shipped in December but contract provides that title and risk of loss remain with seller until January 1; income does not accrue until January 1]

(b) Time payment is due [§1012]

The fact that the debtor has to have a positive cash flow before it is obligated to pay is not a contingency that allows the creditor to postpone accrual of income. Similarly, the fact that the debt to the creditor is subordinated to other debts would not prevent accrual. Both of these contractual provisions relate only to the time when payment must be made, not to the debtor's liability to make the payment. [**Harmont Plaza, Inc. v. Commissioner,** 64 T.C. 632 (1976), *aff'd,* 549 F.2d 414 (6th Cir. 1977)]

(c) Insolvent debtor [§1013]

If the debtor is insolvent, however, the income need not be accrued. [**H. Liebes & Co. v. Commissioner,** 90 F.2d 932 (9th Cir. 1937)]

1) Proof of insolvency [§1014]

The taxpayer must make a strong showing to establish doubts about collectibility. [*See* **Georgia School Book Depository v. Commissioner,** 1 T.C. 463 (1943)—taxpayer required to accrue commissions earned on sale to state, even though payment was to be made only from a special fund, which had no assets at the time, but which ultimately was likely to be funded]

(2) Prepaid income [§1015]

A problem exists where an accrual basis taxpayer is paid in the current tax year for services to be rendered, or goods to be supplied, in future tax years. The issue is whether the income should all be taxable in the year of receipt or whether it can be spread out over the tax years in which the services or goods are to be provided.

(a) Court position—taxed when received [§1016]

The Supreme Court cases (all dealing with prepayments for services, but apparently applicable to prepayments for goods as well) hold that prepaid income is taxable **when received**. Although this is contrary to proper accounting practice, the Court felt that Congress had mandated this result because it repealed legislation that would have allowed accrual basis taxpayers to defer prepaid income. [**American Automobile Association v. United States,** 367 U.S. 687 (1961)—dealing with prepaid dues to automobile club; **Schlude v. Commissioner,** 372 U.S. 128 (1963)—dealing with prepaid dance lesson fees]

1) Majority rule

Since the Supreme Court cases, the lower court cases have generally held that an accrual basis taxpayer cannot defer prepaid income from goods or services. [*See* **Hagen Advertising Displays v. Commissioner,** 407 F.2d 1105 (6th Cir. 1969)—dealing with prepayments for goods]

2) Minority rule

A few cases have held that taxpayers who make a strong showing can avoid the rule that prepayments are always included in income when received. These cases seem to be of dubious validity as long as the Supreme Court sticks to *American Automobile* and *Schlude*.

---

e.g. **Example:** A professional *baseball team* can defer prepaid season ticket income since it can predict precisely when the games will be played. [**Artnell Co. v. Commissioner,** 400 F.2d 981 (7th Cir. 1968)]

---

e.g. **Example:** A taxpayer who is prepaid for *some* engineering jobs, but is paid after rendering services for other jobs, was allowed to defer inclusion of the prepayments. The IRS wanted the taxpayer to include prepayments when received and also to accrue income on the other jobs before payment. The court thought that this was an improper hybrid method of accounting. [**Boise Cascade Corp. v. United States,** 530 F.2d 1367 (Ct. Cl.), *cert. denied,* 429 U.S. 867 (1976)]

(b) Statutory relief in certain situations [§1017]

Congress enacted special remedial legislation to allow deferral of *certain* types of prepaid income. (I.R.C. section 456 allows automobile clubs to spread their membership income over the period in which they are obligated to render services to their members; and I.R.C.

section 455 allows newspaper and magazine publishers to spread subscription income over the period of the subscription.)

(c) IRS position—deferral allowed [§1018]

More recently, the IRS has reversed itself. It now permits an accrual basis taxpayer to defer advance payments from the sale of goods. It also permits a *limited* deferral of advance payments for services.

1) Goods [§1019]

An accrual basis taxpayer now has the *choice* of reporting advance payments for goods in the year of *receipt, or whenever properly accruable* under her regular method of accounting. However, advance payments for goods held in *inventory* cannot be deferred past the second taxable year following receipt. [Treas. Reg. §1.451-5]

2) Services [§1020]

Advance payments for services, however, must still be reported in the year of receipt, with this exception: If the services are to be *completed by the end of the following year*, the taxpayer can *defer to the following year* whatever portion of the advance payment is attributable to that year's services. [Rev. Proc. 71-21] But prepaid *rent* must be reported in the year received.

(3) Dividends [§1021]

Since a dividend becomes a fixed obligation of the corporation when declared, it would seem that accrual basis shareholders should report income from dividends as of the date of declaration. However, due to administrative considerations (particularly, the difficulty of determining the date of declaration in every case), the taxpayer is treated as having no income from dividends until actually received—the same as if he were on the cash basis. [**Commissioner v. American Light & Traction,** 156 F.2d 398 (7th Cir. 1946); Treas. Reg. §1.301-1(b)]

(4) Increasing rents [§1022]

Under certain leases, both the lessor and lessee must account consistently for the rents on the accrual basis, even if either or both of them normally use the cash method. This provision applies only to "section 467 rental agreements," which are leases calling for increasing payments with total rent payments in excess of $250,000. [I.R.C. §467]

(a) General rule [§1023]

If the lease allocates particular payments to particular periods, the parties must accrue income and deductions for that period.

> **e.g.** **Example:** If a five-year lease allocates $0 rent to Year 1 and $100,000 rent to Years 2 through 5, both the lessor and lessee accrue no income or deduction in Year 1 and accrue income or deduction of $100,000 in Years 2 through 5. [I.R.C. §467(b)(1)(A)]

(b) Exception [§1024]

In certain circumstances (*e.g.*, a lease calling for the payment of rent during a year after the year to which the rent applies), the Code calls for an accrual of a constant amount during each year of the lease computed according to present value principles. [I.R.C. §467(b), (e)(1)]

c. Deductions under the accrual method [§1025]

As indicated above, the criteria for deductibility are whether: (i) *all the events* have occurred that establish an *unconditional duty to pay*; (ii) *economic performance* has occurred; and (iii) the amount is *reasonably ascertainable*. [I.R.C. §461(h)(4); **United States v. Anderson,** 269 U.S. 422 (1926); Treas. Reg. §461(a)(2)] Note that the courts refuse to consider the likelihood of actual payment as a factor in determining deductibility. Thus, taxpayers who are insolvent have been allowed to deduct unpaid expenses even though in all probability these items will never be paid. [**Zimmerman Steel Co. v. Commissioner,** 130 F.2d 1011 (8th Cir. 1942)]

(1) Fixed duty to pay

(a) Contested liabilities [§1026]

If the taxpayer disputes its liability for an expense, the taxpayer recognizes no unconditional obligation and hence is not permitted to accrue the item as a deduction. [**Dixie Pine Products v. Commissioner,** 320 U.S. 516 (1944)]

1) *If the taxpayer transfers money to provide for satisfaction of the disputed liability,* she is entitled to deduct it. For example, she might make a payment under protest and immediately sue for recovery. [I.R.C. §461(f); **Chernin v. Commissioner,** 149 F.3d 805 (8th Cir. 1998)—"transfer" to creditor occurred when taxpayer's bank account was garnished]

2) *However, payment of the disputed amount into a trust* does not meet the requirements of section 461(f) where the other parties to the dispute were not parties to the trust agreement. [**Poirier & McLane Corp. v. Commissioner,** 547 F.2d 161 (2d Cir.), *cert. denied,* 431 U.S. 967 (1977)—trust assets would (and in fact did) revert to taxpayer if it was successful in the litigation; *but see* **Varied Investments Inc. v. United States,** 31

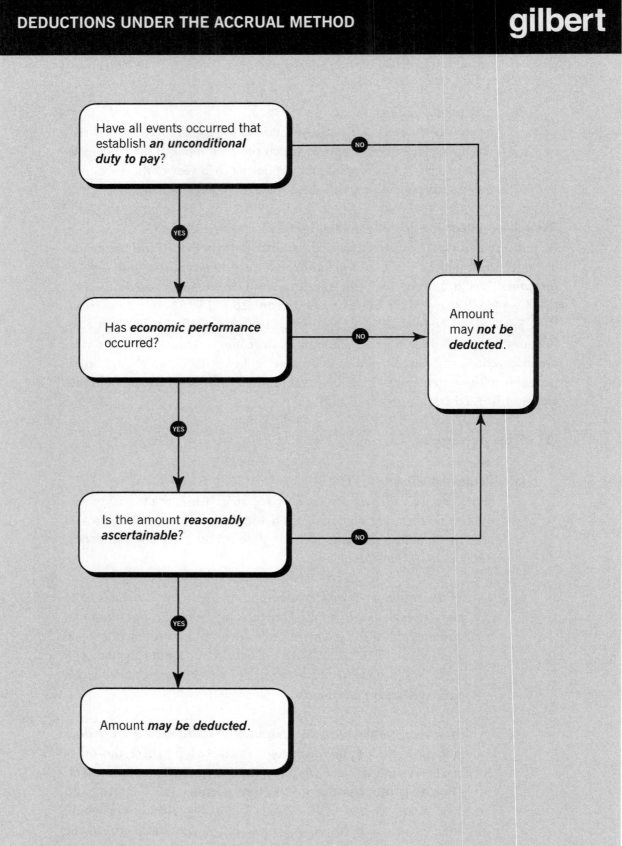

Have all events occurred that establish *an unconditional duty to pay*?

NO

YES

Has *economic performance* occurred?

NO

YES

Is the amount *reasonably ascertainable*?

NO

YES

Amount may *not be deducted*.

Amount *may be deducted*.

F.3d 651 (8th Cir. 1994)—disagreeing with *Poirier & McLane* and allowing deduction for transfer of funds into an escrow account where claimant did not sign the escrow agreement]

(b) Contingent liabilities [§1027]

A deduction cannot be accrued if liability is contingent and the contingency has not occurred.

---

e.g. **Example:** An employer pays the medical expenses incurred by its employees. At the end of the year, some employees have received medical treatment but have not yet filed their claims. Although the employer can predict quite accurately the amount of claims that will ultimately be filed, it cannot deduct these costs. The filing of a claim is an "event" that has not yet occurred; until it does, the employer's obligation to pay remains contingent. Because some employees never do file the claims, the "event" is not an "extremely remote and speculative possibility." [**United States v. General Dynamics Corp.**, 481 U.S. 239 (1987)]

---

1) Recipient of payment [§1028]

However, a taxpayer can deduct an obligation to make payment when all the events have occurred to establish liability, even if the identity of the recipient cannot be ascertained.

---

e.g. **Example:** A gambling casino pays "progressive jackpots," meaning that the amount of a slot machine jackpot keeps rising until somebody finally wins it. At the end of the year, the jackpot has risen to $25,000. Casino can accrue a deduction for the jackpot because state law requires that it ultimately be paid—even though the recipient cannot be identified and it is not known when the jackpot will be won. [**United States v. Hughes Properties, Inc.**, 476 U.S. 593 (1986)] However, the result in this case has been reversed by the economic performance rules (*see infra*, §1030). [I.R.C. §461(h); Treas. Reg. §1.461-4(g)(8), example (4)]

(c) Very long-term obligations [§1029]

If an obligation is to be paid many years in the future, a conflict arises: The taxpayer wants to accrue the deduction immediately, thus producing an immediate tax saving, but the IRS wants to defer the deduction until the amount is actually paid. The case law is uncertain. In many situations, however, the economic performance rule will require deferral until the year of payment (*see, e.g., infra*, §1033).

Example: Mooney Aircraft, Inc., sold an airplane and promised to refund $1,000 to the owner of the plane when the plane was retired (called a "Mooney bond"). The IRS exercised its discretion to switch Mooney Aircraft to the cash method with respect to deducting the $1,000. The court held this was not an abuse of the IRS's discretion, because an immediate deduction would not clearly reflect income. The length of time before payment (20 to 30 years) was just too long. [**Mooney Aircraft, Inc. v. United States,** 420 F.2d 400 (5th Cir. 1969)] The same result (deduction deferred until year of payment) is now required by regulations adopted under the economic performance rule, discussed below. [Treas. Reg. §1.461-4(g)(3)]; *and see* **Ford Motor Co. v. Commissioner,** 71 F.3d 209 (6th Cir. 1995)—tort liabilities to be paid out over 58 years; accrual of entire amount of payment in single year does not clearly reflect income]

(2) Economic performance rule [§1030]

The "all events" test will not be met for purposes of deducting expenses any earlier than the time that "economic performance" occurs with respect to any item.

(a) Purchase of property or services [§1031]

If someone provides services or property to the taxpayer, economic performance does not occur until the services or property are actually provided or used by the taxpayer.

Example: Suppose that in Year 1 Taxpayer agrees to pay $5,000 for stationery to be delivered in Year 3. The cost of the stationery is not deductible until Year 3. [I.R.C. §461(h)(2)(A)]

(b) Sale of property or services [§1032]

When a taxpayer is obligated to provide services or property to someone else, economic performance does not occur until the services or property are actually provided. [I.R.C. §461(h)(2)(B)]

(c) Tort liability [§1033]

If the taxpayer is obligated through judgment or settlement agreement to make installment payments arising out of tort or workers' compensation liability, no deduction can be taken until the payments are actually made. [I.R.C. §461(h)(2)(C)] Prior to enactment of this section, there was authority for allowing the full deduction in the year the obligation became a fixed duty to pay, even if the installment payments were to be made over many years. [*See* **Burnham Corp. v. Commissioner,** 90 T.C. 953, *aff'd,* 878 F.2d 86 (2d Cir.

1989)—total estimated amount of monthly payments to be made for the balance of the plaintiff's life were immediately deductible in the year of the tort settlement] Even before enactment of section 461(h)(2), however, the IRS could reach the same result by switching the taxpayer to the cash method. [*See* **Ford Motor Co. v. Commissioner,** 102 T.C. No. 6 (1994)]

(d) Exception for recurring items [§1034]

To simplify accounting for recurring items, a deduction can be taken in the year before it would be permitted under the above rules if performance will occur within a reasonable time after the close of the year, or within eight and one-half months after the close of the year, whichever comes first. The item must be recurring in nature, consistently treated by the taxpayer, and either not material in amount or (if material) accrual in the earlier year would promote better matching of income and expenses. For this purpose, it helps the taxpayer's case if the item is deducted in the earlier year on its *financial statements.* [I.R.C. §461(h)(3)]

(3) Ascertainable amount [§1035]

Deduction is not permitted unless the amount of the item is reasonably ascertainable.

(4) Disallowance of deduction for amount owed to related taxpayer [§1036]

The Code disallows the accrual of deductions for any item owed to a related cash basis taxpayer until the item is *actually paid.* [I.R.C. §267(a)(2)]

(a) Related persons [§1037]

The above rule applies to a long list of relationships. [I.R.C. §267(b)] For example, it applies to payments between members of a family, and payments between an individual and a corporation of which the individual owns more than 50% of the stock (directly or indirectly). [I.R.C. §267(b)(1), (b)(2), (c)(4); *see supra,* §514]

---

e.g. Example: In December of Year 1, the directors of Widgets Corp. (an accrual method taxpayer) vote a bonus to Bernie (a 51% shareholder who uses the cash method). The bonus is paid on June 6 of Year 2. Although Widgets Corp. ordinarily could accrue the salary in Year 1, it is prevented from doing so until actual payment in Year 2.

---

cf. Compare: Under these facts, Bernie might be found to be in constructive receipt of the salary in Year 1 because he had both a right and power to collect it (*see supra,* §§955-960). If so, Widgets

Corp. could deduct it in Year 1. [**Hyplains Dressed Beef Inc. v. Commissioner,** *56* T.C. 119 (1971)]

(b) Pass-thru entities [§1038]

A stricter rule applies to deductions claimed by pass-thru (so spelled in the Code) entities (S corporations or partnerships). If an amount is owed by an accrual method pass-thru entity to any cash method shareholder or partner (regardless of the percentage of that person's interest), the entity cannot deduct the item until actually paid. [I.R.C. §267(e)—pass-thru entities are discussed in detail in the Tax II Summary]

d. Inventories [§1039]

Whenever inventories are an income-producing factor of the business, the taxpayer *must* account for purchases by using an *inventory*. [Treas. Reg. §1.471-1] This means that the cost of goods sold deduction is increased by the merchandise on hand at the beginning of the tax year and decreased by the merchandise on hand at the end of the year. The basic effect is that the taxpayer cannot deduct the cost of goods or materials in the year he purchases them *unless he sells them that year.*

(1) Methods of computing inventory [§1040]

There are two primary methods by which the taxpayer may take his inventory.

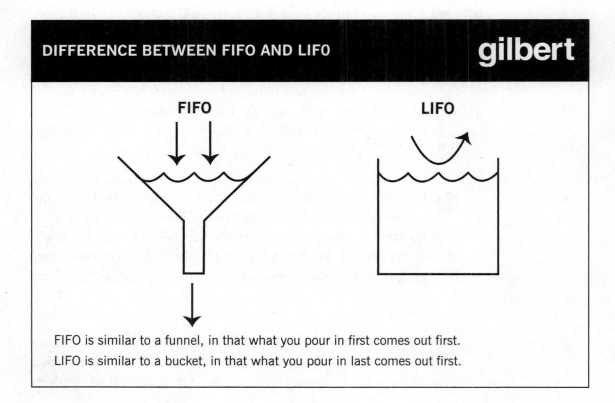

DIFFERENCE BETWEEN FIFO AND LIFO — gilbert

FIFO

LIFO

FIFO is similar to a funnel, in that what you pour in first comes out first.
LIFO is similar to a bucket, in that what you pour in last comes out first.

(a) First in, first out ("FIFO") [§1041]

If the same type of merchandise was purchased at various prices during the year, and so intermingled that the items cannot readily be identified, the "cost" (for inventory purposes) of the goods on hand at the close of the taxable year is the cost of the goods *last* purchased. The theory is that the *goods first acquired* were those that were *first sold*.

---

e.g. **Example:** Athletic Co. sells running shoes. In its first year of operation, it buys 500 pairs of shoes for $20 per pair and later 300 pairs for $25 per pair (a total of $17,500). At the end of the year, it has only 100 pairs of shoes remaining. Under FIFO, the 100 shoes would be valued at $25 each (or $2,500), since it is assumed that Athletic Co. sold the shoes that it bought first, and the remaining shoes are part of the 300 bought for $25 per pair. Thus, cost of goods sold would be $15,000 (purchases of $17,500 less closing inventory of $2,500). The opening inventory for the next year would also be $2,500.

---

1) Valuation [§1042]

Taxpayers using FIFO can, if they wish, value the assets in inventory at cost or at market value, whichever is lower. [Treas. Reg. §§1.471-2, -4]

a) Exception [§1043]

For purposes of determining market value, the taxpayer is not permitted to follow generally accepted accounting principles by writing down its inventory arbitrarily. "Market" means the replacement value of the inventory unless management is offering it for sale at a lower price or unless it is damaged. [**Thor Power Tool Co. v. Commissioner,** 439 U.S. 522 (1979)—spare parts cannot be written down to scrap value as long as they are still held for sale at normal prices]

(b) Last in, first out ("LIFO") [§1044]

Under LIFO, inventory is computed at cost, but the goods on hand at the end of the year are treated as if they had been the earliest items purchased or produced. [I.R.C. §472] (In other words, the last items placed in inventory are assumed to be the first sold.) LIFO can be used for tax purposes only if it is also used for financial reporting purposes. [I.R.C. §472(c)]

---

e.g. **Example:** In the preceding example, the closing inventory would be only $2,000 instead of $2,500. The 100 pairs of shoes in inventory would be considered to be from the *earliest* lot purchased (at $20 per pair). Thus, the cost of goods sold would be $15,500 instead of $15,000, and taxable income would be $500 lower than if FIFO were used.

1) Tax planning [§1045]

In a time of inflation, taxpayers prefer to use LIFO. As the example indicates, when prices are rising, LIFO will produce a lower taxable income. The reverse is true when prices are falling.

(2) Limitation on altering computation method [§1046]

A taxpayer cannot change his inventory method without the approval of the IRS.

EXAM TIP　　　　　　　　　　　　　　　　　　　　　**gilbert**

If you encounter a fact pattern on your exam in which the taxpayer has *switched (or wants to switch) inventory accounting* methods, be sure to check for the *required IRS approval*. Without IRS approval, a taxpayer may not switch inventory accounting methods.

---

4. Installment Method [§1047]

The installment method of taxation is intended to allow sellers of *property* who are receiving payment on a deferred basis to pay tax on their gain only as they receive cash from the sale. The basic idea is that the profit is recognized ratably as payments are made. The installment method can be used only for a sale of property, not services, and only if the sale produced a gain, not a loss. [I.R.C. §453]

a. Election [§1048]

No election is required to use the installment method. It is automatic. A taxpayer who wishes *not* to use the installment method must elect out of it on her tax return for the year in which the disposition occurred. [I.R.C. §453(d)] If an election out occurs, a cash method taxpayer would include in income all cash and the value of cash equivalents received. (*See supra*, §§952-954.) An accrual method taxpayer would include the entire gross profit in income.

b. Mechanics of installment method [§1049]

To use the installment method, compute a fraction: "gross profit" (selling price less basis) over "total contract price." Multiply that fraction times each payment to determine how much of that payment must be taken into income.

---

e.g. **Example:** Taxpayer sells stock of Omega Corp. with a basis of $30 and a value of $150 for $25 down and the balance of $125 in 10 payments of $12.50 each, plus interest on the unpaid balance of 9% per year. The fraction is gross profit of $120 over total contract price of $150, or 4/5. Therefore, 4/5 of the down payment is gross profit ($20) and 4/5 of each later principal payment will also be gross profit ($10).

---

(1) Interest separately treated [§1050]

Of course, payments of interest are separately treated. In the previous example, the interest element of each payment is entirely included in income. If the contract failed to provide for interest at the currently required rate, interest would be imputed under section 483 or 1274 (*see supra,* §915).

(2) Depreciation recapture [§1051]

Often, property sold on the installment method has been depreciated by the seller, and depreciation must be recaptured under section 1245 or 1250 (*supra,* §§925-930). The recapturable amount is ordinary income in the year of sale. It cannot be deferred even though the sale is accounted for under the installment method. The amount recaptured as ordinary income is added to the basis of the property for purposes of determining the fraction that will be used under the installment method. [I.R.C. §453(i)]

---

e.g. Example: Tom Taxpayer sells a truck, which he bought earlier for $1,000, for $2,500. The buyer pays Tom $500 down, with the balance paid in 10 payments of $200 each, plus interest of 9% on the unpaid balance. Assume that Tom must recapture $700 of depreciation. The $700 is ordinary income in the year of the sale. The basis of the property is increased from $1,000 to $1,700. The fraction is now $800/$2,500 (0.32). Therefore, only $160 of the down payment is taxable (probably as a gain under section 1231). Only $64 of each later payment of $200 is taxable.

---

c. Indeterminate sale price [§1052]

The installment method can be used even though the sale price is not fixed. [I.R.C. §453(j); Treas. Reg. §15A.453-l(c)] There are three possibilities:

(1) *The sale price is not fixed but will be payable over a defined period of time* (*e.g.,* five years). In this case, taxpayer recovers a pro rata portion of her basis equally over each year. [Treas. Reg. §15A.453-l(c)(3)]

---

e.g. Example: Suppose in the example *supra,* §1048, Taxpayer sells the stock for $25 down and an additional amount equal to 30% of the profits of Omega Corp. for five years. Under the installment method, Taxpayer recovers 1/5 of her basis each year ($6). Thus, in the year of the sale, she has income of $19 ($25 amount realized less $6 recovery of basis).

---

(2) *The sale price is not fixed, but there is a maximum amount that the buyer must pay*. In this case, the maximum amount is treated as the amount realized for purposes of measuring gross profit and total contract price.

---

e.g. **Example:** Suppose that in the previous example, Taxpayer sells the stock for $25 down and an additional amount equal to 30% of the profits of Omega Corp., but the sale price is capped at $125. The total contract price is $150 and the gross profit is $120. If in a later year it becomes clear that the maximum amount will never be paid, an appropriate adjustment is made in the formula. [Treas. Reg. §1.15A.453-1(c)(2), (7)]

---

(3) *The sale price is not fixed, and there is neither a fixed term nor a maximum amount*. The IRS will scrutinize such deals to make sure a sale really occurred. If it did, basis is recovered equally each year over an arbitrary period of 15 years unless taxpayer persuades the IRS that a different period would be more appropriate. [Treas. Reg. §15A.453-1(c)(4), (7)]

d. Restrictions on use of installment method

(1) Debt payable on demand or readily transferable [§1053]
If, instead of an ordinary promissory note secured by a mortgage, the seller receives a debt instrument that is payable on demand, or is issued by a corporation or government and is readily tradable, such instrument is treated as a cash payment, thus preventing use of the installment method. [I.R.C. §453(f)(4), (5)]

(2) Sale to related person [§1054]
When the seller sells to a related person on a deferred payment basis, and the related person resells the property for cash within two years, the original seller is treated as if she received the cash for purposes of accounting under the installment method. Related persons include family members, related corporations, etc. [I.R.C. §453(e), (f)(1)]

(3) Dealer property [§1055]
The installment method does not apply to "dealer property." This means personal property in the hands of a person who regularly sells or otherwise disposes of the same type of property on the installment plan. It also means real property held by a taxpayer for sale to customers in the ordinary course of trade or business. [I.R.C. §453(b)(2), (1); *see supra*, §§823-828]

e. Interest on deferred income [§1056]

In the case of very large installment sales, the taxpayer is required to pay interest to the government on the deferred tax liability. [I.R.C. §453A]

(1) Sale price must exceed $150,000 [§1057]

The interest rule applies only to an installment sale where the sale price exceeds $150,000. In addition, the face amount of *all* such obligations held by the taxpayer that arose during, and are outstanding at the close of, the taxable year must exceed *$5 million*. [I.R.C. §453A(b)(2)]

(2) Computation of interest [§1058]

Compute the interest obligation as follows: The deferred tax liability is the amount of tax that would be due if all of the unrecognized gain on the obligations were recognized at the close of the year. The applicable percentage is the fraction determined by dividing the face amount of obligations outstanding in excess of $5 million by the aggregate face value of the obligations. The interest rate charged is the rate currently being charged on tax underpayments.

---

e.g. **Example:** During the year, Sam Seller made a single installment sale in which the sale price was $25 million. The deferred gain on the sale was $16 million. Assume Sam's tax bracket is 28%. The deferred tax liability would be 28% of $16 million, or $4,480,000. The applicable fraction is 4/5 ($20,000,000/$25,000,000). Four-fifths of $4,480,000 is $3,584,000. Assume an interest rate of 10%. Thus, Sam must pay the government $358,400.

---

(3) Pledges [§1059]

If an installment obligation falls under the rules of section 453A (*i.e.,* the sale price exceeds $150,000 and the total installment sales exceeded $5 million), and the taxpayer pledges the installment obligation as security for a loan, the pledge is treated as a disposition of the obligation and deferred gain is recognized under the disposition rules. (*See infra,* §1062.)

f. Mortgaged property [§1060]

Often a buyer will assume or take subject to a mortgage or trust deed on the property owing to a third party. The amount of this mortgage is always taken into account in determining the seller's gross profit, but it is not taken into account under section 453 for purposes of determining either payments received in the year of sale or total contract price. [Treas. Reg. §1.453-4(c)] As a result, the seller does not have to worry about when or whether the buyer makes payments on the debt to the third party.

(1) Illustration

Sue sells Blackacre to Barb for $10,000. The basis of Blackacre is $3,000, and it is subject to a $2,000 first mortgage in favor of Bank. Barb pays $1,000 down, takes subject to the mortgage to Bank, and gives Sue a note for $7,000, secured by a second mortgage on Blackacre, which provides for two payments in future years of $3,500, plus interest on the unpaid balance at the rate of 15%.

(2) Calculation

The gross profit is $7,000; both mortgages are taken into account in measuring gross profit. However, the first mortgage is ignored for purposes of measuring both payments and total contract price. Thus, the fraction is $7,000/$8,000, or 7/8. The only current payment is the $1,000 down payment, of which $875 is taxable. Of the $3,500 payments, $3,062.50 is taxable. Thus, the entire $7,000 gross profit will be taxed. [Treas. Reg. §1.453-4(c)]

(3) Exception [§1061]

If the first mortgage exceeds the basis, the excess is considered a payment received in the year of sale and is part of the total contract price.

Example: If the first mortgage in the previous problem were $5,000 (and the second mortgage was therefore reduced to $4,000), the current payments would be $3,000 (the $1,000 down payment plus the $2,000 excess of mortgage over basis) and the total contract price would be $7,000 (*i.e.,* the down payment, the excess of first mortgage over basis, and the second mortgage). The fraction would be $7,000/$7,000, or 1. Thus the entire $3,000 of payments in the year of sale (*i.e.,* the down payment plus the excess of mortgage over basis) would be taxable as would the entire amount of payments as they are made on the second mortgage.

---

g. Disposition of installment obligations [§1062]

Disposition of an installment obligation is a taxable event, whether the disposition is a sale or any other kind of disposition, including a gift. In the case of a disposition, the transferor is deemed to immediately receive the amount realized in the case of a sale (or a satisfaction of the debt by the debtor) and thus to immediately recognize part or all of the previously unrecognized gain. In the case of a gift, the transferor is deemed to receive the fair market value of the installment obligation. [I.R.C. §453B(a)]

(1) Exception—death of taxpayer [§1063]

If the taxpayer dies, the deferred gain is not recognized, and the estate or legatees are permitted to continue accounting for payments on the installment obligation. However, they do not get a stepped-up basis for the obligation since it is considered income in respect of a decedent. [I.R.C. §§453B(c), 691(a)(4), (5)]

(2) Exception—transfer between spouses [§1064]

Transfer of installment obligations between spouses (or former spouses if the transfer is incident to divorce) are excepted from the disposition rule. Suppose at the time of Harold and Wanda's divorce, Wanda transfers an installment obligation to Harold. Wanda does not recognize the deferred gain and Harold continues to account for collections by using the installment method. This rule does not apply to a transfer *in trust* for a spouse or former spouse—a transfer in trust is a disposition. [I.R.C. §453B(g)]

ACCOUNTING METHODS—SUMMARY	**gilbert**
CASH RECEIPT AND DISBURSEMENT METHOD	Income is included in the year in which the taxpayer *receives the equivalent of cash*; deductions are taken in the year in which *payment is made*.
ACCRUAL METHOD	Income is included in the year in which *it is earned*; deductions are taken in the year in which the *expense is incurred*.
INSTALLMENT METHOD	For *sales of property*, a taxpayer (whether he uses the *cash or accrual method*) must include a *percentage of the payments as gain* in the year in which he receives the payment. Note that the taxpayer may opt out of this method and that it *cannot be used for losses*.

B. The Annual Accounting Period

1. Introduction [§1065]

The determination of income and deductions is based on an annual, not a transactional, basis. Hence, even though a taxpayer is engaged in transactions stretching over several years, he ordinarily must pay a tax each year based on his income that year. Items of income and deductions are therefore allocated to a particular year, not to a particular transaction.

2. Selection of Taxable Year [§1066]

Most individual taxpayers report on a calendar year basis (January to December). Other entities (which previously could choose different reporting years) have been required to switch to the calendar year (unless they establish, to the satisfaction of the IRS, a business purpose for a different period). These include partnerships, S corporations (corporations that have elected to be taxed like partnerships), and personal service corporations. [I.R.C. §§443(i), 706(b)(1)(B), 1378] Corporations that are neither S corporations nor personal service corporations are entitled to elect to use a non-calendar year when they file their first returns; they cannot change that year without IRS approval. [I.R.C. §442]

3. **Repayment of Income Reported in Prior Year [§1067]**

As seen above (*see supra,* §991), payments made to the taxpayer during the tax year that he receives under a "claim of right," are taxed as income to him that year, even though he may have to pay it back in a later tax year. The repayment in the later year does *not* reopen the tax computation for the year the income was received. Rather, *a deduction is allowed in the year repayment is made.* This results from the annual accounting concept. [*See* **United States v. Lewis,** *supra,* §992— employee forced to repay portion of bonus paid in prior year]

a. **Choice of brackets [§1068]**

Of course, this could be quite unfair to the taxpayer if he was in a high bracket in the year in which the income was paid to him, but in a low bracket when he had to repay it. To ameliorate this, a special provision allows the taxpayer to deduct the amount at the tax bracket of *either* the current year or the earlier year in which the payment was received. [I.R.C. §1341] However, the amount repaid must be at least $3,000 to merit this special treatment.

Example: Tom Taxpayer is employed by Omega Corp. In Year 1, assume Tom is in a 30% tax bracket. He receives a large salary, but Tom's employment contract obligates him to return to Omega Corp. any portion of the salary that the IRS disallows as unreasonable compensation (*see supra,* §§415-423). In Year 3, Tom returns $30,000 to Omega Corp. Tom has negative income in Year 3. Tom can use section 1341 in Year 3 and thus receive a tax saving of $9,000 rather than zero (*i.e.,* 30% of $30,000 rather than no benefit). [**Van Cleave v. United States,** 718 F.2d 193 (6th Cir. 1983)]

---

(1) **Distinguish—reducing income in later years [§1069]**

Section 1341 generally applies only to situations in which the taxpayer is required to *repay* an amount that she previously reported. If the taxpayer is ordered to reduce its price in later years because of its actions in prior tax years, section 1341 is not applicable. [**Wicor, Inc. v. United States,** 263 F.3d. 659 (7th Cir. 2001)]

Example: Gas Co. is regulated by the state public utility commission ("PUC"). In Year 1, Gas Co. was permitted to charge its customers $160,000 on the assumption that its federal taxes in Year 1 would be $40,000. However, the income tax rate for Year 1 was reduced; therefore, Gas Co. was required to pay federal taxes of only $32,000. As a result, PUC required Gas Co. to reduce its rates in Year 3 by $8,000. The Year 1 tax rates were also much higher than the Year 3 tax rates. The court held that section 1341 does not cover a mandated reduction of income in Year 3, only an actual repayment in Year 3. In other words, section 1341 would have applied if Gas Co. had refunded $8,000 to its customers, but it does not apply when Gas Co. is compelled to reduce its price by $8,000. [**Wicor, Inc. v. United States,** *supra*]

---

b. Tax benefit offset [§1070]
If the taxpayer elects to claim a deduction in the year of repayment, he must *offset* any *tax benefit* he obtained in the year he reported the income.

 Example: Skelly Oil Co. was a producer of natural gas and was ordered to refund to its customers overcharges it had made in prior years (and reported as income). It was entitled to deduct the refunds in the year made, *but* the deduction was reduced by the *depletion allowance* Skelly Oil Co. had claimed with respect to the income in the years of the overcharge. [**United States v. Skelly Oil Co.,** 394 U.S. 678 (1969)]

---

(1) Note
When the income was taxed as a capital gain in the earlier year, a taxpayer can deduct the repayment only as a capital loss. [**Arrowsmith v. Commissioner,** 344 U.S. 6 (1952)] However, by using section 1341, a taxpayer can treat the capital loss as if it had occurred in the year of the capital gain.

4. Tax Benefit Rule [§1071]
When a deduction in an earlier year is followed by a recovery in a later year of the amount deducted, the taxpayer must include the amount previously deducted as income in the later year. [**Hillsboro National Bank v. Commissioner,** 457 U.S. 1103 (1983)] However, the recovery is *not* includible in income to the extent that the earlier deduction *did not reduce the amount of tax*. [I.R.C. §111(a)] This is referred to as the "tax benefit rule"—a recovery is not income unless the earlier outlay produced a tax benefit.

a. "Recovery" [§1072]
A "recovery" means an event *inconsistent* with the earlier deduction.

 Example: Bruce Wayne gives a building to Gotham City as a charitable contribution and deducts its fair market value (which furnishes Bruce a tax benefit). However, the gift provides that the building must be used for a hospital. In a later year, the city decides not to convert the building into a hospital and returns the building to Bruce, an event inconsistent with the prior deduction. The return of the asset is treated as income in the year of return. [**Alice Phelan Sullivan Corp. v. United States,** 381 F.2d 399 (Ct. Cl. 1967)]

 Example: Tilly pays on December 15 of Year 1 (and deducts under I.R.C. section 162, thereby receiving a tax benefit) 90 days' rental on office space for her business. However, on January 5 of Year 2, she converts the space to her residence. The prepayment of rent was deductible in Year 1, because of its short term (*see supra,* §1001). However, the conversion to personal use was inconsistent with having deducted the item as a business expense. She must include in income in Year 2 the amount of the prepaid rent applicable to the period for which the space is not used for business. [**Hillsboro National Bank v. Commissioner,** *supra*—dictum]

Example: Ranch Corp. paid on December 15 of Year 1 (and correctly deducted in Year 1, thereby receiving a tax benefit) the cost of cattle feed that would not be used up until some time in Year 2. On January 20 of Year 2, Ranch Corp. was completely liquidated, and all assets (including the unconsumed portion of the feed) were distributed to Farmer Brown, the sole shareholder. Although I.R.C. section 336 (under prior law) provided that a corporation realized no gain on the transfer of its assets to shareholders in complete liquidation, the tax benefit rule requires that Ranch Corp. include as income in its final tax return for Year 2 the amount of unconsumed feed. The distribution to Farmer Brown is inconsistent with the assumptions that made the Year 1 deduction appropriate for Ranch Corp. Note that the tax benefit rule can even override explicit statutory nonrecognition provisions like section 336. [**Hillsboro National Bank v. Commissioner,** *supra*]

---

b. Erroneous deduction [§1073]

A recovery is income even if the amount deducted in the earlier year was not legally deductible. [**Unvert v. Commissioner,** 656 F.2d 483 (9th Cir. 1981)]

c. Measuring tax benefit [§1074]

Under the tax benefit rule, it is necessary to see whether a prior deduction reduced income tax.

(1) Carryforwards [§1075]

In considering whether a deduction reduced income tax, it is necessary to take the unexpired net operating loss carryforwards or capital loss carryforwards into account. If the deduction created an unexpired carryforward, it is treated as having reduced tax. [I.R.C. §111(c)]

d. Brackets [§1076]

Suppose that the taxpayer is in the 15% bracket in Year 1, and she deducts a loss of $5,000. Her taxable income was $12,000; therefore, she received a tax benefit from the entire $5,000 deduction. In Year 5, she recovers the $5,000 item and is in the 30% bracket. The *amount* of tax saving in Year 1 is *irrelevant*; the entire item is taxed at the applicable bracket in Year 5, even though the result is that it will cost much more in taxes than was saved in Year 1. [**Alice Phelan Sullivan Corp. v. United States,** *supra,* §1072]

5. Net Operating Loss Deduction [§1077]

If all of the business deductions available to a taxpayer—expenses, depreciation, depletion, losses, and bad debts—exceed his income, he has a net operating loss ("NOL"). [I.R.C. §172]

a. Distinguish "loss" from NOL [§1078]

Note that this is a different meaning for the word "loss" than was previously employed. The word "loss" in tax parlance usually means a failure to recover basis when a transaction comes to an end. Here, the word "loss" means an excess of deductions over income.

b. Use of NOL [§1079]

The NOL can be *carried back* and used as a deduction for the two years preceding the loss year. The taxes for those years are then refigured, and the taxpayer is entitled to a refund. If some of the NOL has not been used up by the carryback, it is *carried forward* into the 20 years after the loss year and used as a deduction. It must be carried to the earliest of the 22 possible years before the balance can be used in any later year.

(1) Stimulus legislation

Legislation adopted in 2002 provides that in the case of taxpayers incurring an NOL in 2001 or 2002, the carryback period is five years rather than the usual two years.

c. Amount of NOL [§1080]

The amount of an NOL that may be carried forward or back is equal to a negative taxable income figure adjusted as follows:

(1) *No deduction for capital losses in excess of capital gains* is allowed.

(2) *Personal exemptions* are disallowed.

(3) *Deductions not attributable to a trade or business* are allowed only to the extent of income that is not attributable to a trade or business. The result of this computation is to confine the NOL to trade or business rather than personal or investment losses.

Review Questions
and Answers

Review Questions

1. In Year 1, Angelo borrowed $100 from Bobbi, which Angelo used to go on a vacation. In Year 2, Angelo repaid the $100 to Bobbi, with $6 interest. The loan bears interest at a rate in excess of the applicable federal rate.

   a. Is anything included in Angelo's or Bobbi's gross income? _____

   b. Does either Angelo or Bobbi have any deductions? _____

2. Calvin, a theater critic, receives free tickets to plays and gives them to his friends. Must he include the value of the tickets in income? _____

3. Don, an accountant, is getting divorced. Edna, an attorney, needs accounting services for her law practice. Edna agrees that she will represent Don; for each hour she spends on Don's case, Don will give Edna an hour-and-a-half of accounting services. Thereafter, Edna provides 30 hours of legal services for Don (worth $1,500) and Don provides 45 hours of accounting services for Edna (also worth $1,500).

   a. Do Don and Edna have income from these transactions? _____

   b. Does either of them get any deductions? _____

4. French has been George's valet for many years and they have become close personal friends. When French retires, George unexpectedly presents him with a check for $25,000.

   a. Is the $25,000 includible in French's income? _____

   b. Can George deduct the $25,000? _____

   c. Would French be taxed if George had left him $25,000 in his will? _____

5. The Zero Manufacturing Co. has a custom of paying $8,000 to the widows or widowers of deceased employees. Horace died and Zero paid Iris, his widow, $8,000.

   a. Must Iris include the full $8,000 in income? _____

   b. Can Zero deduct the $8,000? _____

6. Home Magazine gives an annual $10,000 prize to persons who create the most ingenious new interior decorating scheme for their homes. It is necessary to submit a photograph of the rooms involved. Lem wins the prize this year.

a. Must Lem include the $10,000 in income? _____

b. If entering the contest cost Lem $100 for making photos and $40 as an entry fee, could he deduct the $140? _____

7. Mildred attends University. She received a $9,000 scholarship of which $4,200 was applied to her tuition and books. Is any amount of the scholarship taxable? _____

8. Norm takes out a life insurance policy on his life, naming Oona (his cousin) as the beneficiary. Norm pays premiums of $2,000 and Oona pays premiums of $3,500. When Norm dies, Oona collects $10,000.

a. Must Oona include anything in income? _____

b. Could Norm or Oona deduct the premiums they paid? _____

c. Would the answer to question a. have been different if Oona had purchased an existing policy from Norm for $2,000 and then paid $3,500 more in premiums? _____

9. Paul, the surviving spouse of Rhea, is the beneficiary of a $100,000 life insurance policy on her life. He elects to have the company pay out the proceeds in 10 annual payments of $15,000 each. Must Paul include any part of the $15,000 payment in income? _____

10. Steve purchases an annuity policy for $10,000 that will pay him annual payments of $1,000 per year beginning at age 65 until his death. His life expectancy at age 65 is 16 years.

a. How much of each annuity payment is taxable? _____

b. Steve dies at age 66 after receiving only one payment. Is he entitled to a loss deduction in the year of his death? _____

11. Tom buys a $20,000 bond issued by Dubuque, Iowa. He pays $1,000 down, promising to pay the additional $19,000 in the future. In Year 1, he pays $1,900 interest on his debt obligation. He also pays $20 for a safe deposit box to store the bond in. He receives $1,400 of interest income on the bond.

a. Is the $1,400 of interest income taxable? _____

b. Is either the $1,900 interest expense or the $20 for the safe deposit box deductible? _____

12. Indicate whether any of the following items received by Vera (who is single and whose adjusted gross income is $23,000) are taxable:

a. Social Security retirement benefits of $7,000. _____

b. Payments of Supplemental Security Income ("SSI") based on need amounting to $1,300. _____

13. The *San Francisco Chronicle* writes an article describing Silvio as a hired killer for the Mafia. Silvio sues for defamation, recovering $20,000 as actual damages (which include damages to his business as a babysitter) and $50,000 as punitive damages.

a. Is the $20,000 taxable to Will? _____

b. The $50,000? _____

c. Can the *Chronicle* deduct the payments? _____

14. Zero Manufacturing Corp. sued Scratch Electric Co. for antitrust violations, based on price fixing by Scratch of certain materials purchased by Zero. In previous years, Zero had deducted its payments to Scratch and received a tax benefit. The lawsuit was settled for $400,000: $150,000 allocated as damages to Zero's goodwill, $200,000 as damages for lost profits, and $50,000 as punitive damages. Zero had no basis for its goodwill, which had been completely destroyed. Scratch had previously been convicted of criminal antitrust violations by reason of the same conduct alleged in Zero's lawsuit.

a. Must Zero include the $150,000 in income? _____

b. Must Zero include the $200,000? _____

c. The $50,000? _____

d. Can Scratch deduct all of its payments to Zero? _____

15. Cowboy is given bunkhouse facilities and meals on the ranch so that Rancher can have him available for emergencies at all times. The annual value of the lodging is $1,200 and the annual value of the meals is $1,000. Must Cowboy include these amounts in income? _____

16. Alpha Manufacturing Co. owes $10,000 to Piedmont Corp. for services rendered. It offers to settle the debt for $6,000. Piedmont accepts because Alpha's financial condition is so poor that Piedmont does not think Alpha can ever pay the debt in full. Prior to the settlement, Alpha's assets were $34,000 and its liabilities were $37,000. Both Alpha and Piedmont use the accrual method of accounting; thus, Alpha had previously deducted the $10,000, and Piedmont had included it in income.

a. Does Alpha have gross income from this transaction? If so, how much? _____

b. Does Piedmont get a deduction? _____

17. Law Firm gives free legal services to any of its employees who need them. Joe (a paralegal) needs a new will. Carol (a young associate) drafts one for him free of charge. At Law Firm's usual rates, the will would have cost $500. Carol's salary for the time she spent on this job was $120.

    a.   Should Joe include the $500 in income?   _____

    b.   Assuming the $500 is includible, can Joe deduct it?   _____

18. The divorce agreement between H and W calls for H to pay W $40,000 per year for five years (terminable on W's death) plus $12,000 in child support per year.

    a.   How much can H deduct when he pays $52,000 in the first year?   _____

    b.   How much should W include in income?   _____

19. The divorce agreement between H and W calls for H to pay $40,000 per year for 10 years, terminable on W's death. In the first year, H pays the $40,000 but in the second and third years he pays nothing. What consequences to H in the third year?   _____

20. Diego owned a vegetable farm. He gave his son, Sam, the right to harvest and sell the vegetables on the farm. But Diego reserved the right to sell the land and keep the proceeds of sale (as it was located close to a city, it was very valuable real estate). This year, Sam harvests and sells artichokes worth $20,000. Is Sam taxed on the $20,000?   _____

21. Gordon set up a trust, giving the income to Kent for life, remainder to Wayne. Kent receives about $10,000 per year from this trust. In Year 1, Kent gave Lois one-half of his life estate. He also gave Jimmy the remaining one-half of the income for the next five years. In Year 2, Lois receives $5,000 and Jimmy receives $5,000.

    a.   Is Lois taxed on the $5,000 she received?   _____

    b.   Is Jimmy taxed on the $5,000 he received?   _____

22. Miguel, an attorney, tells his clients to pay legal fees to his child, Rafael. In that tax year, Rafael receives $21,000. Is he taxed on the $21,000?   _____

23. Luanne, an attorney, has been working for years on a big personal injury case; if she wins it, she will get one-third of the recovery. Needing cash, she sells her rights to the fee in Year 1 to Tex for $30,000, even though the case has not yet gone to trial. In Year 3, she tries and wins the case, getting a judgment for $300,000. However, before the judgment is collected, Tex gives his rights to the $100,000 contingent fee to his son, Jake. Shortly thereafter, Jake receives $100,000.

    a.   Does Luanne's sale result in her being entitled to capital gain?   _____

b.   Is the $100,000 taxed to Jake?   _____

24.   Jean owns a plastics molding factory. She transfers the factory to a partnership, making herself a general partner, and creates newly formed trusts for her children as limited partners. Independent trustees are used. Jean pays herself a reasonable $60,000 per year salary. After payment of the salary, the partnership has a profit of $100,000. Trust A, which has a 10% interest in the partnership, receives $10,000. Is Trust A taxed on the $10,000?   _____

25.   Paulie is a 10-year-old child movie star. By contract, his earnings are paid to his father, Phil, who completely controls the choice of movies Paulie works in and Paulie's working conditions. This year, Phil receives $50,000 from Paulie's earnings and spends $15,000 on such items as singing lessons for Paulie. Phil also keeps $5,000 for himself since his contract with Paulie entitles Phil to a 10% management fee.

       a.   Is Paulie taxed on the $50,000?   _____

       b.   Can Paulie deduct the $15,000 spent on singing lessons and the like?   _____

       c.   Can Paulie deduct the $5,000 retained by Phil?   _____

26.   Harold and Wilma are husband and wife. They live in a community property state. This year, Wilma earns $28,000 of gross income, which is classified as community property over which she has the power of control. Wilma and Harold file separate returns. Must Wilma report $28,000 on her return?   _____

27.   On January 1 of Year 1, X Corp. loans $250,000 interest free to Enrique, its sole shareholder. Enrique uses the loan proceeds in his separate business as a photographer. The loan is repayable when X Corp. demands it. The applicable federal rate is 6%. (Assume only annual compounding is required.)

       a.   What consequences to Enrique in Year 1?   _____

       b.   What consequences to X Corp. in Year 1?   _____

28.   Giovanna puts some GM stock in trust with the income payable to her minor son Carlo for 12 years, reversion to Giovanna. Must Carlo include the dividends on the stocks in his income?   _____

29.   Ken places property in trust for Barbie and Teresa for life, remainder to Kelly. In each of the following cases, will Ken be taxed on the income from the trust?

       a.   Ken, as the trustee, can invade corpus for either Barbie or Teresa if money is required for educational or medical needs.   _____

       b.   Ken has power, as trustee, to apportion the income of the trust between Barbie and Teresa, depending on their medical and educational needs.   _____

c.   Matt, Ken's grandfather, will have the exclusive power as trustee to apportion income between Barbie and Teresa as required for educational and medical needs.

d.   The Bank of America and Matt (Ken's grandfather) have power to apportion income or principal among the beneficiaries in any manner that they wish.

e.   Ken is the trustee and has power either to distribute income currently to Barbie and Teresa or to accumulate the income. However, the accumulated income must be paid to Barbie or Teresa during their lifetimes or to their estates or appointees.

30. Sam puts property in trust for Tom for life, remainder to Natalie. However, Sam can revoke the trust any time after one year.

a.   Will the income of the trust be taxed to Sam?

b.   Would the answer be different if Sam can revoke only with the consent of Tom?

31. Aaron puts property in trust with the income to be accumulated during the life of his wife, Beth, remainder to Clem. The trustee is the Bank of America. It can pay any of the accumulated income to Beth if, in the Bank's discretion, she is in need of it.

a.   If Beth does not receive any income, is Aaron taxed on it?

b.   Suppose that the income could, in the Bank's discretion, be used only for the support of Aaron's minor son, Don. If Don does not receive any money, is the income taxed to Aaron?

32. Ella puts property in trust, with the income to Fred for life, remainder to George. In the following cases, will the income from the trust be taxed to Ella?

a.   Jack, a business partner of Ella, has the power to borrow interest-free from the corpus of the trust.

b.   Ella, acting as a trustee in a fiduciary capacity, has the power to vote stock in the trust.

33. Ivan sets up a trust with the income payable to Oleg for life, remainder to Igor. Nicolai has the power to assign the trust assets to himself at any time.

a.   Is Nicolai taxable on the trust income, even though he does not assign the corpus to himself?

b.   Suppose that Ivan had the power to distribute corpus to Oleg at any time before Nicolai assigns the trust to himself. Is Nicolai taxable on the income?

34. The terms of Trust A require that all income be currently distributed to the life beneficiary, Mary. However, capital gains are allocated to the corpus. This year the trust has ordinary taxable income of $25,000. However, the trustee did not distribute it to Mary. The trust also has a $12,000 long-term capital gain. Is the trust taxable on:

    a.   The $25,000?   _____

    b.   The $12,000?   _____

35. The beneficiaries of Trust B are Paul and Roy. Paul is entitled to receive $5,000 per year, or the entire income of the trust, whichever is less. The trustee can also distribute income to Roy in his discretion. This year the trust has $14,000 of income. The trustee distributed $5,000 to Paul and $15,000 to Roy. On what portion is Roy taxed?   _____

36. Are the following expenditures deductible to the person who pays them?

    a.   Arnie, a shareholder of Zero Corp., pays $250, which represents the salary Zero owed to one of its employees.   _____

    b.   Roger moves from Newark to Miami to take a new job as an engineer. The cost of moving his furniture and personal belongings is $1,000. He also incurs a $2,000 real estate broker's commission when selling his old house in Newark and has costs of $180 while searching for a new place to live in Miami. Are all of these costs deductible?   _____

37. Are any of the following costs of travel deductible?

    a.   Karen is a private duty nurse and works at the home of different patients every day, to whom she is referred by the nurse's registry. The distance from her house to the nurse's registry is one mile. She goes directly from her home to the home of Mathilda (20 miles).   _____

    b.   Ron is a bass player in the local symphony orchestra. He must transport his instrument with him when he goes to symphony hall to play a concert. But for the need to transport the bass, he would take the subway. Can Ron deduct his auto expenses?   _____

    c.   Tom is a self-employed attorney. He travels from New York to Washington. The primary purpose of the trip is business. However, he spent one of the three days in Washington as a tourist, visiting places of interest. The airfare to Washington is $80. His cost of meals in Washington is $180. His lodging cost is $360. How much, if anything, is deductible?   _____

    d.   Richard has no permanent residence. He is employed as an announcer in the Ringling Bros. Circus. He travels with the circus from place to place. He pays $2,000 for lodging.   _____

e.   George is a philosophy professor at UCLA. He takes a job teaching for one year at Michigan. His cost of meals and lodging while there is $8,000.   _____

38.   Ralph (a full-time veterinarian) has adjusted gross income of $118,000. He owns a house, which he rents to tenants. This year the income from the house was $12,000, but the total deductions were $30,000. He had no other investments except for some stocks that brought in dividend income of $21,000. What portion of the $30,000 is deductible?   _____

39.   Proceedings are brought by Paul's relatives to commit him to a mental institution. Paul knows that if this occurs, it would totally destroy his business as a salesman. Therefore, he incurs legal fees in an effort to resist the commitment. Are these costs deductible?   _____

40.   Are any of the following educational costs deductible?

a.   Wilhelm wishes to become a professional violinist and therefore attends the Juilliard School of Music.   _____

b.   Barbara, a professional pianist who is employed by the Boston Symphony, takes some additional piano lessons from a famous pianist.   _____

41.   Zero Manufacturing Co. has a group life insurance policy on which it pays the premiums. All of the employees of Zero participate in the plan, and they are allowed to name the beneficiaries of the policy. Arthur is an employee of Zero and has life insurance in the amount of $50,000 under the plan.

a.   Is Arthur taxable on the premiums Zero pays on his policy?   _____

b.   Can Zero deduct the premiums?   _____

42.   Ripoff Corp. engages in the following transactions this year. Is it entitled to current deductions?

a.   At a cost of $50,000, it grades and paves an empty lot to be used for employee parking.   _____

b.   Ripoff owns a bulldozer that it purchased in earlier years. The depreciation on the bulldozer allocable to the taxable year is $15,000. The bulldozer is used during the entire year by Ripoff in preparing sites for new factory buildings for its own operations.   _____

43.   Carol is an attorney who uses the cash basis. The lease on her new office is for five years at $40,000 per year. Carol prepays the five years' rent although the lease calls for payments each month. Lee is the landlord who uses the accrual basis.

a. Can Carol deduct her entire rent prepayment in this tax year? _____

b. Must Lee take the entire rent prepayment into income in this tax year? _____

44. For use in his accounting business, Zeke leases a used bookkeeping machine. Although the usual rent for this machine is $1,000 per year, Zeke's arrangement provides for rent of $1,400 per year. At the end of a five-year period, he has an option to purchase the machine by paying an additional $200. The amount of the rental payments, plus the option payment, is about 25% more than the value of the machine when Zeke signs the agreement. Can Zeke deduct his rental payments? _____

45. Are any of the following outlays deductible currently?

a. Amounts paid to an employment agency that fails to find the taxpayer (who is a salesperson) a new sales job? _____

b. The amounts paid to develop a new invention by someone who is not otherwise in business but hopes to make money from the invention? _____

c. The costs of searching for a city in which to locate a new law practice where no appropriate location is found? _____

46. Theda decided to take over a defunct advertising agency that had previously gone out of business with many unpaid debts. To recapture some of the previous clients, Theda began to pay off these debts. In Year 4, she pays $10,000. Larry was a creditor of the former advertising agency. The agency owed him $2,000, which Larry deducted as a bad debt in Year 1. This deduction resulted in a substantial tax saving to Larry. In Year 4, Larry receives $2,000 from Theda.

a. Can Theda deduct the $2,000 payment to Larry? _____

b. Must Larry include this repayment in his gross income? _____

47. Defco, a drug company, produced a new drug called R20. Paula took R20 to deal with allergies and was severely injured when R20 was discovered to cause permanent lung damage. Paula's lawsuit against Defco is settled by Defco's agreement to pay Paula $40,000 per year for the rest of her life without interest. Her life expectancy is estimated at 25 years. The case is settled in Year 1, and Defco makes the first payment in Year 1. Paula uses the cash method and Defco uses the accrual method.

a. Must Paula include any part of the $40,000 in income? _____

b. Can Defco deduct the entire obligation in Year 1? _____

48. Spinoff Recording Co. wishes to have certain songs by its artists played on a specific radio station. It pays the program director of the station $5,000 in return for his

promise to play certain songs during the year. This form of payment is illegal under state law but the law has apparently never been enforced.

a. Can Spinoff deduct these payments? _____

b. Is the $5,000 taxable to the program director? _____

49. Pierre, a personal injury attorney, pays $5,000 to nurses in the X Hospital to refer cases to him. This practice violates the rules of the applicable Bar Association and, if Pierre is caught, he is in danger of professional discipline. This disciplinary rule is frequently enforced. Can Pierre deduct the payments? _____

50. Acme slaughters and sells pork at a packing house. Because of unavoidable failures in equipment, the pork is often short-weighted—that is, a customer would be charged for more than he actually received. Department of Agriculture inspectors frequently discover that Acme has violated the statute against short-weighting. Acme has to pay many criminal fines of $50 each. This law is applicable even to unintentional violations.

a. Can Acme deduct these fines? _____

b. Can Acme deduct legal fees that it incurs in resisting these fines? _____

51. Raoul is a self-employed doctor who is very interested in trying to resist the passage of national health insurance legislation. Can Raoul deduct any of the following expenditures?

a. He gives $5,000 to the campaign of a candidate for the Senate who is opposed to such legislation. _____

b. He travels to Washington to make an appearance before a committee of the House of Representatives considering such legislation, in order to try to influence the legislative product. _____

52. Rex feels he was cheated by Sasha in their joint effort to locate and develop a tungsten mine. Although Rex found the right place to dig, Sasha recorded it in his own name and has been working the claim by himself. He refuses to let Rex have any part of the proceeds from the sale of the metal. Rex sues Sasha to establish his one-half interest in the mine and for damages to recover his part of $150,000 in ore already sold by Sasha.

a. Are attorneys' fees from this litigation deductible by Rex? _____

b. If Rex wins, is the $150,000 taxable to him? _____

53. Lloyd, an attorney, leases an office in a building owned by Red. Can Lloyd claim depreciation on the following assets?

a. The building? _____

b. Walls within the office suite which Lloyd builds to create separate offices for the different attorneys and secretaries? _____

c. Paintings that he hangs on the wall? _____

54. Ralph owns real property and leases it to Sara. The lease is for 25 years. Sara constructs an office building thereon with a useful life of 40 years.

a. Does Ralph have income because of the construction of this building? _____

b. Over what period of time should Sara depreciate the building? _____

c. Ralph sells his interest in the land and building to Vic. Vic allocates $250,000 of this purchase price to the building, which was constructed by the tenant. Is Vic entitled to depreciate this portion of the purchase price? _____

55. Bess acquires a photocopier for use in her law firm. It costs $24,000. She purchases it on December 1 of Year 1. For tax purposes, it is five-year property. Ignore the special allowance under section 179.

a. If Bess uses the straight-line method of depreciation, how much can she deduct in Year 1? _____

b. If she uses accelerated depreciation, how much can she deduct in Year 1? _____

c. How much depreciation would Bess be entitled to in Year 2 under the straight-line method? _____

d. Under the accelerated method? _____

e. How much could Bess deduct under section 179 (assuming this is the only property she purchased in Year 1)? _____

56. In Year 1, Jake purchased an oil well for $100,000. It was estimated to contain 100,000 barrels of oil. In Year 2, the oil well produced a gross income of $40,000. The various costs of operation of the well, including depreciation of physical facilities, totaled $30,000. The well produced 8,000 barrels of oil this year. (Assume Jake qualifies for percentage depletion.)

a. How much cost depletion can Jake collect? _____

b. How much would be available if percentage depletion is claimed? _____

c. Assume that in Year 12, Jake would like to claim percentage depletion of $10,000 on his well. He has previously claimed depletion equal to the entire basis of the property. Is the percentage depletion nevertheless deductible? _____

d.   Assume that Jake claims $10,000 of percentage depletion and basis has been exhausted. Is the amount claimed included as a "tax preference" for purposes of the alternative minimum tax on tax preferences? _____

57.   David acquires a piece of land for $30,000, allocating $12,000 to the purchase of the land and $18,000 to a building on the land. Assume David planned to tear down the building to construct an office building on the property. When he tears down the building, can he deduct the $18,000 allocated to the building as a loss? _____

58.   Floyd purchased a barber shop last year, allocating $30,000 of the purchase price to goodwill. This year, Floyd decides that the goodwill has declined in value to $0 since business is terrible. Can he claim a loss deduction? _____

59.   Leon owned 500 shares of General Motors stock that he purchased 20 years ago for $50,000. At present, the stock is worth only $22,000, and so he sells it to his brother Julius for $22,000 in cash. Two months later, Leon repurchases the property from Julius for its then fair market value of $19,000. Can Leon deduct the $28,000 loss on the sale to Julius? _____

60.   Mike wished to borrow $5,000 to purchase a car. Because of his poor credit, he could not get a loan. Therefore, Gloria guaranteed Mike's loan. Mike did not pay for the car, and Gloria had to make good on her guarantee in the amount of $5,000. Gloria and Mike were personal friends. In the year in which she makes the payment, can Gloria deduct the entire payment? _____

61.   In the course of her banana business, Chiquita makes a $10,000 loan to Dole, one of her customers. In Year 2, it is determined that $6,000 of this debt is no longer collectible and it is realistic to expect Dole to repay only $4,000.

a.   Can Chiquita deduct $6,000? _____

b.   In Year 3, Chiquita accepts $4,000 from Dole in total satisfaction of the debt. Does Dole have income on this transaction? _____

62.   Larry owns 20% of the stock of Zero Corp. He also loans $50,000 to the corporation. Larry works for the corporation and gets a salary. The other stockholders are members of Larry's close family. The debt is uncollectible. Is it deductible as a business bad debt? _____

63.   Nhu is an accountant who uses the cash basis. She does $20,000 worth of work for John in Year 1. By Year 3, it has become clear that the debt is entirely uncollectible. Can Nhu deduct $20,000 in Year 3? _____

64.   Rich (who is single) has gross income of $16,000. He has a short-term capital loss of $600 and alimony of $500, which are deductible. He has employee business expenses such as union dues and the cost of uniforms of $400. How much is Rich's adjusted gross income? _____

65. Jim is a successful lawyer. In Year 1, he has net investment income from stocks and bonds of $60,000. On January 2 of Year 1, he borrowed $500,000 for the purpose of buying bonds. He prepaid $400,000 of interest on the loan. This was interest for 10 years, and was the only interest he paid in Year 1. How much interest can he deduct in Year 1? _____

66. Ray (an attorney) owns a part interest in a restaurant. He works at the restaurant 296 hours during the year and his wife works another 207 hours. His share of the restaurant's losses were $60,000. Can he deduct this amount? _____

67. Are the following state or local taxes deductible to a taxpayer who is not in business?

   a. State gift tax? _____

   b. State gasoline tax? _____

   c. Federal import duties on imported merchandise? _____

   d. State sales tax? _____

68. Barbara gives her farm to her child, Carol, for life, remainder to the Red Cross.

   a. Is the actuarial value of the remainder deductible as a charitable contribution? _____

   b. Suppose instead that the gift was $100,000 in cash in a trust for Carol for life, remainder to the Red Cross. Is the remainder deductible? _____

69. Alison purchased General Motors stock for $10,000 on July 1 of Year 2. By September, the stock has gone up to $14,000 and she donates it to Public University. Her adjusted gross income is $100,000.

   a. How much of a deduction is Alison entitled to? _____

   b. Suppose that Alison had owned the stock for three years. Now how much would be deductible? _____

   c. How much would be deductible if Alison's gift to University was an antique automobile? Assume that the automobile was purchased for $10,000, it is now worth $14,000, and Alison has owned it for four years. _____

70. Glen bought stock for $5,000 which is now worth $25,000. He sells it to the University of Illinois for $5,000. He has held it for four years.

   a. How much is deductible? _____

   b. Does Glen have any capital gain on the sale? _____

71. Bruce has adjusted gross income of $22,000. During this year, he pays medical insurance premiums of $250. He has expenses for prescription drugs of $400 and doctor bills of $1,100. How much is his medical expense deduction? _____

72. Mike and Susan are married and file a joint return showing AGI of $37,000. They have two children, Bob and Carol. Bob is 17 years old and earned $4,600 this year. His parents applied $6,000 toward his support. Carol is age 24 and does not live with her parents. She is not a student. She earned $4,600 during the year, but her parents supplied $6,000 toward her support.

   a.   On Mike and Susan's joint return how many personal exemptions can be claimed? _____

   b.   Can Bob claim himself as an exemption on his own return? _____

73. Harold and Wanda are divorced. They have one child, Clarissa, who lives with Wanda. In this tax year, Harold supplied child support of $4,000. Wanda contributed $2,500 to Clarissa's support.

   a.   The divorce agreement contains no provision with respect to who receives the personal exemption. Can Wanda claim the exemption? _____

   b.   Suppose the family court judge allocated the exemption to Harold. Can he take the exemption? _____

74. Mary is an employed single parent with one child. In 2003, Mary's earned income and adjusted gross income are both $26,000. Mary pays $400 per month for nursery school to care for her child while she is at work. Is she entitled to any deduction or credit for her child care costs? _____

75. Morris purchased a used car for $1,000, which he used for nonbusiness purposes. At a time when the value of the car was $700, it was damaged in an accident. The car was a total loss. Morris's AGI was $4,000. How much can Morris deduct? _____

76. Rex owns a home having a basis of $150,000. The home is damaged by a volcanic eruption. Prior to the eruption, its value was $425,000. After the eruption, its value was $200,000. Rex collected insurance of $60,000. Rex's AGI was $60,000. How much is his casualty loss deduction? _____

77. Vladimir purchases an apartment house, paying $5,000 down and executing a mortgage for $95,000. He also pays a brokerage fee of $3,000 on this purchase. In addition, there is some pending litigation in which a tenant in the apartment house sued the previous owner for personal injuries incurred in the swimming pool. Vladimir promises to pay the judgment in that case, if there is one. The risk of such a judgment's occurring is estimated at $12,000. What is Vladimir's basis for the apartment house after he buys it? _____

78. Sarah purchased real property in 1975 for $10,000. This year, when its value is $100,000, she gives it to her daughter, Deborah. Deborah holds it for one month and sells it for $96,000. Assume that Sarah paid a $4,000 gift tax on the transfer to Deborah.

    a.   How should Deborah account for the sale? _____

    b.   Assume in the previous transaction that the fair market value of the property was only $8,000 at the time of the gift, and that Deborah sells the property for $1,000. How should she account for this transaction? _____

    c.   Assume that in the preceding example, Deborah sells the property for $9,250. How should she account for this transaction? _____

79. Zeke died this year. His sole asset was Blackacre, which had a basis of $200,000 and a value of $1 million. He left it to Kojak.

    a.   What is Kojak's basis for the property? _____

    b.   Assume Zeke also owned furniture and clothing having a basis of $16,000. The value was $9,000. What is Kojak's basis for this property? _____

80. Aidan dies leaving property to John for life, remainder to Colin. The basis to John and Colin is $100,000. Based on actuarial calculations, John's interest is worth 40% and Colin's interest is worth 60%.

    a.   Can John amortize his basis for his life estate over his life expectancy? _____

    b.   John sells his life estate for $41,000. How does he account for this transaction? _____

    c.   Suppose that John and Colin together sell their interests, John receiving $41,000 therefor. How does John account for this transaction? _____

    d.   Assume that in paragraph b., Alice was the person who purchased John's interest for $41,000. Can she amortize her basis over John's life? _____

81. Herbert and Wilma, who are married, live in California (which uses the community property system) and purchased property in 1968 for $50,000. When Herbert died this year, the property was worth $200,000. Assume that the property was purchased with community property funds so that Herbert and Wilma each contributed $25,000.

    a.   Assume that the property was held as community property. Assume further that Herbert left his share of the property to their children and Wilma still owns her community one-half. What is the basis of Wilma's one-half? _____

    b.   Suppose instead that the property was held in joint tenancy. Under the applicable estate tax rules, one-half of the fair market value at the date of death is subject to estate tax in Herbert's estate. What is the basis for income tax purposes of Wilma's one-half?

c.   What will be the basis for income tax purposes, under the assumptions in paragraph b., of Herbert's one-half?

82.   Tim was a movie star who was entitled to 10% of the gross box office receipts from a certain picture. He died on February 16 of Year 1. The amount payable for the six-month period ending June 30 of Year 1 was $15,000, and was paid to Tim's estate on July 6 of Year 1. The amount of these royalties was quite predictable, and the fair market value of the right to receive royalties for this period was $13,500 on the date of Tim's death.

a.   How much must the estate include in its gross income for Year 1?

b.   Assume that the estate tax attributable to this item is $2,000. How much should the estate include in income?

83.   Pablo purchased a punch press for use in his factory for $19,500. He deducted $10,000 in depreciation on this property. The correct amount allowable was only $8,000. However, the statute of limitations has now run on the years in which excessive depreciation was claimed and the IRS cannot correct it. Pablo received a tax benefit for all depreciation he claimed.

a.   What is the basis of the punch press?

b.   Suppose in the preceding problem that only $3,000 in depreciation was claimed. Because the statute of limitations has run, the additional depreciation to which Pablo is entitled cannot now be deducted. What is the basis of the asset?

84.   David purchased a building for $100,000. He sold the air rights over the building for $16,000. This enabled the purchaser who owned the parcels on both sides of David's property to connect his two buildings on top of David's building. Should David report income on the sale of the air rights?

85.   Miriam purchases a factory building, paying $5,000 down and incurring a $95,000 nonrecourse purchase money mortgage. She is not personally liable on this mortgage. While she holds the property, she correctly deducts $18,000 of depreciation on it.

a.   Assume she made no payments on the mortgage and the mortgage is foreclosed. Does she have a gain on the mortgage foreclosure?

b.   Assume that instead of selling the property, Miriam borrows an additional $100,000, giving a second mortgage on the property. Does she have income on this transaction?

86. Winston owns all the shares of stock of Zero Corp. He sells them to Joan for $15,000 cash plus 25% of the profits earned by Zero Corp. in the next 10 years. After consulting with their accountants, Winston and Joan believe that this profit interest is worth $80,000. Winston had a $22,000 basis for his stock. If Winston elects out of the installment method, should he report gain on the sale to Joan? _____

87. Herbert and Wilma are getting divorced. Their marital property is worth $100,000.

   a.   Assume that Herbert and Wilma live in a state in which the divorce court has discretionary power to award some of the marital property held in the name of one spouse to the other spouse. The court awards $20,000 to Wilma, which consists of their home. This house has a basis of $8,000 and is held in Herbert's name. Does Herbert have gain on the transfer of this house to Wilma? _____

   b.   In the transaction described in paragraph a., does Wilma have income? _____

   c.   What is Wilma's basis for the house? _____

88. Bob owns an apartment house having an adjusted basis of $200,000 and a fair market value of $350,000. He exchanges it for a factory building having a fair market value of $290,000. Joyce, the owner of the factory, pays Bob $60,000 in cash as part of the transaction.

   a.   How much gain does Bob recognize on this transaction? _____

   b.   Suppose that the adjusted basis of the apartment house was $330,000. How much gain would Bob recognize? _____

   c.   Suppose that Bob's basis was $420,000 for the apartment house. How much loss can he recognize? _____

   d.   What will be the basis for the factory building received in problem a.? _____

   e.   What will be the basis for the factory building received in problem b.? _____

   f.   What will be the basis for the factory building received in problem c.? _____

89. Lois owns a vacation cottage that has a basis of $4,000 and a value of $9,000. It is destroyed by a flood. Lois collects insurance proceeds of $9,000 and 20 months later purchases another cabin for $7,500.

   a.   Must Lois recognize a $5,000 gain in the collection of the insurance proceeds? _____

   b.   Suppose Lois invested the entire $9,000 proceeds in a new Ferrari. Must she recognize the entire gain? _____

90. Martha, who is single, owns a house that she has lived in for seven years. She purchased it for $75,000 and it is now worth $160,000. On February 9 of Year 1, she buys a new house for $220,000. On January 3 of Year 3, she sells her old house for $160,000.

   a. What portion of the gain on sale of the old house is taxable to Martha? _____

   b. What is the basis of the new house? _____

91. At the time of their divorce, Harry and Wanda had owned and used their home as a principal residence for one year. They bought it for $200,000 and took title as joint tenants. As provided by the divorce decree, Wanda stayed in the house. Harry moved out. The decree provided that when the house is sold, Harry and Wanda would split the proceeds. Five years later, Wanda sold the house for $1,400,000. Harry and Wanda each took $700,000. By this time, Harry had married Mary, and Harry and Mary filed a joint return.

   a. How much gain should Wanda report in the year of sale? _____

   b. How much gain should Harry report in the year of sale? _____

92. Over the years, Regis has purchased many large farms and subdivided them into lots suitable for building purposes. This year he sold 24 lots on three different farms. In each case, Regis had built roads and utility outlets on the property. He engaged in extensive advertising to sell the property. Are his gains on these properties capital gains? _____

93. Luis acquired a piece of real estate in Texas four years ago, which he has held without any development activities. He feels the market is now ripe since a nearby town has expanded close to the property. He lists it for sale with a broker and it is sold. Is this gain treated as long-term capital gain? _____

94. Vicky is a land developer who has held many parcels of property primarily for sale to customers. She acquires land suitable for a shopping center site. She intends to develop the property and rent it out. However, if the appropriate zoning cannot be obtained, she intends to sell the property. As feared, appropriate zoning is not available, and Vicky sells the property at a large gain. Is she entitled to capital gains treatment? _____

95. Warren is heavily involved in the stock market. During the year, he purchases stocks and sells stocks on more than 300 occasions. He spends part of every day at his brokerage house watching the tape and subscribes to many different stock market journals.

   a. Are his gains and losses on the sale of stock capital? _____

   b. Can Warren deduct the price of the investment advisories and newsletters to which he subscribes? _____

96. Betty composes a folk song and sells all substantial rights in it to a publisher for $20,000. This is the first song she has ever sold.

    a.   Is Betty entitled to capital gains treatment on this sale?   _____

    b.   Suppose instead that Betty had invented an improved amplification system for rock music. She sells it to a musical instrument manufacturing company. Is she entitled to capital gains treatment?   _____

97. The President of the United States has many letters and memoranda written to and by him that are worth $500,000. He donates them to the National Archives (a branch of the United States government). Is he entitled to a charitable contribution deduction?   _____

98. Zero Manufacturing Co. purchases all of the stock of a company that manufactures a particular copper part, which is essential for Zero's business. On many occasions, Zero has had difficulty obtaining these parts. Therefore, it purchases the stock exclusively for the purpose of ensuring itself of a source of supply of this vitally needed part. Later, it sells the stock at a loss because it has discovered other means of ensuring itself a source of supply. Is this a capital loss?   _____

99. An investor in a stage play receives percentages of the gross box office receipts. The play is very successful. He sells his rights to the next $17,500 of box office receipts for $15,000. Is he entitled to capital gain?   _____

100. Zahi has an interest for life in all of the profits of a farm. This was given to him by his grandfather. Zahi does not manage the farm; he simply receives the annual proceeds from the manager. He sells his entire right in these proceeds. Is he entitled to capital gain?   _____

101. Allen owned a shopping center. One of the stores was leased to Leonard for use in selling tropical fish. The terms of this lease were unfavorable to the lessee and Leonard wanted to relocate his store.

    a.   Leonard pays Allen $10,000 to be released from the terms of the lease. Is this amount taxable to Allen as ordinary income?   _____

    b.   Suppose instead that Allen wanted to use the store to lease to the May Co., which had adjoining space, and which would pay a high rent. Allen pays Leonard $10,000 to surrender his rights under the lease. Does Leonard have capital gain?   _____

102. Bill wishes to sell the Fresno franchise of a professional football league. He is looking for a buyer. Fred, an attorney, comes to Bill and explains that a client of his (Del) is willing to buy the team. As compensation for his services in putting the deal together, Fred will be entitled to 1% of the gross receipts from the sale of season tickets during the next season. Before any money is received, Fred sells

his right to receive this percentage to Paul for $15,000. Is this amount taxed as capital gain? _____

103. Tess sold some shares of stock, correctly reporting a long-term capital loss of $90,000. Later, as the result of a class action, it was determined that there was a securities fraud occurring at the time of the sale. Tess receives $3,000 by way of damages. Is this taxable as a capital gain? _____

104. Dan wishes to purchase a piece of real property now held by Paul. It is a capital asset in the hands of both of them. Dan first purchases an option for $5,000, which provides that he can purchase the property at any time during the following six months. Paul has held the property for 10 years.

   a. Assume Dan purchases the property, paying an additional $90,000. What is his basis for the property? _____

   b. Assume that Dan decides not to purchase the property and lets the option lapse. Can Dan treat the $5,000 he paid for the option as an ordinary loss? _____

   c. If the option lapsed, is the $5,000 treated as capital gain to Paul? _____

   d. Assume that Dan sold his option to Ed for $12,000. Would the $7,000 gain be treated as a capital gain? _____

105. Donna is a lawyer who sells her practice for $28,000. The entire basis of the practice is $3,000. All of this basis is attributable to the furniture and law books. These were originally purchased for $12,000 and have been depreciated down to $3,000; they are now worth $5,000. The other assets sold are accounts receivable (zero basis, $12,000 value), goodwill (zero basis, $5,000 value), and a covenant not to compete ($6,000). Can Donna treat her $25,000 as a capital gain? _____

106. Thomas Manufacturing Co. sells two parcels of real property used in its trade or business in Year 4. Thomas obtained the two parcels in Year 1. One has a basis of $10,000 and a value of $4,000, and the second has a basis of $18,000 and a fair market value of $21,000. Is the gain on the second parcel taxed as capital gain? _____

107. Mary, a dentist, has the following transactions this year. She sells a dentist's chair and other dental equipment, having a basis of $9,000, for $5,000. During this year, a house held for investment (not personal use) burns down; the insurance proceeds exceeded her basis by $6,000. She also owned a small apartment building, which was condemned by the city of Newark; the proceeds from the condemnation were $9,000 less than her basis. She did not reinvest the proceeds from either the fire or the condemnation. Is her gain by reason of the fire taxed as a capital gain? (Assume that Mary held all assets for more than one year.) _____

108. Bob has a store that sells auto mufflers and shock absorbers. He decides to "franchise" the idea to others in other towns, using the same name. Bob retains the right to control such things as advertising, business hours, prices, and other aspects of the franchisee's operation. The franchisee pays Bob $15,000 for the franchise.

    a.   Is this capital gain to Bob?   _____

    b.   Can the franchisee deduct any part of the $15,000?   _____

109. Bill owes $100 evidenced by a promissory note. Roy acquires this note for $65 from Fred, who had previously loaned the $100 to Bill. Bill pays Roy $95 in full settlement of this debt. Both Fred and Roy can be treated as investors.

    a.   Does Fred have a capital loss when he sells the note to Roy?   _____

    b.   Does Roy have a capital gain when Bill pays off the debt?   _____

    c.   Does Bill have income when he pays off the debt?   _____

110. Laura sells her trucking business to Arnold for $100,000. However, Laura will continue to operate the business and is entitled to all of the profits until the entire purchase price has been paid. Thereafter, Arnold can keep the profits. Does Laura have capital gain when she receives these profits?   _____

111. In Year 1, which was after 2000, Jomo purchased stock for $200,000 in S Company, a new computer software venture with total assets of $5 million. In Year 6, Jomo sold the stock for $4 million. Does he receive any special tax benefit for this gain beyond the normal benefit for long-term capital gain?   _____

112. Sanjay has taxable income of $10,000, apart from any capital transactions. He has long-term capital gain of $6,000 and short-term capital loss of $26,000. What is his taxable income?   _____

113. Rory sells investment land to Ryan for $10,000. Ryan is to pay for it by cash payment due 18 months after the date of the sale. Rory does not elect out of the installment method. Assume that Rory's basis for the land is $1,000 and it is a capital asset. When Ryan makes her $10,000 payment, will Rory's entire gain be treated as capital gain?   _____

114. In Year 6, Zeke, a farmer, sells a tractor he had purchased in Year 1. The original purchase price was $9,000. Zeke deducted depreciation of $8,000. He now sells it for $2,200.

    a.   Is Zeke's gain ordinary income?   _____

    b.   Suppose that Zeke was able to sell the tractor for $11,000 because Zeke discovered the tractor was a rare model having value to collectors. Is his entire gain ordinary income?   _____

c. Suppose that in paragraph a. Zeke sells the tractor for $400. Assume also that he has gains under I.R.C. section 1231 in the same year aggregating $10,000. Is his $600 loss ordinary loss?

_____

d. Suppose that in paragraph a. the tractor was exchanged for a new plow also worth $2,200. Is there any ordinary income on this transaction?

_____

115. Don is married and reported adjusted gross income of $200,000 on his joint return. He exercised an incentive stock option. The difference between the value of the stock and the amount he paid was $80,000. He paid income tax of $57,000. Does Don owe alternative minimum tax ("AMT")?

_____

116. Paul owns Blackacre, having a basis of $1,000 and a value of $10,000. In Year 1, he sells it to Steve for $10,000. Steve furnishes his nonnegotiable promissory note due in Year 3, bearing 10% interest. Assume that the fair market value of this note is $8,500 and that 10% is above the applicable federal rate.

a. If Paul uses the cash basis of accounting and elects out of the installment method, does he have income in Year 1?

_____

b. Suppose Paul was an accrual basis taxpayer and elects out of the installment method. Would he have income in Year 1?

_____

c. Suppose Paul, who uses the cash method, received stock worth $10,000 instead of the promissory note. He does not sell the stock until Year 3. Does he have income in Year 1?

_____

117. Cassie is a cash basis attorney who drafts a will for a client. The work is completed and a bill is sent out in October of Year 1. In November, the client comes in offering to pay the $200 fee. Cassie asks the client not to remit until January of Year 2.

a. Does Cassie have income in Year 1?

_____

b. Assume that in the preceding problem, before drafting the will, Cassie and her client agreed that payment would not be made until Year 2. Nevertheless, the client was entirely willing to pay the money in Year 1. Is Cassie taxed in Year 1?

_____

118. Suman is an employee of the Zero Manufacturing Co. In addition to his normal salary, it is agreed that he will receive $8,000 in Year 6 when he retires. He is concerned about the solvency of Zero and therefore insists that the $8,000 be placed in trust for his benefit beyond the reach of Zero's creditors, with the money in the trust to be distributed to him in Year 6. Is Suman taxed in Year 1 (the year the $8,000 is placed in trust)?

_____

119. Zero Manufacturing Co. has a qualified pension plan. In Year 1, it pays $400 into the plan on behalf of Ling, an employee. Ling is entitled to a pension when

she retires. The $400 paid in that year is the amount necessary to fund the pension. Ling's rights are vested and nonforfeitable.

a.   Must Ling include the $400 income in Year 1? _____

b.   Can Zero Manufacturing Co. deduct the $400 in Year 1? _____

c.   During Year 2, the pension plan trust earns $25,000 in interest and dividends. Must the plan pay tax on these amounts currently? _____

120. Acme Corp. has a stock option plan (which does not meet the requirements for an incentive stock option plan). In Year 1, Pete, an employee, receives an option to purchase 100 shares of Acme stock at $100 per share. The fair market value of Acme stock, on the day the option is granted, is $100. Although the fair market value of the option is estimated to be $2,500, the market value is not easily and clearly ascertainable. In Year 3, when the stock is worth $130 per share, Pete exercises his option.

a.   Does Pete have income in Year 1? _____

b.   In Year 3, does Pete have income? _____

c.   In what year does Acme get a deduction? _____

d.   What is Pete's basis for the shares he acquires in Year 3? _____

e.   Assume that the stock which Pete received in Year 3 was nontransferable for five years. Furthermore, the stock would have to be resold back to Acme at its purchase price ($100 per share) for a five-year period if Pete was no longer employed at Acme during that five-year period. Is Pete taxed in Year 3? _____

f.   Under the facts described in paragraph e., assume that in Year 4 the stock became transferable and the forfeiture provision was removed. At that time, the stock was worth $220 per share. Would Pete be taxed in Year 4? _____

121. Kendra, an attorney, hires Lloyd, another attorney, as her employee. Kendra is in a high tax bracket in Year 1 and, in December of that year, pays Lloyd both his December and January salaries. Both Kendra and Lloyd use the calendar year and the cash method.

a.   Must Lloyd include the money in gross income in Year 1? _____

b.   If Lloyd is an accrual basis taxpayer, must he include the payment in gross income in Year 1? _____

c.   Suppose in this problem Kendra had paid Lloyd for three years of services in advance. Assuming that Lloyd is an accrual basis taxpayer, must he include the entire amount in gross income in Year 1? _____

122. R Corp. declares a dividend on December 1 of Year 1, payable on January 15 of Year 2, to holders of record on December 15. Jalisa is an accrual basis taxpayer who owns stock in the corporation. Must she include the dividend in gross income in Year 1?

    _____

123. Paul, a contractor, is building a house for Roy. Paul uses the accrual method of accounting. In Year 1, Paul completes 90% of Roy's house. Assume that state law provides that even if Paul had stopped working, he could sue and receive 90% of the agreed compensation for building the house.

  a.   Must Paul include in gross income in Year 1, 90% of the total amount of compensation he is contractually entitled to receive?

    _____

  b.   In Year 2, Paul finishes the house for Roy. However, it is then discovered that Roy is insolvent and his liabilities far exceed his assets. Must Paul accrue the compensation due him under the contract?

    _____

124. Louis operates a travel service and uses the accrual method of accounting. In Year 1, a charter flight he had promoted strands 100 tourists in Europe. It seems very likely that Louis will be liable for damages for breach of contract to these tourists in the amount of about $25,000. He is resisting these claims, but feels that he has little chance of success. Can Louis deduct $25,000 in Year 1?

    _____

125. Laura owns 80% of the stock of Zero Corp. She is also the president. Zero Corp. uses the accrual method of accounting; Laura uses the cash method. Both use the calendar year. In Year 1, Laura fails to collect her salary of $50,000, which is payable in December. The treasurer of the corporation does not write a check to her. This amount is finally paid in June of Year 2.

  a.   Must Laura include the unpaid salary in gross income in Year 1?

    _____

  b.   Can Zero Corp. accrue the salary?

    _____

126. Jerry is in the business of wholesaling certain plumbing parts. In his first year of operation, he purchases (in order of time) 100 of the parts at $1.00, 100 at $1.25, 100 at $1.50, and 100 at $1.60. Thus his total purchases are $535. At the end of the year, 120 of the parts still remain. How much is Jerry allowed to deduct as the cost of his goods sold if he uses:

  a.   FIFO?

    _____

  b.   LIFO?

    _____

127. Jack owns Blackacre, which has a basis of $6,000 and a value of $10,000. In Year 1, he sells it to Carla for $10,000, with a down payment of $2,000. The balance is payable in eight annual installments of $1,000 each. Each payment will also bear interest on the unpaid balance at the rate of 12% (which exceeds the applicable federal rate). Assume that Jack uses the cash method of accounting. The obligation is secured by Blackacre. Assume that Jack does not elect out of the installment

method of accounting. In Year 1, he receives only the $2,000 down payment. How much is includible in gross income?

_____

128. Mutt and Jeff render services for Rocky in Year 1 for which Rocky is obligated to pay $50,000. He pays all of the money to Mutt. Mutt knows that Jeff is asserting a claim for some of this money, but Mutt intends to resist the claim. However, it is very likely that he will have to pay over half the money to Jeff. Finally, in Year 3, Jeff sues and recovers $25,000 from Mutt.

    a.   Must Mutt include the entire $50,000 in gross income in Year 1?

_____

    b.   In Year 3, Mutt pays $25,000 to Jeff. Assume, however, that his Year 1 tax bracket was far higher than his Year 3 tax bracket. Is he allowed to amend his Year 1 return claiming a deduction for the payment to Jeff in that year?

_____

    c.   Must Mutt claim the Year 3 deduction only at Year 3 tax rates?

_____

129. Black & White ("B & W"), an accrual basis professional law corporation, was owed $100,000 by C, a cash basis client for work on a tax case. Had C paid the bill, C could have deducted it. In Year 1, B & W properly wrote off $100,000 as a bad debt because C was insolvent and could not pay. B & W's taxable income in Year 1 was $1 million. In Year 4, C found buried treasure and paid the debt.

    a.   What are the tax consequences to B & W in Year 1?

_____

    b.   What are the tax consequences to C in Year 1?

_____

    c.   What are the tax consequences to B & W in Year 4?

_____

    d.   What are the tax consequences to C in Year 4?

_____

130. X Co. is drilling for oil. It contracts in Year 1 with Hughes to drill a new well for $25,000. X Co. is an accrual method taxpayer. Hughes drills the well in Year 3. X Co. pays Hughes in Year 4. In what year can X Co. deduct the intangible drilling expense?

_____

Answers to Review Questions

1.a. **YES**   The $6 interest is included in Bobbi's income. Receiving loan proceeds is not income to Angelo and repayment of the principal of the loan is not income to Bobbi. [§§12-14, 17] The provision for imputed interest on gift loans [I.R.C. §7872] is not applicable because the interest rate exceeds the applicable federal rate. (If it were, Bobbi would have additional interest income.) [§239] An additional exception to section 7872 may also apply: When a gift loan is less than $10,000 and the proceeds are not invested in income-producing assets, interest is not imputed. [§241]

  b. **NO**   The $6 interest is not deductible to Angelo because personal interest is not deductible. The cost of his vacation is not deductible. Making a loan is not deductible by Bobbi and repaying the principal of the loan is not deductible by Angelo. [§§293, 572]

2. **PROBABLY NOT**   The IRS does not seek to tax such items unless the taxpayer seeks a double deduction by donating them to charity. However, the IRS could tax these items under *Haverly* if it chose to do so. [§21]

3.a. **YES**   An exchange of services generates income. Both Don and Edna must include $1,500 in income. [§26]

  b. **YES**   Don cannot deduct the cost of getting divorced, except for that part relating to tax advice. Since the problem does not indicate how much, if any, of Edna's services were for tax advice, Don cannot deduct anything. However, Edna can deduct the cost of accounting services for her practice as section 162 trade or business expense. [§§296, 337-340, 446-449]

4.a. **YES**   Regardless of George's motivation, payments by employers to employees are not excludible gifts. [§§31-34]

  b. **NO**   Even if the payment was intended as compensation for services, the services of a valet are personal, not business, and would not be deductible. [§302]

  c. **YES**   Bequests to employees are taxable under I.R.C. section 102(c). [§45]

5.a. **YES**   Under I.R.C. section 102(c), the amount would probably be treated as income regardless of the employer's motivation. In any event, since Zero has custom of paying such benefits, they are part of the decedent's compensation, not a gift. [§36]

  b. **YES**   It would appear to be an ordinary and necessary business expense—reasonable compensation. No facts are given to suggest that it is unreasonable compensation or a dividend. [§§37, 336]

6.a. **YES**   Prizes are includible in income under I.R.C. section 74. [§§49-50]

   b. **YES**   These would seem to qualify as deductible expenses (under section 212)—incurred to produce income, although not part of a trade or business. [§437] Had Lem lost the contest, there is a chance that his deductions would have been disallowed as hobby losses under section 183. [§319] Note that if Lem's deduction is under section 212 instead of 162, it is a miscellaneous itemized deduction and subject to reduction under section 67. [§562]

7. **YES**   The amount not applied to tuition and books is taxable. [§§53-54]

8.a. **NO**   Life insurance proceeds are excludible under I.R.C. section 101(a). [§58]

   b. **NO**   These are amounts paid to obtain excludible income and are consequently nondeductible—even if they are paid in a business or investment setting. [*See* I.R.C. §265(1)] [§§345, 601, 603]

   c. **YES**   Life insurance policies purchased from an existing holder do not qualify for the exclusion. Oona's profit of $4,500 ($10,000 minus her basis of $5,500) would be taxable. [§65]

9. **YES**   Paul will be receiving a total of $150,000 over the 10 years. Clearly, $50,000 of this is interest; $100,000 is principal. Each payment would be broken down into one-third interest ($5,000) and two-thirds principal ($10,000). Thus, $5,000 of each payment is taxable. [§67]

10.a. **$375**   The investment in the contract is $10,000. The expected return is $16,000. The exclusion ratio is 10/16, or 0.625. Thus, $625 of each payment is excluded and $375 is taxable. [§69]

   b. **YES, $9,375**   Steve recovered $625 of basis against the first payment, leaving $9,375 unrecovered. This is a loss deduction on the tax return for the year of his death. [§§70-71]

11.a. **NO**   Interest on state and municipal bonds is not taxable. [I.R.C. §103(a)] [§75]

   b. **NO**   These are classed as nondeductible costs of obtaining tax-exempt income. [*See* I.R.C. §265(1), (2)] [§§601-602]

12.a. **NO**   Her income is below the threshold for including Social Security benefits in income. [§§78-80]

   b. **NO**   SSI payments are excludible. [§79]

13.a. **YES**   Damages for defamation are taxable because they are not personal physical injuries under section 104(a)(2). [§89]

   b. **YES**   Punitive damages are taxable whether arising from physical or nonphysical torts. [§89]

c. **YES** These seemingly would be an ordinary and necessary business expense. There are no public policy restrictions on deducting this item. [§§408-414, 424-436]

14.a. **YES** Under *Raytheon*, such payments are taxable (as capital gains) since the basis for the destroyed goodwill was zero. [§101]

b. **YES** Payments for lost profits are taxable. The section 186 exclusion does not apply to the payments since Zero got a tax benefit for its overpayments in past years. [§§101, 104]

c. **YES** Punitive damages are taxable. [§101]

d. **NO** It can deduct only $133,333. Under section 162(g), two-thirds of payments of civil damages in antitrust cases are not deductible if there has been a previous criminal conviction. [§436]

15. **NO** These items clearly fall within the exclusion of I.R.C. section 119 for meals and lodging furnished to the employee on employer's premises for the convenience of the employer. [§§111-117]

16.a. **YES** Cancellation of debt produces taxable income. Here, Alpha was insolvent before the cancellation to the extent of $3,000. Consequently, instead of $4,000 income, it has income of only $1,000. Alpha must reduce various tax benefits such as loss carryovers by the amount of the debt cancellation income that was not recognized. [§§144-147]

b. **YES** It has a business bad debt deduction of $4,000. Since Piedmont is an accrual basis taxpayer, it had a basis for the debt of $10,000. [§§533-534]

17.a. **YES** $500 is taxable since this is not a "no additional cost service" as defined in I.R.C. section 132(b). It is too large to be considered a de minimis fringe benefit under section 132(e). The employer incurred substantial additional costs in rendering service. [§§136, 140]

b. **NO** This is a personal item and nondeductible. [§302]

18.a. **$40,000** Child support is not deductible. The $40,000 payments are deductible alimony. [§§163, 171]

b. **$40,000** The rule of reciprocity controls: What is deductible to H is taxable to W. [§162]

19. **$25,000 INCOME** Under recapture, where first-year payments exceed average second- and third-year payments by more than $15,000, the excess over $15,000 is income to the payor (and deductible to the payee) in the third year. [§168]

20. **NO** This is an example of the principle of *Horst*; Diego has retained the property, giving up only the right to income from it. Consequently, he must be taxed on the income. [§193]

21.a.	**YES**	This is the rule in *Blair*. [§§187, 196]
b.	**NO**	This is the rule in *Harrison v. Schaffner*. [§196]
22.	**NO**	This is an example of *Lucas v. Earl*—income is taxed to the person who earns it. [§203]
23.a.	**NO**	Sale of rights to compensation for personal services yields ordinary income, not capital gain. [§§197, 856]
b.	**NO**	Although Tex could give away the contract and shift the income (since Tex's personal services were not involved), he waited too long to do it. The contract is no longer contingent, and it is too late to shift the income through a transfer. [§191]
24.	**YES**	This appears to comply with the requirements of section 704(e) for shifting income in family partnership. Capital is a material income-producing factor, Jean is receiving a reasonable salary, and the transfers to trusts for the children appear bona fide, assuming the trustees are truly independent. [§§218-221]
25.a.	**YES**	Required by I.R.C. section 73. [§222]
b.	**YES**	Also required by I.R.C. section 73; this seems to be an appropriate ordinary and necessary expense for an actor. [§224]
c.	**YES**	This appears to be reasonable compensation for services. [§§415-417]
26.	**NO**	In a community property state, the community property income of spouses must be divided equally between them if they file separate returns. [§§230-231]
27.a.	**INCOME $15,000, DEDUCTION $15,000**	Under section 7872, interest is imputed when a corporation loans a shareholder money and fails to charge the applicable federal rate. This means that the appropriate amount of interest is treated as if it were paid by the corporation as a dividend, then repaid by the shareholder as interest. Thus, Enrique receives a $15,000 dividend (ordinary income) and an offsetting interest deduction (trade or business interest is deductible). [§§239-243]
b.	**INCOME OF $15,000**	The imputed dividend is not deductible, but X Corp. has imputed interest income of $15,000. [§§240, 243]
28.	**NO**	The grantor, Giovanna, must treat the trust property as hers and pay tax on the income because she retained a reversionary interest. [I.R.C. §673] [§253]
29.a.	**NO**	Powers to invade corpus limited by reasonably definite standards will not cause the income to be taxed to the grantor. [I.R.C. §674(b)(5)(A)] [§259]

b.	**YES**	The grantor may not have powers to apportion income. [I.R.C. §674(a)] [§254]
c.	**NO**	If a reasonably definite external standard of apportionment is spelled out, the grantor is not taxed on the trust income if he is not the trustee—even if the trustee is a relative of the grantor. [I.R.C. §674(d)] [§258]
d.	**NO**	An independent trustee (such as the bank) may have power to apportion income or principal among the beneficiaries. The grantor will not be taxed as long as he is not a trustee and not more than half the trustees are his relatives or subordinates subservient to his wishes. [I.R.C. §674(c)] [§257]
e.	**NO**	Income is not taxed to the grantor simply because he has the power to either distribute currently or accumulate income, provided that the accumulated income must eventually be paid to the person who would have received it currently, or to his estate or appointees. [I.R.C. §674(b)(6)] [§259]
30.a.	**YES**	The grantor is taxed if he has the power to revoke. [I.R.C. §676] [§260]
b.	**YES**	Tom is an "adverse party." The grantor is not taxed on the income if an adverse party must agree to revocation. [I.R.C. §676(a)] [§260]
31.a.	**YES**	If the income either is or may be distributable to the grantor's spouse in the discretion of a nonadverse party, it is taxable to the grantor. [I.R.C. §677(a)] [§§261-262]
b.	**NO**	Where income could be used for the support of someone whom the grantor is obligated to support other than his spouse, it is taxed to him only in the event that it is actually so used. [I.R.C. §677(b)] [§§266-268]
32.a.	**YES**	If the grantor or a nonadverse party has the power to borrow corpus or the income without adequate interest or security, the income is taxed to the grantor. [I.R.C. §675(2)] [§271]
b.	**NO**	As long as she has administrative powers of this kind only in a fiduciary capacity, she is not taxed on the income. [I.R.C. §675(4)] [§276]
33.a.	**YES**	If someone has a general power of appointment over trust corpus, meaning that he could vest the trust income or corpus in himself, he is taxed on the income. [I.R.C. §678] [§277]
b.	**NO**	Ivan is taxed on the income under section 674(a), since his powers to distribute corpus to the beneficiary are not limited by an ascertainable standard. Section 674 prevails over section 678, so Ivan is taxed, not Nicolai. [§277]
34.a.	**NO**	Mary is taxable on the $25,000 as ordinary income. Under a simple trust, the amount required to be distributed to the beneficiaries is taxed to them whether or not distributed. [§282]

b. **YES**   The capital gain is taxed to the trust. [§282]

35. **$9,000**   In this complex trust, Paul is a "first tier" beneficiary whose distribution is taxable to the extent that distributable net income ("DNI") is equal to it. Consequently, Paul is taxed on his entire distribution. The remaining DNI of $9,000 is allocated to Roy. Consequently, $9,000 of the distribution to him is taxable. The remaining $6,000 distribution to him is treated as a tax-free distribution of corpus. [§§283-287]

36.a. **NO**   One can deduct only his own expenses, not the expenses of someone else. Furthermore, a stockholder is not treated as being in a trade or business, even though the corporation is. The expenditure would correctly be added to the basis of Arnie's stock and be deductible by the corporation. [§§294, 300]

b. **NO**   The move is clearly far enough to qualify, and the cost of moving household goods is deductible. The other items are not deductible, but the $1,000 commission reduces the amount realized on the sale of the home. [§§325-330]

37.a. **YES**   Under Rev. Rul. 99-7, the cost of the trip is deductible if we assume the registry is a regular place of business. [§§308-309]

b. **NO**   No part of the cost is deductible even though part of it would be allocated to transporting the bass. [§310]

c. **$300**   Since the trip was primarily for business, the entire cost of the airfare ($80) is deductible. However, one-third of the cost of the meals and lodging is not deductible since that part was travel for pleasure. Thus, only $240 of the lodging and $120 of the meals are deductible. In addition, the $120 must be reduced to $60 because only 50% of the cost of meals is deductible. [§311]

d. **NO**   Richard has neither a permanent residence nor a permanent place of business. Therefore, no matter how the word "home" is defined, he has no home from which to be away. [§§314-315]

e. **YES**   George is viewed as being away from home "temporarily," rather than "indefinitely." Therefore, he is entitled to deduct his lodging and 50% of his meals as well as his travel to Michigan. [§318]

38. **$28,000**   Under the passive loss rules, with the exception of the activities of a real estate professional (which Ralph is not), rental activity is always passive. The general rule is that passive loss can be deducted only against passive income (the dividends are portfolio, not passive, income). However, Ralph qualifies for the $25,000 allowance in section 469(i) (assuming he actively participates). This provision allows deduction of up to $25,000 loss on rental real estate if the taxpayer's adjusted gross income ("AGI") is under $100,000. The $25,000 allowance is phased out at a rate of 50 cents for each dollar by which AGI exceeds $100,000. Here, Ralph is $18,000 over, so the allowance

is reduced by $9,000 to $16,000. Thus, Ralph can deduct expenses up to his passive income ($12,000) plus $16,000, or $28,000. The remaining $2,000 of deductions are carried forward to be deducted against future passive income or when there is a taxable disposition of the house. [§§543-551]

39. **NO**

The origin of the dispute—Paul's mental state—is a personal matter, and the amount must be treated as personal rather than a business expense. It is not relevant that the results of losing would be destructive to one's business. (*See* the *Gilmore* case.) [§339]

40.a. **YES**

Part of the tuition cost would be deductible under I.R.C. 222. Wilhelm could deduct $3,000 in 2002 and 2003, and $4,000 in 2004 and 2005, provided that his AGI does not exceed certain levels. Also note that this deduction is scheduled to be eliminated after 2005. Alternatively, the tuition may be subject to either the HOPE scholarship credit or the Lifetime Learning Credit. However, the educational expenses would not be deductible as a business expense because the education would qualify Wilhelm for a new trade or business. [§§341, 343, 717-720]

b. **YES**

This is training that maintains or improves skills required in Barbara's job. It does not qualify her for a new job. It is a miscellaneous itemized deduction subject to the 2% floor. [§§342, 562]

41.a. **NO**

The premiums on group term life insurance paid by an employer for an employee are exempt under I.R.C. section 79. The exclusion applies only with respect to life insurance up to $50,000. [§§110, 345]

b. **YES**

The employer is not allowed to deduct the premiums on insurance if it is the beneficiary, but it is entitled to deduct them if the employee is the beneficiary and (together with all other compensation) the compensation is reasonable. [§345]

42.a. **NO**

This creates an asset that will last for many years and is therefore not deductible as a business expense. It must be capitalized. [§§365-367]

b. **NO**

Under the I.R.C. section 263A and the *Idaho Power* case, the depreciation on the bulldozer is not currently deductible but must be added to the basis of the newly constructed building. [§§380-383]

43.a. **NO**

This must be capitalized as it creates an asset having a useful life of five years. She can amortize the prepayment and allocate it to the years during which she occupies the premises. [§387]

b. **PROBABLY YES**

Accrual basis taxpayers who receive prepayments must include them all in income when received, unless they fall within the Commissioner's rule permitting deferral of amounts received for services to be performed in the following year. A few cases cast doubt on this conclusion. [§§1015-1016] Note that in certain cases of increasing rents required by a lease, both the landlord and tenant must use the accrual method. [§1022]

44. **NO**   Under these facts, the so-called lease would be treated as a purchase. Therefore, the payments are not deductible as rent, but Zeke could claim depreciation on the machine. If he can prove that part of the payment should be treated as interest, he can deduct that part. [§388]

45.a. **YES**   The courts have held that fees paid to an employment agency are deductible business expenses even though no job is found, as long as the taxpayer is already employed in the same kind of business. [§398]

  b. **YES**   Under I.R.C. section 174 and the *Snow* case, these amounts are currently deductible. [§401]

  c. **NO**   The courts have held that the cost of searching for a new business to purchase is currently nondeductible. I.R.C. section 195 does not apply if no business is found. [§§396-397]

46.a. **NO**   This is treated as a nondeductible capital outlay, akin to the purchase of goodwill. The facts are similar to *Welch v. Helvering*. [§404]

  b. **YES**   Although the payment of the debt is ordinarily not income to the creditor (assuming his basis for the debt is equal to the amount repaid), the fact that it was deducted as a bad debt in a prior year creates a different situation. This is an application of the "tax benefit rule." Assuming that the entire amount of the debt provided a tax benefit in a prior year, all of it is includible in income when it is repaid. [I.R.C. §111] [§§536-537, 1073-1079]

47.a. **NO**   Under I.R.C. section 104(a)(2), amounts received as damages for personal physical injury are excluded whether paid in a lump sum or periodic payments. [§89]

  b. **NO**   Defco can deduct only $40,000 in Year 1. Under I.R.C. section 461(h)(2)(C), tort damages cannot be deducted by an accrual method taxpayer until they are paid, regardless of when the obligation arose. [§1033]

48.a. **YES**   Although payments that are illegal under state law are not usually deductible, this is true only if the law against them is generally enforced. Since this law is not generally enforced, the payment would appear to be deductible if it is "ordinary" for such payments to be made. [I.R.C. §162(c)] [§426]

  b. **YES**   Illegal income is taxable the same as legal income. Even though the program director might have an obligation to turn the money over to the station, he nevertheless has taken it under claim of right and it is taxable to him. [§§160-161]

49. **NO**   Under section 162(c)(2), a payment that would subject the payor to professional discipline is not deductible, assuming that the statute or rule is generally enforced. [§426]

50.a. **NO**   Fines are not deductible, even though they otherwise would qualify as business expenses and even though no fault is involved. [I.R.C. §162(f)] [§§431-432]

b. **YES**   Attorneys' fees incurred in resisting criminal prosecution are deductible, assuming that the criminal act involved arose in business. This was clearly established by the *Tellier* case. [§§431-432]

51.a. **NO**   No deduction or credit for political contributions is allowed. [§433]

b. **NO**   Lobbying is not deductible. [§434]

52.a. **NO**   Although he is also trying to get damages, the primary aspect of his lawsuit is to establish title. Consequently, the acquisition costs (including litigation expenditures) must be capitalized. This seems clearly established by the *Woodward* case. Presumably, however, if the litigation proves unsuccessful, Rex can deduct the amounts incurred both in looking for the mine and unsuccessfully suing as a business loss under I.R.C. section 165. [§§443-445, 493 *et seq.*]

b. **YES**   This appears to be in lieu of lost profits and therefore would be taxed as ordinary income. [§§101-107]

53.a. **NO**   Only the lessor is entitled to claim depreciation on the building since he paid for it. [§§459-460]

b. **YES**   The tenant has made an economic investment in the building and is entitled to depreciate those assets. However, he must use the useful life of the improvement as the depreciation period, regardless of the term of the lease. [§460]

c. **NO**   They have an unlimited useful life. [§458]

54.a. **NO**   Under I.R.C. section 109, he does not realize or recognize any income on the construction of this building. [§753]

b. **39 YEARS**   Although one must use the useful life of the building in this situation [§460], the lessee depreciates the property over the recovery period normally used for nonresidential real property under I.R.C. section 168(c)(1) [§465]. Thus, Sara should depreciate the building over 39, rather than 40, years.

c. **YES**   Vic is entitled to depreciate this part of the purchase price, even though the tenant on the property is also depreciating exactly the same property. [§460]

55.a. **$2,400**   Under straight-line depreciation, she can deduct one-fifth of cost, or 20%, per year. The half-year convention means only one-half of a full year's depreciation is deductible in the year of purchase. [§471]

b. **$4,800**   Double-declining balance—twice the straight-line rate, or 40%. She can take half in the year of purchase. [§§468-469]

c. **$4,800**   *See* a., above.

d. **$7,680**   Subtract the first year's depreciation ($4,800 *see* b., above) from the copier's basis ($24,000) and multiply the difference ($19,200) by 40%. [§469]

e. **$24,000 (in 2002) or $25,000 (in 2003)**   Special allowance for expensing small purchases. Amount is $24,000 in 2002, $25,000 in 2003 and subsequent years. [§477]

56.a. **$8,000**   Since the well cost $100,000, and was estimated to contain 100,000 barrels of oil, $1 is allocated to each barrel. Therefore, since 8,000 barrels were pumped, the cost depletion would be $8,000. [§486]

b. **$5,000**   Ordinarily, percentage depletion is based on 15% of the gross income (which would here produce a deduction of $6,000). However, the amount deductible is limited to 50% of the net income from the property. Here the net income is $10,000 ($40,000 gross income less $30,000 expenses), and 50% of that is $5,000. [§§487-489]

c. **YES**   Percentage depletion is not limited to basis. [§489]

d. **YES**   Percentage depletion in excess of basis is treated as a tax preference. [*See* I.R.C. §57(a)(1)] [§§489, 948]

57. **NO**   Demolition of a building produces no deductible loss whether or not the taxpayer intended to demolish a purchased building. [§502]

58. **NO**   Goodwill is amortized over a 15-year period; thus, Floyd is allowed an amortization deduction of $2,000 per year for purchased goodwill. However, even if it is now worthless, there is no closed and completed transaction that would allow a loss of the remaining $28,000 of basis to be realized. Probably only a sale or an abandonment of the entire business would satisfy this requirement. [§§473-474, 504-509]

59. **NO**   There are two potential grounds for attacking this transaction:

1) Losses incurred on sales between siblings (and other family members) are not deductible under I.R.C. section 267. [§§511, 514]

2) Another theory on which the Commissioner could disallow the loss might be that the whole transaction was a sham in the sense that Julius was always

holding the property for Leon and there had been no real shift of ownership. However, this theory could be refuted by the fact that Julius actually lost $3,000 on the resale to Leon. [§518]

3) Note that the repurchase from Julius after two months does not invoke the wash sale provision of I.R.C. section 1091, which comes into play only upon a sale and repurchase within 30 days. [§517] Incidentally, Julius could not deduct his loss on the sale to Leon—I.R.C. section 267 prevents it. It may well be that neither Julius nor Leon can ever deduct these losses since I.R.C. section 267 permits disallowed losses to be used only to offset gains on the property in the event it is later sold at a gain. [§§513-516]

60.	**DEPENDS**	The loss on a guarantee is treated as a bad debt. The theory is that Gloria makes payment to the bank and then by reason of subrogation, becomes a creditor of Mike. Assuming that Mike is insolvent, Gloria then can write off the claim as a bad debt. However, this appears to be a nonbusiness bad debt, which is deductible only as a short-term capital loss. If Gloria has no other capital transactions in this year, she will be limited to only a $3,000 deduction. [§§520-530, 818]
61.a.	**YES**	If she can prove partial worthlessness in Year 2 of a business bad debt, she can deduct the amount that becomes worthless in that year. [§528]
b.	**YES**	This is debt cancellation income. Assuming the exception for insolvency is not applicable, Dole must include $6,000 in income. [§§144-145, 536]
62.	**PROBABLY NOT**	Loans made by persons who are also stockholders are treated as nonbusiness bad debts (capital loss) since they arise in investment rather than in business. The fact that a corporation is in business does not mean that the creditor is in business. The facts of this case suggest that Larry did not need to make the loan to keep his job, since close family members controlled the corporation. Therefore, he cannot rely on the exception that gives business bad debt treatment to employees who make loans to the corporation to protect their jobs. [§§531-532]
63.	**NO**	As a cash basis taxpayer, she has no basis for this debt and therefore nothing is deductible by reason of its worthlessness. If she were on the accrual basis, she could deduct the amount of her basis (presumably the $20,000). Similarly, if she had actually loaned cash to John, she could deduct her basis. But as a cash basis taxpayer, she has no basis in a receivable obtained through the rendering of her services. [§534]
64.	**$14,900**	Certain deductions are subtracted from gross income to reach "adjusted gross income." These include capital losses and alimony. These two items total $1,100, and, consequently, adjusted gross income is $14,900. Other employee business expenses, such as union dues and uniforms, are deductible only from adjusted gross income and subject to the 2% floor. [§§554-555, 561]

65. **$40,000**   Interest prepayments are not deductible immediately and must be amortized over the period for which the interest was prepaid. That provides a $40,000 deduction. Investment interest is deductible only to the extent of net investment income, but Jim has sufficient net investment income to absorb the interest. [I.R.C. §§163(d), 461(g)] [§§605-609]

66. **YES**   Under the passive loss rules, Ray meets the material participation standards of the regulations and can deduct the loss. Spouses can combine their participation, and if their participation exceeds 500 hours, they meet the test. This assumes, however, that all of their participation was in fact appropriate for owners (not extra hours spent dishwashing just to get over 500). [§§543-548]

67.a. **NO**   I.R.C. section 164(a). [§§612-616]

b. **NO**   I.R.C. section 164(a). [§615]

c. **NO**   I.R.C. section 164(a). [§615]

d. **NO**   I.R.C. section 164(a). [§612]

68.a. **YES**   It is permissible to deduct the gift of a remainder in a personal residence or a farm. The actuarial value of that remainder interest is deductible currently, assuming that depreciation on the property during the income beneficiary's lifetime is taken into account. [§624]

b. **NO**   Such charitable remainders are deductible only if in the form of a "fixed annuity trust," or a "unitrust." A fixed annuity trust will pay a fixed dollar amount for Carol's lifetime, not merely all the income. A unitrust will pay a fixed percentage of the fair market value of the assets of the trust each year. The trust described in this problem does not qualify under either standard. A third form of interest in trust that is deductible is a "pooled income fund" in which many donors make contributions to the same trust, which has a charitable remainder. In this situation, it is permissible for all the income produced by the donor's assets to be paid to the income beneficiary for life. [§625]

69.a. **$10,000**   Since this would be short-term capital gain, she must reduce the amount deductible by the entire amount of the short-term capital gain. [§§633-635]

b. **$14,000**   Since this would be long-term capital gain, the entire amount is deductible. However, it should be noted that such gifts of long-term capital gain property cannot be deducted in excess of 30% of adjusted gross income, even though the gift is to a publicly supported charity like Public University. [§§628-629]

c. **$10,000**   Even though long-term capital gain property is involved, the gift was of tangible personal property unrelated to the exempt purpose of the recipient. Consequently, the amount of the gain must be removed from the amount deductible. [§§630-632]

70.a. **$20,000**   This is computed by subtracting the amount the charity paid from the full fair market value of the property. [§§637-638]

b. **YES**   In this case of a bargain sale to charity, he cannot allocate his entire basis against the amount received from the charity. Since the charity paid only one-fifth of the fair market value, he can apply only one-fifth of his basis against the amount received. Therefore, the basis usable is only $1,000, and he has long-term capital gain of $4,000. [§638]

71. **$100**   Total expenses equal $1,750. Seven and one-half percent of AGI is $1,650. Excess is $100. [§661]

72.a. **THREE**   Mike and Susan have exemptions for themselves, and they can claim an exemption for Bob. Although he earned over the exemption amount, that is not disqualifying since he is under age 19 and his parents supplied more than one-half of his support. The fact that Carol earned more than the exemption amount is disqualifying since she is neither a student nor under 19. Even though her parents supplied more than one-half of her support, they cannot claim her as an exemption. [§664]

b. **NO**   The fact that his parents claim him as a dependent prevents him from claiming an exemption for himself. [§664]

73.a. **YES**   The custodial parent is entitled to the exemption. [§668]

b. **NO**   The noncustodial parent may claim the exemption only if the custodial parent signs a waiver and the noncustodial parent attaches it to his return. [§669]

74. **$870 CREDIT**   Mary receives a credit (not a deduction) equal to 29% of $3,000, or $870. Although Mary has child care costs of $4,800, her credit is subject to a $3,000 statutory cap. Additionally, the maximum percentage of 35% (for 2003, this figure is increased from 30%) is reduced by 1% for each $2,000 or fraction thereof by which AGI exceeds $15,000 (for 2003, this figure is increased from $10,000). Mary has AGI of $26,000; thus, the reduction to the maximum percentage is 6% ($26,000 - $15,000 = $11,000 ÷ $2,000 = 5.5%, which is rounded up to 6%). [§§700-706]

75. **$200**   He can deduct the lesser of the adjusted basis ($1,000) or the difference between the value before ($700) and after ($0). Furthermore, the loss must be reduced by $100, leaving a $600 deduction. However, casualty losses are deductible only to the extent they exceed 10% of AGI (10% of $4,000 equals $400). [§§679-681]

76. **$83,900**   Casualty loss deduction is: the lesser of adjusted basis ($150,000) or decline in value ($225,000) less insurance recovery, less $100, and less 10% of AGI. Thus, the calculation here is as follows: $150,000 (adjusted basis) - $60,000

(insurance recovery) = $90,000; $90,000 - $100 = $89,900; $89,900 - $6,000 (10% of AGI) = $83,900. [§§679-681]

| 77. | **$103,000** | The mortgage and the brokerage commission are included in basis. However, the contingent liability is not. If he later has to pay the contingent liability, it would be added to basis at that time. [§§724-727] |

78.a. **$82,400 GAIN**

This is a long-term capital gain. Deborah's basis, for the purposes of computing both gain and loss, is the same as Sarah's—$10,000. However, she is entitled to add a portion of the gift tax paid to basis. The portion is a fraction based on the net appreciation in the gift; 4,000 × 90,000/100,000, or $3,600. Thus Deborah's basis is $13,600. When the property is sold for $96,000, it produces a gain of $82,400. Deborah's gain is long term because she "tacks" Sarah's holding period onto her own. [§§732-733]

b. **$7,000 LOSS**

This is a long-term capital loss. Where the property is worth less than Sarah's basis at the time of the gift, the basis for determining *loss* is the fair market value at the date of the gift ($8,000). (The basis for determining *gain* would be $10,000.) Also in this situation the gift tax (if any) cannot be added to basis since there is no unrealized appreciation in the property. [§732]

c. **NEITHER GAIN NOR LOSS**

Her basis for determining loss is $8,000. Since she sells the property for $9,250, there is no loss. Her basis for determining gain is $10,000, so there is no gain. [§732]

79.a. **$1 MILLION**

Kojak's basis would be $1 million since basis equals fair market value at date of death. Note that in 2010, this rule is slated to change so that the legatee's basis for inherited property is the same as the decedent's basis (subject to many exceptions). [§§735-736]

b. **$9,000**

Basis equals fair market value at date of death. [§§735-736]

80.a. **NO**

Amortization of a life interest or a term interest received by gift or inheritance is not allowed. [I.R.C. §273] [§744]

b. **CAPITAL GAIN OF $41,000**

He is not allowed any basis for the sale of this interest. [I.R.C. §1001(e)] However, he does have capital gain under the *McAllister* case. [§742]

c. **$1,000 CAPITAL GAIN**

He is allowed to use the basis of $40,000 when both life tenant and remainderman together sell their interests. [§743]

d. **YES**

The purchaser of a life estate is entitled to amortize it over the useful life of the asset—which would be the life expectancy of the income beneficiary. [§745]

81.a. **$100,000**   Both halves of the community property receive a new basis under I.R.C. section 1014(b)(6). Note that in 2010, this rule is slated to change so that the legatee's basis for inherited property is the same as the decedent's basis (subject to many exceptions). [§§737-738]

b. **$25,000**   The portion of the joint tenancy property that is not included in the decedent's estate does not receive a new basis. [§740]

c. **$100,000**   Since Herbert's one-half was included in his estate for tax purposes, it receives a new basis. [§740]

82.a. **$15,000**   This item is called "income in respect of a decedent" and is fully taxed to whomever receives it. [*See* I.R.C. §691] The item does not receive a new basis under I.R.C. section 1014. The effect of labeling it "income in respect of a decedent" is to assure that it has the same basis as it had to the decedent—that is, zero. This item is clearly income in respect of a decedent because it represents payment for services rendered by the decedent prior to his death but which, under his method of accounting, was not taxable to him at that time. [§§746-748]

b. **$13,000**   The estate is allowed to deduct for income tax purposes the estate tax paid in respect to this item. [§749]

83.a. **$9,500**   Basis is reduced by the greater of the depreciation allowed or allowable. In this case, more was "allowed" than was allowable, so the entire $10,000 claimed reduces basis. [§751]

b. **$11,500**   In this case the amount allowable ($8,000) was greater than the amount allowed ($3,000); therefore, basis is reduced by the amount allowable. [§751]

84. **NO**   The amount of the overall basis that can be attributed to the air rights is indeterminable. Consequently, David should reduce his basis for the building to $84,000. Later, when the building is sold, this adjustment will cause his ultimate gain to increase or his ultimate loss to decrease. [§754]

85.a. **YES**   She is deemed to have realized $95,000 on the foreclosure, and, consequently, has a $13,000 long-term capital gain (or section 1231 gain). [§762]

b. **NO**   Mortgaging property is not a realizing transaction, even though the amount borrowed is in excess of basis. [§758]

86. **PROBABLY NOT**   This is an example of an "open transaction," although the IRS is likely to dispute this. Since the amount of the profits to be received is not readily determinable (although it can be roughly estimated), Winston should offset $15,000 received against his basis, which will reduce it to $7,000. The next $7,000 he receives on account of the profits' interest will reduce his basis to zero. Thereafter, each dollar will be taxed as capital gain. [§777] This transaction can be

accounted for under the installment method of section 453 since the installment method is available for open transactions. This would be done by equally apportioning Winston's basis over the 10-year payment period. Indeed, the installment method would be used unless the taxpayer elected out of it. [§§774, 777, 1047, 1051] Note also that interest must be imputed here since the parties failed to provide for it. [§915] The IRS's position would be that Winston has a capital gain of $73,000 ($95,000 amount realized less $22,000 basis).

87.a. **NO** This is a nonrecognizing transfer under I.R.C. section 1041. [§808]

b. **NO** Transfers between spouses (or between former spouses incident to a divorce) are treated as gifts to the recipient. [§§808-811]

c. **$8,000** Basis stays the same after a transfer described in I.R.C. section 1041. [§810]

88.a. **$60,000** Although his realized gain is $150,000, this is a transaction described in I.R.C. section 1031—exchange of property of a "like kind" to that given up. Consequently, gain or loss is recognized only to the extent of the "boot" received, which is the $60,000 in cash. [§§781, 789]

b. **$20,000** This again is an I.R.C. section 1031 exchange, but the boot received ($60,000) exceeds the realized gain ($20,000). No more than the realized gain could ever be recognized. [§789]

c. **NONE** Since this is a section 1031 exchange, no loss can be recognized. [§789]

d. **$200,000** The formula is old basis ($200,000) plus gain recognized ($60,000) minus boot received ($60,000), or $200,000. [§§789-791]

e. **$290,000** The formula is old basis ($330,000) minus boot received ($60,000) plus gain recognized ($20,000), or $290,000. [§§789-791]

f. **$360,000** The formula is old basis ($420,000) minus boot received ($60,000), or $360,000. [§§789-791]

89.a. **NO** If she elects to use section 1033 and the reinvestment occurred within two years, she need not recognize the gain. However, she failed to reinvest $1,500 of the proceeds, so $1,500 gain would be recognized. [§796]

b. **YES** The vacation cottage and the Ferrari are not property that is "similar or related in service or use." Consequently the entire gain is recognized. [§797]

90.a. **NONE** Under I.R.C. section 121, a single person can exclude up to $250,000 of gain on sale of a principal residence if during the five-year period ending on the date of the sale it has been both owned and used as a principal residence for two years or more. [§§802-803]

b. **$220,000**   The basis of the new house is its purchase price. [§724]

91.a. **$350,000**   Wanda meets the requirements of I.R.C. section 121 for her share. She is single and can exclude $250,000. However, her share of the gain was $600,000 (her half of the difference between the $1,400,000 sales price and the $200,000 purchase price), so $350,000 is taxable. [§§802-803]

b. **$350,000**   Under I.R.C. section 121(d)(3)(B), Harry is allowed to treat the house as his principal residence during the years he no longer lived there. Therefore he qualifies for exclusion under section 121. However, he cannot exclude $500,000, even though he filed a joint return with Mary, because Mary does not meet the ownership and use requirements of section 121. [§§802-807]

92. **NO**   This is a clear case in which the property is held primarily for sale to customers in the ordinary course of business. This is evidenced by the large number of sales, the fact that he purchased large pieces of property and split them up into smaller pieces, the improvements he made, his practices in prior years, and his personal involvement in selling the property. This is not a case in which he appears to have had several purposes, such as farming, as opposed to selling. It is simply a case in which the nature of his activities clearly shows that the property is being held primarily for sale rather than for investment. [§§823-825]

93. **YES**   This seems to be clearly an investment. None of the facts point to Luis's having held the property primarily for sale to customers in the ordinary course of business. As far as we know, this is the only transaction of this type that he has entered into. He has no personal involvement in improving or in selling the land. The increase in value occurred because of extrinsic factors, not his efforts. This is clearly a capital gain. [§825]

94. **YES**   Under *Malat v. Riddell*, even though Vicky holds other property for sale to customers, it is possible to establish a different purpose for a particular parcel. Here one must measure whether her purpose of developing and leasing the property was more important than her purpose of selling it. Since it seems clear that her primary purpose was development, not sale, it is a capital gain. [§827]

95.a. **YES**   Different standards are applied to stock traders than to land dealers. Despite the volume of his trading, Warren is still treated as holding capital assets; his stocks are not held primarily for sale to customers in the ordinary course of business. The result would be different if Warren were a "dealer" of securities (for example, by acting as a floor specialist on the exchange or by holding stocks in inventory and selling to customers for a commission). [§§829-832]

b. **YES**   These would be deductible under I.R.C. section 212(1) as expenses incurred for the production or collection of income, or under section 212(2) as expenses incurred for the management, conservation, or maintenance of property held for the production of income. However, the 2% floor is applicable. [§§437, 561]

96.a. **NO**   Copyrights and other literary, musical, or artistic property are not capital assets in the hands of the taxpayer whose personal efforts created them. [I.R.C. §1221(3)] [§838]

b. **YES**   Under I.R.C. section 1235, inventors are entitled to long-term capital gain on the sale of their invention. It would not matter whether the purchase price was to be paid in the form of a royalty based upon the number of instruments manufactured; the royalties would still be capital gains. Further, it would not matter how many such inventions Betty previously had made. They would still be capital gains. [§841]

97. **NO**   These assets are classified as ordinary income assets under section 1221(3), meaning that if the President had sold them he would receive ordinary income. Therefore, he is entitled to deduct only their basis, not their market value, when he gives them to charity. Presumably his basis in these letters and memoranda is zero, and, therefore, he would be entitled to no deduction. [§§633, 839]

98. **YES**   Under *Arkansas Best*, this stock is a capital asset regardless of the business reason for buying it. [§835]

99. **NO**   This is similar to the *P.G. Lake* case. When the taxpayer anticipates ordinary income by selling the rights to income while keeping the underlying income-producing asset, he receives ordinary income, not capital gain. [§847]

100. **YES**   Unlike the previous case, he has sold his entire interest. Even though it is only a right to income, the fact that he sells the entire interest, without retaining anything, is sufficient to give him capital gain under the *McAllister* case. Note that under I.R.C. section 1001(e), Zahi is given a zero basis. [§§848-849]

101.a. **YES**   Allen is treated as having sold the right to collect rent, while retaining the reversion, and this is taxable as ordinary income without basis recovery. This was established in the *Hort* case. [§854]

b. **YES**   The lessee has sold his entire interest in the property, and it is treated as a capital asset. Section 1241 establishes that the lessee has a sale or exchange for capital gain purposes. [§§853, 893]

102. **NO**   The contingent right to money was received for personal services. The sale of the right to compensation for personal services produces ordinary income. [§856]

103.	**YES**	Under the "lookback" rule, the money is treated as capital gain because it is referable to a previous transaction that produced capital loss. [§863]
104.a.	**$95,000**	The amount paid for the option is part of his purchase price. [§730]
b.	**NO**	Since it is an option to purchase a capital asset, its lapse is treated as capital loss under I.R.C. section 1234. [§844]
c.	**NO**	It is ordinary income because Paul has not sold or exchanged a capital asset. [§844]
d.	**YES**	The option to purchase a capital asset is itself a capital asset. [§842]
105.	**NO**	The consideration must be fragmented and the analysis must be made asset by asset. The gain on the furniture and books ($2,000) is ordinary income because of depreciation recaptured under I.R.C. section 1245. The accounts receivable produce ordinary income since they are payment for services. [*See* I.R.C. §1221(4)] The goodwill produces capital gain. The covenant not to compete produces ordinary income. Therefore, the gain is $20,000 ordinary income and $5,000 capital gain. [§§836, 865-868, 925-926]
106.	**NO**	These are both section 1231 assets. Since the losses ($6,000) on section 1231 assets exceed the gains ($3,000), both the loss and the gain are given ordinary, not capital, treatment. [§§873-879]
107.	**NO**	If gains on casualties involving business or investment assets exceed losses, both gains and losses are within section 1231. Here the only casualty transaction produces a gain. However, the net of all section 1231 transactions is a loss: consequently, the casualty gain is ordinary income. [§§873-884]
108.a.	**NO**	I.R.C. section 1253 provides that if the franchisor retains these kinds of controls, it is treated as ordinary income to him. [§891]
b.	**YES**	A franchise is amortizable over a 15-year term. Hence, $1,000 per year is deductible. [§474]
109.a.	**YES**	Fred did not collect on the note, but rather sold it. [§899] The note appears to be a capital asset [§821], and the sale to Roy is treated as a sale or exchange. [§888]
b.	**YES**	Collection of a debt instrument (such as a promissory note) is treated as a sale or exchange to the creditor. [§§899-900]
c.	**YES**	He appears to have $5 of debt cancellation income. [§131]
110.	**YES IN PART**	These were the facts in the *Brown* case, which held that the seller was entitled to capital gain. This was so even though the seller continued to manage the business and had all the risks of loss if the business failed. However, part of

the money received by Laura in fact would be treated as ordinary income in this situation because it is a sale with the price to be paid in the future, but without providing for interest. This requires that interest be imputed under I.R.C. section 483. Consequently, each payment would be treated as ordinary income to Laura. [§§903-905, 915]

111. **YES** Jomo can deduct 50% of his $3,800,000 gain under section 1202. Thus, only $1,900,000 is included in income. However, 28% of the excluded amount is treated as a tax preference under the alternative minimum tax. [§§910-913]

112. **$7,000** The capital gain is includible in income; the capital loss is deductible to the extent of capital gain plus $3,000. The remainder of the capital loss ($17,000) will be a carryforward to future years. [§§813-819]

113. **NO** This requires the application of section 483—imputed interest. (Section 1274 does not apply to any transaction under $250,000.) The parties have failed to provide for any interest and therefore it will be imputed. Assume the applicable rate is 10% (and ignore the requirement of semi-annual compounding). Interest at the rate of 10% on $10,000 for 18 months is about $1,500. Consequently, $1,500 will be interest income (ordinary) to Rory, and Ryan will have a $1,500 interest deduction (subject to the limit of the investment interest limitation or the passive loss rules, whichever is applicable). Rory's capital gain will be the amount realized ($8,500) minus basis ($1,000), or $7,500. [§915]

114.a. **YES** Although ordinarily the tractor would presumably be considered section 1231 property, on which the gains would be capital (if it were the only section 1231 transaction that year), the provision for recapture of depreciation would apply here. Section 1245 requires the entire $1,200 gain to be taxed as ordinary income regardless of whether the depreciation was straight-line or accelerated. [§§925-928]

b. **NO** It is ordinary income only up to the amount of the depreciation ($8,000). The balance of the gain of $2,000 would be taxed under section 1231 and (assuming there are no section 1231 losses) would be capital gain. [§927]

c. **NO** It is capital loss because the section 1231 gains exceed the section 1231 losses. Therefore, all transactions are capital. Recapture of depreciation has no application if the property is sold at a loss. [§§926-928]

d. **NO** This is a section 1031 exchange of property for like-kind property. No gain or loss is recognized, and therefore there is no opportunity for depreciation to be recaptured. If Zeke had received any "boot" in this transaction, it would have been treated as ordinary income because of the recapture of depreciation. [§930]

| 115. | **YES** | Don's AMTI is $280,000, because the bargain element in an incentive stock option is a tax preference. The exemption on a joint return is $49,000, which is phased out at a rate of 25% of the excess of AMTI over $150,000. In Don's case, this means that the $49,000 exemption is reduced by $32,500 (25% of $130,000) to $16,500, making the amount subject to AMT $263,500 ($280,000 - $16,500). The AMT is 26% of the first $175,000 plus 28% of the amount over $175,000. Thus, Don's AMT would be $70,280 (26% × $175,000 = $45,500, 28% × $88,500 ($263,500 - $175,000) = $24,780, $45,500 + $24,780 = $70,280). Given that his regular tax was only $57,000, he must pay the AMT instead (an additional $13,280). [§§937-949] |

| 116.a. | **YES** | Paul has capital gain equal to the fair market value of the note less his basis. The regulations require that the note be valued at $10,000 (the value of the property given up) rather than its actual fair market value of $8,500. Thus, Paul has capital gain of $9,000. [§775] |

| b. | **YES** | To an accrual basis taxpayer, the date of actual payment and the value of the note are irrelevant. Paul acquired a right to be paid in Year 1, and therefore must accrue the $9,000 capital gain in that year. [§1006] |

| c. | **YES** | The stock is treated as the equivalent of cash and thus is income when received by a cash basis taxpayer. [§§952, 1006] |

| 117.a. | **YES** | This is an example of constructive receipt. The money was available; Cassie had a right to it and the power to obtain it, but she turned her back on the money. It is taxable in Year 1. [§955] |

| b. | **NO** | It is permissible for a cash basis taxpayer to contract not to receive money until a later year. No income is recognized until the money is paid. [§§961-962] |

| 118. | **YES** | The placing of the money in trust, beyond Zero's control, causes it to be treated as the equivalent of cash to Suman. Thus, it is taxed in Year 1. [§966] |

| 119.a. | **NO** | Under a *qualified* pension or profit-sharing plan, the amounts paid into the plan are not taxable until ultimately received by the employee. [§§969, 971] |

| b. | **YES** | Contributions to a qualified plan are deductible in the year paid. [§969] |

| c. | **NO** | The trust is a tax-exempt entity. [§970] |

| 120.a. | **NO** | In almost all cases, the grant of a stock option is not a taxable event. In the absence of an established market for options, the market value would not generally be clearly ascertainable. [§987] |

| b. | **YES** | The exercise of a stock option is a taxable event (assuming that the earlier grant of the option was not taxed). Pete has purchased 100 shares for $100 |

per share when the real value is $130. Therefore, he has income of $3,000. This is ordinary income since it is compensation for services. [§988]

c. **YEAR 3**   It receives a $3,000 deduction in Year 3. [§929]

d. **$13,000**   His basis consists of the amount paid plus the amount included in income. [§988]

e. **NO**   Under I.R.C. section 83, the stock received would be nontransferable and subject to a substantial risk of forfeiture. It would not be currently taxable. [§§975-976]

f. **YES**   Under the terms of section 83, the stock is taxable as ordinary income at its fair market value when it first becomes transferable or nonforfeitable. Thus, Pete would have $12,000 of income in Year 4 (fair market value of $22,000 less the amount paid—$10,000). [§976]

121.a. **YES**   Lloyd, a cash basis taxpayer, must include money in income when it is received. [§994]

b. **NO**   Although the Supreme Court has established the general rule that prepayments of income must be included by accrual basis taxpayers in the year in which they receive the money, the Code has established a relatively narrow area in which deferral is permitted. As to advance payments for services, if the services are to be performed by the end of the year following payment, the taxpayer can defer to that year the portion of the payment attributable to it. [§§1015-1020]

c. **YES**   The general rule requiring an accrual basis taxpayer to include immediately all prepayments for services applies to this situation. The special exemption provided by the IRS applies only if the services are to be completed by the end of the following year. Since this is more than a one-year prepayment, the IRS's special dispensation does not apply. [§§1015-1020]

122. **NO**   There is a special rule concerning dividends to an accrual basis taxpayer. They are included in income only when received, even though the dividend in this case would accrue on December 15 by ordinary accounting standards. [§1021]

123.a. **NO**   Under the accrual method, nothing is accrued until all the events have occurred that establish the right to the income. The contract would be viewed as a single right to payment, and nothing would be accrued until all the events had occurred that establish the right to receive all of the compensation. [§1010]

b. **NO**   It is not necessary to accrue as income money due from an insolvent debtor. [§§1013-1014]

124. **NO** Even though it is likely that Louis will have to pay the money, all the events have not occurred that establish his obligation to do so. It is not permissible to accrue estimated future expenses, even though under accounting practice, it might be mandatory to do so. In this case, not only is the obligation not yet fixed, but the amount of the damages is also probably not reasonably ascertainable—which is also required before an expense can be accrued. [§§1026, 1035]

125.a. **YES** She will probably be treated as in constructive receipt. The corporation is obligated to pay her the salary, and she has the power to require the treasurer to write the check. [§§955, 958]

b. **YES** Ordinarily, the rule under I.R.C. section 267 is that an accrual basis taxpayer may not accrue an expense payable to a related person (including an owner of more than 50% of its stock) if the creditor is on the cash basis, until payment is actually made. This rule would be applicable here except for the fact that Laura was probably required to include the amount in income under the doctrine of constructive receipt. Consequently, it would follow that Zero Corp. is entitled to a deduction in Year 1. [§§1036-1037]

126.a. **$345** Under FIFO, the inventory is considered to consist of the last item purchased, which is 100 parts at $1.60 ($160) and 20 at $1.50 ($30). Thus, the $535 cost of goods sold is reduced by the inventory of $190. [§§1041-1043]

b. **$410** Under LIFO, the ending inventory is considered to be the first items purchased. Consequently, there are 100 parts at $1 ($100) and 20 purchased at $1.25 ($25), or a total of $125. Thus, cost of goods sold would be $410. [§§1044-1045]

127. **$800** Compute a fraction in which the gross profit ($4,000) is the numerator and the total contract price ($10,000) is the denominator. This fraction is multiplied by the payments received each year to compute the amount includible in income. The interest payments, as they are received, are all ordinary income. [§§1047-1051]

128.a. **YES** He has received it under claim of right and must include it in income notwithstanding the risk that he will not be able to retain it. [§§991-992]

b. **NO** This would be a violation of the annual accounting concept. Since the repayment occurred in Year 3, it can be deducted only in that year. [§1066]

c. **NO** Under I.R.C. section 1341, he has an option: either deduct on his Year 3 return or reduce his Year 3 taxes by the amount of tax he would have saved if he had deducted in Year 1. [§1067]

129.a. **$100,000 DEDUCTION** As an accrual basis taxpayer, B & W had included the $100,000 in income; it had a basis of $100,000. When the debt became worthless, it was a business bad debt (ordinary deduction). [§534]

b. **NONE**

There is no debt cancellation income if debtor could have deducted the payment if he had made it. [§149]

c. **$100,000 INCOME**

Recovery of amount previously deducted is income in the year of recovery if the prior deduction resulted in a tax saving. Contra if no tax benefit. [§§1070-1073]

d. **$100,000 DEDUCTION**

A cash basis taxpayer gets a deduction when the amount is paid. [§951]

130. **YEAR 3**

Under I.R.C. section 461(h)(2)(A), no deduction is allowed to an accrual taxpayer until economic performance occurs—which means when the services are actually performed. In Year 3, economic performance had occurred and also all events had occurred that establish X's obligation to pay; the actual date of payment is irrelevant. Note that drilling expenses for an oil well are deductible immediately; they do not have to be capitalized and depreciated over the useful life of the well. [§§490, 1030-1034]

Exam Questions
and Answers

QUESTION I

Barnes is a Native American. More than 30 years ago, he bought a house in Butte, Montana, where he has lived ever since. He is unmarried. He paid $20,000 for the house, paying $500 down and executing a note and first mortgage for the $19,500 balance. He has made timely payments of principal and interest on the note and has reduced its principal balance to $14,500. The house became very valuable because of development in the area. On June 15 of Year 5, Barnes sold it for $280,000 cash plus assumption of the mortgage.

Spence owns 60 rented houses in Helena, Montana. He spends all of his working time taking care of the houses and looking for profitable sales. There are no "for sale" signs on the houses. Interested buyers are referred to Spence's broker. The broker is self-employed, working for Spence consumes about 5% of his time. Because the Helena housing market has been poor, Spence has sold only one house during the last three years, but has purchased 16 houses during that time.

Spence's house on Oak St. was purchased for $40,000 in Year 1. In Year 2, Spence leased it to Tennant for $400 per month. The lease runs until December 31 of Year 6. Spence has claimed $5,000 in depreciation on the house on Oak St.

Barnes had to move to Helena and began looking for a house there in April of Year 5. He discovered from Spence's broker that the house on Oak St. could be purchased for $75,000. After speaking to Tennant, Barnes discovered that Tennant would surrender his lease for $750. Spence refused to sell to Barnes. Barnes suspects racial discrimination.

Under Montana law, the housing commission can order a house to be sold to a buyer if it finds that the seller refused to sell because of racial discrimination. The commission can also order the seller to pay a $3,000 penalty to the buyer. After holding a hearing, the commission ordered Spence to sell the house on Oak St. to Barnes for $75,000 and ordered him to pay a $3,000 penalty to Barnes.

On June 5 of Year 5, Barnes, Spence, and Tennant settled their affairs. Barnes handed Tennant $750 and paid Spence $72,000 (that is, $75,000 less the $3,000 penalty). Barnes handed Spence a deed to the Oak St. house. On June 10, Barnes moved into the house.

What are the income tax consequences in Year 5 to Barnes, Spence, and Tennant?

QUESTION II

Oliver W. Holmes, a prominent Boston lawyer, had great difficulty in recruiting law school graduates for his exciting practice (which consisted of making claims against railroads for damaged freight). He felt that recruiting might improve if he financed a scholarship program. Consequently, he arranged to fund a scholarship for one needy law student throughout his or her three years of law school. The scholarship would pay $800 per month (during the school year) to the recipient to cover living expenses, not tuition. The recipient's only obligations were to work at Holmes's office the summers between the first and second years and the second and third years of law school and to do research for Holmes on request. (For such research, the recipient would be compensated at the rate of $10 per hour.) In June of Year 1, Holmes sent Harvard Law School a check for $19,200 (*i.e.*, $800 per month for eight months a year for three years).

In Year 1 through Year 5, Holmes's adjusted gross income was $25,000 before taking into account any of the transactions mentioned in this problem.

Paul Prolific, who entered Harvard Law School in the Fall of Year 1, was selected by the Dean as the first recipient of the Oliver W. Holmes Scholarship. He had a wife and five young children and was broke. Each month during the school year from October of Year 1 to May of Year 2, Harvard issued a check to Prolific for $800. He was never asked to do any research during the school year.

Prolific worked at Holmes's office during the summers of Year 2 and Year 3, receiving a salary of $1,500 per month. (You may assume that the $1,500 payments are taxable to Prolific as ordinary income and deductible by Holmes.)

In October of Year 2, Ann Allen, who had been Prolific's secretary at Holmes's office, found herself pregnant and accused Prolific of being the father. She brought a paternity suit to compel Prolific to support the child. Holmes investigated Ms. Allen's charges and decided that they were unwarranted. He thereupon fired her. Holmes assumed the burden of Prolific's defense without charge, since he felt himself somewhat at fault in exposing someone of Prolific's tender years to a person like Ms. Allen.

The costs of the defense (all of which were paid by Holmes in Year 3) were $8,000 (court costs, investigator's fees, and the salaries of attorneys in Holmes's office who worked on the matter). In June of Year 3, the court held that Prolific was not the father of Ms. Allen's child.

After he graduated in June of Year 4, Prolific rejected Holmes's offer of permanent employment and took a job with Penn Central Railway in the freight claims department. In Year 5, Prolific wrote to Holmes, stating his appreciation for all Holmes had done for him. He enclosed a check for $1,000 to partially reimburse Holmes for the costs of defending the paternity suit.

What are the income tax consequences to Holmes and to Prolific in Year 1, Year 2, Year 3, and Year 5? (Ignore consequences to Ann Allen.) Discuss.

QUESTION III

Laura has been a tenant for 10 years in the Hilgard Arms, a 100-unit apartment house; she occupies her apartment on a month-to-month rental agreement. Rex, owner of the Hilgard Arms, decided to convert the building to condominiums, which he plans to offer for sale. Local law allows apartments to be converted to condominiums, but requires the owner to pay each tenant $2,500 to reimburse them for the inconvenience of moving and the possibly higher rent they must pay. Rex pays Laura $2,500 in pursuance of this law.

A. How should Laura treat the $2,500 for tax purposes?

B. How should Rex treat the $2,500?

QUESTION IV

Tailor Corporation, which tailor-makes business suits, made a contract with Grunt Steel Company, which provided that Tailor would make suits for Grunt executives. Each suit has a fair market value of $500. Tailor Corporation will lease these suits to Grunt for $200 per year, and Grunt will provide them free of charge to its executives. The leases run for three years. At the end of the term, Grunt will return the suits to Tailor Corporation, but (since they will be worn out and since they were custom-made) you can assume that they would be worthless at the end of the lease term. Ray, vice president of Grunt, got a new tailor-made suit in Year 1 worth $500. Grunt paid Tailor Corporation $200 as rental in Year 1 on Ray's suit. Tailor's costs of making the suit were $240. All taxpayers use the cash method of accounting.

A. What income tax consequences to Ray in Year 1?

B. What income tax consequences to Grunt in Year 1?

C. What income tax consequences to Tailor Corporation in Year 1?

QUESTION V

Turbo Corporation manufactures hydraulic grunches and has earned substantial profits for the last 20 years. Turbo has a large physical plant with expensive and sophisticated machinery. It has accumulated earnings and profits equal to $400,000, and has never paid a dividend. It uses the accrual method of accounting and the calendar year. Its current policy is to pay out most of its profits as salary and bonus to its executives. All of the executives use the cash method of accounting and the calendar year.

All of the executives of Turbo are the sons and daughters of Max Kirk. Max has been the chief executive officer of Turbo for 10 years. He works a 12-hour day, six days a week. Max owns 25% of the stock of Turbo, and his sons and daughters own the balance. In Year 1, Max was 62 years old and single. He plans to retire in Year 3.

In Year 1, Max received a salary of $125,000. He also was voted a $50,000 bonus in December of Year 1 by the directors. The bonus was payable immediately. However, Max did not get around to requesting that a check be drawn for $50,000 until June 15, Year 2. Max was also entitled to $24,000 of additional salary in Year 1, which he deferred until later years under the deferred compensation plan (described below). Research indicates that the chief executive officers of other hydraulic grunch companies earn between $50,000 and $100,000 per year.

In March of Year 1, the directors of Turbo adopted a deferred compensation plan. Under this plan, each executive can elect to defer up to $3,000 per month of current salary to a future year or years. The election must be made by the 15th of a month, with respect to the salary payable during the immediately following month. Pursuant to this plan, Max elected in April of Year 1 that $3,000 per month of each month's salary should be retained by the corporation and paid to him in 10 installments beginning in Year 4. Thus, $24,000 ($3,000 per month for eight months) of Max's salary was not paid to him in Year 1.

What are the income tax consequences to Max and Turbo in Year 1 and Year 2?

QUESTION VI

Blackacre and Whiteacre are both unimproved parcels of land. Beth purchased Whiteacre in 1992 for $74,000. In 2001, when it was worth $56,000, she transferred it to her friend, Marc. Whiteacre was Beth's only significant asset and she wanted to get on welfare, so she had to divest herself of her property. Beth and Marc understood that if Beth wanted to get Whiteacre back, she only had to ask. The transfer was not recorded.

Hal and Gretel acquired Blackacre as community property in 1984 by exchanging their home for it. The home had a basis of $25,000 and a value of $70,000. Blackacre was worth $70,000 in 1984. In 1995, Hal died at the age of 42, leaving his community one-half interest in Blackacre to Gretel. The value of Blackacre in 1995 was $66,000.

In 2002, Marc and Gretel exchanged Whiteacre for Blackacre. Marc and Beth discussed the exchange and Beth approved of it. In 2002, Whiteacre was worth $61,000. Blackacre was worth $40,000. Gretel transferred $10,000 in cash and an AT&T bond worth $11,000 (basis $13,200) to Marc. What are the income tax consequences of the facts above to Beth, Marc, Hal, and Gretel?

QUESTION VII

Jenny operates a tree surgery business. Paul is going to purchase the entire business for $20,000 in cash. In addition, he will assume $9,200 of Jenny's business liabilities.

The following is a table of the assets of Jenny's business (all of which have been held more than one year):

ASSET	BASIS	VALUE
Lease on office*	$ 0	$ 5,000
Office furniture**	4,000	7,200
Trucks***	16,000	9,000
Goodwill	0	8,000
Total	$20,000	$29,200

*Assume the lease is treated as real property used in the business.

**$5,000 is the depreciation on the furniture.

***$9,000 is the depreciation on the trucks.

Assuming that Jenny's taxable income (without reference to the above) was $30,000, what is her taxable income after taking account of the sale of her business?

QUESTION VIII

On January 1 of Year 2, Bill bought an apartment house (the "Dallas Arms") from Sam. Bill put $20,000 down and took the property subject to a $100,000 nonrecourse first mortgage loan owed to Coast Savings. Bill also gave Sam a note for an additional $30,000, payable on July 1 of Year 5. This was Sam's only asset sale in Year 2.

The note to Sam is nonrecourse and is secured by a second mortgage on Dallas Arms. The note to Coast Savings bears interest at 10%, and the note to Sam bears interest at 18%. Bill made payments to Coast Savings as they became due. In Year 2, principal payments to Coast Savings totaled $2,000 and interest payments to Coast Savings totaled $10,000.

Sam's adjusted basis for Dallas Arms was $60,000. He had claimed straight-line depreciation of $50,000 during his 12 years of ownership.

Tina, a tenant in Dallas Arms, signed a lease on January 1 of Year 1. Tina is rather eccentric and likes to pay bills before they are due. Consequently, in Year 1, she prepaid two years' rent. The total prepayment was $12,000. To account for the fact that a year still remained for which Tina had prepaid rent, Sam paid Bill $6,000 at the time of the sale of Dallas Arms.

On December 31 of Year 2, Tina asked Bill if she could renew her lease for another two years (for Years 3 and 4) at the same rental price, and Tina stated that she desired to prepay the two years' rent ($12,000) immediately. Bill said he did not want to discuss the rent payment until January of Year 3.

Also on December 31 of Year 2, Bill gave Sam a promissory note for $5,400—the amount that Bill owed in interest for Year 2. The note is payable on April 1 of Year 3, bears an interest rate of 20%, and is secured by a third mortgage on Dallas Arms. The note had a fair market value of $5,000 on December 31 of Year 2.

Both Bill and Sam use the cash method of accounting and the calendar year. What are the income tax consequences to Bill and Sam of the facts above? Ignore consequences to Tina and ignore imputed interest.

QUESTION IX

On December 31 of Year 2, Ellen (who is not a professional bicycle thief) stole Rick's racing bike, which was then worth $1,400. The bike was not insured. Rick had bought the bike new on March 15 of Year 1 for $1,000. The bike was so good, and so few were made, that used bikes rose in value. The useful life of the bike was about seven years. Rick used the bike both for pleasure and for riding in bicycle races in which money prizes were given. In the typical bike race, 1,000 people would enter and the top five finishers would get prizes. Rick never finished in the top 200 in a bike race. Rick's AGI in Year 2 was $6,000. Because his itemized deductions did not exceed the standard deduction in Year 2, Rick got no benefit from the resulting casualty loss deduction.

Ellen tried to fence the bike but decided to wait until the market improved. In the meantime, she used the bike for pleasure riding. One day, in Year 3, as she was riding at the beach, Rick saw her and, after a brief struggle, reclaimed the bike, which by then was worth $1,600. Rick also called the police. Ellen was prosecuted for petty theft and paid an attorney $500 in Year 3 to defend her. Ellen resisted the theft charge because, if found guilty, she would probably lose her job as a probation officer. Ellen was acquitted.

What are the tax consequences to Rick and Ellen by reason of the facts above?

ANSWER TO QUESTION I

A. Barnes

Sale and Purchase of House: Barnes's basis for his Butte house is $20,000 (original purchase price, including mortgage). The amount realized on the sale is $294,500 (assumption of mortgage plus cash). The realized gain is $274,500. Under I.R.C. section 121, because the property has been Barnes's principal residence for at least two of the five years preceding the sale, Barnes can exclude $250,000 of his gain. The remaining $24,500 is taxable as long-term capital gain. The fact that he reinvested in another house is irrelevant.

The basis of the Oak St. house is its purchase price ($75,000) plus the amount paid to buy Tennant's rights as a lessee ($750). Thus the total basis is $75,750. The purchase of the house and the penalty are treated separately even though they were netted out by the parties.

Taxation of the Penalty: The $3,000 penalty is taxable. Since racial discrimination is not a physical injury, section 104(a)(2) is inapplicable.

B. Tennant

Tennant's sale of his leasehold interest produces a $750 long-term capital gain. A leasehold is a capital asset to the tenant, provided he sells his entire interest therein. Since the lease is being sold to a third party, not the lessor, it is clear that there is a sale or exchange. (And even if it were sold to the lessor, section 1241 makes it clear that there is a sale or exchange.)

C. Spence

Sale of the House: It is important to treat the sale of the house and payment of the penalty as separate transactions. Spence's adjusted basis for the house is $35,000 ($45,000 purchase price less $5,000 depreciation). The sale price was $75,000; thus, the realized gain is $40,000.

If the house were held for sale to customers in the ordinary course of business, the gain would be ordinary income, not capital gain under section 1231(b)(1)(B) (if rental is treated as being a trade or business) or section 1221 (if rental is not a trade or business).

Factors to Consider: Spence seems more interested in renting the houses than in selling them—all of them are rented, and he spends a great deal of time on renting. This suggests they are not being held for sale. Moreover, Spence has not made any strong efforts to sell, since he does not display any signs and uses an independent broker (rather than an employee) to transact sales. Also, only one sale has been made in three years, further suggesting that the houses are not being held for sale. On the other hand, it could be argued that Spence is renting the houses only to pay his costs and that he is in fact primarily interested in buying and selling as fast as possible (the lack of sales recently being due to the stagnant market). On balance, it appears that Spence has a strong case for capital gains.

Payment of the Penalty: Is the penalty a deductible expense (under section 162 if Spence is in a trade or business or section 212 if he is an investor)? Presumably the payment of such penalties by housing dealers is ordinary (*i.e.*, customary) and necessary (in the sense that payment of the penalty once it was assessed was a necessity). It might be argued that it arose out of Spence's personal life, rather than his business life, since evidently he allows his prejudices to get in the way of business, but this argument seems weak since the penalty is traceable to a business transaction. It might also be argued that the penalty should be treated as a selling expense, which would reduce capital gain rather than allow for a deduction, but this also seems weak since Spence would have had to pay the penalty even if the sale had not gone through (*i.e.,* had Barnes bought a different house).

There is no public policy obstacle to deduction—section 162(f) disallows only fines or penalties paid to a government; section 162(g) disallows only treble damage payments under the antitrust laws; and section 162(c) disallows only deduction of illegal payments (obviously payment of the penalty was not illegal; indeed, it was required by state law). Thus, payment of the penalty is probably deductible by Spence.

ANSWER TO QUESTION II

A. Scholarship

Holmes: The payment of $19,200 to Harvard might qualify as a charitable contribution. If so, it would be deductible, but only in an amount equal to 50% of adjusted gross income, or $12,500. The balance ($6,700) is not currently deductible, but could be carried forward and deducted in 1995.

On the other hand, this is arguably *not* a charitable contribution, in the sense that the donor expects a significant quid pro quo (a guaranteed research assistant and summer clerk as well as a likely permanent recruit). Where there is a direct business benefit to be gained, the outlay is not a charitable contribution, but might be deducted as a business expense under section 162(b). Moreover, it could be argued that this was a grant from Holmes directly to Prolific rather than Harvard—in which case, it would be disallowed because it was not a gift to an organized charity.

Analyzing the payment under section 162, it is seemingly not ordinary for lawyers in Boston to arrange for scholarships; on the contrary, it is extraordinary and unusual. Moreover, the payment probably should be capitalized: It does not yield an immediate benefit—the primary benefit will be realized only after three years when Prolific graduates from law school. Thus, the deduction would have to wait for three years. On the other hand, perhaps it could be amortized over the three-year period, since it does provide some advantages during that time (*e.g.*, a summer clerk and availability of a research assistant).

When Prolific finally turned down Holmes's offer of employment, the $19,200 (if previously capitalized and not amortized) could be deducted as an ordinary business loss under section 165.

Prolific: Scholarships are taxable unless applied directly to tuition or books. Even if this payment were applied to tuition, it could be argued that it is really a payment for services, not a payment for studying. However, since Prolific was being adequately compensated for any work he did for Holmes, it would appear that the payment would qualify as a scholarship (if it were applied to tuition).

B. Paternity Suit

Holmes: Deduction of the $8,000 might be disallowed for the reason that Holmes is paying someone else's expenses, not his own; however, since the dispute arose out of an employment situation, perhaps this rule would not be applied. It would seem appropriate for an employer to pay an employee's litigation costs where the litigation is traceable to the employment. By the same token, these payments were probably "ordinary" within the meaning of section 162. They produce an immediate benefit and hence would not have to be capitalized. (If held to be a gift to Prolific (below), only $25 could be deducted under section 274(b).)

Prolific: Since the litigation costs related to freeing him from child-support liabilities, they would seem to be Prolific's expenses, and the payment of his expenses by his employer should be treated as gross income. Paul might argue that the payments are gifts, excludible under section 102, but that argument will not prevail. Payments by an employer on behalf of an employee cannot be treated as gifts.

Prolific could also argue that these payments were for the convenience of the employer, similar to reimbursement of an employee's travel costs. However, these expenses hardly seem to be within the narrow scope of the "convenience of the employer doctrine," which does not seem to encompass any more than travel, entertainment, and meals and lodging that are closely related to the employment situation and necessarily must be borne to keep the business going.

In any event, Prolific **cannot deduct** the costs. Under *Gilmore,* a paternity dispute surely arises out of the personal part of his life (not the business part), even though there were some connections to the business setting (Ann was his secretary).

C. Repayment

Holmes: If Holmes deducted the $8,000 in the past, the unexpected recovery of $1,000 would be taxable income, unless he did not receive a tax benefit from the deduction. Presumably, however, there was a tax benefit (either in Year 3 or, by way of a net operating loss carryover or carryback, in some other year). Thus, the recovery is taxable.

Prolific: Prolific could argue that reimbursing Holmes for the litigation costs was an ordinary and necessary expense—*i.e.*, it will help Prolific in business by establishing his good character. But this would suggest that the payments should be capitalized, as in *Welch v. Helvering,* as analogous to the purchase of goodwill of indeterminate life. In response, Paul would contend that the payments were akin to deductible advertising. On balance, however, the payments are probably not deductible—either because they are not ordinary, because they have to be capitalized, or because they are only personal (*i.e.*, traceable to the earlier paternity suit that arose out of the personal part of Paul's life).

Assuming Paul can deduct the payment, he would obviously prefer to deduct it in Year 5 (when he is in a higher bracket) than in Year 3. Since Year 5 is the payment year, it is the correct year to deduct the payment (it is improper to reopen Year 3). In the unlikely event that Paul was in a higher bracket in Year 3 than Year 5, he might try to apply section 1341, which allows the payor to select the tax bracket of the payment year or the income year. However, section 1341 is inapplicable because it was never "established" that Paul had to return the money. In addition, section 1341 applies only to payments over $3,000.

ANSWER TO QUESTION III

A.   Laura

Laura has been enriched by $2,500 and at first glance would seem to have gross income of that amount. She has received a windfall, and windfalls produced by statutory policies are taxable under *Glenshaw Glass*. To avoid including the $2,500, Laura might argue that she has received a gift, but this argument clearly fails—Rex was forced by statute to make the payment, so it cannot meet the disinterested generosity standard of *Duberstein*.

A more plausible argument might analogize the payment to a government subsidy or welfare payment. When these are paid by the government and are responsive to the recipient's need, they are not included in income—even though no statute so provides. Here the payment is made by an individual, not the government, but the same argument could be made. However, this argument seems unpersuasive—after all, Rex and Laura are simply contracting parties and a payment required by law made by one party to another seems quite remote from the welfare analogy. Besides, there is no way of knowing whether Laura is really needy at all or how seriously she will be harmed by the eviction.

Another argument Laura might offer is that her moving costs, and her higher rent, are nondeductible outlays (moving costs are deductible only in connection with changing jobs). The refund of a nondeductible outlay should not be taxable under the tax benefit rule. Of course, she receives the reimbursement here before incurring the costs, so perhaps the tax benefit rule would not apply. Moreover, the $2,500 is an arbitrary amount, not related at all to the actual moving cost or higher rent. Perhaps Laura might try, under this theory, to exclude the portion of the $2,500 that in fact is spent on moving costs and higher rent (although for what period she should measure the rent is not clear).

Still another argument Laura might offer is that the payment should be analogized to a personal injury recovery. Under the pre-section-104 case law, tort recoveries for intangible injuries, such as defamation and invasion of privacy, were not taxed, based on a dubious theory that they were a recovery of capital. Here, the law creates a sort of tort (condominium conversion) and awards arbitrary damages that are supposed to approximate the victim's losses. However, this argument is undercut by the fact that the parties' relationship seems more a function of contract than tort. In addition, Laura received the $2,500 before she had incurred the costs of moving—which is not typical of tort recoveries and which ordinarily precludes exclusion of damages either under the case law or statutory personal injury exclusions. On the other hand, the payment is made after the tort had occurred—the decision to evict the tenant and convert to condominiums—so perhaps the personal injury cases could still be used. Probably, section 104(a)(2) would be viewed as overruling the prior case law. Since Laura did not suffer a physical injury, she would not be permitted to exclude the payment under that section.

If the $2,500 is taxable to Laura, she could argue that it is taxable as long-term capital gain. A lease is a capital asset in the hands of the tenant and, if one argues that a month-to-month tenancy is the same as a lease, the $2,500 could certainly be considered an amount realized in a sale or exchange of the lease (an asset held more than one year). Section 1241 makes it clear that the amount received on cancellation of a lease is treated as a sale or exchange to the lessee. However, the month-to-month agreement falls far short of a lease—it is the antithesis of a lease—and might well not be held to be "property" under section 1221. On the other hand, the statute has conferred a sort of property-like protection on the tenancy, and so arguably has turned it into a property for capital gain purposes.

B. Rex

Rex cannot deduct the $2,500 payment. It clearly must be capitalized and added to the basis of the apartment. It is an acquisition cost of an asset held for sale. (But for the capitalization problem, the payment would be deductible as an ordinary and necessary business expense, the deductibility of which is not barred by any public policy provision.)

ANSWER TO QUESTION IV

A.   Ray

If the form of the transaction is given effect, Ray would be treated as receiving the free use of the business suit by reason of his employment with Grunt, and he should include the fair rental value of the suit in income (presumably $200 of ordinary income in Year 1). Although many fringe benefits are excluded from income, this one does not seem to fit. The amount is hardly de minimis, and it is not a "working condition fringe" because the employee cannot deduct it (*see* below). Thus, section 132 is of no help. And if the $200 is includible in income, Ray has no offsetting deduction since business suits are not deductible as a business expense—only clothing not suitable for street wear can be treated as business expense.

However, the transaction probably should be recharacterized as an outright transfer of the suit to Grunt, followed by an outright transfer to Ray—not as a lease by Grunt. The economics of the transfer suggest: the suit will be worthless at the end of the "lease" term, the transaction seems peculiar (nobody leases suits, they buy them), and there is at least the possibility of tax avoidance purpose here (*i.e.*, it is a way of giving an employee immediate use of valuable property without an immediate tax or with tax spread out over the time the property is used). Thus the transaction should be treated in accordance with its true substance, not its form, as an outright transfer by Tailor to Grunt and by Grunt to Ray. In that case, Ray has income of $500 (*see* section 83(a)).

B.   Grunt

If the transaction is treated as a lease by Grunt, followed by a transfer that makes the suits available to Ray, Grunt should deduct the $200 rental it pays as ordinary and necessary business expense (or as compensation to Ray). If the transaction is treated as if Grunt purchased, rather than leased the suits (as explained above), it would have bought an asset for $500. If one assumes that Grunt continued to own the suit and made it available to Ray, the suit could be depreciated over a three-year useful life. Accelerated depreciation under ACRS would be $166.75 (0.67 rate for one-half year) in Year 1. Since Grunt is obligated to pay $600 over three years, the extra $100 should be treated as interest and deducted. It is not clear just how the $200 payment made in Year 1 should be broken down into principal and interest, but it would be logical to treat the interest as payable in equal amounts in each of the three years, in which case, Grunt gets a $33 interest deduction in Year 1.

If Grunt is treated as having purchased the suit, then transferred it outright to Ray, it would not depreciate the suit since Grunt would not own it. Instead Grunt should be treated as if it sold the suit to Ray in discharge of his claim for compensation. Since the suit has a value of $500, which is also its basis, Grunt has no gain or loss on the transfer. In addition, it should take a $500 deduction for compensation (assuming that it is reasonable compensation). (To see this more clearly, pretend that Grunt had sold the suit for cash—which would produce no gain or loss—and transferred the cash to Ray; the latter cash transfer is a payment of compensation.)

C. Tailor Corporation

Tailor Corporation would have rental income of $200 in Year 1 and would depreciate the suit over a three-year useful life. However, if the transaction is recharacterized as a sale, rather than a lease, Tailor Corporation has income of $260 in Year 1 ($500 sale price minus $240 manufacturing costs). (This assumes that Grunt's promise to pay in the future is worth its face value.) In addition, it will have interest income in an amount that matches Grunt's deduction. Tailor cannot use the installment method because it is holding the suits for sale. The income would certainly be ordinary income, as the suits were held for sale to customers in the ordinary course of Tailor's business.

ANSWER TO QUESTION V

A. Excessive Compensation

Max was entitled to Year 1 compensation of $175,000, although $24,000 was deferred. However, Turbo Corporation may deduct compensation costs only if the compensation is deemed reasonable. In this case, "reasonable compensation" may be less. Other hydraulic grunch manufacturers pay their chief executive officers only $50,000 to $100,000 per year. However, these companies may not be comparable, given that Max works long hours and has been very successful for Turbo Corporation. Additionally, under *Exacto Spring*, the test is whether an independent investor, considering the investor's return on equity, would have been willing to pay Max $175,000. Given Turbo's high profits, the answer may be yes, in which case the compensation would be deemed reasonable and Turbo would be able to deduct the compensation costs. On the other hand, under *McCandless*, Turbo has failed to pay dividends, suggesting that part of the salary must be allocated to a reasonable return on capital (and thus taxed as a dividend). The year-end bonus is particularly suspicious in this regard. If any part of the compensation was unreasonable, Turbo is denied a deduction for that part, and that part of the compensation is taxed as a dividend (ordinary income) to Max.

B. Deductibility of Bonus

Under I.R.C. section 267, Max is treated as owning 100% of the stock. Therefore, Turbo is subject to the rule denying deduction for accrued compensation until it is paid. Under that rule, the $50,000 bonus is deductible by Turbo in Year 2. Max is taxed on the $50,000 bonus in Year 2 when he receives it.

It is arguable that Max constructively received the entire bonus in Year 1, since it was immediately payable and as chief operating officer he had both the right and the power to have the check drawn immediately. If it was constructively received in Year 1, it was taxable to Max in Year 1 and Turbo can deduct it in Year 1.

C. Deferred Compensation

The unfunded deferred compensation plan is effective to delay taxation of the deferred compensation until the years in which it is paid. IRS rulings allow elective plans, provided the election is made before the year in which the work is done. Presumably the same principle would apply to a monthly deferral. Under this approach, Max would not be taxed until the money was actually received in Year 4 and Turbo cannot deduct it until it is actually paid in Year 4. [I.R.C. §404(a)(5)]

ANSWER TO QUESTION VI

A. Beth-Marc 2001

If the transfer to Marc is given effect for tax purposes, Beth does not realize her loss because a gift is not a realizing transfer. Similarly, Marc does not include the value of Whiteacre in income since a gift is excluded under I.R.C. section 102. However, it is likely that the transfer would not be given effect for tax purposes, since Beth can get it back anytime she wants and simply made the transfer to commit welfare fraud. Failure to record the transfer is very relevant to this determination. For economic purposes, she would still be considered the owner of the property; her transfer would be a sham (which is defined as a transaction in which, for practical purposes, nothing really happened). At most, the transfer would be considered to create a revocable trust, the income of which is taxed to the grantor. [I.R.C. §676]

B. Hal-Gretel 1984

The exchange of the home for Blackacre was not a nonrecognition exchange under I.R.C. section 1031 because that section requires both properties to be held for investment or business. Since the home was used for personal purposes, the exchange does not qualify. The exchange also did not qualify for rollover under the now repealed section 1034, since Blackacre was investment property, not a principal residence. Thus the sale of the home was taxable; Hal and Gretel had a capital gain of $45,000. They are treated as if they purchased Blackacre for cash. Thus its basis was $70,000.

C. Hal-Gretel 1995

Neither Hal nor his estate recognizes gain upon transferring property by reason of death, and Gretel does not include the value of inherited property. However, in the case of community property, both the decedent's and the survivor's halves are given a new basis of the value of the property at the date of death. [I.R.C. §1014(b)(6)] Consequently, Gretel's basis for Blackacre is $66,000.

D. 2002 Exchange

Here there is a clear I.R.C. section 1031 exchange of like kind property.

Gretel: Gretel has a realized loss of $26,000 on Blackacre (basis is $66,000, value is $40,000). However, she cannot recognize this loss because of section 1031. She does recognize the loss on her AT&T bond since it is not like kind property. Thus, she has a capital loss of $2,200. Her basis for Whiteacre is her old basis for all the property transferred ($66,000 + $13,200), plus cash paid out ($10,000), plus gain recognized ($0), less loss recognized ($2,200), or a total of $87,000. (*Check the answer:* If she now sold Whiteacre for its value of $61,000, she would have a recognized loss of $26,000; this is exactly the amount of the realized loss on the exchange that she previously could not deduct. Thus, $87,000 is the correct basis for Whiteacre.)

Beth: Assuming that Beth, and not Marc, is the owner of Whiteacre for tax purposes, any tax consequences should be attributed to Beth. Beth has a realized loss of $13,000 on the exchange ($74,000 basis less $61,000 value) but cannot recognize it because of I.R.C. section 1031, even though she receives boot.

Her basis for Blackacre and for the AT&T bond is her old basis ($74,000), less cash received ($10,000), or $64,000. This amount is allocated first to the AT&T bond in its fair market value ($11,000); the balance is allocated to Blackacre ($53,000). (*Check the result:* If Blackacre is now sold for its value of $40,000, she will have a $13,000 recognized loss—exactly the amount she was not allowed to recognize on the exchange.)

ANSWER TO QUESTION VII

The amount realized on the sale is $29,200—assumption of liabilities is the same as receiving cash. It is necessary to break down the transaction asset-by-asset; a business is not treated as a single unit for tax purposes.

The sale of the lease produces $5,000 of gain under I.R.C. section 1231 (since it is real property used in a trade or business). The furniture produces $3,200 of ordinary income because of depreciation recapture. The trucks produce $7,000 of section 1231 loss. (They are depreciable property used in business, and there is no depreciation recapture when property is sold at a loss.) The goodwill produces a long-term capital gain of $8,000 (goodwill is not a section 1231 asset since it is not subject to depreciation under section 167—although it is depreciable in Paul's hands under section 197).

Thus, taxable income is $39,200: Add to $30,000 taxable income, the ordinary income ($3,200) and the gains ($13,000); subtract the loss ($7,000). The sum is $39,200. Since section 1231 losses exceed gains, both section 1231 transactions are ordinary and the loss is fully deductible.

ANSWER TO QUESTION VIII

A.   Sam

Purchase: Sam's realized gain is $90,000 (amount realized, which includes both the note to Coast and to himself, of $150,000; basis of $60,000). To avoid recognizing all of the gain, he will probably choose to use the installment method of taxation. (He must use that method unless he affirmatively elects out of it.) Under the installment method, he must include the excess of the Coast note ($100,000) over his basis ($60,000) in both the payments and the total contract price. The total contract price therefore is $40,000 (excess of Coast note over basis) + cash received ($20,000) + note received ($30,000) or $90,000. The gross profit is also $90,000. Thus, 100% of payments received are taxable. In Year 2, he receives $20,000 in cash and $40,000 representing excess of mortgage over basis, or a total of $60,000. Consequently, Sam has long-term capital gain of $60,000. He has no depreciation recapture under section 1250 since he used straight-line depreciation. Because Sam does not have $5 million in installment sales during Year 2, he does not pay interest on the deferred tax. Note that Sam's capital gain is taxed at a rate of 25% (compared with the usual rate of 20%) to the extent of depreciation taken on the property ($50,000). The balance of his gain ($40,000) would be taxed at a rate of 20%.

B.   Tina's Prepaid Rent in Year 1

When Tina prepaid $12,000 in rent to Sam in Year 1, Sam had to take the entire amount into income. However, when Sam repays the $6,000 unearned portion to Bill, he is entitled to deduct $6,000. He should not, however, be required to reduce the sale price by $6,000 (which would have the effect of denying him a deduction but reducing his capital gain on the sale). The rent item is logically separate from the purchase of the building and should be accounted for separately.

The amount was taken into income on the theory that Sam would retain it. When he has to transfer it to a buyer of the building, he no longer has that use, and a deduction under either I.R.C. section 162 or section 165 is appropriate.

Compare, for example, the treatment of amounts received under claim of right that must later be repaid; the payor can deduct the repayment. It seems unlikely, however, that Sam can take advantage of section 1341 on the repayment since it was never established that he did not have an "unrestricted right" to such item. [I.R.C. §1341(a)(2)]

Bill should take the $6,000 received from Sam into income as prepaid rent. He should not treat it as a reduction in his purchase price. From his point of view, it is just rental received.

C. Tina's Prepaid Rent for Years 3 and 4

The issue is whether Bill constructively received $12,000 in prepaid rent on December 31 of Year 2 from Tina. Although he did "turn his back" on income, it could be strongly argued that the constructive receipt doctrine is not applicable. This situation is akin to deferred compensation in which an employer is willing to pay an employee immediately but the employee insists on a contract deferring the amount. The employee is not currently taxed. [Rev. Rul. 60-31] Here, until a new lease is signed, Bill has no right to any money from Tina and no agreement has yet been signed. Notwithstanding Tina's willingness to prepay rent immediately, it is likely that Bill has successfully deferred the income until Year 3.

D. Interest Payments

Bill can deduct the $10,000 in interest paid to Coast but not the $2,000 in principal. As to the interest due to Sam, Bill cannot deduct it. Giving a note—even a negotiable one—is not considered a payment by a cash basis taxpayer. However, Sam must include in income the fair market value of the note. A secured promissory note is the equivalent of cash; so, Sam has interest income of $5,000 upon receipt of this note. Sam has additional income in Year 3 of $400 when the note is paid (plus interest income on the note).

ANSWER TO QUESTION IX

A. Rick—Basis

Rick bought the bike for $1,000. If the bike was an asset used in his trade or business, he can claim depreciation. Under ACRS, presumably the bike is five-year property (since its useful life is seven years). Thus if Rick used straight-line depreciation, he could claim $100 of depreciation in both Year 1 and Year 2 (half-year convention for year of acquisition and disposition).

However, it is unlikely that the bike would be treated as a depreciable asset because it is unlikely that bike racing would be considered Rick's trade or business. Rick has never come close to making any money at it. The problem specifies that he uses the bike partly for pleasure. Under section 183, the test is whether there was a significant profit motivation. Based on the facts given us, which should be analyzed carefully under the section 183 regulations, it would probably be found that Rick had no such intention. Consequently, he cannot depreciate the bike and its basis remains $1,000.

B. Theft Deduction

When the bike is stolen, Rick can deduct its adjusted basis ($1,000) or its fair market value ($1,400), whichever is less, as a casualty loss. He must reduce this amount by an additional $100 and by 10% of AGI (or $600). (If the bike were a business asset, he would not reduce it by $100 or 10% of AGI.) Thus, Rick would have had a $300 casualty loss deduction in 1994 but does not because his itemized deductions are less than the standard deduction. If the bike is considered a business asset, Rick would have an above-the-line loss deduction equal to the adjusted basis of the bike (probably $800). He could deduct this item in addition to the standard deduction.

C. Theft Income

When Ellen steals the bike, she has income of $1,400, despite the obligation to return the bike. *James* has firmly established the taxability of stolen goods. (Her basis for the bike is $1,400.)

D. Return of the Bike

When Ellen returns the bike in Year 3, she should deduct the amount previously included in income. It is not likely that she can deduct $1,600 (the value of the bike at the date of return). Because essentially accounting adjustments are involved, it would seem more reasonable to allow a deduction that simply offsets the earlier income item. However, she cannot use section 1341 for the repayment since it never "appeared that the taxpayer had an unrestricted right to such item" as required by section 1341(a) and also the amount is less than $3,000. Another approach would be to treat the return as a realization of $1,600, producing $200 of short-term capital gain and a $1,600 loss, which would be a nondeductible personal loss.

Rick would ordinarily have to include $300 in income; under the tax benefit rule, when an item previously deducted has been returned, it produces income. The measure of the income is the amount deducted, not the value of the bike at the time it is returned. However, Rick received no tax benefit from the deduction in Year 2, so would not include anything in income in Year 3. [I.R.C. §111] If Rick had been entitled to treat the theft as a business loss of $800, which would have produced a tax benefit, he would be required to include $800 in income in Year 3.

E. Ellen's Attorneys' Fees

These might be deductible under section 212(1). Under *Gilmore*, the fact that she paid the costs to keep her job is irrelevant. She is not in the trade or business of bike theft, so she cannot deduct them under section 162. However, the theft was a profit-seeking transaction so the origin of the later criminal case was an attempt to produce income, which would make the legal fees deductible under section 212. No public policy rule bars deduction of attorneys' fees.

Tables of Citations

CITATIONS TO INTERNAL REVENUE CODE (I.R.C.)

I.R.C.	Text Reference	I.R.C.	Text Reference	I.R.C.	Text Reference
1	§§690, 937	56(b)(1)(F)	§946	73	§222
1(d)	§237	57	§948	73(b)	§224
1(f)	§691	57(a)(7)	§913	74(a)	§50
1(g)	§226	57(a)(8)	§489	74(b)	§51
1(h)	§813	57(a)(11)	§491	74(c)	§52
1(h)(2)	§816	61	§§19, 27	79	§110
1(h)(4)(A)	§817	62	§§279, 554	82	§§141, 329
1(h)(6)	§815	62(a)(1)	§555	83	§§967, 975, 988
2	§229	62(a)(2)(A)	§555	83(a)	§§42, 983
2(b)	§238	62(a)(2)(B)	§555	83(b)	§982
2(c)	§238	62(a)(2)(D)	§555	83(c)(3)	§981
21	§700	62(a)(3)	§555	83(d)	§978
21(b)	§701	62(a)(4)	§§440, 555	83(e)(3)	§42
21(c)	§705	62(a)(5)	§555	83(h)	§§927, 977, 983
21(d)(2)	§706	62(a)(7)	§686	84	§201
21(e)(5)	§707	62(a)(10)	§§163, 555, 685	85	§83
21(e)(9)	§703	62(a)(17)	§§555, 600	86	§79
22	§§695, 697	62(a)(18)	§§343, 555	86(d)(1)(A)	§79
23	§716	62(b)	§555	101(a)	§§58, 59
24	§708	63	§566	101(a)(2)	§65
24(b)	§709	63(c)(3)	§569	101(c)	§67
24(c)(1)(C)	§710	63(c)(5)	§570	101(d)	§67
24(d)	§711	63(c)(7)	§§234, 568	101(g)	§62
25A	§717	63(f)	§569	102	§§34, 188, 336
27	§694	67	§§297, 321, 340, 440, 562	102(a)	§28
31	§693			102(b)(1)	§47
32	§713			102(b)(2)	§§48, 744
32(c)(3)(B)	§710	67(b)	§944	102(c)	§§31, 33, 34, 45
38(b)	§699	68	§§565, 946	103	§75
44F	§401	68(f)(2)	§565	103(b)	§77
51	§699	71	§§268, 685	103(b)(1)	§75
55	§937	71(a)	§163	104(a)	§91
55(b)(3)	§940	71(b)(1)(B)	§165	104(a)(2)	§§89, 94, 96, 97, 100, 601
55(d)(3)	§939	71(b)(1)(C)	§166		
56(a)(1)	§943	71(b)(1)(D)	§167	104(a)(3)	§84
56(b)(1)(A)(i)	§944	71(b)(2)	§164	105(a)	§88
56(b)(1)(A)(ii)	§945	71(c)	§535	105(c)	§87
56(b)(1)(B)	§942	71(c)(1)	§171	105(d)	§86
56(b)(1)(C)	§947	72	§68	105(g)	§86
56(b)(1)(E)	§946	72(b)(3)	§71	106	§86

I.R.C.	Text Reference	I.R.C.	Text Reference	I.R.C.	Text Reference
107	§125	152(e)(2)	§669	168(d)(2)	§476
108(a)	§145	162	§§296, 297, 336, 424,	168(d)(3)	§470
108(a)(1)(D)	§148		431, 438, 439, 440,	168(d)(4)(B)	§476
108(b)	§147		519, 1072	168(e)(3)(A)	§465
108(c)	§148	162(a)	§§318, 615	168(i)(6)	§460
108(d)(3)	§145	162(a)(1)	§415	168(i)(14)	§465
108(e)(2)	§149	162(a)(2)	§118	168(k)	§472
108(e)(5)	§156	162(a)(3)	§386	170(a)(3)	§626
108(e)(6)	§156	162(c)(1)	§425	170(b)(1)	§617
108(f)(1)	§151	162(c)(2)	§426	170(b)(1)(D)	§629
108(f)(2)	§151	162(c)(3)	§427	170(b)(2)	§619
109	§§120, 753	162(e)	§434	170(d)	§§617, 618
111	§§537, 862	162(e)(2)	§433	170(e)(1)(A)	§§633, 819
111(a)	§1071	162(f)	§§431, 519	170(e)(1)(B)(i)	§631
111(c)	§1075	162(g)	§436	170(e)(1)(B)(ii)	§632
112	§125	162(l)	§662	170(e)(2)	§638
113	§125	162(m)	§423	170(e)(3)	§635
117	§53	163	§579	170(e)(4)	§635
117(b)	§54	163(d)	§607	170(e)(5)	§631
117(c)	§54	163(h)	§244	170(f)(2)	§625
117(d)	§55	163(h)(3)	§592	170(f)(2)(B)	§627
118(a)	§56	163(h)(3)(B)	§593	170(f)(3)	§§624, 644
118(b)	§57	163(h)(4)	§592	170(f)(8)	§622
119	§§118, 133	163(h)(4)(A)	§595	170(i)	§642
119(a)	§111	163(h)(4)(C)	§594	170(j)	§649
119(b)(3)	§119	164	§612	170(l)	§646
119(b)(4)	§115	164(b)	§616	172	§1077
121(a)	§803	164(d)	§613	172(d)(4)	§297
121(b)(2)	§805	165	§§493, 519	174	§§401, 494
121(b)(3)	§804	165(c)	§933	179	§§477, 480, 481
121(d)(1)	§805	165(c)(1)	§§297, 497, 672	182	§898
121(d)(3)(A)	§806	165(c)(2)	§§297, 472	183	§§319, 323, 454, 898
121(d)(3)(B)	§807	165(d)	§§160, 298, 501	183(b)	§321
123	§122	165(e)	§510	183(d)	§320
131	§125	165(h)	§510	186	§102
132	§§135, 143	165(h)(1)	§672	195	§§392, 393, 394, 400
132(b)	§136	165(h)(2)(A)	§§683, 882	195(a)	§393
132(c)	§§42, 137	165(h)(2)(B)	§§682, 882	195(b)	§393
132(d)	§138	165(h)(4)	§681	195(c)	§393
132(e)	§140	166(a)	§528	195(c)(1)	§395
132(f)	§139	166(a)(2)	§528	197	§§405, 456, 457, 473,
132(f)(4)	§139	166(d)	§528		474, 475, 867, 868
132(g)	§§141, 329	167	§450	198	§378
132(h)(1)	§137	167(a)(1)	§297	212	§§300, 339, 354, 437,
132(h)(2)	§143	167(a)(2)	§297		438, 440, 441, 442,
132(h)(5)	§140	167(c)(2)	§460		490, 555, 615
132(m)	§142	167(f)	§457	212(1)	§§297, 448
135	§123	167(g)	§457	212(2)	§297
141	§75	167(h)	§§463, 464	212(3)	§§340, 449
151(c)	§664	168	§450	213	§§650, 651
152(a)	§664	168(a)(3)(C)	§471	213(a)	§661
152(b)(5)	§664	168(a)(5)	§471	213(b)	§651
152(c)	§666	168(b)	§469	213(d)(1)(A)	§651
152(e)(1)	§668	168(d)	§470	213(d)(1)(B)	§651

I.R.C.	Text Reference	I.R.C.	Text Reference	I.R.C.	Text Reference
213(d)(1)(C)	§655	274(d)	§333	448(d)(1)	§1009
213(d)(2)	§§651, 653	274(h)	§312	448(d)(2)	§1009
213(d)(3)	§650	274(h)(7)	§442	448(d)(3)	§1009
213(d)(9)	§651	274(j)	§52	453	§§1046, 1060
213(e)(1)(C)	§651	274(k)	§334	453(b)(2)	§1055
213(e)(2)	§651	274(m)(2)	§311	453(d)	§1048
215	§§163, 685	274(m)(3)	§313	453(e)	§1054
215(c)	§169	274(n)	§§304, 317, 331, 334	453(f)(1)	§1054
217	§§325, 555	275	§616	453(f)(4)	§1053
217(b)	§328	278	§1003	453(f)(5)	§1053
217(c)	§326	279	§609	453(i)	§1051
217(c)(2)	§327	280A	§347	453(j)	§1052
219(b)(5)	§686	280A(c)(1)	§§348, 351, 353	453A	§1058
219(f)(1)	§686	280A(c)(2)	§352	453A(b)(2)	§1056
219(g)	§687	280A(c)(4)	§352	453B(a)	§1060
221	§596	280A(c)(5)	§§355, 362	453B(c)	§1062
222	§343	280A(d)	§358	453B(g)	§1063
222(e)	§343	280A(d)(1)	§595	454	§123
248	§400	280A(d)(3)	§§359, 360	455	§1017
262	§§302, 933	280A(e)	§361	456	§1017
263	§365	280A(g)	§363	461(f)	§1026
263(c)	§491	280B	§502	461(g)	§§605, 1002
263A	§§380, 383, 386	280E	§428	461(g)(2)	§§606, 1002
263A(b)(2)	§384	280F	§478	461(h)	§1028
263A(f)	§382	280F(a)	§480	461(h)(2)	§§100, 1033
263A(h)	§386	280F(b)	§479	461(h)(2)(A)	§1031
264	§577	280F(c)	§386	461(h)(2)(B)	§1032
264(a)(1)	§344	280F(d)(3)	§481	461(h)(2)(C)	§1033
264(a)(2)	§603	336	§1072	461(h)(3)	§1034
264(a)(3)	§603	341	§872	461(h)(4)	§1025
264(c)	§603	351(d)	§155	461(i)(3)	§1009
265(a)(1)	§601	401	§969	464	§1003
265(a)(2)	§602	401(a)(4)	§972	465	§§452, 936
267	§§511, 513, 514,	401(a)(5)	§972	465(a)	§538
	516, 518, 932	402(a)	§969	465(b)	§539
267(a)(2)	§1036	402(a)(1)	§74	465(c)	§540
267(b)	§§793, 1037	402(b)(1)	§967	467	§§608, 1022
267(b)(1)	§1037	404	§969	467(b)	§1024
267(b)(2)	§§514, 794, 1037	404(a)(3)	§973	467(b)(1)(A)	§1023
267(b)(4)	§514	404(a)(5)	§963	467(e)(1)	§1024
267(b)(6)	§514	407	§969	469	§§451, 543, 610, 935
267(b)(7)	§514	408(m)	§817	469(c)(7)	§550
267(b)(9)	§514	408A	§688	472	§1044
267(c)(4)	§1037	410	§972	472(c)	§1044
267(d)	§516	422A	§999	475(a)	§831
267(e)	§1038	442	§1066	475(d)(3)	§831
273	§744	443(i)	§1066	475(f)	§832
274	§35	446	§950	482	§§208, 209, 210
274(a)	§331	446(b)	§950	483	§§25, 248, 588, 915, 919,
274(a)(1)(B)	§332	446(c)	§950		921, 1049
274(a)(2)(A)	§332	448	§1009	483(d)(2)	§922
274(a)(3)	§332	448(b)(1)	§1009	483(e)	§923
274(b)	§336	448(b)(3)	§1009	501	§173
274(b)(1)	§37	448(c)	§1009	501(c)(3)	§173

I.R.C.	Text Reference	I.R.C.	Text Reference	I.R.C.	Text Reference
501(c)(4)	§176	682	§§170, 268	1060	§869
501(c)(5)	§176	691	§746	1091	§§517, 518, 934
501(c)(6)	§176	691(a)(4)	§1062	1202(a)	§910
508(e)	§181	691(a)(5)	§1062	1202(b)(1)	§911
509	§181	691(c)	§749	1202(c)	§912
511	§178	704(e)	§§218, 220, 221	1202(d)	§912
514	§§180, 905	704(e)(2)	§218	1202(e)	§912
527	§182	706(b)(1)(B)	§1066	1211	§555
530	§689	741	§872	1211(b)	§818
611	§§483, 486	751	§872	1212	§818
612	§486	901	§694	1221	§§821, 860
613(b)	§487	902	§694	1221(1)	§§823, 827, 829, 840
613(A)	§488	903	§694		
615	§492	904	§694	1221(3)	§838
616	§492	905	§694	1221(4)	§836
642(b)	§288	911	§§109, 227	1221(7)	§833
642(c)	§620	911(c)	§109	1221(8)	§873
643(a)	§280	1001	§757	1221(b)(2)	§833
651(a)	§281	1001(b)	§764	1222(11)	§814
652(a)	§282	1001(c)	§779	1231	§§837, 873, 876, 877, 878, 879, 880, 882, 883, 887, 902, 928, 1050
662(a)(1)	§284	1001(e)	§849		
662(a)(2)	§285	1001(e)(2)	§742		
663(a)	§286	1001(e)(3)	§743		
665	§290	1002	§779	1231(a)(4)C	§880
666	§290	1012	§§723, 724	1231(b)	§876
667	§§290, 291	1013	§723	1234	§§842, 843, 894
668	§290	1014	§§723, 735, 736, 746	1234(A)	§894
669	§290	1014(b)(6)	§738	1235	§841
671	§§250, 251	1014(c)	§746	1235(a)	§841
672(a)	§255	1015	§§723, 732	1235(d)	§841
672(b)	§255	1015(d)(6)	§733	1236	§828
672(e)	§253	1016	§750	1239	§885
673	§253	1016(a)(2)(B)	§752	1241	§894
674	§§254, 255	1019	§§120, 753	1245	§§482, 928, 1050
674(b)	§259	1022	§736	1245(a)	§927
674(b)(3)	§259	1031	§§495, 788, 793, 800, 929	1245(a)(1)	§928
674(b)(5)	§259			1245(a)(2)	§928
674(b)(6)	§259	1031(a)(3)	§787	1245(b)	§930
674(b)(7)	§259	1031(b)	§789	1250	§§929, 1050
674(c)	§257	1031(c)	§789	1250(d)	§930
674(d)	§258	1031(d)	§791	1253(a)	§891
675	§269	1031(f)(1)	§793	1253(e)	§892
675(1)	§270	1031(f)(2)	§794	1254	§491
675(2)	§271	1032	§56	1256(b)(3)(B)	§1009
675(3)	§272	1033	§§796, 798, 799, 800, 881, 930	1271	§900
675(4)	§276			1271(a)(1)	§§899, 900
676	§260	1033(a)	§797	1271(b)(1)	§899
677	§261	1033(g)	§801	1272	§901
677(a)(1)	§268	1034	§802	1273	§901
677(a)(3)	§265	1038	§812	1274	§§25, 248, 588, 901, 915, 919, 920, 1049
678	§277	1041	§§66, 511, 512, 518, 806, 808, 809		
678(b)	§277			1274(c)(4)	§917
678(c)	§277	1041(b)(2)	§810	1275	§901
678(d)	§277	1041(c)	§811	1275(a)(1)	§900

I.R.C.	Text Reference	I.R.C.	Text Reference	I.R.C.	Text Reference
1275(b)	§924	6013(d)	§235	7702B(c)	§62
1286	§194	6015(b)	§236	7703(b)	§238
1341	§§993, 1068, 1069	6015(c)	§236	7872	§§25, 239, 240, 241, 242, 243, 245, 587
1378	§1066	6015(d)	§236		
2040	§740	6115	§648	7872(a)	§§244, 246
2040(c)(9)	§740	6201(c)	§223	7872(b)	§247
4940	§181	6315	§693	7872(c)	§240
4941	§181	6511(d)(1)	§526	7872(c)(2)	§241
4942	§181	6661(b)(2)(C)(ii)	§1009	7872(c)(3)	§241
4943	§181	6676(c)	§169	7872(d)	§241
4944	§181	6714	§648		
4945	§181	7701(g)	§768		
6013	§229	7702B	§655		

CITATIONS TO REVENUE RULINGS

Rev. Rul.	Text Reference	Rev. Rul.	Text Reference	Rev. Rul.	Text Reference
53-162	§640	70-54	§61	79-24	§26
56-531	§853	71-425	§82	79-220	§100
57-418	§396	73-529	§315	82-94	§575
60-31	§961	74-22	§18	82-149	§429
64-328	§346	74-23	§18	89-23	§383
65-57	§59	74-77	§95	90-16	§772
65-261	§860	74-323	§426	92-99	§157
66-7	§908	75-120	§398	93-86	§318
66-167	§46	75-380	§310	94-12	§376
67-297	§584	75-432	§314	94-38	§379
69-188	§585	76-75	§573	99-7	§309
69-650	§962	78-38	§1005	99-23	§394
70-45	§867	78-39	§1005		

Table of Cases

Cummings, Commissioner v. - §864
Curtis Co. v. Commissioner - §826

D

Danielson, Commissioner v. - §866
Davis v. United States - §§621, 643
Davis, United States v. - §§294, 449, 759, 809
Dexsil Corp. v. Commissioner - §419
Diedrich v. Commissioner - §761
Diez-Arguelles v. Commissioner - §535
Disney, United States v. - §313
Dixie Pine Products v. Commissioner - §1026
Dosher v. United States - §678
Doyle v. Mitchell Bros. - §16
Drescher, United States v. - §§73, 968
Duberstein, Commissioner v. - §§29, 32, 33, 34, 35
Ducros v. Commissioner - §64
Dunn & McCarthy, Inc. v. Commissioner - §406
Dyke v. Commissioner - §908

E

Eisner v. Macomber - §§4, 10, 22, 756
Encyclopaedia Britannica v. Commissioner - §368
Estate of - see name of party
Exacto Spring Corp. v. Commissioner - §419

F

Fairbanks v. United States - §899
Farmers & Merchants Bank v. Commissioner - §101
Fausner v. Commissioner - §310
Ferguson v. Commissioner - §200
Ferrer, Commissioner v. - §§851, 857, 893
Flowers, Commissioner v. - §306
Fogarty v. United States - §206
Fogelsong v. Commissioner - §210
Ford Motor Co. v. Commissioner (1995) - §1029
Ford Motor Co. v. Commissioner (1994) - §1033
Frank v. Commissioner - §396
Frank Lyon Co. v. United States - §461
Franklin, Estate of v. Commissioner - §§453, 578, 727
Freedman v. Commissioner - §303
Friedman v. Commissioner - §191
Friedman v. Delaney - §411
Fritschle v. Commissioner - §222

G

Galt v. Commissioner - §195
General Artists Corp. v. Commissioner - §856
General Dynamics Corp., United States v. - §1027
Generes, United States v. - §532
Georator Corp. v. United States - §367

Georgia School Book Depository v. Commissioner - §1014
Gerstacker v. Commissioner - §657
Gevirtz v. Commissioner - §500
Gilbert v. Commissioner - §160
Gilmore, United States v. - §§339, 447
Glassell v. Commissioner - §1004
Glenshaw Glass Co., Commissioner v. - §§11, 20, 94
Goldman v. Commissioner - §330
Goldstein v. Commissioner - §§579, 580
Goodstein v. Commissioner - §575
Gotcher, United States v. - §129
Gould v. Commissioner - §295
Graphic Press, Inc. v. Commissioner - §799
Groetzinger, Commissioner v. - §298

H

H. Liebes & Co. v. Commissioner - §1013
Haag v. Commissioner - §210
Hagar v. Commissioner - §39
Hagen Advertising Displays v. Commissioner - §1016
Hallmark Cards Inc. v. Commissioner - §1011
Hamlin's Trust v. Commissioner - §868
Handelman v. Commissioner - §889
Hantzis v. Commissioner - §318
Harmon, Commissioner v. - §231
Harmont Plaza, Inc. v. Commissioner - §1012
Harold's Club v. Commissioner - §§416, 418
Harris v. Commissioner - §654
Harris, United States v. - §34
Harrison v. Schaffner - §196
Haverly v. United States - §21
Heim v. Fitzpatrick - §§207, 214
Helvering v. Clifford - §§211, 212, 501
Helvering v. Eubank - §204
Helvering v. Hammel - §895
Helvering v. Lazarus - §459
Helvering v. Le Gierse - §59
Henderson v. Commissioner - §§315, 318
Hernandez v. Commissioner - §645
Hillsboro National Bank v. Commissioner - §§1071, 1072
Hochschild v. Commissioner - §444
Horne, Estate of v. Commissioner - §64
Hort v. Commissioner - §854
Hughes Properties, Inc., United States v. - §1028
Hutchinson Baseball Enterprises, Inc. v. Commissioner - §174
Hyplains Dressed Beef Inc. v. Commissioner - §1037

I

Idaho Power Co., Commissioner v. - §§383, 659
Inaja Land Co. v. Commissioner - §754
Indianapolis Power & Light Co., Commissioner v. - §995

Winters v. Commissioner - **§645**
Wisconsin Cheeseman v. United States - **§602**
Witte v. Commissioner - **§950**
Wood v. United States - **§890**
Woodsam Association, Inc. v. Commissioner - **§758**
Woodward v. Commissioner - **§§391, 445**

Y

Yaeger, Estate of v. Commissioner - **§354**
Yosha v. Commissioner - **§324**

Z

Zaninovich v. Commissioner - **§1001**
Zarin v. Commissioner - **§§158, 159**
Zimmerman Steel Co. v. Commissioner - **§1025**

Index

Subject	I.R.C. Section	Text Section
legal fees, organization of business	195; 248	§§400, 445
litigation costs related to property		§§443-445
patents, copyrights, trademarks, purchase of	174	§401
property produced or sold	263A	§§380-385
qualified creative expense exception	263(A)(h)	§385
rental prepayments		§387
search for business, successful	195	§§393-394

CAPITAL GAINS AND LOSSES

Subject	I.R.C. Section	Text Section
alternative minimum tax	55; 56; 57	§§837, 940
business interests, sale of	197; 341; 751	§§865-872
capital assets, defined	1221	§821
capital loss, deduction of	1211(b); 1212	§818
charitable contributions	170(e)(1)(A)	§819
collectibles	1(h)(4)(A); 408(m)	§817
contract rights, sale of		§§850-858
depreciable property used in trade or business. *See also* Quasi-capital assets	1221(2); 1231	§§837, 873-875
gift to political organization	84	§201
goodwill, sale of	197; 1060	§§867, 869, 875
holding period of capital assets, determination of	1222	§§907-909
involuntary conversions	1033; 1231	§§795-801, 881, 902
life estates, sale of		§849
long-term gains, defined	1221; 1222	§§907-908
noncapital gains or losses, sale or exchange of		
personal services		§856
right to income		§§845-847
options	1234	§§842-844
patents	1235	§841
property held more than five years	1(h)(2)	§816
real property subdivided and sold exception	1237	§828
real property used in trade or business	1221(2); 1231	§§837, 873-875
sale or exchange, requirement of		§§888-906
sales of real estate	1(h)(6)	§815
short-term gains, defined	1221; 1222	§907
small business stock	57(a)(7); 1202(a)-(d)	§§910-913
special computations		
disallowed losses. *See also* Losses, nondeductible	165(c); 262; 267; 465; 469; 1091	§§931-936
imputed interest	483; 1274	§§915-924
recapture of depreciation	1245	§§925-930
tax rates	1(h); 408(m)	§§813-818

CASH BASIS

Subject	I.R.C. Section	Text Section
		§§951-1005
cash equivalents		§§952-954
promissory note or deferred payment		§954
stock or property as compensation		§§953, 975-990
claim of right doctrine	1341	§§991-993
repayment in later year. *See also* Annual accounting periods		§§1067-1070
constructive receipt doctrine	402; 404	§§955-968
deferred compensation		§§961-968
interest not withdrawn		§957
uncashed checks		§957
unpaid corporate salaries		§958
when mandatory		§960

Subject	I.R.C. Section	Text Section
CHILD CARE EXPENSES, CREDIT FOR	21	§§700-707
amount and limitations	21(c), (d)(2)	§§704-706
divorced parents	21(e)(5)	§707
qualifying individuals	21(b)	§701
transportation costs excluded		§702
CHILD SUPPORT	71(c)(1), (2)	§§162, 171-172, 535
CHILDREN		
income of. *See* Gross income		
CLAIM OF RIGHT		
income received under	1341	§§991-993, 1067-1070
"CLIFFORD" TRUSTS	671	§§211-212, 250-277
See also Trusts		
COMPENSATION FOR PERSONAL SERVICES		
See also Gross income		
assignment of		§§205, 856
bargain purchase from employer as		§§41-42
deduction by employer		
disallowance of in certain cases	162(a)(1)	§§415-423
family partnerships. *See* Partnerships		
frequent flier miles as		§134
fringe benefits	132	§§135-143
gift and leaseback		§215
gift, distinguished from		§31
meals and lodging furnished by employer as	119	§§111, 113-119, 130-133
payment of employee's income taxes		§128
reasonable, requirement of for deduction	162(a)(1)	§§415-423
reimbursements in connection with employment		§§129-134
stock options as	83	§§42, 984-990
transfer of property to employee	83	§§975-983
CONSTITUTIONAL BACKGROUND		
Article I tax provision unconstitutional		§§1-2, 7
due process		§6
Sixteenth Amendment tax provision		§§3-4
invalid tax procedures		§8
CONSTRUCTIVE RECEIPT DOCTRINE	402(b)	§§955-968
See also Cash basis		
CONTRIBUTIONS		
See Charitable contributions		
CORPORATIONS		
accrual method	448	§1009
charitable deduction by	170(b)(2)	§619
sale of		§§870-872
CREDITS AGAINST TAX		
adoption credit	23	§716
child care expense credit. *See also* Child care expenses,		
credit for	21	§§700-707
child tax credit	24	§§708-712
"child" defined	24(c)(1)(C); 32(c)(3)(B)	§710
divorced parents		§712
phaseouts	24(b)	§709
refundable	24(d)	§711

Subject	I.R.C. Section	Text Section
disallowed		§§590-610
accrued unpaid		§604
excess investment	163(d)	§§607-609
exempt income expenses	265(a)(1)	§601
loan to purchase insurance	264(a)(2), (3)	§603
passive activity	469	§610
personal		§§591-600
education loan exception	221; 62(a)(17)	§§596-600
residence loan exception	163(h)(3), (4); 280A(d)(1)	§§592-595
prepaid	461(g)(1), (2)	§§605-606
tax-exempt interest	265(a)(2)	§602
items not deductible. See Nondeductible items		
losses. See Losses		
medical expenses. See also Medical expenses	213	§§650-662
particular items. See appropriate headings this index		
personal		§552
personal exemption	151; 152	§663
phaseout	55(d)(3)	§§565, 670-671, 709, 720
recovery of items previously deducted, tax treatment of	111	§§1071-1077
retirement plans		§§686-688
IRAs	62(a)(7); 219(b)(5), (f)(1)	§§686-687
Roth IRAs	408A	§688
shifting of		§§294-295
standard deduction	63	§§566-571
amount		§567
dependents	63(c)(5)	§570
elderly and blind taxpayers	63(c)(3), (f)	§569
marriage penalty	63(c)(7)	§568
taxes		§§611-616
disability insurance		§614
in connection with business investment	162(a); 212	§615
nondeductible	164(b); 275	§616
two percent floor	67	§§561-562, 564

DEFERRED COMPENSATION	402(b); 404(a)(5)	§§961-968

DEPENDENT		
defined	151-152	§664
divorced parents, agreement concerning	152(e)	§§668-669
exemption for. See also Exemptions	151-152	§§664-669

DEPLETION		
by whom deductible		§485
cost method	611-612	§486
deduction for wasting asset	611	§483
depletable property		§484
drilling costs	263(c); 615-616	§§480-492
mineral deposits	615-616	§492
percentage method	613	§§487-489
tax advantages		§489

DEPRECIATION AND AMORTIZATION		
accelerated cost recovery system ("ACRS")	168	§450
computation of		§§465-476
accelerated method	168(b), (d)(3)	§§468-470
intangibles, amortization of	197	§§473-475
real property	168(d)(2), (4)(B)	§476

Subject	I.R.C. Section	Text Section
recovery periods	168(3)(A), (i)(14)	§465
salvage value		§466
stimulus bill—extra depreciation		§472
straight line method	168(a)(3)(C), (5)	§§467, 471
consumer items limited deductions	280F	§§478-481
depreciable property		§§455-458
books, films, sound recordings, software	167(f), (g); 197	§457
intangibles	197	§456
"limited useful life"		§455
works of art		§458
election to expense	179	§477
limitations		§§451-454
"at risk"	465	§452
generic tax shelters	183	§454
passive loss rules	469	§451
property worth less than debt		§453
recapture of .	1245; 1250	§§925-930
reduction of basis effect		§482
who may deduct		§§459-464
future interest holder	167(h)	§463
landlord-tenant	167(c)(2); 168(i)(b)	§460
purchaser		§462
sale-leaseback		§461
trustee-beneficiary	167(h)	§464

DIVORCE

See also Support payments

exemption for children	152(e)	§§668-669
deductibility of expenses of	212(1), (3)	§§446-449
no gain or loss	1041	§§512, 808-812
marital property divisions	121(d)(3); 1041	§§806-812
sales between spouses	1041	§§808-811

E

EARNED INCOME CREDIT	32	§§713-715
EDUCATIONAL EXPENSES	222	§§341-343
EMPLOYEE STOCK OPTIONS	83; 422a	§§975-981, 984-990
ENTERTAINMENT EXPENSES	82; 132; 217; 274	§§331-335

EXCHANGES

See also Gain or loss on sale or exchange; "Sale or exchange" of capital assets

as income		§26
between related persons	1031(f)	§§793-794
boot, effect of		§§789-791
deferred exchange	103(a)(3)	§§786-787
like-kind exchanges	1031	§§781-794
defined	1031(h)	§§782-783
no gain or loss	103(a)	§781
losses		§509
mortgage, effect of		§792
noninventory tangible property		§784
realization	1001(c); 1031(b), (f)(1); 267(b)	§§763, 779, 789, 793
residence property		§763

Subject	I.R.C. Section	Text Section
GROSS INCOME		
See also Exclusions from gross income		
adjusted. *See* Adjusted gross income, defined		
alimony and separate maintenance	62; 71; 215; 682; 6676(c)	§§162-170
assignment of		§205
awards and prizes	74(a)	§§49-52
bargain purchases		§§41-42
cancellation of indebtedness. *See* Cancellation of indebtedness		
change in form		§12
children, earnings of, to whom taxable	1(g); 73; 911; 6201(c)	§§222-226
claim of right, income received under	1341	§§991-993, 1067-1070
compensation as. *See* Compensation for personal services		
defined	61	§§9-22
exclusions from. *See* Exclusions from gross income		
gratuities		§38
husbands and wives, earnings of, to whom taxable. *See also* Husband and wife, joint return	1(d); 2; 6013	§§229-232
illegal income		§§160-161
imputed		§§23-26
exchange of services and goods		§26
self-employment		§24
includible items		
alimony, separate maintenance and child support	62(a)(10); 71(a), (c); 215; 682; 6676(c)	§§162-170
any increase in net worth		§126
cancellation of indebtedness	108	§§144-159
compensation for services rendered		§127
expenses of employees. *See also* Expenses		§§130-134
frequent flier miles		§134
meals and lodgings		§§118, 132-133
reimbursements		§131
unreimbursed		§132
fringe benefits	82; 132	§§135-143
"employee" defined	132(h)(2)	§143
moving expenses	82; 132(g)	§141
retirement advice	132(m)	§142
transportation	132(f)	§139
income from illegal activities		§§160-161
payment of employee's income taxes		§128
reimbursements		§§99, 118, 129-132
kiddie tax	1(g)	§§226-228
net worth concept		§§11-22
no income		
borrowing		§21
loan repayment		§§13-15
return of capital		§16
unsolicitated property		§21
noncash income		§19
punitive damages	104(a)	§§89, 93
strike benefits		§§39-40
windfalls		§20
GROUP TERM LIFE INSURANCE	79	§110

Subject	I.R.C. Section	Text Section
H		
HEAD OF HOUSEHOLD, TAX ON	2(b), (c); 7703(b)	§238
HOLDING PERIOD OF CAPITAL ASSETS	1(h); 1221	§§814, 902-909
HOME OFFICES, EXPENSE DEDUCTIONS	280A	§§347-355
HUSBAND AND WIFE, JOINT RETURN	1(d); 2; 6013	§§232-237
effect of	6013	§232
joint and several liability	6013(d)	§§235-236
divorced or separated spouse	6015(c), (d)	§236
innocent spouse rule	6015(b)	§236
marriage and single penalty		§§233-234
gradual elimination	63(c)(7)	§234
not mandatory	1(d)	§237
right to file	2, 6013	§229
sale of residence exclusion	121(b)(2), (d)(1)	§805
sales between	1041	§§808-811
I		
IMPUTED INCOME		§§23-26
INCOME		
See Gross income		
INCOME IN RESPECT OF DECEDENTS	691; 1014(c)	§§746-749
INCOME SPLITTING BY GIFTS		
common control of two businesses	482	§§208-210
intercorporate transactions		§209
services of individuals		§210
excessive controls retained		§§211-216
gift and leaseback		§215
transfers of patents		§§213-214
family partnerships		§§216-221
reasonable compensation	704(e)(2)	§219
sham transfers		§220
income-producing property, in general		§§47-48, 185-202
accrued income		§189
contingent contracts		§191
dividend income		§190
excludible gift	102	§188
gift tax		§188
transfer shifts income	102(b)(1), (2)	§§47-48, 186
no gain or loss to donor		§§198-202
charitable contributions		§199
gifts to political organization exception	84	§201
mortgaged property exception		§202
"ripened" gifts		§200
personal service income		§§203-210
charity, working for		§206
obligatory assignments		§205
working for oneself		§207
sham transfers		§192
transfer of income only		§§193-197
assignments for consideration		§197
assignments of trust income		§196

Subject	I.R.C. Section	Text Section
coupon bonds	1286	§194
general rule		§§193-194
rental income		§195
INDIVIDUAL RETIREMENT ACCOUNTS	62(a); 219; 408	§§686-689
education IRAs	530	§689
Roth IRA	408A	§688
INHERITANCE	102(c); 1014	§§43-46, 735
INSTALLMENT METHOD		§§1047-1064
computation		§§1049-1051
depreciation recapture	453(i); 1245; 1250	§1051
imputed interest	483; 1274	§1050
election out	453(d)	§1048
indeterminate sale price	453(j)	§1052
installment obligation, disposition of	453B(a)	§§1062-1064
restrictions		§§1053-1055
dealer property	453(b)(1), (2)	§1055
payable on demand debts	453(f)(4), (5)	§1053
sale to related person	453(e), (f)(1)	§1054
sale of property only	453	§1047
INTEREST		
below-market interest on loans. *See also* Below-market interest on loans	483; 7872	§§239-248
deductibility of	163; 189; 264; 265; 279; 461(g)	§§572-610
business purpose	163	§§579-580
excess investment interest	163(d); 279	§§607-609
family loans		§581
imputed interest	483; 1274; 7872	§§239-241, 248, 586-588
below-market interest on loans. *See also* Below-market interest on loans	7872	§§239-248
computation	483; 1274	§§918-924
deductibility for business debts		§§586-588
deferred payments on property sales	483; 1274	§§915-924
farms and residences	483	§917
installment payments on property sales	483; 1274	§1050
included in gross income		§14
nondeductibility of	163(d); 189; 264; 265; 279; 461(g)	§§590-610
personal interest	163(h)	§§591-600
prepaid interest	461(g)	§§605-606, 1002
residence loans	56(b)(1)(C), (e); 163(h)(3), (4)	§§592-595, 947
tax-free		
higher education	135; 454	§123
state and local bonds	103	§§75-77
INVENTORIES		
methods of computing	472	§§1039-1046
not capital assets	1221(1)	§§822-835
INVESTOR EXPENSES		
See Nonbusiness expenses for production of income		
INVOLUNTARY CONVERSIONS	1033; 1231	§§795-801
See also Gain or loss on sale or exchange		

Subject	I.R.C. Section	Text Section
J		
JOINT RETURNS	1(d); 2; 121(b)(2); 121(b)(2), (d)(1); 6013	§§229-232, 805
K		
KICKBACKS	162	§§424-430
KIDDIE TAX	1(g)	§§226-228
L		
LESSEE, IMPROVEMENTS BY		
adjusted basis	109	§753
basis of property to lessor	1019	§§120-121
depreciation on	167(c)(2); 168(i)(6)	§460
not income to lessor	109	§§120, 753
LIABILITIES, EFFECT ON BASIS		§§726-727
LIFE INSURANCE		
accelerated death benefits	101(g); 7702B(c)	§62
benefits excluded from gross income	101(a)	§58
corporation owned policy		§64
debtor's insurance by creditor		§61
defined		§59
employer-paid benefits		
distinguished		§60
group term	79	§110
installment payments	101(c), (d)	§67
premium payments, deductibility of	264	§§344-346
deductibility of	264(a)(1)	§344
trust, paid by	677	§§264-265
who pays not relevant		§§63-64
purchasers of existing policies not excluded	101(a)(2)	§§65-66
purchase by insured		§66
LIKE KIND EXCHANGES	1031	§§781-794
LITIGATION EXPENSE	195; 212(3); 248	§§97-98, 337-340, 400, 443-445
primary purpose test		§444
LONG-TERM CAPITAL GAINS		
See Capital gains and losses		
LOSSES		
"at risk" limitation	465	§§538-542
casualty and theft	165(c), (h)	§§672-683
amount deductible		§679
anticipated physical losses		§676
deduction limitations	165(c)(1), (2), (h)(1)	§672
gains and losses in same year	165(h)(2)(A), (B)	§§682-683
insurance, effect of	165(h)(4)	§681
local law defines "theft"		§677
taxpayer's property		§678
closed transaction		§508
defined	165	§§494-495
individuals, deductible by		§§496-503
casualty or abandonment. *See also* Deductions	165(c), (h)	§§502, 672-683
demolition costs nondeductible	280(B)	§502

Subject	I.R.C. Section	Text Section
NONBUSINESS EXPENSES FOR PRODUCTION OF INCOME	212	§§437-449
NONDEDUCTIBLE ITEMS		
bribes and illegal payments	162(c)	§§425-430
capital expenditures	263	§365
clothing		§364
commissions paid on sale of property		§403
fines and penalties	162(f)	§431
insurance premiums in certain cases	264(a)(1)	§§345-346
lobbying costs	162(e)	§434
losses between closely related taxpayers	267; 1041	§§511-516, 932
personal expenses	262	§302
purchase of goodwill	197	§§404-405
running for office		§§339, 399
unreasonable compensation	162(a)(1), (m)	§§415-423
NONRECOGNITION OF GAIN OR LOSS		
See Gain or loss on sale or exchange		
NONTAXABLE ITEMS		
See Exclusions from gross income		

O

Subject	I.R.C. Section	Text Section
OBSOLESCENCE		
See Depreciation and amortization		
OFFICE AT HOME	280A	§§347-355
See also Expenses		
OPTIONS, GAIN OR LOSS ON	1234	§§842-844
ORDINARY AND NECESSARY EXPENSE		§§408-423
defined		§409
determinative factors		§§410-414

P

Subject	I.R.C. Section	Text Section
PARTNERSHIPS		
family partnerships	704(e)	§§216-221
sale of	741; 751	§§870-872
PASSIVE LOSSES		§§543-551, 610, 935
See also Losses		
interest on disallowed	469	§§610, 935
PATENTS		
character of asset	1235	§841
shifting royalty income		§§213-214
PENSIONS AND PROFIT-SHARING PLANS, QUALIFIED	401-407	§§969-974
PERSONAL EXEMPTIONS		§663
PERSONAL SERVICE INCOME		
See Compensation for personal services		
PRIVATE FOUNDATIONS	170(b), (e)	§§618, 631
PUBLIC POLICY		
expenses disallowed by reason of	162	§§424-436

Subject	I.R.C. Section	Text Section
losses disallowed by reason of	165	§519

Q

QUASI-CAPITAL ASSETS	1231; 1221(2), (8)	§§873-887
casualties, special rules for		§§880-882
computation of gain and loss	1231(c)	§§878-879
property used in trade or business		§§875-877
recapture of depreciation		§883
related taxpayers, sales between	1239	§§885-887

R

RATES OF TAX		
capital gains. *See also* Capital gains and losses	1(h); 408(m); 1222(11)	§§814-817
claim of right, income restored, limitation of tax	1341	§§991-993, 1067-1070
head of household	2	§238
husband and wife	2; 6013; 1(d)	§§229-234
in general	1	§§690-691
minimum tax. *See also* Alternative minimum tax	55; 56; 57	§§913, 937-949
REALIZATION		
amount realized on mortgaged property	1001(b)	§§764-772
Crane rule		§§766
nonrecourse loan		§§768-771
recourse loan		§§770, 772
as constitutional limitation		§756
exchanges		§763
extent of	1002	§779
future payments		§§773-778
losses	165(e), (h)	§§504-510
no realization to gift donor		§§198-202
property transactions	1001	§§757-762
as debt payment		§757
mortgage foreclosures		§762
mortgages and gifts		§§758, 760-762
required for taxation on increase in net worth		§§22, 756
Sixteenth Amendment, required by		§§4, 756
RECAPTURE OF DEPRECIATION		
personal property	1245	§§926-928
real property	1250	§929
transfers not subject to depreciation recapture		§930
RECOVERY OF ITEMS PREVIOUSLY DEDUCTED, TAX TREATMENT OF	111	§§1071-1076
See also Tax benefit rule		
REPAIRS		§§376-380
RETIREMENT PLANS, CONTRIBUTIONS TO	219; 408	§§686-688
RETURNS, JOINT	2; 121(b)(2), (d)(1); 6013	§§229-232

S

SALARY		
See Compensation for personal services		

Subject	I.R.C. Section	Text Section
"SALE OR EXCHANGE" OF CAPITAL ASSETS		
See also Gain or loss on sale or exchange		
contract rights	1234; 1234A; 1241	§§893-894
foreclosure		§895
franchises, trademarks and trade names	1253(a), (e)	§§891-892
involuntary conversion	1231	§902
mineral interests		§890
not affected by seller's retention of control	514	§§903-906
payment to creditor	1271(a)(1), (b)(1); 1275(a)(1)	§§899-901
worthless debts or securities	182-183	§896
SCHOLARSHIPS	117	§§53-55
SOLE PROPRIETORSHIPS, SALE OF	197	§§865-869
STOCK OPTIONS, EMPLOYEE'S	83; 422A	§§42, 975-981, 984-990
SUPPORT PAYMENTS		
child support	71(c)(1), (2)	§§171-172
spousal		§§162-170
alimony trusts	682	§170
cohabitation between parties	71(b)(1)(C)	§166
general rule	71(a); 62(a)(10)	§163
judicial decree required	71(b)(2)	§164
payments cease at death	71(b)(1)(D)	§167
recapture of payments		§168

T

Subject	I.R.C. Section	Text Section
TAX BENEFIT RULE		
carry forwards	111(c)	§1075
classification of assets		§862
erroneous deduction		§1073
"recovery" defined		§1072
recovery of bad debts	111	§537
statement of rule	111(a)	§1071
tax brackets		§1076
TAX EXEMPT ORGANIZATIONS	501	§§173-184
charitable	501(c)(3)	§§174-175
description of	501(c)	§§173-174
political organizations	527	§§182-184
private foundations	508(e); 509; 4940-4945	§181
racial discrimination disqualification		§177
unions, fraternities, civic leagues	501(c)(4)-(6)	§176
unrelated business income	511	§§178-180
debt-financed property	514	§180
rental		§179
TAX PREFERENCE, ITEMS OF	57	§§948-949
TAX RATES		
See Rates of tax		
TAX SHELTERS		
accrual method required	448(d), (c); 461(i)(3); 1256(b)(3)(B); 6661(b)(2)(C)(ii)	§1009
"at risk" limitations	465(a)	§§538-542

Subject	I.R.C. Section	Text Section
business operated for pleasure	183	§§322-324
flagrant		§301
generic		§§322-324, 580

TAXES

See also Alternative minimum tax

deduction for	162(a); 164; 212; 275	§§565-570
business and investment expense	162; 212	§615
disability insurance		§614
property taxes	164(d)	§613
foreign, credit for	27; 901-905	§694
nondeductible	56(b)(1)(A)(ii); 164(b); 275	§§616, 945

TRAVEL EXPENSE — 162(a)(2) — §§304-318

"away from home"		§§314-318
business reason for home		§318
homeless persons		§315
several offices		§316
"sleep or rest" rule		§317
"temporary vs. indefinite" rule	162(a)	§318
meals		§317
"pursuit of trade or business"	274(h), (m)(2), (3)	§§305-313
combined business and pleasure	274(m)(2)	§311
commuting		§§306-310
foreign meetings	274(h)	§312
spouse expenses	274(m)(3)	§313
stockholder's travel	212; 274(h)(7)	§442

TRUSTS

alimony trusts	682	§§170, 268
assignments of income		§196
beneficiary, tax to	667	§§279, 283-285, 291
"Clifford trusts"	671; 678	§§211-212, 250-277
distributable net income, defined	643(a)	§280
estate and gift taxes		§252
loans to grantor	675	§§271-275
separate taxable entity		§§278-291
beneficiary or trust taxed		§279
complex trusts	642(b); 662(a)(1), (2); 663(a)	§§283-288
decedent's estates as		§283
simple trusts	651(a); 652(a)	§§281-282
throwback rule	665-669	§§289-291
tax effect	671	§§251-252
trusts taxable to grantor	671	§§250-278
administrative control by grantor	675	§§269-276
borrowing from trust	675(1)-(3)	§§271-275
income for benefit of grantor or spouse	677; 682	§§261-268
support of dependents		§§266-267
power to alter beneficiary	674	§§254-259
external standards exception	674(d)	§258
independent trustees' powers exception	674(c)	§257
reasonable alterations exception	674(b)	§259
power to revoke	676	§260
reversionary interest	672(e); 673	§253
trusts taxable to person other than grantor	678	§277

Subject	I.R.C. Section	Text Section
U		
UNADJUSTED BASIS *See* Basis of property		
VWXYZ		
VACATION HOMES	280A	§§356-363